'... this novel with its s[...]
humour, intelligence, a[...]
spirit, is a tribute and a t[...]

'This novel, so vast and [...]
sweet, sleepless pilgrimage to life. ... Such writing reminds us that there are secrets beyond technique, beyond
even style, which have to do with a quality of soul on the
part of the writer, a giving of oneself. ... His novel
deserves thousands of long marriages and suitable
readers.'

JAMES WOOD *Guardian*

'A phenomenon, a prodigy, a marvel of 19th century-style
storytelling in the language of today. ... It is hard to
believe that Seth is only one man. ... This is quite a
novel.'

PATRICK SKENE CATLING *Evening Standard*

'*A Suitable Boy* modulates unawkwardly from moments
of delicate emotional and psychological accuracy to scenes
of panoramic drama ... it lines up with its eminent 19th-
century predecessors in combining depth of imagination
with breadth of appeal.'

PETER KEMP *Sunday Times*

'No-one, surely, could wish this novel shorter. ... the
greatness of the novel, its unassailable truthfulness, owes
less to research than to imagination, an instinctive knowledge of the human heart.'

SALLY LAIRD *Observer*

'A big book in more than size. *A Suitable Boy* will win
readers for decades to come.'

Macleans

'... vastly entertaining.'

Ottawa Citizen

'. . . a wide-ranging, eminently readable epic work.'

Toronto Star

'If you study a map of India you will not find the city of Brahmpur, but if you travel to India you will find it almost everywhere. . . . This is . . . fiction on the grand scale. . . . By the time you reach the 1349th and last page you will have absorbed a splendid story, full of the tangle and perfume of India.'

TREVOR FISHLOCK *Sunday Telegraph*

'Vivid, evocative and beautifully written, *A Suitable Boy* casts its net far and wide across the country. . . . Seth has a wonderful sense of place and the (fictional) city of Brahmpur is almost a character in its own right. . . . The cast of *A Suitable Boy* is as vast and various as that of any 19th-century novel.'

SUSAN ALICE WATKINS *Literary Review*

'*A Suitable Boy* is not merely one of the longest novels in English: it may also prove to be the most fecund as well as the most prodigious work of the latter half of this century – perhaps even the book to restore the serious reading public's faith in the contemporary novel. . . . Vikram Seth is already the best writer of his generation. . . . You should make time for it. It will keep you company for the rest of your life.'

DANIEL JOHNSON *The Times*

'This mammoth novel takes to its heart the maxim that literature must delight and instruct.'

Montreal Gazette

'When I think of *A Suitable Boy*, a smile of sheer pleasure rises to my face. I do not expect to read another novel this lovely in my lifetime, so I will read *A Suitable Boy* again and again and again.'

Toronto Sun

ABOUT THE AUTHOR

Vikram Seth was born in 1952. He trained as an economist and has lived for several years each in the UK, California, China and India. He is the author of *The Golden Gate: A Novel in Verse*, described by Gore Vidal as 'The Great Californian Novel', *From Heaven Lake: Travels through Sinkiang and Tibet*, and four volumes of poetry.

BY THE SAME AUTHOR

Mappings (*poems*)
From Heaven Lake: Travels through Sinkiang and Tibet
The Humble Administrator's Garden (*poems*)
The Golden Gate: A Novel in Verse
All You Who Sleep Tonight (*poems*)
Three Chinese Poets (*translations*)
Beastly Tales From Here and There (*poems*)
Arion and the Dolphin (*libretto*)

A Suitable Boy
Volume One

VIKRAM SETH

Little, Brown & Company (Canada) Limited
Boston   London   Toronto

© Copyright Vikram Seth, 1993

Canadian Cataloguing in Publication Data

Seth, Vikram, 1952–
A suitable boy: a novel

ISBN 0–316–78153–3
I. Title.

PR9499.3.S39S95   1993   823   C93–093137–8

Printed in England by Clays Ltd, St Ives plc

Little, Brown & Company (Canada) Limited
148 Yorkville Avenue, Toronto, Ontario, Canada

This Canadian edition dedicated to
Christine Cooke MacGregor
1950–1992
A very suitable girl

To
Papa and Mama
and
the memory of Amma

A WORD OF THANKS

To these I owe a debt past telling:
My several muses, harsh and kind;
My folks, who stood my sulks and yelling,
And (in the long run) did not mind;
Dead legislators, whose orations
I've filched to mix my own potations;
Indeed, all those whose brains I've pressed,
Unmerciful, because obsessed;
My own dumb soul, which on a pittance
Survived to weave this fictive spell;
And, gentle reader, you as well,
The fountainhead of all remittance.
Buy me before good sense insists
You'll strain your purse and sprain your wrists.

CONTENTS

ACKNOWLEDGEMENTS

The author and publishers would like to thank the following for permission to quote copyright material:

The Ministry of Human Resources Development, Govt. of India for extracts from *Letters to Chief Ministers*, Vol. 2, 1950–1952 by Jawaharlal Nehru, general editor G. Parthasarathi (Jawaharlal Nehru Memorial Fund, distributed by Oxford University Press, 1986)

HarperCollins Publishers Ltd. for extracts from *The Koran Interpreted* by A.J. Arberry (George Allen & Unwin Ltd.; and Oxford University Press, 1964)

Oxford University Press for an extract from *The Select Nonsense of Sukumar Ray* translated by Sukanta Chaudhuri (Oxford University Press, 1987)

Faber & Faber for an extract from the poem 'Law, Say the Gardeners' published in *W.H. Auden: Collected Poems* edited by Edward Mendelson (Faber & Faber)

Penguin Books Ltd. for extracts from *Selected Poems* by Rabindranath Tagore, translated by William Radice (Penguin Books, 1985)

Bantam Books Inc. for extracts from *The Bhagavad-Gita* translated by Barbara Stoler Miller (Bantam Books, 1986)

The Sahitya Akademi for extracts from *Mir Anis* by Ali Jawad Zaidi published in the series 'Makers of Indian Literature' (Sahitya Akademi, 1986)

The Gita Press, Gorakhpur for extracts from *Sri Ramacharitamanasa* translated into English (Gita Press, 1968)

MEHRAS

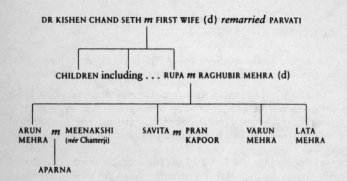

DR KISHEN CHAND SETH *m* FIRST WIFE (d) *remarried* PARVATI

CHILDREN including . . . RUPA *m* RAGHUBIR MEHRA (d)

ARUN MEHRA *m* MEENAKSHI (née Chatterji)   SAVITA *m* PRAN KAPOOR   VARUN MEHRA   LATA MEHRA

APARNA

KAPOORS

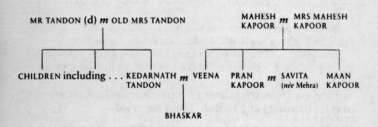

MR TANDON (d) *m* OLD MRS TANDON

MAHESH KAPOOR *m* MRS MAHESH KAPOOR

CHILDREN including . . . KEDARNATH TANDON *m* VEENA   PRAN KAPOOR *m* SAVITA (née Mehra)   MAAN KAPOOR

BHASKAR

KHANS

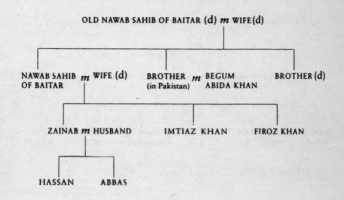

OLD NAWAB SAHIB OF BAITAR (d) *m* WIFE (d)

NAWAB SAHIB *m* WIFE (d)   BROTHER *m* BEGUM   BROTHER (d)
OF BAITAR   (in Pakistan) ABIDA KHAN

ZAINAB *m* HUSBAND   IMTIAZ KHAN   FIROZ KHAN

HASSAN   ABBAS

CHATTERJIS

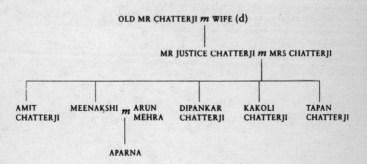

OLD MR CHATTERJI *m* WIFE (d)

MR JUSTICE CHATTERJI *m* MRS CHATTERJI

AMIT   MEENAKSHI *m* ARUN   DIPANKAR   KAKOLI   TAPAN
CHATTERJI   MEHRA   CHATTERJI CHATTERJI   CHATTERJI

APARNA

(d)=deceased

The superfluous, that very necessary thing . . .
VOLTAIRE

The secret of being a bore is to say everything.
VOLTAIRE

Part One

'YOU too will marry a boy I choose,' said Mrs Rupa Mehra firmly to her younger daughter.

Lata avoided the maternal imperative by looking around the great lamp-lit garden of Prem Nivas. The wedding-guests were gathered on the lawn. 'Hmm,' she said. This annoyed her mother further.

'I know what your hmms mean, young lady, and I can tell you I will not stand for hmms in this matter. I do know what is best. I am doing it all for you. Do you think it is easy for me, trying to arrange things for all four of my children without His help?' Her nose began to redden at the thought of her husband, who would, she felt certain, be partaking of their present joy from somewhere benevolently above. Mrs Rupa Mehra believed, of course, in reincarnation, but at moments of exceptional sentiment, she imagined that the late Raghubir Mehra still inhabited the form in which she had known him when he was alive: the robust, cheerful form of his early forties before over-work had brought about his heart attack at the height of the Second World War. Eight years ago, eight years, thought Mrs Rupa Mehra miserably.

'Now, now, Ma, you can't cry on Savita's wedding day,' said Lata, putting her arm gently but not very concernedly around her mother's shoulder.

'If He had been here, I could have worn the tissue-patola sari I wore for my own wedding,' sighed Mrs Rupa Mehra. 'But it is too rich for a widow to wear.'

'Ma!' said Lata, a little exasperated at the emotional capital her mother insisted on making out of every possible circumstance. 'People are looking at you. They want to congratulate you, and they'll think it very odd if they see you crying in this way.'

Several guests were indeed doing namasté to Mrs Rupa Mehra and smiling at her; the cream of Brahmpur society, she was pleased to note.

'Let them see me!' said Mrs Rupa Mehra defiantly, dabbing at her eyes hastily with a handkerchief perfumed with 4711 eau-de-Cologne. 'They will only think it is because of my happiness at Savita's wedding. Everything I do is for you, and no one appreciates me. I have chosen such a good boy for Savita, and all everyone does is complain.'

Lata reflected that of the four brothers and sisters, the only one who hadn't complained of the match had been the sweet-tempered, fair-complexioned, beautiful Savita herself.

'He is a little thin, Ma,' said Lata a bit thoughtlessly. This was putting it mildly. Pran Kapoor, soon to be her brother-in-law, was lank, dark, gangly, and asthmatic.

'Thin? What is thin? Everyone is trying to become thin these days. Even I have had to fast the whole day and it is not good for my diabetes. And if Savita is not complaining, everyone should be happy with him. Arun and Varun are always complaining: why didn't they choose a boy for their sister then? Pran is a good, decent, cultured khatri boy.'

There was no denying that Pran, at thirty, was a good boy, a decent boy, and belonged to the right caste. And, indeed, Lata did like Pran. Oddly enough, she knew him better than her sister did – or, at least, had seen him for longer than her sister had. Lata was studying English at Brahmpur University, and Pran Kapoor was a popular lecturer there. Lata had attended his class on the Elizabethans, while Savita, the bride, had met him for only an hour, and that too in her mother's company.

'And Savita will fatten him up,' added Mrs Rupa Mehra. 'Why are you trying to annoy me when I am so happy? And Pran and Savita will be happy, you will see. They will be happy,' she continued emphatically. 'Thank you, thank you,' she now beamed at those who were coming up to greet her. 'It is so wonderful – the boy of my dreams, and such a good family. The Minister Sahib has been very kind to us. And Savita is so happy. Please eat something, please eat: they have made such delicious gulab-jamuns, but owing to my diabetes I cannot eat them even after the ceremonies. I am not even allowed gajak, which is so difficult to resist in winter. But please eat, please eat. I must go in to check what is happening: the time that the pandits have given is coming up, and there is no sign of either bride or groom!' She looked at Lata, frowning. Her younger daughter was going to prove more difficult than her elder, she decided.

'Don't forget what I told you,' she said in an admonitory voice.

'Hmm,' said Lata. 'Ma, your handkerchief's sticking out of your blouse.'

'Oh!' said Mrs Rupa Mehra, worriedly tucking it in. 'And tell Arun to please take his duties seriously. He is just standing there in a corner talking to that Meenakshi and his silly friend from Calcutta. He should see that everyone is drinking and eating properly and having a gala time.'

'That Meenakshi' was Arun's glamorous wife and her own disrespectful daughter-in-law. In four years of marriage Meenakshi's only worthwhile act, in Mrs Rupa Mehra's eyes, had been to give birth to her beloved granddaughter, Aparna, who even now had found her way to her grandmother's brown silk sari and was tugging it for attention. Mrs Rupa Mehra was delighted. She gave her a kiss and told her:

'Aparna, you must stay with your Mummy or with Lata Bua, otherwise you will get lost. And then where would we be?'

'Can't I come with you?' asked Aparna, who, at three, naturally had views and preferences of her own.

'Sweetheart, I wish you could,' said Mrs Rupa Mehra, 'but I have to make sure that your Savita Bua is ready to be married. She is so late already.' And Mrs Rupa Mehra looked once again at the little gold watch that had been her husband's first gift to her and which had not missed a beat for two-and-a-half decades.

'I want to see Savita Bua!' said Aparna, holding her ground.

Mrs Rupa Mehra looked a little harassed and nodded vaguely at Aparna.

Lata picked Aparna up. 'When Savita Bua comes out,

5

we'll go over there together, shall we, and I'll hold you up like this, and we'll both get a good view. Meanwhile, should we go and see if we can get some ice-cream? I feel like some too.'

Aparna approved of this, as of most of Lata's suggestions. It was never too cold for ice-cream. They walked towards the buffet table together, three-year-old and nineteen-year-old hand in hand. A few rose-petals wafted down on them from somewhere.

'What is good enough for your sister is good enough for you,' said Mrs Rupa Mehra to Lata as a parting shot.

'We can't both marry Pran,' said Lata, laughing.

1.2

THE other chief host of the wedding was the groom's father, Mr Mahesh Kapoor, who was the Minister of Revenue of the state of Purva Pradesh. It was in fact in his large, C-shaped, cream-coloured, two-storey family house, Prem Nivas, situated in the quietest, greenest residential area of the ancient, and – for the most part – over-populated city of Brahmpur, that the wedding was taking place.

This was so unusual that the whole of Brahmpur had been buzzing about it for days. Mrs Rupa Mehra's father, who was supposed to be the host, had taken sudden umbrage a fortnight before the wedding, had locked up his house, and had disappeared. Mrs Rupa Mehra had been distraught. The Minister Sahib had stepped in ('Your honour is our honour'), and had insisted on putting on the wedding himself. As for the ensuing gossip, he ignored it.

There was no question of Mrs Rupa Mehra helping to pay for the wedding. The Minister Sahib would not hear of it. Nor had he at any time asked for any dowry. He was an old friend and bridge partner of Mrs Rupa Mehra's father and he had liked what he had seen of her daughter Savita (though he could never remember the girl's name). He was sympathetic to economic hardship, for he too had tasted it. During the several years he had spent in British jails during the struggle for Independence, there had been no one to run his farm or his cloth business. As a result very little income had come in, and his wife and family had struggled along with great difficulty.

Those unhappy times, however, were only a memory for the able, impatient, and powerful Minister. It was the early winter of 1950, and India had been free for over three years. But freedom for the country did not mean freedom for his younger son, Maan, who even now was being told by his father:

'What is good enough for your brother is good enough for you.'

'Yes, Baoji,' said Maan, smiling.

Mr Mahesh Kapoor frowned. His younger son, while succeeding to his own habit of fine dress, had not succeeded to his obsession with hard work. Nor did he appear to have any ambition to speak of.

'It is no use being a good-looking young wastrel forever,' said his father. 'And marriage will force you to settle down and take things seriously. I have written to the Banaras people, and I expect a favourable answer any day.'

Marriage was the last thing on Maan's mind; he had caught a friend's eye in the crowd and was waving at him. Hundreds of small coloured lights strung through the hedge came on all at once, and the silk saris and jewellery of the women glimmered and glinted even more brightly. The high, reedy shehnai music burst into a pattern of speed and brilliance. Maan was entranced. He noticed Lata making her way through the guests. Quite an attractive girl, Savita's sister, he thought. Not very tall and not very fair, but attractive, with an oval face, a shy light in her dark eyes and an affectionate manner towards the child she was leading by the hand.

'Yes, Baoji,' said Maan obediently.

'What did I say?' demanded his father.

'About marriage, Baoji,' said Maan.

'What about marriage?'

Maan was nonplussed.

'Don't you listen?' demanded Mahesh Kapoor, wanting

to twist Maan's ear. 'You are as bad as the clerks in the Revenue Department. You were not paying attention, you were waving at Firoz.'

Maan looked a little shamefaced. He knew what his father thought of him. But he had been enjoying himself until a couple of minutes ago, and it was just like Baoji to come and puncture his light spirits.

'So that's all fixed up,' continued his father. 'Don't tell me later that I didn't warn you. And don't get that weak-willed woman, your mother, to change her mind and come telling me that you aren't yet ready to take on the responsi-bilities of a man.'

'No, Baoji,' said Maan, getting the drift of things and looking a trifle glum.

'We chose well for Veena, we have chosen well for Pran, and you are not to complain about our choice of a bride for you.'

Maan said nothing. He was wondering how to repair the puncture. He had a bottle of Scotch upstairs in his room, and perhaps he and Firoz could escape for a few minutes before the ceremony – or even during it – for refreshment.

His father paused to smile brusquely at a few well-wishers, then turned to Maan again.

'I don't want to have to waste any more time with you today. God knows I have enough to do as it is. What has happened to Pran and that girl, what's her name? It's getting late. They were supposed to come out from opposite ends of the house and meet here for the jaymala five minutes ago.'

'Savita,' prompted Maan.

'Yes, yes,' said his father impatiently. 'Savita. Your superstitious mother will start panicking if they miss the correct configuration of the stars. Go and calm her down. Go! Do some good.'

And Mahesh Kapoor went back to his own duties as a host. He frowned impatiently at one of the officiating priests, who smiled weakly back. He narrowly avoided being butted in the stomach and knocked over by three children, offspring of his rural relatives, who were careering joyfully around the garden as if it were a field of stubble. And he greeted, before he had walked ten steps, a professor of literature (who could be useful for Pran's career); two influential members of the state legislature from the Congress Party (who might well agree to back him in his perennial power-struggle with the Home Minister); a judge, the very last Englishman to remain on the bench of the Brahmpur High Court after Independence; and his old friend the Nawab Sahib of Baitar, one of the largest landowners in the state.

1.3

LATA, who had heard a part of Maan's conversation with his father, could not help smiling to herself as she walked past.

'I see you're enjoying yourself,' said Maan to her in English.

His conversation with his father had been in Hindi, hers with her mother in English. Maan spoke both well.

Lata was struck shy, as she sometimes was with strangers, especially those who smiled as boldly as Maan. Let him do the smiling for both of us, she thought.

'Yes,' she said simply, her eyes resting on his face for just a second. Aparna tugged at her hand.

'Well, now, we're almost family,' said Maan, perhaps sensing her awkwardness. 'A few minutes more, and the ceremonies will start.'

'Yes,' agreed Lata, looking up at him again more confidently. She paused and frowned. 'My mother's concerned that they won't start on time.'

'So is my father,' said Maan.

Lata began smiling again, but when Maan asked her why she shook her head.

'Well,' said Maan, flicking a rose-petal off his beautiful tight white achkan, 'you're not laughing at me, are you?'

'I'm not laughing at all,' said Lata.

'Smiling, I meant.'

'No, not at you,' said Lata. 'At myself.'

'That's very mysterious,' said Maan. His good-natured face melted into an expression of exaggerated perplexity.

'It'll have to remain so, I'm afraid,' said Lata, almost laughing now. 'Aparna here wants her ice-cream, and I must supply it.'

'Try the pistachio ice-cream,' suggested Maan. His eyes followed her pink sari for a few seconds. Good-looking girl – in a way, he thought again. Pink's the wrong colour for her complexion, though. She should be dressed in deep green or dark blue . . . like that woman there. His attention veered to a new object of contemplation.

A few seconds later Lata bumped into her best friend, Malati, a medical student who shared her room at the student hostel. Malati was very outgoing and never lost her tongue with strangers. Strangers, however, blinking into her lovely green eyes, sometimes lost their tongues with her.

'Who was that Cad you were talking to?' she asked Lata eagerly.

This wasn't as bad as it sounded. A good-looking young man, in the slang of Brahmpur University girls, was a Cad. The term derived from Cadbury's chocolate.

'Oh, that's just Maan, he's Pran's younger brother.'

'Really! But he's so good-looking and Pran's so, well, not ugly, but, you know, dark, and nothing special.'

'Maybe he's a dark Cad,' suggested Lata. 'Bitter but sustaining.'

Malati considered this.

'And,' continued Lata, 'as my aunts have reminded me five times in the last hour, I'm not all that fair either, and will therefore find it impossible to get a suitable husband.'

'How can you put up with them, Lata?' asked Malati, who had been brought up, fatherless and brotherless, in a circle of very supportive women.

'Oh, I like most of them,' said Lata. 'And if it wasn't for this sort of speculation it wouldn't be much of a wedding for them. Once they see the bride and groom together, they'll have an even better time. Beauty and the Beast.'

'Well, he's looked rather beast-like whenever I've seen him on the university campus,' said Malati. 'Like a dark giraffe.'

'Don't be mean,' said Lata, laughing. 'Anyway, Pran's very popular as a lecturer,' she continued. 'And I like him. And you're going to have to visit me at his house once I leave the hostel and start living there. And since he'll be my brother-in-law you'll have to like him too. Promise me you will.'

'I won't,' said Malati firmly. 'He's taking you away from me.'

'He's doing nothing of the sort, Malati,' said Lata. 'My mother, with her fine sense of household economy, is dumping me on him.'

'Well, I don't see why you should obey your mother. Tell her you can't bear to be parted from me.'

'I always obey my mother,' said Lata. 'And besides, who will pay my hostel fees if she doesn't? And it will be very nice for me to live with Savita for a while. I refuse to lose you. You really must visit us – you must keep visiting us. If you don't, I'll know how much value to put on your friendship.'

Malati looked unhappy for a second or two, then recovered. 'Who's this?' she asked. Aparna was looking at her in a severe and uncompromising manner.

'My niece, Aparna,' said Lata. 'Say hello to Malati Aunty, Aparna.'

'Hello,' said Aparna, who had reached the end of her patience. 'Can I have a pistachio ice-cream, please?'

'Yes, kuchuk, of course, I'm sorry,' said Lata. 'Come, let's all go together and get some.'

1.4

LATA soon lost Malati to a clutch of college friends, but before she and Aparna could get much further, they were captured by Aparna's parents.

'So there you are, you precious little runaway,' said the resplendent Meenakshi, implanting a kiss on her daughter's forehead. 'Isn't she precious, Arun? Now where have you been, you precious truant?'

'I went to find Daadi,' began Aparna. 'And then I found her, but she had to go into the house because of Savita Bua, but I couldn't go with her, and then Lata Bua took me to have ice-cream, but we couldn't because –'

But Meenakshi had lost interest and had turned to Lata.

'That pink doesn't really suit you, Luts,' said Meenakshi. 'It lacks a certain – a certain –'

'Je ne sais quoi?' prompted a suave friend of her husband's, who was standing nearby.

'Thank you,' said Meenakshi, with such withering charm that the young fellow glided away for a while and pretended to stare at the stars.

'No, pink's just not right for you, Luts,' re-affirmed Meenakshi, stretching her long, tawny neck like a relaxed cat and appraising her sister-in-law.

She herself was wearing a green-and-gold sari of Banaras silk, with a green choli that exposed more of her midriff than Brahmpur society was normally privileged or prepared to see.

'Oh,' said Lata, suddenly self-conscious. She knew she didn't have much dress sense, and imagined she looked rather drab standing next to this bird-of-paradise.

'Who was that fellow you were talking to?' demanded her brother Arun, who, unlike his wife, had noticed Lata talking to Maan. Arun was twenty-five, a tall, fair, intelligent, pleasant-looking bully who kept his siblings in place by pummelling their egos. He was fond of reminding them that after their father's death, he was 'in a manner of speaking', in loco parentis to them.

'That was Maan, Pran's brother.'

'Ah.' The word spoke volumes of disapproval.

Arun and Meenakshi had arrived just this morning by overnight train from Calcutta, where Arun worked as one of the few Indian executives in the prestigious and largely white firm of Bentsen & Pryce. He had had neither the time nor the desire to acquaint himself with the Kapoor family – or clan, as he called it – with whom his mother had contrived a match for his sister. He cast his eyes balefully around. Typical of their type to overdo everything, he thought, looking at the coloured lights in the hedge. The crassness of the state politicians, white-capped and effusive, and of Mahesh Kapoor's contingent of rustic relatives excited his finely-tuned disdain. And the fact that neither the brigadier from the Brahmpur Cantonment nor the Brahmpur representatives of companies like Burmah Shell, Imperial Tobacco, and Caltex were represented in the crowd of invitees blinded his eyes to the presence of the larger part of the professional elite of Brahmpur.

'A bit of a bounder, I'd say,' said Arun, who had noticed Maan's eyes casually following Lata before he had turned them elsewhere.

Lata smiled, and her meek brother Varun, who was a nervous shadow to Arun and Meenakshi, smiled too in a kind of stifled complicity. Varun was studying – or trying to study mathematics at Calcutta University, and he lived with Arun and Meenakshi in their small ground-floor flat. He was thin, unsure of himself, sweet-natured and shifty-eyed; and he was Lata's favourite. Though he was a year older than her, she felt protective of him. Varun was terrified, in different ways, of both Arun and Meenakshi, and in some ways even of the precocious Aparna. His enjoyment of mathematics was mainly limited to the calculation of odds and handicaps on the racing form. In winter, as Varun's excitement rose with the racing season, so did his elder brother's ire. Arun was fond of calling him a bounder as well.

And what would you know about bounding, Arun Bhai? thought Lata to herself. Aloud she said: 'He seemed quite nice.'

'An Aunty we met called him a Cad,' contributed Aparna.

'Did she, precious?' said Meenakshi, interested. 'Do point him out to me, Arun.' But Maan was now nowhere to be seen.

'I blame myself to some extent,' said Arun in a voice which implied nothing of the sort; Arun was not capable of blaming himself for anything. 'I really should have done something,' he continued. 'If I hadn't been so tied up with work, I might have prevented this whole fiasco. But once Ma got it into her head that this Kapoor chap was suitable, it was impossible to dissuade her. It's impossible to talk reason with Ma; she just turns on the water-works.'

What had also helped deflect Arun's suspicions had been the fact that Dr Pran Kapoor taught English. And yet, to Arun's chagrin, there was hardly an English face in this whole provincial crowd.

'How fearfully dowdy!' said Meenakshi wearily to her-self, encapsulating her husband's thoughts. 'And how ut-terly unlike Calcutta. Precious, you have smut on your nose,' she added to Aparna, half looking around to tell an imaginary ayah to wipe it off with a handkerchief.

'I'm enjoying it here,' Varun ventured, seeing Lata look hurt. He knew that she liked Brahmpur, though it was clearly no metropolis.

'You be quiet,' snapped Arun brutally. His judgment was being challenged by his subordinate, and he would have none of it.

Varun struggled with himself; he glared, then looked down.

'Don't talk about what you don't understand,' added Arun, putting the boot in.

Varun glowered silently.

'Did you hear me?'

'Yes,' said Varun.

'Yes, what?'

'Yes, Arun Bhai,' muttered Varun.

This pulverization was standard fare for Varun, and Lata was not surprised by the exchange. But she felt very bad for him, and indignant with Arun. She could not understand either the pleasure or the purpose of it. She decided she would speak to Varun as soon after the wed-ding as possible to try to help him withstand – at least internally – such assaults upon his spirit. Even if I'm not very good at withstanding them myself, Lata thought.

'Well, Arun Bhai,' she said innocently, 'I suppose it's too late. We're all one big happy family now, and we'll have to put up with each other as well as we can.'

The phrase, however, was not innocent. 'One big happy family' was an ironically used Chatterji phrase. Meenakshi Mehra had been a Chatterji before she and Arun had met at a cocktail party, fallen in torrid, rapturous and elegant love, and got married within a month, to the shock of both families. Whether or not Mr Justice Chatterji of the Calcutta High Court and his wife were happy to welcome the non-Bengali Arun as the first appendage to their ring of five children (plus Cuddles the dog), and whether or not Mrs Rupa Mehra had been delighted at the thought of her first-born, the apple of her eye, marrying outside the khatri caste (and to a spoilt supersophisticate like Meenakshi at that), Arun certainly valued the Chatterji connection greatly. The Chatterjis had wealth and position and a grand Calcutta house where they threw enormous (but tasteful) parties. And even if the big happy family, especially Meenakshi's brothers and sisters, sometimes bothered him with their endless, unchokable wit and improvised rhyming couplets, he accepted it precisely because it appeared to him to be undeniably urbane. It was a far cry from this provincial capital, this Kapoor crowd and these garish light-in-the-hedge celebrations – with pomegranate juice in lieu of alcohol!

'What precisely do you mean by that?' demanded Arun of Lata. 'Do you think that if Daddy had been alive we would have married into this sort of a family?'

Arun hardly seemed to care that they might be overheard. Lata flushed. But the brutal point was well made. Had Raghubir Mehra not died in his forties but continued his meteoric rise in the Railway Service, he would – when the British left Indian government service in droves in 1947 – certainly have become a member of the Railway Board. His excellence and experience might even have made him the Chairman. The family would not have had to struggle, as it had had to for years and was still forced to, on Mrs Rupa Mehra's depleted savings, the kindness of friends and, lately, her elder son's salary. She would not have had to sell most of her jewellery and even their small house in Darjeeling to give her children the schooling which she felt that, above everything else, they must have. Beneath her pervasive sentimentality – and her attachment to the seemingly secure physical objects that reminded her of her beloved husband – lay a sense of sacrifice and a sense of values that determinedly melted them down into the insecure, intangible benefits of an excellent English-medium boarding-school education. And so Arun and Varun had continued to go to St George's School, and Savita and Lata had not been withdrawn from St Sophia's Convent.

The Kapoors might be all very well for Brahmpur society, thought Arun, but if Daddy had been alive, a constellation of brilliant matches would have been strewn at the feet of the Mehras. At least he, for one, had overcome their circumstances and done well in the way of in-laws. What possible comparison could there be between Pran's brother, that ogling fellow whom Lata had just been talking to – who ran, of all things, a cloth shop in Banaras, from what Arun had heard – and, say, Meenakshi's elder brother, who had been to Oxford, was studying law at Lincoln's Inn, and was, in addition, a published poet?

Arun's speculations were brought down to earth by his daughter, who threatened to scream if she didn't get her ice-cream. She knew from experience that screaming (or even the threat of it) worked wonders with her parents. And, after all, they sometimes screamed at each other, and often at the servants.

Lata looked guilty. 'It's my fault, darling,' she said to Aparna. 'Let's go at once before we get caught up in something else. But you mustn't cry or yell, promise me that. It won't work with me.'

Aparna, who knew it wouldn't, was silent.

But just at that moment the bridegroom emerged from one side of the house, dressed all in white, his dark, rather nervous face veiled with hanging strings of white flowers; everyone crowded forward towards the door from which the bride would emerge; and Aparna, lifted into her Lata Bua's arms, was forced to defer once again both treat and threat.

1.5

IT was a little untraditional, Lata couldn't help thinking, that Pran hadn't ridden up to the gate on a white horse with a little nephew sitting in front of him and with the groom's party in tow to claim his bride; but then Prem Nivas was the groom's house after all. And no doubt if he had followed the convention, Arun would have found further cause for mockery. As it was, Lata found it difficult to imagine the lecturer on Elizabethan Drama under that veil of tuberoses. He was now placing a garland of dark red, heavily fragrant roses around her sister Savita's neck – and Savita was doing the same to him. She looked lovely in her red-and-gold wedding sari, and quite subdued; Lata thought she might even have been crying. Her head was covered, and she looked down at the ground as her mother had doubtless instructed her to do. It was not proper, even when she was putting the garland round his neck, that she should look full in the face of the man with whom she was to live her life.

The welcoming ceremony completed, bride and groom moved together to the middle of the garden, where a small platform, decorated with more white flowers and open to the auspicious stars, had been erected. Here the priests, one from each family, and Mrs Rupa Mehra and the parents of the groom sat around the small fire that would be the witness of their vows.

Mrs Rupa Mehra's brother, whom the family very rarely met, had earlier in the day taken charge of the bangle ceremony. Arun was annoyed that he had not been allowed to take charge of anything. He had suggested to his mother after the crisis brought on by his grandfather's inexplicable actions, that they should move the wedding to Calcutta. But it was too late for that, and she would not hear of it.

Now that the exchange of garlands was over, the crowd paid no great attention to the actual wedding rites. These would go on for the better part of an hour while the guests milled and chattered round the lawns of Prem Nivas. They laughed; they shook hands or folded them to their foreheads; they coalesced into little knots, the men here, the women there; they warmed themselves at the charcoal-filled clay stoves placed strategically around the garden while their frosted, gossip-laden breath rose into the air; they admired the multicoloured lights; they smiled for the photographer as he murmured 'Steady, please!' in English; they breathed deeply the scent of flowers and perfume and cooked spices; they exchanged births and deaths and politics and scandal under the brightly-coloured cloth canopy at the back of the garden beneath which long tables of food had been laid out; they sat down exhaustedly on chairs with their plates full and tucked in inexhaustibly. Servants, some in white livery, some in khaki, brought around fruit juice and tea and coffee and snacks to those who were standing in the garden: samosas, kachauris, laddus, gulab-jamuns, barfis and gajak and ice-cream were consumed and replenished along with puris and six kinds of vegetables. Friends who had not met each other for months fell upon each other with loud cries, relatives who met only at weddings and funerals embraced tearfully and exchanged the latest news of third cousins thrice removed. Lata's aunt from Kanpur, horrified by the complexion of the groom, was talking to an aunt from Lucknow about 'Rupa's black grandchildren', as if they already existed. They made much of Aparna, who was obviously going to be Rupa's last fair grandchild, and praised her even when she spooned pistachio ice-cream down the front of her pale yellow cashmere sweater. The barbaric children from rustic Rudhia ran around yelling as if they were playing pitthu on the farm. And though the plaintive, festive music of the shehnai had now ceased, a happy babble of convivial

18

voices rose to the skies and quite drowned out the irrelevant chant of the ceremonies.

Lata, however, stood close by and watched with an attentive mixture of fascination and dismay. The two bare-chested priests, one very fat and one fairly thin, both apparently immune to the cold, were locked in mildly insistent competition as to who knew a more elaborate form of the service. So, while the stars stayed their courses in order to keep the auspicious time in abeyance, the Sanskrit wound interminably on. Even the groom's parents were asked by the fat priest to repeat something after him. Mahesh Kapoor's eyebrows were quivering; he was about to blow his rather short fuse.

Lata tried to imagine what Savita was thinking. How could she have agreed to get married without knowing this man? Kind-hearted and accommodating though she was, she did have views of her own. Lata loved her deeply and admired her generous, even temper; the evenness was certainly a contrast to her own erratic swings of mood. Savita was free from any vanity about her fresh and lovely looks; but didn't she rebel against the fact that Pran would fail the most lenient test of glamour? Did Savita really accept that Mother knew best? It was difficult to speak to Savita, or sometimes even to guess what she was thinking. Since Lata had gone to college, it was Malati rather than her sister who had become her confidante. And Malati, she knew, would never have agreed to be married off in this summary manner by all the mothers in the world conjoined.

In a few minutes Savita would relinquish even her name to Pran. She would no longer be a Mehra, like the rest of them, but a Kapoor. Arun, thank God, had never had to do that. Lata tried 'Savita Kapoor' on her tongue, and did not like it at all.

The smoke from the fire – or possibly the pollen from the flowers – was beginning to bother Pran, and he coughed a little, covering his mouth with his hand. His mother said something to him in a low voice. Savita too looked up at him very quickly, with a glance, Lata thought, of gentle concern. Savita, it was true, would have been concerned about anyone who was suffering from anything; but there was a special tenderness here that irritated and confused Lata. Savita had only met this man for an hour! And now he was returning her affectionate look. It was too much.

Lata forgot that she had been defending Pran to Malati just a short while ago, and began to discover things to irritate herself with.

'Prem Nivas' for a start: the abode of love. An idiotic name, thought Lata crossly, for this house of arranged marriages. And a needlessly grandiloquent one: as if it were the centre of the universe and felt obliged to make a philosophical statement about it. And the scene, looked at objectively, was absurd: seven living people, none of them stupid, sitting around a fire intoning a dead language that only three of them understood. And yet, Lata thought, her mind wandering from one thing to another, perhaps this little fire was indeed the centre of the universe. For here it burned, in the middle of this fragrant garden, itself in the heart of Pasand Bagh, the pleasantest locality of Brahmpur, which was the capital of the state of Purva Pradesh, which lay in the centre of the Gangetic plains, which was itself the heartland of India ... and so on through the galaxies to the outer limits of perception and knowledge. The thought did not seem in the least trite to Lata; it helped her control her irritation at, indeed resentment of Pran.

'Speak up! Speak up! If your mother had mumbled like you, we would never have got married.'

Mahesh Kapoor had turned impatiently towards his dumpy little wife, who became even more tongue-tied as a result.

Pran turned and smiled encouragingly at his mother, and quickly rose again in Lata's estimation.

Mahesh Kapoor frowned, but held his peace for a few minutes, after which he burst out, this time to the family priest:

'Is this mumbo-jumbo going to go on for ever?'

The priest said something soothing in Sanskrit, as if

blessing Mahesh Kapoor, who felt obliged to lapse into an irked silence. He was irritated for several reasons, one of which was the distinct and unwelcome sight of his arch political rival, the Home Minister, deep in conversation with the large and venerable Chief Minister S.S. Sharma. What could they be plotting? he thought. My stupid wife insisted on inviting Agarwal because our daughters are friends, even though she knew it would sour things for me. And now the Chief Minister is talking to him as if no one else exists. And in my garden!

His other major irritation was directed at Mrs Rupa Mehra. Mahesh Kapoor, once he had taken over the arrangements, had set his heart on inviting a beautiful and renowned singer of ghazals to perform at Prem Nivas, as was the tradition whenever anyone in his family got married. But Mrs Rupa Mehra, though she was not even paying for the wedding, had put her foot down. She could not have 'that sort of person' singing love-lyrics at the wedding of her daughter. 'That sort of person' meant both a Muslim and a courtesan.

Mahesh Kapoor muffed his responses, and the priest repeated them gently.

'Yes, yes, go on, go on,' said Mahesh Kapoor. He glowered at the fire.

But now Savita was being given away by her mother with a handful of rose-petals, and all three women were in tears.

Really! thought Mahesh Kapoor. They'll douse the flames. He looked in exasperation at the main culprit, whose sobs were the most obstreperous.

But Mrs Rupa Mehra was not even bothering to tuck her handkerchief back into her blouse. Her eyes were red and her nose and cheeks were flushed with weeping. She was thinking back to her own wedding. The scent of 4711 eau-de-Cologne brought back unbearably happy memories of her late husband. Then she thought downwards one generation to her beloved Savita who would soon be walking around this fire with Pran to begin her own married life. May it be a longer one than mine, prayed Mrs

Rupa Mehra. May she wear this very sari to her own daughter's wedding.

She also thought upwards a generation to her father, and this brought on a fresh gush of tears. What the septuagenarian radiologist Dr Kishen Chand Seth had taken offence at, no one knew: probably something said or done by his friend Mahesh Kapoor, but quite possibly by his own daughter; no one could tell for sure. Apart from repudiating his duties as a host, he had chosen not even to attend his granddaughter's wedding, and had gone furiously off to Delhi 'for a conference of cardiologists', as he claimed. He had taken with him the insufferable Parvati, his thirty-five-year-old second wife, who was ten years younger than Mrs Rupa Mehra herself.

It was also possible, though this did not cross his daughter's mind, that Dr Kishen Chand Seth would have gone mad at the wedding had he attended it, and had in fact fled from that specific eventuality. Short and trim though he had always been, he was enormously fond of food; but owing to a digestive disorder combined with diabetes his diet was now confined to boiled eggs, weak tea, lemon squash, and arrowroot biscuits.

I don't care who stares at me, I have plenty of reasons to cry, said Mrs Rupa Mehra to herself defiantly. I am so happy and heartbroken today. But her heartbreak lasted only a few minutes more. The groom and bride walked around the fire seven times, Savita keeping her head meekly down, her eyelashes wet with tears; and Pran and she were man and wife.

After a few concluding words by the priests, everyone rose. The newly-weds were escorted to a flower-shrouded bench near a sweet-smelling, rough-leafed harsingar tree in white and orange bloom; and congratulations fell on them and their parents and all the Mehras and Kapoors present as copiously as those delicate flowers fall to the ground at dawn.

Mrs Rupa Mehra's joy was unconfined. She gobbled the congratulations down like forbidden gulab-jamuns. She looked a little speculatively at her younger daughter, who appeared to be laughing at her from a distance. Or was she laughing at her sister? Well, she would find out soon enough what the happy tears of matrimony were all about!

Pran's much-shouted-at mother, subdued yet happy, after blessing her son and daughter-in-law, and failing to see her younger son Maan anywhere, had gone over to her daughter Veena. Veena embraced her; Mrs Mahesh Kapoor, temporarily overcome, said nothing, but sobbed and smiled simultaneously. The dreaded Home Minister and his daughter Priya joined them for a few minutes, and in return for their congratulations, Mrs Mahesh Kapoor had a few kind words to say to each of them. Priya, who was married and virtually immured by her in-laws in a house in the old, cramped part of Brahmpur, said, rather wistfully, that the garden looked beautiful. And it was true, thought Mrs Mahesh Kapoor with quiet pride: the garden was indeed looking beautiful. The grass was rich, the gardenias were creamy and fragrant, and a few chrysanthemums and roses were already in bloom. And though she could take no credit for the sudden, prolific blossoming of the harsingar tree, that was surely the grace of the gods whose prized and contested possession, in mythical times, it used to be.

1.6

HER lord and master the Minister of Revenue was meanwhile accepting congratulations from the Chief Minister of Purva Pradesh, Shri S.S. Sharma. Sharmaji was rather a hulking man with a perceptible limp and an unconscious and slight vibration of the head, which was exacerbated when, as now, he had had a long day. He ran the state with a mixture of guile, charisma and benevolence. Delhi was far away and rarely interested in his legislative and administrative fief. Though he was uncommunicative about his discussion with his Home Minister, he was nevertheless in good spirits.

Noticing the rowdy kids from Rudhia, he said in his slightly nasal voice to Mahesh Kapoor:

'So you're cultivating a rural constituency for the coming elections?'

Mahesh Kapoor smiled. Ever since 1937 he had stood from the same urban constituency in the heart of Old Brahmpur – a constituency that included much of Misri Mandi, the home of the shoe trade of the city. Despite his farm and his knowledge of rural affairs – he was the prime mover of a bill to abolish large and unproductive landholdings in the state – it was unimaginable that he would desert his electoral home and choose to contest from a rural constituency. By way of answer, he indicated his garments; the handsome black achkan he was wearing, the tight off-white pyjamas, and the brilliantly embroidered white jutis with their up-turned toes would present an incongruous picture in a rice field.

'Why, nothing is impossible in politics,' said Sharmaji slowly. 'After your Zamindari Abolition Bill goes through, you will become a hero throughout the countryside. If you chose, you could become Chief Minister. Why not?' said Sharmaji generously and warily. He looked around, and his eye fell on the Nawab Sahib of Baitar, who was stroking his beard and looking around perplexedly. 'Of course, you might lose a friend or two in the process,' he added.

Mahesh Kapoor, who had followed his glance without turning his head, said quietly: 'There are zamindars and zamindars. Not all of them tie their friendship to their land. The Nawab Sahib knows that I am acting out of principle.' He paused, and continued: 'Some of my own relatives in Rudhia stand to lose their land.'

The Chief Minister nodded at the sermon, then rubbed his hands, which were cold. 'Well, he is a good man,' he said indulgently. 'And so was his father,' he added.

Mahesh Kapoor was silent. The one thing Sharmaji could not be called was rash; and yet here was a rash statement if ever there was one. It was well known that the Nawab Sahib's father, the late Nawab Sahib of Baitar, had been an active member of the Muslim League; and though he had not lived to see the birth of Pakistan, that above all was what he had dedicated his life to.

The tall, grey-bearded Nawab Sahib, noticing four eyes on him, gravely raised his cupped hand to his forehead in polite salutation, then tilted his head sideways with a quiet smile, as if to congratulate his old friend.

'You haven't seen Firoz and Imtiaz anywhere, have you?' he asked Mahesh Kapoor, after walking slowly over.

'No, no — but I haven't seen my son either, so I assume....'

The Nawab Sahib raised his hands slightly, palms forward, in a gesture of helplessness.

After a while he said: 'So Pran is married, and Maan is next. I would imagine you will find him a little less tractable.'

'Well, tractable or not, there are some people in Banaras I have been talking to,' said Mahesh Kapoor in a determined tone. 'Maan has met the father. He's also in the cloth business. We're making enquiries. Let's see. And what about your twins? A joint wedding to two sisters?'

'Let's see, let's see,' said the Nawab Sahib, thinking rather sadly about his wife, buried these many years; 'Inshallah, all of them will settle down soon enough.'

1.7

'TO the law,' said Maan, raising his third glass of Scotch to Firoz, who was sitting on his bed with a glass of his own. Imtiaz was lounging in a stuffed chair and examining the bottle.

'Thank you,' said Firoz. 'But not to new laws, I hope.'

'Oh, don't worry, don't worry, my father's bill will never pass,' said Maan. 'And even if it does, you'll be much richer than me. Look at me,' he added, gloomily. 'I have to work for a living.'

Since Firoz was a lawyer and his brother a doctor, it was

not as if they fitted the popular mould of the idle sons of aristocracy.

'And soon,' went on Maan, 'if my father has his way, I'll have to work on behalf of two people. And later for more. Oh God!'

'What – your father isn't getting you married off, is he?' asked Firoz, halfway between a smile and a frown.

'Well, the buffer zone disappeared tonight,' said Maan disconsolately. 'Have another.'

'No, no thanks, I still have plenty,' said Firoz. Firoz enjoyed his drink, but with a slightly guilty feeling; his father would approve even less than Maan's. 'So when's the happy hour?' he added uncertainly.

'God knows. It's at the enquiry stage,' said Maan.

'At the first reading,' Imtiaz added.

For some reason, this delighted Maan. 'At the first reading!' he repeated. 'Well, let's hope it never gets to the third reading! And, even if it does, that the President withholds his assent!'

He laughed and took a couple of long swigs 'And what about your marriage?' he demanded of Firoz.

Firoz looked a little evasively around the room. I˙ was as bare and functional as most of the rooms in Prem Nivas – which looked as if they expected the imminent arrival of a herd of constituents. 'My marriage!' he said with a laugh.

Maan nodded vigorously.

'Change the subject,' said Firoz.

'Why, if you were to go into the garden instead of drinking here in seclusion –'

'It's hardly seclusion.'

'Don't interrupt,' said Maan, throwing an arm around him. 'If you were to go down into the garden, a good-looking, elegant fellow like you, you would be surrounded within seconds by eligible young beauties. And ineligible ones too. They'd cling to you like bees to a lotus. Curly locks, curly locks, will you be mine?'

Firoz flushed. 'You've got the simile slightly wrong,' he said. 'Men are bees, women lotuses.'

Maan quoted a couplet from an Urdu ghazal to the

effect that the hunter could turn into the hunted, and Imtiaz laughed.

'Shut up, both of you,' said Firoz, attempting to appear more annoyed than he was; he had had enough of this sort of nonsense. 'I'm going down. Abba will be wondering where on earth we've got to. And so will your father. And besides, we ought to find out if your brother is formally married yet – and whether you really do now have a beautiful sister-in-law to scold you and curb your excesses.'

'All right, all right, we'll all go down,' said Maan genially. 'Maybe some of the bees will cling to us too. And if we get stung to the heart, Doctor Sahib here can cure us. Can't you, Imtiaz? All you would have to do would be to apply a rose-petal to the wound, isn't that so?'

'As long as there are no contra-indications,' said Imtiaz seriously.

'No contra-indications,' said Maan, laughing as he led the way down the stairs.

'You may laugh,' said Imtiaz. 'But some people are allergic even to rose-petals. Talking of which, you have one sticking to your cap.'

'Do I?' asked Maan. 'These things float down from nowhere.'

'So they do,' said Firoz, who was walking down just behind him. He gently brushed it away.

1.8

BECAUSE the Nawab Sahib had been looking somewhat lost without his sons, Mahesh Kapoor's daughter Veena had drawn him into her family circle. She asked him about his eldest child, his daughter Zainab, who was a childhood friend of hers but who, after her marriage, had disappeared into the world of purdah. The old man talked about her rather guardedly, but about her two children with transparent delight. His grandchildren were the only two beings in the world who had the right to interrupt him when he was studying in his library. But now the great yellow ancestral mansion of Baitar House, just a few minutes' walk from Prem Nivas, was somewhat run down, and the library too had suffered. 'Silverfish, you know,' said the Nawab Sahib. 'And I need help with cataloguing. It's a gigantic task, and in some ways not very heartening. Some of the early editions of Ghalib can't be traced now; and some valuable manuscripts by our own poet Mast. My brother never made a list of what he took with him to Pakistan....'

At the word Pakistan, Veena's mother-in-law, withered old Mrs Tandon, flinched. Three years ago, her whole family had had to flee the blood and flames and unforgettable terror of Lahore. They had been wealthy, 'propertied' people, but almost everything they had owned was lost, and they had been lucky to escape with their lives. Her son Kedarnath, Veena's husband, still had scars on his hands from an attack by rioters on his refugee convoy. Several of their friends had been butchered.

The young, old Mrs Tandon thought bitterly, are very resilient: her grandchild Bhaskar had of course only been six at the time; but even Veena and Kedarnath had not let those events embitter their lives. They had returned here to Veena's hometown, and Kedarnath had set himself up in a small way in – of all polluting, carcass-tainted things – the shoe trade. For old Mrs Tandon, the descent from a decent prosperity could not have been more painful. She had been willing to tolerate talking to the Nawab Sahib though he was a Muslim, but when he mentioned comings and goings from Pakistan, it was too much for her imagination. She felt ill. The pleasant chatter of the garden in Brahmpur was amplified into the cries of the blood-mad mobs on the streets of Lahore, the lights into fire. Daily, sometimes hourly, in her imagination she returned to what she still thought of as her city and her home. It had been beautiful before it had become so suddenly hideous; it had appeared completely secure so shortly before it was lost for ever.

The Nawab Sahib did not notice that anything was the matter, but Veena did, and quickly changed the subject even at the cost of appearing rude. 'Where's Bhaskar?' she asked her husband.

'I don't know. I think I saw him near the food, the little frog,' said Kedarnath.

'I wish you wouldn't call him that,' said Veena. 'He is your son. It's not auspicious....'

'It's not my name for him, it's Maan's,' said Kedarnath with a smile. He enjoyed being mildly henpecked. 'But I'll call him whatever you want me to.'

Veena led her mother-in-law away. And to distract the old lady she did in fact get involved in looking for her son. Finally they found Bhaskar. He was not eating anything but simply standing under the great multicoloured cloth canopy that covered the food tables, gazing upwards with pleased and abstract wonderment at the elaborate geometrical patterns – red rhombuses, green trapeziums, yellow squares and blue triangles – from which it had been stitched together.

1.9

THE crowds had thinned; the guests, some chewing paan, were departing at the gate; a heap of gifts had grown by the side of the bench where Pran and Savita had been sitting. Finally only they and a few members of the family were left – and the yawning servants who would put away the more valuable furniture for the night, or pack the gifts in a trunk under the watchful eye of Mrs Rupa Mehra.

The bride and groom were lost in their thoughts. They avoided looking at each other now. They would spend the night in a carefully prepared room in Prem Nivas, and leave for a week's honeymoon in Simla tomorrow.

Lata tried to imagine the nuptial room. Presumably it would be fragrant with tuberoses; that, at least, was Malati's confident opinion. I'll always associate tuberoses with Pran, Lata thought. It was not at all pleasant to follow her imagination further. That Savita would be sleeping with Pran tonight did not bear thinking of. It did not strike her as being at all romantic. Perhaps they would be too exhausted, she thought optimistically.

'What are you thinking of, Lata?' asked her mother.

'Oh, nothing, Ma,' said Lata automatically.

'You turned up your nose. I saw it.'

Lata blushed.

'I don't think I ever want to get married,' she said emphatically.

Mrs Rupa Mehra was too wearied by the wedding, too exhausted by emotion, too softened by Sanskrit, too cumbered with congratulations, too overwrought, in short, to do anything but stare at Lata for ten seconds. What on earth had got into the girl? What was good enough for her mother and her mother's mother and her mother's mother's mother should be good enough for her. Lata, though, had always been a difficult one, with a strange will of her own, quiet but unpredictable – like that time in St Sophia's when she had wanted to become a nun! But Mrs Rupa Mehra too had a will, and she was determined to have her own way, even if she was under no illusions as to Lata's pliability.

And yet, Lata was named after that most pliable thing, a vine, which was trained to cling: first to her family, then to her husband. Indeed, when she was a baby, Lata's fingers had had a strong and coiling grasp which even now came back with a sweet vividness to her mother. Suddenly Mrs Rupa Mehra burst out with the inspired remark:

'Lata, you are a vine, you must cling to your husband!'

It was not a success.

'Cling?' said Lata. 'Cling?' The word was pronounced with such quiet scorn that her mother could not help bursting into tears. How terrible it was to have an ungrateful daughter. And how unpredictable a baby could be.

Now that the tears were running down her cheeks, Mrs Rupa Mehra transferred them fluidly from one daughter to the other. She clasped Savita to her bosom and wept loudly. 'You must write to me, Savita darling,' she said. 'You must write to me every day from Simla. Pran, you are like my own son now, you must be responsible and see to it. Soon I will be all alone in Calcutta – all alone.'

This was of course quite untrue. Arun and Varun and Meenakshi and Aparna would all be crowded together with her in Arun's little flat in Sunny Park. But Mrs Rupa Mehra was one who believed with unformulated but absolute conviction in the paramountcy of subjective over objective truth.

1.10

THE tonga clip-clopped along the road, and the tonga-wallah sang out:

'A heart was shattered into bits – and one fell here, and one fell there. . . .'

Varun started to hum along, then sang louder, then suddenly stopped.

'Oh, don't stop,' said Malati, nudging Lata gently. 'You have a nice voice. Like a bulbul.'

'In a china-china-shop,' she whispered to Lata.

'Heh, heh, heh.' Varun's laugh was nervous. Realizing that it sounded weak, he tried to make it slightly sinister. But it didn't work. He felt miserable. And Malati, with her green eyes and sarcasm – for it had to be sarcasm – wasn't helping.

The tonga was quite crowded: Varun was sitting with young Bhaskar in the front, next to the tonga-wallah; and back-to-back with them sat Lata and Malati – both dressed in salwaar-kameez – and Aparna in her ice-cream-stained sweater and a frock. It was a sunny winter morning.

The white-turbaned old tonga-wallah enjoyed driving furiously through this part of town with its broad, relatively uncrowded streets – unlike the cramped madness of Old Brahmpur. He started talking to his horse, urging her on.

Malati now began to sing the words of the popular film song herself. She hadn't meant to discourage Varun. It was pleasant to think of shattered hearts on a cloudless morning.

Varun didn't join in. But after a while he took his life in his hands and said, turning around:

'You have a – a wonderful voice.'

It was true. Malati loved music, and studied classical singing under Ustad Majeed Khan, one of the finest singers in north India. She had even got Lata interested in Indian classical music during the time they had lived together in the student hostel. As a result, Lata often found herself humming some tune or other in one of her favourite raags.

Malati did not disclaim Varun's compliment.

'Do you think so?' she said, turning around to look deeply into his eyes. 'You are very sweet to say so.'

Varun blushed to the depths of his soul and was speechless for a few minutes. But as they passed the Brahmpur Race-course, he gripped the tonga-wallah's arm and cried:

'Stop!'

'What's the matter?' asked Lata.

'Oh – nothing – nothing – if we're in a hurry, let's go on. Yes, let's go on.'

'Of course we're not, Varun Bhai,' she said. 'We're only going to the zoo. Let's stop if you want.'

After they had got down, Varun, almost uncontrollably excited, wandered to the white palings and stared through.

'It's the only anti-clockwise race-course in India other than Lucknow,' he breathed, almost to himself, awe-struck. 'They say it's based on the Derby,' he added to young Bhaskar, who happened to be standing next to him.

'But what's the difference?' asked Bhaskar. 'The distance is the same, isn't it, whether you run clockwise or anti-clockwise?'

Varun paid no attention to Bhaskar's question. He had started walking slowly, dreamily, by himself, anti-clockwise along the fence. He was almost pawing the earth.

Lata caught up with him: 'Varun Bhai?' she said.

'Er – yes? Yes?'

'About yesterday evening.'

'Yesterday evening?' Varun dragged himself back to the two-legged world. 'What happened?'

'Our sister got married.'

'Ah. Oh. Yes, yes, I know. Savita,' he added, hoping to imply alertness by specificity.

'Well,' said Lata, 'don't let yourself be bullied by Arun Bhai. Just don't.' She stopped smiling, and looked at him as a shadow crossed his face. 'I really hate it, Varun Bhai, I really hate seeing him bully you. I don't mean that you should cheek him or answer back or anything, just that you shouldn't let it hurt you the way that – well, that I can see it does.'

'No, no –' he said, uncertainly.

'Just because he's a few years older doesn't make him your father and teacher and sergeant-major all rolled into one.'

Varun nodded unhappily. He was too well aware that while he lived in his elder brother's house he was subject to his elder brother's will.

'Anyway, I think you should be more confident,' continued Lata. 'Arun Bhai tries to crush everyone around him like a steamroller, and it's up to us to remove our egos from his path. I have a hard enough time, and I'm not even in Calcutta. I just thought I'd say so now, because at the house I'll hardly get the chance to talk to you alone. And tomorrow you'll be gone.'

Lata spoke from experience, as Varun well knew. Arun, when angry, hardly cared what he said. When Lata had taken it into her head to become a nun – a foolish, adolescent notion, but her own – Arun, exasperated with the lack of success of his bludgeoning attempts at dissuasion, had said: 'All right, go ahead, become a nun, ruin your life, no one would have married you anyway, you look just like the Bible – flat in front and flat at the back.' Lata thanked God that she wasn't studying at Calcutta University; for most of the year at least, she was outside the range of Arun's blunderbuss. Even though those words were no longer true, the memory of them still stung.

'I wish you were in Calcutta,' said Varun.

'Surely you must have some friends –' said Lata.

'Well, in the evening Arun Bhai and Meenakshi Bhabhi are often out and I have to mind Aparna,' said Varun, smiling weakly. 'Not that I mind,' he added.

'Varun, this won't do,' said Lata. She placed her hand firmly on his slouching shoulder and said: 'I want you to go out with your friends – with people you really like and who like you – for at least two evenings a week. Pretend you have to attend a coaching session or something.' Lata didn't care for deception, and she didn't know whether Varun would be any good at it, but she didn't want things to continue as they were. She was worried about Varun. He had looked even more jittery at the wedding than when she had seen him a few months previously.

A train hooted suddenly from alarmingly close, and the tonga horse shied.

'How amazing,' said Varun to himself, all thoughts of everything else obliterated.

He patted the horse when they got back into the tonga.

'How far is the station from here?' he asked the tonga-wallah.

'Oh, it's just over there,' said the tonga-wallah, indicating vaguely the built-up area beyond the well-laid-out gardens of the race-course. 'Not far from the zoo.'

I wonder if it gives the local horses an advantage, Varun said to himself. Would the others tend to bolt? What difference would it make to the odds?

1.11

WHEN they got to the zoo, Bhaskar and Aparna joined forces and asked to ride on the children's railway, which, Bhaskar noted, also went around anti-clockwise. Lata and Malati wanted a walk after the tonga ride, but they were overruled. All five of them sat in a small, post-box-red compartment, squashed together and facing each other this time, while the little green steam engine puffed along on its one-foot-wide track. Varun sat opposite Malati, their knees

34

almost touching. Malati enjoyed the fun of this, but Varun was so disconcerted that he looked desperately around at the giraffes, and even stared attentively at the crowds of schoolchildren, some of whom were licking huge bobbins of pink spun candy. Aparna's eyes began to shine with anticipation.

Since Bhaskar was nine, and Aparna a third of his age, they did not have much to say to each other. They attached themselves to their most-favoured adults. Aparna, brought up by her socialite parents with alternating indulgence and irritation, found Lata reassuringly certain in her affection. In Lata's company she behaved in a less brat-like manner. Bhaskar and Varun got on famously once Bhaskar succeeded in getting him to concentrate. They discussed mathematics, with special reference to racing odds.

They saw the elephant, the camel, the emu, the common bat, the brown pelican, the red fox, and all the big cats. They even saw a smaller one, the black-spotted leopard-cat, as he paced frenziedly across the floor of his cage.

But the best stop of all was the reptile house. Both children were eager to see the snake pit, which was full of fairly sluggish pythons, and the glass cases with their deadly vipers and kraits and cobras. And also, of course, the cold, corrugated crocodiles onto whose backs some schoolchildren and visiting villagers were throwing coins – while others, as the white, serrated mouths opened lazily far below, leaned over the railings and pointed and squealed and shuddered. Luckily Varun had a taste for the sinister, and took the kids inside. Lata and Malati refused to go in.

'I see enough horrifying things as a medical student,' said Malati.

'I wish you wouldn't tease Varun,' said Lata after a while.

'Oh, I wasn't teasing him,' said Malati. 'Just listening to him attentively. It's good for him.' She laughed.

'Mm – you make him nervous.'

'You're very protective of your elder brother.'

'He's not – oh, I see – yes, my younger elder brother.

35

Well, since I don't have a younger brother, I suppose I've given him the part. But seriously, Malati, I am worried about him. And so is my mother. We don't know what he's going to do when he graduates in a few months. He hasn't shown much aptitude for anything. And Arun bullies him fearfully. I wish some nice girl would take him in charge.'

'And I'm not the one? I must say, he has a certain feeble charm. Heh, heh!' Malati imitated Varun's laugh.

'Don't be facetious, Malati. I don't know about Varun, but my mother would have a fit,' said Lata.

This was certainly true. Even though it was an impossible proposition geographically, the very thought of it would have given Mrs Rupa Mehra nightmares. Malati Trivedi, apart from being one of a small handful of girls among the almost five hundred boys at the Prince of Wales Medical College, was notorious for her outspoken views, her participation in the activities of the Socialist Party, and her love affairs – though not with any of those five hundred boys, whom, by and large, she treated with contempt.

'Your mother likes me, I can tell,' said Malati.

'That's beside the point,' said Lata. 'And actually, I'm quite amazed that she does. She usually judges things by influences. I would have thought you're a bad influence on me.'

But this was not entirely true, even from Mrs Rupa Mehra's viewpoint. Malati had certainly given Lata more confidence than she had had when she had emerged wet-feathered from St Sophia's. And Malati had succeeded in getting Lata to enjoy Indian classical music, which (unlike ghazals) Mrs Rupa Mehra approved of. That they should have become room-mates at all was because the government medical college (usually referred to by its royal title) had no provision for housing its small contingent of women and had persuaded the university to accommodate them in its hostels.

Malati was charming, dressed conservatively but attractively, and could talk to Mrs Rupa Mehra about everything from religious fasts to cooking to genealogy, matters that her own westernized children showed very little interest in. She was also fair, an enormous plus in Mrs Rupa Mehra's subconscious calculus. Mrs Rupa Mehra was convinced that Malati Trivedi, with her dangerously attractive greenish eyes, must have Kashmiri or Sindhi blood in her. So far, however, she had not discovered any.

Though they did not often talk about it, the bond of paternal loss also tied Lata and Malati together.

Malati had lost her adored father, a surgeon from Agra, when she was eight. He had been a successful and handsome man with a wide acquaintance and a varied history of work: he had been attached to the army for a while and had gone to Afghanistan; he had taught in Lucknow at the medical college; he had also been in private practice. At the time of his death, although he had not been very good at saving money, he had owned a fair amount of property – largely in the form of houses. Every five years or so he would uproot himself and move to another town in U.P. – Meerut, Bareilly, Lucknow, Agra. Wherever he lived he built a new house, but without disposing of the old ones. When he died, Malati's mother went into what seemed like an irreversible depression, and remained in that state for two years.

Then she pulled herself together. She had a large family to take care of, and it was essential that she think of things in a practical way. She was a very simple, idealistic, upright woman, and she was concerned more with what was right than with what was convenient or approved of or monetarily beneficial. It was in that light that she was determined to bring up her family.

And what a family! – almost all girls. The eldest was a proper tomboy, sixteen years old when her father died, and already married to a rural landlord's son; she lived about twenty miles away from Agra in a huge house with twenty servants, lichi orchards, and endless fields, but even after her marriage she joined her sisters in Agra for months at a time. This daughter had been followed by two sons, but they had both died in childhood, one aged five, the other three. The boys had been followed by Malati herself, who was eight years younger than her sister. She also grew up as a sort of boy – though not by any means like the tomboy her sister was – for a variety of reasons connected with her infancy: the direct gaze in her unusual eyes, her boyish look, the fact that the boys' clothes were at hand, the sadness that her parents had experienced at the death of their two sons. After Malati came three girls, one after another; then another boy; and then her father died.

Malati had therefore been brought up almost entirely among women; even her little brother had been like a little sister; he had been too young to be treated as anything different. (After a while, perhaps out of perplexity, he had gone the way of his brothers.) The girls grew up in an atmosphere where men came to be seen as exploitative and threatening; many of the men Malati came into contact with were precisely that. No one could touch the memory of her father. Malati was determined to become a doctor like him, and never allowed his instruments to rust. She intended one day to use them.

Who were these men? One was the cousin who did them out of many of the things that her father had collected and used, but which were lying in storage after his death. Malati's mother had cleared out what she had seen as inessentials from their life. It was not necessary now to have two kitchens, one European and one Indian. The china and fine cutlery for western food was put away, together with a great deal of furniture, in a garage. The cousin came, got the keys from the grieving widow, told her he would manage matters, and cleaned out whatever had been stored. Malati's mother never saw a rupee of the proceeds. 'Well,' she had said philosophically, 'at least my sins have lessened.'

Another was the servant who acted as an intermediary for the sale of the houses. He would contact property agents or other prospective buyers in the towns where the houses were located, and make deals with them. He had something of a reputation as a cheat.

Yet another was her father's younger brother, who still lived in the Lucknow house, with his wife downstairs and a dancing girl upstairs. He would happily have cheated them, if he had been able to, over the sale of that house. He needed money to spend on the dancing girl.

Then there was the young – well, twenty-six-year-old – but rather sleazy college teacher who had lived downstairs in a rented room when Malati was fifteen or so. Malati's mother wanted her to learn English, and had no compunction, no matter what the neighbours said (and they said a great deal, not much of it charitable) about sending Malati to learn from him – though he was a bachelor. Perhaps in this case the neighbours were right. He very soon fell madly in love with Malati, and requested her mother for permission to marry her. When Malati was asked by her mother for her views on the matter, she was amazed and shocked, and refused point-blank.

At the medical college in Brahmpur, and before that, when she had studied Intermediate Science in Agra, Malati had had a lot to put up with: teasing, gossip, the pulling of the light chunni around her neck, and remarks such as 'She wants to be a boy.' This was very far from the truth. The remarks were unbearable and only diminished when, provoked by one boy beyond endurance, she had slapped his face hard in front of his friends.

Men fell for her at a rapid rate, but she saw them as beneath her attention. It was not as if she truly hated men; most of the time she didn't. It was just that her standards were too high. No one came near the image she and her sisters had of their father, and most men struck her as being immature. Besides, marriage was a distraction for someone who had set her sights upon the career of medicine, and she was not enormously concerned if she never got married.

She over-filled the unforgiving minute. As a girl of twelve or thirteen, she had been a loner, even in her crowded family. She loved reading, and people knew better than to talk to her when she had a book in her hands. When this happened, her mother did not insist that she help with cooking and housework. 'Malati's reading,' was enough for people to avoid the room where she lay or sat crouched, for she would pounce angrily on anyone who dared disturb her. Sometimes she would actually hide from people, seeking out a corner where no one would be likely to find her. They got the message soon enough. As the years passed, she guided the education of her younger sisters. Her elder sister, the tomboy, guided them all – or, rather, bossed them around – in other matters.

Malati's mother was remarkable in that she wished her daughters to be independent. She wanted them, apart from their schooling at a Hindi medium school, to learn music and dancing and languages (and especially to be good at English); and if this meant that they had to go to someone's house to learn what was needed, they would go – regardless of what people said. If a tutor had to be called to the house of the six women, he would be called. Young men would look up in fascination at the first floor of the house, as they heard five girls singing along undemurely together. If the girls wanted ice-cream as a special treat, they would be allowed to go to the shop by themselves and eat it. When neighbours objected to the shamelessness of letting young girls go around by themselves in Agra, they were allowed occasionally to go to the shop after dark instead – which, presumably, was worse, though less detectable. Malati's mother made it clear to the girls that she would give them the best education possible, but that they would have to find their own husbands.

Soon after she came to Brahmpur, Malati fell in love with a married musician, who was a socialist. She remained involved with the Socialist Party even when their affair ended. Then she had another rather unhappy love affair. At the moment she was unattached.

Though full of energy most of the time, Malati would fall ill every few months or so, and her mother would come down from Agra to Brahmpur to cure her of the evil eye, an influence that lay outside the province of western medicine. Because Malati had such remarkable eyes herself, she was a special target of the evil eye.

A dirty, grey, pink-legged crane surveyed Malati and Lata with its small, intense red eyes; then a grey film blinked sideways across each eyeball, and it walked carefully away.

'Let's surprise the kids by buying some of that spun candy for them,' said Lata as a vendor went past. 'I wonder what's keeping them. What's the matter, Malati? What are you thinking of?'

'Love,' said Malati.

'Oh, love, what a boring subject,' said Lata. 'I'll never fall in love. I know you do from time to time. But –' She lapsed into silence, thinking once again, with some distaste, of Savita and Pran, who had left for Simla. Presumably they would return from the hills deeply in love. It was intolerable.

'Well, sex then.'

'Oh please, Malati,' said Lata looking around quickly. 'I'm not interested in that either,' she added, blushing.

'Well, marriage then. I'm wondering whom you'll get married to. Your mother will get you married off within a year, I'm sure of it. And like an obedient little mouse, you'll obey her.'

'Quite right,' said Lata.

This rather annoyed Malati, who bent down and plucked three narcissi growing immediately in front of a sign that read, *Do not pluck the flowers*. One she kept, and two she handed to Lata, who felt very awkward holding such illegally gotten gains. Then Malati bought five sticks of flossy pink candy, handed four to Lata to hold with her two narcissi, and began to eat the fifth.

Lata started to laugh.

'And what will happen then to your plan to teach in a small school for poor children?' demanded Malati.

'Look, here they come,' said Lata.

Aparna was looking petrified and holding Varun's hand tightly. For a few minutes they all ate their candy, walking towards the exit. At the turnstile a ragged urchin looked longingly at them, and Lata quickly gave him a small coin. He had been on the point of begging, but hadn't yet done so, and looked astonished.

One of her narcissi went into the horse's mane. The

41

tonga-wallah again began to sing of his shattered heart. This time they all joined in. Passers-by turned their heads as the tonga trotted past.

The crocodiles had had a liberating effect on Varun. But when they got back to Pran's house on the university campus, where Arun and Meenakshi and Mrs Rupa Mehra were staying, he had to face the consequences of returning an hour late. Aparna's mother and grandmother were looking anxious.

'You damn irresponsible fool,' said Arun, dressing him down in front of everyone. 'You, as the man, are in charge, and if you say twelve-thirty, it had better be twelve-thirty, especially since you have my daughter with you. And my sister. I don't want to hear any excuses. You damned idiot.' He was furious. 'And you —' he added to Lata, 'you should have known better than to let him lose track of the time. You know what he's like.'

Varun bowed his head and looked shiftily at his feet. He was thinking how satisfying it would be to feed his elder brother, head first, to the largest of the crocodiles.

1.12

ONE of the reasons why Lata was studying in Brahmpur was because this was where her grandfather, Dr Kishen Chand Seth, lived. He had promised his daughter Rupa when Lata first came to study here that he would take very good care of her. But this had never happened. Dr Kishen Chand Seth was far too preoccupied either with bridge at the Subzipore Club or feuds with the likes of the Minister of Revenue or passion for his young wife Parvati to be capable of fulfilling any guardian-like role towards Lata. Since it was from his grandfather that Arun had inherited his atrocious temper, perhaps this was, all in all, not a bad thing. At any rate, Lata did not mind living in the university dormitory. Far better for her studies, she thought, than under the wing of her irascible Nana.

Just after Raghubir Mehra had died, Mrs Rupa Mehra

and her family had gone to live with her father, who at that stage had not yet remarried. Given her straitened finances, this seemed to be the only thing to do; she also thought that he might be lonely, and hoped to help him with his household affairs. The experiment had lasted a few months, and had been a disaster. Dr Kishen Chand Seth was an impossible man to live with. Tiny though he was, he was a force to reckon with not only at the medical college, from which he had retired as Principal, but in Brahmpur at large: everyone was scared of him and obeyed him tremblingly. He expected his home life to run on similar lines. He overrode Rupa Mehra's writ with respect to her own children. He left home suddenly for weeks on end without leaving money or instructions for the staff. Finally, he accused his daughter, whose good looks had survived her widowhood, of making eyes at his colleagues when he invited them home – a shocking accusation for the heartbroken though sociable Rupa.

The teenaged Arun had threatened to beat up his grandfather. There had been tears and yells and Dr Kishen Chand Seth had pounded the floor with his stick. Then Mrs Rupa Mehra had left, weeping and determined, with her brood of four, and had sought refuge with sympathetic friends in Darjeeling.

Reconciliation had been effected a year later in a renewed bout of weeping. Since then things had jolted along. The marriage with Parvati (which had shocked not just his family but Brahmpur at large because of the disparity of age), Lata's enrolment at Brahmpur University, Savita's engagement (which Dr Kishen Chand Seth had helped arrange), Savita's wedding (which he had almost wrecked and from which he had wilfully absented himself): all these were landmarks along an extremely bumpy road. But family was family, and, as Mrs Rupa Mehra continually told herself, one had to take the rough with the smooth.

Several months had now passed since Savita's wedding. Winter had gone and the pythons in the zoo had emerged from hibernation. Roses had replaced narcissi, and had been replaced in their turn by the purple-wreath creeper, whose five-bladed flowers helicoptered gently to the ground in the hot breeze. The broad, silty-brown Ganga, flowing due east past the ugly chimneys of the tannery and the marble edifice of the Barsaat Mahal, past Old Brahmpur with its crowded bazaars and alleys, temples and mosques, past the bathing ghats and the cremation ghat and the Brahmpur Fort, past the whitewashed pillars of the Subzipore Club and the spacious estate of the university, had shrunken with the summer, but boats and steamers still plied busily up and down its length, as did trains along the parallel railway line that bounded Brahmpur to the south.

Lata had left the hostel and had gone to live with Savita and Pran, who had descended from Simla to the plains very much in love. Malati visited Lata often, and had grown to like the lanky Pran, of whom she had formed such an unfavourable first impression. Lata too liked his decent, affectionate ways, and was not too upset to learn that Savita was pregnant. Mrs Rupa Mehra wrote long letters to her daughters from Arun's flat in Calcutta, and complained repeatedly that no one replied to her letters either soon enough or often enough.

Though she did not mention this in any of her letters for fear of enraging her daughter, Mrs Rupa Mehra had tried – without success – to find a match for Lata in Calcutta. Perhaps she had not made enough effort, she told herself: she was, after all, still recovering from the excitement and exertion of Savita's wedding. But now at last she was going back to Brahmpur for a three-month stint at what she had begun to call her second home: her daughter's home, not her father's. As the train puffed along towards Brahmpur, the propitious city which had yielded her one son-in-law already, Mrs Rupa Mehra promised herself that she would make another attempt. Within a day or two of her arrival she would go to her father for advice.

1.13

IN the event, it was not necessary to go to Dr Kishen Chand Seth for advice. He drove to the university the next day in a fury and arrived at Pran Kapoor's house.

It was three in the afternoon, and hot. Pran was at the department. Lata was attending a lecture on the Metaphysical Poets. Savita had gone shopping. Mansoor, the young servant, tried to soothe Dr Kishen Chand Seth by offering him tea, coffee or fresh lime juice. All this was brushed brusquely aside.

'Is anyone at home? Where is everyone?' asked Dr Kishen Chand Seth in a rage. His short, compressed and very jowly appearance made him look a little like a fierce and wrinkled Tibetan watchdog. (Mrs Rupa Mehra's good looks had been the gift of her mother.) He carried a carved Kashmiri cane which he used more for emphasis than for support. Mansoor hurried inside.

'Burri Memsahib?' he called, knocking at the door of Mrs Rupa Mehra's room.

'What? . . . Who?'

'Burri Memsahib, your father is here.'

'Oh. Oh.' Mrs Rupa Mehra, who had been enjoying an afternoon nap, woke into a nightmare. 'Tell him I will be with him immediately, and offer him some tea.'

'Yes, Memsahib.'

Mansoor entered the drawing room. Dr Seth was staring at an ashtray.

'Well? Are you dumb as well as half-witted?' asked Dr Kishen Chand Seth.

'She's just coming, Sahib.'

'Who's just coming? Fool!'

'Burri Memsahib, Sahib. She was resting.'

That Rupa, his mere chit of a daughter, could ever somehow have been elevated into not just a Memsahib but a Burri Memsahib puzzled and annoyed Dr Seth.

Mansoor said, 'Will you have some tea, Sahib? Or coffee?'

'Just now you offered me nimbu pani.'

'Yes, Sahib.'

'A glass of nimbu pani.'

'Yes, Sahib. At once.' Mansoor made to go.

'And oh –'

'Yes, Sahib?'

'Are there any arrowroot biscuits in this house?'

'I think so, Sahib.'

Mansoor went into the back garden to pluck a couple of limes, then returned to the kitchen to squeeze them into juice.

Dr Kishen Chand Seth picked up a day-old *Statesman* in preference to that day's *Brahmpur Chronicle*, and sat down to read in an armchair. Everyone was half-witted in this house.

Mrs Rupa Mehra dressed hurriedly in a black and white cotton sari and emerged from her room. She entered the drawing room, and began to apologize.

'Oh, stop it, stop it, stop all this nonsense,' said Dr Kishen Chand Seth impatiently in Hindi.

'Yes, Baoji.'

'After waiting for a week I decided to visit you. What kind of daughter are you?'

'A week?' said Mrs Rupa Mehra palely.

'Yes, yes, a week. You heard me, Burri Memsahib.'

Mrs Rupa Mehra didn't know which was worse, her father's anger or his sarcasm.

'But I only arrived from Calcutta yesterday.'

Her father seemed ready to explode at this patent fiction when Mansoor came in with the nimbu pani and a plate of arrowroot biscuits. He noticed the expression on Dr Seth's face and stood hesitantly by the door.

'Yes, yes, put it down here, what are you waiting for?'

Mansoor set the tray down on a small glass-topped table and turned to leave. Dr Seth took a sip and bellowed in fury –

'Scoundrel!'

Mansoor turned, trembling. He was only sixteen, and was standing in for his father, who had taken a short leave. None of his teachers during his five years at a village school had inspired in him such erratic terror as Burri Memsahib's crazy father.

'You rogue – do you want to poison me?'

'No, Sahib.'

'What have you given me?'

'Nimbu pani, Sahib.'

Dr Seth, jowls shaking, looked closely at Mansoor. Was he trying to cheek him?

'Of course it's nimbu pani. Did you think I thought it was whisky?'

'Sahib.' Mansoor was nonplussed.

'What have you put in it?'

'Sugar, Sahib.'

'You buffoon! I have my nimbu pani made with salt, not sugar,' roared Dr Kishen Chand Seth. 'Sugar is poison for me. I have diabetes, like your Burri Memsahib. How many times have I told you that?'

Mansoor was tempted to reply, 'Never,' but thought better of it. Usually Dr Seth had tea, and he brought the milk and sugar separately.

Dr Kishen Chand Seth rapped his stick on the floor. 'Go. Why are you staring at me like an owl?'

'Yes, Sahib. I'll make another glass.'

'Leave it. No. Yes – make another glass.'

'With salt, Sahib.' Mansoor ventured to smile. He had quite a nice smile.

'What are you laughing at like a donkey?' asked Dr Seth. 'With salt, of course.'

'Yes, Sahib.'

'And, idiot –'

'Yes, Sahib?'

'With pepper too.'

'Yes, Sahib.'

Dr Kishen Chand Seth veered around towards his daughter. She wilted before him.

'What kind of daughter do I have?' he asked rhetorically. Rupa Mehra waited for the answer, and it was not long in coming. 'Ungrateful!' Her father bit into an arrowroot biscuit for emphasis. 'Soggy!' he added in disgust.

Mrs Rupa Mehra knew better than to protest.

Dr Kishen Chand Seth went on:

'You have been back from Calcutta for a week and you haven't visited me once. Is it me you hate so much or your stepmother?'

Since her stepmother, Parvati, was considerably younger than herself, Mrs Rupa Mehra found it very difficult to think of her other than as her father's nurse and, later, mistress. Though fastidious, Mrs Rupa Mehra did not entirely resent Parvati. Her father had been lonely for three decades after her mother had died. Parvati was good to him and (she supposed) good for him. Anyway, thought Mrs Rupa Mehra, this is the way things happen in the world. It is best to be on good terms with everyone.

'But I only arrived here yesterday,' she said. She had told him so a minute ago, but he evidently did not believe her.

'Hunh!' said Dr Seth dismissively.

'By the Brahmpur Mail.'

'You wrote in your letter that you would be coming last week.'

'But I couldn't get reservations, Baoji, so I decided to stay in Calcutta another week.' This was true, but the pleasure of spending time with her three-year-old granddaughter Aparna had also been a factor in her delay.

'Have you heard of telegrams?'

'I thought of sending you one, Baoji, but I didn't think it was so important. Then, the expense. . . .'

'Ever since you became a Mehra you have become completely evasive.'

This was an unkind cut, and could not fail to wound. Mrs Rupa Mehra bowed her head.

'Here. Have a biscuit,' said her father in a conciliatory manner.

Mrs Rupa Mehra shook her head.

'Eat, fool!' said her father with rough affection. 'Or are you still keeping those brainless fasts that are so bad for your health?'

'It is Ekadashi today.' Mrs Rupa Mehra fasted on the eleventh day of each lunar fortnight in memory of her husband.

'I don't care if it's ten Ekadashis,' said her father with some heat. 'Ever since you came under the influence of the Mehras you have become as religious as your ill-fated mother. There have been too many mismatched marriages in this family.'

The combination of these two sentences, loosely coupled in several possible wounding interpretations, was too much for Mrs Rupa Mehra. Her nose began to redden. Her husband's family was no more religious than it was evasive. Raghubir's brothers and sisters had taken her to their heart in a manner both affecting and comforting to a sixteen-year-old bride, and still, eight years after her husband's death, she visited as many of them as possible in the course of what her children called her Annual Trans-India Rail-Pilgrimage. If she was growing to be 'as religious as her mother' (which she was not – at least not yet), the operative influence was probably the obvious one: that of her mother, who had died in the post-First-World-War influenza epidemic, when Rupa was very young. A faded image now came before her eyes: the soft spirit of Dr Kishen Chand Seth's first wife could not have been more distant from his own freethinking, allopathic soul. His comment about mismatched marriages injured the memory of two loved ghosts, and was possibly even intended as an insult to the asthmatic Pran.

'Oh don't be so sensitive!' said Dr Kishen Chand Seth brutally. Most women, he had decided, spent two-thirds of their time weeping and whimpering. What good did they think it did? As an afterthought he added, 'You should get Lata married off soon.'

Mrs Rupa Mehra's head jerked up. 'Oh? Do you think so?' she said. Her father seemed even more full of surprises than usual.

'Yes. She must be nearly twenty. Far too late. Parvati got married when she was in her thirties, and see what she got. A suitable boy must be found for Lata.'

'Yes, yes, I was just thinking the same,' said Mrs Rupa Mehra. 'But I don't know what Lata will say.'

Dr Kishen Chand Seth frowned at this irrelevance.

'And where will I find a suitable boy?' she continued. 'We were lucky with Savita.'

'Lucky – nothing! I made the introduction. Is she preg-

49

nant? No one tells me anything,' said Dr Kishen Chand Seth.

'Yes, Baoji.'

Dr Seth paused to interpret the yes. Then he said: 'It's about time. I hope I get a great-grandson this time.' He paused again. 'How is she?'

'Well, a bit of morning sickness,' began Mrs Rupa Mehra.

'No, idiot, I mean my great-granddaughter, Arun's child,' said Dr Kishen Chand Seth impatiently.

'Oh, Aparna? She's very sweet. She's grown very attached to me,' said Mrs Rupa Mehra happily. 'Arun and Meenakshi send their love.'

This seemed to satisfy Dr Seth for the moment, and he bit his arrowroot biscuit carefully. 'Soft,' he complained. 'Soft.'

Things had to be just so for her father, Mrs Rupa Mehra knew. When she was a child she had not been allowed to drink water with her meals. Each morsel had to be chewed twenty-four times to aid digestion. For a man so particular about, indeed so fond of, his food, it was sad to see him reduced to biscuits and boiled eggs.

'I'll see what I can do for Lata,' her father went on. 'There's a young radiologist at the Prince of Wales. I can't remember his name. If we had thought about it earlier and used our imaginations we could have captured Pran's younger brother and had a double wedding. But now they say he's got engaged to that Banaras girl. Perhaps that is just as well,' he added, remembering that he was supposed to be feuding with the Minister.

'But you can't go now, Baoji. Everyone will be back soon,' protested Mrs Rupa Mehra.

'Can't? Can't? Where is everyone when I want them?' retorted Dr Kishen Chand Seth. He clicked his tongue impatiently. 'Don't forget your stepmother's birthday next week,' he added as he walked to the door.

Mrs Rupa Mehra looked wistfully and worriedly from the doorway at her father's back. On the way to his car he paused by a bed of red and yellow cannas in Pran's front garden, and she noticed him get more and more agitated. Bureaucratic flowers (among which he also classified marigolds, bougainvillaea and petunias) infuriated him. He had banned them at the Prince of Wales Medical College as long as he had wielded supreme power there; now they were making a comeback. With one swipe of his Kashmiri walking-stick he lopped off the head of a yellow canna. As his daughter tremblingly watched, he got into his ancient grey Buick. This noble machine, a Raja among the rabble of Austins and Morrises that plied the Indian roads, was still slightly dented from the time when, ten years ago, Arun (on a visit during his vacation from St George's) had taken it for a catastrophic joyride. Arun was the only one in the family who could defy his grandfather and get away with it, indeed was loved the more for it. As Dr Kishen Chand Seth drove off, he told himself that this had been a satisfying visit. It had given him something to think about, something to plan.

Mrs Rupa Mehra took a few moments to recover from her father's bracing company. Suddenly realizing how hungry she was, she began to think of her sunset meal. She could not break her fast with grain, so young Mansoor was dispatched to the market to buy some raw bananas to make into cutlets. As he went through the kitchen to get the bicycle key and the shopping bag, he passed by the counter, and noticed the rejected glass of nimbu pani: cool, sour, inviting.

He swiftly gulped it down.

1.14

EVERYONE who knew Mrs Rupa Mehra knew how much she loved roses and, particularly, pictures of roses, and therefore most of the birthday cards she received featured roses of various colours and sizes, and various degrees of copiousness and blatancy. This afternoon, sitting with her reading-glasses on at the desk in the room she shared with Lata, she was going through old cards for a practical purpose, although the project threatened to overwhelm her with its resonances of ancient sentiment. Red roses, yellow roses, even a blue rose here and there combined themselves with ribbons, pictures of kittens and one of a guilty-looking puppy. Apples and grapes and roses in a basket; sheep in a field with a foreground of roses; roses in a misty pewter mug with a bowl of strawberries resting nearby; violet-flushed roses graced with unrose-like, unserrated leaves and mild, even inviting, green thorns: birthday cards from family, friends and assorted well-wishers all over India, and even some from abroad – everything reminded her of everything, as her elder son was apt to remark.

Mrs Rupa Mehra glanced in a cursory manner over her piles of old New Year cards before returning to the birth-day roses. She took out a small pair of scissors from the recesses of her great black handbag, and tried to decide which card she would have to sacrifice. It was very rarely that Mrs Rupa Mehra bought a card for anyone, no matter how close or dear the person was. The habit of necessary thrift had sunk deep into her mind, but eight years of the deprivation of small luxuries could not reduce for her the sanctity of the birthday greeting. She could not afford cards, so she made them. In fact she enjoyed the creative challenge of making them. Scraps of cardboard, shreds of ribbon, lengths of coloured paper, little silver stars and adhesive golden numerals lay in a variegated trove at the bottom of the largest of her three suitcases, and these were now pressed into service. The scissors poised, descended. Three silver stars were parted from their fellows and pasted (with the help of borrowed glue – this was the only constituent Mrs Rupa Mehra did not, for fear of leakage, carry with her) onto three corners of the front of the folded blank white piece of cardboard. The fourth corner, the northwest corner, could contain two golden numerals indicating the age of the recipient.

But now Mrs Rupa Mehra paused – for surely the age of the recipient would be an ambivalent detail in the present case. Her stepmother, as she could never cease to remem-ber, was fully ten years younger than she was, and the accusing '35', even – or perhaps especially – in gold, could be seen – would be seen – as implying an unacceptable disparity, possibly even an unacceptable motivation. The golden numerals were put aside, and a fourth silver star joined its fellows in a pattern of innocuous symmetry.

Postponing the decision of illustration, Mrs Rupa Mehra now looked for assistance in building up a rhyming text for her card. The rose-and-pewter card contained the following lines:

> May the gladness you have scattered
>   Along life's shining way
> And the little deeds of kindness
>   That are yours from day to day
> And the happiness you've showered
>   On others all life through
> Return to swell your blessings
>   In this birthday hour for you.

This would not do for Parvati, Mrs Rupa Mehra decided. She turned to the card illustrated with grapes and apples.

> 'Tis a day for hugs and kisses,
>   For cakes and candles too,
> A day for all who love you
>   To renew their love anew,
> A day for sweet reflection
>   Along life's shining way,
> And a day for all to tell you:
>   Have the wonderfullest day.

This showed promise but there was something wrong with the fourth line, Mrs Rupa Mehra instinctively felt. Also, she would have to alter 'hugs and kisses' to 'special greetings'; Parvati might very well deserve hugs and kisses but Mrs Rupa Mehra was incapable of giving them to her.

Who had sent her this card? Queenie and Pussy Kapadia, two unmarried sisters in their forties whom she had not met for years. Unmarried! The very word was like a knell.

Mrs Rupa Mehra paused in her thoughts for a moment, and moved resolutely on.

The puppy yapped an unrhymed and therefore unusable text – a mere 'Happy Birthday and Many Happy Returns' – but the sheep bleated in rhymes identical to, but sentiment marginally distinct from, the others:

> It's not a standard greeting
>> For just one joyful day
> But a wish that's meant to cover
>> Life's bright and shining way –
> To wish you all the special things
>> That mean the most to you
> So that this year and every year
>> Your fondest dreams come true.

Yes! Life's shining way, a concept dear to Mrs Rupa Mehra, was here polished to an even finer lustre. Nor did the lines commit her to any deep protestation of affection for her father's second wife. At the same time the greeting was not accusably distant. She got out her black and gold Mont Blanc fountain pen, Raghubir's present to her when Arun was born – twenty-five years old and still going strong, she reflected with a sad smile – and began to write.

Mrs Rupa Mehra's handwriting was very small and well-formed, and this presented her in the present instance with a problem. She had chosen too large a size of card in proportion to her affection, but the silver stars had been stuck and it was too late to change that parameter. She now wished to fill as much space as possible with the rhymed message so that she would not have to inscribe more than a few words in her own right to supplement the verse. The first three couplets were therefore laid out – with as much white space in between as would not appear too obvious – on the left hand side; an ellipsis of seven dots spoored across the page in a semblance of suspense; and the concluding couplet was allowed to crash down with thunderous blandness on the right.

'To dear Parvati – a very happy birthday, much love,

54

Rupa,' wrote Mrs Rupa Mehra with a dutiful expression. Then, repenting, she added 'est' to the 'Dear'. It looked a little cramped now, but only a careful eye would perceive it as an afterthought.

Now came the heartbreaking part: not the mere transcription of a stanza but the actual sacrifice of an old card. Which of the roses would have to be transplanted? After some thought, Mrs Rupa Mehra decided that she could not bear to part with any of them. The dog, then? He looked mournful, even guilty – besides, the picture of a dog, however appealing his appearance, was open to misinterpretation. The sheep perhaps – yes, they would do. They were fluffy and unemotional. She did not mind parting with them. Mrs Rupa Mehra was a vegetarian, whereas both her father and Parvati were avid meat-eaters. The roses in the foreground of the old card were preserved for future use, and the three sheared sheep were driven carefully towards new pastures.

Before she sealed the envelope Mrs Rupa Mehra got out a small writing pad, and wrote a few lines to her father:

Dearest Baoji,

Words cannot express how much happiness it gave me to see you yesterday. Pran and Savita and Lata were very disappointed. They did not get the chance to be there, but such is life. About the radiologist, or any other prospect for Lata, please pursue enquiries. A good khatri boy would be best of course, but after Arun's marriage I am capable of considering others. Fair or dark, as you know, one cannot be choosy. I have recovered from my journey and remain, with much affection,

Your everloving daughter,
Rupa

The house was quiet. She asked Mansoor for a cup of tea, and decided to write a letter to Arun. She unfolded a green inland letter form, dated it carefully in her minute and lucid script, and began.

*

My darling Arun,

I hope you are feeling much better and the pain in your back as well as the toothache is much less. I was very sad and upset in Calcutta as we did not have much time to spend at the station together due to the traffic on Strand and Howrah Bridge and you having to leave before the train left because Meenakshi wanted you home early. You don't know how very much you are in my thoughts – much more than words can say. I thought maybe the preparations for the party could have been postponed by ten minutes but it was not to be. Meenakshi knows best. Anyway whatever it all was the net result was that we didn't have long at the station and tears rolled down my cheeks due to disappointment. My dear Varun also had to go back because he came in your car to see me off. Such is life one doesn't often get the things one wants. Now I only pray for you to get well soon and keep good health wherever you are and have no more trouble with your back so that you can play golf again which you are so fond of. If it be God's will we will meet again very soon. I love you lots and wish you all the happiness and success you well deserve. Your Daddy would have been so proud to see you in Bentsen and Pryce, and now with wife and child. Love and kisses to darling Aparna.

The journey passed peacefully and as planned, but I must admit I could not resist having some mihidana at Burdwan. If you had been there you would have scolded me, but I could not resist my sweet tooth. The ladies in my Ladies' Reserve compartment were very friendly and we played rummy and three-two-five and had a good chat. One of the ladies knew the Miss Pal we used to visit in Darjeeling, the one who was engaged to the army captain but he died in the War. I had the set of cards that Varun gave me for my last birthday in my bag, and they helped to while away the journey. Whenever I travel I remember our saloon days with your Daddy. Please give him my love and tell him to study hard in the good traditions of his father.

Savita is looking very well, and Pran is a first-class husband except for his asthma and most caring. I think that he is having some difficulty with his department but he does not like to talk about it. Your grandfather visited yesterday and could have given him some medical advice but unfortunately only I was at home. By the way it is the birthday of your step-grandmother next week, and maybe you should send her a card. Better late than sorry.

I am suffering some pain in my foot but that is expected. Monsoons will be here in two three months and then my joints will play up. Unfortunately Pran cannot afford a car on his lecturer's salary and the transport situation is not good. I take a bus or tonga to go here and there and sometimes I walk. As you know, the Ganges is not far from the house and Lata also goes walking quite a lot, she seems to enjoy it. It is quite safe as far as the dhobi-ghat near the university, though there is a bit of a monkey menace.

Has Meenakshi had Daddy's gold medals set yet? I like the idea of a neck-pendant for one and the lid of a little cardamom-container for the other. That way you can read what is written on both sides of the medal.

Now Arun mine, do not be cross with me for what I am saying, but I have been thinking a lot about Lata lately, and I think you should build up her confidence which she is lacking despite her brilliant record of studies. She is quite afraid of your comments, sometimes even I am afraid of them. I know you do not mean to be harsh, but she is a sensitive girl and now that she is of marriageable age she is super-sensitive. I am going to write to Mr Gaur's daughter Kalpana in Delhi – she knows everyone, and may help us find a suitable match for Lata. Also I think it is time for you to help in the matter. I could see how busy you were with work, so I mentioned it very rarely when I was in Calcutta but it was always on my mind. Another covenanted boy from a good family, does not have to be khatri, would be a dream come true. Now that the college year is almost over Lata will have time. I may have many faults but I think I am a loving mother, and I long to see all my children well settled.

Soon it will be April and I am afraid I will again be very depressed and lonely at heart because that month will bring back memories of your father's illness and death as if they happened only the other day and it is eight long years that have gone by and so much has happened under the bridge in this period. I know there are thousands who have had and are having much more to suffer but to every human being one's own sufferings seem the most and I am still very much human and have not risen very much above the usual feelings of sorrow and disappointments. I am trying very hard though believe me to rise above all this, and (D.V.) I will.

Here the inland letter form ended, and Mrs Rupa Mehra began to fill in – transversely – the space left blank near the head of the letter:

Anyway space is short so my darling Arun I will end now. Do not worry at all about me, my blood sugar level is OK I am sure, Pran is making me go for a test at the university clinic tomorrow morning, and I have been careful about my diet except for one glass of very sweet nimbu pani when I arrived tired after my journey.

Here she went on to write on the non-adhesive flap:

After I have written to Kalpana I will play a game of patience with Varun's cards. Lots and lots of love to you and to Varun and a big hug and lots of kisses to my little sweetheart Aparna, and of course to Meenakshi also.

Yours everloving,
Ma

Fearing that her pen might run out during the course of her next letter, Mrs Rupa Mehra opened her handbag and took out an already opened bottle of ink – Parker's Quink Royal Washable Blue – effectively separated from the other contents of the handbag by several layers of rags and cellophane. A bottle of glue she habitually carried had once leaked from its slit rubber cap with disastrous consequences, and glue had thenceforth been banished from her handbag, but ink had so far caused her only minor problems.

Mrs Rupa Mehra took out another inland letter form, then decided that this would be a false economy in the present case, and began writing on a well-husbanded pad of cream-coloured cambric bond:

Dearest Kalpana,

You have always been like a daughter to me so I will speak from the heart. You know how worried I have been about Lata this last year or so. As you know, since your Uncle Raghubir died I have had a hard time in many ways, and your father – who was so close to Uncle during his lifetime – has been as good to me after his sad demise. Whenever I come to Delhi which is sadly not often of late I feel happy when I am with you, despite the jackals that bark all night behind your house, and since your dear mother passed away I have felt like a mother to you.

Now the time has come to get Lata well settled, and I must look all out for a suitable boy. Arun should shoulder some responsibility in the matter but you know how it is, he is so occupied with work and family. Varun is too young to help and is quite unsteady also. You my dear Kalpana are a few years older to Lata and I hope you can suggest some suitable names among your old college friends or others in Delhi. Maybe in October in the Divali holidays – or in December in the Christmas-New Year holidays – Lata and I can come to Delhi to look into things? I only mention this to mention it. Do please say what you think?

How is your dear father? I am writing from Brahmpur where I am staying with Savita and Pran. All is well but the heat is already very delapidating and I am dreading April-May-June. I wish you could have come to their wedding but what with Pimmy's appendix operation I can understand. I was worried to know she had not been well. I hope it is all resolved now. I am in good health and my blood sugar is fine. I have taken your advice and had new glasses made and can read and write without strain.

Please write soonest to this address. I will be here throughout March and April, maybe even in May till Lata's results for this year are out.

With fondest love,
Yours ever,
Ma (Mrs Rupa Mehra)

P.S. Lata sometimes comes up with the idea that she will not get married. I hope you will cure her of such theories. I know how you feel about early marriage after what happened with your engagement, but in a different way I also feel that 'tis better to have loved and lost etc. Not that love is always an unmixed blessing.

P.S. Divali would be better than New Year for us to come to Delhi, because it fits in better with my annual travel plans, but whichever time you say is fine.

Lovingly, Ma

Mrs Rupa Mehra looked over her letter (and her signature – she insisted on all young people calling her Ma), folded it neatly in four, and sealed it in a matching envelope. She fished out a stamp from her bag, licked it thoughtfully, stuck it on the envelope, and wrote Kalpana's address (from memory) as well as Pran's address on the back. Then she closed her eyes and sat perfectly still for a few minutes. It was a warm afternoon. After a while she took out the pack of playing cards from her bag. When Mansoor came in to take away the tea and to do the accounts, he found she had dozed off over a game of patience.

THE IMPERIAL BOOK DEPOT was one of the two best book-shops in town, and was located on Nabiganj, the fashion-able street that was the last bulwark of modernity before the labyrinthine alleys and ancient, cluttered neighbour-hoods of Old Brahmpur. Though it was a couple of miles away from the university proper it had a greater following among students and teachers than the University and Allied Bookshop, which was just a few minutes away from campus. The Imperial Book Depot was run by two broth-ers, Yashwant and Balwant, both almost illiterate in Eng-lish, but both (despite their prosperous roundness) so ener-getic and entrepreneurial that it apparently made no differ-ence. They had the best stock in town, and were extremely helpful to their customers. If a book was not available in the shop, they asked the customer himself to write down its name on the appropriate order form.

Twice a week an impoverished university student was paid to sort new arrivals onto the designated shelves. And since the bookshop prided itself on its academic as well as general stock, the proprietors unashamedly collared univer-sity teachers who wandered in to browse, sat them down with a cup of tea and a couple of publishers' lists, and made them tick off titles that they thought the bookshop should consider ordering. These teachers were happy to ensure that books they needed for their courses would be readily available to their students. Many of them resented the University and Allied Bookshop for its entrenched, lethargic, unresponsive and high-handed ways.

After classes, Lata and Malati, both dressed casually in their usual salwaar-kameez, went to Nabiganj to wander around and have a cup of coffee at the Blue Danube coffee house. This activity, known to university students as 'gan-jing', they could afford to indulge in about once a week. As they passed the Imperial Book Depot, they were drawn magnetically in. Each wandered off to her favourite shelves and subjects. Malati headed straight for the novels, Lata went for poetry. On the way, however, she paused by the science shelves, not because she understood much science, but, rather, because she did not. Whenever she opened a scientific book and saw whole paragraphs of incomprehensible words and symbols, she felt a sense of wonder at the great territories of learning that lay beyond her – the sum of so many noble and purposive attempts to make objective sense of the world. She enjoyed the feeling; it suited her serious moods; and this afternoon she was feeling serious. She picked up a random book and read a random paragraph:

> It follows from De Moivre's formula that $z^n = r^n (\cos n + i \sin n)$. Thus, if we allow complex number z to describe a circle of radius r about the origin, z^n will describe n complete times a circle of radius r^n as z describes its circle once. We also recall that r, the modulus of z, written $|z|$, gives the distance of z from O, and that if $z' = x' + iy'$, then $|z - z'|$ is the distance between z and z'. With these preliminaries we may proceed to the proof of the theorem.

What exactly it was that pleased her in these sentences she did not know, but they conveyed weight, comfort, inevitability. Her mind strayed to Varun and his mathematical studies. She hoped that her brief words to him the day after the wedding had done him some good. She should have written to him more often to bolster his courage, but with exams coming up she had very little time for anything. It was at the insistence of Malati – who was even busier than she was – that she had gone ganjing at all.

She read the paragraph again, looking serious. 'We also recall' and 'with these preliminaries' drew her into a compact with the author of these verities and mysteries. The words were assured, and therefore reassuring: things were what they were even in this uncertain world, and she could proceed from there.

She smiled to herself now, not aware of her surroundings. Still holding the book, she looked up. And this was how a young man, who had been standing not far from her, was included, unintentionally, in her smile. He was pleasantly startled, and smiled back at her. Lata frowned at him and looked down at the page again. But she could not concentrate on it, and after a few moments, replaced it on the shelf before making her way to Poetry.

Lata, whatever she thought of love itself, liked love poetry. 'Maud' was one of her favourite poems. She began to flip through a volume of Tennyson.

The tall young man, who had (Lata noticed) slightly wavy black hair and very good, rather aquiline, looks, seemed to be as interested in poetry as in mathematics, because a few minutes later Lata was aware that he had shifted his attention to the poetry shelves, and was glancing through the anthologies. Lata felt that his eyes were on her from time to time. This annoyed her and she did not look up. When, despite herself, she did, she noticed him innocently immersed in his reading. She could not resist glancing at the cover of his book. It was a Penguin: *Contemporary Verse*. He now looked up, and the tables were turned. Before she could glance down again, he said: 'It's unusual for someone to be interested in both poetry and mathematics.'

'Is that so?' said Lata severely.

'Courant and Robbins – it's an excellent work.'

'Oh?' said Lata. Then, realizing that the young man was referring to the mathematics book she had picked randomly off the shelf, she said, 'Is it?' by way of closure.

But the young man was eager to continue the conversation.

'My father says so,' he went on. 'Not as a text but as a broad introduction to various, well, facets of the subject. He teaches maths at the university.'

Lata looked around to see if Malati was listening. But Malati was intent on her browsing in the front of the shop. Nor was anyone else eavesdropping; the shop was not busy at this time of year – or this time of day.

'Actually, I'm not interested in mathematics,' said Lata with an air of finality. The young man looked a little downcast before he rallied and confided, genially: 'You know, nor am I. I'm a history student myself.'

Lata was amazed at his determination and, looking straight at him, said, 'I must go now. My friend is waiting for me.' Even as she was saying this, however, she could not help noticing how sensitive, even vulnerable, this wavy-haired young man looked. This appeared to contradict his determined, bold behaviour in speaking to an unknown, unintroduced, girl in a bookshop.

'I'm sorry, I suppose I've been disturbing you?' he apologized, as if reading her thoughts.

'No,' said Lata. She was about to go to the front of the shop when he added quickly, with a nervous smile, 'In that case, may I ask you your name?'

'Lata,' said Lata shortly, though she didn't see the logic of 'in that case'.

'Aren't you going to ask me mine?' asked the young man, his smile broadening amiably.

'No,' said Lata, quite kindly, and rejoined Malati, who had a couple of paperback novels in her hand.

'Who's he?' whispered Malati conspiratorially.

'Just someone,' said Lata, glancing back a bit anxiously. 'I don't know. He just came up to me and began a conversation. Hurry up. Let's go. I'm feeling hungry. And thirsty. It's hot in here.'

The man at the counter was looking at Lata and Malati with the energetic friendliness he showered on regular customers. The little finger of his left hand was searching for wax in the crevices of his ear. He shook his head with reproving benevolence and said in Hindi to Malati:

'Exams are coming up, Malatiji, and you are still buying novels? Twelve annas plus one rupee four annas makes two rupees altogether. I should not allow this. You are like daughters to me.'

'Balwantji, you would go out of business if we did not read your novels. We are sacrificing our examination results at the altar of your prosperity,' said Malati.

'I'm not,' said Lata. The young man must have disappeared behind a bookshelf, because she couldn't see him anywhere.

'Good girl, good girl,' said Balwant, possibly referring to both of them.

'Actually, we were going to get some coffee and came into your shop unplanned,' said Malati, 'so I didn't bring – ' She left the sentence unfinished and flung a winning smile at Balwant.

'No, no, that is not necessary – you can give it later,' said Balwant. He and his brother extended terms of easy credit to many students. When asked whether this wasn't bad for business, they would reply that they had never lost money trusting anyone who bought books. And, certainly, they were doing very well for themselves. They reminded Lata of the priests of a well-endowed temple. The reverence with which the brothers treated their books supported the analogy.

'Since you suddenly feel famished, we are going straight to the Blue Danube,' said Malati decisively once they were outside the shop. 'And there you will tell me exactly what happened between that Cad and you.'

'Nothing,' said Lata.

'Hah!' said Malati in affectionate scorn. 'So what did you two talk about?'

'Nothing,' said Lata. 'Seriously, Malati, he just came up and started talking nonsense, and I said nothing in reply. Or monosyllables. Don't add chillies to boiled potatoes.'

They continued to stroll down Nabiganj.

'Quite tall,' said Malati, a couple of minutes later.

Lata said nothing.

'Not exactly dark,' said Malati.

Lata did not think this was worth responding to either. 'Dark', as she understood it, referred in novels to hair, not skin.

'But very handsome,' persisted Malati.

Lata made a wry face at her friend, but she was, to her own surprise, quite enjoying her description.

'What's his name?' continued Malati.

'I don't know,' said Lata, looking at herself in the glass front of a shoe shop.

Malati was astonished at Lata's ineptness. 'You talked to him for fifteen minutes and you don't know his name?'

'We did not talk for fifteen minutes,' said Lata. 'And I hardly talked at all. If you're so keen on him, why don't you go back to the Imperial Book Depot and ask him his name? Like you, he has no compunctions about talking to anyone.'

'So you don't like him?'

Lata was silent. Then she said, 'No, I don't. I've no reason to like him.'

'It's not all that easy for men to talk to us, you know,' said Malati. 'We shouldn't be so hard on them.'

'Malati defending the weaker sex!' said Lata. 'I never thought I'd see the day.'

'Don't change the subject,' said Malati. 'He didn't seem the brazen type. I know. Trust my five-hundredfold experience.'

Lata flushed. 'It seemed pretty easy for him to talk to me,' she said. 'As if I was the sort of girl who . . .'

'Who what?'

'Who can be talked to,' ended Lata uncertainly. Visions of her mother's disapproval floated across her mind. She made an effort to push these away.

'Well,' said Malati, a little more quietly than usual as they entered the Blue Danube, 'he really does have nice looks.'

They sat down.

'Nice hair,' continued Malati, surveying the menu.

'Let's order,' said Lata. Malati appeared to be in love with the word 'nice'.

They ordered coffee and pastries.

'Nice eyes,' said Malati, five minutes later, laughing now at Lata's studied unresponsiveness.

Lata remembered the young man's temporary nervousness when she had looked straight at him.

'Yes,' she agreed. 'But so what? I have nice eyes too, and one pair is enough.'

66

WHILE his mother-in-law was playing patience and his sister-in-law was fending off Malati's leading questions, Dr Pran Kapoor, that first-class husband and son-in-law, was battling with the departmental problems he was reticent about burdening his family with.

Pran, though a calm man by and large, and a kind man, regarded the head of the English Department, Professor Mishra, with a loathing that made him almost ill. Professor O.P. Mishra was a huge, pale, oily hulk, political and manipulative to the very depths of his being. The four members of the syllabus committee of the English Department were seated this afternoon around an oval table in the staff room. It was an unusually warm day. The single window was open (to the view of a dusty laburnum tree), but there was no breeze; everyone looked uncomfortable, but Professor Mishra was sweating in profuse drops that gathered on his forehead, wet his thin eyebrows, and trickled down the sides of his large nose. His lips were sweetly pursed and he was saying in his genial, high-pitched voice, 'Dr Kapoor, your point is well taken, but I think that we will need a little convincing.'

The point was the inclusion of James Joyce on the syllabus for the paper on Modern British Literature. Pran Kapoor had been pressing this on the syllabus committee for two terms – ever since he had been appointed a member – and at last the committee had decided to agree whether to consider it.

Why, Pran wondered, did he dislike Professor Mishra so intensely? Although Pran had been appointed to his lectureship five years ago under the headship of his predecessor, Professor Mishra, as a senior member of the department, must have had a say in hiring him. When he first came to the department, Professor Mishra had gone out of his way to be gracious to him, even inviting him to tea at his house. Mrs Mishra was a small, busy, worried woman, and Pran had liked her. But despite Professor Mishra's open-armed avuncularity, his Falstaffian bulk and charm,

Pran detected something dangerous: his wife and two young sons were, so it seemed to him, afraid of their father.

Pran had never been able to understand why people loved power, but he accepted it as a fact of life. His own father, for instance, was greatly attracted by it: his enjoyment in its exercise went beyond the pleasure of being able to realize his ideological principles. Mahesh Kapoor enjoyed being Revenue Minister, and he would probably be happy to become either Chief Minister of Purva Pradesh or a Minister in Prime Minister Nehru's Cabinet in Delhi. The headaches, the overwork, the responsibility, the lack of control over one's own time, the complete absence of opportunity to contemplate the world from a calm vantage point: these mattered little to him. Perhaps it was true to say that Mahesh Kapoor had contemplated the world sufficiently long from the calm vantage point of his cell in a prison in British India, and now required what he had in fact acquired: an intensely active role in running things. It was almost as if father and son had exchanged between themselves the second and third stages of the accepted Hindu scheme of life: the father was entangled in the world, the son longed to separate himself into a life of philosophical detachment.

Pran, however, whether he liked it or not, was what the scriptures would call a householder. He enjoyed Savita's company, he basked in her warmth and care and beauty, he looked forward to the birth of their child. He was determined not to depend on his father for financial support, although the small salary of a department lecturer – 200 rupees per month – was barely enough to subsist on – 'to subside on', as he told himself in moments of cynicism. But he had applied for a readership that had recently fallen open in the department; the salary attached to that post was less pitiful, and it would be a step up in terms of the academic hierarchy. Pran did not care about titular prestige, but he realized that designations helped one's designs. He wanted to see certain things done, and being a reader would help him do them. He believed that he deserved the job, but he had also learned that merit was only one criterion among several.

His experience of the recurrent asthmatic illness that had afflicted him since childhood had made him calm. Excitement disturbed his breathing, and caused him pain and incapacitation, and he had therefore almost dispensed with excitability. This was the simple logic of it, but the path itself had been difficult. He had studied patience, and by slow practice he had become patient. But Professor O.P. Mishra had got under his skin in a way Pran had not been able to envisage.

'Professor Mishra,' said Pran, 'I am pleased that the committee has decided to consider this proposal, and I am delighted that it has been placed second on the agenda today and has at last come up for discussion. My main argument is quite simple. You have read my note on the subject' – he nodded around the table to Dr Gupta and Dr Narayanan – 'and you will, I am sure, appreciate that there is nothing radical in my suggestion.' He looked down at the pale blue type of the cyclostyled sheets before him. 'As you can see, we have twenty-one writers whose works we consider it essential for our B.A students to read in order for them to obtain a proper understanding of Modern British Literature. But there is no Joyce. And, I might add, no Lawrence. These two writers –'

'Wouldn't it be better,' interrupted Professor Mishra, wiping an eyelash away from the corner of his eye, 'wouldn't it be better if we were to concentrate on Joyce for the moment? We will take up Lawrence at our session next month – before we adjourn for the summer vacation.'

'The two matters are interlinked, surely,' said Pran, looking around the table for support. Dr Narayanan was about to say something when Professor Mishra pointed out:

'But not on this agenda, Dr Kapoor, not on this agenda.' He smiled at Pran sweetly, and his eyes twinkled. He then placed his huge white hands, palms down, on the table and said, 'But what were you saying when I so rudely interrupted?'

Pran looked at the large white hands emanating from

the grand pulp of Professor Mishra's round body, and thought, I may look thin and fit, but I am not, and this man, for all his slug-like pallor and bulk, has a great deal of stamina. If I am to get agreement on this measure I must remain calm and collected.

He smiled around the table, and said: 'Joyce is a great writer. This is now universally acknowledged. He is, for instance, the subject of increasing academic study in America. I do think he should be on our syllabus too.'

'Dr Kapoor,' the high voice responded, 'each point in the universe must make up its own mind on the question of acknowledgement before acknowledgement can be considered to be universal. We in India pride ourselves on our Independence – an Independence won at great expense by the best men of several generations, a fact I need not emphasize to the illustrious son of an even more illustrious father. We should hesitate before we blindly allow the American dissertation mill to order our priorities. What do you say, Dr Narayanan?'

Dr Narayanan, who was a Romantic Revivalist, seemed to look deep into his soul for a few seconds. 'That is a good point,' he said judiciously, shaking his head sideways for emphasis.

'If we do not keep pace with our companions,' continued Professor Mishra, 'perhaps it is because we hear a different drummer. Let us step to the music that we hear, we in India. To quote an American,' he added.

Pran looked down at the table and said quietly: 'I say Joyce is a great writer because I believe he is a great writer, not because of what the Americans say.' He remembered his first introduction to Joyce: a friend had lent him *Ulysses* a month before his Ph.D. oral examination at Allahabad University and he had, as a result, ignored his own subject to the point where he had jeopardized his academic career.

Dr Narayanan looked at him and came out suddenly in unexpected support. '"The Dead",' said Dr Narayanan. 'A fine story. I read it twice.'

Pran looked at him gratefully.

Professor Mishra looked at Dr Narayanan's small, bald head almost approvingly. 'Very good, very good,' he said, as if applauding a small child. 'But' – and his voice assumed a cutting edge – 'there is more to Joyce than "The Dead". There is the unreadable *Ulysses*. There is the worse than unreadable *Finnegan's Wake*. This kind of writing is unhealthy for our students. It encourages them, as it were, in sloppy and ungrammatical writing. And what about the ending of *Ulysses*? There are young and impressionable women whom in our courses it is our responsibility to introduce to the higher things of life, Dr Kapoor – your charming sister-in-law for example. Would you put a book like *Ulysses* into her hands?' Professor Mishra smiled benignly.

'Yes,' said Pran simply.

Dr Narayanan looked interested. Dr Gupta, who was mainly interested in Anglo-Saxon and Middle English, looked at his nails.

'It is heartening to come across a young man – a young lecturer' – Professor Mishra looked over at the rank-conscious reader, Dr Gupta – 'who is so, shall I say, so, well, direct in his opinions and so willing to share them with his colleagues, however senior they may be. It is heartening. We may disagree of course; but India is a democracy and we can speak our minds. . . .' He stopped for a few seconds, and stared out of the window at the dusty laburnum. 'A democracy. Yes. But even democracies are faced with hard choices. There can be only one head of department, for example. And when a post falls open, of all the deserving candidates only one can be selected. We are already hardpressed to teach twenty-one writers in the time we allot to this paper. If Joyce goes in, what comes out?'

'Flecker,' said Pran without a moment's hesitation.

Professor Mishra laughed indulgently. 'Ah, Dr Kapoor, Dr Kapoor . . .' he intoned,

'Pass not beneath, O Caravan, or pass not singing. Have you heard
That silence where the birds are dead yet something pipeth like a bird?

James Elroy Flecker, James Elroy Flecker.' That seemed to settle it in his mind.

Pran's face became completely impassive. Does he believe this? he thought. Does he really believe what he is implying? Aloud he said, 'If Fletcher – Flecker – is indispensable, I suggest we include Joyce as our twenty-second writer. I would be pleased to put it to the committee for a vote.' Surely, thought Pran, the ignominy of being known to have turned Joyce down (as opposed to merely having deferred the decision indefinitely) would be something that the committee would not be willing to face.

'Ah, Dr Kapoor, you are angry. Do not get angry. You want to pin us down,' said Professor Mishra playfully. He turned his palms up on the table to display his own helplessness. 'But we did not agree to decide the matter at this meeting, only to decide whether to decide it.'

This was too much for Pran in his present mood, though he knew it was true.

'Please do not misunderstand me, Professor Mishra,' he said, 'but that line of argument may be taken by those of us not well-versed in the finer forms of parliamentary byplay to be a species of quibbling.'

'A species of quibbling . . . a species of quibbling.' Professor Mishra appeared delighted by the phrase, while both his colleagues looked appalled at Pran's insubordination. (This is like playing bridge with two dummies, thought Pran.) Professor Mishra continued: 'I will now order coffee, and we will collect ourselves and approach the issues calmly, as it were.'

Dr Narayanan perked up at the prospect of coffee. Professor Mishra clapped his hands, and a lean peon in a threadbare green uniform came in.

'Is coffee ready?' asked Professor Mishra in Hindi.

'Yes, Sahib.'

'Good.' Professor Mishra indicated that it should be served.

The peon brought in a tray with a coffee pot, a small jug of hot milk, a bowl of sugar, and four cups. Professor Mishra indicated that he should serve the others first. The peon did so in the usual manner. Then Professor Mishra was offered coffee. As Professor Mishra poured coffee into his cup, the peon moved the tray deferentially backwards. Professor Mishra made to set down the coffee pot, and the peon moved the tray forward. Professor Mishra picked up the milk jug and began to add milk to his coffee, and the peon moved the tray backwards. And so on for each of three spoons of sugar. It was like a comic ballet. It would have been merely ridiculous, thought Pran, this display of the naked gradient of power and obsequiousness between the department head and the department peon, if it had only been some other department at some other university. But it was the English Department of Brahmpur University – and it was through this man that Pran had to apply to the selection committee for the readership he both wanted and needed.

This same man whom in my first term I considered jovial, bluff, expansive, charming, why have I transformed him in my mind into such a caricature of a villain? thought Pran looking into his cup. Does he loathe me? No, that is his strength: he doesn't. He just wants his own way. In effective politics hatred is just not useful. For him all this is like a game of chess – on a slightly vibrating board. He is fifty-eight – he has two more years until he retires. How will I be able to put up with him for so long? A sudden murderous impulse seized Pran, whom murderous impulses never seized, and he realized his hands were trembling slightly. And all this over Joyce, he said to himself. At least I haven't had a bronchial attack. He looked down at the pad on which he, as the junior member of the committee, was taking the minutes of the meeting. It read simply:

Present: Professor O.P. Mishra (head); Dr R.B. Gupta;
Dr T.R. Narayanan; Dr P. Kapoor.

1. The Minutes of the last meeting were read and approved.

We have got nowhere, and we will get nowhere, he thought.

A few well-known lines from Tagore came into his head in Tagore's own English translation:

Where the clear stream of reason has not lost its way into
        the dreary desert sand of dead habit;
Where the mind is led forward by Thee into ever-widening
        thought and action –
Into that heaven of freedom, my Father, let my country
  awake.

At least his own mortal father had given him principles, thought Pran, even if he had given him almost no time or company when he was younger. His mind wandered back home, to the small whitewashed house, to Savita, her sister, her mother – the family that he had taken into his heart and that had taken him into theirs; and then to the Ganges flowing close by the house. (When he thought in English, it was the Ganges, rather than the Ganga, to him.) He followed it first downstream to Patna and Calcutta, then upstream past Banaras till it divided at Allahabad; there he chose the Yamuna and followed it to Delhi. Are things as closed-minded in the capital? he asked himself. As mad, as mean, as silly, as rigid? How will I be able to live in Brahmpur all my life? And Mishra will doubtless give me an excellent report just to see the back of me.

1.17

BUT now Dr Gupta was laughing at a remark of Dr Narayanan's, and Professor Mishra was saying, 'Consensus – consensus is the goal, the civilized goal – how can we vote when we might be divided two votes against two? There were five Pandavas, they could have voted if they chose, but even they did everything by consensus. They even took a wife by consensus, ha, ha, ha! And Dr Varma is indisposed as usual, so we are only four.'

Pran looked at the twinkling eyes, the great nose, the sweetly pursed lips with reluctant admiration. University statutes required that the syllabus committee, like departmental committees of any kind, should consist of an odd number of members. But Professor Mishra, as head of the department, appointed the members of each committee within his purview in such a way as always to include someone who for reasons of health or research was likely to be indisposed or absent. With an even number of members present, committees were more reluctant than ever to bring things to the climax of a vote. And the head, with his control over the agenda and the pacing of a meeting, could in the circumstances gather even more effective power into his hands.

'I think we have, as it were, expended enough time on item two,' said Professor Mishra. 'Shall we go on to chiasmus and anacoluthia?' He was referring to a proposal, put forward by himself, that they eliminate too detailed a study of traditional figures of speech for the paper in Literary Theory and Criticism. 'And then we have the question of symmetrical auxiliaries proposed by the junior member of the committee. Though this will, of course, depend upon other departments agreeing to our proposals. And finally, since the shades of night are falling,' continued Professor Mishra, 'I think we should, without prejudice to items five, six, and seven, wind up the meeting. We can take up those items next month.'

But Pran was unwilling to be dissuaded from pressing on with the unresolved question of Joyce. 'I think we have now collected ourselves,' he said, 'and can approach the issue under discussion quite calmly. If I were willing to accept that *Ulysses* might be a bit, well, difficult for B.A students, would the committee agree to include *Dubliners* on the syllabus as a first step? Dr Gupta, what do you think?'

Dr Gupta looked up at the slowly circulating fan. His ability to get speakers on Old and Middle English invited to the departmental seminar depended upon Professor Mishra's goodwill: outside speakers entailed incidental expenses, and funds had to be approved by the head of the department. Dr Gupta knew as well as anyone what 'as a first step' implied. He looked up at Pran and said, 'I would be willing —'

But he was swiftly interrupted in his sentence, whatever that might have been. 'We are forgetting,' Professor Mishra cut in, 'something that even I, I must admit, did not bear in mind earlier in this discussion. I mean that, by tradition, the Modern British Literature paper does not include writers who were living at the time of the Second World War.' This was news to Pran, who must have looked astonished, because Professor Mishra felt compelled to explain: 'This is not altogether a matter for surprise. We need the distance of time objectively to appraise the stature of modern writers, to include them in our canon, as it were. Do remind me, Dr Kapoor . . . when did Joyce die?'

'1941,' said Pran sharply. It was clear that the great white whale had known this all along.

'Well, there you are . . .' said Professor Mishra helplessly. His finger moved down the agenda.

'Eliot, of course, is still alive,' said Pran quietly, looking at the list of prescribed authors.

The head of the department looked as if he had been slapped across the face. He opened his mouth slightly, then pursed his lips together. The jolly twinkle appeared again in his eyes. 'But Eliot, Eliot, surely – we have objective criteria enough in his case – why, even Dr Leavis –'

Professor Mishra clearly responded to a different drummer from the Americans, reflected Pran. Aloud he said, 'Dr Leavis, as we know, greatly approves of Lawrence too. . . .'

'We have agreed to discuss Lawrence next time,' Professor Mishra expostulated.

Pran gazed out of the window. It was getting dark and the leaves of the laburnum now looked cool, not dusty. He went on, not looking at Professor Mishra: '. . . and, besides,

Joyce has a better claim as a British writer in Modern British Literature than Eliot. So if we –'

'That, my young friend, if I may say so,' cut in Professor Mishra, 'could be considered a species of quibbling.' He was recovering quickly from his shock. In a minute he would be quoting Prufrock.

What is it about Eliot, thought Pran irrelevantly, his mind wandering from the subject at hand, that makes him such a sacred cow for us Indian intellectuals? Aloud he said: 'Let us hope that T.S. Eliot has many more years of life, of productive life. I am glad that, unlike Joyce, he did not die in 1941. But we are now living in 1951, which implies that the pre-war rule you mentioned, even if it is a tradition, could not be a very ancient one. If we can't do away with it, why not update it? Surely its purpose is that we should revere the dead above the living – or, to be less sceptical, appraise the dead before the living. Eliot, who is alive, has been granted a waiver. I propose we grant Joyce one. A friendly compromise.' Pran paused, then added: 'As it were.' He smiled: 'Dr Narayanan, are you for "The Dead"?'

'Yes, well, I think so,' said Dr Narayanan with the faintest of responding smiles, before Professor Mishra could interrupt.

'Dr Gupta?' asked Pran.

Dr Gupta could not look Professor Mishra in the eye.

'I agree with Dr Narayanan,' said Professor Gupta.

There was silence for a few seconds. Pran thought, I can't believe it. I've won. I've won. I can't believe it.

And indeed, it seemed that he had. Everyone knew that the approval of the Academic Council of the university was usually a formality once the syllabus committee of a department had decided matters.

As if nothing in the least untoward had occurred, the head of the department gathered together the reins of the meeting. The great soft hands scuttled across the cyclostyled sheets. 'The next item . . .' said Professor Mishra with a smile, then paused and began again: 'But before we go on to the next item, I should say that I personally have always greatly admired James Joyce as a writer. I am delighted, needless to say –'

A couple of lines of poetry came terrifyingly unbidden to Pran's mind:

> Pale hands I loved beside the Shalimar,
> Where are you now? Who lies beneath your spell?

and he burst into a fit of sudden laughter, incomprehensible even to himself, which went on for twenty seconds and ended in a spasm of coughing. He bent his head and tears streamed down his cheeks. Professor Mishra rewarded him with a look of unfeigned fury and hatred.

'Sorry, sorry,' muttered Pran as he recovered. Dr Gupta was thumping him vigorously on the back, which was not helpful. 'Please continue – I was overcome – it sometimes happens. . . .' But to offer any further explanation was impossible.

The meeting was resumed and the next two points discussed quickly. There was no real disagreement. It was dark now; the meeting was adjourned. As Pran left the room Professor Mishra put a friendly arm around his shoulder. 'My dear boy, that was a fine performance.' Pran shuddered at the memory. 'You are clearly a man of great integrity, intellectual and otherwise.' Oh, oh, what is he up to now? thought Pran. Professor Mishra continued: 'The Proctor has been badgering me since last Tuesday to submit a member of my department – it's our turn, you know – to join the student welfare committee of the university. . . .' Oh no, thought Pran, there goes one day every week. '. . . and I have decided to volunteer you.' I didn't know the verb was transitive, thought Pran. In the darkness – they were now walking across the campus – it was difficult for Professor Mishra entirely to disguise the active dislike in his high voice. Pran could almost see the pursed lips, the specious twinkle. He was silent, and that, to the head of the English Department, implied acceptance.

'I realize you are busy, my dear Dr Kapoor, what with your extra tutorials, the Debating Society, the Colloquium, putting on plays, and so on. . . .' said Professor Mishra. 'The sort of thing that makes one deservedly popular with students. But you are comparatively new here, my dear fellow – five years is not a long time from the perspective of an old fogey like me – and you must allow me to give you a word of advice. Cut down on your unacademic activities. Don't tire yourself out unnecessarily. Don't take things so seriously. What were those wonderful lines of Yeats?

> She bid me take life easy as the leaves grown on the tree,
> But I being young and foolish with her did not agree.

I'm sure your charming wife would endorse that. Don't drive yourself so hard – your health depends on it. And your future, I dare say. . . . In some ways you are your own worst enemy.'

But I am only my metaphorical enemy, thought Pran. And obstinacy on my part has earned me the actual enmity of the formidable Professor Mishra. But was Professor Mishra more dangerous or less dangerous to him – in this matter of the readership, for instance, now that Pran had won his hatred?

What was Professor Mishra thinking, wondered Pran. He imagined his thoughts went something like this: I should never have got this uppity young lecturer onto the syllabus committee. It's too late, however, to regret all that. But at least his presence here has kept him from working mischief in, say, the admissions committee; there he could have brought up all kinds of objections to students I wanted to bring in if they weren't selected entirely on the basis of merit. As for the university's selection committee for the readership in English, I must rig this somehow before I allow it to meet –

But Pran got no further clues to the inner working of that mysterious intelligence. For at this point the paths of the two colleagues diverged and, with expressions of great mutual respect, they parted from each other.

MEENAKSHI, Arun's wife, was feeling utterly bored, so she decided to have her daughter Aparna brought to her. Aparna was looking even more pretty than usual: round and fair and black-haired with gorgeous eyes, as sharp as those of her mother. Meenakshi pressed the electric buzzer twice (the signal for the child's ayah) and looked at the book in her lap. It was Thomas Mann's *Buddenbrooks*, and it was unutterably dull. She didn't know how she was going to get through another five pages of it. Arun, delighted though he normally was with her, had the irksome habit of throwing an improving book her way now and then, and Meenakshi felt his suggestions were more in the way of subtle commands. 'A wonderful book. ...' Arun would say some evening, laughing, in the company of the oddly flippant crowd they mixed with, a crowd that Meenakshi felt convinced could not possibly be more interested than she was in *Buddenbrooks* or any other such clotted Germanic construct. '... I have been reading this marvellous book by Mann, and I'm now getting Meenakshi involved in it.' Some of the others, especially the languid Billy Irani, would look from Arun to Meenakshi in momentary wonderment, and the topic would pass to office matters or the social world or racing or dancing or golf or the Calcutta Club or complaints about 'these bloody politicians' or 'these brainless bureaucrats', and Thomas Mann would be quite forgotten. But Meenakshi would now feel obliged to read enough of the book to convey an acquaintance with its contents, and it seemed to make Arun happy to see her do so.

How wonderful Arun was, thought Meenakshi, and how pleasant it was to live in this nice flat in Sunny Park, not far from her father's house on Ballygunge Circular Road, and why did they have to have all these furious tiffs? Arun was incredibly hotheaded and jealous, and she had only to look languidly at the languid Billy for Arun to start smouldering somewhere deep inside. It might be wonderful to have a smouldering husband in bed later,

Meenakshi reflected, but such advantages did not come unadulterated. Sometimes Arun would go off into a smouldering sulk, and was quite spoilt for love-making. Billy Irani had a girlfriend, Shireen, but that made no difference to Arun, who suspected Meenakshi (quite correctly) of harbouring a casual lust for his friend. Shireen for her part occasionally sighed amidst her cocktails and announced that Billy was incorrigible.

When the ayah arrived in answer to the bell, Meenakshi said, 'Baby lao!' in a kind of pidgin Hindi. The aged ayah, most of whose reactions were slow, turned creakingly to fulfil her mistress's behest. Aparna was fetched. She had been having her afternoon nap, and yawned as she was brought in to her mother. Her small fists were rubbing her eyes.

'Mummy!' said Aparna in English. 'I'm sleepy, and Miriam woke me up.' Miriam, the ayah, upon hearing her name spoken, although she could understand no English, grinned at the child with toothless goodwill.

'I know, precious baby doll,' said Meenakshi, 'but Mummy had to see you, she was so bored. Come and give – yes – and now on the other side.'

Aparna was wearing a mauve dress of flouncy fluffy stuff and was looking, thought her mother, inexcusably enchanting. Meenakshi's eyes went to her dressing-table mirror and she noticed with a surge of joy what a wonderful mother-and-child pair they made. 'You are looking *so* lovely,' she informed Aparna, 'that I think I will have a whole line of little girls.... Aparna, and Bibeka, and Charulata, and –'

Here she was cut off by Aparna's glare. 'If another baby comes into this house,' announced Aparna, 'I will throw it straight into the waste-paper basket.'

'Oh,' said Meenakshi, more than a little startled. Aparna, living among so many opinionated personalities, had quite early developed a powerful vocabulary. But three-year-olds were not supposed to express themselves so lucidly, and in conditional sentences at that. Meenakshi looked at Aparna and sighed.

'You are *so* scrumptious,' she told Aparna. 'Now have

81

your milk.' To the ayah she said, 'Dudh lao. Ek dum!' And Miriam creaked off to get a glass of milk for the little girl.

For some reason the ayah's slow-moving back irritated Meenakshi and she thought: We really ought to replace the T.C. She's quite needlessly senile. This was her and Arun's private abbreviation for the ayah and Meenakshi laughed with pleasure as she remembered the occasion over the breakfast table when Arun had turned from the *Statesman* crossword to say, 'Oh, do get the toothless crone out of the room. She quite puts me off my omelette.' Miriam had been the T.C ever since. Living with Arun was full of sudden delightful moments like that, thought Meenakshi. If only it could all be that way.

But the trouble was that she also had to run the house, and she hated it. The elder daughter of Mr Justice Chatterji had always had everything done for her – and she was now discovering how trying it could be to handle things on her own. Managing the staff (ayah, servant-cum-cook, part-time sweeper, part-time gardener; Arun supervised the driver, who was on the company payroll); doing the accounts; buying those items that one simply couldn't trust the servant or the ayah to buy; and making sure that everything fitted within the budget. This last she found especially difficult. She had been brought up in some luxury, and though she had insisted (against her parents' advice) on the romantic adventure of standing after marriage entirely on their own four feet, she had found it impossible to curb her taste for certain items (foreign soap, foreign butter, and so on) that were intrinsic to the fabric of a civilized life. She was very conscious of the fact that Arun helped support everyone in his own family and often commented to him about the fact.

'Well,' Arun had said just recently, 'now that Savita's married, that's one less, you'll agree, darling.' Meenakshi had sighed, replying in a couplet:

'Marry one – and what's my fate?
Every Mehra on my plate.'

Arun had frowned. He had been reminded once again of the fact that Meenakshi's elder brother was a poet. It was from long familiarity – almost obsession – with rhyme that most of the younger Chatterjis had learned to improvise couplets, sometimes of surpassing puerility.

The ayah brought the milk and left. Meenakshi turned her lovely eyes back to *Buddenbrooks* while Aparna sat on the bed drinking her milk. With a sound of impatience Meenakshi threw Thomas Mann onto the bed and followed him there, closed her eyes and went off to sleep. She was awakened with a shock twenty minutes later by Aparna, who was pinching her breast.

'Don't be horrid, Aparna precious. Mummy's trying to sleep,' said Meenakshi.

'Don't sleep,' said Aparna. 'I want to play.' Unlike other children of her age, Aparna never used her name in the Caesarean third person, though her mother did.

'Darling sweetheart, Mummy is tired, she's been reading a book and she doesn't want to play. Not now, anyway. Later, when Daddy comes home, you can play with him. Or you can play with Uncle Varun when he returns from college. What have you done with your glass?'

'When will Daddy come home?'

'I'd say in about an hour,' replied Meenakshi.

'I'd say in about an hour,' said Aparna speculatively, as if she liked the phrase. 'I want a necklace too,' she added, and tugged at her mother's gold chain.

Meenakshi gave her daughter a hug. 'And you shall have one,' she said, and dismissed the subject. 'Now go to Miriam.'

'No.'

'Then stay here if you want. But do be quiet, darling.'

Aparna was quiet for a while. She looked at *Buddenbrooks*, at her empty glass, at her sleeping mother, at the quilt, at the mirror, at the ceiling. Then she said, 'Mummy?' tentatively. There was no response.

'Mummy?' Aparna attempted a few notches louder.

'Mmm?'

'MUMMY!' yelled Aparna at the top of her lungs.

Meenakshi sat bolt upright and shook Aparna. 'Do you want me to spank you?' she asked.

'No,' replied Aparna definitively.

'Then what is it? Why are you shouting? What were you going to say?'

'Have you had a hard day, darling?' asked Aparna, hoping to arouse a response to her imitative charm.

'Yes,' said Meenakshi shortly. 'Now, darling, pick up that glass and go to Miriam at once.'

'Shall I comb your hair?'

'No.'

Aparna got down reluctantly from the bed and made her way to the door. She toyed with the idea of saying, 'I'll tell Daddy!' though what she could have complained about was left unformulated. Her mother meanwhile was once again sleeping sweetly, her lips slightly parted, her long black hair spread across the pillow. It was so hot in the afternoon, and everything tilted her towards a long and languorous sleep. Her breasts rose and fell gently, and she dreamed about Arun, who was handsome and dashing and covenanted, and who would be coming home in an hour. And after a while she began to dream about Billy Irani, whom they would be meeting later that evening.

When Arun arrived, he left his briefcase in the drawing room, walked into the bedroom, and closed the door. Seeing Meenakshi asleep, he paced up and down for a while, then took off his coat and tie, and lay down beside her without disturbing her sleep. But after a while his hand moved to her forehead and then down her face to her breasts. Meenakshi opened her eyes and said, 'Oh.' She was momentarily bewildered. After a while she asked, 'What's the time?'

'Five-thirty. I came home early just as I promised – and I found you asleep.'

'I couldn't sleep earlier, darling. Aparna woke me up every few minutes.'

'What's the programme for the evening?'

'Dinner and dancing with Billy and Shireen.'

'Oh yes, of course.' After a pause Arun continued: 'To tell you the truth, darling, I'm rather tired. I wonder whether we shouldn't simply call it off tonight?'

'Oh, you'll revive quickly enough after you've had a drink,' said Meenakshi brightly. 'And a glance or two from Shireen,' she added.

'I suppose you're right, dear.' Arun reached out for her. He had had a little trouble with his back a month ago, but had quite recovered.

'Naughty boy,' said Meenakshi, and pushed his hand away. After a while she added, 'The T.C has been cheating us on the Ostermilk.'

'Ah? Has she?' said Arun indifferently, then swerved off to a subject that interested him – 'I discovered today that we were being overcharged sixty thousand on the new paper project by one of our local businessmen. We've asked him to revise his estimates, of course, but it does rather shock one.... No sense of business ethics – or personal ethics either. He was in the office the other day, and he assured me that he was making us a special offer because of what he called our long-standing relationship. Now I find, after talking to Jock Mackay, that that's the line he took with them as well – but charged them sixty thousand less than us.'

'What will you do?' Meenakshi asked dutifully. She had switched off a few sentences ago.

Arun talked on for five minutes or so, while Meenakshi's mind wandered. When he stopped and looked at her questioningly, she said, yawning a little from residual sleepiness:

'How has your boss reacted to all this?'

'Difficult to say. With Basil Cox it's difficult to say anything, even when he's delighted. In this case I think he's as annoyed by the possible delay as pleased by the definite saving.' Arun unburdened himself for another five minutes while Meenakshi began to buff her nails.

The bedroom door had been bolted against interruption, but when Aparna saw her father's briefcase she knew that he had returned and insisted upon being admitted. Arun

85

opened the door and gave her a hug, and for the next hour or so they did a jigsaw featuring a giraffe, which Aparna had seen in a toyshop a week after being taken to the Brahmpur Zoo. They had done the jigsaw several times before, but Aparna had not yet tired of it. Nor had Arun. He adored his daughter and occasionally felt it was a pity that he and Meenakshi went out almost every evening. But one simply couldn't let one's life come to a standstill because one had a child. What, after all, were ayahs for? What, for that matter, were younger brothers for?

'Mummy has promised me a necklace,' said Aparna.

'Has she, darling?' said Arun. 'How does she imagine she's going to buy it? We can't afford it at the moment.'

Aparna looked so disappointed at this latest intelligence that Arun and Meenakshi turned to each other with transferred adoration.

'But she will,' said Aparna, quietly and determinedly. 'Now I want to do a jigsaw.'

'But we've just done one,' protested Arun.

'I want to do another.'

'You handle her, Meenakshi,' said Arun.

'You handle her, darling,' said Meenakshi. 'I must get ready. And please clear the bedroom floor.'

So for a while Arun and Aparna, banished to the drawing room this time, lay on the carpet putting together a jigsaw of the Victoria Memorial while Meenakshi bathed and dressed and perfumed and ornamented herself.

Varun returned from college, slid past Arun into his tiny box of a room, and sat down with his books. But he seemed nervous, and could not settle down to studying. When Arun went to get ready, Aparna was transferred to him; and the rest of Varun's evening was spent at home trying to keep her amused.

The long-necked Meenakshi turned numerous heads when their party of four entered Firpos for dinner. Arun told Shireen she was looking gorgeous and Billy looked with soulful languor at Meenakshi and said that she looked divine, and things went wonderfully well and were followed

86

by some pleasantly titillating dancing at the 300 Club. Meenakshi and Arun were not really able to afford all this – Billy Irani had independent means – but it seemed intolerable that they, for whom this kind of life was so obviously intended, should be deprived of it by a mere lack of funds. Meenakshi could not help noticing, through dinner and beyond, the lovely little gold danglers that Shireen was wearing, and that hung so becomingly from her little velvety ears.

It was a warm evening. In the car on the way back home Arun said to Meenakshi, 'Give me your hand, darling,' and Meenakshi, placing one red nail-polished fingertip on the back of his hand, said, 'Here!' Arun thought that this was delightfully elegant and flirtatious. But Meenakshi had her mind on something else.

Later, when Arun had gone to bed, Meenakshi unlocked her jewellery case (the Chatterjis did not believe in giving their daughter great quantities of jewellery but she had been given quite enough for her likely requirements) and took out the two gold medals so precious to Mrs Rupa Mehra's heart. She had given these to Meenakshi at the time of her wedding as a gift to the bride of her elder son. This she felt was the appropriate thing to do; she had nothing else to give, and she felt that her husband would have approved. On the back of the medals was engraved: 'Thomasson Engineering College Roorkee. Raghubir Mehra. Civil Engg. First. 1916' and 'Physics. First. 1916' respectively. Two lions crouched sternly on pedestals on each medal. Meenakshi looked at the medals, then balanced them in her hands, then held the cool and precious discs to her cheeks. She wondered how much they weighed. She thought of the gold chain she had promised Aparna and the gold drops she had virtually promised herself. She had examined them quite carefully as they hung from Shireen's little ears. The danglers were shaped like tiny pears.

When Arun rather impatiently called her to bed, she murmured, 'Just coming.' But it was a minute or two before she joined him. 'What are you thinking of, darling?' he asked her. 'You look dangerously preoccupied.' But

Meenakshi instinctively realized that to mention what had passed through her head — what she planned to do with those dowdy medals — would not be a good idea, and she avoided the subject by nibbling at the lobe of his left ear.

1.19

THE next morning at ten o'clock Meenakshi phoned her younger sister Kakoli.

'Kuku, a friend of mine from the Shady Ladies — my club, you know — wants to find out where she can get some gold melted down discreetly. Do you know of a good jeweller?'

'Well, Satram Das or Lilaram, I suppose,' yawned Kuku, barely awake.

'No, I am not talking of Park Street jewellers — or any jewellers of that kind,' said Meenakshi with a sigh. 'I want to go somewhere where they don't know me.'

'*You* want to go somewhere?'

There was a short silence at the other end. 'Well, you may as well know,' said Meenakshi: 'I've set my heart on a pair of earrings — they look adorable — just like tiny little pears — and I want to melt down those fat ugly medals that Arun's mother gave me for my wedding.'

'Oh, don't do that,' said Kakoli in a kind of alarmed warble.

'Kuku, I want your advice about the place, not about the decision.'

'Well, you could go to Sarkar's. No — try Jauhri's on Rashbehari Avenue. Does Arun know?'

'The medals were given to me,' said Meenakshi. 'If Arun wants to melt his golf clubs down to make a back brace I won't object.'

When she got to the jeweller's, she was astonished to meet opposition there as well.

'Madam,' said Mr Jauhri in Bengali, looking at the medals won by her father-in-law, 'these are beautiful medals.' His fingers, blunt and dark, slightly incongruous for someone who held and supervised work of such fineness and beauty, touched the embossed lions lovingly, and circled around the smooth, unmilled edges.

Meenakshi stroked the side of her neck with the long, red-polished nail of the middle finger of her right hand.

'Yes,' she said indifferently.

'Madam, if I might advise you, why not order these earrings and this chain and pay for them separately? There is really no need to melt down these medals.' A well-dressed and evidently wealthy lady would presumably not find any difficulty in this suggestion.

Meenakshi looked at the jeweller with cool surprise. 'Now that I know the approximate weight of the medals, I propose to melt down one, not both,' she said. Somewhat annoyed by his impertinence – these shopkeepers some-times got above themselves – she went on: 'I came here to get a job done; I would normally have gone to my regular jewellers. How long do you think it will take?'

Mr Jauhri did not dispute the issue further. 'It will take two weeks,' he said.

'That's rather a long time.'

'Well, you know how it is, Madam. Artisans of the requisite skill are scarce, and we have many orders.'

'But it is March. The wedding season is virtually over.'

'Nevertheless, Madam.'

'Well, I suppose that will have to do,' Meenakshi said. She picked up one medal – it happened to be the Physics one – and popped it back in her purse. The jeweller looked somewhat regretfully at the Engineering Medal lying on a small velvet square on his table. He had not dared to ask whose it was, but when Meenakshi took a receipt for the medal after it had been weighed exactly on his scales, he had deduced from her name that it must have been awarded to her father-in-law. He was not to know that Meenakshi had never known her father-in-law and felt no particular closeness to him.

As Meenakshi turned to leave, he said, 'Madam, if you happen to change your mind . . .'

Meenakshi turned to him, and snapped: 'Mr Jauhri, if I

89

wish for your advice I will ask for it. I came to you specifically because you were recommended to me.'

'Quite right, Madam, quite right. Of course it is entirely up to you. In two weeks then.' Mr Jauhri frowned sadly at the medal before summoning his master artisan.

Two weeks later, Arun discovered through a casual conversational slip what Meenakshi had done. He was livid.

Meenakshi sighed. 'It's pointless talking to you when you are as cross as this,' she said. 'You behave quite heartlessly. Come, Aparna darling, Daddy's angry with us, let's go into the other room.'

A few days later Arun wrote – or, rather, scrawled – a letter to his mother:

Dear Ma,

Sorry not written to you earlier in response to your letter re Lata. Yes, by all means, will look for someone. But don't be sanguine, the covenanted are almost twice-born and get dowry offers in the tens of thousands, even lakhs. Still, situation not entirely hopeless. Will try, but I suggest Lata come to Calcutta in the summer. Will effect introductions &c. But she must cooperate. Varun lacka-daisical, studies hard only when I take a hand. Shows no interest in girls, only the fourfooted as usual, and dread-ful songs. Aparna in fine fettle, asks after her Daadi continually so rest assured she misses you. Daddy's Engg. Medal melted down for ear-drops and chain by M, but I've placed injunction on Physics, not to worry. All else well, back OK, Chatterjis much the same, will write at length when time.

Love and xxx from all,
Arun

This brief note, written in Arun's illegible telegraphese (the upright lines of the letters tilting at angles of thirty degrees randomly to left or right), landed like a grenade in Brahm-pur by the second post one afternoon. When Mrs Rupa Mehra read it, she burst into tears without even (as Arun might have been tempted to remark had he been there) the customary preliminary of a reddening nose. In fact, not to make cynical light of the matter, she was deeply upset, and for every obvious reason.

The horror of the melted medal, the callousness of her daughter-in-law, her disregard of every tender feeling as evidenced by this shallow act of vanity upset Mrs Rupa Mehra more than anything had in years, more even than Arun's marriage to Meenakshi in the first place. She saw before her very eyes her husband's golden name being physically melted away in a crucible. Mrs Rupa Mehra had loved and admired her husband almost to excess, and the thought that one of the few things that tied his presence to the earth was now maliciously – for what was such wounding indifference but a kind of malice – and irretrievably lost made her weep tears of bitterness, anger and frustration. He had been a brilliant student at the Roorkee College and his memories of his student days had been happy ones. He had hardly studied, yet had done extremely well. He had been liked by both his fellow students and his teachers. The only subject he had been weak in had been Drawing. In that he had barely scraped through. Mrs Rupa Mehra remembered his little sketches in the children's autograph books and felt that the examiners had been ignorant and unjust.

Collecting herself after a while and dabbing her forehead with eau-de-Cologne, she went out into the garden. It was a warm day, but a breeze was blowing from the river. Savita was sleeping, and all the others were out. She looked over at the unswept path past the bed of cannas. The young sweeper-woman was talking to the gardener in the shade of a mulberry tree. I must speak to her about this, thought Mrs Rupa Mehra absently.

Mansoor's father, the far shrewder Mateen, came out onto the verandah with the account book. Mrs Rupa Mehra was in no mood for the accounts, but felt it was her duty to do them. Wearily she returned to the verandah, got her spectacles out of her black bag and looked at the book.

The sweeper-woman took up a broom and started sweeping up the dust, dried leaves, twigs, and fallen flowers from the path. Mrs Rupa Mehra glanced unseeingly at the open page of the account book.

'Should I come back later?' asked Mateen.

'No, I'll do them now. Wait a minute.' She got out a blue pencil and looked at the lists of purchases. Doing the accounts had become much more of a strain since Mateen's return from his village. Quite apart from his odd variant of the Hindi script, Mateen was more experienced than his son at cooking the books.

'What is this?' asked Mrs Rupa Mehra. 'Another four-seer tin of ghee? Do you think we are millionaires? When did we order our last tin?'

'Must be two months ago, Burri Memsahib.'

'When you were away loafing in the village, didn't Mansoor buy a tin?'

'He may have, Burri Memsahib. I don't know; I didn't see it.'

Mrs Rupa Mehra started riffling back through the pages of the account book until she came upon the entry in Mansoor's more legible hand. 'He bought one a month ago. Almost twenty rupees. What happened to it? We're not a family of twelve to go through a tin at such a rate.'

'I've just returned, myself,' Mateen ventured, with a glance at the sweeper-woman.

'You'd buy us a sixteen-seer tin of ghee a week if given half the chance,' said Mrs Rupa Mehra. 'Find out what happened to the rest of it.'

'It goes in puris and parathas and on the daal – and Memsahib likes Sahib to put some ghee every day on his chapatis and rice –' began Mateen.

'Yes, yes,' Mrs Rupa Mehra interrupted. 'I can work out how much should go into all that. I want to find out what happened to the rest of it. We don't keep open house – nor has this become the shop of a sweetseller.'

'Yes, Burri Memsahib.'

'Though young Mansoor seems to treat it like one.'

Mateen said nothing, but frowned, as if in disapproval.

'He eats the sweets and drinks the nimbu pani that is kept aside for guests,' continued Mrs Rupa Mehra.

'I'll speak to him, Burri Memsahib.'

'I'm not sure about the sweets,' said Mrs Rupa Mehra scrupulously. 'He is a self-willed boy. And you – you never bring my tea regularly. Why does no one take care of me in this house? When I am at Arun Sahib's house in Calcutta his servant brings me tea all the time. No one even asks here. If I had my own house, it would have been different.'

Mateen, understanding that the accounts session was over, went to get Mrs Rupa Mehra her tea. About fifteen minutes later, Savita, who had emerged from her afternoon nap looking groggily beautiful, came onto the verandah to find her mother re-reading Arun's letter in tears, and saying, 'Ear-drops! He even calls them ear-drops!' When Savita found out what the matter was she felt a rush of sympathy towards her mother and indignation towards Meenakshi.

'How could she have done that?' she asked. Savita's fierce defensiveness towards those whom she loved was masked by her gentle nature. She was independent-spirited but in such a low key that only those who knew her very well got any sense that her life and desires were not entirely determined by the easy drift of circumstance. She held her mother close and said, 'I am amazed at Meenakshi. I will make sure that nothing happens to the other medal. Daddy's memory is worth a great deal more than her small-minded whims. Don't cry, Ma. I'll send a letter off immediately. Or if you want we can write one together.'

'No, no.' Mrs Rupa Mehra looked down sadly at her empty cup.

When Lata returned and heard the news, she too was shocked. She had been her father's darling and had loved looking at his academic medals; indeed she had been very unhappy when they had been given to Meenakshi. What could they mean to her, Lata had wondered, compared to what they would mean to his daughters? She was now most unpleasantly being proved right. She was angry too with Arun who, she felt, had permitted this sorry business by his consent or indulgence and who now made light of the event in his fatuously casual letter. His brutal little attempts to shock or tease his mother made Lata fume. As to his suggestion that she go to Calcutta and cooperate in his introductions – Lata decided that that would be the last thing in the world she would do.

Pran returned late from his first meeting of the student welfare committee to a household that was clearly not itself, but he was too exhausted to inquire immediately what the matter was. He sat in his favourite chair – a rocking-chair requisitioned from Prem Nivas – and read for a few minutes. After a while he asked Savita if she wanted to go for a walk, and during the course of it he was briefed on the crisis. He asked Savita whether he could look over the letter she had written to Meenakshi. It was not that he lacked faith in his wife's judgment – quite the contrary. But he hoped that he, not being a Mehra and therefore less taut with a sense of injury, might be of help in preventing irretrievable words from exacerbating irretrievable acts. Family quarrels, whether over property or sentiment, were bitter things; their prevention was almost a public duty.

Savita was happy to show him the letter. Pran looked it over, nodding from time to time. 'This is fine,' he said rather gravely, as if approving a student's essay. 'Diplomatic but deadly! Soft steel,' he added in a different tone. He looked at his wife with an expression of amused curiosity. 'Well, I'll see it goes off tomorrow.'

Malati came over later. Lata told her about the medal. Malati described some experiments that they had been required to perform at the medical college, and Mrs Rupa Mehra was sufficiently disgusted to be distracted – at least for a while.

Savita noticed for the first time over dinner that Malati had a crush on her husband. It was evident in the way the girl looked at him over the soup and avoided looking at him over the main course. Savita was not at all annoyed. She assumed that but to know Pran was to love him; Malati's affection was both natural and harmless. Pran, it was clear, was unaware of this; he was talking about the play that he had put on for Annual Day the previous year: *Julius Caesar* – a typical university choice (Pran was saying) since so few parents wanted their daughters to act on stage ... but, on the other hand, the themes of violence, patriotism and a change of regime had given it a freshness in the present historical context that it would not otherwise have had.

The obtuseness of intelligent men, thought Savita with a smile, is half of what makes them lovable. She closed her eyes for a second to say a prayer for his health and her own and that of her unborn child.

Part Two

2.1

ON the morning of Holi, Maan woke up smiling. He drank
not just one but several glasses of thandai laced with
bhang and was soon as high as a kite. He felt the ceiling
floating down towards him – or was it he who was
floating up towards it? As if in a mist he saw his friends
Firoz and Imtiaz together with the Nawab Sahib arrive at
Prem Nivas to greet the family. He went forward to wish
them a happy Holi. But all he could manage was a continu-
ous stream of laughter. They smeared his face with colour
and he went on laughing. They sat him down in a corner
and he continued laughing until the tears rolled down his
cheeks. The ceiling had now floated away entirely, and it
was the walls that were pulsing in and out in an immensely
puzzling way. Suddenly he got up and put his arms around
Firoz and Imtiaz and made for the door, pushing them
along with him.

'Where are we going?' asked Firoz.

'To Pran's,' Maan replied. 'I have to play Holi with my
sister-in-law.' He grabbed a couple of packets of coloured
powder and put them in the pocket of his kurta.

'You'd better not drive your father's car in this state,'
Firoz said.

'Oh, we'll take a tonga, a tonga,' Maan said, waving his
arms around, and then embracing Firoz. 'But first drink
some thandai. It's got an amazing kick.'

They were lucky. There weren't many tongas out this
morning, but one trotted up just as they got onto Cornwal-
lis Road. The horse was nervous as he passed the crowds
of stained and shouting merry-makers on the way to the
university. They paid the tonga-wallah double his regular
fare and smeared his forehead pink and that of his horse
green for good measure. When Pran saw them dismounting
he went up and welcomed them into the garden. Just
outside the door on the verandah of the house was a large
bathtub filled with pink colour and several foot-long
copper syringes. Pran's kurta and pyjama were soaked and
his face and hair smeared with yellow and pink powder.

99

'Where's my bhabhi?' shouted Maan.

'I'm not coming out –' said Savita from inside.

'That's fine,' shouted Maan, 'we'll come in.'

'Oh no you won't,' said Savita. 'Not unless you've brought me a sari.'

'You'll get your sari, what I want now is my pound of flesh,' Maan said.

'Very funny,' said Savita. 'You can play Holi as much as you like with my husband, but promise me you'll only put a bit of colour on me.'

'Yes, yes, I promise! Just a smidgeon, no more, of powder – and then a bit on your pretty little sister's face – and I'll be satisfied – until next year.'

Savita opened the door cautiously. She was wearing an old and faded salwaar-kameez and looked lovely: laughing and cautious, half-poised for flight.

Maan held the packet of pink powder in his left hand. He now smeared a bit on his sister-in-law's forehead. She reached into the packet to do the same to him.

'– and a little bit on each cheek –' Maan continued as he smeared more powder on her face.

'Good, that's fine,' said Savita. 'Very good. Happy Holi!'

'– and a little bit here –' said Maan, rubbing more on her neck and shoulders and back, holding her firmly and fondling her a bit as she struggled to get away.

'You're a real ruffian, I'll never trust you again,' said Savita. 'Please let me go, please stop it, no, Maan, please – not in my condition. . . .'

'So I'm a ruffian, am I?' said Maan, reaching for a mug and dipping it in the tub.

'No, no, no –' said Savita. 'I didn't mean it. Pran, please help me,' said Savita, half laughing and half crying. Mrs Rupa Mehra was peeping in alarm through the window. 'No wet colour, Maan, please –' cried Savita, her voice rising to a scream.

But despite all her pleading Maan poured three or four mugs of cold pink water over her head, and rubbed the moist powder onto her kameez over her breasts, laughing all the while.

Lata was looking out of the window too, amazed by Maan's bold, licentious attack – the licence presumably being provided by the day. She could almost feel Maan's hands on her and then the cold shock of the water. To her surprise, and to that of her mother, who was standing next to her, she gave a gasp and a shiver. But nothing would induce her to go outside, where Maan was continuing his polychrome pleasures.

'Stop –' cried Savita, outraged. 'What kind of cowards are you? Why don't you help me? He's had bhang, I can see it – just look at his eyes –'

Firoz and Pran managed to distract Maan by squirting several syringes full of coloured water at him, and he fled into the garden. He was not very steady on his feet as it was, and he stumbled and fell into the bed of yellow cannas. He raised his head among the flowers long enough to sing the single line: 'Oh revellers, it's Holi in the land of Braj!' and sat down again, disappearing from view. A minute later, like a cuckoo-clock, he got up to repeat the same line and sat down once more. Savita, bent on revenge, filled a small brass pot with coloured water and came down the steps into the garden. She made her way stealthily to the bed of cannas. Just at that moment Maan got up once again to sing. As his head appeared above the cannas he saw Savita and the lota of water. But it was too late. Savita, fierce and determined, threw the entire contents on his face and chest. Looking at Maan's astonished expression she began to giggle. But Maan had sat down once again and was now crying, 'Bhabhi doesn't love me, my bhabhi doesn't love me.'

'Of course I don't,' said Savita. 'Why should I?'

Tears rolled down Maan's cheeks and he was inconsolable. When Firoz tried to get him onto his feet he clung to him. 'You're my only real friend,' he wept. 'Where are the sweets?'

Now that Maan had neutralized himself, Lata ventured out and played a little mild Holi with Pran, Firoz and Savita. Mrs Rupa Mehra got smeared with a bit of colour too.

But all the while Lata kept wondering what it would have felt like to be rubbed and smeared by the cheerful Maan in such a public and intimate way. And this was a man who was engaged! She had never seen anyone behave even remotely like Maan – and Pran was very far from furious. A strange family, the Kapoors, she thought.

Meanwhile Imtiaz, like Maan, had got fairly stoned on the bhang in his thandai and was sitting on the steps, smiling at the world and murmuring repeatedly to himself a word that sounded like 'myocardial'. Sometimes he murmured it, sometimes he sang it, at other times it seemed to be a question both profound and unanswerable. Occasionally he would touch the small mole on his cheek in a thoughtful manner.

A group of about twenty students – multicoloured and almost unrecognizable – appeared along the road. There were even a few girls in the group – and one of them was the now purple-skinned (but still green-eyed) Malati. They had induced Professor Mishra to join them; he lived just a few houses away. His whale-like bulk was unmistakable, and besides, he had very little colour on him.

'What an honour, what an honour,' said Pran, 'but I should have come to your house, Sir, not you to mine.'

'Oh, I don't stand on ceremony in such matters,' said Professor Mishra, pursing his lips and twinkling his eyes. 'Now, do tell me, where is the charming Mrs Kapoor?'

'Hello, Professor Mishra, how nice of you to have come to play Holi with us,' Savita said, advancing with a little powder in her hand. 'Welcome, all of you. Hello, Malati, we were wondering what had happened to you. It's almost noon. Welcome, welcome –'

A little colour was applied to the Professor's broad forehead as he bent downwards.

But Maan, who had been leaning, downcast, on Firoz's shoulder now dropped a canna he had been toying with and advanced with an open-hearted smile towards Professor Mishra. 'So you are the notorious Professor Mishra,' he said in delighted welcome. 'How wonderful to meet so infamous a man.' He embraced him warmly. 'Tell me, are you really an Enemy of the People?' he asked encouragingly. 'What a remarkable face, what a mobile expression!' he murmured in awed appreciation as Professor Mishra's jaw dropped.

'Maan,' said Pran, startled.

'So nefarious!' said Maan, in whole-hearted approval.

Professor Mishra stared at him.

'My brother calls you Moby-Dick, the great white whale,' continued Maan in a friendly way. 'Now I see why. Come for a swim,' he invited Professor Mishra generously, indicating the tub full of pink water.

'No, no, I don't think –' began Professor Mishra weakly.

'Imtiaz, give me a hand,' said Maan.

'Myocardial,' said Imtiaz to indicate his willingness. They lifted Professor Mishra by the shoulders and led him physically to the tub.

'No, no, I'll get pneumonia!' cried Professor Mishra in anger and bewilderment.

'Stop it, Maan!' said Pran sharply.

'What do you say, Doctor Sahib?' Maan asked Imtiaz.

'No contra-indications,' said Imtiaz, and the two pushed the unprepared professor into the tub. He splashed around, wet to the bone, submerged in pinkness, wild with rage and confusion. Maan looked on, helpless with happy laughter, while Imtiaz grinned beneficently. Pran sat down on a step with his head in his hands. Everyone else looked on horrified.

When Professor Mishra got out of the tub he stood on the verandah for a second, trembling with wetness and emotion. Then he looked around the company like a bull at bay, and walked dripping down the steps and out of the garden. Pran was too taken aback even to apologize. With indignant dignity the great pink figure made its way out of the gate and disappeared along the road.

Maan looked around at the assembled company for approval. Savita avoided looking at him, and everyone else was quiet and subdued, and Maan felt that for some reason he was in the dog-house again.

DRESSED in a fresh, clean kurta-pyjama after a long bath, happy under the influence of bhang and a warm afternoon, Maan had gone to sleep back in Prem Nivas. He dreamed an unusual dream: he was about to catch a train to Banaras to meet his fiancée. He realized that if he did not catch this train he would be imprisoned, but under what charge he did not know. A large body of policemen, from the Inspector-General of Purva Pradesh down to a dozen constables, had formed a cordon around him, and he, together with a number of mud-spattered villagers and about twenty festively dressed women students, was being herded into a compartment. But he had left something behind and was pleading for permission to go and get it. No one was listening to him and he was becoming more and more vehement and upset. And he was falling at the feet of the policemen and the ticket examiner and pleading that he be allowed to go out: he had left something somewhere else, perhaps at home, perhaps on another platform, and it was imperative that he be allowed to go and get it. But now the whistle was blowing and he had been forced onto the train. Some of the women were laughing at him as he got more and more desperate. 'Please let me out,' he kept insisting, but the train had left the station and was picking up speed. He looked up and saw a small red and white sign: *To Stop Train Pull Chain. Penalty for Improper Use Rupees 50.* He leapt onto a berth. The villagers tried to stop him as they saw what he was about to do, but he struggled against them and grabbed hold of the chain and pulled it down with all his might. But it had no effect. The train kept gathering speed, and now the women were laughing even more openly at him. 'I've left something there,' he kept repeating, pointing in the general direction from which they had come, as if somehow the train would listen to his explanation and consent to stop. He took out his wallet and begged the ticket examiner: 'Here is fifty rupees. Just stop the train. I beg you – turn it back. I don't mind going to jail.' But the man kept examining everyone else's ticket and shrugging off Maan as if he was a harmless madman.

Maan woke up, sweating, and was relieved to return to the familiar objects of his room in Prem Nivas – the stuffed chair and the overhead fan and the red rug and the five or six paperback thrillers.

Quickly dismissing the dream from his mind, he went to wash his face. But as he looked at his startled expression in the mirror a picture of the women in the dream came vividly back to him. Why were they laughing at me? he asked himself. Was the laughter unkind ...? It was just a dream, he went on, reassuringly. But though he kept splashing water on his face, he could not get the notion out of his head that there was an explanation, and that it lay just beyond his reach. He closed his eyes to recapture something of the dream once more, but it was all extremely vague now, and only his unease, the sense that he had left something behind, remained. The faces of the women, the villagers, the ticket collector, the policemen, had all been washed away. What could I have left behind? he wondered. Why were they laughing at me?

From somewhere in the house he could hear his father calling sharply: 'Maan, Maan – are you awake? The guests will start arriving for the concert in half an hour.' He did not answer and looked at himself in the mirror. Not a bad face, he thought: lively, fresh, strong-featured, but balding slightly at the temples – which struck him as being a bit unfair, considering that he was only twenty-five. A few minutes later a servant was sent to inform him that his father wished to see him in the courtyard. Maan asked the servant if his sister Veena had arrived yet, and heard that she and her family had come and gone. Veena had in fact come to his room but, finding him asleep, had not let her son Bhaskar disturb him.

Maan frowned, yawned, and went to the clothes' cupboard. He wasn't interested in guests and concerts and he wanted to go to sleep again, dreamlessly this time. That was how he usually spent the evening of Holi when he was in Banaras – sleeping off his bhang.

Downstairs the guests had started coming in. They were most of them dressed in new clothes and, apart from a little red under the nails and in the hair, were not outwardly coloured by the morning's revels. But they were all in excellent humour, and smiling, not just from the effect of the bhang. Mahesh Kapoor's Holi concerts were an annual ritual, and had been going on at Prem Nivas for as long as anyone could remember. His father and grandfather had hosted them as well, and the only years that anyone could remember that they had not been held were when their host had been in jail.

Saeeda Bai Firozabadi was the singer tonight, as she had been for the last two years. She lived not far from Prem Nivas, came from a family of singers and courtesans, and had a fine, rich, and powerfully emotional voice. She was a woman of about thirty-five, but her fame as a singer had already spread outwards from Brahmpur and nowadays she was called for recitals as far away as Bombay and Calcutta. Many of Mahesh Kapoor's guests this evening had come not so much to enjoy their host's – or, more accurately, their unobtrusive hostess's – excellent hospitality as to listen to Saeeda Bai. Maan, who had spent his previous two Holis in Banaras, knew of her fame but had not heard her sing.

Rugs and white sheets were spread over the semi-circular courtyard, which was bounded by whitewashed rooms and open corridors along the curve, and was open to the garden on the straight side. There was no stage, no microphone, no visible separation of the singer's area from the audience. There were no chairs, just pillows and bolsters to lean on, and a few potted plants around the edge of the sitting area. The first few guests were standing around sipping fruit juice or thandai and nibbling kababs or nuts or traditional Holi sweets. Mahesh Kapoor stood greeting his guests as they came into the courtyard, but he was waiting for Maan to come down to relieve him so that he could spend a little time talking to some of his guests instead of merely exchanging perfunctory pleasantries with all of them. If he doesn't come down in five minutes, said

Mahesh Kapoor to himself, I'll go upstairs and shake him awake myself. He may as well be in Banaras for all his usefulness. Where is the boy? The car's already been sent for Saeeda Bai.

2.3

THE car had in fact been sent for Saeeda Bai and her musicians more than half an hour ago, and Mahesh Kapoor was just beginning to be concerned. Most of the audience had by now sat down, but some were still standing around and talking. Saeeda Bai was known on occasion to have committed to sing somewhere and then simply gone off on an impulse somewhere else – perhaps to visit an old or a new flame, or to see a relative, or even to sing to a small circle of friends. She behaved very much to suit her own inclinations. This policy, or rather tendency, could have done her a great deal of harm professionally if her voice and her manner had not been as captivating as they were. There was even a mystery to her irresponsibility if seen in a certain light. This light had begun to dim for Mahesh Kapoor, however, when he heard a buzz of muted exclamation from the door: Saeeda Bai and her three accompanists had finally arrived.

She looked stunning. If she had not sung a word all evening but had kept smiling at familiar faces and looking appreciatively around the room, pausing whenever she saw a handsome man or a good-looking (if 'modern') woman, that would have been enough for most of the men present. But very shortly she made her way to the open side of the courtyard – the part bordering the garden – and sat down near her harmonium, which a servant of the house had carried from the car. She moved the pallu of her silk sari further forward over her head: it tended to slip down, and one of her most charming gestures – to be repeated throughout the evening – was to adjust her sari to ensure that her head was not left uncovered. The musicians – a tabla player, a sarangi player, and a man who strummed the tanpura – sat down and started tuning their instruments as she pressed down a black key with a heavily ringed right hand, gently forcing air through the bellows with an equally bejewelled left. The tabla player used a small silver hammer to tauten the leather straps on his right-hand drum, the sarangi player adjusted his tuning-pegs and bowed a few phrases on the strings. The audience adjusted itself and found places for new arrivals. Several boys, some as young as six, sat down near their fathers or uncles. There was an air of pleasant expectancy. Shallow bowls filled with rose and jasmine petals were passed around: those who, like Imtiaz, were still somewhat high on bhang, lingered delightedly over their enhanced fragrance.

Upstairs on the balcony two of the (less modern) women looked down through the slits in a cane screen and discussed Saeeda Bai's dress, ornament, face, manner, antecedents and voice.

'Nice sari, but nothing special. She always wears Banarasi silk. Red tonight. Last year it was green. Stop and go.'

'Look at that zari work in the sari.'

'Very flashy, very flashy – but I suppose all that is necessary in her profession, poor thing.'

'I wouldn't say "poor thing". Look at her jewels. That heavy gold necklace with the enamel work –'

'It comes down a bit too low for my taste –'

'– well, anyway, they say it was given to her by the Sitagarh people!'

'Oh.'

'And many of those rings too, I should think. She's quite a favourite of the Nawab of Sitagarh. They say he's quite a lover of music.'

'And of music-makers?'

'Naturally. Now she's greeting Maheshji and his son Maan. He looks very pleased with himself. Is that the Governor he's –'

'Yes, yes, all these Congress-wallahs are the same. They talk about simplicity and plain living, and then they invite this kind of person to the house to entertain their friends.'

'Well, she's not a dancer or anything like that.'

'No, but you can't deny what she is!'

'But your husband has come as well.'

'My husband!'

The two ladies – one the wife of an ear, nose and throat specialist, one the wife of an important middleman in the shoe trade – looked at each other in exasperated resignation at the ways of men.

'She's exchanging greetings with the Governor now. Look at him grinning. What a fat little man – but they say he's very capable.'

'Aré, what does a Governor have to do except snip a few ribbons here and there and enjoy the luxuries of Government House? Can you hear what she's saying?'

'No.'

'Every time she shakes her head the diamond on her nose-pin flashes. It's like the headlight of a car.'

'A car that has seen many passengers in its time.'

'What time? She's only thirty-five. She's guaranteed for many more miles. And all those rings. No wonder she loves doing adaab to anyone she sees.'

'Diamonds and sapphires mainly, though I can't see clearly from here. What a large diamond that is on her right hand –'

'No, that's a white something – I was going to say a white sapphire, but it isn't that – I was told it was even more expensive than a diamond, but I can't remember what they call it.'

'Why does she need to wear all those bright glass bangles among the gold ones. They look a bit cheap!'

'Well, she's not called Firozabadi for nothing. Even if her forefathers – her foremothers – don't come from Firozabad, at least her glass bangles do. Oh-hoh, look at the eyes she's making at the young men!'

'Shameless.'

'That poor young man doesn't know where to look.'

'Who is he?'

'Doctor Durrani's younger son, Hashim. He's just eighteen.'

'Hmm. . . .'

'Very good-looking. Look at him blush.'

'Blush! All these Muslim boys might look innocent, but they are lascivious in their hearts, let me tell you. When we used to live in Karachi –'

But at this point Saeeda Bai Firozabadi, having exchanged salutations with various members of the audience, having spoken to her musicians in a low tone, having placed a paan in the corner of her right cheek, and having coughed twice to clear her throat, began to sing.

2.4

ONLY a few words had emerged from that lovely throat when the 'wah! wahs!' and other appreciative comments of the audience elicited an acknowledging smile from Saeeda Bai. Lovely she certainly was, and yet in what did her loveliness lie? Most of the men there would have been hard-pressed to explain it; the women sitting above might have been more perceptive. She was no more than pleasing-looking, but she had all the airs of the distinguished courtesan – the small marks of favour, the tilt of the head, the flash of the nose-pin, a delightful mixture of directness and circuitousness in her attentions to those whom she was attracted by, a knowledge of Urdu poetry, especially of the ghazal, that was by no means viewed as shallow even in an audience of cognoscenti. But more than all this, and more than her clothes and jewels and even her exceptional natural talent and musical training, was a touch of heartache in her voice. Where it had come from, no one knew for sure, though rumours about her past were common enough in Brahmpur. Even the women could not say that this sadness was a device. She seemed somehow to be both bold and vulnerable, and it was this combination that was irresistible.

It being Holi, she began her recital with a few Holi songs. Saeeda Bai Firozabadi was Muslim, but sang these happy descriptions of young Krishna playing Holi with the milkmaids of his foster-father's village with such charm and energy that one would have had to be convinced that she saw the scene before her own eyes. The little boys in the audience looked at her wonderingly. Even Savita, whose first Holi this was at her parents-in-law's house, and who had come more out of duty than from the expectation of pleasure, began to enjoy herself.

Mrs Rupa Mehra, torn between the need to protect her younger daughter and the inappropriateness of one of her generation, particularly a widow, forming a part of the downstairs audience, had (with a strict admonition to Pran to keep an eye on Lata) disappeared upstairs. She was looking through a gap in the cane screen and saying to Mrs Mahesh Kapoor, 'In my time, no women would have been allowed in the courtyard for such an evening.' It was a little unfair of Mrs Rupa Mehra to make such an objection known to her quiet, much-put-upon hostess, who had in fact spoken about this very matter to her husband, and had been impatiently overruled by him on the grounds that the times were changing.

People came in and out of the courtyard during the recital, and, as Saeeda Bai's eye caught a movement somewhere in the audience, she acknowledged the new guest with a gesture of her hand that broke the line of her self-accompaniment on the harmonium. But the mournful bowed strings of the sarangi were more than a sufficient shadow to her voice, and she often turned to the player with a look of appreciation for some particularly fine imitation or improvisation. Most of her attention, however, was devoted to young Hashim Durrani, who sat in the front row and blushed beetroot whenever she broke off singing to make some pointed remark or address some casual couplet towards him. Saeeda Bai was notorious for choosing a single person in the audience early in the evening and addressing all her songs to that one person – he would become for her the cruel one, the slayer, the hunter, the executioner and so on – the anchor, in fact, for her ghazals.

Saeeda Bai enjoyed most of all singing the ghazals of

Mir and Ghalib, but she also had a taste for Vali Dakkani – and for Mast, whose poetry was not particularly distinguished, but who was a great local favourite because he had spent much of his unhappy life in Brahmpur, reciting many of his ghazals for the first time in the Barsaat Mahal for the culture-stricken Nawab of Brahmpur before his incompetent, bankrupt, and heirless kingdom was annexed by the British. So her first ghazal was one of Mast's, and no sooner had the first phrase been sung than the enraptured audience burst into a roar of appreciation.

'I do not stoop, yet find my collar torn ...' she began, and half-closed her eyes.

'I do not stoop, yet find my collar torn.
The thorns were here, beneath my feet, not there.'

'Ah,' said Mr Justice Maheshwari helplessly, his head vibrating in ecstasy on his plump neck. Saeeda Bai continued:

'Can I be blameless when no voice will blame
The hunter who has caught me in this snare?'

Here Saeeda Bai shot a half-melting, half-accusing look at the poor eighteen-year-old. He looked down immediately, and one of his friends nudged him and repeated delightedly, 'Can you be blameless?' which embarrassed him yet further.

Lata looked at the young fellow with sympathy, and at Saeeda Bai with fascination. How can she do this? she thought, admiring and slightly horrified – she's just moulding their feelings like putty, and all those men can do is grin and groan! And Maan's the worst of the lot! Lata liked more serious classical music as a rule. But now she – like her sister – found herself enjoying the ghazal too, and also – though it was strange to her – the transformed, romantic atmosphere of Prem Nivas. She was glad her mother was upstairs.

Meanwhile, Saeeda Bai, extending an arm to the guests, sang on:

> 'The pious people shun the tavern door –
> But I need courage to outstare their stare.'

'Wah! wah!' cried Imtiaz loudly from the back. Saeeda Bai graced him with a dazzling smile, then frowned as if startled. However, gathering herself together, she continued:

> 'After a wakeful night outside that lane,
> The breeze of morning stirs the scented air.
>
> Interpretation's Gate is closed and barred
> But I go through and neither know nor care.'

'And neither know nor care,' was sung simultaneously by twenty voices.

Saeeda Bai rewarded their enthusiasm with a tilt of her head. But the unorthodoxy of this couplet was out-done by that of the next:

> 'I kneel within the Kaaba of my heart
> And to my idol raise my face in prayer.'

The audience sighed and groaned; her voice almost broke at the word 'prayer'; one would have had to be an unfeeling idol oneself to have disapproved.

> 'Though blinded by the sun I see, O Mast,
> The moonlight of the face, the clouds of hair.'

Maan was so affected by Saeeda Bai's recitation of this final couplet that he raised his arms helplessly towards her. Saeeda Bai coughed to clear her throat, and looked at him enigmatically. Maan felt hot and shivery all over, and was speechless for a while, but drummed a tabla beat on the head of one of his rustic nephews, aged seven.

'What will you listen to next, Maheshji?' Saeeda Bai asked his father. 'What a grand audience you always provide in your house. And so knowledgeable that I sometimes feel myself redundant. I need only sing two words and you gentlemen complete the rest of the ghazal.'

There were cries of 'No, no!', 'What are you saying?' and 'We are your mere shadows, Saeeda Begum!'

'I know that it is not because of my voice but through your grace – and that of the one above –' she added, 'that I am here tonight. I see your son is as appreciative of my poor efforts as you have been for many years. Such things must run in the blood. Your father, may he rest in peace, was full of kindness to my mother. And now I am the recipient of your graciousness.'

'Who has graced whom?' responded Mahesh Kapoor gallantly.

Lata looked at him in some surprise. Maan caught her eye and winked – and Lata could not help smiling back. Now that he was a relative, she felt much easier with him. Her mind flashed back to his behaviour this morning, and again a smile curled up at the corners of her mouth. Lata would never be able to hear Professor Mishra lecturing again without seeing him emerge from the tub as wet and pink and helpless as a baby.

'But some young men are so silent,' Saeeda Bai continued, 'that they might as well themselves be idols in temples. Perhaps they have opened their veins so often that they have no blood left. Hanh?' She laughed delightfully.

'Why should my heart not be tied to him?' she quoted –
'Today he is dressed in colourful clothes.'

Young Hashim looked down guiltily at his blue, embroidered kurta. But Saeeda Bai continued unmercifully:

'How can I praise his fine taste in dress?
In appearance he is like a prince.'

Since much Urdu poetry, like much Persian and Arabic

poetry before it, had been addressed by poets to young men, Saeeda Bai found it mischievously easy to find such references to male dress and demeanour as would make it clear whom she was aiming her shafts at. Hashim might blush and burn and bite his lower lip but her quiver was not likely to run out of couplets. She looked at him and recited:

> 'Your red lips are full of nectar.
> How rightly you have been named Amrit Lal!'

Hashim's friends were by now convulsed with laughter. But perhaps Saeeda Bai realized that he could not take much more amorous baiting for the moment, and she graciously permitted him a little respite. By now the audience felt bold enough to make its own suggestions, and after Saeeda Bai had indulged her taste for one of the more abstruse and referential ghazals of Ghalib – a strongly intellectual taste for so sensuous a singer – someone in the audience suggested one of his simpler favourites, 'Where have those meetings and those partings gone?'

Saeeda Bai assented by turning to the sarangi and tabla players and murmuring a few words. The sarangi began to play an introduction to the slow, melancholy, nostalgic ghazal, written by Ghalib not in his old age but when he was not much older than the singer herself. But Saeeda Bai invested each of its questioning couplets with such bitterness and sweetness that even the hearts of the oldest in the audience were moved. When they joined in at the end of a familiar sentimental line it was as if they were asking a question of themselves rather than displaying their knowledge to their neighbours. And this attentiveness brought forth a yet deeper response from the singer, so that even the difficult last couplet, where Ghalib reverts to his metaphysical abstractions, climaxed rather than ebbed away from the ghazal as a whole.

After this wonderful rendition, the audience was eating out of the palm of Saeeda Bai's hand. Those who had planned to leave at the latest by eleven o'clock found themselves unable to tear themselves away, and soon it was past midnight.

Maan's little nephew had gone off to sleep in his lap, as had many of the other young boys, and they had been taken off to bed by the servants. Maan himself, who had been in love often enough in the past and was therefore prone to a sort of cheerful nostalgia, was overwhelmed by Saeeda Bai's last ghazal, and popped a thoughtful cashew nut into his mouth. What could he do? – he felt he was falling irresistibly in love with her. Saeeda Bai had now reverted to her playfulness with Hashim, and Maan felt a little jab of jealousy as she tried to get a response out of the boy. When:

'The tulip and the rose, how do they compare with you?
They are no more than incomplete metaphors'

produced no result beyond a restless shifting in his place, she attempted the bolder couplet:

'Your beauty was that which once bewitched the world –
Even after the first down came on your cheeks it was a wonder.'

This found its mark. There were two puns here, one mild and one not so mild: 'world' and 'wonder' were the same word – aalam – and 'the first down' could possibly be taken as meaning 'a letter'. Hashim, who had a very light down on his face, tried his best to act as if 'khat' simply meant letter, but it cost him a great deal of discomfiture. He looked around at his father for support in his suffering – his own friends were less than no help, having long ago decided to join in teasing him – but the absent-minded Dr Durrani was half-asleep somewhere at the back. One of his friends rubbed his palm gently along Hashim's cheek and sighed strickenly. Blushing, Hashim got up to leave the courtyard and take a walk in the garden. He was only half on his feet when Saeeda Bai fired a barrel of Ghalib at him:

'At the mere mention of my name in the gathering she
    got up to go. . . .'

Hashim, almost in tears, did adaab to Saeeda Bai, and walked out of the courtyard. Lata, her eyes shining with quiet excitement, felt rather sorry for him; but soon she too had to leave with her mother and Savita and Pran.

2.5

MAAN, on the other hand, did not feel at all sorry for his lily-livered rival. He came forward, and with a nod to the left and the right, and a respectful salutation to the singer, seated himself in Hashim's place. Saeeda Bai, happy to have a prepossessing if not quite so sprig-like a volunteer as her source of inspiration for the rest of the evening, smiled at him and said:

'By no means forsake constancy, O heart,
For love without constancy has weak foundations.'

To which Maan replied instantly and stoutly:

'Wherever Dagh has sat down he has sat down.
Others may quit your assembly, not he!'

This met with laughter from the audience, but Saeeda Bai decided to have the last word by repaying him in his own poet:

'Dagh is ogling and peeping once more.
He will trip up and get ensnared somewhere.'

At this just response the audience burst into spontaneous

applause. Maan was as delighted as anyone that Saeeda Bai Firozabadi had trumped his ace or, as she would have put it, tenned his nine. She was laughing as hard as anyone, and so were her accompanists, the fat tabla player and his lean counterpart on the sarangi. After a while, Saeeda Bai raised her hand for silence and said, 'I hope that half that applause was intended for my witty young friend here.'

Maan replied with playful contrition: 'Ah, Saeeda Begum, I had the temerity to banter with you but – all my arrangements were in vain.'

The audience laughed again, and Saeeda Bai Firozabadi rewarded this quotation from Mir with a lovely rendition of the appropriate ghazal:

'All my arrangements were in vain, no drug could cure my
    malady.
It was an ailment of my heart that made a final end of me.

My term of youth I passed in tears, in age I closed my eyes
    at last;
That is: I lay awake long nights till dawn and sleep came
    finally.'

Maan looked at her, bewitched, entranced and enraptured. What would it be like to lie awake long nights till dawn, listening to her voice in his ear?

'We who were helpless were accused of independent
    thought and deed.
They did whatever they desired, and us they smeared with
                                                    calumny.

Here in this world of darkness and of light this is my only
    part:
To somehow pass from day to night and night to day in
    misery.

Why do you ask what has become of Mir's religion, his
    Islam?
Wearing the brahmin's mark he haunts the temples of
    idolatry.'

The night continued with alternating banter and music. It
was very late now; the audience of a hundred had thinned
to a dozen. But Saeeda Bai was now so deep in the flow of
music that those who remained, remained spellbound. They
moved forward into a more intimate group. Maan did not
know whether he was held there more by his ears or by his
eyes. From time to time Saeeda Bai paused in her singing
and talked to the surviving faithful. She dismissed the
sarangi and tanpura players. Finally she even dismissed her
tabla player, who could hardly keep his eyes open. Her
voice and the harmonium were all that were left, and they
provided enchantment enough. It was near dawn when she
herself yawned and rose.
    Maan looked at her with half-longing, half-laughing
eyes. 'I'll arrange for the car,' he said.
    'I'll walk in the garden till then,' said Saeeda Bai. 'This
is the most beautiful time of night. Just have this' – she
indicated the harmonium – 'and the other things – sent
back to my place tomorrow morning. Well, then,' she
continued to the five or six people left in the courtyard:

'Now Mir takes his leave from the temple of idols –
We shall meet again . . .'

Maan completed the couplet: '. . . if it be God's will.'
    He looked at her for an acknowledging nod, but she had
turned towards the garden already.
    Saeeda Bai Firozabadi, suddenly weary 'of all this' (but
what was 'all this'?) strolled for a minute or two through
the garden of Prem Nivas. She touched the glossy leaves of
a pomelo tree. The harsingar was no longer in bloom, but
a jacaranda flower dropped downwards in the darkness.
She looked up and smiled to herself a little sadly. Everything was quiet: not even a watchman, not even a dog. A

few favourite lines from a minor poet, Minai, came to her mind, and she recited, rather than sang, them aloud:

'The meeting has dispersed; the moths
 Bid farewell to the candle-light.
Departure's hour is on the sky.
Only a few stars mark the night. . . .'

She coughed a little – for the night had got chilly all of a sudden – wrapped her light shawl more closely around her, and waited for someone to escort her to her own house, also in Pasand Bagh, no more than a few minutes away.

2.6

THE day after Saeeda Bai sang at Prem Nivas was Sunday. The light-hearted spirit of Holi was still in the air. Maan could not get her out of his mind.

He wandered about in a daze. He arranged for her harmonium to be sent on to her house early in the afternoon, and was tempted to get into the car himself. But that was hardly the time to visit Saeeda Bai – who had, anyway, given him no indication that she would be pleased to see him again.

Maan had nothing as such to do. That was part of his problem. In Banaras there was business of a kind to keep him busy; in Brahmpur he had always felt himself to be at a loose end. He didn't really mind, though. Reading was not something he enjoyed much, but he did like wandering around with friends. Perhaps he should visit Firoz, he thought.

Then, thinking of the ghazals of Mast, he jumped into a tonga, and told the tonga-wallah to take him to the Barsaat Mahal. It had been years since Maan had been there, and the thought of seeing it appealed to him today.

The tonga passed through the green residential 'colonies' of the eastern part of Brahmpur, and came to Nabiganj, the commercial street that marked the end of spaciousness and the start of clutter and confusion. Old Brahmpur lay beyond it, and, almost at the western end of the old town, on the Ganges itself, stood the beautiful grounds and the still more beautiful marble structure of the Barsaat Mahal.

Nabiganj was the fashionable shopping street where the quality of Brahmpur were to be seen strolling up and down of an evening. At the moment, in the heat of the afternoon, there were not many shoppers about, and only a few cars and tongas and bicycles. The signs of Nabiganj were painted in English, and the prices matched the signs. Bookshops like the Imperial Book Depot, well-stocked general stores such as Dowling & Snapp (now under Indian management), fine tailors such as Magourian's where Firoz had all his clothes (from suits to achkans) made, the Praha shoe shop, an elegant jeweller's, restaurants and coffee houses such as the Red Fox, Chez Yasmeen, and the Blue Danube, and two cinema-halls – Manorma Talkies (which showed Hindi films) and the Rialto (which leaned towards Hollywood and Ealing): each of these places had played some minor or major role in one or another of Maan's romances. But today, as the tonga trotted through the broad street, Maan paid them no attention. The tonga turned off onto a smaller road, and almost immediately onto a yet smaller one, and they were now in a different world.

There was just enough room for the tonga to get through among the bullock-carts, rickshaws, cycles and pedestrians who thronged both the road and the pavement – which they shared with barbers plying their trade out of doors, fortune-tellers, flimsy tea-stalls, vegetable-stands, monkey-trainers, ear-cleaners, pickpockets, stray cattle, the odd sleepy policeman sauntering along in faded khaki, sweat-soaked men carrying impossible loads of copper, steel rods, glass or scrap paper on their backs as they yelled 'Look out! Look out!' in voices that somehow pierced through the din, shops of brassware and cloth (the owners attempting with shouts and gestures to entice uncertain shoppers in), the small carved stone entrance of the Tinny

Tots (English Medium) School which opened out onto the courtyard of the reconverted haveli of a bankrupt aristocrat, and beggars – young and old, aggressive and meek, leprous, maimed or blinded – who would quietly invade Nabiganj as evening fell, attempting to avoid the police as they worked the queues in front of the cinema-halls. Crows cawed, small boys in rags rushed around on errands (one balancing six small dirty glasses of tea on a cheap tin tray as he weaved through the crowd), monkeys chattered in and bounded about a great shivering-leafed pipal tree and tried to raid unwary customers as they left the well-guarded fruit-stand, women shuffled along in anonymous burqas or bright saris, with or without their menfolk, a few students from the university lounging around a chaat-stand shouted at each other from a foot away either out of habit or in order to be heard, mangy dogs snapped and were kicked, skeletal cats mewed and were stoned, and flies settled everywhere: on heaps of foetid, rotting rubbish, on the uncovered sweets at the sweetseller's in whose huge curved pans of ghee sizzled delicious jalebis, on the faces of the sari-clad but not the burqa-clad women, and on the horse's nostrils as he shook his blinkered head and tried to forge his way through Old Brahmpur in the direction of the Barsaat Mahal.

Maan's thoughts were suddenly interrupted by the sight of Firoz standing by a pavement stall. He halted the tonga at once and got down.

'Firoz, you'll have a long life – I was just thinking about you. Well, half an hour ago!'

Firoz said that he was just wandering about, and had decided to buy a walking-stick.

'For yourself or for your father?'

'For myself.'

'A man who has to buy himself a walking-stick in his twenties might not have such a long life after all,' said Maan.

Firoz, after leaning at various angles on various sticks, decided upon one and, without haggling about the price, bought it.

'And you, what are you doing here? Paying a visit to Tarbuz ka Bazaar?' he asked.

'Don't be disgusting,' said Maan cheerfully. Tarbuz ka Bazaar was the street of singing girls and prostitutes.

'Oh, but I forgot,' said Firoz slyly: 'Why should you consort with mere melons when you can taste the peaches of Samarkand?'

Maan frowned.

'What further news of Saeeda Bai?' continued Firoz, who, from the back of the audience, had enjoyed the previous night. Though he had left by midnight, he had sensed that Maan's engagement notwithstanding, romance was once again entering his friend's life. More, perhaps, than anyone else, he knew and understood Maan.

'What do you expect?' asked Maan, a little glumly. 'Things will happen the way they will. She didn't even allow me to escort her back.'

This was quite unlike Maan, thought Firoz, who had very rarely seen his friend depressed. 'So where are you going?' he asked him.

'To the Barsaat Mahal.'

'To end it all?' inquired Firoz tenderly. The parapet of the Barsaat Mahal faced the Ganges and was the venue of a number of romantic suicides every year.

'Yes, yes, to end it all,' said Maan impatiently. 'Now tell me, Firoz, what do you advise?'

Firoz laughed. 'Say that again. I can't believe it,' he said. 'Maan Kapoor, beau of Brahmpur, at whose feet young women of good families, heedless of reputation, hasten to fling themselves like bees on a lotus, seeks the advice of the steely and stainless Firoz on how to proceed in a matter of the heart. You're not asking for my legal advice, are you?'

'If you're going to act like that –' began Maan, disgruntled. Suddenly a thought struck him. 'Firoz, why is Saeeda Bai called Firozabadi? I thought she came from these parts.'

Firoz replied: 'Well, her people did in fact originally come from Firozabad. But that's all history. In fact her mother Mohsina Bai settled in Tarbuz ka Bazaar, and

Saeeda Bai was brought up in this part of the city.' He pointed his stick towards the disreputable quarter. 'But naturally Saeeda Bai herself, now that she's made good and lives in Pasand Bagh – and breathes the same air as you and I – doesn't like people to talk about her local origins.'

Maan mused over this for a few moments. 'How do you know so much about her?' he asked, puzzled.

'Oh, I don't know,' said Firoz, waving away a fly. 'This sort of information just floats around in the air.' Not reacting to Maan's look of astonishment, he went on, 'But I must be off. My father wants me to meet someone boring who's coming to tea.' Firoz leaped into Maan's tonga. 'It's too crowded to ride a tonga through Old Brahmpur; you're better off on foot,' he told Maan, and drove off.

Maan wandered along, mulling – but not for long – over what Firoz had said. He hummed a bit of the ghazal that had embedded itself in his mind, stopped to buy a paan (he preferred the spicier, darker green leaves of the desi paan to the paler Banarasi), manoeuvred his way across the road through a crowd of cycles, rickshaws, push-carts, men and cattle, and found himself in Misri Mandi, near a small vegetable-stall, close to where his sister Veena lived.

Feeling guilty for having been asleep when she came to Prem Nivas the previous afternoon, Maan decided impulsively to visit her – and his brother-in-law Kedarnath and nephew Bhaskar. Maan was very fond of Bhaskar and liked throwing arithmetical problems at him like a ball to a performing seal.

As he entered the residential areas of Misri Mandi, the alleys became narrower and cooler and somewhat quieter, though there were still plenty of people getting about from place to place and others just lounging around or playing chess on the ledge near the Radhakrishna Temple, whose walls were still bright with the stains of Holi colours. The strip of bright sunlight above his head was now thin and unoppressive, and there were fewer flies. After turning into a still narrower alley, just three feet across, and avoiding a urinating cow, he arrived at his sister's house.

It was a very narrow house: three storeys and a flat rooftop, with about a room-and-a-half on each storey and a central grating in the middle of the stairwell that allowed light from the sky all the way through to the bottom. Maan entered through the unlocked door and saw old Mrs Tandon, Veena's mother-in-law, cooking something in a pan. Old Mrs Tandon disapproved of Veena's taste for music, and it was because of her that the family had had to come back the previous evening without listening to Saeeda Bai. She always gave Maan the shivers; and so, after a perfunctory greeting, he went up the stairs, and soon found Veena and Kedarnath on the roof – playing chaupar in the shade of a trellis and evidently deep in an argument.

2.7

VEENA was a few years older than Maan, and she took after her mother in shape – she was short and a bit dumpy. When Maan appeared on the roof, her voice had been raised, and her plump, cheerful face was frowning, but when she saw Maan she beamed at him. Then she remembered something and frowned again.

'So you've come to apologize. Good! And not a moment too soon. We were all very annoyed with you yesterday. What kind of brother are you, sleeping for hours on end when you know that we're bound to visit Prem Nivas?'

'But I thought you'd stay for the singing –' said Maan.

'Yes, yes,' said Veena nodding her head. 'I'm quite sure you thought of all that when you dozed off. It had nothing to do with bhang, for instance. And it simply slipped your mind that we had to get Kedarnath's mother home before the music began. At least Pran came early and met us at Prem Nivas, with Savita and his mother-in-law and Lata –'

'Oh, Pran, Pran, Pran –' said Maan in exasperation. 'He's always the hero and I'm always the villain.'

'That's not true, don't dramatize things,' said Veena, thinking of Maan as a small boy trying to shoot pigeons with a catapult in the garden and claiming to be an archer

125

in the Mahabharata. 'It's just that you have no sense of responsibility.'

'Anyway, what were you quarrelling about when I came up the stairs? And where's Bhaskar?' asked Maan, thinking of his father's recent remarks and trying to change the subject.

'He's out with his friends flying kites. Yes, he was annoyed as well. He wanted to wake you up. You'll have to have dinner with us today to make up.'

'Oh – uh –' said Maan undecidedly, wondering whether he might not risk visiting Saeeda Bai's house in the evening. He coughed. 'But what were you quarrelling about?'

'We weren't quarrelling,' said the mild Kedarnath, smiling at Maan. He was in his thirties, but already greying. A worried optimist, he, unlike Maan, had – if anything – too strong a sense of his responsibilities, and the difficulties of starting from scratch in Brahmpur after Partition had aged him prematurely. When he was not on the road somewhere in south India drumming up orders, he was working till late at night in his shop in Misri Mandi. It was in the evenings that business was conducted there, when middlemen like him bought baskets of shoes from the shoemakers. His afternoons, though, were fairly free.

'No, not quarrelling, not quarrelling at all. Just arguing about chaupar, that's all,' said Veena hastily, throwing the cowrie-shells down once more, counting her tally, and moving her pieces forward on the cross-shaped cloth board.

'Yes, yes, I'm quite sure,' said Maan.

He sat down on the rug and looked around at the flowerpots filled with leafy plants, which Mrs Mahesh Kapoor had contributed to her daughter's roof garden. Veena's saris were hanging up to dry on one side of the roof, and there were bright splashes of Holi colour all over the terrace. Beyond the roof a jumble of rooftops, minarets, towers and temple-tops stretched out as far as the railway station in 'New' Brahmpur. A few paper kites, pink, green and yellow, like the colours of Holi, fought each other in the cloudless sky.

'Don't you want something to drink?' asked Veena quickly. 'I'll get you some sherbet – or will you have tea? I'm afraid we don't have any thandai,' she added gratuitously.

'No, thank you.... But you can answer my question. What was the debate about?' demanded Maan. 'Let me guess. Kedarnath wants to keep a second wife, and he naturally wants your consent.'

'Don't be stupid,' said Veena, a little sharply. 'I want a second child and I naturally want his consent. Oh!' she exclaimed, realizing her indiscretion and looking at her husband. 'I didn't mean to – anyway, he's my brother – we can ask his advice, surely.'

'But you don't want my mother's advice in the matter, do you?' countered Kedarnath.

'Well, it's too late now,' said Maan genially. 'What do you want a second child for? Isn't Bhaskar enough?'

'We can't afford a second child,' said Kedarnath, with his eyes closed – a habit that Veena still found bothersome. 'Not at the moment, at any rate. My business is – well, you know how it is. And now there's the possibility of a shoemakers's strike.' He opened his eyes. 'And Bhaskar is so bright that we want to send him to the very best schools. And they don't come cheap.'

'Yes, we wish he was stupid, but unfortunately –'

'Veena is being witty as usual,' said Kedarnath. 'Just two days before Holi she reminded me that it was difficult to make ends meet, what with the rent and the rise in food prices and everything. And the cost of her music lessons and my mother's medicines and Bhaskar's special maths books and my cigarettes. Then she said that we had to count the rupees, and now she's saying that we should have another child because every grain of rice it will eat has already been marked with its name. The logic of women! She was born into a family of three children, so she thinks that having three children is a law of nature. Can you imagine how we'll survive if they're all as bright as Bhaskar?'

Kedarnath, who was usually quite henpecked, was putting up a good fight.

'Only the first child is bright as a rule,' said Veena. 'I guarantee that my next two will be as stupid as Pran and Maan.' She resumed her sewing.

Kedarnath smiled, picked up the speckled cowries in his scarred palm, and threw them onto the board. Normally he was a very polite man and would have given Maan his full attention, but chaupar was chaupar, and it was almost impossible to stop playing once the game had begun. It was even more addictive than chess. Dinners grew cold in Misri Mandi, guests left, creditors threw tantrums, but the chaupar players pleaded for just one more game. Old Mrs Tandon had once thrown the cloth board and the sinful shells into a disused well in a neighbouring lane, but, despite the family finances, another set had been procured, and the truant couple now played on the roof, even though it was hotter there. In this way they avoided Kedarnath's mother, whose gastric and arthritic problems made climbing stairs difficult. In Lahore, both because of the horizontal geography of the house and because of her role as the confident matriarch of a wealthy and unscattered family, she had exercised tight, even tyrannical, control. Her world had collapsed with the trauma of Partition.

Their conversation was interrupted by a scream of outrage from a neighbouring rooftop. A large, middle-aged woman in a scarlet cotton sari was shouting down from her roof at an invisible adversary:

'They want to suck my blood, it's clear! Neither can I lie down anywhere nor can I sit anywhere in peace. The sound of the thumping of balls is driving me mad.... Of course what takes place on the roof can be heard downstairs! You wretched kahars, you useless washers of dishes, can't you keep your children under control?'

Noticing Veena and Kedarnath on their roof, she walked over the connecting rooftops, clambering through a low gap in the far wall. With her piercing voice, wild teeth and large, spreading, sagging breasts, she made a powerful impression on Maan.

After Veena had introduced them, the woman said with a fierce smile:

'Oh, so this is the one who isn't getting married.'

'He's the one,' admitted Veena. She didn't tempt fate by mentioning Maan's tentative engagement to the girl from Banaras.

'But didn't you tell me you'd introduced him to that girl – what's her name, remind me – the one who came here from Allahabad to visit her brother?'

Maan said: 'Amazing how it is with some people. You write "A" and they read "Z".'

'Well, it's quite natural,' said the woman in a predatory manner. 'A young man, a young woman. . . .'

'She was very pretty,' Veena said. 'With eyes like a deer.'

'But she doesn't have her brother's nose – luckily,' added the woman.

'No – it's much finer. And it even quivers a bit like a deer's.'

Kedarnath, despairing of his game of chaupar, got up to go downstairs. He couldn't stand visits from this over-friendly neighbour. Ever since her husband had got a telephone installed in their house, she had become even more self-confident and strident.

'What shall I call you?' Maan asked the woman.

'Bhabhi. Just bhabhi,' said Veena.

'So – how did you like her?' asked the woman.

'Fine,' said Maan.

'Fine?' said the woman, pouncing delightedly on the word.

'I meant, fine that I should call you bhabhi.'

'He's very cunning,' said Veena.

'I'm no less so,' asserted her neighbour. 'You should come here, meet people, meet nice women,' she told Maan. 'What is the charm of living in the colonies? I tell you, when I visit Pasand Bagh or Civil Lines my brain goes dead in four hours. When I return to the lanes of our neighbourhood it starts whirring again. People here care for each other; if someone falls ill the whole neighbourhood asks about them. But it may be difficult to fix you up. You should get a slightly taller girl than average –'

'I'm not concerned about all that,' said Maan, laughing. 'A short one is fine by me.'

'So you don't mind whether she's tall or short, dark or fair, thin or fat, ugly or beautiful?'

'Z for A again,' said Maan, glancing in the direction of her roof. 'By the way, I like your method of drying your blouses.'

The woman gave a short hoot of laughter, which might have been self-deprecatory if it hadn't been so loud. She looked back at the rack-like arrangement of steel on the top of her water-tank.

'There's no other place on my roof,' she said. 'You've got lines all over on your side.... You know,' continued the woman, off on a tangent, 'marriage is strange. I read in *Star-Gazer* that a girl from Madras, well-married, with two children, saw *Hulchul* five times – five times! – and got completely besotted with Daleep Kumar – to the extent that she went off her head. She went down to Bombay, clearly not knowing what she was doing, because she didn't even have his address. Then she found it with the help of one of these filmi fan magazines, took a taxi there, and confronted him with all kinds of mad, obsessed remarks. Eventually he gave her a hundred rupees to help her get back, and threw her out. But she returned.'

'Daleep Kumar!' said Veena, frowning. 'I don't think much of his acting. I think he must have made it all up for publicity.'

'Oh no, no! Have you seen him in *Deedar*? He is amazing! And *Star-Gazer* says he's such a nice man – he would never go after publicity. You must tell Kedarnath to beware of Madrasi women, he spends so much time there, they're very fierce.... I hear that they don't even wash their silk saris gently, they just go dhup! dhup! dhup! like washerwomen under the tap – Oh! my milk!' cried the woman in sudden alarm. 'I must go – I hope it hasn't – my husband –' And she rushed off like a great red apparition across the rooftops.

Maan burst out laughing.

'Now I'm off as well,' he said. 'I've had enough of life outside the colonies. My brain's whirring too much.'

'You can't go,' said Veena sternly and sweetly. 'You've just come. They said you played Holi the whole morning with Pran and his professor and Savita and Lata, so you can certainly spend this afternoon with us. And Bhaskar will be very annoyed if he misses you again. You should have seen him yesterday. He looked like a black imp.'

'Will he be at the shop this evening?' asked Maan, coughing a bit.

'Yes. I suppose so. Thinking about the patterns of the shoe-boxes. Strange boy,' said Veena.

'Then I'll visit him on my way back.'

'On your way back from where?' asked Veena. 'And aren't you coming for dinner?'

'I'll try – I promise,' said Maan.

'What's wrong with your throat?' asked Veena. 'You've been up till late, haven't you? How late, I wonder? Or is it just from getting soaked at Holi? I'll give you some jushanda to cure it.'

'No – that vile stuff! Take it yourself as a preventative,' exclaimed Maan.

'So – how was the singing? And the singer?' asked Veena.

Maan shrugged so indifferently that Veena got worried.

'Be careful, Maan,' she warned him.

Maan knew his sister too well to try to protest his innocence. Besides, Veena would soon enough hear about his public flirting.

'It's not her that you're going to visit?' asked Veena sharply.

'No – heaven forbid,' said Maan.

'Yes, heaven forbid. So where are you going?'

'To the Barsaat Mahal,' said Maan. 'Come along with me! You remember we used to go there for picnics as children? Come. All you're doing is playing chaupar.'

'So that's how you think I fill my days, do you? Let me tell you, I work almost as hard as Ammaji. Which reminds me, I saw yesterday that they'd chopped the top of the neem tree down, the one you used to climb to get to the upstairs window. It makes a difference to Prem Nivas.'

'Yes, she was very angry,' said Maan, thinking of his mother. 'The Public Works Department were just supposed to trim it to get rid of the vulture's roost, but they hired a contractor who chopped down as much wood as possible and made off with it. But you know Ammaji. All she said was, "What you have done is really not right."'

'If Baoji had been in the least concerned about these matters, he'd have done to that man what he did to that tree,' said Veena. 'There's so little greenery in this part of town that you really learn to appreciate it when you see it. When my friend Priya came to Pran's wedding, the garden was looking so beautiful that she said to me: "I feel as if I've been let out of a cage." She doesn't even have a roof garden, poor thing. And they hardly ever let her out of the house. "Come in the palanquin, leave on the bier": that's the way it is with the daughters-in-law in that house.' Veena looked darkly over the rooftops towards her friend's house in the next neighbourhood. A thought struck her. 'Did Baoji talk to anyone about Pran's job yesterday evening? Doesn't the Governor have something to do with these appointments? In his capacity as Chancellor of the university?'

'If he did I didn't hear him,' said Maan.

'Hmm,' said Veena, not very pleased. 'If I know Baoji, he probably thought about it, and then pushed the thought aside as being unworthy of him. Even we had to wait in line for our turn to get that pitiful compensation for the loss of our business in Lahore. And that too when Ammaji was working day and night in the refugee camps. I sometimes think he cares for nothing but politics. Priya says her father's equally bad. All right, eight o'clock. I'll make your favourite alu paratha.'

'You can bully Kedarnath, but not me,' said Maan with a smile.

'All right, go, go!' said Veena, tossing her head. 'You'd think we were still in Lahore from the amount we get to see you.'

Maan made a propitiatory sound, a tongue-click followed by a half-sigh.

'With all his sales trips, I sometimes feel I have a quarter of a husband,' continued Veena. 'And an eighth of a brother each.' She rolled up the chaupar board. 'When are you returning to Banaras to do an honest day's work?'

'Ah, Banaras,' said Maan with a smile, as if Veena had suggested Saturn. And Veena left it at that.

2.8

IT was evening by the time Maan got to the Barsaat Mahal, and the grounds were not crowded. He walked through the arched entrance in the boundary wall, and passed through the outer grounds, a sort of park which was for the most part covered with dry grass and bushes. A few antelope browsed under a large neem tree, bounding lazily away as he approached.

The inner wall was lower, the arched entranceway less imposing, more delicate. Verses from the Quran in black stone and bold geometrical patterns in coloured stone were embedded in its marble façade. Like the outer wall, the inner wall ran along three sides of a rectangle. The fourth side was common to both: a sheer drop from a stone platform – protected only by a balustrade – to the waters of the Ganga below.

Between the inner entrance and the river was the celebrated garden and the small but exquisite palace. The garden itself was a triumph as much of geometry as of horticulture. It was unlikely in fact that the flowers with which it was now planted – other than jasmine and the dark red, deep-scented Indian rose – were the same as those for which it had been planned more than two centuries ago. What few flowers remained now looked exhausted from the daily heat. But the well-tended, well-watered lawns, the great, shady neem trees dispersed symmetrically about the grounds, and the narrow sandstone strips that divided the flowerbeds and lawns into octagons and squares provided an island of calm in a troubled and crowded town. Most beautiful of all was the small, perfectly shaped pleasure-palace of the Nawabs of Brahmpur, set in the exact centre of the inner gardens, a filigreed jewel box of white marble, its spirit compounded equally of extravagant dissipation and architectural restraint.

In the days of the Nawabs, peacocks used to roam the grounds, and their raucous voices would on occasion compete with the musical entertainments laid on for those reclining and declining rulers: a performance by dancing girls, a more serious performance of khyaal by a court musician, a poetry competition, a new ghazal by the poet Mast.

The thought of Mast brought the wonder of the previous evening back into Maan's mind. The clear lines of the ghazal, the soft lines of Saeeda Bai's face, her banter, which now seemed to Maan to be both lively and tender, the way she would pull her sari over her head as it threatened to slip off, the special attentions she had granted Maan, all these came back to him as he wandered up and down along the parapet with thoughts very far from suicide. The river breeze was pleasant, and Maan began to feel encouraged by events. He had been wondering whether to stop by Saeeda Bai's house in the evening, and he felt suddenly optimistic.

The great red sky covered the burnished Ganga like an inflamed bowl. On the far shore the sands stretched endlessly away.

As he looked at the river he was struck by a remark he had heard from the mother of his fiancée. She, pious woman, was convinced that on the festival of Ganga Dussehra the obedient river would begin to rise again and would cover, on that particular day, one of the steps along the ghats of her native Banaras. Maan began to think about his fiancée and her family and became depressed about his engagement, as he usually did when he gave it any thought. His father had arranged it, as he had threatened to do; Maan, taking the path of least resistance, had gone along with it; and now it was an ominous fact of life.

He would sooner or later have to get married to her. Maan felt no affection for her – they had hardly met each other except in the company of their families – and he did not really want to think about her. He was much happier thinking about Samia, who was now in Pakistan with her family but who wanted to return to Brahmpur just to visit Maan, or Sarla, the daughter of the former Inspector-General of Police, or any of his other earlier passions. A later flame, however brightly it burned, did not douse an earlier one in Maan's heart. He continued to feel sudden throbs of warmth and goodwill at the thought of almost any of them.

2.9

IT was dark by the time Maan walked back into the crowded town, uncertain once again about whether he should try his luck at Saeeda Bai's. He was in Misri Mandi in a few minutes. It was a Sunday, but not a holiday here. The shoe-market was full of bustle, light and noise: Kedarnath Tandon's shop was open, as were all the other shops in the arcade – known as the Brahmpur Shoe Mart – that was located just off the main street. The so-called basket-wallahs ran hastily from shop to shop with baskets on their heads, offering their wares to the wholesalers: shoes that they and their families had made during the day and that they would have to sell in order to buy food as well as leather and other materials for their next day's work. These shoemakers, mainly members of the 'untouchable' jatav caste or a few lower-caste Muslims, a large number of whom had remained in Brahmpur after Partition, were gaunt and poorly clad, and many of them looked desperate. The shops were elevated three feet or so above street level to enable them to place their baskets at the edge of the cloth-covered floor for examination by a possible buyer. Kedarnath, for instance, might take a pair of shoes out of a basket submitted for his inspection. If he rejected the basket, the seller would have to run to the next wholesaler

– or to one in another arcade. Or Kedarnath might offer a lower price, which the shoemaker might or might not accept. Or Kedarnath might husband his funds by offering the shoemaker the same price but less cash, making up the remainder with a credit note or 'chit' that would be accepted by a discount agent or a seller of raw materials. Even after the shoes were sold, the material for the next day remained to be bought, and the basket-wallahs were virtually forced to sell to someone not too late in the evening, even on unfavourable terms.

Maan did not understand the system, the large turn-over of which depended on an effective network of credit in which chits were everything and banks played almost no role. Not that he wanted to understand it; the cloth business in Banaras was dependent on different financial structures. He had merely dropped in for a social chat, a cup of tea, and a chance to meet his nephew. Bhaskar, who was dressed in a white kurta-pyjama like his father, was sitting barefoot on the white cloth spread out on the floor of the shop. Kedarnath would occasionally turn to him and ask him to calculate something – sometimes to keep the boy entertained, sometimes because he was of real help. Bhaskar found the shop very exciting – what with the pleasure of working out discount rates or postal rates for distant orders, and the intriguing geo-metrical and arithmetical relationships of the stacked shoe-boxes. He would delay going to bed as long as possible in order to remain with his father, and Veena sometimes had to send word more than once that he should come home.

'How's the frog?' asked Maan, holding Bhaskar's nose. 'Is he awake? He's looking very neat today.'

'You should have seen him yesterday morning,' said Kedarnath. 'You could only see his eyes.'

Bhaskar's face lit up. 'What have you brought me?' he asked Maan. 'You were the one who was sleeping. You have to pay me a forfeit.'

'Son –' began his father reprovingly.

'Nothing,' said Maan gravely, releasing his nose and

clapping his hand over his mouth. 'But tell me – what do you want? Quickly!'

Bhaskar furrowed his forehead in thought.

Two men walked past, talking about the impending strike by the basket-wallahs. A radio blared. A policeman shouted. The shop-boy brought in two glasses of tea from the market and, after blowing on the surface for a minute, Maan began drinking.

'Is everything going well?' he asked Kedarnath. 'We didn't get much chance to talk this afternoon.'

Kedarnath shrugged, then nodded.

'Everything's fine. But you look preoccupied.'

'Preoccupied? Me? Oh, no, no –' Maan protested. 'But what's this I hear about the basket-wallahs threatening to go on strike?'

'Well –' said Kedarnath.

He could imagine the havoc that the threatened strike would spell, and didn't want to get onto the subject. He passed his hand through his greying hair in an anxious gesture and closed his eyes.

'I'm still thinking,' said Bhaskar.

'That's a good habit,' said Maan. 'Well, tell me your decision next time – or send me a postcard.'

'All right,' said Bhaskar, with the faintest of smiles.

'Bye, now.'

'Bye, Maan Maama ... oh, did you know that if you have a triangle like this, and if you draw squares on the sides like this, and then add up these two squares you get that square,' Bhaskar gesticulated. 'Every time,' he added.

'Yes, I do know that.' Smug frog, thought Maan.

Bhaskar looked disappointed, then cheered up. 'Shall I tell you why?' he asked Maan.

'Not today. I have to go. Do you want a goodbye sum?'

Bhaskar was tempted to say, 'Not today,' but changed his mind. 'Yes,' he said.

'What is 256 times 512?' asked Maan, who had worked this out beforehand.

'That's too easy,' said Bhaskar. 'Ask me another one.'

'Well, what's the answer, then?'

'One lakh, thirty-one thousand and seventy-two.'

'Hmm. What's 400 times 400?'

Bhaskar turned away, hurt.

'All right, all right,' said Maan. 'What's 789 times 987?'

'Seven lakhs, seventy-eight thousand, seven hundred and forty-three,' said Bhaskar after a pause of a few seconds.

'I'll take your word for it,' said Maan. The thought had suddenly entered his mind that perhaps he had better not risk his luck with Saeeda Bai, who was so notoriously temperamental.

'Aren't you going to check?' asked Bhaskar.

'No, genius, I have to be off.' He tousled his nephew's hair, gave his brother-in-law a nod, and walked out onto the main street of Misri Mandi. There he hailed a tonga to go back home.

On the way he changed his mind yet again and went straight to Saeeda Bai's instead.

The khaki-turbaned watchman at the entrance appraised him for a moment and told him that Saeeda Bai was not in. Maan thought of writing her a note, but was faced with a problem. Which language should he write it in? Saeeda Bai would certainly not be able to read English and would almost certainly not be able to read Hindi, and Maan could not write Urdu. He tipped the watchman a rupee and said, 'Please inform her that I came to pay my respects.'

The watchman raised his right hand to his turban in a salute, and said:

'And Sahib's name?'

Maan was about to give his name when he thought of something better.

'Tell her that I am one who lives in love,' he said. This was an atrocious pun on Prem Nivas.

The watchman nodded impassively.

Maan looked at the small, two-storeyed, rose-coloured house. Some lights were on inside, but that might not mean anything. With a sinking heart and a sense of deep frustration he turned away and walked in the general direction of home. But then he did what he usually did when he was feeling low or at a loose end – he sought out the company of friends. He told the tonga-wallah to take him to the house of the Nawab Sahib of Baitar. Upon finding that Firoz and Imtiaz were out till late, he decided to pay a visit to Pran. Pran hadn't been pleased about the ducking of the whale, and Maan felt he should smooth his ruffled feathers. His brother struck him as being a decent fellow, but a man of tepid, unboisterous affections. Maan thought cheerfully that Pran just did not have it in him to be as love-struck and miserable as he was.

2.10

RETURNING later to the sadly ill-maintained mansion of Baitar House, Maan chatted till late with Firoz and Imtiaz, and then stayed overnight.

Imtiaz went out very early on a call, yawning and cursing his profession.

Firoz had some urgent work with a client, went into the section of his father's vast library that served as his chambers, remained closeted in there for a couple of hours, and emerged whistling in time for a late breakfast.

Maan, who had deferred having breakfast until Firoz could eat with him, was still sitting in his guest bedroom, looking over the *Brahmpur Chronicle*, and yawning. He had a slight hangover.

An ancient retainer of the Nawab Sahib's family appeared before him and, after making his obeisance and salutation, announced that the younger Sahib – Chhoté Sahib – would be coming for breakfast immediately, and would Maan Sahib be pleased to go downstairs? All this was pronounced in stately and measured Urdu.

Maan nodded. After about half a minute he noticed that the old servant was still standing a little distance away and gazing expectantly at him. Maan looked at him quizzically.

'Any other command?' asked the servant, who – Maan noticed – looked at least seventy years old, but quite spry. He would have to be fit, thought Maan, in order to negotiate the stairs of the Nawab Sahib's house several times a day. Maan wondered why he had never seen him before.

'No,' said Maan. 'You can go. I'll be down shortly.' Then, as the old man raised his cupped palm to his forehead in polite salutation and turned to leave, Maan said, 'Er, wait. . . .'

The old man turned around and waited to hear what Maan had to say.

'You must have been with the Nawab Sahib for many years,' said Maan.

'Yes, Huzoor, that I have. I am an old servitor of the family. Most of my life I have worked at Baitar Fort, but now in my old age it has pleased him to bring me here.'

Maan smiled to see how unselfconsciously and with what quiet pride the old man referred to himself in the very words – 'purana khidmatgar' – that Maan had used mentally to classify him.

Seeing Maan silent, the old man went on. 'I entered service when I was, I think, ten years old. I came from the Nawab Sahib's village of Raipur on the Baitar Estate. In those days I would get a rupee a month, and it was more than sufficient for my needs. This war, Huzoor, has raised the price of things so much that with many times such a salary people find the going difficult. And now with Partition – and all its troubles, and with the Nawab Sahib's brother going to Pakistan and all these laws threatening the property – things are uncertain, very' – he paused to find another word, but in the end merely repeated himself – 'very uncertain.'

Maan shook his head in the hope of clearing it and said, 'Is there any aspirin available here?'

The old man looked pleased that he could be of some use, and said, 'Yes, I believe so, Huzoor. I will go and get some for you.'

'Excellent,' said Maan. 'No, don't get it for me,' he added, having second thoughts about making the old man exert himself. 'Just leave a couple of tablets near my plate when I come downstairs for breakfast. Oh, by the way,' he went on, as he visualized the two small tablets at the side of his plate, 'why is Firoz called Chhoté Sahib, when he and Imtiaz were born at the same time?'

The old man looked out of the window at the spreading magnolia tree which had been planted a few days after the twins had been born. He coughed for a second, and said, 'Chhoté Sahib, that is Firoz Sahib, was born seven minutes after Burré Sahib.'

'Ah,' said Maan.

'That is why he looks more delicate, less robust, than Burré Sahib.'

Maan was silent, pondering this physiological theory.

'He has his mother's fine features,' said the old man, then stopped, as if he had transgressed some limit of explanation.

Maan recalled that the Begum Sahiba – the Nawab of Baitar's wife and the mother of his daughter and twin sons – had maintained strict purdah throughout her life. He wondered how a male servant could have known what she looked like, but could sense the old man's embarrassment and did not ask. Possibly a photograph, much more likely discussion among the servants, he thought.

'Or so they say,' added the old man. Then he paused, and said, 'She was a very good woman, rest her soul. She was good to us all. She had a strong will.'

Maan was intrigued by the old man's hesitant but eager incursions into the history of the family to which he had given his life. But he was – despite his headache – quite hungry now, and decided that this was not the time to talk. So he said, 'Tell Chhoté Sahib I will be down in, well, in seven minutes.'

If the old man was puzzled by Maan's unusual sense of timing, he did not show it. He nodded and was about to go.

'What do they call you?' asked Maan.

'Ghulam Rusool, Huzoor,' said the old servant.

Maan nodded and he left.

'DID you sleep well?' asked Firoz, smiling at Maan.

'Very. But you rose early.'

'Not earlier than usual. I like to get a great deal of work done before breakfast. If it hadn't been a client, it would have been my briefs. It seems to me that you don't work at all.'

Maan looked at the two little pills lying on his quarter-plate, but said nothing, so Firoz went on.

'Now, I don't know anything about cloth —' began Firoz.

Maan groaned. 'Is this a serious conversation?' he asked.

'Yes, of course,' said Firoz, laughing. 'I've been up at least two hours.'

'Well, I have a hangover,' said Maan. 'Have a heart.'

'I do,' said Firoz, reddening a bit. 'I can assure you.' He looked at the clock on the wall. 'But I'm due at the Riding Club. One day I'm going to teach you polo, you know, Maan, all your protests notwithstanding.' He got up and walked towards the corridor.

'Oh, good,' said Maan, more cheerfully. 'That's more in my line.'

An omelette came. It was lukewarm, having had to traverse the vast distance between the kitchens and the breakfast room in Baitar House. Maan looked at it for a while, then gingerly bit a slice of unbuttered toast. His hunger had disappeared again. He swallowed the aspirins.

Firoz, meanwhile, had just got to the front door when he noticed his father's private secretary, Murtaza Ali, argu-ing with a young man at the entrance. The young man wanted to meet the Nawab Sahib. Murtaza Ali, who was not much older, was trying, in his sympathetic, troubled way, to prevent him from doing so. The young man was not dressed very well – his kurta was of homespun white cotton – but his Urdu was cultured in both accent and expression. He was saying:

'But he told me to come at this time, and here I am.'

The intensity of expression on his lean features made Firoz pause.

'What seems to be the matter?' asked Firoz.

Murtaza Ali turned and said: 'Chhoté Sahib, it appears that this man wants to meet your father in connection with a job in the library. He says he has an appointment.'

'Do you know anything about this?' Firoz asked Murtaza Ali.

'I'm afraid not, Chhoté Sahib.'

The young man said: 'I have come from some distance and with some difficulty. The Nawab Sahib told me expressly that I should be here at ten o'clock to meet him.'

Firoz, in a not unkindly tone, said: 'Are you sure he meant today?'

'Yes, quite sure.'

'If my father had said he was to be disturbed, he would have left word,' said Firoz. 'The problem is that once my father is in the library, well, he's in a different world. You will, I am afraid, have to wait till he comes out. Or could you perhaps come back later?'

A strong emotion began to work at the corners of the young man's mouth. Clearly he needed the income from the job, but equally clearly he had a sense of pride. 'I am not prepared to run around like this,' he said clearly but quietly.

Firoz was surprised. This definiteness, it appeared to him, bordered on incivility. He had not said, for example: 'The Nawabzada will appreciate that it is difficult for me ...' or any such ameliorative phrase. Simply: 'I am not prepared....'

'Well, that is up to you,' said Firoz, easily. 'Now, forgive me, I have to be somewhere very soon.' He frowned slightly as he got into the car.

2.12

THE previous evening, when Maan had stopped by, Saeeda Bai had been entertaining an old but gross client of hers:

the Raja of Marh, a small princely state in Madhya Pradesh. The Raja was in Brahmpur for a few days, partly to supervise the management of some of his Brahmpur lands, and partly to help in the construction of a new temple to Shiva on the land he owned near the Alamgiri Mosque in Old Brahmpur. The Raja was familiar with Brahmpur from his student days twenty years ago; he had frequented Mohsina Bai's establishment when she was still living with her daughter Saeeda in the infamous alley of Tarbuz ka Bazaar.

Throughout Saeeda Bai's childhood she and her mother had shared the upper floor of a house with three other courtesans, the oldest of whom, by virtue of the fact that she owned the place, had acted for years as their madam. Saeeda Bai's mother did not like this arrangement, and as her daughter's fame and attractiveness grew she was able to assert their independence. When Saeeda Bai was seventeen or so, she came to the attention of the Maharaja of a large state in Rajasthan, and later the Nawab of Sitagarh; and from then on there had been no looking back.

In time, Saeeda Bai had been able to afford her present house in Pasand Bagh, and had gone to live there with her mother and young sister. The three women, separated by gaps of about twenty and fifteen years respectively, were all attractive, each in her own way. If the mother had the strength and brightness of brass, Saeeda Bai had the tarnishable brilliance of silver, and young, soft-hearted Tasneem, named after a spring in Paradise, protected by both mother and sister from the profession of their ancestors, had the lively elusiveness of mercury.

Mohsina Bai had died two years ago. This had been a terrible blow for Saeeda Bai, who sometimes still visited the graveyard and lay weeping, stretched out on her mother's grave. Saeeda Bai and Tasneem now lived alone in the house in Pasand Bagh with two women servants: a maid and a cook. At night the calm watchman guarded the gate. Tonight Saeeda Bai was not expecting to entertain visitors; she was sitting with her tabla player and sarangi player, and amusing herself with gossip and music.

Saeeda Bai's accompanists were a study in contrast. Both were about twenty-five, and both were devoted and skilled musicians. Both were fond of each other, and deeply attached – by economics and affection – to Saeeda Bai. But beyond that the resemblance ended. Ishaq Khan, who bowed his sarangi with such ease and harmoniousness, almost self-effacement, was a slightly sardonic bachelor. Motu Chand, so nicknamed because of his plumpness, was a contented man, already a father of four. He looked a bit like a bulldog with his large eyes and snuffling mouth, and was benignly torpid, except when frenziedly drumming his tabla.

They were discussing Ustad Majeed Khan, one of the most famous classical singers of India, a notoriously aloof man who lived in the old city, not far from where Saeeda Bai had grown up.

'But what I don't understand, Saeeda Begum,' said Motu Chand, leaning awkwardly backwards because of his paunch, 'is why he should be so critical of us small people. There he sits with his head above the clouds, like Lord Shiva on Kailash. Why should he open his third eye to burn us up?'

'There is no accounting for the moods of the great,' said Ishaq Khan. He touched his sarangi with his left hand and went on, 'Now look at this sarangi – it's a noble instrument – yet the noble Majeed Khan hates it. He never allows it to accompany him.'

Saeeda Bai nodded; Motu Chand made reassuring sounds. 'It is the loveliest of all instruments,' he said.

'You kafir,' said Ishaq Khan, smiling twistedly at his friend. 'How can you pretend to like this instrument? What is it made of?'

'Well, wood of course,' said Motu Chand, now leaning forward with an effort.

'Look at the little wrestler,' laughed Saeeda Bai. 'We must feed him some laddus.' She called out for her maid, and sent her to get some sweets.

Ishaq continued to wind the coils of his argument around the struggling Motu Chand.

'Wood!' he cried. 'And what else?'

'Oh, well, you know, Khan Sahib – strings and so on,' said Motu Chand, defeated as to Ishaq's intention.

'And what are these strings made of?' continued Ishaq Khan relentlessly.

'Ah!' said Motu Chand, getting a glimpse of his meaning. Ishaq was not a bad fellow, but he appeared to get a cruel pleasure from worsting Motu Chand in an argument.

'Gut,' said Ishaq. 'These strings are made of gut. As you well know. And the front of a sarangi is made of skin. The hide of a dead animal. Now what would your brahmins of Brahmpur say if they were forced to touch it? Would they not be polluted by it?'

Motu Chand looked downcast, then rallied. 'Anyway, I'm not a brahmin, you know ...' he began.

'Don't tease him,' said Saeeda Bai to Ishaq Khan.

'I love the fat kafir too much to want to tease him,' said Ishaq Khan.

This was not true. Since Motu Chand was of an alarmingly equable bent of mind, what Ishaq Khan liked more than anything else was to upset his balance. But this time Motu Chand reacted in an irksomely philosophical manner.

'Khan Sahib is very kind,' he said. 'But sometimes even the ignorant have wisdom, and he would be the first to acknowledge this. Now for me the sarangi is not what it is made of but what it makes – these divine sounds. In the hands of an artist even this gut and this skin can be made to sing.' His face wreathed with a contented, almost Sufi, smile. 'After all, what are we all but gut and skin? And yet'– his forehead creased with concentration – 'in the hands of one who – the One. . . .'

But the maid now came in with the sweets and Motu Chand's theological meanderings halted. His plump and agile fingers quickly reached for a laddu as round as himself and popped it whole into his mouth.

After a while Saeeda Bai said, 'But we were not discussing the One above' – she pointed upwards – 'but the One to the West.' She pointed in the direction of Old Brahmpur.

'They are the same,' said Ishaq Khan. 'We pray both westwards and upwards. I am sure Ustad Majeed Khan would not take it amiss if we were mistakenly to turn to him in prayer one evening. And why not?' he ended ambiguously. 'When we pray to such lofty art, we are praying to God himself.' He looked at Motu Chand for approval, but Motu appeared to be either sulking or concentrating on his laddu.

The maid re-entered and announced: 'There is some trouble at the gate.'

Saeeda Bai looked more interested than alarmed.

'What sort of trouble, Bibbo?' she asked.

The maid looked at her cheekily and said, 'It seems that a young man is quarrelling with the watchman.'

'Shameless thing, wipe that expression off your face,' said Saeeda Bai. 'Hmm,' she went on, 'what does he look like?'

'How would I know, Begum Sahiba?' protested the maid.

'Don't be troublesome, Bibbo. Does he look respectable?'

'Yes,' admitted the maid. 'But the street-lights were not bright enough for me to see anything more.'

'Call the watchman,' said Saeeda Bai. 'There's only us here,' she added, as the maid looked hesitant.

'But the young man?' asked the maid.

'If he's as respectable as you say, Bibbo, he'll remain outside.'

'Yes, Begum Sahiba,' said the maid and went to do her bidding.

'Who do you think it could be?' mused Saeeda Bai aloud, and was silent for a minute.

The watchman entered the house, left his spear at the front entrance, and climbed heavily up the stairs to the gallery. He stood at the doorway of the room where they were sitting, and saluted. With his khaki turban, khaki uniform, thick boots and bushy moustache, he was completely out of place in that femininely furnished room. But he did not seem at all ill at ease.

'Who is this man and what does he want?' asked Saeeda Bai.

'He wants to come in and speak with you,' said the watchman phlegmatically.

'Yes, yes, I thought as much – but what is his name?'

'He won't say, Begum Sahiba. Nor will he take no for an answer. Yesterday too he came, and told me to give you a message, but it was so impertinent, I decided not to.'

Saeeda Bai's eyes flashed. 'You decided not to?' she asked.

'The Raja Sahib was here,' said the watchman calmly.

'Hmmh. And the message?'

'That he is one who lives in love,' said the watchman impassively.

He had used a different word for love and had thus lost the pun on Prem Nivas.

'One who lives in love? What can he mean?' remarked Saeeda Bai to Motu and Ishaq. The two looked at each other, Ishaq Khan with a slight smirk of disdain.

'This world is populated by donkeys,' said Saeeda Bai, but whom she was referring to was unclear. 'Why didn't he leave a note? So those were his exact words? Neither very idiomatic nor very witty.'

The watchman searched his memory and came out with a closer approximation to the actual words Maan had used the previous evening. At any rate, 'prem' and 'nivas' both figured in his sentence.

All three musicians solved the riddle immediately.

'Ah!' said Saeeda Bai, amused. 'I think I have an admirer. What do you say? Shall we let him in? Why not?'

Neither of the others demurred – as, indeed, how could they? The watchman was told to let the young man in. And Bibbo was told to tell Tasneem to stay in her room.

MAAN, who was fretting by the gate, could hardly believe his good fortune at being so speedily admitted. He felt a surge of gratitude towards the watchman and pressed a rupee into his hand. The watchman left him at the door of the house, and the maid pointed him up to the room.

As Maan's footsteps were heard in the gallery outside Saeeda Bai's room, she called out, 'Come in, come in, Dagh Sahib. Sit down and illumine our gathering.'

Maan stood outside the door for a second, and looked at Saeeda Bai. He was smiling with pleasure, and Saeeda Bai could not help smiling back at him. He was dressed simply and immaculately in a well-starched white kurta-pyjama. The fine chikan embroidery on his kurta complemented the embroidery on his fine white cotton cap. His shoes – slip-on jutis of soft leather, pointed at the toe – were also white.

'How did you come?' asked Saeeda Bai.

'I walked.'

'These are fine clothes to risk in the dust.'

Maan said simply, 'It is just a few minutes away.'

'Please – sit down.'

Maan sat cross-legged on the white-sheeted floor.

Saeeda Bai began to busy herself making paan. Maan looked at her wonderingly.

'I came yesterday too, but was less fortunate.'

'I know, I know,' said Saeeda Bai. 'My fool of a watchman turned you away. What can I say? We are not all blessed with the faculty of discrimination. . . .'

'But I'm here today,' said Maan, rather obviously.

'Wherever Dagh has sat down, he has sat down?' asked Saeeda Bai, with a smile. Her head was bent, and she was spreading a little white dab of lime on the paan leaves.

'He may not quit your assembly at all this time,' said Maan.

Since she was not looking directly at him, he could look at her without embarrassment. She had covered her head with her sari before he had come in. But the soft, smooth skin of her neck and shoulders was exposed, and Maan found the tilt of her neck as she bent over her task indescribably charming.

Having made a pair of paans she impaled them on a little silver toothpick with tassels, and offered them to him. He took them and put them in his mouth, pleasantly surprised at the taste of coconut, which was an ingredient Saeeda Bai was fond of adding to her paan.

'I see you are wearing your own style of Gandhi cap,' said Saeeda Bai, after popping a couple of paans into her mouth. She did not offer any to Ishaq Khan or Motu Chand, but then they seemed to have virtually melted into the background.

Maan touched the side of his embroidered white cap nervously, unsure of himself.

'No, no, Dagh Sahib, don't trouble yourself. This isn't a church, you know.' Saeeda Bai looked at him and said, 'I was reminded of other white caps one sees floating around in Brahmpur. The heads that wear them have grown taller recently.'

'I am afraid you are going to accuse me of the accident of my birth,' said Maan.

'No, no,' said Saeeda Bai. 'Your father has been an old patron of the arts. It is the other Congress-wallahs I was thinking of.'

'Perhaps I should wear a cap of a different colour the next time I come,' said Maan.

Saeeda Bai raised an eyebrow.

'Assuming I am ushered into your presence,' Maan added humbly.

Saeeda Bai thought to herself: What a well-brought-up young man. She indicated to Motu Chand that he should bring the tablas and harmonium that were lying in the corner of the room.

To Maan she said, 'And now what does Hazrat Dagh command us to sing?'

'Why, anything,' said Maan, throwing banter to the winds.

'Not a ghazal, I hope,' said Saeeda Bai, pressing down a

key on the harmonium to help the tabla and sarangi tune up.

'No?' asked Maan, disappointed.

'Ghazals are for open gatherings or the intimacy of lovers,' said Saeeda Bai. 'I'll sing what my family is best known for and what my Ustad best taught me.'

She began a thumri in Raag Pilu, 'Why then are you not speaking to me?' and Maan's face brightened up. As she sang he floated off into a state of intoxication. The sight of her face, the sound of her voice, and the scent of her perfume were intertwined in his happiness.

After two or three thumris and a dadra, Saeeda Bai indicated that she was tired, and that Maan should leave.

He left reluctantly, showing, however, more good humour than reluctance. Downstairs, the watchman found a five-rupee note pressed into his hand.

Out on the street Maan trod on air.

She will sing a ghazal for me sometime, he promised himself. She will, she certainly will.

2.14

IT was Sunday morning. The sky was bright and clear. The weekly bird market near the Barsaat Mahal was in full swing. Thousands of birds – mynas, partridges, pigeons, parakeets – fighting birds, eating birds, racing birds, talking birds – sat or fluttered in iron or cane cages in little stalls from which rowdy hawkers cried out the excellence and cheapness of their wares. The pavement had been taken over by the bird market, and buyers or passers-by like Ishaq had to walk on the road surface, bumping against rickshaws and bicycles and the occasional tonga.

There was even a pavement stall with books about birds. Ishaq picked up a flimsy, blunt-typed paperback about owls and spells, and looked idly through to see what uses this unlucky bird could be put to. It appeared to be a book of Hindu black magic, *The Tantra of Owls*, though it was printed in Urdu. He read:

Sovereign Remedy to Obtain Employment
Take the tail-feathers of an owl and a crow, and burn them together in a fire made from mango wood until they form ash. Place this ash on your forehead like a caste-mark when you go to seek employment, and you will most certainly obtain it.

He frowned and read on:

Method of Keeping a Woman in Your Power
If you want to keep a woman in your control, and wish to prevent her from coming under the influence of anyone else, then use the technique described below:
    Take the blood of an owl, the blood of a jungle fowl and the blood of a bat in equal proportions, and after smearing the mixture on your penis have intercourse with the woman. Then she will never desire another man.'

Ishaq felt almost sick. These Hindus! he thought. On an impulse he bought the book, deciding that it was an excellent means of provoking his friend Motu Chand.

'I have one on vultures as well,' said the bookseller helpfully.

'No, this is all I want,' said Ishaq, and walked on.

He stopped at a stall where a large number of tiny, almost formless grey-green balls of stubbly flesh lay imprisoned in a hooped cage.

'Ah!' he said.

His look of interest had an immediate effect on the white-capped stall-keeper, who appraised him, glancing at the book in his hand.

'These are not ordinary parakeets, Huzoor, these are hill parakeets, Alexandrine parakeets as the English sahibs say.'

The English had left more than three years ago, but Ishaq let it pass.

'I know, I know,' he said.

'I can tell an expert when I see one,' said the stall-keeper in a most friendly manner. 'Now, why not have this one? Only two rupees – and it will sing like an angel.'

'A male angel or a female angel?' said Ishaq severely.

The stall-keeper suddenly became obsequious.

'Oh, you must forgive me, you must forgive me. People here are so ignorant, one can hardly bear to part with one's most promising birds, but for one who knows parakeets I will do anything, anything. Have this one, Huzoor.' And he picked out one with a larger head, a male.

Ishaq held it for a few seconds, then placed it back in the cage. The man shook his head, then said:

'Now for a true fancier, what can I provide that is better than this? Is it a bird from Rudhia District that you want? Or from the foothills in Horshana? They talk better than mynas.'

Ishaq simply said, 'Let's see something worth seeing.'

The man went to the back of the shop and opened a cage in which three little half-fledged birds sat huddled together. Ishaq looked at them silently, then asked to see one of them.

He smiled, thinking of parakeets he had known. His aunt was very fond of them, and had one who was still alive at the age of seventeen. 'This one,' he said to the man. 'And you know by now that I will not be fooled about the price either.'

They haggled for a while. Until the money changed hands the stall-keeper seemed a bit resentful. Then, as Ishaq was about to leave – with his purchase nestled in his handkerchief – the stall-keeper said in an anxious voice, 'Tell me how he is doing when you come by next time.'

'What do they call you?' asked Ishaq.

'Muhammad Ismail, Huzoor. And how are you addressed?'

'Ishaq Khan.'

'Then we are brothers!' beamed the stall-keeper. 'You must always get your birds from my shop.'

'Yes, yes,' agreed Ishaq, and walked hurriedly away. This was a good bird he had got, and would delight the heart of young Tasneem.

ISHAQ went home, had lunch, and fed the bird a little flour mixed with water. Later, carrying the parakeet in his handkerchief, he made his way to Saeeda Bai's house. From time to time he looked at it in appreciation, imagining what an excellent and intelligent bird it potentially was. He was in high spirits. A good Alexandrine parakeet was his favourite kind of parrot. As he walked towards Nabiganj he almost bumped into a hand-cart.

He arrived at Saeeda Bai's house at about four and told Tasneem that he had brought something for her. She was to try and guess what it was.

'Don't tease me, Ishaq Bhai,' she said, fixing her beautiful large eyes on his face. 'Please tell me what it is.'

Ishaq looked at her and thought that 'gazelle-like' really did suit Tasneem. Delicate-featured, tall and slender, she did not greatly resemble her elder sister. Her eyes were liquid and her expression tender. She was lively, but always seemed to be on the point of taking flight.

'Why do you insist on calling me Bhai?' he asked.

'Because you are virtually my brother,' said Tasneem. 'I need one, too. And your bringing me this gift proves it. Now please don't keep me in suspense. Is it something to wear?'

'Oh no – that would be superfluous to your beauty,' said Ishaq, smiling.

'Please don't talk that way,' said Tasneem, frowning. 'Apa might hear you, and then there will be trouble.'

'Well, here it is. . . .' And Ishaq took out what looked like a soft ball of fluffy material wrapped in a handkerchief.

'A ball of wool! You want me to knit you a pair of socks. Well, I won't. I have better things to do.'

'Like what?' said Ishaq.

'Like . . .' began Tasneem, then was silent. She glanced uncomfortably at a long mirror on the wall. What did she do? Cut vegetables to help the cook, talk to her sister, read novels, gossip with the maid, think about life. But before she could meditate too deeply on the subject, the ball moved, and her eyes lit up with pleasure.

'So you see –' said Ishaq, 'it's a mouse.'

'It is not –' said Tasneem with contempt. 'It's a bird. I'm not a child, you know.'

'And I'm not exactly your brother, you know,' said Ishaq. He unwrapped the parakeet and they looked at it together. Then he placed it on a table near a red lacquer vase. The stubbly ball of flesh looked quite disgusting.

'How lovely,' said Tasneem.

'I selected him this morning,' said Ishaq. 'It took me hours, but I wanted to have one that would be just right for you.'

Tasneem gazed at the bird, then stretched out her hand and touched it. Despite its stubble it was very soft. Its colour was very slightly green, as its feathers had only just begun to emerge.

'A parakeet?'

'Yes, but not a regular one. He's a hill parakeet. He'll talk as well as a myna.'

When Mohsina Bai died, her highly talkative myna had quickly followed her. Tasneem had been even lonelier without the bird, but she was glad that Ishaq had not got her another myna but something quite different. That was doubly considerate of him.

'What is he called?'

Ishaq laughed. 'Why do you want to call him anything? Just "tota" will do. He's not a warhorse that he should be called Ruksh or Bucephalas.'

Both of them were standing and looking at the baby parakeet. At the same moment each stretched out a hand to touch him. Tasneem swiftly drew her hand back.

'You go ahead,' said Ishaq. 'I've had him all day.'

'Has he eaten anything?'

'A bit of flour mixed with water,' said Ishaq.

'How do they get such tiny birds?' asked Tasneem.

Their eyes were level, and Ishaq, looking at her head, covered with a yellow scarf, found himself speaking without paying any attention to his words.

'Oh, they're taken from their nests when they're very young – if you don't get them young they don't learn to speak – and you should get a male one – he'll develop a lovely rose-and-black ring around his neck – and males are more intelligent. The best talkers come from the foothills, you know. There were three of them in the stall from the same nest, and I had to think quite hard before I decided –'

'You mean, he's separated from his brothers and sisters?' Tasneem broke in.

'But of course,' said Ishaq. 'He had to be. If you get a pair of them, they don't learn to imitate anything we say.'

'How cruel,' said Tasneem. Her eyes grew moist.

'But he had already been taken from his nest when I bought him,' said Ishaq, upset that he had caused her pain. 'You can't put them back or they'll be rejected by their parents.' He put his hand on hers – she didn't draw back at once – and said: 'Now it's up to you to give him a good life. Put him in a nest of cloth in the cage in which your mother's myna used to be kept. And for the first few days feed him a little parched gram flour moistened with water or a little daal soaked overnight. If he doesn't like that cage, I'll get him another one.'

Tasneem withdrew her hand gently from under Ishaq's. Poor parakeet, loved and unfree! He could change one cage for another. And she would change these four walls for a different four. Her sister, fifteen years her senior, and experienced in the ways of the world, would arrange all that soon enough. And then –

'Sometimes I wish I could fly....' She stopped, embarrassed.

Ishaq looked at her seriously. 'It is a good thing we can't, Tasneem – or can you imagine the confusion? The police have a hard enough time controlling traffic in Chowk – but if we could fly as well as walk it would be a hundred times worse.'

Tasneem tried not to smile.

'But it would be worse still if birds, like us, could only walk,' continued Ishaq. 'Imagine them strolling up and down Nabiganj with their walking-sticks in the evenings.'

Now she was laughing. Ishaq too started laughing, and the two of them, delighted by the picture they had conjured up, felt the tears rolling down their cheeks. Ishaq wiped his away with his hand, Tasneem hers with her yellow dupatta. Their laughter sounded through the house.

The baby parakeet sat quite still on the table-top near the red lacquer vase; his translucent gullet worked up and down.

Saeeda Bai, roused from her afternoon nap, came into the room, and in a surprised voice, with something of a stern edge, said: 'Ishaq — what's all this? Is one not to be permitted to rest even in the afternoon?' Then her eyes alighted on the baby parakeet, and she clicked her tongue in irritation.

'No – no more birds in this house. That miserable myna of my mother's caused me enough trouble.' She paused, then added: 'One singer is enough in any establishment. Get rid of it.'

2.16

NO ONE spoke. After a while Saeeda Bai broke the silence. 'Ishaq, you are here early,' she said.

Ishaq looked guilty. Tasneem looked down with half a sob. The parakeet made a feeble attempt to move. Saeeda Bai, looking from one to the other, suddenly said:

'Where is your sarangi anyway?'

Ishaq realized he had not even brought it. He flushed.

'I forgot. I was thinking of the parakeet.'

'Well?'

'Of course I'll go and get it immediately.'

'The Raja of Marh has sent word he will be coming this evening.'

'I'm just going,' said Ishaq. Then he added, looking at Tasneem, 'Shall I take the parakeet?'

'No, no –' said Saeeda Bai, 'why should you want to take it? Just get your sarangi. And don't be all day about it.'

Ishaq left hurriedly.

Tasneem, who had been close to tears, looked gratefully at her sister. Saeeda Bai, however, was far away. The business of the bird had woken her up from a haunting and peculiar dream involving the death of her mother and her own earlier life – and when Ishaq left, its atmosphere of dread and even guilt had surged back over her.

Tasneem, noticing her sister suddenly sad, held her hand.

'What's the matter, Apa?' she asked, using the term of endearment and respect she always used for her elder sister.

Saeeda Bai began to sob, and hugged Tasneem to her, kissing her forehead and cheeks.

'You are the only thing I care for in the world,' she said. 'May God keep you happy....'

Tasneem hugged her and said, 'Why, Apa, why are you crying? Why are you so overwrought? Is it Ammi-jaan's grave you are thinking of?'

'Yes, yes,' said Saeeda Bai quickly, and turned away. 'Now go inside, get the cage lying in Ammi-jaan's old room. Polish it and bring it here. And soak some daal – some chané ki daal – for him to eat later.'

Tasneem went in towards the kitchen. Saeeda Bai sat down, looking a bit dazed. Then she held the small parakeet in her hands to keep him warm. She was sitting like this when the maidservant came in to announce that someone had arrived from the Nawab Sahib's place, and was waiting outside.

Saeeda Bai pulled herself together and dried her eyes. 'Let him in,' she said.

But when Firoz walked in, handsome and smiling, gripping his elegant walking-stick lightly in his right hand, she gave a startled gasp.

'You?'

'Yes,' said Firoz. 'I've brought an envelope from my father.'

'You've come late.... I mean, he usually sends someone in the morning,' murmured Saeeda Bai, trying to still the confusion in her mind. 'Please sit down, please sit down.'

Until now the Nawab Sahib had sent a servant with the monthly envelope. For the last two months, Saeeda Bai remembered it had been just a couple of days after her period. And this month too, of course. . . .

Her thoughts were interrupted by Firoz, who said: 'I happened to bump into my father's private secretary, who was coming –'

'Yes, yes.' Saeeda Bai looked upset. Firoz wondered why his appearance should have distressed her so much. That many years ago there must have been something between the Nawab Sahib and Saeeda Bai's mother – and that his father continued to send a little something each month to support the family – surely there was nothing in this to cause her such agitation. Then he realized that she must have been upset even before his arrival by something quite different.

I have come at a bad time, he thought, and decided to go.

Tasneem walked in with the copper birdcage and, seeing him, suddenly stopped.

They looked at each other. For Tasneem, Firoz was just another handsome admirer of her sister's – but startlingly so. She lowered her eyes quickly, then looked at him again.

She stood there with her yellow dupatta, the birdcage in her right hand, her mouth slightly open in astonishment – perhaps at his astonishment. Firoz was staring at her, transfixed.

'Have we met before?' he asked gently, his heart beating fast.

Tasneem was about to reply when Saeeda Bai said, 'Whenever my sister goes out of the house she goes in purdah. And this is the first time that the Nawabzada has graced my poor lodgings with his presence. So it is not possible that you could have met. Tasneem, put the cage down, and go back to your Arabic exercises. I have not got you a new teacher for nothing.'

'But . . .' began Tasneem.

'Go back to your room at once. I will take care of the bird. Have you soaked the daal yet?'

'I . . .'

'Go and do so immediately. Do you want the bird to starve?'

When the bewildered Tasneem had left, Firoz tried to orient his thoughts. His mouth was dry. He felt strangely disturbed. Surely, he felt, even if we have not met on this mortal plane, we have met in some former life. The thought, counter to the religion he nominally adhered to, affected him the more powerfully for all that. The girl with the birdcage had in a few short moments made the most profound and unsettling impression on him.

After abridged pleasantries with Saeeda Bai, who seemed to be paying as little attention to his words as he to hers, he walked slowly out of the door.

Saeeda Bai sat perfectly still on the sofa for a few minutes. Her hands still cradled the little parakeet gently. He appeared to have gone off to sleep. She wrapped him up warmly in a piece of cloth and set him down near the red vase again. From outside she heard the call to evening prayer, and she covered her head.

All over India, all over the world, as the sun or the shadow of darkness moves from east to west, the call to prayer moves with it, and people kneel down in a wave to pray to God. Five waves each day – one for each namaaz – ripple across the globe from longitude to longitude. The component elements change direction, like iron filings near a magnet – towards the house of God in Mecca. Saeeda Bai got up to go to an inner room where she performed the ritual ablution and began her prayers:

In the Name of God, the Merciful, the Compassionate

Praise belongs to God, the Lord of all Being,
the All-Merciful, the All-Compassionate,
    the Master of the Day of Doom.
Thee only we serve; to Thee alone we pray for succour.
    Guide us in the straight path,
the path of those whom Thou hast blessed,
    not those against whom Thou art wrathful,
    nor of those who are astray.

But through this, and through her subsequent kneelings and prostrations, one terrifying line from the Holy Book recurred again and again to her mind:

> And God alone knows what you keep secret
> and what you publish.

2.17

SAEEDA BAI'S pretty young maidservant, Bibbo, sensing her mistress was distressed, thought she would try to cheer her up by talking of the Raja of Marh, who was to visit that evening. With his tiger hunts and mountain fastnesses, his reputation as temple-builder and tyrant, and his strange tastes in sex, the Raja was not the ideal subject for comic relief. He had come to lay the foundation of the Shiva temple, his latest venture, in the centre of the old town. The temple was to stand cheek by jowl with the grand mosque constructed by order of the Emperor Aurangzeb two-and-a-half centuries ago on the ruins of an earlier temple to Shiva. If the Raja of Marh had had his way, the foundation of his temple would have stood on the rubble of the mosque itself.

Given this background, it was interesting that the Raja of Marh had once been so utterly besotted with Saeeda Bai that he had some years ago proposed to marry her even though there was no question of her renouncing her beliefs as a Muslim. The thought of being his wife made Saeeda Bai so uneasy that she set impossible conditions upon him. Any possible heirs of the Raja's present wife were to be dispossessed, and Saeeda Bai's eldest son by him — assuming she had any — was to inherit Marh. Saeeda Bai made this demand of the Raja despite the fact that the Rani of Marh and the Dowager Rani of Marh had both treated her with kindness when she had been summoned to the state to perform at the wedding of the Raja's sister; she liked the Ranis, and knew that there was no possibility of her conditions being accepted. But the Raja thought with his crotch rather than his brain. He accepted these demands, and Saeeda Bai, trapped, had to fall seriously ill and be told by compliant doctors that to move her away from the city to a princely hill state would very likely kill her.

The Raja, whose looks resembled those of a huge water-buffalo, pawed the earth dangerously for a while. He suspected duplicity and fell into a drunken and – literally – bloodshot rage; probably the main factor that prevented his hiring someone to get rid of Saeeda Bai was the knowledge that the British, if they discovered the truth, would probably depose him – as they had other Rajas, and even Maharajas, for similar scandals and killings.

Not a great deal of this was known to the maidservant Bibbo, who was, however, keyed into the gossip that the Raja had some years previously proposed to her mistress. Saeeda Bai was talking to Tasneem's bird – rather prematurely, considering how tiny it was, but Saeeda Bai felt that this was how birds learned best – when Bibbo appeared.

'Are any special arrangements to be made for the Raja Sahib?' she asked.

'Why? No, of course not,' said Saeeda Bai.

'Perhaps I should get a garland of marigolds –'

'Are you crazy, Bibbo?'

'– for him to eat.'

Saeeda Bai smiled.

Bibbo went on: 'Will we have to move to Marh, Rani Sahiba?'

'Oh do be quiet,' said Saeeda Bai.

'But to rule a state –'

'No one really rules their states now; Delhi does,' said Saeeda Bai. 'And listen, Bibbo, it would not be the crown I would have to marry but the buffalo underneath. Now go – you are ruining the education of this parakeet.'

The maidservant turned to leave.

'Oh, yes, and get me a little sugar, and see if the daal that you soaked earlier is soft yet. It probably isn't.'

Saeeda Bai continued to talk to the parakeet, who was

sitting on a little nest of clean rags in the middle of the brass cage that had once held Mohsina Bai's myna.

'Now, Miya Mitthu,' said Saeeda Bai rather sadly to the parakeet, 'You had better learn good and auspicious things at an early age, or you'll be ruined for life, like that foul-mouthed myna. As they say, if you don't learn your alif-be-pe-te clearly, you'll never amount to a calligrapher. What do you have to say for yourself? Do you want to learn?'

The small, unfeathered ball of flesh was in no position to answer, and didn't.

'Now look at me,' said Saeeda Bai. 'I still feel young, though I admit I am naturally not as young as you. I am waiting to spend the evening with this disgustingly ugly man who is fifty-five years old, who picks his nose and belches, and who is going to be drunk even before he gets here. Then he'll want me to sing romantic songs to him. Everyone feels that I am the epitome of romance, Miya Mitthu, but what about my feelings? How can I feel anything for these ancient animals, whose skin hangs from their jaws – like that of the old cattle straying around Chowk?'

The parakeet opened his mouth.

'Miya Mitthu,' said Saeeda Bai.

The parakeet rocked a little from side to side. His big head looked unsteady.

'Miya Mitthu,' repeated Saeeda Bai, trying to imprint the syllables on his mind.

The parakeet closed his mouth.

'What I really want tonight is not to entertain but to be entertained. By someone young and handsome,' she added.

Saeeda Bai smiled at the thought of Maan.

'What do you think of him, Miya Mitthu?' continued Saeeda Bai. 'Oh, I'm sorry, you haven't yet met Dagh Sahib, you have just brought your presence here today. And you must be hungry, that's why you are refusing to talk to me – you can't sing bhajans on an empty stomach. I'm sorry the service is so slow in this establishment, but Bibbo is a very scatterbrained girl.'

But soon Bibbo came in and the parakeet was fed.

The old cook had decided that a little daal should be boiled and then cooled, rather than merely soaked, for the bird. Now she too came to look at him.

Ishaq Khan came in with his sarangi, looking a little shamefaced.

Motu Chand came in and admired the parakeet.

Tasneem put down the novel she was reading, and came in to say 'Miya Mitthu' and 'Mitthu Miya' several times to the parakeet, delighting Ishaq with each iteration. At least she loved his bird.

And in due course the Raja of Marh was announced.

2.18

HIS HIGHNESS THE RAJA OF MARH was less drunk on arrival than he usually was, but rapidly remedied the situation. He had brought along a bottle of Black Dog, his favourite whisky. This immediately reminded Saeeda Bai of one of his more unpleasant characteristics, the fact that he would get incredibly excited when he saw dogs copulating. In Marh, when Saeeda Bai had visited, he had twice got dogs to mount a bitch in heat. This was the prelude to his flinging his own gross body on Saeeda Bai.

This took place a couple of years before Independence; despite Saeeda Bai's revulsion she had not been able immediately to escape from Marh, where the crass Raja, restrained only by a succession of disgusted but tactful British Residents, held ultimate sway. Afterwards, she was too frightened of the sluggish and brutal man and his hired ruffians to cut off relations completely with him. She could only hope that his visits to Brahmpur would become less frequent with time.

The Raja had degenerated from his student days in Brahmpur, when he had given the impression of being tolerably presentable. His son, who had been protected from his father's way of life by the Rani and Dowager Rani, was now himself a student at Brahmpur University;

no doubt he too, upon returning to feudal Marh as an adult, would shake off the maternal influence and grow to be as tamasic as his father: ignorant, brutal, slothful, and rank.

The father ignored the son during his stay in town and visited a series of courtesans and prostitutes. Today, once again, it was Saeeda Bai's turn. He arrived adorned with diamond ear-tops and a ruby in his silk turban, and smelling strongly of attar of musk. He placed a small silken pouch containing five hundred rupees on a table near the door of the upstairs room where Saeeda Bai entertained. The Raja then stretched out against a long white bolster on the white-sheeted floor, and looked around for glasses. They were lying on the low table where the tablas and harmonium stood. The Black Dog was opened and the whisky poured into two glasses. The musicians remained downstairs.

'How long it has been since these eyes last saw you —' said Saeeda Bai, sipping her whisky and restraining a grimace at its strong taste.

The Raja was too involved with his drink to think of answering.

'You have become as difficult to sight as the moon at Id.'

The Raja grunted at the pleasantry. After he had downed a few whiskies, he became more affable, and told her how beautiful she was looking — before pushing her thickly towards the door that led into the bedroom.

After half an hour, they came out, and the musicians were summoned. Saeeda Bai was looking slightly sick.

He made her sing the same set of ghazals he always did; she sang them with the same break in her voice at the same heartrending phrases — something she had learned to do without difficulty. She nursed her glass of whisky. The Raja had finished a third of his bottle by now, and his eyes were becoming red. From time to time he shouted, 'wah! wah!' in indiscriminate praise, or belched or snorted or gaped or scratched his crotch.

WHILE the ghazals were proceeding upstairs, Maan was walking towards the house. From the street he could not make out the sound of singing. He told the watchman he was there to see Saeeda Bai, but the stolid man told him that she was indisposed.

'Oh,' said Maan, his voice filled with concern. 'Let me go in – I'll see how she is – perhaps I can fetch a doctor.'

'Begum Sahiba is not admitting anyone today.'

'But I have something for her with me here,' said Maan. He had a large book in his left hand. He reached into his pocket with his right and extracted his wallet. 'Would you see she gets it?'

'Yes, Huzoor,' said the watchman, accepting a five-rupee note.

'Well, then –' said Maan and, with a disappointed look at the rose-coloured house beyond the small green gate, walked slowly away.

The watchman carried the book a couple of minutes later to the front door and gave it to Bibbo.

'What – for me?' said Bibbo flirtatiously.

The watchman looked at her with such a lack of expression it was almost an expression in itself.

'No. And tell Begum Sahiba it was from that young man who came the other day.'

'The one who got you into such trouble with Begum Sahiba?'

'I was not in trouble.'

And the watchman walked back to the gate.

Bibbo giggled and closed the door. She looked at the book for a few minutes. It was very handsome and – apart from print – contained pictures of languid men and women in various romantic settings. One particular picture took her fancy. A woman in a black robe was kneeling by a grave. Her eyes were closed. There were stars in the sky behind a high wall in the background. In the foreground was a short, gnarled, leafless tree, its roots entwined among large stones. Bibbo stood wondering for a few moments.

Then, without thinking about the Raja of Marh, she closed the book to take it up to Saeeda Bai.

Like a spark on a slow fuse, the book now moved from the gate to the front door, across the hall, up the stairs and along the gallery to the open doorway of the room where Saeeda Bai was entertaining the Raja. When she saw him, Bibbo stopped abruptly and tried to retreat along the gallery. But Saeeda Bai had spotted her. She broke off the ghazal she was singing.

'Bibbo, what's the matter? Come in.'

'Nothing, Saeeda Begum. I'll come back later.'

'What's the matter with the girl? First she interrupts, then it's "Nothing, Saeeda Begum, I'll come back later!" What's that in your hands?'

'Nothing, Begum Sahiba.'

'Let's have a look at that nothing,' said Saeeda Bai.

Bibbo entered with a frightened salaam, and handed the book to her. On the brown cover in gold letters it said in Urdu: *The Poetical Works of Ghalib. An Album of Pictures by Chughtai.*

It was clearly no ordinary collected poems of Ghalib. Saeeda Bai could not resist opening it. She turned the pages. The book contained a few words of introduction and an essay by the artist Chughtai, the entire collected Urdu poems of the great Ghalib, a group of plates of the most beautiful paintings in the Persian style (each illustrating a line or two of Ghalib's poetry), and some text in English. This English text was probably a foreword when seen from the other side, thought Saeeda Bai, who was still amused by the fact that books in English opened at the wrong end.

So delighted was she by the gift that she placed it on the harmonium and began to leaf through the illustrations. 'Who sent it?' she asked, when she noticed that there was no inscription. In her pleasure she had forgotten the presence of the Raja, who was simmering with anger and jealousy.

Bibbo, with a quick glance around the room for inspiration, said, 'It came with the watchman.'

She had sensed the Raja's dangerous rage, and did not wish her mistress to display the involuntary joy she might if her admirer's name were mentioned directly. Besides, the Raja would not be tenderly disposed towards the sender of the book; and Bibbo, though mischievous, did not wish Maan ill. Far from it, in fact.

Meanwhile, Saeeda Bai, her head down, was looking at a picture of an old woman, a young woman and a boy praying before a window towards a new moon at sunset. 'Yes, yes –' she said '– but who sent it?' She looked up and frowned.

Bibbo, now under duress, tried to name Maan as elliptically as possible. Hoping that the Raja would not notice, she pointed to a spot on the white-sheeted floor where he had spilt some of his whisky. Aloud she said, 'I don't know. No name was left. May I go?'

'Yes, yes – what a fool –' said her mistress, impatient with Bibbo's enigmatic behaviour.

But the Raja of Marh had had enough of this insolent interruption. With an ugly snort he moved forward to snatch the book from Saeeda Bai's hands. If she had not moved it swiftly away at the last moment he would have ripped it from her grasp.

Now, breathing heavily, he said: 'Who is he? How much is his life worth? What is his name? Is this exhibition to be part of my entertainment?'

'No – no –' said Saeeda Bai, 'please forgive the silly girl. It is impossible to teach etiquette and discrimination to these unsophisticated things.' Then, to mollify him, she added: 'But look at this picture – how lovely it is – their hands raised in prayer – the sunset, the white dome and minaret of the mosque –'

It was the wrong word to use. With a guttural grunt of rage, the Raja of Marh ripped out the page she was showing him. Saeeda Bai stared at him, petrified.

'Play!' he roared at Motu and Ishaq. And to Saeeda Bai he said, moving his face forward in threat: 'Sing! Finish the ghazal – No! begin it again. Remember who has reserved you for the evening.'

Saeeda Bai replaced the ragged page in the book, closed it, and set it by the harmonium. Then, closing her eyes, she began again to sing the words of love. Her voice was trembling and there was no life to the lines. Indeed, she was not even thinking of them. Beneath her tears she was in a white rage. If she had had the freedom to, she would have lashed out against the Raja – flung her whisky at his bulging red eyes, slashed his face, thrown him out onto the street. But she knew that, for all her worldly wisdom, she was utterly powerless. To avoid these thoughts her mind strayed to Bibbo's gestures.

Whisky? Liquor? Floor? Sheet? she wondered to herself.

Then suddenly she realized what Bibbo had tried to say to her. It was the word for stain – 'dagh'.

With a song now in her heart, not only on her lips, Saeeda Bai opened her eyes and smiled, looking at the whisky stain. As of a black dog pissing! she thought. I must give that quick-thinking girl a gift.

She thought of Maan, one man – the only man, in fact – whom she both liked and felt she could have almost complete control over. Perhaps she had not treated him well enough – perhaps she had been too cavalier with his infatuation.

The ghazal she was singing bloomed into life. Ishaq Khan was startled and could not understand it. Even Motu Chand was puzzled.

It certainly also had charms to soothe the savage breast. The Raja of Marh's head sank gently onto his chest, and in a while he began snoring.

2.20

THE next evening, when Maan asked the watchman about Saeeda Bai's health, he was told that she had left instructions that he was to be sent up. This was wonderful, considering that he had neither left word nor sent a note to say that he would be coming.

As he walked up the stairs at the end of the hall he paused to admire himself in the mirror, and greeted himself with a sotto voce 'Adaab arz, Dagh Sahib,' raising his cupped hand to his forehead in happy salutation. He was dressed as smartly as ever in a starched and immaculate kurta-pyjama; he wore the same white cap that had drawn a comment from Saeeda Bai.

When he got to the upstairs gallery that fringed the hall below, he stopped. There was no sound of music or talk. Saeeda Bai would probably be alone. He was filled with a pleased expectation; his heart began beating hard.

She must have heard his footsteps: she had put down the slim novel she had been reading – at least it appeared to be a novel from the illustration on the cover – and had stood up to greet him.

As he entered the doorway she said, 'Dagh Sahib, Dagh Sahib, you did not need to do that.'

Maan looked at her – she appeared a little tired. She was wearing the same red silk sari that she had worn in Prem Nivas. He smiled and said: 'Every object strives for its proper place. A book seeks to be near its truest admirer. Just as this helpless moth seeks to be near the candle that infatuates him.'

'But, Maan Sahib, books are chosen with care and treated with love,' said Saeeda Bai, addressing him tenderly by his own name for – was it? – the first time, and entirely disregarding his conventionally gallant remark. 'You must have had this book in your library for many years. You should not have parted with it.'

Maan had in fact had the book on his bookshelf, but in Banaras. He had remembered it for some reason, had thought immediately of Saeeda Bai, and after some search had obtained a perfect secondhand copy from a bookseller in Chowk. But in the pleasure of hearing himself so gently addressed, all he now said was, 'The Urdu, even of those poems that I know by heart, is wasted on me. I cannot read the script. Did you like it?'

'Yes,' said Saeeda Bai very quietly. 'Everyone gives me jewels and other glittering things, but nothing has caught my eyes or my heart like your gift. But why are we standing? Please sit down.'

Maan sat down. There was the same slight fragrance that he had noticed before in this room. But today attar of roses was slightly interfused with attar of musk, a combination which made the robust Maan almost weak with longing.

'Will you have some whisky, Dagh Sahib?' asked Saeeda Bai. 'I am sorry that this is the only kind we have got,' she added, indicating the half-empty bottle of Black Dog.

'But this is excellent whisky, Saeeda Begum,' said Maan.

'We've had it for some time,' she said, handing him the glass.

Maan sat silent for a while, leaning against a long cylindrical bolster and sipping his Scotch. Then he said, 'I've often wondered about the couplets that inspired Chughtai's paintings, but have never got around to asking someone who knows Urdu to read them to me. For instance, there is one picture that has always intrigued me. I can describe it even without opening the book. It shows a watery landscape in orange and brown, with a tree, a withered tree, rising out from the water. And somewhere in the middle of the water floats a lotus on which a small, smoky oil lamp is resting. Do you know the one I'm talking about? I think it's somewhere at the beginning of the book. On the page of tissue that covers it is the single word "Life!" That's all there is in English, and it is very mysterious — because there is a whole couplet underneath in Urdu. Perhaps you could tell me how it reads?'

Saeeda Bai fetched the book. She sat down on Maan's left, and as he turned the pages of his magnificent gift, she prayed that he would not come upon the torn page that she had carefully patched together. The English titles were oddly succinct. After flipping past 'Around the Beloved', 'The Brimming Cup', and 'The Wasted Vigil', Maan came to 'Life!'

'This is the one,' he said, as they re-examined the mysterious painting. 'Ghalib has plenty of couplets dealing with lamps. I wonder which one this is.'

Saeeda Bai turned back to the covering sheet of tissue, and as she did their hands touched for a moment. With a slight intake of breath, Saeeda Bai looked down at the Urdu couplet, then read it out:

'The horse of time is galloping fast: let us see where he halts.
Neither is the hand on the reins nor the foot in the stirrup.'

Maan burst out laughing. 'Well,' he said, 'that should teach me how dangerous it is to come to conclusions based on shaky assumptions.'

They went through a couple of other couplets, and then Saeeda Bai said: 'When I looked through the poems this morning, I wondered what the few pages in English at the end of the book were all about.'

The beginning of the book from my point of view, thought Maan, still smiling. Aloud, he said: 'I suppose it's a translation of the Urdu pages at the other end – but why don't we make sure?'

'Certainly,' said Saeeda Bai. 'But to do so you will have to change places with me and sit on my left. Then you can read a sentence in English and I can read its translation in Urdu. It will be like having a private tutor,' she added, a slight smile forming on her lips.

The very nearness of Saeeda Bai in these last few minutes, delightful as it had been, now created a small problem for Maan. Before he got up to change places with her he had to make a slight adjustment to his clothing in order not to let her see how aroused he was. But when he sat down again it seemed to him that Saeeda Bai was more amused than ever. She's a real sitam-zareef, he thought to himself – a tyrant with a smile.

'So, Ustad Sahib, let's begin our lesson,' she said, raising an eyebrow.

'Well,' said Maan, not looking at her, but acutely conscious of her closeness. 'The first item is an introduction by a certain James Cousins to Chughtai's illustrations.'

'Oh,' said Saeeda Bai, 'the first item from the Urdu side is an explanation by the artist himself of what he hoped to do by having this book printed.'

'And,' continued Maan, 'my second item is a foreword by the poet Iqbal to the book as a whole.'

'And mine,' said Saeeda Bai, 'is a long essay, again by Chughtai himself, on various matters, including his views on art.'

'Look at this,' said Maan, suddenly involved in what he was reading. 'I'd forgotten what a pompous foreword Iqbal wrote. All he seems to talk about is his own books, not the one that he's introducing. "In this book of mine I said this, in that book of mine I said that" – and only a few patronizing remarks about Chughtai and how young he is –'

He stopped indignantly.

'Dagh Sahib,' said Saeeda Bai, 'you're getting heated all right.'

They looked at each other, Maan thrown a little off balance by her directness. It seemed to him that she was trying to refrain from laughing outright. 'Perhaps I should cool you down with a melancholy ghazal,' continued Saeeda Bai.

'Yes, why don't you try?' said Maan, remembering what she had once said about ghazals. 'Let's see what effect it has on me.'

'Let me summon my musicians,' said Saeeda Bai.

'No,' said Maan, placing his hand on hers. 'Just you and the harmonium, that'll be enough.'

'At least the tabla player?'

'I'll keep the beat with my heart,' said Maan.

With a slight inclination of the head – a gesture that made Maan's heart almost skip a beat – Saeeda Bai acquiesced. 'Would you be capable of standing up and getting it for me?' she asked slyly.

'Hmm,' said Maan, but remained seated.

'And I also see that your glass is empty,' added Saeeda Bai.

Refusing this time to be embarrassed by anything, Maan

got up. He fetched her the harmonium and himself another drink. Saeeda Bai hummed for a few seconds and said, 'Yes, I know which one will do.' She began to sing the enigmatic lines:

'No grain of dust in the garden is wasted.
Even the path is like a lamp to the tulip's stain.'

At the word 'dagh' Saeeda Bai shot Maan a quick and amused glance. The next couplet was fairly uneventful. But it was followed by:

'The rose laughs at the activities of the nightingale –
What they call love is a defect of the mind.'

Maan, who knew these lines well, must have shown a very transparent dismay; for as soon as Saeeda Bai looked at him, she threw back her head and laughed with pleasure. The sight of her soft white throat exposed, her sudden, slightly husky laughter, and the piquancy of not knowing whether she was laughing with or at him made Maan completely forget himself. Before he knew it and despite the hindrance of the harmonium, he had leaned over and kissed her on the neck, and before she knew it she was responding.

'Not now, not now, Dagh Sahib,' she said, a little out of breath.

'Now – now –' said Maan.

'Then we'd better go to the other room,' said Saeeda Bai. 'You are getting into the habit of interrupting my ghazals.'

'When else have I interrupted your ghazals?' asked Maan as she led him to her bedroom.

'I'll tell you some other time,' said Saeeda Bai.

Part Three

SUNDAY breakfast at Pran's house was usually a bit later than during the week. The *Brahmpur Chronicle* had arrived and Pran had his nose fixed in the Sunday Supplement. Savita sat to one side eating her toast and buttering Pran's. Mrs Rupa Mehra came into the room and asked, in a worried tone, 'Have you seen Lata anywhere?'

Pran shook his head behind his newspaper.

'No, Ma,' said Savita.

'I hope she's all right,' said Mrs Rupa Mehra anxiously. She looked around and said to Mateen: 'Where's the spice-powder? I am always forgotten when you lay the table.'

'Why wouldn't she be all right, Ma?' said Pran. 'This is Brahmpur, not Calcutta.'

'Calcutta's very safe,' said Mrs Rupa Mehra, defending the city of her only grandchild. 'It may be a big city, but the people are very good. It's quite safe for a girl to walk about at any time.'

'Ma, you're just homesick for Arun,' said Savita. 'Everyone knows who your favourite child is.'

'I don't have favourites,' said Mrs Rupa Mehra.

The phone rang. 'I'll take it,' said Pran casually. 'It's probably something to do with tonight's debating contest. Why do I consent to organize all these wretched activities?'

'For the looks of adoration in your students' eyes,' said Savita.

Pran picked up the phone. The other two continued with their breakfast. A sharp, exclamatory tone in Pran's voice, however, told Savita that it was something serious. Pran looked shocked, and glanced worriedly at Mrs Rupa Mehra.

'Ma –' said Pran, but could say nothing further.

'It's about Lata,' said Mrs Rupa Mehra, reading his face. 'She's had an accident.'

'No –' said Pran.

'Thank God.'

'She's eloped –' said Pran.

'Oh my God,' said Mrs Rupa Mehra.

'With whom?' asked Savita, transfixed, still holding a piece of toast in her hand.

'– with Maan,' said Pran, shaking his head slowly back and forth in disbelief. 'How –' he went on, but was temporarily unable to speak.

'Oh my God,' said Savita and her mother almost simultaneously.

For a few seconds there was stunned silence.

'He phoned my father from the railway station,' continued Pran, shaking his head. 'Why didn't he talk it over with me? I don't see any objection to the match as such, except for Maan's previous engagement –'

'No objection –' whispered Mrs Rupa Mehra in astonishment. Her nose had gone red and two tears had started helplessly down her cheeks. Her hands were clasped together as if in prayer.

'Your brother –' began Savita indignantly, 'may think he is the cat's whiskers, but how you can think that we –'

'Oh my poor daughter, oh my poor daughter,' wept Mrs Rupa Mehra.

The door opened, and Lata walked in.

'Yes, Ma?' said Lata. 'Were you calling me?' She looked at the dramatic tableau in surprise, and went over to comfort her mother. 'Now what's the matter?' she asked, looking around the table. 'Not the other medal, I hope.'

'Say it isn't true, say it isn't true,' cried Mrs Rupa Mehra. 'How could you think of doing this? And with Maan! How can you break my heart like this?' A thought suddenly occurred to her. 'But – it can't be true. The railway station?'

'I haven't been to any station,' said Lata. 'What's going on, Ma? Pran told me you were going to have a long session by yourselves about plans and prospects for me' – she frowned a little – 'and that it would only embarrass me to be here. He told me to come back late for breakfast. What have I done that has upset you all so much?'

Savita looked at Pran in angry astonishment; now, to her outrage, he simply yawned.

'Those who aren't conscious of the date,' said Pran, tapping the head of the paper, 'must take the consequences.'

It was the 1st of April.

Mrs Rupa Mehra had stopped weeping but was still bewildered. Savita looked at her husband and her sister in severe reproof and said, 'Ma, this is Pran and Lata's idea of an April Fool joke.'

'Not mine,' said Lata, beginning to understand what had happened in her absence. She began to laugh. Then she sat down and looked at the others. 'Really, Pran,' said Savita. She turned to her sister: 'It's not so funny, Lata.'

'Yes,' said Mrs Rupa Mehra. 'And at exam time – it will disturb your studies – and all this time and money will have gone down the drain. Don't laugh.'

'Cheer up, cheer up, everyone. Lata is still unmarried. God's in his Heaven,' Pran said unrepentantly, and hid behind his newspaper again. He too was laughing, but silently to himself. Savita and Mrs Rupa Mehra looked daggers at the *Brahmpur Chronicle*.

A sudden thought struck Savita. 'I could have had a miscarriage,' she said.

'Oh, no,' said Pran unconcernedly. 'You're robust. I'm the frail one. Besides, this was done entirely for your benefit: to liven up your Sunday morning. You're always complaining about how dull Sunday is.'

'Well, I prefer boredom to this. Aren't you at least going to apologize to us?'

'Of course,' said Pran readily. Though he was not very happy with himself for having brought his mother-in-law to tears, he was delighted at the way the trick had come off. And Lata at least had enjoyed it. 'Sorry, Ma. Sorry, darling.'

'I should hope so. Say sorry to Lata too,' Savita said.

'Sorry, Lata,' said Pran, laughing. 'You must be hungry. Why don't you order your egg?'

'Though actually,' continued Pran, undoing most of the goodwill he had salvaged, 'I don't see why I should apologize. I don't enjoy these April fooleries. It's because I've married into a westernized family that I decided, well, Pran, you have to keep your end up or they'll think you are a peasant, and you'll never be able to face Arun Mehra again.'

'You can stop making snide remarks about my brother,' said Savita. 'You've been doing so ever since the wedding. Yours is equally vulnerable. More so, in fact.'

Pran considered this for a moment. People had begun talking about Maan.

'Come on, darling, forgive me,' he said with a little more genuine contrition in his voice. 'What do I have to do to make up?'

'Take us to see a film,' Savita said immediately. 'I want to see a Hindi film today – just to emphasize how western-ized I am.' Savita enjoyed Hindi movies (the more sentimen-tal the better); she also knew that Pran, for the most part, detested them.

'A Hindi film?' said Pran. 'I thought the strange tastes of expecting mothers extended only to food and drink.'

'All right, that's fixed then,' said Savita. 'Which one should we see?'

'Sorry,' said Pran, 'impossible. There's that debate this evening.'

'A matinée then,' said Savita, flicking the butter off the end of her toast in a decisive manner.

'Oh, all right, all right, I suppose I've brought this upon myself,' said Pran. He turned to the appropriate page in the newspaper. 'How about this? *Sangraam*. At the Odeon. "Acclaimed by all – a greatest movie marvel. For adults only." Ashok Kumar's acting in it – he makes Ma's heart beat faster.'

'You're teasing me,' Mrs Rupa Mehra said, somewhat appeased. 'But I do like his acting. Still, somehow, you know, all these adult movies, I feel –'

'All right,' said Pran. 'Next one. No – there's no after-noon show for that. Um, um, here's something that looks interesting. *Kaalé Badal*. An epic of love and romance. Meena, Shyam, Gulab, Jeewan, etcetera, etcetera, even

Baby Tabassum! Just right for you in your present condition,' he added to Savita.

'No,' said Savita. 'I don't like any of the actors.'

'This family is very particular,' Pran said. 'First they want a film, then they reject all the options.'

'Keep reading,' said Savita, rather sternly.

'Yes, Memsahib,' said Pran. 'Well, then we have *Hulchul*. Great Gala Opening. Nargis –'

'I like her,' said Mrs Rupa Mehra. 'She has such expressive features –'

'Daleep Kumar –'

'Ah!' said Mrs Rupa Mehra.

'Restrain yourself, Ma,' said Pran. '– Sitara, Yaqub, K.N. Singh and Jeevan. "Great in story. Great in stars. Great in music. In 30 years of Indian films no picture like this." Well?'

'Where's it showing?'

'At the Majestic. "Renovated, luxuriously furnished and fitted with fresh air circulating device for cool comfort."'

'That sounds right in every way,' said Mrs Rupa Mehra with careful optimism, as if she were discussing a prospective match for Lata.

'But wait!' said Pran, 'Here's an ad that's so big I missed it: it's for *Deedar*. Showing in the, let's see, in the equally well-appointed Manorma Talkies which also has a fresh air circulating device. Here's what it says: "It's a star-studded! Playing for 5th week. Punched with Lusty Songs & Romance To Warm Your Cockles. Nargis, Ashok Kumar –"'

He paused for the expected exclamation from his mother-in-law.

'You are always teasing me, Pran,' said Mrs Rupa Mehra happily, all her tears forgotten.

'"– Nimmi, Daleep Kumar –" (amazing luck, Ma) "– Yaqub, Baby Tabassum –" (we've hit the jackpot) "– Musical-Miracle songs which are sung in every street of the city. Acclaimed, Applauded, Admired by All. The only Picture for Families. A Storm of Movie. A Rainfall of Melody. Filmkar's *Deedar*! Star-studded Gem amongst

Pictures! No Greater Picture will come your Way for So Many Years." Well, what do you say?'

He looked around him at three wondering faces. 'Thunderstruck!' said Pran approvingly. 'Twice in one morning.'

3.2

THAT afternoon the four of them went to warm their cockles at Manorma Talkies. They bought the best tickets in the balcony section, high above the hoi polloi, and a bar of Cadbury's chocolate of which Lata and Savita ate the major portion. Mrs Rupa Mehra was allowed one square despite her diabetes and Pran wanted no more than one. Pran and Lata were almost dry-eyed, Savita sniffed, and Mrs Rupa Mehra sobbed broken-heartedly. The film was indeed very sad, and the songs were sad too, and it was not clear whether it was the piteous fate of the blind singer or the tenderness of the love story that had most affected her. An entirely good time would have been had by all had it not been for a man a row or two behind them who, every time the blind Daleep Kumar appeared on the screen, burst into a horrific frenzy of weeping and once or twice even knocked his stick on the floor to indicate perhaps an outraged protest against Fate or the director. Eventually Pran could bear it no longer, turned around and exclaimed: 'Sir, do you think you could refrain from knocking that —'

He stopped suddenly as he saw that the culprit was Mrs Rupa Mehra's father. 'Oh, my God,' he said to Savita, 'it's your grandfather! I'm so sorry, Sir! Please don't mind what I said, Sir. Ma is here as well, Sir, I mean Mrs Rupa Mehra. Terribly sorry. And Savita and Lata are here too. We do hope you will meet us after the film is over.'

By this time Pran himself was being shushed by others in the audience, and he turned back to the screen, shaking his head. The others were equally horror-struck. All this had no apparent effect on the emotions of Dr Kishen Chand Seth, who wept with as much clamour and energy through the last half-hour of the movie as before.

'How was it we didn't meet during the interval?' Pran asked himself. 'And didn't he notice us either? We were sitting in front of him.' What Pran could not know was that Dr Kishen Chand Seth was impervious to any extraneous visual or auditory stimulus once he was involved in a film. As for the matter of the interval, that was – and was to remain – a mystery, especially since Dr Kishen Chand Seth and his wife Parvati had come together.

When the movie was over and they had been extruded out of the hall like the rest of the crowd, everyone met in the lobby. Dr Kishen Chand Seth was still streaming copious tears, the others were dabbing at their eyes with handkerchiefs.

Parvati and Mrs Rupa Mehra made a couple of brave but hopeless attempts to pretend liking for each other. Parvati was a strong, bony, rather hard-boiled woman of thirty-five. She had brown, sun-hardened skin, and an attitude towards the world that seemed to be an extension of her attitude to her more enfeebled patients: it was as if she had suddenly decided she was not going to empty anyone's bedpans any more. She was wearing a georgette sari with what looked like pink pine-cones printed all over it. Her lipstick, however, was not pink but orange.

Mrs Rupa Mehra, shrinking from this impressive vision, tried to explain why she had not been able to visit Parvati for her birthday.

'How nice to meet you here, though,' she added.

'Yes, isn't it?' said Parvati. 'I was saying to Kishy just the other day . . .'

But the rest of the sentence was lost on Mrs Rupa Mehra, who had never heard her seventy-year-old father referred to in terms of such odious triviality. 'My husband' was bad enough; but 'Kishy'? She looked at him, but he seemed still to be locked in a globe of celluloid.

Dr Kishen Chand Seth emerged from this sentimental aura in a minute or two. 'We must go home,' he announced.

'Please come over to our place for tea, and then go back,' suggested Pran.

'No, no, impossible, impossible today. Some other time. Yes. Tell your father we expect him for bridge tomorrow evening. At seven-thirty sharp. Surgeon's time, not politician's.'

'Oh,' said Pran, smiling now, 'I'd be glad to. I'm glad your misunderstanding has been sorted out.'

Dr Kishen Chand Seth realized with a start that of course it hadn't. Under the filmy mist that had engulfed him – for in *Deedar* good friends had spoken bitter words to each other – he had forgotten about his falling out with Mahesh Kapoor. He looked at Pran with annoyance. Parvati came to a sudden decision.

'Yes, it's been sorted out in my husband's mind. Please tell him we look forward to seeing him.' She looked at Dr Seth for confirmation; he gave a disgusted grunt, but thought it best to let things be. Suddenly his attention shifted.

'When?' he demanded, indicating Savita's stomach with the handle of his cane.

'August or September, that's what we've been told,' said Pran, rather vaguely, as if afraid that Dr Kishen Chand Seth might decide to take over things again.

Dr Kishen Chand Seth turned to Lata. 'Why aren't you married yet? Don't you like my radiologist?' he asked her.

Lata looked at him and tried to hide her amazement. Her cheeks burned.

'You haven't introduced her to the radiologist yet,' Mrs Rupa Mehra interposed quickly. 'And now it is almost time for her exams.'

'What radiologist?' asked Lata. 'It's still the 1st of April. Is that it?'

'Yes, the radiologist. Call me tomorrow,' said Dr Kishen Chand Seth to his daughter. 'Remind me, Parvati. Now we must go. I must see this film again next week. So sad,' he added approvingly.

On the way to his grey Buick Dr Kishen Chand Seth noticed a wrongly parked car. He yelled at the policeman on duty at the busy intersection. The policeman, who recognized the terrifying Dr Seth, as did most of the forces

of order and disorder in Brahmpur, left the traffic to fend
for itself, came over promptly, and took down the number
of the car. A beggar limped alongside and asked for a
couple of pice. Dr Kishen Chand Seth looked at him in
fury and gave him a brutal whack on the leg with his stick.
He and Parvati got into the car and the policeman cleared
the traffic for them.

3.3

'NO talking, please,' said the invigilator.

'I was just borrowing a ruler, Sir.'

'If you have to do that, do it through me.'

'Yes, Sir.'

The boy sat down and applied himself once more to the
question-paper in front of him.

A fly buzzed against the window-pane of the examination hall. Outside the window the red crown of a gul-
mohur tree could be seen below the stone steps. The fans
whirled slowly around. Row after row of heads, row after
row of hands, drop after drop of ink, words and yet more
words. Someone got up to have a drink of water from the
earthenware pitcher near the exit. Someone leaned back
against his chair and sighed.

Lata had stopped writing about half an hour ago, and
had been staring at her paper sightlessly since. She was
trembling. She could not think of the questions at all. She
was breathing deeply and the sweat stood out on her
forehead. Neither of the girls on either side of her noticed.
Who were they? She didn't recognize them from the English
lectures.

What do these questions mean? she asked herself. And
how was I managing to answer them just a little while
ago? Do Shakespeare's tragic heroes deserve their fates?
Does anyone deserve her fate? She looked around again.
What is the matter with me, I who am so good at taking
exams? I don't have a headache, I don't have a period,
what is my excuse? What will Ma say –

An image of her bedroom in Pran's house came to her mind. In it she saw her mother's three suitcases, filled with most of what she owned in the world. Standard appendages of her Annual Rail-Pilgrimage, they lay in a corner, with her large handbag resting like a self-confident black swan upon them. Nearby lay a small square dark green copy of the Bhagavad Gita and a glass that contained her false teeth. She had worn them ever since a car accident ten years ago.

What would my father have thought? wondered Lata – with his brilliant record – his gold medals – how can I fail him like this? It was in April that he died. Gul-mohurs were in bloom then too.... I must concentrate. I must concentrate. Something has happened to me and I must not panic. I must relax and things will be all right again.

She fell into a reverie once more. The fly buzzed in a steady drone.

'No humming. Please be silent.'

Lata realized with a start that it was she who had been humming softly to herself and that both her neighbours were now looking at her: one appeared puzzled, the other annoyed. She bent her head towards her answer-book. The pale blue lines stretched out without any potential meaning across the blank page.

'If at first you don't succeed –' she heard her mother's voice say.

She quickly turned back to a previous question she had already answered, but what she had written made no sense to her.

'The disappearance of Julius Caesar from his own play as early as Act III would seem to imply ...'

Lata rested her head on her hands.

'Are you feeling all right?'

She raised her head and looked at the troubled face of a young lecturer from the Philosophy Department who happened to be on invigilation duty that day.

'Yes.'

'You're quite sure?' he murmured.

Lata nodded.

She picked up her pen and began to write something in her answer-book. A few minutes passed, and the invigilator announced: 'Half an hour left.' Lata realized that at least an hour of her three-hour paper had vanished into nothingness. She had answered only two questions so far. Activated by sudden alarm, she began to write answers to the two remaining questions – she chose them virtually at random – in a rapid, panic-stricken scrawl, smearing her fingers with ink, smudging the answer-book, hardly conscious of what she was writing. The buzzing of the fly seemed to her to have entered her brain. Her normally attractive handwriting now looked worse than Arun's, and this thought almost made her seize up again.

'Five minutes left.'

Lata continued to write, hardly aware of what it was she was writing.

'Pens down, please.'

Lata's hand continued to move across the page.

'No more writing, please. Time's up.'

Lata put her pen down and buried her head in her hands.

'Bring your papers to the front of the hall. Please make sure that your roll numbers are correctly inscribed on the front and that your supplementary booklets, if you have any, are arranged in the right order. No talking, please, until you have left the hall.'

Lata handed in her booklet. On the way out she rested her right wrist for a few seconds against the cool earthenware pitcher.

She did not know what had come over her.

3.4

LATA stood outside the hall for a minute. Sunlight poured onto the stone steps. The edge of her middle finger was smeared with dark blue ink, and she looked at it, frowning. She was close to tears.

Other English students stood on the steps and chatted. A

post-mortem of the paper was being held, and it was dominated by an optimistic and chubby girl who was ticking off on her fingers the various points she had answered correctly.

'This is one paper I know I have done really well,' she said. 'Especially the *King Lear* question. I think that the answer was "Yes".' Others were looking excited or depressed. Everyone agreed that several of the questions were far harder than they had needed to be. A knot of history students stood not far away, discussing their paper, which had been held simultaneously in the same building. One of them was the young man who had brought himself to Lata's attention in the Imperial Book Depot, and he was looking a little worried. He had spent a great deal of time these last few months in extra-curricular activities – particularly cricket – and this had taken its toll upon his performance.

Lata walked to a bench beneath the gul-mohur tree, and sat down to collect herself. When she got home for lunch she would be pestered with a hundred questions about how well she had done. She looked down at the red flowers that lay scattered at her feet. In her head she could still hear the buzzing of the fly.

The young man, though he had been talking to his classmates, had noticed her walking down the steps. When she sat down on the far bench under the tree, he decided to have a word with her. He told his friends that he had to go home for lunch – that his father would be waiting for him – and hurried along the path past the gul-mohur. As he came to the bench, he uttered an exclamation of surprise and stopped.

'Hello,' he said.

Lata raised her head and recognized him. She flushed with embarrassment that he should see her in her present visible distress.

'I suppose you don't remember me?' he said.

'I do,' said Lata, surprised that he should continue to talk to her despite her obvious wish that he should walk on. She said nothing further, nor did he for a few seconds.

'We met at the bookshop,' he said.

'Yes,' said Lata. Then, quickly, she added: 'Please, just let me be. I don't feel like talking to anyone.'

'It's the exam, isn't it?'

'Yes.'

'Don't worry,' he said. 'You'll have forgotten all about it in five years.'

Lata became indignant. She did not care for his glib philosophy. Who on earth did he think he was? Why didn't he just buzz off – like that wretched fly?

'I say that,' he continued, 'because a student of my father's once tried to kill himself after he had done badly in his final exams. It's a good thing he didn't succeed, because when the results came out he found he'd got a first.'

'How can you think you've done badly in mathematics when you've done well?' asked Lata, interested despite herself. 'Your answers are either right or wrong. I can understand it in history or English, but ...'

'Well, that's an encouraging thought,' said the young man, pleased that she had remembered something about him. 'Both of us have probably done less badly than we think.'

'So you've done badly too?' asked Lata.

'Yes,' he said, simply.

Lata found it hard to believe him, as he didn't appear distressed in the least.

There was silence for a few moments. Some of the young man's friends passed by the bench but very tactfully forebore from greeting him. He knew, however, that this would not prevent them from taxing him later about the beginnings of a grand passion.

'But look, don't worry ...' he went on. 'One paper in six is bound to be difficult. Do you want a dry handkerchief?'

'No, thank you.' She glared at him, then looked away.

'When I was standing there, feeling low,' he said, pointing to the top of the steps, 'I noticed you here looking even worse, and that cheered me up. May I sit down?'

'Please don't,' said Lata. Then, realizing how rude her words had sounded, she said, 'No, do. But I have to be off. I hope you've done better than you think.'

'I hope you'll feel better than you do,' said the young man, sitting down. 'Has it helped to talk to me?'

'No,' said Lata. 'Not at all.'

'Oh,' said the young man, a bit disconcerted. 'Anyway, remember,' he went on, 'there are more important things in the world than exams.' He stretched backwards on the bench, and looked up at the reddish-orange flowers.

'Like what?' asked Lata.

'Like friendship,' he said, a little severely.

'Really?' said Lata, smiling a little now despite herself.

'Really,' he said. 'Talking to you has certainly cheered me up.' But he continued to look stern.

Lata stood up and started to walk away from the bench.

'You don't have any objection to my walking along with you for a bit?' he said, getting up himself.

'I can't very well stop you,' said Lata. 'India is a free country now.'

'All right. I'll sit on this bench and think of you,' he said melodramatically, sitting down again. 'And of that attractive and mysterious ink-stain near your nose. It's been some days since Holi.'

Lata made a sound of impatience and walked away. The young man's eyes were following her, and she was aware of it. She rubbed her stained middle finger with her thumb to control her awkwardness. She was annoyed with him and with herself, and unsettled by her unexpected enjoyment of his unexpected company. But these thoughts did have the effect of replacing her anxiety – indeed, panic – about how badly she'd done in the paper on Drama with the wish to look at a mirror at once.

3.5

LATER that afternoon, Lata and Malati and a couple of their friends – all girls, of course – were taking a walk together to the jacaranda grove where they liked to sit and study. The jacaranda grove by tradition was open only to girls. Malati was carrying an incongruously fat medical textbook.

It was a hot day. The two wandered hand in hand among the jacaranda trees. A few soft mauve flowers drifted down to earth. When they were out of earshot of the others, Malati said, with quiet amusement:

'What is on your mind?'

When Lata looked at her quizzically, Malati continued, undeterred: 'No, no, it's no use looking at me like that, I know that something is bothering you. In fact I know what it is that's bothering you. I have my sources of information.'

Lata responded: 'I know what you're going to say, and it's not true.'

Malati looked at her friend and said: 'All that Christian training at St Sophia's has had a bad influence on you, Lata. It's made you into a terrible liar. No, I don't mean that exactly. What I mean is that when you do lie, you do it terribly.'

'All right, then, what were you going to say?' said Lata.

'I've forgotten now,' said Malati.

'Please,' said Lata, 'I didn't get up from my books for this. Don't be mean, don't be elliptical, and don't tease me. It's bad enough as it is.'

'Why?' said Malati. 'Are you in love already? It's high time, spring is over.'

'Of course not,' said Lata indignantly. 'Are you mad?'

'No,' said Malati.

'Then why do you have to ask such astonishing questions?'

'I heard about the way he walked familiarly up to you while you were sitting on the bench after the exam,' said Malati, 'so I assumed that you must have been meeting off and on since the Imperial Book Depot.' From her informant's description Malati had assumed that it had been the same fellow. And she was pleased she was right.

Lata looked at her friend with more exasperation than

affection. News travels much too fast, she thought, and Malati listens in on every line.

'We have not been meeting either off or on,' she said. 'I don't know where you get your information from, Malati. I wish you would talk about music or the news or something sensible. Even your socialism. This is only the second time we've met, and I don't even know his name. Here, give me your textbook, and let's sit down. If I read a paragraph or two of something I don't understand, I'll be all right.'

'You don't even know his name?' said Malati, now looking at Lata as if she was the one who was mad. 'Poor fellow! Does he know yours?'

'I think I told him at the bookshop. Yes, I did. And then he asked me if I was going to ask him his – and I said no.'

'And you wish you hadn't,' said Malati, watching her face closely.

Lata was silent. She sat down and leaned against a jacaranda.

'And I suppose he would like to have told you,' said Malati, sitting down as well.

'I suppose he would,' said Lata laughing.

'Poor boiled potatoes,' said Malati.

'Boiled – what?'

'You know – "Don't put chillies on boiled potatoes."' Malati imitated Lata.

Lata blushed.

'You do like him, don't you?' said Malati. 'If you lie, I'd know it.'

Lata did not respond immediately. She had been able to face her mother with reasonable calmness at lunch, despite the strange, trance-like event of the Drama paper. Then she said:

'He could see that I was upset after the paper. I don't think it was easy for him to come up and talk to me when I had, well, in a way rebuffed him at the bookshop.'

'Oh, I don't know,' said Malati casually. 'Boys are such louts. He could very well have done it for the challenge. They're always daring each other to do idiotic things – for instance, storming the Women's Hostel at Holi. They think they are such heroes.'

'He is not a lout,' said Lata, bridling. 'And as for heroism, I think it does take at least a little courage to do something when you know that your head can be bitten off as a result. You said something to the same effect in the Blue Danube.'

'Not courage, boldness,' said Malati, who was thoroughly enjoying her friend's reactions. 'Boys aren't in love, they're just bold. When the four of us were walking to the grove just now, I noticed a couple of boys on bicycles following us in a pathetic sort of way. Neither really wanted to brave an encounter with us, but neither could say so. So it was quite a relief to them when we entered the grove and the question became moot.'

Lata was silent. She lay down on the grass and stared up at the sky through the jacaranda branches. She was thinking of the smear on her nose, which she had washed off before lunch.

'Sometimes they'll come up to you together,' continued Malati, 'and grin more at each other than at you. At other times they're so afraid that their friends will come up with a better "line" than they themselves can think of that they'll actually take their life in their hands and come up to you alone. And what are their lines? Nine times out of ten it is "May I borrow your notes?" perhaps tempered with a lukewarm, feeble-minded "Namasté". What, incidentally, was the introductory line of the Potato Man?'

Lata kicked Malati.

'Sorry – I meant the apple of your heart.'

'What did he say?' said Lata, almost to herself. When she tried to recall exactly how the conversation had begun, she realized that, although it had taken place just a few hours ago, it had already grown hazy in her mind. What remained, however, was the memory that her initial nervousness at the young man's presence had ended in a sense of confused warmth: at least someone, if only a good-looking stranger, had understood that she had been bewildered and upset, and had cared enough to do something to lift her spirits.

<h2 style="text-align:center">3.6</h2>

A couple of days later there was a music recital in the Bharatendu Auditorium, one of the two largest auditoriums in town. One of the performers was Ustad Majeed Khan.

Lata and Malati both managed to get tickets. So did Hema, a tall, thin, and high-spirited friend of theirs who lived with innumerable cousins – boys and girls – in a house not far from Nabiganj. They were all under the care of a strict elder member of the family who was referred to by everyone as 'Tauji'. Hema's Tauji had quite a job on his hands, as he was not only responsible for the well-being and reputation of the girls of the family but also had to make sure that the boys did not get into the countless kinds of mischief that boys are prone to. He had often cursed his luck that he was the sole representative in a university town of a large and far-flung family. He had on occasion threatened to send everyone straight back home when they had caused him more trouble than he could bear. But his wife, 'Taiji' to everyone, though she herself had been brought up with almost no liberty or latitude, felt it was a great pity that her nieces and grandnieces should be similarly constrained. She managed to obtain for the girls what they could not obtain by a more direct approach.

This evening Hema and her cousins had thus succeeded in reserving the use of Tauji's large maroon Packard, and went around town collecting their friends for the concert. No sooner was Tauji out of sight than they had entirely forgotten his outraged parting comment: 'Flowers? Flowers in your hair? Rushing off in exam time – and listening to all this pleasure-music! Everyone will think you are completely dissolute – you will never get married.'

Eleven girls, including Lata and Malati, emerged from the Packard at Bharatendu Auditorium. Strangely enough, their saris were not crushed, though perhaps they looked slightly dishevelled. They stood outside the auditorium re-arranging their own and each other's hair, chattering excitedly. Then in a busy shimmer of colour they streamed inside. There was no place for all of them to sit together, so they broke up into twos and threes, and sat down, rapt but no less voluble. A few fans whirled round over-head, but it had been a hot day, and the auditorium was stuffy. Lata and her friends started fanning themselves with their programmes, and waited for the recital to begin.

The first half consisted of a disappointingly indifferent sitar recital by a well-known musician. At the interval, Lata and Malati were standing by the staircase in the lobby when the Potato Man walked towards them.

Malati saw him first, nudged Lata's attention in his direction, and said:

'Meeting number three. I'm going to make myself scarce.'

'Malati, please stay here,' said Lata in sudden desperation, but Malati had disappeared with the admonition: 'Don't be a mouse. Be a tigress.'

The young man approached her with fairly assured steps.

'Is it all right to interrupt you?' he said, not very loudly.

Lata could not make out what he was saying in the noise of the crowded lobby, and indicated as much.

This was taken by the young man as permission to approach. He came closer, smiled at her, and said:

'I wondered if it was all right to interrupt you.'

'To interrupt me?' said Lata. 'But I was doing nothing.' Her heart was beating fast.

'I meant, to interrupt your thoughts.'

'I wasn't having any,' said Lata, trying to control a sudden overload of them. She thought of Malati's comment about her being a poor liar and felt the blood rush to her cheeks.

'Quite stuffy in there,' said the young man. 'Here too, of course.'

Lata nodded. I'm not a mouse or a tigress, she thought, I'm a hedgehog.

'Lovely music,' he said.

'Yes,' agreed Lata, though she hadn't thought so. His presence so close to her was making her tingle. Besides, she was embarrassed about being seen with a young man. She knew that if she looked around she would see someone she recognized looking at her. But having been unkind to him twice already she was determined not to rebuff him again. Holding up her side of the conversation, however, was difficult when she was feeling so distracted. Since it was hard for her to meet his eye, she looked down instead.

The young man was saying: '... though, of course, I don't often go there. How about you?'

Lata, nonplussed, because she had either not heard or not registered what went before, did not reply.

'You're very quiet,' he said.

'I'm always very quiet,' said Lata. 'It balances out.'

'No, you aren't,' said the young man with a faint smile. 'You and your friends were chattering like a flock of jungle babblers when you came in – and some of you continued to chatter while the sitar player was tuning up.'

'Do you think,' Lata said, looking up a little sharply, 'that men don't chatter and babble as much as women?'

'I do,' said the young man airily, happy that she was talking at last. 'It's a fact of nature. Shall I tell you a folk-tale about Akbar and Birbal? It's very relevant to this subject.'

'I don't know,' said Lata. 'Once I've heard it I'll tell you if you should have told it.'

'Well, maybe at our next meeting?'

Lata took this remark quite coolly.

'I suppose there will be one,' she said. 'We seem to keep meeting by chance.'

'Does it have to be by chance?' asked the young man. 'When I talked about you and your friends, the fact is that I had eyes mostly for you. The moment I saw you enter, I thought how lovely you looked – in a simple green sari with just a white rose in your hair.'

The word 'mostly' bothered Lata, but the rest was music. She smiled.

He smiled back, and suddenly became very specific.

'There's a meeting of the Brahmpur Literary Society at five o'clock on Friday evening at old Mr Nowrojee's house – 20 Hastings Road. It should be interesting – and it's open to anyone who feels like coming. With the university vacations coming up, they seem to want to welcome outsiders to make up the numbers.'

The university vacations, thought Lata. Perhaps we won't see each other again after all. The thought saddened her.

'Oh, I know what I wanted to ask you,' she said.

'Yes?' asked the young man, looking puzzled. 'Go ahead.'

'What's your name?' asked Lata.

The young man's face broke into a happy grin. 'Ah!' he said, 'I thought you would never ask. I'm Kabir, but very recently my friends have started calling me Galahad.'

'Why?' asked Lata, surprised.

'Because they think that I spend my time rescuing damsels in distress.'

'I was not in such distress that I needed rescuing,' said Lata.

Kabir laughed. 'I know you weren't, you know you weren't, but my friends are such idiots,' he said.

'So are mine,' said Lata disloyally. Malati had, after all, left her in the lurch.

'Why don't we exchange last names as well?' said the young man, pursuing his advantage.

Some instinct of self-preservation made Lata pause. She liked him, and she very much hoped she would meet him again – but he might ask her for her address next. Images of Mrs Rupa Mehra's interrogations came to mind.

'No, let's not,' said Lata. Then, feeling her abruptness and the hurt she might have caused him, she quickly blurted out the first thing she could think of. 'Do you have any brothers and sisters?'

'Yes, a younger brother.'

'No sisters?' Lata smiled, though she did not quite know why.

'I had a younger sister till last year.'

'Oh – I am so sorry,' said Lata in dismay. 'How terrible that must have been for you – and for your parents.'

'Well, for my father,' said Kabir quietly. 'But it looks as if Ustad Majeed Khan has begun. Maybe we should go in?'

Lata, moved by a rush of sympathy and even tenderness, hardly heard him; but as he walked towards the door, so did she. Inside the hall the maestro had begun his slow and magnificent rendition of Raag Shri. They separated, resumed their previous places, and sat down to listen.

3.7

NORMALLY Lata would have been transfixed by Ustad Majeed Khan's music. Malati, sitting next to her, was. But her encounter with Kabir had set her mind wandering in so many different directions, often simultaneously, that she might as well have been listening to silence. She felt suddenly light-hearted and started smiling to herself at the thought of the rose in her hair. A minute later, remembering the last part of their conversation, she rebuked herself for being so unfeeling. She tried to make sense of what he had meant by saying – and so quietly at that – 'Well, for my father.' Was it that his mother had already died? That would place him and Lata in a curiously symmetrical position. Or was his mother so estranged from the family that she was unconscious of or not much distressed by the loss of her daughter? Why am I thinking such impossible thoughts? Lata wondered. Indeed, when Kabir had said, 'I had a younger sister till last year,' did that have to imply the conclusion to which Lata had automatically jumped? But, poor fellow, he had grown so tense and subdued by the last few words that had passed between them that he had himself suggested that they return to the hall.

Malati was kind enough and smart enough neither to

glance at her nor to nudge her. And soon Lata too sank into the music and lost herself in it.

3.8

THE next time Lata saw Kabir, he was looking the very opposite of tense and subdued. She was walking across the campus with a book and a file under her arm when she saw him and another student, both wearing cricket clothes, sauntering along the path that led to the sports fields. Kabir was casually swinging a bat as he walked and the two of them appeared to be engaged in relaxed and occasional conversation. Lata was too far behind them to make out anything of what they were saying. Suddenly Kabir leaned his head back and burst out laughing. He looked so handsome in the morning sunlight and his laughter was so open-hearted and free from tension that Lata, who had been about to turn towards the library, found herself continuing to follow him. She was astonished by this, but didn't rebuke herself. 'Well, why shouldn't I?' she thought. 'Since he's approached me three times already, I don't see why I shouldn't follow him for once. But I thought the cricket season was over. I didn't know there was a match on in the middle of exams.'

As it happened, Kabir and his friend were off for a bit of practice at the nets. It was his way of taking a break from studies. The far end of the sports fields, where the practice nets had been set up, was close to a small stand of bamboos. Lata sat down in the shade and – herself unobserved – watched the two take turns with bat and ball. She did not know the first thing about cricket – even Pran's enthusiasm had not affected her at all – but she was drowsily entranced by the sight of Kabir, dressed completely in white, shirt unbuttoned at the collar, capless and with ruffled hair, running in to bowl – or standing at the crease wielding his bat with what seemed like easy skill. Kabir was an inch or two under six feet, slim and athletic, with a 'fair to wheatish' complexion, an aquiline nose, and black, wavy hair. Lata did not know how long she sat there, but it must have been for more than half an hour. The sound of bat on ball, the rustle of a slight breeze in the bamboo, the twittering of a few sparrows, the calls of a couple of mynas, and, above all, the sound of the young men's easy laughter and indistinct conversation all combined to make her almost oblivious of herself. It was quite a while before she came to.

I'm behaving like a fascinated gopi, she thought. Soon, instead of feeling jealous of Krishna's flute I'll start envying Kabir's bat! She smiled at the thought, then got up, brushed a few dried leaves from her salwaar-kameez, and – still unnoticed – walked back the way she had come.

'You have to find out who he is,' she told Malati that afternoon, plucking a leaf and absent-mindedly running it up and down her arm.

'Who?' said Malati. She was delighted.

Lata made a sound of exasperation.

'Well, I could have told you something about him,' said Malati, 'if you'd allowed me to after the concert.'

'Like what?' said Lata expectantly.

'Well, here are two facts to begin with,' said Malati tantalizingly. 'His name is Kabir, and he plays cricket.'

'But I know that already,' protested Lata. 'And that's about all I do know. Don't you know anything else?'

'No,' said Malati. She toyed with the idea of inventing a streak of criminality in his family, but decided that that was too cruel.

'But you said "to begin with". That means you must have something else.'

'No,' said Malati. 'The second half of the concert began just as I was about to ask my informant a few more questions.'

'I'm sure you can find out everything about him if you put your mind to it.' Lata's faith in her friend was touching.

Malati doubted it. She had a wide circle of acquaintance. But it was nearly the end of term and she didn't know where to begin enquiries. Some students – those whose exams were over – had already left Brahmpur; these included her informant at the concert. She herself would be leaving in a couple of days to go back to Agra for a while.

'The Trivedi Detective Agency needs a clue or two to start with,' she said. 'And time is short. You've got to think back over your conversations. Isn't there anything else you know about him that could help me?'

Lata thought for a while but came up with a blank. 'Nothing,' she said. 'Oh, wait – his father teaches maths.'

'At Brahmpur University?' asked Malati.

'I don't know,' said Lata. 'And another thing: I think he's fond of literature. He wanted me to come to the Lit Soc meeting tomorrow.'

'Then why don't you go there and ask him about himself,' said Malati, who believed in the Approach Audacious. 'Whether he brushes his teeth with Kolynos, for instance. "There's magic in a Kolynos smile."'

'I can't,' said Lata, so forcefully that Malati was a little taken aback.

'Surely you're not falling for him!' she said. 'You don't know the first thing about him – his family, or even his full name.'

'I feel I know more important things about him than the first thing,' said Lata.

'Yes, yes,' said Malati, 'like the whiteness of his teeth and the blackness of his hair. "She floated on a magical cloud high in the sky, sensing his strong presence around her with every fibre of her being. He was her whole universe. He was the be-all and end-all and catch-all and hold-all of her existence." I know the feeling.'

'If you're going to talk nonsense –' said Lata, feeling the warmth rise to her face.

'No, no, no, no, no,' said Malati, still laughing. 'I'll find out whatever I can.'

Several thoughts went through her mind: cricket reports in the university magazine? The Mathematics Department? The Registrar's Office?

Aloud she said, 'Leave Boiled Potatoes to me. I'll smother him with chillies and present him to you on a platter.

Anyway, Lata, from your face, no one would know you still had a paper left. Being in love is good for you. You must do it more often.'

'Yes, I will,' said Lata. 'When you become a doctor, prescribe it to all your patients.'

3.9

LATA arrived at 20 Hastings Road at five o'clock the next day. She had finished her last paper that morning. She was convinced she had not done well in it, but when she started to feel upset, she thought of Kabir and instantly cheered up. Now she looked around for him among the group of about fifteen men and women who were sitting in old Mr Nowrojee's drawing room – the room in which the weekly meetings of the Brahmpur Literary Society had been held from as far back as anyone could remember. But either Kabir had not yet arrived or else he had changed his mind about coming.

The room was full of stuffed chairs with flowery prints and overstuffed cushions with flowery prints.

Mr Nowrojee, a thin, short and gentle man, with an immaculate white goatee beard and an immaculate light grey suit, presided over the occasion. Noticing that Lata was a new face, he introduced himself and made her feel welcome. The others, who were sitting or standing in small groups, paid no attention to her. Feeling awkward at first, she walked over to a window and gazed out towards a small, well-tended garden with a sundial in the middle. She was looking forward so much to seeing him that she vehemently pushed aside the thought that he might not turn up.

'Good afternoon, Kabir.'

'Good afternoon, Mr Nowrojee.'

Lata turned around at the mention of Kabir's name and the sound of his low, pleasant voice, and gave him such a happy smile that he put his hand to his forehead and staggered back a few steps.

Lata did not know what to make of his buffoonery, which luckily no one else had noticed. Mr Nowrojee was now seated at the oblong table at the end of the room and was coughing mildly for attention. Lata and Kabir sat down on an empty sofa near the wall farthest from the table. Before they could say anything to each other, a middle-aged man with a plump, bright-eyed, cheerful face handed them each a sheaf of carbon copies which appeared to be covered with poetry.

'Makhijani,' he said mysteriously as he passed.

Mr Nowrojee took a sip of water from one of the three glasses in front of him. 'Fellow members of the Brahmpur Literary Society – and friends,' he said in a voice that barely carried to where Lata and Kabir were sitting, 'we have gathered here for the 1,698th meeting of our society. I now declare the meeting open.'

He looked wistfully out of the window, and rubbed his glasses with a handkerchief. Then he continued: 'I remember when Edmund Blunden addressed us. He said – and I remember his words to this very day – he said –'

Mr Nowrojee stopped, coughed, and looked down at the sheet of paper in front of him. His skin itself appeared to be as thin as paper.

He went on: '1,698th meeting. Poetry recitation of their own poetry by members of the society. Copies, I see, have been handed out. Next week Professor O.P. Mishra of the English Department will present to us a paper on the subject: "Eliot: Whither?"'

Lata, who enjoyed Professor Mishra's lectures despite the pinkness with which he was now invested in her mind, looked interested, though the title was a bit mystifying.

'Three poets will be reading from their own work today,' continued Mr Nowrojee, 'following which I hope you will join us for tea. I am sorry to see that my young friend Mr Sorabjee has not been able to make the time to come,' he added in tones of gentle rebuke.

Mr Sorabjee, fifty-seven years old, and – like Mr Nowrojee himself – a Parsi, was the Proctor of Brahmpur University. He rarely missed a meeting of the literary societies of either the university or the town. But he always managed to avoid meetings where members read out their own literary efforts.

Mr Nowrojee smiled indecisively. 'The poets reading today are Dr Vikas Makhijani, Mrs Supriya Joshi –'

'Shrimati Supriya Joshi,' said a booming female voice. The broad-bosomed Mrs Joshi had stood up to make the correction.

'Er, yes, our, er, talented poetess Shrimati Supriya Joshi – and, of course, myself, Mr R.P. Nowrojee. As I am already seated at the table I will avail myself of the chairman's prerogative of reading my own poems first – by way of an apéritif to the more substantial fare that is to follow. Bon appetit.' He allowed himself a sad, rather wintry, chuckle before clearing his throat and taking another sip of water.

'The first poem that I would like to read is entitled "Haunting Passion",' said Mr Nowrojee primly. And he read the following poem:

> I'm haunted by a tender passion,
>   The ghost of which will never die.
> The leaves of autumn have grown ashen:
> I'm haunted by a tender passion.
> And spring-time too, in its own fashion,
>   Burns me with love's sweet song – so I –
> I'm haunted by a tender passion,
>   The ghost of which will never die.

As Mr Nowrojee completed his poem, he seemed to be manfully holding back his tears. He looked out towards the garden, towards the sundial, and, pulling himself together, said:

'That is a triolet. Now I will read you a ballade. It is called "Buried Flames".'

After he had read this and three other poems in a similar vein with diminishing vigour, he stopped, spent of all emotion. He then got up like one who had completed an infinitely distant and exhausting journey, and sat down on a stuffed chair not far from the speaker's table.

In the brief interval between him and the next reader Kabir looked inquiringly at Lata and she looked quizzically back at him. They were both trying to control their laughter, and looking at each other was not helping them do this.

Luckily, the happy, plump-faced man who had handed them the poems that he planned to read now rushed forward energetically to the speaker's table and, before sitting down, said the single word:

'Makhijani.'

After he had announced his name, he looked even more delighted than before. He riffled through his sheaf of papers with an expression of intense and pleasurable concentration, then smiled at Mr Nowrojee, who shrank in his chair like a sparrow cowering in a niche before a gale. Mr Nowrojee had tried at one stage to dissuade Dr Makhijani from reading, but had met with such good-natured outrage that he had had to give in. But having read a copy of the poems earlier in the day, he could not help wishing that the banquet had ended with the apéritif.

'A Hymn to Mother India,' said Dr Makhijani sententiously, then beamed at his audience. He leaned forward with the concentration of a burly blacksmith and read his poem through, including the stanza numbers, which he hammered out like horseshoes.

1. Who a child has not seen drinking milk
   At bright breasts of Mother, rags she wears or silks?
   Love of mild Mother like rain-racked gift of cloud.
   In poet's words, Mother to thee I bow.

2. What poor gift when doctor patient treats.
   Hearts he hears but so much his heart bleats?
   Where is doctor that can cure my pains?
   Why suffers Mother? Where to base the blame?

3. Her raiments rain-drenched with May or Monsoon,
   Like Savitri sweet she wins from Yama her sons,

Cheating death with millions of population,
Leading to chaste and virtuous nation.

4. From shore of Kanyakumari to Kashmir,
From tiger of Assam to rampant beast of Gir,
Freedom's dawn now bathing, laving her face,
Tremble of jetty locks is Ganga's grace.

5. How to describe bondage of Mother pure
By pervert punies chained through shackles of law?
British cut-throat, Indian smiling and slave:
Such shame will not dispense till a sweating grave.

While reading the above stanza, Dr Makhijani became
highly agitated, but he was restored to equanimity by the
next one:

6. Let me recall history of heroes proud,
Mother-milk fed their breasts, who did not bow.
Fought they fiercely, carrying worlds of weight,
Establishing firm foundation of Indian state.

Nodding at the nervous Mr Nowrojee, Dr Makhijani now
lauded his namesake, one of the fathers of the Indian
freedom movement:

7. Dadabhai Naoroji entered Parliament,
As MP from Finsbury, grace was heaven-sent.
But he forgot not Mother's plumpy breasts:
Dreams were of India, living in the West.

Lata and Kabir looked at each other in mingled delight
and horror.

8. B.G. Tilak from Maharashtra hailed.
'Swaraj my birthright is' he ever wailed.
But cruel captors sent him to the sweltry jail
In Forts of Mandalay, a six-year sail.

9. Shame of the Mother bold Bengal reviled.
    Terrorist pistol in hand of the Kali child.
    Draupadi's sari twirling off and off –
    White Duryodhanas laugh to scorn and scoff.

Dr Makhijani's voice trembled with belligerence at these vivid lines. Several stanzas later he descended on figures of the immediate past and present:

26. Mahatma came to us like summer 'andhi',
    Sweeping the dungs and dirt, was M.K. Gandhi.
    Murder has mayhemed peace beyond understanding.
    Respect and sorrow leave me soiled and standing.

At this point Dr Makhijani stood up as a mark of veneration, and remained standing for the final three stanzas:

27. Then when the British left after all,
    We had as PM our own Jawahar Lal.
    Like rosy shimmers to the throne he came,
    And gave to our India a glorious name.

28. Muslim, Hindu, Sikh, Christian, revere him.
    Parsis, Jains, Buddhists also endear him.
    Cynosure of eyes, he stalks with regal mien
    Breathing spirit of a splendid scene.

29. We are all masters, each a Raja or Rani.
    No slave, or high or low, says Makhijani.
    Liberty equality fraternity justice as in Constitution.
    In homage of Mother we will find all solutions.

In the tradition of Urdu or Hindi poetry, the bard had imbedded his own name in the last stanza. He now sat down, wiping the sweat from his forehead, and beaming.

Kabir had been scribbling a note. He passed it on to Lata; their hands touched accidentally. Though she was in pain with her attempt to suppress her laughter, she felt a shock of excitement at his touch. It was he who, after a few seconds, moved his hand away, and she saw what he had written:

> Prompt escape from 20 Hastings Road
> Is my desire, although prized poets' abode.
> Desert not friendship. Renegade with me
> From raptured realm of Mr Nowrojee.

It was not quite up to Dr Makhijani's efforts, but it got its point across. Lata and Kabir, as if at a signal, got up quickly and, before they could be intercepted by a cheated Dr Makhijani, got to the front door.

Out on the sober street they laughed delightedly for a few minutes, quoting back at each other bits of Dr Makhijani's patriotic hymn. When the laughter had died down, Kabir said to her:

'How about a coffee? We could go to the Blue Danube.'

Lata, worried that she might meet someone she knew and already thinking of Mrs Rupa Mehra, said, 'No, I really can't. I have to go back home. To my Mother,' she added mischievously.

Kabir could not take his eyes off her.

'But your exams are over,' he said. 'You should be celebrating. It's I who have two papers left.'

'I wish I could. But meeting you here has been a pretty bold step for me.'

'Well, won't we at least meet here again next week? For "Eliot: Whither?"' Kabir made an airy gesture, rather like a foppish courtier, and Lata smiled.

'But are you going to be in Brahmpur next Friday?' she asked. 'The holidays . . .'

'Oh yes,' said Kabir. 'I live here.'

He was unwilling to say goodbye, but did so at last.

'See you next Friday then – or before,' he said, getting onto his bike. 'Are you sure I can't drop you anywhere – on my bicycle made for two? Smudged or unsmudged, you do look beautiful.'

Lata looked around, blushing.

'No, I'm sure. Goodbye,' she said. 'And – well – thank you.'

3.10

WHEN Lata got home she avoided her mother and sister and went straight to the bedroom. She lay on the bed and stared at the ceiling just as, a few days before, she had lain on the grass and stared at the sky through the jacaranda branches. The accidental touch of his hand as he had passed her the note was what she most wanted to recall.

Later, during dinner, the phone rang. Lata, sitting closest to the telephone, went to pick up the receiver.

'Hello?' said Lata.

'Hello – Lata?' said Malati.

'Yes,' said Lata happily.

'I've found out a couple of things. I'm going away tonight for a fortnight, so I thought I'd better tell you at once. Are you by yourself?' Malati added cautiously.

'No,' said Lata.

'Will you be by yourself within the next half-hour or so?'

'No, I don't think so,' said Lata.

'It isn't good news, Lata,' said Malati, seriously. 'You had better drop him.'

Lata said nothing.

'Are you still there?' asked Malati, concerned.

'Yes,' said Lata, glancing at the other three seated around the dining table. 'Go on.'

'Well, he's on the university cricket team,' said Malati, reluctant to break the ultimate bad news to her friend. 'There's a photograph of the team in the university magazine.'

'Yes?' said Lata, puzzled. 'But what –'

'Lata,' said Malati, unable to beat about the bush any further. 'His surname is Durrani.'

So what? thought Lata. What does that make him? Is he a Sindhi or something? Like – well – Chetwani or Advani – or . . . or Makhijani?'

'He's a Muslim,' said Malati, cutting into her thoughts. 'Are you still there?'

Lata was staring straight ahead. Savita put down her knife and fork, and looked anxiously at her sister.

Malati continued: 'You haven't a chance. Your family will be dead set against him. Forget him. Put it down to experience. And always find out the last name of anyone with an ambiguous first name. ... Why don't you say something? Are you listening?'

'Yes,' said Lata, her heart in turmoil.

She had a hundred questions, and more than ever she needed her friend's advice and sympathy and help. She said, slowly and evenly, 'I'd better go now. We're in the middle of dinner.'

Malati said, 'It didn't occur to me – it just didn't occur to me – but didn't it occur to you either? With a name like that – though all the Kabirs I know are Hindu – Kabir Bhandare, Kabir Sondhi –'

'It didn't occur to me,' said Lata. 'Thanks, Malu,' she added, using the form of Malati's name she sometimes used out of affection. 'Thank you for – well –'

'I'm so sorry. Poor Lata.'

'No. See you when you return.'

'Read a P.G. Wodehouse or two,' said Malati by way of parting advice. 'Bye.'

'Bye,' said Lata and put down the receiver carefully.

She returned to the table but she could not eat. Mrs Rupa Mehra immediately tried to find out what the matter was. Savita decided not to say anything at all for the moment. Pran looked on, puzzled.

'It's nothing,' Lata said, looking at her mother's anxious face.

After dinner, she went to the bedroom. She couldn't bear to talk with the family or listen to the late news on the radio. She lay face down on her bed and burst into tears – as quietly as she could – repeating his name with love and with angry reproach.

IT did not need Malati to tell her that it was impossible. Lata knew it well enough herself. She knew her mother and the deep pain and horror she would suffer if she heard that her daughter had been seeing a Muslim boy.

Any boy was worrisome enough, but this was too shameful, too painful, to believe. Lata could hear Mrs Rupa Mehra's voice: 'What did I do in my past life that I have deserved this?' And she could see her mother's tears as she faced the horror of her beloved daughter being given over to the nameless 'them'. Her old age would be embittered and she would be past consoling.

Lata lay on the bed. It was getting light. Her mother had gone through two chapters of the Gita that she recited every day at dawn. The Gita asked for detachment, tranquil wisdom, indifference to the fruits of action. This was a lesson that Mrs Rupa Mehra would never learn, could never learn. The lesson did not suit her temperament, even if its recitation did. The day she learned to be detached and indifferent and tranquil she would cease to be herself.

Lata knew that her mother was worried about her. But perhaps she attributed Lata's undisguisable misery over the next few days to anxiety about the results of the exams.

If only Malati were here, Lata said to herself.

If only she had not met him in the first place. If only their hands had not touched. If only.

If only I could stop acting like a fool! Lata said to herself. Malati always insisted that it was boys who behaved like morons when they were in love, sighing in their hostel rooms and wallowing in the Shelley-like treacle of ghazals. It was going to be a week before she met Kabir again. If she had known how to get in touch with him before then, she would have been even more torn with indecision.

She thought of yesterday's laughter outside Mr Nowrojee's house and angry tears came to her eyes again. She went to Pran's bookshelf and picked up the first P.G.

Wodehouse she saw: *Pigs Have Wings*. Malati, though flippant, both meant and prescribed well.

'Are you all right?' asked Savita.

'Yes,' said Lata. 'Did it kick last night?'

'I don't think so. At least I didn't wake up.'

'Men should have to bear them,' said Lata, apropos of nothing. 'I'm going for a walk by the river.' She assumed, correctly, that Savita was in no state to join her down the steep path that led from the campus to the sands.

She changed her slippers for sandals, which made walking easier. As she descended the clayey slope, almost a mud cliff, to the shore of the Ganga, she noticed a troupe of monkeys cavorting in a couple of banyan trees – two trees that had fused into one through the intertwining of their branches. A small orange-smeared statue of a god was jammed between the central trunks. The monkeys were usually pleased to see her – she brought them fruits and nuts whenever she remembered to. Today she had forgotten, and they made clear their displeasure. A couple of the smaller ones pulled at her elbow in request, while one of the larger ones, a fierce male, bared his teeth in annoyance – but from a distance.

She needed to be distracted. She suddenly felt very gentle towards the animal world – which seemed to her, probably incorrectly, to be a simpler place than the world of humans. Though she was halfway down the cliff, she walked back up again, went to the kitchen, and got a paper bag full of peanuts and another filled with three large musammis for the monkeys. She knew they did not like them as much as oranges, but in the summer only the thicker-skinned green sweet-limes were available.

They were, however, entirely delighted. Even before she said 'Aa! Aa!' – something she had once heard an old sadhu say to entice them – the monkeys noticed the paper bags. They gathered around, grabbing, grasping, pleading, clambering up the trees and down the trees in excitement, even hanging down from the branches and suspended roots and stretching their arms. The little ones squeaked, the big ones growled. One brute, possibly the one who had bared his teeth at her earlier, stored some of the peanuts in his cheekpads while he tried to grab more. Lata scattered a few, but fed them mainly by hand. She even ate a couple of peanuts herself. The two smallest monkeys, as before, grabbed – and even stroked – her elbow for attention. When she kept her hands closed to tease them, they opened them quite gently, not with their teeth but with their fingers.

When she tried to peel the musammis, the biggest monkeys would have none of it. She usually succeeded in a democratic distribution, but this time all three musammis were grabbed by fairly large monkeys. One went a little farther down the slope, and sat on a large root to eat it: he half peeled it, then ate it from the inside. Another, less particular, ate his skin and all.

Lata, laughing, finally swung what was left of the bag of peanuts around her head, and it flew off into the tree; it was caught in a high branch, but then came free, fell a little more, and got caught on a branch again. A great red-bottomed monkey climbed towards it, turning around at intervals to threaten one or two others who were climbing up the other root-branches that hung down from the main body of the banyan tree. He grabbed the whole packet and climbed higher to enjoy his monopoly. But the mouth of the bag suddenly came open and the nuts scattered all around. Seeing this, a thin baby monkey leaped in its excitement from one branch to another, lost its hold, banged its head against the trunk, and dropped down to the ground. It ran off squeaking.

Instead of going down to the river as she had planned, Lata now sat down on the exposed root where the monkey had just been eating his musammi, and tried to address herself to the book in her hands. It did not succeed in diverting her thoughts. She got up, climbed the path up the slope again, then walked to the library.

She looked through the last season's issues of the university magazine, reading through with intense interest what she had never so much as glanced at before: the cricket reports and the names beneath the team photographs. The writer of the reports, who signed himself 'S.K.', had a style of lively formality. He wrote, for example, not about Akhilesh and Kabir but about Mr Mittal and Mr Durrani and their excellent seventh wicket stand.

It appeared that Kabir was a good bowler and a fair batsman. Though he was usually placed low in the batting order, he had saved a number of matches by remaining unflappable in the face of considerable odds. And he must have been an incredibly swift runner, because he had sometimes run three runs, and on one occasion, had actually run four. In the words of S.K.:

This reporter has never seen anything like it. It is true that the outfield was not merely sluggish but torpid with the morning's rain. It is undeniable that the mid-wicket boundary at our opponents' field is more than ordinarily distant. It is irrefutable that there was confusion in the ranks of their fielders, and that one of them actually slipped and fell in pursuit of the ball. But what will be remembered are not these detracting circumstances. What will be remembered by Brahmpurians in time to come is the quicksilver crossing of two human bullets ricocheting from crease to crease and back again with a velocity appropriate more to the track than the pitch, and unusual even there. Mr Durrani and Mr Mittal ran four runs where no four was, on a ball that did not even cross the boundary; and that they were home and dry with more than a yard to spare attests to the fact that theirs was no flamboyant or unseasoned risk.

Lata read and relived matches that had been layered over by the pressure of recency even for the participants themselves, and the more she read the more she felt herself in love with Kabir – both as she knew him and as he was revealed to her by the judicious eye of S.K.

Mr Durrani, she thought, this should have been a different world.

If, as Kabir said, he lived in the town, it was more than likely that it was at Brahmpur University that his father taught. Lata, with a flair for research that she did not know she possessed, now looked up the fat volume of the Brahmpur University Calendar, and found what she was seeking under 'Faculty of Arts: Department of Mathematics'. Dr Durrani was not the head of his department, but the three magic letters after his name that indicated that he was a Fellow of the Royal Society outgloried twenty 'Professors'.

And Mrs Durrani? Lata said the two words aloud, appraising them. What of her? And of Kabir's brother and the sister he had had 'until last year'? Over the last few days her mind had time and again recurred to these elusive beings and those few elusive comments. But even if she had thought about them in the course of the happy conversation outside Mr Nowrojee's – and she hadn't – she could not have brought herself to ask him about them at the time. Now, of course, it was too late. If she did not want to lose her own family, she would have to shade herself from the bright beam of sudden sunlight that had strayed into her life.

Outside the library she tried to take stock of things. She realized that she could not now attend next Friday's meeting of the Brahmpur Literary Society.

'Lata: Whither?' she said to herself, laughed for a second or two, and found herself in tears.

Don't! she thought. You might attract another Galahad. This made her laugh once again. But it was a laughter that swept nothing away and unsettled her still further.

3.12

KABIR confronted her next Saturday morning not far from her house. She had gone out for a walk. He was on his bicycle, leaning against a tree. He looked rather like a horseman. His face was grim. When she saw him her heart went into her mouth.

It was not possible to avoid him. He had clearly been waiting for her. She put on a brave front.

'Hello, Kabir.'

'Hello. I thought you'd never come out of your house.'

'How did you find out where I live?'

'I instituted inquiries,' he said unsmilingly.

'Whom did you ask?' said Lata, feeling a little guilty for the inquiries she herself had 'instituted'.

'That doesn't matter,' said Kabir with a shake of his head.

Lata looked at him in distress. 'Are your exams over?' she asked, her tone betraying a touch of tenderness.

'Yes. Yesterday.' He didn't elaborate.

Lata stared at his bicycle unhappily. She wanted to say to him: 'Why didn't you tell me? Why didn't you tell me about yourself as soon as we exchanged words in the bookshop, so that I could have made sure I didn't feel anything for you?' But how often had they in fact met, and were they in any sense of the word intimate enough for such a direct, almost despairing, question? Did he feel what she felt for him? He liked her, she knew. But how much more could be added to that?

He pre-empted any possible question of hers by saying:

'Why didn't you come yesterday?'

'I couldn't,' she said helplessly.

'Don't twist the end of your dupatta, you'll crumple it.'

'Oh, sorry.' Lata looked at her hands in surprise.

'I waited for you. I went early. I sat through the whole lecture. I even chomped through Mrs Nowrojee's rock-hard little cakes. I had built up a good appetite by then.'

'Oh – I didn't know there was a Mrs Nowrojee,' said Lata, seizing upon the remark. 'I wondered about the inspiration for his poem, what was it called – "Haunted Passion"? Can you imagine her reaction to that? What does she look like?'

'Lata –' said Kabir with some pain, 'you're going to ask me next if Professor Mishra's lecture was any good. It was, but I didn't care. Mrs Nowrojee is fat and fair, but I couldn't care less. Why didn't you come?'

'I couldn't,' said Lata quietly. It would be better all around, she reflected, if she could summon up some anger to deal with his questions. All she could summon up was dismay.

'Then come and have some coffee with me now at the university coffee house.'

'I can't,' she said. He shook his head wonderingly. 'I really can't,' she repeated. 'Please let me go.'

'I'm not stopping you,' he said.

Lata looked at him and sighed: 'We can't stand here.'

Kabir refused to be affected by all these can'ts and couldn'ts.

'Well, let's stand somewhere else, then. Let's go for a walk in Curzon Park.'

'Oh no,' said Lata. Half the world walked in Curzon Park.

'Where then?'

They walked to the banyan trees on the slope leading down to the sands by the river. Kabir chained his bike to a tree at the top of the path. The monkeys were nowhere to be seen. Through the scarcely moving leaves of the gnarled trees they looked out at the Ganges. The wide brown river glinted in the sunlight. Neither said anything. Lata sat down on the upraised root, and Kabir followed.

'How beautiful it is here,' she said.

Kabir nodded. There was a bitterness about his mouth. If he had spoken, it would have been reflected in his voice.

Though Malati had warned her sternly off him, Lata just wanted to be with him for some time. She felt that if he were now to get up and go, she would try to dissuade him. Even if they were not talking, even in his present mood, she wanted to sit here with him.

Kabir was looking out over the river. With sudden eagerness, as if he had forgotten his grimness of a moment ago, he said: 'Let's go boating.'

Lata thought of Windermere, the lake near the High Court where they sometimes had department parties. Friends hired boats there and went out boating together. On Saturdays it was full of married couples and their children.

'Everyone goes to Windermere,' Lata said. 'Someone will recognize us.'

'I didn't mean Windermere. I meant up the Ganges. It always amazes me that people go sailing or boating on that foolish lake when they have the greatest river in the world at their doorstep. We'll go up the Ganges to the Barsaat Mahal. It's a wonderful sight by night. We'll get a boatman to keep the boat still in midstream, and you'll see it reflected by moonlight.' He turned to her.

Lata could not bear to look at him.

Kabir could not understand why she was so aloof and depressed. Nor could he understand why he had so suddenly fallen out of favour.

'Why are you so distant? Is it something to do with me?' he asked. 'Have I said something?'

Lata shook her head.

'Have I done something then?'

For some reason the thought of him running that impossible four runs came to her mind. She shook her head again.

'You'll forget about all this in five years,' she said.

'What sort of answer is that?' said Kabir, alarmed.

'It's what you said to me once.'

'Did I?' Kabir was surprised.

'Yes, on the bench, when you were rescuing me. I really can't come with you, Kabir, I really can't,' said Lata with sudden vehemence. 'You should know better than to ask me to come boating with you at midnight.' Ah, here was that blessed anger.

Kabir was about to respond in kind, but stopped himself. He paused, then said with surprising quietness:

'I won't tell you that I live from our one meeting to the next. You probably know that. It doesn't have to be by moonlight. Dawn is fine. If you're concerned about other people, don't worry. No one will see us; no one we're likely to know goes out in a boat at dawn. Bring a friend along. Bring ten friends along if you like. I just wanted to show you the Barsaat Mahal reflected in the water. If your mood has nothing to do with me, you must come.'

'Dawn –' said Lata, thinking aloud. 'There's no harm in dawn.'

'Harm?' Kabir looked at her incredulously. 'Don't you trust me?'

Lata said nothing. Kabir went on:

'Don't you care for me at all?'

She was silent.

'Listen,' said Kabir. 'If anyone asks you, it was just an educational trip. By daylight. With a friend, or as many friends as you wish to bring. I'll tell you the history of the Barsaat Mahal. The Nawab Sahib of Baitar has given me access to his library, and I've found out quite a few surprising facts about the place. You'll be the students. I'll be the guide: "a young history student, I can't remember his name now – he came with us and pointed out the spots of historical interest – provided quite a passable commentary – really quite a nice chap."'

Lata smiled ruefully.

Feeling that he had almost broken through some unseen defence, Kabir said:

'I'll see you and your friends here at this very spot on Monday morning at six sharp. Wear a sweater; there'll be a river breeze.' He burst into Makhijanian doggerel:

> 'Oh Miss Lata, meet me here
> Far from banks of Windermere.
> On the Ganga we will skim –
> Many hers and single him.'

Lata laughed.

'Say you'll come with me,' said Kabir.

'All right,' said Lata, shaking her head, not – as it appeared to Kabir – in partial denial of her own decision but in partial regret at her own weakness.

LATA did not want ten friends to accompany her, and even
if she had she would not have been able to round up half
that number. One was enough. Malati unfortunately had
left Brahmpur. Lata decided to go over to Hema's place to
persuade her to come. Hema was very excited at the
prospect, and readily agreed. It sounded romantic and
conspiratorial. 'I'll keep it a secret,' she said, but made the
mistake of confiding it on pain of lifelong enmity to one of
her innumerable cousins, who confided it to another cousin
on similarly strict terms. Within a day it had come to
Taiji's ears. Taiji, normally lenient, saw grave dangers in
this enterprise. She did not know – nor for that matter did
Hema – that Kabir was Muslim. But going out with any
boy in a boat at six in the morning: even she baulked here.
She told Hema she would not be allowed to go out. Hema
sulked but succumbed, and phoned Lata on Sunday
evening. Lata went to bed in great anxiety, but, having
made up her mind, did not sleep badly.

She could not let Kabir down again. She pictured him
standing in the banyan grove, cold and anxious, without
even the granitic sustenance of Mrs Nowrojee's little cakes,
waiting for her as the minutes passed and she did not
come. At a quarter to six the next morning she got out of
bed, dressed quickly, pulled on a baggy grey sweater that
had once belonged to her father, told her mother she was
going for a long walk in the university grounds, and went
to meet Kabir at the appointed place.

He was waiting for her. It was light, and the whole
grove was filled with the sound of waking birds.

'You're looking very unusual in that sweater,' he said
approvingly.

'You look just the same as ever,' she said, also approvingly. 'Have you been waiting long?'

He shook his head.

She told him about the confusion with Hema.

'I hope you're not going to call it off because you don't
have a chaperone,' he said.

'No,' said Lata. She felt as bold as Malati. She had not had much time to think about things this morning, and did not want to either. Despite her evening's anxiety, her oval face looked fresh and attractive, and her lively eyes were no longer sleepy.

They got down to the river and walked along the sand for a while until they came to some stone steps. A few washermen were standing in the water, beating clothes against the steps. On a small path going up the slope at this point stood a few bored little donkeys overburdened with bundles of clothes. A washerman's dog barked at them in uncertain, staccato yaps.

'Are you sure we'll get a boat?' said Lata.

'Oh, yes, there's always someone. I've done this often enough.'

A small, sharp pulse of pain went through Lata, though Kabir had meant merely that he enjoyed going out on the Ganga at dawn.

'Ah, there's one,' he said. A boatman was scouting up and down with his boat in midstream. It was April, so the river was low and the current sluggish. Kabir cupped his hands and shouted:

'Aré, mallah!'

The boatman, however, made no attempt to row towards them.

'What's the matter?' he yelled in Hindi that had a strong Brahmpuri accent; he gave the verb 'hai' an unusual emphasis.

'Can you take us to a point where we can see the Barsaat Mahal and its reflection?' said Kabir.

'Sure!'

'How much?'

'Two rupees.' He was now approaching the shore in his old flat-bottomed boat.

Kabir got annoyed. 'Aren't you ashamed to ask so much?' he said angrily.

'It's what everyone charges, Sahib.'

'I'm not some outsider that you can cheat me,' said Kabir.

'Oh,' said Lata, 'please don't quarrel over nothing –'

She stopped short; presumably Kabir would insist on paying, and he, like her, probably did not have much money.

Kabir went on angrily, shouting to be heard over the sound of the clothes hitting the steps of the ghat:

'We come empty-handed into this world and go out empty-handed. Do you have to lie so early in the morning? Will you take this money with you when you go?'

The boatman, presumably intrigued at being so philo-sophically addressed, said:

'Sahib, come down. Whatever you think is appropriate I will accept.' He guided Kabir towards a spot a couple of hundred yards away where the boat could come close to the shore. By the time Lata and Kabir had reached the spot, he had gone up the river.

'He's gone away,' said Lata. 'Perhaps we'll find another one.'

Kabir shook his head. He said:

'We've spoken. He'll return.'

The boatman, after rowing upstream and to the far shore, got something from the bank, and rowed back.

'Do you swim?' he asked them.

'I do,' said Kabir, and turned towards Lata.

'No,' said Lata, 'I don't.'

Kabir looked surprised.

'I never learned,' explained Lata. 'Darjeeling and Mussourie.'

'I trust your rowing,' said Kabir to the boatman, a brown, bristle-faced man dressed in a shirt and lungi with a woollen bundi to cover his chest. 'If there's an accident, you handle yourself, I'll handle her.'

'Right,' said the boatman.

'Now, how much?'

'Well, whatever you –'

'No,' said Kabir, 'let's fix a price. I've never dealt with boatmen any other way.'

'All right,' said the boatman, 'what do you think is right?'

'One rupee four annas.'

'Fine.'

Kabir stepped on board, then stretched his hand out for Lata. With an assured grip he pulled her onto the boat. She looked flushed and happy. For an unnecessary second he did not release her hand. Then, sensing she was about to pull away, he let her go.

There was still a slight mist on the river. Kabir and Lata sat facing the boatman as he pulled on the oars. They were more than two hundred yards from the dhobi-ghat, but the sound of the beating of clothes, though faint, was still audible. The details of the bank disappeared in the mist.

'Ah,' said Kabir. 'It's wonderful to be here on the river surrounded by mist – and it's rare at this time of year. It reminds me of the holiday we once spent in Simla. All the problems of the world slipped away. It was as if we were a different family altogether.'

'Do you go to a hill station every summer?' asked Lata. Though she had been schooled at St Sophia's in Mussourie, there was no question now of being able to afford to take a house in the hills whenever they chose.

'Oh yes,' said Kabir. 'My father insists on it. We usually go to a different hill station every year – Almora, Nainital, Ranikhet, Mussourie, Simla, even Darjeeling. He says that the fresh air "opens up his assumptions", whatever that means. Once, when he came down from the hills, he said that like Zarathustra he had gained enough mathematical insight on the mountainside in six weeks to last a lifetime. But of course, we went up to the hills the next year as usual.'

'And you?' asked Lata. 'What about you?'

'What about me?' said Kabir. He seemed troubled by some memory.

'Do you like it in the hills? Will you be going this year as usual?'

'I don't know about this year,' said Kabir. 'I do like it up there. It's like swimming.'

'Swimming?' asked Lata, trailing a hand in the water.

A thought suddenly struck Kabir. He said to the boatman: 'How much do you charge local people to take them all the way up to the Barsaat Mahal from near the dhobi-ghat?'

'Four annas a head,' said the boatman.

'Well then,' said Kabir, 'We should be paying you a rupee – at the most – considering that half your journey is downstream. And I'm paying you a rupee and four annas. So it's not unfair.'

'I'm not complaining,' said the boatman, surprised.

The mist had cleared, and now before them on the bank of the river stood the grand grey edifice of the Brahmpur Fort, with a broad reach of sand stretching out in front of it. Near it, and leading down to the sands was a huge earthen ramp, and above it a great pipal tree, its leaves shimmering in the morning breeze.

'What did you mean by "swimming"?' asked Lata.

'Oh yes,' said Kabir. 'What I meant was that you're in a completely different element. All your movements are different – and, as a result, all your thoughts. When I went tobogganing in Gulmarg once, I remember thinking that I didn't really exist. All that existed was the clean, pure air, the high snows, this rush of swift movement. The flat, drab plains bring you back to yourself. Except, perhaps, well, like now on the river.'

'Like music?' said Lata.

The question was addressed as much to herself as to Kabir.

'Mmm, yes, I think so, in a way,' Kabir mused. 'No, not really,' he decided.

He had been thinking of a change of spirit brought about by a change of physical activity.

'But,' said Lata, following her own thoughts, 'music really does do that to me. Simply strumming the tanpura, even if I don't sing a single note, puts me into a trance. Sometimes I do it for fifteen minutes before I come back to myself. When things get to be too much for me, it's the first thing I turn to. And when I think that I only took up singing under Malati's influence last year I realize how lucky I've been. Do you know that my mother is so unmusical that when I was a child and she would sing lullabies to me, I would beg her to stop and let my ayah sing them instead?'

Kabir was smiling. He put his arm around her shoulder and, instead of protesting, she let it remain. It seemed to be in the right place.

'Why aren't you saying anything?' she said.

'I was just hoping that you'd go on talking. It's unusual to hear you talking about yourself. I sometimes think I don't know the first thing about you. Who is this Malati, for instance?'

'The first thing?' said Lata, recalling a shred of conversation she'd had with Malati. 'Even after all the inquiries you've instituted?'

'Yes,' said Kabir. 'Tell me about yourself.'

'That's not much use as a request. Be more specific. Where should I begin?'

'Oh, anywhere. Begin at the beginning, go on until you reach the end and then stop.'

'Well,' said Lata, 'it's before breakfast, so you'll have to hear at least six impossible things.'

'Good,' said Kabir, laughing.

'Except that my life probably doesn't contain six impossible things. It's quite humdrum.'

'Begin with the family,' said Kabir.

Lata began to talk about her family – her much-beloved father, who seemed even now to cast a protective aura over her, not least significantly in the shape of a grey sweater; her mother, with her Gita, water-works, and affectionate volubility; Arun and Meenakshi and Aparna and Varun in Calcutta; and of course Savita and Pran and the baby-to-be. She talked freely, even moving a little closer to Kabir. Strangely enough, for one who was sometimes so unsure of herself, she did not at all doubt his affection.

The Fort and the sands had gone past, as had the cremation ghat and a glimpse of the temples of Old Brahmpur and the minarets of the Alamgiri Mosque. Now as they came round a gentle bend in the river they saw before them the delicate white structure of the Barsaat Mahal, at first from an angle, and then, gradually, full face.

The water was not clear, but it was quite calm and its surface was like murky glass. The boatman moved into mid-stream as he rowed. Then he settled the boat dead centre – in line with the vertical axis of symmetry of the Barsaat Mahal – and plunged the long pole that he had earlier fetched from the opposite bank deep into the middle of the river. It hit the bottom, and the boat was still.

'Now sit and watch for five minutes,' said the boatman. 'This is a sight you will never forget in your lives.'

Indeed it was, and neither of them was to forget it. The Barsaat Mahal, site of statesmanship and intrigue, love and dissolute enjoyment, glory and slow decay, was transfigured into something of abstract and final beauty. Above its sheer river-wall it rose, its reflection in the water almost perfect, almost unrippled. They were in a stretch of the river where even the sounds of the old town were dim. For a few minutes they said nothing at all.

3.14

AFTER a little while, without as such being told to, the boatman pulled his pole out of the mud at the bottom of the river. He continued to row upstream, past the Barsaat Mahal. The river narrowed slightly because of a spit of sand jutting almost into mid-stream from the opposite bank. The chimneys of a shoe factory, a tannery and a flour mill came into view. Kabir stretched and yawned, releasing Lata's shoulder.

'Now I'll turn around and we'll drift past it,' said the boatman.

Kabir nodded.

'This is where the easy part begins for me,' said the boatman, turning the boat around. 'It's good it's not too hot yet.' Steering with an occasional stroke of the oar, he let the boat drift downstream on the current.

'Lots of suicides from that place there,' he commented

cheerfully, pointing at the sheer drop from the Barsaat Mahal to the water. 'There was one last week. The hotter the weather, the crazier people get. Crazy people, crazy people.' He gestured along the shore. Clearly, in his mind, the perpetually land-bound could never be quite sane.

As they passed the Barsaat Mahal again, Kabir took a small booklet entitled *Diamond Guide to Brahmpur* out of his pocket. He read out the following to Lata:

Although Fatima Jaan was only third wife of Nawab Khushwaqt still it was to her that he made the nobile edifice of Barsaat Mahal. Her femine grace, dignity of heart and wit proved so powerful that Nawab Khushwaqt's all affections were soon transferred to his new bride, their Impassionate love made them inseparatable companions both in the palaces as well as in the court. To her he built Barsaat Mahal, miracle of marble filligral work, for their life and pleasures.

Once she also accompanied him in the campaign. At that time she gave birth to a weakly son and unfortunately, due to some disorder in the system, she looked despairingly at her lord. At this, the Nawab was shocked too much. His heart was sank with grief and face grew much too pale ... Alas! On the day of 23 April, 1735, Fatima Jaan closed her eyes at a shortage of 33 before her broken-hearted lover.

'But is all this true?' said Lata laughing.

'Every word,' said Kabir. 'Trust your historian.' He went on:

Nawab Khushwaqt was so much grieved that his mind was upset, he was even prepared to die which he, of course, could not do. For a long time he could not forget her though all possible efforts were made. On each Friday he went on foot to the grave of his best-loved and himself read fatiha on final resting spot of her bones.

'Please,' said Lata, 'Please stop. You'll ruin the Barsaat Mahal for me.' But Kabir read mercilessly on:

After her death the palace became sordid and sad. No longer did the tanks full of golden and silvery fish afford sportive amusements to the Nawab. He became lustrious and debauching. He built now a dark room where refractory members of harem were hanged and their bodies were swept away in the river. This left a blot on his personality. During those days these punishments were usual without distinction of sexes. There was no law except the Nawab's orders and the punishments were drastic and furious.

The fountains played still with frangrant water and an unceasing water rolled on the floors. The palace was not less than a heaven where beauty and charms were scattered freely. But after expiry of the One of his life what to him mattered the innumerable blooming ladies? He breathed his last on the 14 January gazzing steadfastly at a picture of F. Jaan.

'Which year did he die in?' asked Lata.

'I believe the *Diamond Guide to Brahmpur* is silent on this subject, but I can supply the date myself. It was 1766. Nor does it tell us why it was called the Barsaat Mahal in the first place.'

'Why was it?' asked Lata. 'Because an unceasing water rolled freely?' she speculated.

'Actually it has to do with the poet Mast,' said Kabir. 'It used to be called the Fatima Mahal. Mast, during one of his recitations there, made a poetic analogy between Khushwaqt's unceasing tears and the monsoon rains. The ghazal containing that particular couplet became popular.'

'Ah,' said Lata, and closed her eyes.

'Also,' continued Kabir, 'the Nawab's successors – including his weakly son – used to be found more often in the pleasure-grounds of the Fatima Mahal during the monsoons than at any other time. Most things stopped during the rains except pleasure. And so its popular name changed.'

'And what was that other story you were about to tell me about Akbar and Birbal?' asked Lata.

'About Akbar and Birbal?' asked Kabir.

'Not today; at the concert.'

'Oh,' said Kabir. 'Did I? But there are so many stories. Which one was I referring to? I mean, what was the context?'

How is it, thought Lata, that he doesn't remember these remarks of his that I remember so well?

'I think it was about me and my friends reminding you of jungle babblers.'

'Oh, yes.' Kabir's face lit up at the memory. 'This is how it goes. Akbar was bored with things, so he asked his court to tell him something truly astonishing – but not something that they had merely heard about, something that they themselves had seen. The most astonishing story would win a prize. All his courtiers and ministers came up with different and astonishing facts – all the usual ones. One said that he had seen an elephant trumpeting in terror before an ant. Another said that he had seen a ship flying in the sky. Another that he had met a Sheikh who could see treasure buried in the earth. Another that he had seen a buffalo with three heads. And so on and so forth. When it came to Birbal's turn, he didn't say anything. Finally, he admitted that he had seen something unusual while riding to court that day: about fifty women sitting under a tree together, absolutely silent. And everyone immediately agreed that Birbal should get the prize.' Kabir threw back his head and laughed.

Lata was not pleased by the story, and was about to tell him so when she thought of Mrs Rupa Mehra, who found it impossible to remain silent for even a couple of minutes in grief, joy, sickness or health, in a railway carriage or at a concert or indeed anywhere at all.

'Why do you always remind me of my mother?' asked Lata.

'Do I?' said Kabir. 'I didn't mean to.' And he put his arm around her again.

He became silent; his thoughts had wandered off to his own family. Lata too was silent; she still could not work out what had caused her to panic in the exam, and it had returned to perplex her.

The shoreline of Brahmpur again drifted past but now there was more activity at the water's edge. The boatman had chosen to keep closer to the shore. They could hear more clearly the oars of other boats; bathers splashing, clearing their throats, coughing and blowing their noses; crows cawing; verses from the scriptures being chanted over a loudspeaker; and beyond the sands the sound of temple bells and conches.

The river flowed due east at this point, and the risen sun was reflected in its surface far beyond the university. A marigold garland floated in the water. Pyres were burning at the cremation ghat. From the Fort came the shouted commands of parade. As they drifted downstream they once more heard the ceaseless sounds of the washermen and the occasional braying of their donkeys.

The boat reached the steps. Kabir offered the boatman two rupees.

He nobly refused it.

'We came to an understanding beforehand. Next time you'll look out for me,' he said.

When the boat stopped moving Lata felt a pang of regret. She thought of what Kabir had said about swimming or tobogganing – about the ease conferred by a new element, a different physical motion. The movement of the boat, their feeling of freedom and distance from the world would soon, she felt, disperse. But when Kabir helped her ashore, she did not pull away, and they walked hand in hand along the edge of the river towards the banyan grove and the minor shrine. They did not say much.

It was more difficult to climb up the path than to walk down it in her slippers, but he helped pull her up. He might be gentle, she thought, but he is certainly strong. It struck her as amazing that they had hardly talked about the university, their exams, cricket, teachers, plans, the world immediately above the cliffs. She blessed the qualms of Hema's Taiji.

They sat on the twisted root of the twin banyan trees. Lata was at a loss as to what to say. She heard herself saying:

'Kabir, are you interested in politics?'

He looked at her in amazement at the unexpected question, then simply said, 'No,' and kissed her.

Her heart turned over completely. She responded to his kiss – without thinking anything out – but with a sense of amazement at herself – that she could be so reckless and happy.

When the kiss was over, Lata suddenly began thinking again, and more furiously than ever.

'I love you,' said Kabir.

When she was silent, he said:

'Well, aren't you going to say anything?'

'Oh, I love you too,' said Lata, stating a fact that was completely obvious to her and therefore should have been obvious to him. 'But it's pointless to say so, so take it back.'

Kabir started. But before he could say anything, Lata said:

'Kabir, why didn't you tell me your last name?'

'It's Durrani.'

'I know.' Hearing him say it so casually brought all the cares of the world back on her head.

'You know?' Kabir was surprised. 'But I remember that at the concert you refused to exchange last names with me.'

Lata smiled; his memory was quite selective. Then she grew serious again.

'You're Muslim,' she said quietly.

'Yes, yes, but why is all this so important to you? Is that why you've been so strange and distant sometimes?' There was a humorous light in his eyes.

'Important?' It was Lata's turn to be amazed. 'It's all-important. Don't you know what it means in my family?'

Was he deliberately refusing to see difficulties, she wondered, or did he truly believe that it made no difference?

Kabir held her hand and said, 'You love me. And I love you. That's all that matters.'

Lata persisted: 'Doesn't your father care?'

'No. Unlike many Muslim families, I suppose we were sheltered during Partition – and before. He hardly thinks of anything except his parameters and perimeters. And an equation is the same whether it's written in red or green ink. I don't see why we have to talk about this.'

Lata tied her grey sweater around her waist, and they walked to the top of the path. They agreed to meet again in three days at the same place at the same time. Kabir was going to be occupied for a couple of days doing some work for his father. He unchained his bike and – looking quickly around – kissed her again. When he was about to cycle off, she said to him:

'Have you kissed anyone else?'

'What was that?' He looked amused.

She was looking at his face; she didn't repeat the question.

'Do you mean ever?' he asked. 'No. I don't think so. Not seriously.'

And he rode off.

3.15

LATER that day, Mrs Rupa Mehra was sitting with her daughters, embroidering a tiny handkerchief with a rose for the baby. White was a sexually neutral colour, but white-on-white was too drab for Mrs Rupa Mehra's tastes, and so she decided on yellow. After her beloved granddaughter Aparna, she wanted – and had predicted – a grandson. She would have embroidered the handkerchief in blue, except that this would certainly have invited Fate to change the sex of the child in the womb.

Rafi Ahmad Kidwai, the Union Minister of Communications, had just announced that postal charges were to be raised. Since replying to her abundant correspondence was what occupied at least a third of Mrs Rupa Mehra's time, this had hit her hard. Rafi Sahib was the most secular-minded, least communally impassioned man possible, but he happened to be Muslim. Mrs Rupa Mehra felt like hitting out, and he presented a direct target. She said:

'Nehru indulges them too much, he only talks to Azad and Kidwai, does he think he's the Prime Minister of Pakistan? Then see what they do.'

Lata and Savita usually let their mother have her say, but today Lata protested:

'Ma, I don't agree at all. He's the Prime Minister of India, not just the Hindus. What's the harm if he has two Muslim Ministers in his Cabinet?'

'You have too many educated ideas,' said Mrs Rupa Mehra, who normally revered education.

Mrs Rupa Mehra may have also been upset because the older women were making no headway in persuading Mahesh Kapoor to agree to a recitation of the Ramcharit-manas in Prem Nivas on the occasion of Ramnavami. The troubles of the Shiva Temple in Chowk weighed upon Mahesh Kapoor's mind, and many of the largest landlords that his Zamindari Abolition Bill would dispossess were Muslim. He felt that he should at least stay clear of exacerbating the situation.

'I know about all these Muslims,' said Mrs Rupa Mehra darkly, almost to herself. At that moment she did not think of Uncle Shafi and Talat Khala, old friends of the family.

Lata looked at her indignantly but said nothing. Savita looked at Lata, but said nothing either.

'Don't make big-big eyes at me,' said Mrs Rupa Mehra fiercely to her younger daughter. 'I know facts. You don't know them like I do. You have no experience of life.'

Lata said, 'I'm going to study.' She got up from Pran's rocking chair, where she had been sitting.

Mrs Rupa Mehra was in a belligerent mood. 'Why?' she demanded. 'Why must you study? Your exams are over. Will you be studying for the next year? All work and no play makes Jack a dull boy. Sit and talk to me. Or go for a walk. It will be good for your complexion.'

'I went for a walk this morning,' said Lata. 'I'm always going for walks.'

'You are a very stubborn girl,' said Mrs Rupa Mehra.

Yes, thought Lata, and, with the faintest shadow of a smile on her face, went to her room.

Savita had observed this little flare-up, and felt that the provocation was too small, too impersonal, to upset Lata in the ordinary course of things. Clearly, something was weighing on her heart. The phone call from Malati which had had such an acute effect on her also came to Savita's mind. The two and two which she put together did not quite make four, but the pair of swan-like digits sitting side by side were still quite disquieting. She was worried for her sister. Lata seemed to be in a volatile state of excitement these days, but did not appear to wish to confide in anyone. Nor was Malati, her friend and confidante, in town. Savita waited for an opportunity to talk to Lata alone, which was not easy. And when she did, she seized it at once.

Lata was lying on the bed, her face cupped in her hands, reading. She had finished *Pigs Have Wings* and had gone on to *Galahad at Blandings*. She thought that the title was appropriate now that she and Kabir were in love. These three days of separation would be like a month, and she would have to distract herself with as much Wodehouse as possible.

Lata was not overjoyed to be disturbed, even by her sister.

'May I sit here on the bed?' asked Savita.

Lata nodded, and Savita sat down.

'What's that you're reading?' asked Savita.

Lata held up the cover for quick inspection, then went back to her reading.

'I've been feeling a bit low today,' said Savita.

'Oh.' Lata sat up promptly and looked at her sister. 'Are you having your period or something?'

Savita started laughing. 'When you're expecting you

don't have periods.' She looked at Lata in surprise. 'Didn't you know that?' It seemed to Savita that she herself had known this elementary fact for a long time, but perhaps that wasn't so.

'No,' said Lata. Since her conversations with the informative Malati were quite wide-ranging, it was surprising that this had never come up. But it struck her as entirely right that Savita should not have to cope with two physical problems at the same time. 'What's the matter, then?'

'Oh, nothing, I don't know what it is. I just feel this way sometimes – lately, quite a lot. Maybe it's Pran's health.' She put her arm gently on Lata's.

Savita was not a moody person, and Lata knew it. She looked at her sister affectionately, and said: 'Do you love Pran?' This suddenly seemed very important.

'Of course I do,' said Savita, surprised.

'Why "of course", Didi?'

'I don't know,' said Savita. 'I love him. I feel better when he's here. I feel worried about him. And sometimes I feel worried about his baby.'

'Oh, he'll be all right,' said Lata, 'judging from his kicking.'

She lay down again, and tried to go back to her book. But she couldn't concentrate even on Wodehouse. After a pause, she said:

'Do you like being pregnant?'

'Yes,' said Savita with a smile.

'Do you like being married?'

'Yes,' said Savita, her smile widening.

'To a man who was chosen for you – whom you didn't really know before your marriage?'

'Don't talk like that about Pran, it's as if you were talking about a stranger,' said Savita, taken aback. 'You're funny sometimes, Lata. Don't you love him too?'

'Yes,' said Lata, frowning at this non sequitur, 'but I don't have to be close to him in the same way. What I can't understand is how – well, it was other people who decided he was suitable for you – but if you didn't find him attractive –'

She was thinking that Pran was not good-looking, and she did not believe that his goodness was a substitute for – what? – a spark.

'Why are you asking me all these questions?' asked Savita, stroking her sister's hair.

'Well, I might have to face a problem like that some day.'

'Are you in love, Lata?'

The head beneath Savita's hand jerked up very slightly and then pretended it hadn't. Savita had her answer, and in half an hour she had most of the details about Kabir and Lata and their various meetings. Lata was so relieved to talk to someone who loved her and understood her that she poured out all her hopes and visions of bliss. Savita saw at once how impossible these were, but let Lata talk on. She felt increasingly sad as Lata grew more elated.

'But what should I do?' said Lata.

'Do?' repeated Savita. The answer that came to her mind was that Lata should give Kabir up immediately before their infatuation went any further, but she knew better than to say so to Lata, who could be very contrary.

'Should I tell Ma?' said Lata.

'No!' said Savita. 'No. Don't tell Ma, whatever you do.' She could imagine her mother's shock and pain.

'Please don't tell anyone either, Didi. Anyone,' said Lata.

'I can't keep any secrets from Pran,' said Savita.

'Please keep this one,' said Lata. 'Rumours get around so easily. You're my *sister*. You've known this man for less than a year.' As soon as the words were out of her mouth, Lata felt bad about the way she had referred to Pran, whom she now adored. She should have phrased it better.

Savita nodded, a little unhappily.

Although she hated the atmosphere of conspiracy that her question might generate, Savita felt that she had to help her sister, even guard her in some way.

'Shouldn't I meet Kabir?' she asked.

'I'll ask him,' said Lata. She felt sure that Kabir would not have any reservations about meeting anyone who was basically sympathetic, but she did not think he would enjoy it particularly. Nor did she want him to meet anyone from her family for some time yet. She sensed that everything would become troubled and confused, and that the carefree spirit of their boat-ride would quickly disappear.

'Please be careful, Lata,' said Savita. 'He may be very good-looking and from a good family, but –'

She left the second half of her sentence unfinished, and later Lata tried to fit various endings to it.

3.16

EARLY that evening, when the heat of the day had somewhat died down, Savita went to visit her mother-in-law, whom she had grown to be very fond of. It had been almost a week since they had seen each other. Mrs Mahesh Kapoor was out in the garden, and rushed over to Savita when she saw the tonga arrive. She was pleased to see her, but concerned that she should be jolting about in a tonga when she was pregnant. She questioned Savita about her own health and Pran's; complained that he came over very rarely; enquired after Mrs Rupa Mehra, who was due to come over to Prem Nivas the next day; and asked Savita whether either of her brothers was by any chance in town. Savita, slightly puzzled by this last question, said that they weren't. Mrs Mahesh Kapoor and she then wandered into the garden.

The garden was looking a bit dry, despite the fact that it had been watered a couple of days previously; but a gulmohur tree was in bloom: its petals were almost scarlet, rather than the usual red-orange. Everything, Savita thought, appeared more intense in the garden at Prem Nivas. It was almost as if the plants understood that their mistress, though she would not overtly complain about a weak performance, would not be happy with less than their best.

The head gardener Gajraj and Mrs Mahesh Kapoor had been at loggerheads for a few days now. They were agreed upon what cuttings to propagate, which varieties to select for seed collection, which shrubs to prune, and when to transplant the small chrysanthemum plants to larger pots. But ever since the ground had begun to be prepared for the sowing of new lawns, an apparently irreconcilable difference had emerged.

This year, as an experiment, Mrs Mahesh Kapoor proposed that a part of the lawn be left unlevelled before sowing. This had struck the mali as being eccentric in the extreme, and utterly at variance with Mrs Mahesh Kapoor's usual instructions. He complained that it would be impossible to water the lawn properly, that mowing it would be difficult, that muddy puddles would form in the monsoons and the winter rains, that the garden would be infested with pond-herons feeding on water-beetles and other insects, and that the Flower Show Judges' Committee would see the lack of evenness as a sign of lack of balance – aesthetically speaking, of course.

Mrs Mahesh Kapoor had replied that she had only proposed an unevenness for the side lawn, not the front lawn; that the unevenness that she proposed was slight; that he could water the higher parts with a hose; that the small proportion of the mowing that proved difficult for the grand, blunt lawnmower dragged by the Public Works Department's placid white bullock could be done with a small foreign-made lawnmower that she would borrow from a friend; that the Flower Show Judges' Committee might look at the garden for an hour in February but that it gave her pleasure all the year round; that level had nothing to do with balance; and, finally, that it was precisely because of the puddles and the pond-herons that she had proposed the experiment.

One day in late December, a couple of months after Savita's wedding, when the honey-scented harsingar had still been in blossom, when the roses were in their first full flush, when the sweet alyssum and sweet william had begun to bloom, when those beds of feathery-leafed larkspur that the partridges had not gobbled down almost to the root were doing their best to recover in front of the tall ranks of equally feathery-leafed but untempting cosmos, there had been a tremendous, almost torrential rainstorm. It had been gloomy, gusty and cold, and there had been no sun for two days, but the garden had been full of birds: pond-herons, partridges, mynas, small puffed-up grey babblers in their chattering groups of seven, hoopoes and parakeets in a combination that reminded her of the colours of the Congress flag, a pair of red-wattled lapwings, and a couple of vultures, flying with huge twigs in their mouths to the neem tree. Despite their heroism in the Ramayana, Mrs Mahesh Kapoor had never been able to reconcile herself to vultures. But what had truly delighted her had been the three plump, dowdy pond-herons, each standing near a separate small pool, almost entirely motionless as they gazed at the water, taking a careful minute over every step they made, and thoroughly content with the squelchiness of their environment. But the pools on the level lawn had quickly dried up when the sun had emerged. Mrs Mahesh Kapoor wanted to offer the hospitality of her lawn to a few more pond-herons this year, and she did not want to leave matters to chance.

All this she explained to her daughter-in-law, gasping a little as she spoke because of her allergy to neem blossoms. Savita reflected that Mrs Mahesh Kapoor looked a bit like a pond-heron herself. Drab, earthy-brown, dumpy unlike the rest of the species, inelegant, hunched-up but alert, and endlessly patient, she was capable of suddenly flashing a brilliant white wing as she rose up in flight.

Savita was amused by her analogy, and began to smile. But Mrs Mahesh Kapoor, though she smiled in response, did not attempt to find out what Savita was so happy about.

How unlike Ma she is, thought Savita to herself as the two continued to walk around the garden. She could see resemblances between Mrs Mahesh Kapoor and Pran, and an obvious physical resemblance between her and the more animated Veena. But how she could have produced such a son as Maan was still to Savita a matter of amusement and amazement.

THE next morning Mrs Rupa Mehra, old Mrs Tandon and Mrs Mahesh Kapoor met in Prem Nivas for a chat. It was fitting that the kind and gentle Mrs Mahesh Kapoor should have acted as host. She was the samdhin – the 'co-mother-in-law' – of both of the others, the link in the chain. Besides, she was the only one whose own husband was still living, the only one who was still mistress in her own house.

Mrs Rupa Mehra loved company of any kind, and this kind was ideal. First they had tea, and matthri with a mango pickle that Mrs Mahesh Kapoor had herself prepared. It was declared delicious all round. The recipe of the pickle was analysed and compared with that of seven or eight other kinds of mango pickle. As for the matthri, Mrs Rupa Mehra said:

'It is just as it should be: crisp and flaky, but it holds together very well.'

'I can't have much because of my digestion,' said old Mrs Tandon, helping herself to another.

'What can one do when one gets old –' said Mrs Rupa Mehra with fellow-feeling. She was only in her mid-forties but liked to imagine herself old in older company; and indeed, having been widowed for several years, she felt that she had partaken of at least part of the experience of old age.

The entire conversation proceeded in Hindi with the occasional English word. Mrs Mahesh Kapoor, for instance, when referring to her husband, often called him 'Minister Sahib'. Sometimes, in Hindi, she even called him 'Pran's father'. To refer to him by name would have been unthinkable. Even 'my husband' was unacceptable to her, but 'my this' was all right.

They compared the prices of vegetables with what they had been at the same time the previous year. Minister Sahib cared more for the clauses of his bill than for his food, but he sometimes got very annoyed when there was too much or too little salt – or the food was too highly spiced. He was particularly fond of karela, the bitterest of all vegetables – and the more bitter the better.

Mrs Rupa Mehra felt very close to old Mrs Tandon. For someone who believed that everyone in a railway carriage existed mainly to be absorbed into a network of acquaintance, a samdhin's samdhin was virtually a sister. They were both widowed, and both had problematical daughters-in-law. Mrs Rupa Mehra complained about Meenakshi; she had already told them some weeks ago about the medal that had been so heartlessly melted down. But, naturally, old Mrs Tandon could not complain about Veena and her fondness for irreligious music in front of Mrs Mahesh Kapoor.

Grandchildren were also discussed: Bhaskar and Aparna and Savita's unborn baby each made an appearance.

Then the conversation moved into a different mode.

'Can't we do something about Ramnavami? Won't Minister Sahib change his mind?' asked old Mrs Tandon, probably the most insistently pious of the three.

'Uff! What can I say, he's so stubborn,' said Mrs Mahesh Kapoor. 'And nowadays he is under so much pressure that he gets impatient at every little thing I say. I get pains these days, but I hardly worry about them, I'm worrying about him so much.' She smiled. 'I'll tell you frankly,' she continued in her quiet voice, 'I'm afraid to say anything to him. I told him, all right, if you don't want the whole Ramcharit-manas to be recited, at least let us get a priest to recite some part of it, maybe just the Sundar Kanda, and all he said was, "You women will burn up this town. Do what you like!" and stalked out of the room.'

Mrs Rupa Mehra and old Mrs Tandon made sympathetic noises.

'Later he was striding up and down the garden in the heat, which is good neither for him nor for the plants. I said to him, we could get Maan's future parents-in-law from Banaras to enjoy it with us. They are also fond of recitations. That will help cement the ties. Maan is getting so' – she searched for the proper word – 'so out of control these days. . . .' She trailed off, distressed.

Rumours of Maan and Saeeda Bai were by now rife in Brahmpur.

'What did he say?' asked Mrs Rupa Mehra, rapt.

'He just waved me away, saying, "All these plots and plans!"'

Old Mrs Tandon shook her head and said:

'When Zaidi's son passed the civil service exam, his wife arranged a reading of the whole Quran in her house: thirty women came, and they each read a – what do they call it? paara; yes, paara.' The word seemed to displease her.

'Really?' said Mrs Rupa Mehra, struck by the injustice of it. 'Should I speak to Minister Sahib?' She had a vague sense that this would help.

'No, no, no –' said Mrs Mahesh Kapoor, worried at the thought of these two powerful wills colliding. 'He will only say this and that. Once when I touched upon the subject he even said: "If you must have it, go to your great friend the Home Minister – he will certainly support this kind of mischief." I was too frightened to say anything after that.'

They all bewailed the general decline of true piety.

Old Mrs Tandon said: 'Nowadays, everyone goes in for big functions in the temples – chanting and bhajans and recitations and discourses and puja – but they don't have proper ceremonies in the home.'

'True,' said the other two.

Old Mrs Tandon continued: 'At least in our neighbourhood we will have our own Ramlila in six months' time. Bhaskar is too young to be one of the main characters, but he can certainly be a monkey-warrior.'

'Lata used to be very fond of monkeys,' reflected Mrs Rupa Mehra vaguely.

Old Mrs Tandon and Mrs Mahesh Kapoor exchanged glances.

Mrs Rupa Mehra snapped out of her vagueness and looked at the others. 'Why – is something the matter?' she asked.

'Before you came we were just talking – you know, just like that,' said old Mrs Tandon soothingly.

'Is it about Lata?' said Mrs Rupa Mehra, reading her tone as accurately as she had read her glance.

The two ladies looked at each other and nodded seriously.

'Tell me, tell me quick,' said Mrs Rupa Mehra, thoroughly alarmed.

'You see, it is like this,' said Mrs Mahesh Kapoor gently, 'please look after your daughter, because someone saw her walking with a boy on the bank of the Ganga near the dhobi-ghat yesterday morning.'

'What boy?'

'That I don't know. But they were walking hand in hand.'

'Who saw them?'

'What should I hide from you?' said Mrs Mahesh Kapoor sympathetically. 'It was Avtar Bhai's brother-in-law. He recognized Lata but he didn't recognize the boy. I told him it must have been one of your sons, but I know from Savita that they are in Calcutta.'

Mrs Rupa Mehra's nose started to redden with unhappiness and shame. Two tears rolled down her cheeks, and she reached into her capacious handbag for an embroidered handkerchief.

'Yesterday morning?' she said in a trembling voice.

She tried to remember where Lata had said she'd gone. This was what happened when you trusted your children, when you let them roam around, taking walks everywhere. Nowhere was safe.

'That's what he said,' said Mrs Mahesh Kapoor gently. 'Have some tea. Don't get too alarmed. All these girls see these modern love films and it has an effect on them, but Lata is a good girl. Only talk to her.'

But Mrs Rupa Mehra was very alarmed, gulped down her tea, even sweetening it with sugar by mistake, and went home as soon as she politely could.

3.18

MRS RUPA MEHRA came breathlessly through the door.

She had been crying in the tonga. The tonga-wallah,

concerned that such a decently dressed lady should be weeping so openly, had tried to keep up a monologue in order to pretend that he hadn't noticed, but she had now gone through not only her embroidered handkerchief but her reserve handkerchief as well.

'Oh my daughter!' she said, 'oh, my daughter.'

Savita said, 'Yes, Ma?' She was shocked to see her mother's tear-streaked face.

'Not you,' said Mrs Rupa Mehra. 'Where is that shameless Lata?'

Savita sensed that their mother had discovered something. But what? And how much? She moved instinctively towards her mother to calm her down.

'Ma, sit down, calm down, have some tea,' said Savita, guiding Mrs Rupa Mehra, who seemed quite distracted, to her favourite armchair.

'Tea! Tea! More and more tea!' said Mrs Rupa Mehra in resistant misery.

Savita went and told Mateen to get some tea for the two of them.

'Where is she? What will become of us all? Who will marry her now?'

'Ma, don't over-dramatize things,' said Savita soothingly. 'It will blow over.'

Mrs Rupa Mehra sat up abruptly. 'So you knew! You knew! And you didn't tell me. And I had to learn this from strangers.' This new betrayal engendered a new bout of sobbing. Savita squeezed her mother's shoulders, and offered her another handkerchief. After a few minutes of this, Savita said:

'Don't cry, Ma, don't cry. What did you hear?'

'Oh, my poor Lata – is he from a good family? I had a sense something was going on. Oh God! What would her father have said if he had been alive? Oh, my daughter.'

'Ma, his father teaches mathematics at the university. He's a decent boy. And Lata's a sensible girl.'

Mateen brought the tea in, registered the scene with deferential interest, and went back towards the kitchen.

Lata walked in a few seconds later. She had taken a

book to the banyan grove, where she had sat down undisturbed for a while, lost in Wodehouse and her own enchanted thoughts. Two more days, one more day, and she would see Kabir again.

She was unprepared for the scene before her, and stopped in the doorway.

'Where have you been, young lady?' demanded Mrs Rupa Mehra, her voice quivering with anger.

'For a walk,' faltered Lata.

'Walk? Walk?' Mrs Rupa Mehra's voice rose to a crescendo. 'I'll give you walk.'

Lata's mouth flew open, and she looked at Savita. Savita shook both her head and her right hand slightly, as if to say that it was not she who had given her away.

'Who is he?' demanded Mrs Rupa Mehra. 'Come here. Come here at once.'

Lata looked at Savita. Savita nodded.

'Just a friend,' said Lata, approaching her mother.

'Just a friend! A friend! And friends are for holding hands with? Is this what I brought you up for? All of you – and is this –'

'Ma, sit down,' said Savita, for Mrs Rupa Mehra had half risen out of her chair.

'Who told you?' asked Lata. 'Hema's Taiji?'

'Hema's Taiji? Hema's Taiji? Is she in this too?' exclaimed Mrs Rupa Mehra with new indignation. 'She lets those girls run around all over the place with flowers in their hair in the evening. Who told me? The wretched girl asks me who told me. No one told me. It's the talk of the town, everyone knows about it. Everyone thought you were a good girl with a good reputation – and now it is too late. Too late,' she sobbed.

'Ma, you always say Malati is such a nice girl,' said Lata by way of self-defence. 'And she has friends like that – you know that – everyone knows that.'

'Be quiet! Don't answer me back! I'll give you two tight slaps. Roaming around shamelessly near the dhobi-ghat and having a gala time.'

'But Malati –'

245

'Malati! Malati! I'm talking about you, not about Malati. Studying medicine and cutting up frogs –' Mrs Rupa Mehra's voice rose once more. 'Do you want to be like her? And lying to your mother. I'll never let you go for a walk again. You'll stay in this house, do you hear? Do you hear?' Mrs Rupa Mehra had stood up.

'Yes, Ma,' said Lata, remembering with a twinge of shame that she had had to lie to her mother in order to meet Kabir. The enchantment was being torn apart; she felt alarmed and miserable.

'What's his name?'

'Kabir,' said Lata, growing pale.

'Kabir what?'

Lata stood still and didn't answer. A tear rolled down her cheek.

Mrs Rupa Mehra was in no mood for sympathy. What were all these ridiculous tears? She caught hold of Lata's ear and twisted it. Lata gasped.

'He has a name, doesn't he? What is he – Kabir Lal, Kabir Mehra – or what? Are you waiting for the tea to get cold? Or have you forgotten?'

Lata closed her eyes.

'Kabir Durrani,' she said, and waited for the house to come tumbling down.

The three deadly syllables had their effect. Mrs Rupa Mehra clutched at her heart, opened her mouth in silent horror, looked unseeingly around the room, and sat down.

Savita rushed to her immediately. Her own heart was beating far too fast.

One last faint possibility struck Mrs Rupa Mehra. 'Is he a Parsi?' she asked weakly, almost pleadingly. The thought was odious but not so calamitously horrifying. But a look at Savita's face told her the truth.

'A Muslim!' said Mrs Rupa Mehra more to herself now than to anyone else. 'What did I do in my past life that I have brought this upon my beloved daughter?'

Savita was standing near her and held her hand. Mrs Rupa Mehra's hand was inert as she stared in front of her.

Suddenly she became aware of the gentle curve of Savita's stomach, and fresh horrors came to her mind.

She stood up again. 'Never, never, never –' she said.

By now Lata, having conjured up the image of Kabir in her mind, had gained a little strength. She opened her eyes. Her tears had stopped and there was a defiant set to her mouth.

'Never, never, absolutely not – dirty, violent, cruel, lecherous –'

'Like Talat Khala?' demanded Lata. 'Like Uncle Shafi? Like the Nawab Sahib of Baitar? Like Firoz and Imtiaz?'

'Do you want to marry him?' cried Mrs Rupa Mehra in a fury.

'Yes!' said Lata, carried away, and angrier by the second.

'He'll marry you – and next year he'll say "Talaq talaq talaq" and you'll be out on the streets. You obstinate, stupid girl! You should drown yourself in a handful of water for sheer shame.'

'I *will* marry him,' said Lata, unilaterally.

'I'll lock you up. Like when you said you wanted to become a nun.'

Savita tried to intercede.

'You go to your room!' said Mrs Rupa Mehra. 'This isn't good for you.' She pointed her finger, and Savita, not used to being ordered about in her own home, meekly complied.

'I wish I had become a nun,' said Lata. 'I remember Daddy used to tell us we should follow our own hearts.'

'Still answering back?' said Mrs Rupa Mehra, infuriated by the mention of Daddy. 'I'll give you two tight slaps.'

She slapped her daughter hard, twice, and instantly burst into tears.

3.19

MRS RUPA MEHRA was not more prejudiced against Muslims than most upper-caste Hindu women of her age and background. As Lata had inopportunely pointed out, she even had friends who were Muslims, though almost all of them were not orthodox at all. The Nawab Sahib was, perhaps, quite orthodox, but then he was, for Mrs Rupa Mehra, more a social acquaintance than a friend.

The more Mrs Rupa Mehra thought, the more agitated she became. Even marrying a non-khatri Hindu was bad enough. But this was unspeakable. It was one thing to mix socially with Muslims, entirely another to dream of polluting one's blood and sacrificing one's daughter.

Whom could she turn to in her hour of darkness? When Pran came home for lunch and heard the story, he suggested mildly that they meet the boy. Mrs Rupa Mehra threw another fit. It was utterly out of the question. Pran then decided to stay out of things and to let them die down. He had not been hurt when he realized that Savita had kept her sister's confidence from him, and Savita loved him still more for that. She tried to calm her mother down, console Lata, and keep them in separate rooms – at least during the day.

Lata looked around the bedroom and wondered what she was doing in this house with her mother when her heart was entirely elsewhere, anywhere but here – a boat, a cricket field, a concert, a banyan grove, a cottage in the hills, Blandings Castle, anywhere, anywhere, so long as she was with Kabir. No matter what happened, she would meet him as planned, tomorrow. She told herself again and again that the path of true love never did run smooth.

Mrs Rupa Mehra wrote a letter on an inland form to Arun in Calcutta. Her tears fell on the letter and blotched the ink. She added: 'P.S. My tears have fallen on this letter, but what to do? My heart is broken and only God will show a way out. But His will be done.' Because the postage had just gone up she had to stick an extra stamp on the prepaid form.

In much bitterness of spirit, she went to see her father. It would be a humiliating visit. She would have to brave his temper in order to get his advice. Her father may have married a crass woman half his age, but that was a heaven-made match compared to what Lata was threatened with.

As expected, Dr Kishen Chand Seth rebuked Mrs Rupa Mehra roundly in front of the dreadful Parvati and told her what a useless mother she was. But then, he added, everyone seemed to be brainless these days. Just last week he had told a patient whom he had seen at the hospital: 'You are a stupid man. In ten to fifteen days you will be dead. Throw away money if you want to on an operation, it'll only kill you quicker.' The stupid patient had been quite upset. It was clear that no one knew how to take or to give advice these days. And no one knew how to discipline their children; that was where all the trouble in the world sprang from.

'Look at Mahesh Kapoor!' he added with satisfaction.

Mrs Rupa Mehra nodded.

'And you are worse.'

Mrs Rupa Mehra sobbed.

'You spoiled the eldest' – he chuckled at the memory of Arun's jaunt in his car – 'and now you have spoiled the youngest, and you have only yourself to blame. And you come to me for advice when it is too late.'

His daughter said nothing.

'And your beloved Chatterjis are just the same,' he added with relish. 'I hear from Calcutta circles that they have no control over their children. None.' This thought gave him an idea.

Mrs Rupa Mehra was now satisfactorily in tears, so he gave her some advice and told her to put it into effect immediately.

Mrs Rupa Mehra went home, got out some money, and went straight to the Brahmpur Junction Railway Station. She bought two tickets for Calcutta by the next evening's train.

Instead of posting her letter to Arun, she sent him a telegram.

Savita tried to dissuade her mother but to no effect. 'At least wait till the beginning of May when the exam results come out,' she said. 'Lata will be needlessly worried about them.'

Mrs Rupa Mehra told Savita that exam results meant nothing if a girl's character was ruined, and that they could be transmitted by mail. She knew what Lata was worried about all right. She then turned the emotional tables on Savita by saying that any scenes between Lata and herself should take place elsewhere, not within earshot of Savita. Savita was pregnant and should stay calm. 'Calm, that's the word,' repeated Mrs Rupa Mehra forcefully.

As for Lata, she said nothing to her mother, simply remaining tight-lipped when she was told to pack her things for the journey. 'We are going to Calcutta tomorrow evening by the 6.22 train – and that is that. Don't you dare say anything,' said Mrs Rupa Mehra.

Lata did not say anything. She refused to show any emotion to her mother. She packed carefully. She even ate something for dinner. The image of Kabir kept her company.

After dinner she sat on the roof, thinking. When she came to bed, she did not say goodnight to Mrs Rupa Mehra, who was lying sleeplessly in the next bed. Mrs Rupa Mehra was heartbroken, but Lata was not feeling very charitable. She went to sleep quite soon, and dreamed, among other things, of a washerman's donkey with the face of Dr Makhijani, chewing up Mrs Rupa Mehra's black handbag and all her little silver stars.

3.20

SHE awoke, rested. It was still dark. She had agreed to meet Kabir at six. She went to the bathroom, locked it from the inside, then slipped out from the back into the garden. She did not dare to take a sweater with her, as this would have made her mother suspicious. Anyway, it was not too cold.

But she was trembling. She walked down towards the

mud cliffs, then down the path. Kabir was waiting for her, sitting on their root in the banyan grove. He got up when he heard her coming. His hair was ruffled, and he looked sleepy. He even yawned while she walked up towards him. In the dawn light his face looked even more handsome than when he had thrown his head back and laughed near the cricket field.

She seemed to him to be very tense and excited, but not unhappy. They kissed. Then Kabir said:

'Good morning.'

'Good morning.'

'Did you sleep well?'

'Very well, thank you,' said Lata. 'I dreamed of a donkey.'

'Oh, not of me?'

'No.'

'I can't remember what I dreamed of,' said Kabir, 'but I didn't have a restful night.'

'I love sleeping,' said Lata. 'I can sleep for nine or ten hours a day.'

'Ah ... aren't you cold? Why don't you wear this?' Kabir made to take off his sweater.

'I've been longing to see you again,' said Lata.

'Lata?' said Kabir. 'What's happened to upset you?' Her eyes were unusually bright.

'Nothing,' said Lata, fighting back her tears. 'I don't know when I'll see you again.'

'What's happened?'

'I'm going to Calcutta tonight. My mother's found out about us. When she heard your name she threw a fit – I told you what my family was like.'

Kabir sat down on the root and said, 'Oh no.'

Lata sat down too. 'Do you still love me?' she said after a while.

'Still?' Kabir laughed bitterly. 'What's the matter with you?'

'You remember what you said the last time: that we loved each other and that that was all that mattered?'

'Yes,' said Kabir. 'It is.'

'Let's go away –'

'Away,' said Kabir sadly. 'Where?'

'Anywhere – to the hills – anywhere, really.'

'And leave everything?'

'Everything. I don't care. I've even packed some things.'

This hint of practicality made him smile instead of alarming him. He said, 'Lata, we don't have a chance if we go away. Let's wait and see how things work out. We'll make them work out.'

'I thought you lived from our one meeting to the next.'

Kabir put an arm around her.

'I do. But we can't decide everything. I don't want to disillusion you, but –'

'You are, you are disillusioning me. How long will we have to wait?'

'Two years, I think. First I have to finish my degree. After that I'm going to apply to get into Cambridge – or maybe take the exam for the Indian Foreign Service –'

'Ah –' It was a low cry of almost physical pain.

He stopped, realizing how selfish he must have sounded.

'I'll be married off in two years,' said Lata, covering her face in her hands. 'You're not a girl. You don't understand. My mother might not even let me come back to Brahmpur –'

Two lines from one of their meetings came to her mind:

Desert not friendship. Renegade with me
From raptured realm of Mr Nowrojee.

She got up. She made no attempt to hide her tears. 'I'm going,' she said.

'Please don't, Lata. Please listen,' said Kabir. 'When will we be able to speak to each other again? If we don't talk now –'

Lata was walking quickly up the path, trying to escape from his company now.

'Lata, be reasonable.'

She had reached the flat top of the path. Kabir walked behind her. She seemed so walled off from him that he didn't touch her. He sensed that she would have brushed him off, maybe with another painful remark.

Halfway to the house was a shrubbery of the most fragrant kamini, some bushes of which had grown as tall as trees. The air was thick with their scent, the branches full of small white blossoms against dark-green leaves, the ground covered with petals. As they passed below, he tousled the leaves gently, and a shower of fragrant petals fell on her hair. If she even noticed this, she gave no indication of it.

They walked on, unspeaking. Then Lata turned around.

'That's my sister's husband there in a dressing-gown. They've been looking for me. Go back. No one's seen us yet.'

'Yes; Dr Kapoor. I know. I'll – I'll talk to him. I'll convince them –'

'You can't run four runs every day,' said Lata.

Kabir stopped dead in his tracks, a look of puzzlement rather than pain on his face. Lata walked on without looking back.

She never wanted to see him again.

At the house, Mrs Rupa Mehra was having hysterics. Pran was grim. Savita had been crying. Lata refused to answer any questions.

Mrs Rupa Mehra and Lata left for Calcutta that evening. Mrs Rupa Mehra kept up a litany of how shameful and inconsiderate Lata was; how she was forcing her mother to leave Brahmpur before Ramnavami; how she had been the cause of unnecessary disruption and expense.

Receiving no response, she finally gave up. For once, she hardly talked to the other passengers.

Lata kept quiet. She looked out of the train window till it became completely dark. She felt heartbroken and humiliated. She was sick of her mother, and of Kabir, and of the mess that was life.

Part Four

4.1

WHILE Lata was falling in love with Kabir, a quite different set of events was taking place in Old Brahmpur, which, however, were to prove not irrelevant to her story. These events involved Pran's sister, Veena, and her family.

Veena Tandon entered her house in Misri Mandi, to be greeted by her son Bhaskar with a kiss, which she happily accepted despite the fact that he had a cold. He then rushed back to the small sofa where he had been sitting – his father on one side and his father's guest on the other – and continued his explanation of the powers of ten.

Kedarnath Tandon looked at his son indulgently but, happy in the consciousness of Bhaskar's genius, did not pay much attention to what he was saying. His father's guest, Haresh Khanna, who had been introduced to Kedarnath by a mutual acquaintance in the shoe business, would have been happier talking about the leather and footwear trade of Brahmpur, but felt it best to indulge his host's son – especially as Bhaskar, carried away by his enthusiasm, would have been very disappointed to lose his indoor audience on a day when he had not been allowed to go out kite-flying. He tried to concentrate on what Bhaskar was saying.

'Well, you see, Haresh Chacha, it's like this. First you have ten, that's just ten, that is, ten to the first power. Then you have a hundred, which is ten times ten, which makes it ten to the second power. Then you have a thousand, which is ten to the third power. Then you have ten thousand, which is ten to the fourth power but this is where the problem begins, don't you see? We don't have a special word for that – and we really should. Ten times that is ten to the fifth power, which is a lakh. Then we have ten to the sixth power, which is a million, ten to the seventh power which is a crore, and then we come to another power for which we don't have a word – which is ten to the eighth. We should have a word for that as well. Then ten to the ninth power is a billion, and then comes ten to the tenth. Now it's amazing that we don't have a word in either English or Hindi for a number that is as important as ten to the tenth. Don't you agree with me, Haresh Chacha?' he continued, his bright eyes fixed on Haresh's face.

'But you know,' said Haresh, pulling something out of his recent memory for the enthusiastic Bhaskar, 'I think there is a special word for ten thousand. The Chinese tanners of Calcutta, with whom we have some dealings, once told me that they used the number ten-thousand as a standard unit of counting. What they call it I can't remember, but just as we use a lakh as a natural measuring point, they use ten-thousand.'

Bhaskar was electrified. 'But Haresh Chacha, you must find that number for me,' he said. 'You must find out what they call it. I have to know,' he said, his eyes burning with mystical fire, and his small frog-like features taking on an astonishing radiance.

'All right,' said Haresh. 'I'll tell you what. When I go back to Kanpur, I'll make enquiries, and as soon as I find out what that number is, I'll send you a letter. Who knows, perhaps they even have a number for ten to the eighth.'

'Do you really think so?' breathed Bhaskar wonderingly. His pleasure was akin to that of a stamp-collector who finds the two missing values in an incomplete series suddenly supplied to him by a total stranger. 'When are you going back to Kanpur?'

Veena, who had just come in bearing cups of tea, rebuked Bhaskar for his inhospitable comment, and asked Haresh how many spoonfuls of sugar he took.

Haresh could not help noticing that when he had seen her a few minutes earlier her head had been uncovered, but now, after returning from the kitchen, she had covered it with her sari. He guessed correctly that it was at her mother-in-law's behest that she had done so. Although Veena was a little older than him, and quite plump, he could not help thinking how animated her features were. The slight touches of anxiety about her eyes only added to her liveliness of character.

Veena, for her part, could not help noticing that her husband's guest was a good-looking young man. Haresh was short, well-built without being stocky, fair in complexion, with a squarish rather than an oval face. His eyes were not large, but they had a directness of gaze which she believed was a key to straightforwardness of character. Silk shirt and agate cuff-links, she observed to herself.

'Now, Bhaskar, go and talk to your grandmother,' said Veena. 'Papa's friend wants to talk to him about important matters.'

Bhaskar looked at the two men in inquiring appeal. His father, though he had closed his eyes, sensed that Bhaskar was waiting for his word.

'Yes. Do as your mother says,' said Kedarnath. Haresh said nothing, but smiled. Bhaskar went off, rather annoyed at being excluded.

'Don't mind him, he's never annoyed for long,' said Veena apologetically. 'He doesn't like being left out of things that interest him. When we play chaupar together – Kedarnath and I – we have to make sure Bhaskar isn't in the house, otherwise he insists on playing and beats both of us. Very bothersome.'

'I can imagine it would be,' said Haresh.

'The trouble is that he has no one to talk to about his maths, and sometimes he becomes very withdrawn. His teachers at school are less proud of him than worried about him. Sometimes it seems he deliberately does badly in maths – if a question annoys him, for instance. Once, when he was very young, I remember Maan – that's my brother – asked him for the answer to 17 minus 6. When he got 11, Maan asked him to subtract 6 again. When he got 5, Maan asked him to subtract 6 yet again. And Bhaskar actually began to cry! "No, no," he said, "Maan Maama is playing a trick on me. Stop him!" And he wouldn't speak to him for a week.'

'Well, for a day or two at least,' said Kedarnath. 'But that was before he learned about negative numbers. Once he did, he insisted on taking bigger things away from smaller things the whole day long. I suppose, the way things are going with my work, he'll get plenty of practice in that line.'

'By the way,' said Veena to her husband anxiously, 'I think you should go out this afternoon. Bajaj came this morning and, when he didn't find you in, he said he would drop by at about three.'

From her expression and his, Haresh guessed that Bajaj might be a creditor.

'Once the strike's over, things will improve,' said Kedarnath a bit apologetically to Haresh. 'I'm a little over-extended at present.'

'The trouble is,' said Veena, 'that there's so much mistrust. And the local leaders make it much worse. Because my father's so busy with his department and the legislature, Kedarnath tries to help him by keeping in touch with his constituency. So when there's trouble of some kind, people often come to him. But this time, when Kedarnath tried to mediate, although – I know I shouldn't be saying this and he doesn't like me to, but it's quite true – although he's quite well-liked and respected by people on both sides, the shoemakers' leaders have undermined all his efforts – just because he's a trader.'

'Well, that's not quite it,' said Kedarnath, but decided to defer his explanation until he and Haresh were alone. He had closed his eyes again. Haresh looked a little concerned.

'Don't worry,' said Veena to Haresh. 'He's not asleep or bored or even praying before lunch.' Her husband opened his eyes quickly. 'He does it all the time,' she explained. 'Even at our wedding – but it was less obvious behind those strings of flowers.'

She got up to see if the rice was ready. After the men had been served and had eaten, old Mrs Tandon came in for a short while to exchange a few words. Upon hearing that Haresh Khanna was originally from Delhi she asked him whether he belonged to the Khannas of Neel Darvaza or those who lived in Lakkhi Kothi. When Haresh said he was from Neel Darvaza, she told him she had visited it once as a girl.

Haresh described a few changes, recounted a few personal anecdotes, praised the simple but tasty vegetarian food that the two women had prepared, and was a hit with the old lady.

'My son has to travel a lot,' she confided to Haresh, 'and no one feeds him properly on the way. Even here, if it wasn't for me –'

'Quite right,' said Veena, attempting to take the wind out of her sails. 'It is so important for a man to be treated as a child. In matters of food, of course. Kedarnath – I mean Bhaskar's father' – she corrected herself as her mother-in-law shot a look at her – 'simply loves the food his mother prepares. It's a pity men don't like being sung to sleep with lullabies.'

Haresh's eyes twinkled and almost disappeared between his eyelids, but he kept his lips steady.

'I wonder if Bhaskar will continue to like the food I prepare,' continued Veena. 'Probably not. When he gets married –'

Kedarnath held up his hand. 'Really,' he said, in mild reproof.

Haresh noticed that Kedarnath's palm was badly scarred.

'Now what have I done?' asked Veena innocently, but she changed the subject. Her husband had a decency which rather frightened her, and she didn't want to be judged badly by him.

'You know, I blame myself for Bhaskar's obsession with mathematics,' she continued. 'I named him Bhaskar after the sun. Then, when he was a year old, someone told me that one of our ancient mathematicians was called Bhaskar, and now our Bhaskar can't live without his mathematics. Names are terribly important. My father wasn't in town when I was born, and my mother named me Veena, thinking it would please him because he's so fond of music. But as a result I've become obsessed with music, and I can't live without it either.'

'Really?' said Haresh. 'And do you play the veena?'

'No,' laughed Veena, her eyes shining. 'I sing. I sing. I can't live without singing.'

Old Mrs Tandon got up and left the room.

After a while, with a shrug, Veena followed her.

4.2

WHEN the men were left alone, Haresh – who had been sent to Brahmpur for a few days to purchase some materials by his employers, the Cawnpore Leather & Footwear Company – turned to Kedarnath and said: 'Well, I've been around the markets during the last couple of days and have got some idea of what goes on there, or at least what is supposed to go on there. But despite all this running around, I don't think I've been able to make complete sense of it. Especially your system of credit – what with all these chits and promissory notes and so on. And why have the small manufacturers – who make shoes in their own homes – gone on strike? Surely it must cause them terrible hardship. And it must be very bad for traders like yourself who buy directly from them.'

'Well,' said Kedarnath, passing his hand through his slightly greyed hair, 'about the chit system – it confused me too at the beginning. As I mentioned, we were forced out of Lahore at the time of Partition and even then I was not exactly in the footwear trade. I did happen to go through Agra and Kanpur on the way here and you're quite right, Kanpur has nothing like the system that we have here. But have you been to Agra?'

'Yes,' said Haresh. 'I have. But that was before I entered the industry.'

'Well, Agra has a system somewhat similar to ours.' And Kedarnath outlined it roughly.

Because they were perennially short of cash, the traders paid the shoemakers partly with post-dated chits. The shoemakers could only get cash to buy raw materials by discounting these chits elsewhere. They had felt for years that the traders had been squeezing a kind of unwarranted credit out of them. Finally, when the traders, as a body, had tried to winch up the proposition of chit to cash, the shoemakers had struck.

'And of course, you're right,' Kedarnath added, 'the strike hurts everyone – they could starve and we could be ruined.'

'I suppose the shoemakers would claim,' said Haresh, with a meditative air, 'that as a result of the chit system they are the ones who are financing your expansion.'

There was no tone of accusation in Haresh's voice, simply the curiosity of a pragmatic man trying to get facts and attitudes straight. Kedarnath responded to his interest and went on:

'That's indeed what they claim,' he agreed. 'But it is also their own expansion, the expansion of the whole market, that they are financing,' he said. 'And, besides, it is only a portion of their payment that is made by post-dated chits. Most of it is still made by cash. I'm afraid that everyone has begun to see matters in black and white, with the traders usually being the ones who are painted black. It's a good thing that the Home Minister, L.N. Agarwal, comes from a trading community. He's the MLA for a part of this area, and he does at least see our side of the matter. My wife's father doesn't get along well with him at all politically – or even personally, really – but, as I tell Veena when she's in a mood to listen, Agarwal understands the ways of business better than her father does.'

'Well, do you think that you could take me around Misri Mandi in the afternoon?' asked Haresh. 'I'll get a more informed perspective that way.'

It was interesting, thought Haresh, that the two powerful – and rival – Ministers should represent contiguous constituencies.

Kedarnath was in two minds as to whether to agree, and Haresh must have seen this in his face. Kedarnath had been impressed by Haresh's technical knowledge of shoe manufacture, and by his enterprising spirit, and was thinking of proposing a business connection. Perhaps, he thought, the Cawnpore Leather & Footwear Company would be interested in buying shoes directly from him.

After all, it sometimes happened that companies like CLFC received small orders from shoe stores, perhaps for 5,000 pairs of a particular kind of shoe, and it was not worth their while to re-tool their own plant to fulfil such orders. In such a case, if Kedarnath could ensure that he got shoes from local Brahmpur shoemakers that fulfilled CLFC's quality requirements, and shipped them to Kanpur, it might work out well both for him and for Haresh's employers.

However, these were disturbed days, everyone was under great financial pressure, and the impression that Haresh might obtain of the reliability or efficiency of the shoe trade in Brahmpur would not be a favourable one.

But Haresh's small kindness to his son and his respectful attitude to his mother tilted the balance. 'All right, we'll go,' he said. 'But the market will really only open later, towards the evening – even at the level to which the strike has reduced it. The Brahmpur Shoe Mart, where I have my stall, opens at six. But I have a suggestion in the meanwhile. I'll take you to see a few places where shoes are actually made. It'll be a change for you from the conditions of manufacture that you've seen in England – or at your Kanpur factory.'

Haresh agreed readily.

As they walked downstairs, with the afternoon sunlight falling on them from above through the layers of grating, Haresh thought how similar in design this house was to his foster-father's house in Neel Darvaza – though of course, much smaller.

At the corner of the alley, where it opened out into a slightly broader and more crowded lane, there was a paan stand. They stopped. 'Plain or sweet?' asked Kedarnath.

'Plain, with tobacco.'

For the next five minutes, as they walked along together, Haresh did not say anything because he kept the paan in his mouth without swallowing it. He would spit it out later into an opening in the small drain that ran along the side of the alley. But for the moment, under the pleasant intoxication of the tobacco, amid the bustle all around him, the shouts and chatter and the sound of bicycle-bells, cow-bells, and bells from the Radhakrishna Temple, he was again reminded of the alley near his foster-father's house in Old Delhi where he had been brought up after his parents died.

As for Kedarnath, though he had got a plain paan for himself, he did not speak much either. He would be taking this silk-shirted young man to one of the poorest parts of the city, where the jatav shoemakers lived and worked in conditions of wretched squalor, and he wondered how he would react. He thought of his own sudden fall from wealth in Lahore to the virtual destitution of 1947; the hard-won security he had obtained for Veena and Bhaskar over the last few years; the problems of the present strike and the dangers it would mean for them. That there was some special spark of genius in his son he believed with utter conviction. He dreamed of sending him to a school like Doon, and perhaps later even to Oxford or Cambridge. But times were hard, and whether Bhaskar would obtain the special education he deserved, whether Veena could keep up with the music she craved, whether they could even continue to afford their modest rent, were questions that troubled and aged him.

But these are the hostages of love, he said to himself, and it is meaningless to ask myself whether I would exchange a head of unworried hair for my wife and child.

4.3

THEY emerged onto a yet broader alley, and then onto a hot, dusty street not far from the high ground of the Chowk. One of the two great landmarks of this crowded area was a huge, pink three-storey building. This was the kotwali or city police station, the largest in Purva Pradesh. The other landmark, a hundred yards away, was the beautiful and austere Alamgiri Mosque, ordered by the Emperor Aurangzeb to be built in the heart of the city upon the ruins of a great temple.

Late Mughal and British records attest to a series of Hindu-Muslim riots around this spot. It is not clear what exactly incurred the wrath of the emperor. He was the least tolerant of the great emperors of his dynasty, true, but the area around Brahmpur had been spared his worst excesses. The re-imposition of the poll-tax on unbelievers, a tax rescinded by his great-grandfather Akbar, affected the citizens of Brahmpur as it did those throughout the empire. But the razing of temples usually required some extraordinary impetus, such as the indication that it was being used as a centre for armed or political resistance. Apologists for Aurangzeb were apt to claim that he had a worse reputation for intolerance than he deserved and that he was as harsh with Shias as he was with Hindus. But for the more orthodox Hindu citizenry of Brahmpur, the previous 250 years of history had not dimmed their loathing for a man who had dared to destroy one of the holiest temples of the great destroyer Shiva himself.

The great Shiva-linga of the inner sanctum of the temple was rumoured to have been preserved by the priests of the so-called Chandrachur Temple on the night before it was reduced to rubble. They sank it not in a deep well as was often the case in those days, but in the shallows and sands near the cremation ground by the Ganga. How the huge stone object was carried there is not known. Apparently the knowledge of its location was secretly maintained and passed on for more than ten generations from head-priest to head-priest in hereditary succession. Of all the common images of Hindu worship it was probably the sacred phallus, the Shiva-linga, which was most despised by the orthodox theologians of Islam. Where they could destroy it, they did so with a particular sense of righteous disgust. While there was any chance that the Muslim peril might resurface, the priests did not act upon their family knowledge. But after Independence and the Partition of Pakistan and India, the priest of the long-since-destroyed Chandrachur Temple – who lived in poverty in a shack near the cremation ghat – felt that it was safe to emerge and identify himself. He tried to get his temple rebuilt and the Shiva-linga excavated and re-installed. At first the Archaeological Survey had refused to believe the particulars he gave of the location of the linga. The rumour of its preservation was unsupported by other records. And even if it were true, the Ganges had changed course, the sands and shallows had shifted, and the unwritten verses or mantras describing its location could themselves have grown inaccurate through repeated transmission. It is also possible that officers of the Archaeological Survey were aware or had been appraised of the possible effects of unearthing the linga and had decided that for the sake of public peace it was safer horizontal under the sand than vertical in a sanctum. At any rate, the priest obtained no help from them.

As they passed below the red walls of the mosque, Haresh, not being a native of Brahmpur, asked why black flags were hanging at the outer gates. Kedarnath replied in an indifferent voice that they had come up just the previous week when the ground had been broken for a temple in the neighbouring plot of land. For one who had lost his house, his land and his livelihood in Lahore, he did not appear to be embittered against Muslims so much as exhausted by religious zealots in general. His mother was very upset at his evenhandedness.

'Some local pujari located a Shiva-linga in the Ganga,' said Kedarnath. 'It is supposed to have come from the Chandrachur Temple, the great Shiva temple that they say Aurangzeb destroyed. The pillars of the mosque do have bits of Hindu carving, so it must have been made out of some ruined temple, God knows how long ago. Mind your step!'

Haresh narrowly avoided stepping into some dog-shit. He was wearing a rather smart pair of maroon brogues, and was very glad to have been warned.

'Anyway,' continued Kedarnath, smiling at Haresh's agility, 'the Raja of Marh has title to the house that stands – stood, rather – beyond the western wall of the mosque. He has had it broken down and is building a temple there. A new Chandrachur Temple. He's a real lunatic. Since he can't destroy the mosque and build on the original site, he's decided to build to the immediate west and install the linga in the sanctum there. For him it's a great joke to think that the Muslims will be bowing down in the direction of his Shiva-linga five times a day.'

Noticing an unoccupied cycle-rickshaw, Kedarnath hailed it, and they got in. 'To Ravidaspur,' he said, and then continued: 'You know, for a supposedly gentle, spiritual people, we seem to delight in rubbing other people's noses in dog-shit, don't you think? Certainly I cannot understand people like the Raja of Marh. He imagines himself to be a new Ganesh whose divine mission in life is to lead the armies of Shiva to victory over the demons. And yet he's besotted with half the Muslim courtesans of the city. When he laid the foundation stone of the temple two people died. Not that this meant anything to him, he's probably had twenty times that number murdered in his own time in his own state. Anyway, one of the two was a Muslim and that's when the mullahs put the black flags up on the gate of the mosque. And if you look carefully, you'll see that there are even some smaller ones on the minarets.'

Haresh turned back to look, but suddenly the cycle-rickshaw, which had been gathering speed downhill, collided with a slowly moving car, and they came to a sudden halt. The car had been crawling along the crowded road, and there was no damage to anyone, but a couple of the bicycle's spokes had got bent. The rickshaw-wallah, who looked thin and unassertive, jumped off the cycle, glanced quickly at his front wheel, and banged aggressively on the window of the car.

'Give me money! Phataphat! Immediately!' he yelled.

The liveried driver and the passengers, who were two middle-aged women, looked surprised at this sudden demand. The driver half-recovered, and put his head out of the window.

'Why?' he shouted. 'You were coming down the slope without control. We weren't even moving. If you want to commit suicide do I have to pay for your funeral?'

'Money! Quickly! Three spokes – three rupees!' said the rickshaw-wallah, as brusquely as a highwayman.

The driver turned his face away. The rickshaw-wallah grew angrier:

'You daughter-fucker! I don't have all day. If you don't pay for my damages, I'll give your car some of its own.'

The driver would probably have responded with some insults in kind, but since he was with his employers, who were getting nervous, he remained tight-lipped.

Another rickshaw-wallah passed, and shouted in encouragement: 'That's right, brother, don't be afraid.' By now about twenty people had gathered round to watch the sport.

'Oh, pay him and let's go on,' said one of the ladies at the back. 'It's too hot to argue.'

'Three rupees!' repeated the rickshaw-wallah.

Haresh was about to leap out of the rickshaw to put an end to this extortion when the driver of the car suddenly flung an eight-anna coin at the rickshaw-wallah. 'Take this – and fuck off!' the driver said, stung to rage by his helplessness.

When the car had gone and the crowd had cleared, the rickshaw-wallah started singing with delight. He bent down and straightened the two bent spokes in twenty seconds, and they were on their way again.

4.4

'I'VE only been a couple of times to Jagat Ram's place, so I'll have to make enquiries once we get to Ravidaspur,' said Kedarnath.

'Jagat Ram?' asked Haresh, still thinking of the incident of the spokes and angry with the rickshaw-wallah.

'The shoemaker whose workshop we're going to see. He's a shoemaker, a jatav. He was originally one of those basket-wallahs I told you about who bring their shoes to Misri Mandi to sell to any trader who'll buy them.'

'And now?'

'Now he has his own workshop. He's reliable, unlike most of these shoemakers who, once they have a bit of money in their pockets, don't care about deadlines or promises. And he's skilled. And he doesn't drink – not much. I began by giving him a small order for a few dozen pairs, and he did a good job. Soon I was ordering from him regularly. Now he's able to hire two or three people in addition to his own family. It's helped both him and me. And perhaps you might want to see if the quality of his work comes up to the standard that your people at CLFC need. If so . . .' Kedarnath left the rest of the sentence in the air.

Haresh nodded, and gave him a comforting smile. After a pause, Haresh said, 'It's hot now that we're out of the alleys. And it smells worse than a tannery. Where are we now? In Ravidaspur?'

'Not yet. That's on the other side of the railway line. It doesn't smell quite so bad there. Yes, there's an area here where they prepare the leather, but it isn't a proper tannery like the one on the Ganga –'

'Perhaps we should get down and see it,' said Haresh with interest.

'But there's nothing to see,' protested Kedarnath, covering his nose.

'Have you been here before?' asked Haresh.

'No!'

Haresh laughed. 'Stop here!' he shouted at the rickshaw-wallah. Over Kedarnath's protests, he got him to dismount, and the two of them entered the warren of stinking paths and low huts, led by their noses towards the tanning pits.

The dirt paths stopped suddenly at a large open area surrounded by shacks and pockmarked by circular pits which had been dug into the ground and lined with hardened clay. A fearsome stench rose from the entire zone. Haresh felt sick; Kedarnath almost vomited with disgust. The sun shone harshly down, and the heat made the stench worse still. Some of the pits were filled with a white liquid, others with a brown tannic brew. Dark, scrawny men dressed only in lungis stood to one side of the pits, scraping off fat and hair from a pile of hides. One of them stood in a pit and seemed to be wrestling with a large hide. A pig was drinking at a ditch filled with stagnant black water. Two children with filthy matted hair were playing in the dust near the pits. When they saw the strangers they stopped abruptly and stared at them.

'If you had wanted to see the whole process from the beginning I could have taken you to see the ground where dead buffaloes are stripped and left to the vultures,' said Kedarnath wryly. 'It's near the unfinished bypass.'

Haresh, slightly regretful for having forced his companion into accompanying him here, shook his head. He looked at the nearest shack, which was empty except for a rudimentary fleshing machine. Haresh went up and examined it. In the next shack was an ancient splitting machine and a wattle pit. Three young men were rubbing a black paste onto a buffalo hide lying on the ground. Next to them was a white pile of salted sheepskins. When they saw the strangers they stopped working and looked at them.

No one said a word, neither the children, nor the three young men, nor the two strangers.

Eventually Kedarnath broke the silence. 'Bhai,' he said, addressing one of the three young men. 'We have just come to see how the leather is prepared. Would you show us around?'

The man looked at him closely, and then stared at Haresh, taking in his off-white silk shirt, his brogues, his briefcase, his businesslike air.

'Where are you from?' he asked Kedarnath.

'We're from the town. We're on our way to Ravidaspur. There's a local man there whom I work with.'

Ravidaspur was almost entirely a shoemaker's neighbourhood. But if Kedarnath imagined that by implying that another leatherworker was a colleague of his he would win acceptance here among the tanners, he was mistaken. Even among the leatherworkers or chamars, there was a hierarchy. The shoemakers – like the man they were going to visit – looked down upon the flayers and tanners. In turn, those who were looked down upon expressed their dislike of the shoemakers.

'That is a neighbourhood we do not like to go to,' said one of the young men shortly.

'Where does the paste come from?' asked Haresh, after a pause.

'From Brahmpur,' said the young man, refusing to be specific.

There was another long silence.

Then an old man appeared with his hands wet and dripping with some dark sticky liquid. He stood at the entrance of the shack and observed them.

'You! This wattle water – pani!' he said in English before lapsing into crude Hindi again. His voice was cracked, and he was drunk. He picked up a piece of rough, red-dyed leather from the ground and said, 'This is better than cherry leather from Japan! Have you heard of Japan? I had a fight with them, and I made them fail. Patent leather from China? I can match them all. I am sixty years old and I have a full knowledge of all pastes, all masalas, all techniques.'

Kedarnath began to get worried, and tried to move out of the shack. The old man barred his way by stretching his hands out sideways in a servile gesture of aggression. 'You cannot see the pits. You are a spy from the CID, from the police, from the bank –' He held his ears in a gesture of shame, then lapsed into English: 'No, no, no, bilkul no!'

By now the stench and the tension had made Kedarnath somewhat desperate. His face was drawn, he was sweating with anxiety as much as heat. 'Let us go, we have to get to Ravidaspur,' he said.

The old man moved towards him and held out his stained and dripping hand: 'Money!' he said. 'Fees! To drink – otherwise you cannot see the pits. You go to Ravidaspur. We don't like the jatavs, we are not like them, they eat the meat of buffaloes. Chhhi!' He spat out a syllable of disgust. 'We only eat goats and sheep.'

Kedarnath shrank back. Haresh began to get annoyed.

The old man sensed that he had got under his skin. This

gave him a perverse sense of encouragement. Mercenary, suspicious and boastful by turn, he now led them towards the pits. 'We get no money from the government,' he whispered. 'We need money, each family, for buying materials, chemicals. The government gives us too little money. You are my Hindu brother,' he said mockingly. 'Bring me a bottle – I will give you samples of the best dyes, the best liquor, the best medicine!' He laughed at his joke. 'Look!' He pointed at a reddish liquid in a pit.

One of the young men, a short man who was blind in one eye, said, 'They stop us from moving raw materials, stop us from getting chemicals. We have to have supporting documents and registration. We are harassed in transit. You tell your government department to exempt us from duty and give us money. Look at our children. Look –' He gestured towards a child who was defecating on a rubbish heap.

To Kedarnath the whole slum was unbearably vile. He said in a low voice: 'We are not from a government department.'

The young man suddenly got annoyed. His lips tightened and he said: 'Where are you from then?' The eyelid over his blind eye began to twitch. 'Where are you from? Why have you come here? What do you want from this place?'

Kedarnath could tell that Haresh was about to flare up. He sensed that Haresh was abrupt and quite fearless, but believed that it was pointless being fearless when there was something to fear. He knew how things could suddenly explode from acrimony into violence. He put one arm around Haresh's shoulder and led him back between the pits. The ground oozed, and the lower part of Haresh's brogues was splattered with black filth.

The young man followed them, and at one point it seemed that he was about to lay his hands on Kedarnath. 'I'll recognize you,' he said. 'You don't come back. You want to make money from our blood. There is more money in leather than in silver and gold – or you wouldn't come to this stinking place.'

'No – no –' said the drunken old man aggressively, 'bilkul no!'

Kedarnath and Haresh re-entered the neighbouring lanes; the stench was hardly better. Just at the opening of a lane, at the periphery of the open, pit-riddled ground, Haresh noticed a large red stone, flat on the top. On it a boy of about seventeen had laid a piece of sheepskin, largely cleaned of wool and fat. With a fleshing knife he was removing the remaining pieces of flesh off the skin. He was utterly intent upon what he was doing. The skins piled up nearby were cleaner than they could have been if they had been fleshed by a machine. Despite what had happened before, Haresh was fascinated. Normally he would have stopped to ask a few questions, but Kedarnath hurried him on.

The tanners had left them. Haresh and Kedarnath, dust-covered and sweating, made their way back through the dirt paths. When they got to their rickshaw on the street they gratefully breathed in the air that had seemed at first unbearably foul. And indeed, compared to what they had taken in for the last half-hour, it was the breath of paradise.

4.5

AFTER waiting in the heat for fifteen minutes for a late, long and very slow goods train to pass a level crossing, they finally got to Ravidaspur. It was somewhat less crowded in the lanes of this outlying neighbourhood than in the old heart of Brahmpur where Kedarnath lived, but far more insanitary, with sluggish sewage trickling along and across the lanes. Picking their way between flea-ridden dogs, grunting filth-spattered pigs and various unpleasant static objects, and crossing an open sewer on a rickety wooden bridge, they found their way to Jagat Ram's small, rectangular, windowless brick-and-mud workshop. At night after the work was cleared away, this was where his six children slept; he and his wife usually slept in a

274

brick-walled room with a corrugated iron roof which he had built on top of the flat roof of the workshop.

Several men and two young boys were working inside by the sunlight entering through the doorway and a couple of dim, bare electric bulbs. They were dressed in lungis for the most part, except for one man, who was dressed in kurta-pyjama, and Jagat Ram himself, who wore a shirt and trousers. They were sitting cross-legged on the ground in front of low platforms – square in shape and made of grey stone – on which their materials were placed. They were intent on their work – cutting, skiving, pasting, folding, trimming or hammering – and their heads were bent down, but from time to time one or the other would make a comment – about work or personal gossip or politics or the world in general – and this would lead to a little ripple of conversation among the sounds of hammers, knives, and the single pedal-operated Singer sewing machine.

When he saw Kedarnath and Haresh, Jagat Ram looked mystified. He touched his moustache in an unconscious gesture. He had expected other visitors.

'Welcome,' he said calmly. 'Come in. What brings you here? I've told you that the strike won't come in the way of fulfilling your order,' he added, anticipating a possible reason for Kedarnath's presence.

A little girl of about five, Jagat Ram's daughter, sat on the step. Now she began singing 'Lovely walé aa gayé! Lovely walé aa gayé!' and clapped her hands.

It was Kedarnath's turn to look surprised – and not entirely pleased. Her father, a little disconcerted, corrected her: 'These are not the people from Lovely, Meera – now go and tell your mother we need some tea.'

He turned to Kedarnath and said, 'Actually, I was expecting the people from Lovely.' He did not feel the need to volunteer any further information.

Kedarnath nodded. The Lovely Shoe Shop, one of the more recent shops to appear just off Nabiganj, had a good selection of women's shoes. Normally the man who ran the shop would have got the Bombay middlemen to supply him, as Bombay was where most women's shoes in the country were produced. Now he was obviously looking close to home for his supplies, and tapping a source that Kedarnath would have been happier tapping – or at least mediating – himself.

Dismissing the subject from his mind for the moment, he said, 'This is Mr Haresh Khanna, who is originally from Delhi, but is working for CLFC in Kanpur. He has studied footwear manufacture in England. And, well, I have brought him here to show him what work our Brahmpur shoemakers are capable of, even with their simple tools.'

Jagat Ram nodded, quite pleased.

There was a small wooden stool near the entrance of the workshop, and Jagat Ram asked Kedarnath to sit down. Kedarnath in turn invited Haresh to sit, but Haresh courteously declined. He sat down instead on one of the small stone platforms at which no one was working. The artisans stiffened, looking at him in displeasure and astonishment. Their reaction was so palpable that Haresh quickly got up again. Clearly he had done something wrong and, being a direct man, he turned to Jagat Ram and said, 'What's the matter? Can't one sit on those?'

Jagat Ram had reacted with similar resentment when Haresh had sat down, but the straightforwardness of Haresh's query – and his obvious lack of intention to offend anyone – caused him to respond mildly.

'A workman calls his work-platform his rozi or "employment"; he does not sit on it,' he said quietly. He did not mention that each man kept his rozi immaculately polished, and even said a brief prayer to it before beginning his day's work. To his son he said, 'Get up – let Haresh Sahib sit down.'

A boy of fifteen got up from the chair near the sewing machine, and despite Haresh's protests that he did not want to interrupt anyone's work he was made to sit down. Jagat Ram's youngest son, who was seven, came in with three cups of tea.

The cups were thick and small, chipped here and there

on their white surface, but clean. There was a little talk of this and that, of the strike in Misri Mandi, of the claim by a newspaper that the smoke from the tannery and the Praha Shoe Factory were damaging the Barsaat Mahal, of the new municipal market-tax, of various local personalities.

After a while, Haresh became impatient, as he tended to do when he was sitting idle. He got up to look around the workshop and find out what everyone was doing. A batch of women's sandals was being made; they looked quite attractive with their green and black plaited leather straps.

Haresh was indeed surprised at the skill of the workmen. With rudimentary tools – chisel and knife and awl and hammer and foot-operated sewing machine – they were producing shoes that were not far below the quality of those made by the machines of CLFC. He told them what he thought of their skill and the quality of their product, given the limitations under which they worked; and they warmed to him.

One of the bolder workmen – Jagat Ram's younger brother, a friendly, round-faced man – asked to see Haresh's shoes, the maroon brogues that he was wearing. Haresh took them off, mentioning that they were not very clean. In fact they were by now completely splattered and caked with mud. They were passed around for general admiration and examination.

Jagat Ram read out the letters painstakingly and spelt 'Saxone'. 'Saksena from England,' he explained with some pride.

'I can see that you make men's shoes as well,' said Haresh. He had noticed a large clump of wooden lasts for men hanging grape-like from the ceiling in a dark corner of the room.

'Of course,' said Jagat Ram's brother with a jovial grin. 'But there's more profit in what few others can do. It's much better for us to make women's shoes –'

'Not necessarily,' said Haresh, whipping out – to everyone's, including Kedarnath's, surprise – a set of paper patterns from his briefcase. 'Now, Jagat Ram, tell me, are your workmen skilled enough to give me a shoe – also a brogue – based on these patterns?'

'Yes,' said Jagat Ram, almost without thinking.

'Don't say yes so quickly,' said Haresh, though he was pleased by the ready and confident response. He too enjoyed taking up challenges as much as he enjoyed throwing them down.

Jagat Ram was looking at the patterns – they were for a size 7 winged brogue – with great interest. Just by looking at the flat pieces of thin cardboard that made up the patterns – the fine punched design, the shape of the toe, the vamp, the quarters – the whole shoe came to vivid, three-dimensional shape before his eyes.

'Who is making these shoes?' he asked, his forehead creased with curiosity. 'They are somewhat different from the brogues you are wearing.'

'We are, at CLFC. And if you do a good job, you may be too – for us.'

Jagat Ram, though clearly very surprised and interested by Haresh's statement, did not say anything for a while in response, but continued to examine the patterns.

Pleased with the dramatic effect of his sudden production of the patterns, Haresh said: 'Keep them. Look over them today. I can see that those lasts hanging there are non-standard, so I'll send you a pair of size 7 standard lasts tomorrow. I've brought a couple of pairs to Brahmpur. Now then, apart from the lasts, what will you need? Let's say, three square feet of leather, calf leather – let's make that maroon as well –'

'And lining leather,' said Jagat Ram.

'Right; suppose we say natural cow, also three square feet – I'll get that from town.'

'And leather for the sole and insole?' asked Jagat Ram.

'No, that's readily available and not very expensive. You can manage that. I'll give you twenty rupees to cover costs and time – and you can get the material for the heels yourself. I've brought a few counters and toe-puffs of decent quality – they are always a problem – and some thread; but they're at the house where I'm staying.'

Kedarnath, though his eyes were closed, raised his eyebrows in admiration at this enterprising fellow who had had the foresight to think of all these details before he left on a brief out-of-town trip intended mainly for purchasing materials. He was, however, concerned that Jagat Ram might be taken over by Haresh and that he himself might be cut out. The mention of the Lovely Shoe Shop came back to worry him as well.

'Now, if I came over tomorrow morning with these things,' Haresh was saying, 'when could you let me have the shoes?'

'I think I could have them ready in five days,' said Jagat Ram.

Haresh shook his head impatiently.

'I can't stay in town for five days just for a pair of shoes. How about three?'

'I'll have to leave them on the lasts for at least seventy-two hours,' said Jagat Ram. 'If you want me to make a pair of shoes which retain their shape, you know that that is a minimum.'

Now that both of them were standing up, he towered over Haresh. But Haresh, who had always treated his shortness with the irritation that befitted an inconvenient but psychologically insignificant fact, was not in the least overpowered. Besides, he was the one ordering the shoes.

'Four.'

'Well, if you send the leather to me tonight, so that we can start with the cutting first thing tomorrow morning –'

'Done,' said Haresh. 'Four days. I'll come over personally tomorrow with the other components to see how you're getting on. Now we'd better go.'

'One more thing strikes me, Haresh Sahib,' said Jagat Ram, as they were leaving. 'Ideally I'd like to have a sample of the shoe that you want me to reproduce.'

'Yes,' said Kedarnath with a smile. 'Why aren't you wearing a pair of brogues manufactured by your own company – instead of these English shoes? Take them off immediately, and I'll have you carried back to the rickshaw.'

'I'm afraid my feet have got used to these,' said Haresh, returning the smile, though he knew as well as anyone that it was more his heart than his feet. He loved good clothes and he loved good shoes, and he felt bad that CLFC products did not achieve the international standards of quality that, both by instinct and by training, he so greatly admired.

'Well, I'll try to get you a sample pair of those,' he continued, pointing at the paper patterns in Jagat Ram's hands, 'by one means or another.'

He had given a pair of CLFC winged brogues as a present to the old college friend whom he was staying with. Now he would have to borrow his own gift back for a few days. But he had no compunction about doing that. When it came to work, he never felt awkward in the least about anything. In fact, Haresh was not given to feeling awkward in general.

As they walked back to the waiting rickshaw, Haresh felt very pleased with the way things were going. Brahmpur had got off to a sleepy start, but was proving to be very interesting, indeed, unpredictable.

He got out a small card from his pocket and noted down in English:

Action Points –
  1. Misri Mandi – see trading.
  2. Purchase leather.
  3. Send leather to Jagat Ram.
  4. Dinner at Sunil's; recover brogues from him.
  5. Tmro: Jagat Ram/Ravidaspur.
  6. Telegram – late return to Cawnpore.

Having made his list, he scanned it through, and realized that it would be difficult to send the leather to Jagat Ram, because no one would be able to find his place, especially at night. He toyed with the idea of getting the rickshaw-wallah to see where Jagat Ram lived and hiring him to take the leather to him later. Then he had a better idea. He walked back to the workshop and told Jagat Ram to send someone to Kedarnath Tandon's shop in the Brahmpur Shoe Mart in Misri Mandi at nine o'clock sharp that night. The leather would be waiting for him there. He had only to pick it up and to begin work at first light the next day.

4.6

IT was ten o'clock, and Haresh and the other young men sitting and standing around Sunil Patwardhan's room near the university were happily intoxicated on a mixture of alcohol and high spirits.

Sunil Patwardhan was a mathematics lecturer at Brahmpur University. He had been a friend of Haresh's at St Stephen's College in Delhi; after that, what with Haresh going to England for his footwear course, they had been out of touch for years, and had heard about each other only through mutual friends. Although he was a mathematician, Sunil had had a reputation at St Stephen's for being one of the lads. He was big and quite plump, but filled as he was with sluggish energy and lazy wit and Urdu ghazals and Shakespearian quotations, many women found him attractive. He also enjoyed drinking, and had tried during his college days to get Haresh to drink – without success, because Haresh used to be a teetotaller then.

Sunil Patwardhan had believed as a student that to get one true mathematical insight a fortnight was enough by way of work; for the rest of the time he paid no attention to his studies, and did excellently. Now that he was teaching students he found it hard to impose an academic discipline on them that he himself had no faith in.

He was delighted to see Haresh again after several years. Haresh, true to form, had not informed him that he would be coming to Brahmpur on work but had landed on his doorstep two or three days earlier, had left his luggage in the drawing room, had talked for half an hour, and had then rushed off somewhere, saying something incomprehensible about the purchase of micro-sheets and leatherboard.

'Here, these are for you,' he had added in parting,

depositing a cardboard shoe-box on the drawing room table.

Sunil had opened it and been delighted. Haresh had said:

'I know you never wear anything except brogues.'

'But how did you remember my size?'

Haresh laughed and said, 'People's feet are like cars to me. I just remember their size – don't ask me how I do it. And your feet are like Rolls-Royces.'

Sunil remembered the time when he and a couple of friends had challenged Haresh – who was being his usual irritatingly overconfident self – to identify from a distance each of the fifty or so cars parked outside the college on the occasion of an official function. Haresh had got every one of them right. Considering his almost perfect memory for objects, it was odd that he had emerged from his English B.A. Honours course with a third, and had messed up his Poetry paper with innumerable misquotations.

God knows, thought Sunil, how he's wandered into the shoe trade, but it probably suits him. It would have been a tragedy for the world and for him if he had become an academic like me. What is amazing is that he should ever have chosen English as a subject in the first place.

'Good! Now that you're here, we'll have a party,' Sunil had said. 'It'll be like old times. I'll get a couple of old Stephanians who are in Brahmpur to join the more lively of my academic colleagues. But if you want soft drinks you'll have to bring your own.'

Haresh had promised to try to come, 'work permitting'. Sunil had threatened him with excommunication if he didn't.

Now he was here, but talking endlessly and enthusiastically about his day's efforts.

'Oh stop it, Haresh, don't tell us about chamars and micro-sheets,' said Sunil. 'We're not interested in all that. What happened to that Sikh girl you used to chase in your headier days?'

'It wasn't a sardarni, it was the inimitable Kalpana Gaur,' said a young historian. He tilted his head to the left

282

as wistfully as he could in exaggerated imitation of Kalpana Gaur's adoring gaze at Haresh from the other side of the room during lectures on Byron. Kalpana had been one of the few women students at St Stephen's.

'Uh —' said Sunil with dismissive authority. 'You don't know the true facts of the matter. Kalpana Gaur was chasing him, and he was chasing the sardarni. He used to serenade her outside the walls of her family's house and send her letters through go-betweens. The Sikh family couldn't bear the thought of their beloved daughter getting married to a Lala. If you want further details —'

'He's intoxicated with his own voice,' said Haresh.

'So I am,' said Sunil. 'But you — you misdirected yours. You should have wooed not the girl but the mother and the grandmother.'

'Thanks,' said Haresh.

'So do you still keep in touch with her? What was her name —'

Haresh did not oblige with any information. He was in no mood to tell these affable idiots that he was still very much in love with her after all these years — and that, together with his toe-puffs and counters, he kept a silver-framed photograph of her in his suitcase.

'Take those shoes off,' he said to Sunil. 'I want them back.'

'You swine!' said Sunil. 'Just because I happened to mention the holiest of holies. . . .'

'You donkey,' replied Haresh. 'I'm not going to eat them — I'll give them back to you in a few days.'

'What are you going to do with them?'

'You'd be bored if I told you. Come on, take them off.'

'What, now?'

'Yes, why not? A few drinks later I'll have forgotten and you'll have gone off to sleep with them on.'

'Oh, all right!' said Sunil obligingly and took off his shoes.

'That's better,' said Haresh. 'It's brought you an inch closer to my height. What glorious socks,' he added, as

Sunil's bright red cotton tartan socks came more fully into view.

'Wah! wah!' There were cries of approval from all sides.

'What beautiful ankles,' continued Haresh. 'Let's have a performance!'

'Light the chandeliers,' cried someone.

'Bring out the emerald goblets.'

'Sprinkle the attar of roses.'

'Lay a white sheet on the floor and charge an entrance fee!'

The young historian, in the affected tones of an official announcer, informed the audience: 'The famous courtesan Sunil Patwardhan will now perform for us her exquisite rendering of the kathak dance. Lord Krishna is dancing with the milkmaids. "Come," he says to the gopis, "Come to me. What is there to fear?"'

'Tha-tha-thai-thai!' said a drunken physicist, imitating the sound of the dance steps.

'Not courtesan, you lout, artiste!'

'Artiste!' said the historian, prolonging the last vowel.

'Come on, Sunil – we're waiting.'

And Sunil, obliging fellow that he was, danced a few clumpish steps of quasi-kathak while his friends rolled around with laughter. He simpered coyly as he twirled his chubby bulk about the room, knocking a book down here and spilling someone's drink there. He then became completely engrossed in what he was doing, and followed his rendition of Krishna and the gopis – in which he played both parts – with an impromptu scene representing the Vice-Chancellor of Brahmpur University (a notorious and indiscriminate womanizer) oilily greeting the poet Sarojini Naidu when she came as the chief guest at the Annual Day ceremonies. Some of his friends, helpless with laughter, begged him to stop, and others, equally helpless, begged him to dance for ever.

INTO this scene walked a tall, white-haired gentleman, Dr
Durrani. He was mildly surprised to see what was going
on inside. Sunil froze in mid-dance, indeed in mid-stance –
but then went forward to greet his unexpected guest.

Dr Durrani was not as surprised as he should have been;
a mathematical problem was occupying the large part of
his cerebrum. He had decided to walk over and discuss it
with his young colleague. In fact it had been Sunil who had
given him the impetus for his idea in the first place.

'Er, I, have I, er, chosen a bad time – er –?' he asked in
his maddeningly slow voice.

'Well, no – not, er, exactly –' said Sunil. He liked Dr
Durrani and was somewhat in awe of him. Dr Durrani
was one of the two Fellows of the Royal Society that
Brahmpur University could boast of, the other being Professor Ramaswami, the well-known physicist.

Dr Durrani did not even notice that Sunil was imitating
his manner of speech; Sunil himself was still in an imitative
mode after his kathak performance, and only noticed it
himself after he had done it.

'Er, well, Patwardhan, er, I do feel that, perhaps, I
am, er, impinging?' continued Dr Durrani. He had a
strong square face, with a handsome white moustache,
but scrunched up his eyes for punctuation every time he
said 'er'. This syllable also caused his eyebrows and the
lower part of the skin on his forehead to move up and
down.

'No, no, Dr Durrani, of course not. Please do join us.'
Sunil led Dr Durrani to the centre of the room, planning to
introduce him to the other guests. Dr Durrani and Sunil
Patwardhan were a study in physical contrast despite the
fact they were both rather tall.

'Well, if you are, er, certain, you know, that I'm not
going to, er, er, be in the way. You see,' went on Dr
Durrani more fluently but just as slowly, 'what has been
troubling me for the last day or so is this question of what
you might call, er, super-operations. I – well, I – you see, I,

um, thought that on the basis of all that, we could come up with several quite surprising series: you see, er –'

Such was the force of Dr Durrani's innocent involvement in his magical world, and so uncensorious was he about the indecorous high jinks of his juniors, that they did not seem greatly put out by the fact that he had intruded on their evening.

'Now you see, Patwardhan,' – Dr Durrani treated the whole world on terms of gentle distance – 'it isn't just a question of $1, 3, 6, 10, 15$ – which would be a, er, trivial series based on the, er, primary combinative operation – or even $1, 2, 6, 24, 120$ – which would be based on the secondary combinative operation. It could go much, er, much further. The tertiary combinative operation would result in $1, 2, 9, 262144$, and then 5 to the power of 262144. And of course that only, er, takes us to the fifth term in the, er, third such operation. Where will the, er, where will the steepness end?' He looked both excited and distressed.

'Ah,' said Sunil, his whisky-rich mind not quite on the problem.

'But of course what I am saying is, er, quite obvious. I didn't mean to, er, er, trouble you with that. But I did think that I, er,' – he looked around the room, his eye alighting on a cuckoo-clock on the wall – 'that I would, well, pick your brains on something that might be quite, er, quite unintuitive. Now take $1, 4, 216, 72576$ and so on. Does that surprise you?'

'Well –' said Sunil.

'Ah!' said Dr Durrani, 'I thought not.' He looked approvingly at his younger colleague, whose brains he often picked in this manner. 'Well, well, well! Now shall I tell you what the impetus, the, er, catalyst, for all this, was?'

'Oh, please do,' said Sunil.

'It was a, er, a remark – a very, er, perceptive remark of yours.'

'Ah!'

'You said, apropos the Pergolesi Lemma, "The concept

will form a tree." It was a, er, a brilliant comment – I never thought of it in those terms before.'

'Oh –' said Sunil.

Haresh winked at him, but Sunil frowned. Making deliberate fun of Dr Durrani was lèse majesté in his eyes.

'And indeed,' went on Dr Durrani generously, 'though I was, er, blind to it at the time' – he scrunched up his deep-set eyes almost into nothingness by way of unconscious illustration – 'it, well, it does form a tree. An unprunable one.'

He saw in his mind's eye a huge, proliferating, and – worst of all – uncontrollable banyan tree spreading over a flat landscape, and continued, with increasing distress and excitement: 'Because whatever, er, method of super-operating is chosen – that is, type 1 or type 2 – it cannot, er, it cannot definitely be applied at each, er, at each stage. To choose a particular, well, clumping of types may, may ... er, yes, it may indeed prune the branches but it will be too, er, arbitrary. The alternative will not yield a, er, consistent algorithm. So this, er, question arose in my, er, mind: how can one generalize it as one moves to higher operations?' Dr Durrani, who tended to stoop slightly, now straightened up. Clearly, action was required in the face of these terrible uncertainties.

'What conclusion did you come to?' said Sunil, tottering a bit.

'Oh, but that is just it. I didn't. Of course, er, super-operation $n + 1$ has to act vis-à-vis super-operation n as n acts to $n - 1$. That goes without saying. What troubles me is, er, the question of iteration. Does the same sub-operation, the same, er, sub-super-operation, if I might call it that' – he smiled at the thought of his terminology – 'does it, er, – would it –'

The sentence was left unfinished as Professor Durrani looked around the room, pleasingly mystified.

'Do join us for dinner, Dr Durrani,' said Sunil. 'It's open house. And may I offer you something to drink?'

'Oh, no, no, er, no,' said Dr Durrani kindly. 'You young people go ahead. Don't mind me.'

Haresh, suddenly thinking of Bhaskar, approached Dr Durrani and said, 'Excuse me, Sir, but I wonder if I might force a very bright young man onto your attention. I think he would very much enjoy meeting you – and I hope you would enjoy meeting him.'

Dr Durrani looked inquiringly at Haresh but did not say anything. What did young people have to do with anything? he wondered. (Or people, for that matter.)

'He was talking of the powers of ten the other day,' said Haresh, 'and he regretted that neither in English nor in Hindi is there a word for ten to the power of four or ten to the power of eight.'

'Yes, er, well, it is a great pity,' said Dr Durrani with some feeling. 'Of course, in the accounts of Al-Biruni one finds. . . .'

'He seemed to feel that something should be done about it.'

'How old is this young man?' said Dr Durrani, quite interested.

'Nine.'

Dr Durrani stooped once more in order to put himself on talking terms with Haresh. 'Ah,' he said. 'Well, er, er, send him along. You know where I, er, live,' he added, and turned to go.

Since neither Haresh nor Dr Durrani had ever seen each other before, this was unlikely. But Haresh thanked him, very pleased to be able to put two like minds into contact with each other. He did not feel uncomfortable that he might be encroaching on the time and energies of the great man. In fact the thought did not even occur to him.

4.8

PRAN, who dropped in a bit later, was not an old Stephanian. He had been invited by Sunil as a friend and colleague. He missed seeing Dr Durrani, with whom he had a nodding acquaintance, and missed hearing about Bhaskar.

In common with almost everyone in the family, he was a little in awe of his nephew, who seemed in certain respects just like any other child – fond of flying kites, fond of playing truant from school, and affectionate most of all towards his grandmothers.

'Why have you come so late?' asked Sunil a little belligerently. 'And why is Savita not here? We were trusting her to leaven our cloddish company. Or is she walking ten paces behind you? No – I don't see her anywhere. Did she think she'd cramp our style?'

'I'll answer the two questions worth answering,' said Pran. 'One – Savita decided she was feeling too tired; she begs you to excuse her. Two – I'm late because I've had dinner before coming. I know how things run in your house. Dinner isn't served until midnight – if you remember to serve it at all – and even then it's inedible. We usually have to get kababs at some wayside stall to fill ourselves up on the way home. You should get married yourself, you know, Sunil – then your household wouldn't run so haphazardly. Besides, there would be someone to darn those atrocious socks. Anyway, why don't you have your shoes on?'

Sunil sighed. 'That's because Haresh decided he needed two pairs of shoes for himself. "My need is greater than thine." There they are in the corner, and I know I'll never see them again. Oh, but you two haven't met,' said Sunil, talking now in Hindi. 'Haresh Khanna – Pran Kapoor. Both of you have studied English literature, and I've never met anyone who knows more about it than the one, or less about it than the other.'

The two men shook hands.

'Well,' said Pran with a smile. 'Why do you need two pairs of shoes?'

'This fellow delights in creating mysteries,' said Haresh, 'but there's a simple explanation. I'm using it as a sample to have another pair made.'

'For yourself?'

'Oh, no. I work with CLFC and I'm in Brahmpur for a few days on work.'

Haresh assumed that the abbreviations he often used were entirely familiar to everyone else.

'CLFC?' asked Pran.

'Cawnpore Leather & Footwear Company.'

'Oh. So you work in the shoe trade,' said Pran. 'That's a far cry from English literature.'

'All I am living by is with the awl,' said Haresh lightly, and offered no more by way of explanation and misquotation.

'My brother-in-law works in the shoe trade as well,' said Pran. 'Perhaps you've met him. He's a trader in the Brahmpur Shoe Mart.'

'I may have,' said Haresh, 'though because of the strike not all the traders have their stalls open. What's his name?'

'Kedarnath Tandon.'

'Kedarnath Tandon! But of course I know him. He's been showing me around all sorts of places –' Haresh was very pleased. 'In fact, it's because of him in a way that Sunil has lost his shoes. So you're his sala – sorry, I mean Veena's brother. Are you the older one or the younger one?'

Sunil Patwardhan had loomed back into the conversation. 'The elder,' he said. 'The younger one – Maan – was invited too, but his evenings nowadays are otherwise occupied.'

'Well, tell me,' said Pran, turning determinedly towards Sunil, 'is there some special occasion for this party? It's not your birthday, is it?'

'No it's not. And you're not very good at changing the subject. But I'll let you wriggle out of this one because I have a question for you, Dr Kapoor. One of my best students has been suffering because of you. Why were you so harsh – you and your disciplinary committee – what do they call it? student welfare committee? – with the boys who indulged in a little high spirits over Holi?'

'A little high spirits?' exclaimed Pran. 'Those girls looked like they had been dyed in red and blue ink. It's lucky they didn't catch pneumonia. And really, there was a lot of, you know, unnecessary rubbing of colour here and there.'

'But throwing the boys out of their hostels and threatening them with expulsion?'

'Do you call that harsh?' said Pran.

'Of course. At the time that they're preparing for their final exams?'

'They certainly weren't preparing for their exams on Holi when they decided – it seems that a few of them had even taken bhang – to storm the Women's Hostel and lock up the warden in the common room.'

'Oh, that steel-hearted bitch!' said Sunil dismissively, then burst out laughing at the image of the women's warden locked up, banging perhaps on the carom board in frustration. The warden was a draconian if rather good-looking woman who kept her charges on a strict leash, wore lots of make-up, and glared at any of the girls who did the same.

'Come on, Sunil, she's quite attractive – I think you have a soft spot for her yourself.'

Sunil snorted at the ridiculous idea.

'I bet she asked for them to be expelled immediately. Or rusticated. Or electrocuted. Like those Russian spies in America the other day. The trouble is that no one remembers their own student days once they are on the other side.'

'What would you have done in her place?' asked Pran. 'Or in our place for that matter? The girls' parents would have been up in arms if we had taken no action. And, quite apart from the question of such repercussions, I don't think the punishment was unfair. A couple of members of the committee wanted them expelled.'

'Who? The Proctor?'

'Well – a couple of members,' said Pran.

'Come on, come on, don't be secretive, you're among friends –' said Sunil, putting a broad arm around Pran's gangly shoulders.

'No, really, Sunil, I've said too much already.'

'You, of course, voted for leniency.'

Pran rebutted the friendly sarcasm seriously. 'As it happens, yes, I did suggest leniency. Besides, I know how things can get out of hand. I thought of what happened when Maan decided to play Holi with Moby-Dick.' The incident with Professor Mishra was by now notorious throughout the university.

'Oh, yes,' said the physicist who had wandered over, 'What's happened to your readership?'

Pran sucked in his breath slowly. 'Nothing,' he said.

'But it's been months that the post has been lying open.'

'I know,' said Pran. 'It's even been advertised, but they don't seem to want to set a date for the selection committee to meet.'

'It's not right. I'll talk to someone at the *Brahmpur Chronicle*,' said the young physicist.

'Yes, yes,' said Sunil enthusiastically. 'It has come to our knowledge that despite the chronic understaffing in the English Department of our renowned university and the availability of a more than suitable local candidate for the post of reader which has been lying unfilled now for an unconscionable length of time –'

'Please –' said Pran, not at all calmly. 'Just let things take their natural course. Don't get the papers involved in all this.'

Sunil looked meditative for a while, as if he was working something out. 'All right, all right, have a drink!' he said suddenly. 'Why don't you have a drink in your hand?'

'First he grills me for half an hour without offering me a drink, then he asks me why I don't have one. I'll have whisky – with water,' said Pran, in a less agitated tone.

As the evening went on, the talk of the party turned to news in the town, to India's consistently poor performance in international cricket ('I doubt we will ever win a Test Match' said Pran with confident pessimism), to politics in Purva Pradesh and the world at large, and to the peculiarities of various teachers, both at Brahmpur University and – for the Stephanians – at St Stephen's in Delhi. To the mystification of the non-Stephanians, they participated in chorus with a querulous: 'In my class I will say one thing:

you may not understand, you may not want to understand, but you will understand!'

Dinner was served, and it was just as rudimentary as Pran had predicted. Sunil, for all his good-natured bullying of his friends, was himself bullied by an old servant whose affection for his master (whom he had served since Sunil was a child) was only equalled by his unwillingness to do any work.

Over dinner there was a discussion – somewhat incoherent because some of the participants were either belligerent or erratic with whisky – about the economy and the political situation. Making complete sense of it was difficult, but a part of it went like this:

'Look, the only reason why Nehru became PM was because he was Gandhi's favourite. Everyone knows that. All he knows how to do is to make those bloody long speeches that never go anywhere. He never seems to take a stand on anything. Just think. Even in the Congress Party, where Tandon and his cronies are pushing him to the wall, what does he do? He just goes along with it, and we have to –'

'But what can he do? He's not a dictator.'

'Do you mind not interrupting? I mean to say, may I make my point? After that you can say whatever you want for as long as you want. So what does Nehru do? I mean to say, what does he do? He sends a message to some society that he's been asked to address and he says, "We often feel a sense of darkness." Darkness – who cares about his darkness or what's going on inside his head? He may have a handsome head and that red rose may look pretty in his buttonhole, but what we need is someone with a stout heart, not a sensitive one. It's his duty as Prime Minister to give a lead to the country, and he's just not got the strength of character to do it.'

'Well –'

'Well, what?'

'You just try to run a country. Try to feed the people, for a start. Keep the Hindus from slaughtering the Muslims –'

'Or vice versa.'

'All right, or vice versa. And try to abolish the zamindars' estates when they fight you every inch of the way.'

'He isn't doing that as PM – land revenue isn't a central subject – it's a state subject. Nehru will make his vague speeches, but you ask Pran who's the real brains behind our Zamindari Abolition Bill.'

'Yes,' admitted Pran, 'it's my father. At any rate, my mother says he works terribly late and sometimes comes back home from the Secretariat after midnight, dog-tired, then reads through the night to prepare for the next day's arguments in the Assembly.' He laughed shortly and shook his head. 'My mother's worried because he's ruining his health. Two hundred clauses, two hundred ulcers, she thinks. And now that the Zamindari Act in Bihar has been declared unconstitutional, everyone's in a panic. As if there's not enough to panic about anyway, what with the trouble in Chowk.'

'What trouble in Chowk?' asked someone, thinking Pran was referring to something that might have happened that day.

'The Raja of Marh and his damned Shiva Temple,' said Haresh promptly. Though he was the only one from out of town, he had just been filled in on the facts by Kedarnath, and had made them his own.

'Don't call it a damned Shiva Temple,' said the historian.

'It is a damned Shiva Temple, it's caused enough deaths already.'

'You're a Hindu, and you call it a damned temple – you should look at yourself in the mirror. The British have left, in case you need reminding, so don't put on their airs. Damned temple, damned natives –'

'Oh God! I'll have another drink after all,' said Haresh to Sunil.

As the discussion rose and subsided over dinner and afterwards, and people formed themselves into small knots or tied themselves into worse ones, Pran drew Sunil aside and inquired casually, 'Is that fellow Haresh married or engaged or anything?'

'Anything.'

'What?' said Pran, frowning.

'He's not married or engaged,' said Sunil, 'but he's certainly "anything".'

'Sunil, don't talk in riddles. It's midnight.'

'This is what comes of turning up late for my party. Before you came we were talking at length about him and that sardarni, Simran Kaur, whom he's still infatuated with. Now why didn't I remember her name an hour ago? There was a couplet about him at college:

> Chased by Gaur and chasing Kaur;
> Chaste before but chaste no more!

I can't vouch for the facts of the second line. But, anyway, it was clear from his face today that he's still in love with her. And I can't blame him. I met her once and she was a real beauty.'

Sunil Patwardhan recited a couplet in Urdu about the black monsoon clouds of her hair.

'Well, well, well,' said Pran.

'But why do you want to know?'

'Nothing,' shrugged Pran. 'I think he's a man who knows his own mind, and I was curious.'

A little later the guests started taking their leave. Sunil suggested that they all visit Old Brahmpur 'to see if anything's going on'.

'Tonight at the midnight hour,' he intoned in a singsong, Nehruvian voice, 'while the world sleeps, Brahmpur will awake to life and freedom.'

As Sunil saw his guests to the door he suddenly became depressed. 'Good night,' he said gently; then in a more melancholy tone: 'Good night, ladies, good night, sweet ladies, good night, good night.' And a little later, as he closed the door, more to himself than anyone else, he mumbled, in the liltingly incomplete cadence with which Nehru ended his Hindi speeches: 'Brothers and sisters – Jai Hind!'

But Pran walked home in high spirits. He had enjoyed

the party, had enjoyed getting away both from work and – he had to admit it – the family circle of wife, mother-in-law, and sister-in-law.

What a pity, he thought, that Haresh was already spoken for. Despite his misquotations, Pran had liked him, and wondered if he might be a possible 'prospect' for Lata. Pran was concerned about her. Ever since she had received a phone call at dinner a few days ago, she had not been herself. But it had become difficult to talk even to Savita about her sister. Sometimes, thought Pran, I feel they all see me as an interloper – a mere meddler among Mehras.

4.9

HARESH, with an effort, woke up early despite a heavy head, and took a rickshaw to Ravidaspur. He had with him the lasts, the other materials he had promised, and Sunil's shoes. People in rags were moving about the lanes among the thatched mud huts. A boy was dragging a piece of wood with a string and another boy was trying to hit it with a stick. As he walked across the unstable bridge, he noticed that a thick, whitish vapour lay over the black water of the open sewer, where people were performing their morning ablutions. How can they live like this? he thought to himself.

A couple of electric wires hung casually from poles or were tangled among the branches of a dusty tree. A few houses tapped illegally into this meagre source by slinging a wire over the main line. From the dark interiors of the other huts came the flicker of makeshift lamps: tins filled with kerosene, whose smoke filled the huts. It was easy for a child or a dog or a calf to knock these over, and fires sometimes started this way, spreading from hut to hut and burning everything hidden in the thatch for safe-keeping, including the precious ration-cards. Haresh shook his head at the waste of it all.

He got to the workshop and found Jagat Ram sitting on

the step by himself, watched only by his small daughter. But to Haresh's annoyance he found that what he was working on was not the brogues but a wooden toy: a cat, it appeared. He was whittling away at it with great concentration, and looked surprised to see Haresh. He set the unfinished cat down on the step and stood up.

'You've come early,' he said.

'I have,' said Haresh brusquely. 'And I find you are working on something else. I am making every effort on my part to supply you with materials as quickly as possible, but I have no intention of working with someone who is unreliable.'

Jagat Ram touched his moustache. His eyes took on a dull glow, and his speech became staccato:

'What I mean to say —' he began, '— have you even asked? What I mean to say is — do you think I am not a man of my word?'

He stood up, went inside, and fetched the pieces he had cut according to the patterns Haresh had given him from the handsome maroon leather that he had fetched the previous night. While Haresh was examining them, he said:

'I haven't punched them with the brogue design yet — but I thought I'd do the cutting myself, not leave it to my cutter. I've been up since dawn.'

'Good, good,' said Haresh, nodding his head and in a kinder tone. 'Let's see the piece of leather I left for you.'

Jagat Ram rather reluctantly took it out from one of the brick shelves embedded in the wall of the small room. Quite a lot of it was still unused. Haresh examined it carefully, and handed it back. Jagat Ram looked relieved. He moved his hand to his greying moustache and rubbed it meditatively, saying nothing.

'Excellent,' said Haresh with generous enthusiasm. Jagat Ram's cutting had been both surprisingly swift and extremely economical of the leather. In fact, he appeared to have an intuitive spatial mastery that was very rare even among trained shoemakers of many years' standing. It had been hinted at yesterday in his comments when he had constructed the shoe in his mind's eye after just a brief glance at the components of the pattern.

'Where's your daughter disappeared to?'

Jagat Ram permitted himself a slight smile. 'She was late for school,' he said.

'Did the people from the Lovely Shoe Shop turn up yesterday?' asked Haresh.

'Well, yes and no,' said Jagat Ram and did not elaborate further.

Since Haresh had no direct interest in the Lovely people, he did not press the question. He thought that perhaps Jagat Ram did not want to talk about one of Kedarnath's competitors in front of Kedarnath's friend.

'Well,' said Haresh. 'Here is all the other stuff you need.' He opened his briefcase and took out the thread and the components, the lasts and the shoes. As Jagat Ram turned the lasts around appreciatively in his hands, Haresh continued: 'I will see you three days from today at two o'clock in the afternoon, and I will expect the brogues to be ready by then. I have bought my ticket for the six-thirty train back to Kanpur that evening. If the shoes are well made, I expect I will be able to get you an order. If they are not, I'm not going to delay my journey back.'

'I will hope to work directly with you if things work out,' said Jagat Ram.

Haresh shook his head. 'I met you through Kedarnath and I'll deal with you through Kedarnath,' he replied.

Jagat Ram nodded a little grimly, and saw Haresh to the door. There seemed to be no getting away from these bloodsucking middlemen. First the Muslims, now these Punjabis who had taken their place. Kedarnath, however, had given him his first break, and was not such a bad man – as such things went. Perhaps he was merely blood-sipping.

'Good,' said Haresh. 'Excellent. Well, I have a lot of things to do. I must be off.'

And he walked off with his usual high energy through the dirty paths of Ravidaspur. Today he was wearing ordinary black Oxfords. In an open but filthy space near a little white shrine he saw a group of small boys gambling with a tattered pack of cards – one of them was Jagat Ram's youngest son – and he clicked his tongue, not so much from moral disapproval as from a feeling of annoyance that this should be the state of things. Illiteracy, poverty, indiscipline, dirt! It wasn't as if people here didn't have potential. If he had his way and was given funds and labour, he would have this neighbourhood on its feet in six months. Sanitation, drinking water, electricity, paving, civic sense – it was simply a question of making sensible decisions and having the requisite facilities to implement them. Haresh was as keen on 'requisite facilities' as he was on his 'To Do' list. He was impatient with himself if anything was lacking in the former or undone in the latter. He also believed in 'following things through'.

Oh yes; Kedarnath's son, what's his name now, Bhaskar! he said to himself. I should have got Dr Durrani's address from Sunil last night. He frowned at his own lack of foresight.

But after lunch he collected Bhaskar anyway and took a tonga to Sunil's. Dr Durrani looked as if he had walked to Sunil's house, reflected Haresh, so he couldn't live all that far away.

Bhaskar accompanied Haresh in silence, and Haresh, for his own part, was happy not to say anything other than where they were going.

Sunil's faithful, lazy servant pointed out Dr Durrani's house, which was a few doors away. Haresh paid off the tonga, and walked over with Bhaskar.

4.10

A tall, good-looking fellow in cricket whites opened the door.

'We've come to see Dr Durrani,' said Haresh. 'Do you think he might be free?'

'I'll just see what my father is doing,' said the young

man in a low, pleasant, slightly rough-edged voice. 'Please come in.'

A minute or two later he emerged and said, 'My father will be out in a minute. He asked me who you were, and I realized I hadn't asked. I'm sorry, I should introduce myself first. My name's Kabir.'

Haresh, impressed by the young man's looks and manner, held out his hand, smiled in a clipped sort of way, and introduced himself. 'And this is Bhaskar, a friend's son.'

The young man seemed a bit troubled about something, but did his best to make conversation.

'Hello, Bhaskar,' said Kabir. 'How old are you?'

'Nine,' said Bhaskar, not objecting to this least original of questions. He was pondering what all this was about.

After a while Kabir said, 'I wonder what's keeping my father,' and went back in.

When Dr Durrani finally came into the drawing room, he was quite surprised to see his visitors. Noticing Bhaskar, he asked Haresh:

'Have you come to see one of my, er, sons?'

Bhaskar's eyes lit up at this unusual adult behaviour. He liked Dr Durrani's strong, square face, and in particular the balance and symmetry of his magnificent white moustache. Haresh, who had stood up, said:

'No indeed, Dr Durrani, it's you we've come to see. I don't know if you remember me – we met at Sunil's party....'

'Sunil?' said Dr Durrani, his eyes scrunched up in utter perplexity, his eyebrows working up and down. 'Sunil ... Sunil ...' He seemed to be weighing something up with great seriousness, and coming closer and closer to a conclusion. 'Patwardhan,' he said, with the air of having arrived at a considerable insight. He appraised this new premise from several angles in silence.

Haresh decided to speed up the process. He said, rather briskly:

'Dr Durrani, you said that we could drop in to see you. This is my young friend Bhaskar, whom I told you about. I think his interest in mathematics is remarkable, and I felt he should meet you.'

Dr Durrani looked quite pleased, and asked Bhaskar what two plus two was.

Haresh was taken aback, but Bhaskar – though he normally rejected considerably more complex sums as unworthy of his attention – was not, apparently, insulted. In a very tentative voice he replied:

'Four?'

Dr Durrani was silent. He appeared to be mulling over this answer. Haresh began to feel ill at ease.

'Well, yes, you can, er, leave him here for a while,' said Dr Durrani.

'Shall I come back to pick him up at four o'clock?' asked Haresh.

'More or less,' said Dr Durrani.

When he and Bhaskar were left alone, both of them were silent. After a while, Bhaskar said:

'Was that the right answer?'

'More or less,' said Dr Durrani. 'You see,' he said, picking up a musammi from a bowl on the dining table, 'it's rather, er, it's rather like the question of the, er, sum of the angles in a – in a triangle. What have they, er, taught you that is?'

'180 degrees,' said Bhaskar.

'Well, more or less,' said Dr Durrani. 'On the, er, surface of it, at least. But on the surface of this, er, musammi, for instance –'

For a while he gazed at the green citrus, following a mysterious train of thought. Once it had served his purpose, he looked at it wonderingly, as if he could not figure out what it was doing in his hand. He peeled it with some difficulty because of its thick skin and began to eat it.

'Would you, er, like some?' he asked Bhaskar matter-of-factly.

'Yes, please,' said Bhaskar, and held out both hands for a segment, as if he were receiving a sanctified offering from a temple.

An hour later, when Haresh returned, he got the sense

that he was an unwelcome interruption. They were now both sitting at the dining table, on which were lying – among other things – several musammis, several peels of musammis, a large number of toothpicks in various configurations, an inverted ashtray, some strips of newspaper stuck together in odd-looking twisted loops, and a purple kite. The remaining surface of the dining room table was covered with equations in yellow chalk.

Before Bhaskar left with Haresh, he took with him the loops of newspaper, the purple kite, and exactly sixteen toothpicks. Neither Dr Durrani nor Bhaskar thanked each other for the time they had spent together. In the tonga back to Misri Mandi, Haresh could not resist asking Bhaskar:

'Did you understand all those equations?'

'No,' said Bhaskar. It was clear from the tone of his answer, however, that he did not think this mattered.

Though Bhaskar did not say anything when he got home, his mother could tell from one glance at his face that he had had a wonderfully stimulating time. She took his various objects off him and told him to wash his gummy hands. Then, almost with tears in her eyes, she thanked Haresh.

'It's so kind of you to have taken this trouble, Haresh Bhai. I can tell what this has meant to him,' Veena said.

'Well,' said Haresh with a smile, 'that's more than I can.'

4.11

MEANWHILE, the brogues were sitting on their lasts in Jagat Ram's workshop. Two days passed. On the appointed day at two o'clock, Haresh came to collect the shoes and the lasts. Jagat Ram's little daughter recognized him, and clapped her hands at his arrival. She was entertaining herself with a song, and since he was there, she entertained him too. The song went as follows:

Ram Ram Shah,	Ram Ram Shah,
Alu ka rasa,	Gravy made from spuds,
Mendaki ki chatni—	Chutney made from female frog—
Aa gaya nasha!	Drink it, and you're drunk!

Haresh looked the shoes over with a practised eye. They
were well made. The uppers had been stitched excellently,
though on the simple sewing machine in front of him. The
lasting had been carefully done – there were no bubbles or
wrinkles. The finishing was fine, down to the coloration of
the leather of the punched brogue. He was well pleased.
He had been strict in his demands, but now he gave Jagat
Ram one-and-a-half times as much as he had promised
him by way of payment.

'You will be hearing from me,' he promised.

'Well, Haresh Sahib, I certainly hope so,' said Jagat
Ram. 'You're really leaving today? A pity.'

'Yes, I'm afraid so.'

'And you stayed on just for this?'

'Yes, I would have left in two days instead of four
otherwise.'

'Well, I hope they like this pair at CLFC.'

With that they parted. Haresh did a few chores, made a
few small purchases, went back to Sunil's, returned his
brogues, packed, said goodbye, and took a tonga to the
station to catch the evening train to Kanpur. On the way
he stopped at Kedarnath's to thank him.

'I hope I can be of some help to you,' said Haresh,
shaking his hand warmly.

'You already have, Veena tells me.'

'I meant, by way of business.'

'I certainly hope so,' said Kedarnath. 'And, well, if I can
help you in any way –'

They shook hands.

'Tell me –' said Haresh suddenly. 'I have been meaning
to ask you this for several days now – how did you get all
those scars on the inside of your hands? They don't look
as if they've been caught in a machine – they'd be scarred
on both sides if they had.'

Kedarnath was silent for a few seconds, as if adjusting

to a change of thought. 'I got those during Partition,' he said. He paused and continued, 'At the time that we were forced to flee from Lahore, I got a place in a convoy of army trucks and we got into the first truck – my younger brother and I. Nothing, I thought, could be safer. But, well, it was a Baluchi regiment. They stopped just before the Ravi Bridge, and Muslim ruffians came from behind the timber yards there and started butchering us with their spears. My younger brother has marks on his back and I have these on my palms and my wrist – I tried to hold onto the blade of the spear.... I was in hospital for a month.'

Haresh's face betrayed his shock. Kedarnath continued, closing his eyes, but in a calm voice:

'Twenty or thirty people were slaughtered in two minutes – someone's father, someone's daughter.... By the greatest of luck a Gurkha regiment was coming from the other side and they began to fire. And, well, the looters fled, and I'm here to tell you the story.'

'Where was the family?' asked Haresh. 'In the other trucks?'

'No – I'd sent them on by train a little earlier. Bhaskar was only six at the time. Not that the trains were safe either, as you know.'

'I don't know if I should have asked these questions,' said Haresh, feeling atypically embarrassed.

'No, no – that's all right. We were fortunate, as these things go. The Muslim trader who used to own my shop here in Brahmpur – well.... Strange, though – after all that happened there, I still miss Lahore,' said Kedarnath. 'But you'd better hurry or you'll miss your train.'

Brahmpur Junction was as crowded and noisy and smelly as ever: hissing clouds of steam, the whistles of incoming trains, hawkers' shouts, the stench of fish, the buzz of flies, the scurrying babble of passengers. Haresh felt tired. Though it was past six o'clock it was still very warm. He touched an agate cuff-link and wondered at its coolness.

Glancing at the crowd, he noticed a young woman in a light blue cotton sari standing near her mother. The English teacher whom he had met at Sunil's party was seeing them off on the down train to Calcutta. The mother's back was turned towards Haresh, so he could not get a proper glimpse of her. The daughter's face was striking. It was not classically beautiful – it did not catch at his heart as did the photograph he kept with him – but it had a quality of such attractive intensity that Haresh stopped for a second. The young woman seemed to be determinedly fighting back some sadness that went beyond the normal sadness of parting at a railway platform. Haresh thought of pausing for a little to re-introduce himself to the young lecturer, but something in the girl's expression of inward-ness, almost despair, stopped him from doing so. Besides, his train was leaving soon, his coolie was already quite far ahead of him, and Haresh, not being tall, was concerned that he might lose him in the crowd.

Part Five

SOME riots are caused, some bring themselves into being. The problems at Misri Mandi were not expected to reach a point of violence. A few days after Haresh left, however, the heart of Misri Mandi – including the area around Kedarnath's shop – was full of armed police.

The previous evening there had been a fight inside a cheap drinking place along the unpaved road that led towards the tannery from Old Brahmpur. The strike meant less money but more time for everyone, so the kalari's joint was about as crowded as usual. The place was mainly frequented by jatavs, but not exclusively so. Drink equalized the drinkers, and they didn't care who was sitting at the plain wooden table next to them. They drank, laughed, cried, then tottered and staggered out, sometimes singing, sometimes cursing. They swore undying friendship, they divulged confidences, they imagined insults. The assistant of a trader in Misri Mandi was in a foul mood because he was having a hard time with his father-in-law. He was drinking alone and working himself into a generalized state of aggressiveness. He overheard a comment from behind him about the sharp practice of his employer, and his hands clenched into a fist. Knocking his bench over as he twisted around to see who was speaking, he fell onto the floor.

The three men at the table behind him laughed. They were jatavs who had dealt with him before. It was he who used to take the shoes from their baskets when they scurried desperately in the evening to Misri Mandi – his employer the trader did not like to touch shoes because he felt they would pollute him. The jatavs knew that the breakdown of the trade in Misri Mandi had particularly hurt those traders who had overextended themselves on the chit system. That it had hurt themselves still more, they also knew – but for them it was not a case of the mighty being brought to their knees. Here, however, literally in front of them, it was.

The locally-distilled cheap alcohol had gone to their

heads, and they did not have the money to buy the pakoras and other snacks that could have settled it. They laughed uncontrollably.

'He's wrestling with the air,' jeered one.

'I bet he'd rather be doing another kind of wrestling,' sneered another.

'But would he be any good at it? They say that's why he has trouble at home –'

'What a reject,' taunted the first man, waving him away with the airy gesture of a trader rejecting a basket on the basis of a single faulty pair.

Their speech was slurred, their eyes contemptuous. The man who had fallen lunged at them, and they set upon him. A couple of people, including the owner or kalari, tried to make peace, but most gathered around to enjoy the fun and shout drunken encouragement. The four rolled around on the floor, fighting.

It ended with the man who had started the fight being beaten unconscious, and all of the others being injured. One was bleeding from the eye and screaming in pain.

That night, when he lost the sight of his eye, an ominous crowd of jatavs gathered at the Govind Shoe Mart, where the trader had his stall. They found the stall closed. The crowd began to shout slogans, then threatened to burn the stall down. One of the other traders tried to reason with the crowd, and they set upon him. A couple of policemen, sensing the crowd's mood, ran to the local police station for reinforcements. Ten policemen now emerged, armed with short stout bamboo lathis, and they began to beat people up indiscriminately. The crowd scattered.

Surprisingly soon, every relevant authority knew about the matter: from the Superintendent of Police of the district to the Inspector-General of Purva Pradesh, from the Home Secretary to the Home Minister. Everyone received different facts and interpretations, and had different suggestions for action or inaction.

The Chief Minister was out of town. In his absence – and because law and order lay in his domain – the Home Minister ran things. Mahesh Kapoor, though Revenue

Minister, and not therefore directly concerned, heard about the unrest because part of Misri Mandi lay in his constituency. He hurried to the spot and talked with the Superintendent of Police and the District Magistrate. The SP and the DM believed that things would blow over if neither side was provoked. However, the Home Minister, L.N. Agarwal, part of whose constituency also lay in Misri Mandi, did not think it necessary to go to the spot. He received a number of phone calls at home and decided that something by way of a salutary example needed to be provided.

These jatavs had disrupted the trade of the city long enough with their frivolous complaints and their mischievous strike. They had doubtless been stirred up by union leaders. Now they were threatening to block the entrance of the Govind Shoe Mart at the point where it joined the main road of Misri Mandi. Many traders there were already in financial straits. The threatened picketing would finish them off. L.N. Agarwal himself came from a shopkeeping family and some of the traders were good friends of his. Others supplied him with election funds. He had received three desperate calls from them. It was a time not for talk but for action. It was not merely a question of law, but of order, the order of society itself. Surely this is what the Iron Man of India, the late Sardar Patel, would have felt in his place.

But what would he have done had he been here? As if in a dream, the Home Minister conjured up the domed and severe head of his political mentor, dead these four months. He sat in thought for a while. Then he told his personal assistant to get him the District Magistrate on the phone.

The District Magistrate, who was in his mid-thirties, was directly in charge of the civil administration of Brahmpur District and, together with the SP – as the Superintendent of Police was referred to by everyone – maintained law and order.

The PA tried to get through, then said: 'Sorry, Sir, DM is out on the site. He is trying to conciliate –'

'Give me the phone,' said the Home Minister in a calm voice. The PA nervously handed him the receiver.

'Who? ... Where? ... I am Agarwal speaking, that's who ... yes, direct instructions ... I don't care. Get Dayal at once. ... Yes, ten minutes ... call me back. ... The SP is there, that is enough surely, is it a cinema show?'

He put down the phone and grasped the grey curls that curved like a horse-shoe around his otherwise bald head.

After a while he made as if to pick up the receiver again, then decided against it, and turned his attention to a file.

Ten minutes later the young District Magistrate, Krishan Dayal, was on the phone. The Home Minister told him to guard the entrance of the Govind Shoe Mart. He was to disperse any pickets forthwith, if necessary by reading out Section 144 of the Criminal Procedure Code – and then firing if the crowd did not disperse.

The line was unclear but the message disturbingly clear. Krishan Dayal said in a strong voice, but one which was fraught with concern: 'Sir, with respect, may I suggest an alternative course of action. We are talking with the leaders of the crowd –'

'So there are leaders, are there, it is not spontaneous?'

'Sir, it is spontaneous, but there are leaders.'

L.N. Agarwal reflected that it was puppies of the ilk of Krishan Dayal who used to lock him up in British jails. He said, calmly:

'Are you being witty, Mr Dayal?'

'No, Sir, I –'

'You have your instructions. This is an emergency. I have discussed things with the Chief Secretary by phone. I understand that the crowd is some three hundred strong. I want the SP to get the police stationed everywhere along the main road of Misri Mandi and to guard all entrances – Govind Shoe Mart, Brahmpur Shoe Mart, and so on – you just do the needful.'

There was a pause. The Home Minister was about to put down the phone when the DM said:

'Sir, we may not be able to spare such a large number of police at short notice. A number of policemen are stationed at the site of the Shiva Temple in case of trouble. Things are very tense, Sir. The Revenue Minister thinks that on Friday –'

'Are they there at the moment? I did not notice them this morning,' said L.N. Agarwal in a relaxed but steely tone.

'No, Sir, but they are in the main police station in the Chowk area, so it is sufficiently close to the temple site. It is best to keep them there for a true emergency.' Krishan Dayal had been in the army during the war, but he was rattled by the Home Minister's calm air of almost dismissive interrogation and command.

'God will take care of the Shiva Temple. I am in close touch with many members of the committee, do you think I do not know the circumstances?' He had been irked by Dayal's reference to 'a true emergency' as much as by his mention of Mahesh Kapoor, his rival and – as abrasive chance would have it – the MLA from the constituency contiguous to his own.

'Yes, Sir,' said Krishan Dayal, his face reddening – which luckily the Home Minister could not see. 'And may I know how long the police are to remain there?'

'Until further notice,' said the Home Minister and put down the phone to pre-empt further backchat. He did not like the way these so-called civil servants answered back to those above them in the chain of command – who were besides, twenty years older than them. It was necessary to have an administrative service, no doubt, but it was equally necessary that it should learn that it no longer ruled this country.

5.2

ON Friday at the midday prayer the hereditary Imam of the Alamgiri Mosque gave his sermon. He was a short, plump man with short breath, but this did not stem his jerky crescendos of oratory. If anything, his breathlessness gave the impression that he was choked with emotion. The construction of the Shiva Temple was going ahead. The Imam's appeals to everyone from the Governor down had fallen on deaf ears. A legal case contesting the Raja of Marh's title to the land contiguous to the mosque had been instituted and was at present going through the lowest court. A stay order on the construction of the temple, however, could not be immediately obtained – indeed, perhaps could not be obtained at all. Meanwhile the dung-heap was growing before the Imam's agonized eyes.

His congregation was tense already. It was with dismay that many Muslims in Brahmpur had, over the months, seen the foundations of the temple rising in the plot to the west of their mosque. Now, after the first part of the prayers, the Imam gave his audience the most stirring and inflammatory speech he had given in years, very far removed from his ordinary sermon on personal morality or cleanliness or alms or piety. His grief and frustration as much as their own bitter anxiety called for something stronger. Their religion was in danger. The barbarians were at the gates. They prayed, these infidels, to their pictures and stones and perpetuated themselves in ignorance and sin. Let them do what they wanted to in their dens of filth. But God could see what was happening now. They had brought their beastliness near the very precincts of the mosque itself. The land that the kafirs sought to build on – why sought? were at this very moment building on – was disputed land – disputed in God's eyes and in man's eyes – but not in the eyes of animals who spent their time blowing conches and worshipping parts of the body whose very names it was shameful to mention. Did the people of the faith gathered here in God's presence know how it was planned to consecrate this Shiva-linga? Naked ash-smeared savages would dance before it – naked! These were the shameless, like the people of Sodom, who mocked at the power of the All-Merciful.

... God guides not the people
of the unbelievers.

> Those – God has set a seal on their
> hearts, and their hearing, and their eyes,
> and those – they are the heedless ones;
> Without a doubt, in the world to come they
>   will be the losers.

They worshipped their hundreds of idols that they claimed were divine – idols with four heads and five heads and the heads of elephants – and now the infidels who held power in the land wanted Muslims, when they turned their faces westwards in prayer to the Kaaba, to face these same idols and these same obscene objects with their heads bowed. 'But,' continued the Imam, 'we who have lived through hard and bitter times and have suffered for our faith and paid for our faith in blood need only remember the fate of the idolaters:

> And they set up compeers to God, that
> they might lead astray from His way.
> Say: "Take your joy! Your homecoming
>   shall be – the Fire!"'

A slow, attentive, shocked expectation filled the silence that followed.

'But even now,' cried the Imam in renewed frenzy, half-gasping for air, 'even as I speak – they could be hatching their designs to prevent our evening devotion by blowing their conches to drown out the call to prayer. Ignorant they may be, but they are full of guile. They are already getting rid of Muslims in the police force so that the community of God will be left defenceless. Then they can attack and enslave us. Now it is too clear to us that we are living not in a land of protection but a land of enmity. We have appealed for justice, and have been kicked down at the very doors where we have gone pleading. The Home Minister himself supports this temple committee – and its guiding spirit is the debauched buffalo of Marh! Let it not happen that our holy places are to be polluted by the proximity of filth – let it not happen – but what can save us now that we are left defenceless before the sword of our enemies in the land of the Hindus, what can save us but our own efforts, our own' – here he struggled for breath and emphasis again – 'our own direct action – to protect ourselves. And not just ourselves, not just our families but these few feet of paved earth that have been given to us for centuries, where we have unrolled our mats and raised our hands in tears to the All-Powerful, which are worn smooth by the devotions of our ancestors and ourselves and – if God so wills – will so be by our descendants also. But have no fear, God does so will, have no fear, God will be with you:

> Hast thou not seen how thy Lord did with Ad,
> > Iram of the pillars,
> the like of which was never created in the land,
> and Thamood, who hollowed the rocks in the valley,
> > and Pharaoh, he of the tent-pegs,
> > who all were insolent in the land
> > and worked much corruption therein?
> Thy Lord unloosed on them a scourge of chastisement;
> > surely thy Lord is ever on the watch.

O God, help those who help the religion of the Prophet Muhammad, peace be upon Him. May we also do the same. Make those weak, who weaken the religion of Muhammad. Praise be to God, the Lord of all Being.'

The plump Imam descended from the pulpit, and led the people in more prayer.

That evening there was a riot.

5.3

BECAUSE of the instructions of the Home Minister, the greater part of the police was stationed at sensitive points in Misri Mandi. There were only about fifteen policemen left in the main police station in Chowk by evening. As the call for prayer from the Alamgiri Mosque trembled across the evening sky, by some unfortunate chance or possibly intentional provocation, the sound of a conch was heard interrupting it several times. Normally such a thing might have been angrily shrugged off, but not today.

No one knew how the men who were gathering in the narrow alleys of the Muslim neighbourhood that lay on one side of Chowk became a mob. One moment they were walking individually or in small groups through the alleys towards the mosque for evening prayer, then they had coalesced into larger clusters, excitedly discussing the ominous signals they had heard. After the midday sermon most were in no mood to listen to any voice of moderation. A couple of the more eager members of the Alamgiri Masjid Hifaazat Committee made a few crowd-rousing remarks, a few local hotheads and toughs stirred themselves and those around them into a state of rage, the crowd increased in size as the alleys joined into larger alleys, its density and speed and sense of indistinct determination increased, and it was no longer a collection but a thing – wounded and enraged, and wanting nothing less than to wound and enrage. There were cries of 'Allah-u-Akbar' which could be heard all the way to the police station. A few of those who joined the crowd had sticks in their hands. One or two even had knives. Now it was not the mosque that they were headed for but the partly constructed temple just next to it. It was from here that the blasphemy had originated, it was this that must be destroyed.

Since the Superintendent of Police of the district was occupied in Misri Mandi, the young District Magistrate, Krishan Dayal, had himself gone to the tall pink edifice of the main police station about an hour earlier to ensure that things would remain stable in the Chowk area. He feared the increased tension that Friday often brought. When he heard about the Imam's sermon, he asked the kotwal – as the Deputy Superintendent of Police for the City was called – what he planned to do to protect the area.

The kotwal of Brahmpur, however, was a lazy man who wanted nothing better than to be left alone to take his bribes in peace.

'There will be no trouble, Sir, believe me,' he assured the District Magistrate. 'Agarwal Sahib himself has phoned me. Now he tells me I am to go to Misri Mandi to join the SP – so I must be off, Sir, with your leave, of course.' And he bustled off in a preoccupied sort of way, taking two other lower officers with him, and leaving the kotwali virtually in the charge of a head constable. 'I will just be sending the Inspector back,' he said in a reassuring manner. 'You should not stay, Sir,' he added ingratiatingly. 'It is late. This is a peaceful time. After the previous troubles at the mosque we have defused the situation, I am glad to say.'

Krishan Dayal, left with a force of about twelve constables, thought he would wait until the Inspector returned before he decided whether to go home. His wife was used to him coming back at odd hours, and would wait for him; it was not necessary to phone her. He did not actually expect a riot; he merely felt that tension was running high and that it was not worth taking a chance. He believed that the Home Minister had his priorities wrong where Chowk and Misri Mandi were concerned; but then the Home Minister was arguably the most powerful man in the state next to the Chief Minister, and he himself was just a DM.

He was sitting and waiting in this unworried but uneasy frame of mind when he heard what was to be recalled by several policemen at the subsequent inquiry – the inquiry by a senior officer that is required to be held after every magisterial order to fire. First he heard the coinciding sounds of the conch and the muezzin's call to prayer. This worried him mildly, but the reports he had had of the Imam's speech had not included his prescient reference to a conch. Then, after a while, came the distant murmur of shouting voices interspersed by high cries. Even before he could make out the individual syllables, he could tell what was being shouted by the direction from which it came and the general shape and fervour of the sound. He sent a policeman to the top of the police station – it was three storeys high – to judge where the mob now was. The mob itself would be invisible – hidden as it was by the intervening houses of the labyrinthine alleys – but the direction of the heads of the spectators from the rooftops would give its position away. As the cries of 'Allah-u-Akbar! Allah-u-Akbar!' came closer, the DM urgently told the small force of twelve constables to stand with him in a line – rifles at the ready – before the foundations and rudimentary walls of the site of the Shiva Temple. The thought flashed through his mind that despite his training in the army he had not learned to think tactically in a terrain of urban lawlessness. Was there nothing better he could do than to perform this mad sacrificial duty of standing against a wall and facing overwhelming odds?

The constables under his effective command were Muslims and Rajputs, mainly Muslims. The police force before Partition was very largely composed of Muslims as the result of the sound imperialist policy of divide and rule: it helped the British that the predominantly Hindu Congress-wallahs should be beaten up by predominantly Muslim policemen. Even after the exodus to Pakistan in 1947 there were large numbers of Muslims in the force. They would not be happy to fire upon other Muslims.

Krishan Dayal believed in general that although it was not always necessary to give effect to maximum force, it was necessary to give the impression that you were prepared to do so. In a strong voice he told the policemen that they were to fire when he gave the order. He himself stood there, pistol in hand. But he felt more vulnerable than ever before in his life. He told himself that a good officer, together with a force on which he could absolutely rely, could almost always carry the day, but he had reservations about the 'absolutely'; and the 'almost' worried him. Once the mob, still a few alleys away, came round the final bend, broke into a charge, and made straight for the temple, the patently, pathetically ineffective police force would be overwhelmed. A couple of men had just come running to tell him that there were perhaps a thousand men in the mob, that they were well-armed, and that –

judging by their speed – they would be upon them in two or three minutes.

Now that he knew he might be dead in a few minutes – dead if he fired, dead if he did not – the young DM gave his wife a brief thought, then his parents, and finally an old schoolmaster of his who had once confiscated a blue toy pistol that he had brought to class. His wandering thoughts were brought back to earth by the head constable who was addressing him urgently.

'Sahib!'

'Yes – yes?'

'Sahib – you are determined to shoot if necessary?' The head constable was a Muslim; it must have struck him as strange that he was about to die shooting Muslims in the course of defending a half-built Hindu temple that was an affront to the very mosque in which he himself often prayed.

'What do you think?' Krishan Dayal said in a voice that made things quite clear. 'Do I need to repeat my orders?'

'Sahib, if you take my advice –' said the head constable quickly, 'we should not stand here where we will be overpowered. We should stand in wait for them just before they turn the last bend before the temple – and just as they turn the bend we should charge and fire simultaneously. They won't know how many we are, and they won't know what's hit them. There's a ninety-nine per cent chance they will disperse.'

The astonished DM said to the head constable: 'You should have my job.'

He turned to the others, who appeared petrified. He immediately ordered them to run with him towards the bend. They stationed themselves on either side of the alley, about twenty feet from the bend itself. The mob was less than a minute away. He could hear it screaming and yelling; he could feel the vibration of the ground as hundreds of feet rushed forward.

At the last moment he gave the signal. The thirteen men roared and charged and fired.

The wild and dangerous mob, hundreds strong, faced

with this sudden terror, halted, staggered, turned and fled. It was uncanny. Within thirty seconds it had melted away. Two bodies were left in the street: one young man had been shot through the neck and was dying or dead; the other, an old man with a white beard, had fallen and been crushed by the retreating mob. He was badly, perhaps fatally, injured. Slippers and sticks were scattered here and there. There was blood in several places in the alley, so it was apparent that there had been other injuries, possibly deaths. Friends or members of their families had probably dragged the bodies back into the doorways of neighbouring houses. No one wanted to be brought to the attention of the police.

The DM looked around at his men. A couple of them were trembling, most of them were jubilant. None of them was injured. He caught the head constable's eye. Both of them started laughing with relief, then stopped. A couple of women were wailing in nearby houses. Otherwise, everything was peaceful or, rather, still.

5.4

THE next day L.N. Agarwal visited his only child, his married daughter Priya. He did so because he liked visiting her and her husband, and also to escape from the panic-stricken MLAs of his faction who were desperately worried about the aftermath of the firing in Chowk, and were making his life miserable with their misery.

L.N. Agarwal's daughter lived in Old Brahmpur in the Shahi Darvaza area, not far from Misri Mandi where her childhood friend Veena Tandon lived. Priya lived in a joint family which included her husband's brothers and their wives and children. Her husband was Ram Vilas Goyal, a lawyer with a practice concentrated mainly in the District Court – though he did appear in the High Court from time to time. He worked mainly on civil, not criminal cases. He was a placid, good-natured, bland-featured man, sparing with his words, and with only a mild interest in politics.

Law and a little business on the side was enough for him; that and a calm family background and the peaceful ratchet of routine, which he expected Priya to provide. His colleagues respected him for his scrupulous honesty and his slow but clear-headed legal abilities. And his father-in-law the Home Minister enjoyed talking to him: he maintained confidences, refrained from giving advice, and had no passion for politics.

Priya Goyal for her part was a fiery spirit. Every morning, winter or summer, she paced fiercely along the roof. It was a long roof, since it covered three contiguous narrow houses, connected lengthways at each of the three storeys. In effect the whole operated as one large house, and was treated as such by the family and the neighbours. It was known locally as the Rai Bahadur's house because Ram Vilas Goyal's grandfather (still alive at eighty-eight), who had been given that title by the British, had bought and restructured the property half a century ago.

On the ground floor were a number of store-rooms and the servants' quarters. On the floor above lived Ram Vilas's ancient grandfather, the Rai Bahadur; his father and stepmother; and his sister. The common kitchen was also located on this floor as was the puja room (which the unpious, even impious Priya rarely visited). On the top floor were the rooms, respectively, of the families of the three brothers; Ram Vilas was the middle brother and he occupied the two rooms of the top floor of the middle 'house'. Above this was the roof with its washing lines and water tanks.

When she paced up and down the roof, Priya Goyal would picture herself as a panther in a cage. She would look longingly towards the small house just a few minutes' walk away – and just visible through the jungle of intervening roofs – in which her childhood friend Veena Tandon lived. Veena, she knew, was not well off any longer, but she was free to do as she pleased: to go to the market, to walk around by herself, to go for music lessons. In Priya's own household there was no question of that. For a daughter-in-law from the house of the Rai Bahadur to be seen in the market would have been disgraceful. That she was thirty-two years old with a girl of ten and a boy of eight was irrelevant. Ram Vilas, ever placid, would have none of it. It was simply not his way; more importantly, it would cause pain to his father and stepmother and grandfather and elder brother – and Ram Vilas sincerely believed in maintaining the decencies of a joint family.

Priya hated living in a joint family. She had never done so until she came to live with the Goyals of Shahi Darvaza. This was because her father, Lakshmi Narayan Agarwal, had been the only son to survive to adulthood, and he in his turn had only had the one daughter. When his wife died, he had been stricken, and had taken the Gandhian vow of sexual abstinence. He was a man of spartan habits. Although Home Minister, he lived in two rooms in a hostel for Members of the Legislative Assembly.

'The first years of married life are the hardest – they require the most adjustment,' Priya had been told; but she felt that in some ways it was getting more and more intolerable as time went on. Unlike Veena, she had no proper paternal – and more importantly, maternal home to run away to with her children for at least a month a year – the prerogative of all married women. Even her grandparents (with whom she had spent the time when her father was in jail) were now dead. Her father loved her dearly as his only child; it was his love that had in a sense spoiled her for the constrained life of the Goyal joint family, for it had imbued her with a spirit of independence; and now, living in austerity as he did, he could not himself provide her with any refuge.

If her husband had not been so kind, she felt she would have gone mad. He did not understand her but he was understanding. He tried to make things easier for her in small ways, and he never once raised his voice. Also, she liked the ancient Rai Bahadur, her grandfather-in-law. There was a spark to him. The rest of the family and particularly the women – her mother-in-law, her husband's sister, and her husband's elder brother's wife – had done their best to make her miserable as a young bride, and she could not stand them. But she had to pretend she did, every day, all the time – except when she paced up and down on the roof – where she was not even permitted to have a garden, on the grounds that it would attract monkeys. Ram Vilas's stepmother had even tried to dissuade her from her daily to-ing and fro-ing ('Just think, Priya, how will it look to the neighbours?'), but for once Priya had refused to go along. The sisters-in-law above whose heads she paced at dawn reported her to their mother-in-law. But perhaps the old witch sensed that she had driven Priya to the limit, and did not phrase her complaint in a direct manner again. Anything indirect on the matter Priya chose not to understand.

L.N. Agarwal came dressed as always in an immaculately starched (but not fancy) kurta, dhoti and Congress cap. Below the white cap could be seen his curve of curly grey hair but not the baldness it enclosed. Whenever he ventured out to Shahi Darvaza he kept his cane handy to scare away the monkeys that frequented, some would say dominated, the neighbourhood. He dismissed his rickshaw near the local market, and turned off the main road into a tiny side-lane which opened out into a small square. In the middle of the square was a large pipal tree. One entire side of the square was the Rai Bahadur's house.

The door below the stairs was kept closed because of the monkeys, and he rapped on it with his cane. A couple of faces appeared at the enclosed wrought-iron balconies of the floors above. His daughter's face lit up when she saw him; she quickly coiled her loose black hair into a bun and came downstairs to open the door. Her father embraced her and they went upstairs again.

'And where has Vakil Sahib disappeared?' he asked in Hindi.

He liked to refer to his son-in-law as the lawyer, although the appellation was equally appropriate to Ram Vilas's father and grandfather.

'He was here a minute ago,' replied Priya, and got up to search for him.

'Don't bother yet,' said her father in a warm, relaxed voice. 'First give me some tea.'

For a few minutes the Home Minister enjoyed home comforts: well-made tea (not the useless stuff he got at the MLA hostel); sweets and kachauris made by the women of his daughter's house – maybe by his daughter herself; some minutes with his grandson and granddaughter, who preferred, however, to play with their friends in the heat on the roof or below in the square (his granddaughter was good at street cricket); and a few words with his daughter, whom he saw rarely enough and missed a great deal.

He had no compunction, as some fathers-in-law had, about accepting food, drink and hospitality at his son-in-law's house. He talked with Priya about his health and his grandchildren and their schooling and character; about how Vakil Sahib was working far too hard, a little about Priya's mother in passing, at the mention of whom a sadness came into both their eyes, and about the antics of the old servants of the Goyal household.

As they talked, other people passed the open door of the room, saw them, and came in. They included Ram Vilas's father, rather a helpless character who was terrorized by his second wife. Soon the whole Goyal clan had dropped by – except for the Rai Bahadur, who did not like climbing stairs.

'But where is Vakil Sahib?' repeated L.N. Agarwal.

'Oh,' said someone, 'he's downstairs talking with the Rai Bahadur. He knows you are in the house and he will come up as soon as he is released.'

'Why don't I go down and pay my respects to the Rai Bahadur now?' said L.N. Agarwal, and got up.

Downstairs, grandfather and grandson were talking in the large room that the Rai Bahadur had reserved as his own – mainly because he was attached to the beautiful peacock tiles that decorated the fireplace. L.N. Agarwal, being of the middle generation, paid his respects and had respects paid to him.

'Of course you'll have tea?' said the Rai Bahadur.

'I've had some upstairs.'

'Since when have Leaders of the People placed a limit on their tea-consumption?' asked the Rai Bahadur in a creaky and lucid voice. The word he used was 'Neta-log', which had about the same level of mock deference as 'Vakil Sahib'.

'Now, tell me,' he continued, 'what is all this killing you've been doing in Chowk?'

It was not meant the way it sounded, it was merely the old Rai Bahadur's style of speech, but L.N. Agarwal could have done without direct examination. He would probably get enough of that on the floor of the House on Monday. What he would have preferred was a quiet chat with his placid son-in-law, an unloading of his troubled mind.

'Nothing, nothing, it will all blow over,' he said.

'I heard that twenty Muslims were killed,' said the old Rai Bahadur philosophically.

'No, not that many,' said L.N. Agarwal. 'A few. Matters are well in hand.' He paused, ruminating on the fact that he had misjudged the situation. 'This is a hard town to manage,' he continued. 'If it isn't one thing it's another. We are an ill-disciplined people. The lathi and the gun are the only things that will teach us discipline.'

'In British days law and order was not such a problem,' said the creaky voice.

The Home Minister did not rise to the Rai Bahadur's bait. In fact, he was not sure that the remark was not delivered innocently.

'Still, there it is,' he responded.

'Mahesh Kapoor's daughter was here the other day,' ventured the Rai Bahadur.

Surely this could not be an innocent comment. Or was it? Perhaps the Rai Bahadur was merely following a train of thought.

'Yes, she is a good girl,' said L.N. Agarwal. He rubbed his perimeter of hair in a thoughtful way. Then, after a pause, he added calmly: 'I can handle the town; it is not the tension that disturbs me. Ten Misri Mandis and twenty Chowks are nothing. It is the politics, the politicians –'

The Rai Bahadur allowed himself a smile. This too was

somewhat creaky, as if the separate plates of his aged face were gradually reconfiguring themselves with difficulty.

L.N. Agarwal shook his head, then went on. 'Until two this morning the MLAs were gathering around me like chicks around their mother. They were in a state of panic. The Chief Minister goes out of town for a few days and see what happens in his absence! What will Sharmaji say when he comes back? What capital will Mahesh Kapoor's faction make out of all this? In Misri Mandi they will emphasize the lot of the jatavs, in Chowk that of the Muslims. What will the effect of all this be on the jatav vote and the Muslim vote? The General Elections are just a few months away. Will these votebanks swing away from the Congress? If so, in what numbers? One or two gentlemen have even asked if there is the danger of further conflagration – though usually this is the least of their concerns.'

'And what do you tell them when they come running to you?' asked the Rai Bahadur. His daughter-in-law – the arch-witch in Priya's demonology – had just brought in the tea. The top of her head was covered with her sari. She poured the tea, gave them a sharp look, exchanged a couple of words, and went out.

The thread of the conversation had been lost, but the Rai Bahadur, perhaps remembering the cross-examinations for which he had been famous in his prime, drew it gently back again.

'Oh, nothing,' said L.N. Agarwal quite calmly. 'I just tell them whatever is necessary to stop them from keeping me awake.'

'Nothing?'

'No, nothing much. Just that things will blow over; that what's done is done; that a little discipline never did a neighbourhood any harm; that the General Elections are still far enough away. That sort of thing.' L.N. Agarwal sipped his tea before continuing: 'The fact of the matter is that the country has far more important things to think about. Food is the main one. Bihar is virtually starving. And if we have a bad monsoon, we will be too. Mere

Muslims threatening us from inside the country or across the border we can deal with. If Nehru were not so soft-hearted we would have dealt with them properly a few years ago. And now these jatavs, these' — his expression conveyed distaste at the words — 'these scheduled caste people are becoming a problem once again. But let's see, let's see. . . .'

Ram Vilas Goyal had sat silent through the whole exchange. Once he frowned slightly, once he nodded.

'That is what I like about my son-in-law,' reflected L.N. Agarwal. 'He's not dumb, but he doesn't speak.' He decided yet again that he had made the right match for his daughter. Priya could provoke, and he would simply not allow himself to be provoked.

5.5

MEANWHILE, upstairs, Priya was talking to Veena, who had come to pay her a visit. But it was more than a social visit, it was an emergency. Veena was very distressed. She had come home and found Kedarnath not merely with his eyes closed but with his head in his hands. This was far worse than his general state of optimistic anxiety. He had not wanted to talk about it, but she had eventually discovered that he was in very grave financial trouble. With the pickets and the stationing of the police in Chowk, the wholesale shoe market had finally ground from a slow-down to a complete halt. Every day now his chits were coming due, and he just did not have the cash to pay them. Those who owed him money, particularly two large stores in Bombay, had deferred paying him for past supplies because they thought he could not ensure future supplies. The supplies he got from people like Jagat Ram, who made shoes to order, were not enough. To fulfil the orders that buyers around the country had placed with him, he needed the shoes of the basket-wallahs, and they did not dare come to Misri Mandi these days.

But the immediate problem was how to pay for the chits

that were coming due. He had no one to go to; all his associates were themselves short of cash. Going to his father-in-law was for him out of the question. He was at his wits' end. He would try once more to talk to his creditors – the moneylenders who held his chits and their commission agents who came to him for payment when they were due. He would try to persuade them that it would do no one any good to drive him and others like him to the wall in a credit squeeze. This situation would surely not last long. He was not insolvent, just illiquid. But even as he spoke he knew what their answer would be. He knew that money, unlike labour, owed no allegiance to a particular trade, and could flow out of shoes and into, say, cold storage facilities without retraining or compunction or doubt. It only asked two questions: 'What interest?' and 'What risk?'

Veena had not come to Priya for financial help, but to ask her how best to sell the jewellery she had got from her mother upon her marriage – and to weep on her shoulder. She had brought the jewellery with her. Only a little had remained from the traumatic days after the family's flight from Lahore. Every piece meant so much to her that she started crying when she thought of losing it. She had only two requests – that her husband not find out until the jewellery had actually been sold; and that for a few weeks at least her father and mother should not know.

They talked quickly, because there was no privacy in the house, and at any moment anyone could walk into Priya's room.

'My father's here,' Priya said. 'Downstairs, talking politics.'

'We will always be friends, no matter what,' said Veena suddenly, and started crying again.

Priya hugged her friend, told her to have courage, and suggested a brisk walk on the roof.

'What, in this heat, are you mad?' asked Veena.

'Why not? It's either heat-stroke or interruption by my mother-in-law – and I know which I'd prefer.'

'I'm scared of your monkeys,' said Veena as a second

line of defence. 'First they fight on the roof of the daal factory, then they leap over onto your roof. Shahi Darvaza should be renamed Hanuman Dwar.'

'You're not scared of anything. I don't believe you,' said Priya. 'In fact, I envy you. You can walk over by yourself any time. Look at me. And look at these bars on the balcony. The monkeys can't come in, and I can't go out.'

'Ah,' said Veena, 'you shouldn't envy me.'

They were silent for a while.

'How is Bhaskar?' asked Priya.

Veena's plump face lit up in a smile, rather a sad one. 'He's very well – as well as your pair, anyway. He insisted on coming along. At the moment they are all playing cricket in the square downstairs. The pipal tree doesn't seem to bother them.... I wish for your sake, Priya, that you had a brother or sister,' Veena added suddenly, thinking of her own childhood.

The two friends went to the balcony and looked down through the wrought-iron grille. Their three children, together with two others, were playing cricket in the small square. Priya's ten-year-old daughter was by far the best of them. She was a fair bowler and a fine batsman. She usually managed to avoid the pipal tree, which gave the others endless trouble.

'Why don't you stay for lunch?' asked Priya.

'I can't,' said Veena, thinking of Kedarnath and her mother-in-law, who would be expecting her. 'Tomorrow perhaps.'

'Tomorrow then.'

Veena left the bag of jewellery with Priya, who locked it up in a steel almirah. As she stood by the cupboard Veena said: 'You're putting on weight.'

'I've always been fat,' said Priya, 'and because I do nothing but sit here all day like a caged bird, I've grown fatter.'

'You're not fat and you never have been,' said her friend. 'And since when have you stopped pacing on the roof?'

'I haven't,' said Priya, 'but one day I'm going to throw myself off it.'

'Now if you talk like that I'm going to leave at once,' said Veena and made to go.

'No, don't go. Seeing you has cheered me up,' said Priya. 'I hope you have lots of bad fortune. Then you'll come running to me all the time. If it hadn't been for Partition you'd never have come back to Brahmpur.'

Veena laughed.

'Come on, let's go to the roof,' continued Priya. 'I really can't talk freely to you here. People are always coming in and listening from the balcony. I hate it here, I'm so unhappy, if I don't tell you I'll burst.' She laughed, and pulled Veena to her feet. 'I'll tell Bablu to get us something cold to prevent heat-stroke.'

Bablu was the weird fifty-year-old servant who had come to the family as a child and had grown more eccentric with each passing year. Lately he had taken to eating everyone's medicines.

When they got to the roof, they sat in the shade of the water-tank and started laughing like schoolgirls.

'We should live next to each other,' said Priya, shaking out her jet black hair, which she had washed and oiled that morning. 'Then, even if I throw myself off my roof, I'll fall onto yours.'

'It would be awful if we lived next to each other,' said Veena, laughing. 'The witch and the scarecrow would get together every afternoon and complain about their daughters-in-law. "O, she's bewitched my son, they play chaupar on the roof all the time, she'll make him as dark as soot. And she sings on the roof so shamelessly to the whole neighbourhood. And she deliberately prepares rich food so that I fill up with gas. One day I'll explode and she'll dance over my bones."'

Priya giggled. 'No,' she said, 'it'll be fine. The two kitchens will face each other, and the vegetables can join us in complaining about our oppression. "O, friend Potato, the khatri scarecrow is boiling me. Tell everyone I died miserably. Farewell, farewell, never forget me." "O friend

Pumpkin, the bania witch has spared me for only another two days. I'll weep for you but I won't be able to attend your chautha. Forgive me, forgive me."'

Veena's laughter bubbled out again. 'Actually, I feel quite sorry for my scarecrow,' she said. 'She had a hard time during Partition. But she was quite horrible to me even in Lahore, even after Bhaskar was born. When she sees I'm not miserable she becomes even more miserable. When we become mothers-in-law, Priya, we'll feed our daughters-in-law ghee and sugar every day.'

'I certainly don't feel sorry for my witch,' said Priya disgustedly. 'And I shall certainly bully my daughter-in-law from morning till night until I've completely crushed her spirit. Women look much more beautiful when they're unhappy, don't you think?' She shook her thick black hair from side to side and glared at the stairs. 'This is a vile house,' she added. 'I'd much rather be a monkey and fight on the roof of the daal factory than a daughter-in-law in the Rai Bahadur's house. I'd run to the market and steal bananas. I'd fight the dogs, I'd snap at the bats. I'd go to Tarbuz ka Bazaar and pinch the bottoms of all the pretty prostitutes. I'd ... do you know what the monkeys did here the other day?'

'No,' said Veena. 'Tell me.'

'I was just going to. Bablu, who is getting crazier by the minute, placed the Rai Bahadur's alarm clocks on the ledge. Well, the next thing we saw was three monkeys in the pipal tree, examining them, saying, "Mmmmmmm", "Mmmmmmmm", in a high-pitched voice, as if to say, "Well? We have your clocks. What now?" The witch went out. We didn't have the little packets of wheat which we usually bribe them with, so she took some musammis and bananas and carrots and tried to tempt them down, saying, "Here, here, come, beautiful ones, come, come, I swear by Hanuman I'll give you lovely things to eat...." And they came down all right, one by one they came down, very cautiously, each with a clock tucked beneath his arm. Then they began to eat the food, first with one hand, like this – then, putting the clocks down, with both hands.

Well – no sooner were all three clocks on the ground than the witch took a stick which she had hidden behind her back and threatened their lives with it – using such filthy language that I was forced to admire her. The carrot and the stick, don't they say in English? So the story has a happy ending. But the monkeys of Shahi Darvaza are very smart. They know what they can hold up to ransom, and what they can't.'

Bablu had come up the stairs, gripping with four dirty fingers of one hand four glasses of cold nimbu pani filled almost to the brim. 'Here!' he said, setting them down. 'Drink! If you sit in the sun like this, you'll catch pneumonia.' Then he disappeared.

'The same as ever?' asked Veena.

'The same, but even more so,' said Priya. 'Nothing changes. The only comforting constant here is that Vakil Sahib snores as loudly as ever. Sometimes at night when the bed vibrates, I think he'll disappear, and all that will be left for me to weep over will be his snore. But I can't tell you some of the things that go on in this house,' she added darkly. 'You're lucky you don't have much money. What people will do for money, Veena, I can't tell you. And what does it go into? Not into education or art or music or literature – no, it all goes into jewellery. And the women of the house have to wear ten tons of it on their necks at every wedding. And you should see them all sizing each other up. Oh, Veena –' she said, suddenly realizing her insensitivity, 'I have a habit of blabbering. Tell me to be quiet.'

'No, no, I'm enjoying it,' said Veena. 'But tell me, when the jeweller comes to your house next time will you be able to get an estimate? For the small pieces – and, well, especially for my navratan? Will you be able to get a few minutes with him alone so that your mother-in-law doesn't come to know? If I had to go to a jeweller myself I'd certainly be cheated. But you know all about these things.'

Priya nodded. 'I'll try,' she said. The navratan was a lovely piece; she had last seen it round Veena's neck at Pran and Savita's wedding. It consisted of an arc of nine square gold compartments, each the setting of a different precious stone, with delicate enamel work at the sides and even on the back, where it could not be seen. Topaz, white sapphire, emerald, blue sapphire, ruby, diamond, pearl, catseye and coral: instead of looking cluttered and disordered, the heavy necklace had a wonderful combination of traditional solidity and charm. For Veena it had more than that: of all her mother's gifts it was the one she loved most.

'I think our fathers are mad to dislike each other so much,' said Priya out of the blue. 'Who cares who the next Chief Minister of Purva Pradesh will be?'

Veena nodded as she sipped her nimbu pani.

'What news of Maan?' asked Priya.

They gossiped on: Maan and Saeeda Bai; the Nawab Sahib's daughter and whether her situation in purdah was worse than Priya's; Savita's pregnancy; even, at secondhand, Mrs Rupa Mehra, and how she was trying to corrupt her samdhins by teaching them rummy.

They had forgotten about the world. But suddenly Bablu's large head and rounded shoulders appeared at the top of the stairs. 'Oh my God,' said Priya with a start. 'My duties in the kitchen – since I've been talking to you, they've gone straight out of my head. My mother-in-law must have finished her stupid rigmarole of cooking her own food in a wet dhoti after her bath, and she's yelling for me. I've got to run. She does it for purity, so she says – though she doesn't mind that we have cockroaches the size of buffaloes running around all over the house, and rats that bite off your hair at night if you don't wash the oil off. Oh, do stay for lunch, Veena, I never get to see you!'

'I really can't,' said Veena. 'The Sleeper likes his food just so. And so does the Snorer, I'm sure.'

'Oh, he's not so particular,' said Priya, frowning. 'He puts up with all my nonsense. But I can't go out, I can't go out, I can't go out anywhere except for weddings and the odd trip to the temple or a religious fair and you know what I think of those. If he wasn't so good, I would go completely mad. Wife-beating is something of a common

334

sport in our neighbourhood, you aren't considered much
of a man if you don't slap your wife around a couple of
times, but Ram Vilas wouldn't even beat a drum at Dussehra. And he's so respectful to the witch it makes me sick,
though she's only his stepmother. They say he's so nice to
witnesses that they tell him the truth – even though they're
in court! Well, if you can't stay, you must come tomorrow.
Promise me again.'

Veena promised, and the two friends went down to the
room on the top floor. Priya's daughter and son were
sitting on the bed, and they informed Veena that Bhaskar
had gone back home.

'What? By himself?' said Veena anxiously.

'He's nine years old, and it's five minutes away,' said the
boy.

'Shh!' said Priya. 'Speak properly to your elders.'

'I'd better go at once,' said Veena.

On the way down, Veena met L.N. Agarwal coming up.
The stairs were narrow and steep. She pressed herself
against the wall and said namasté. He acknowledged the
greeting with a 'Jeeti raho, beti', and went up.

But though he had addressed her as 'daughter', Veena
felt that he had been reminded the instant he saw her of
the ministerial rival whose daughter she really was.

5.6

'IS the Government aware that the Brahmpur Police made
a lathi charge on the members of the jatav community last
week when they demonstrated in front of the Govind Shoe
Mart?'

The Minister for Home Affairs, Shri L.N. Agarwal, got
to his feet.

'There was no lathi charge,' he replied.

'Mild lathi charge, if you like. Is the Government aware
of the incident I am referring to?'

The Home Minister looked across the well of the great
circular chamber, and stated calmly:

'There was no lathi charge in the usual sense. The police were forced to use light canes, one inch thick, when the unruly crowd had stoned and manhandled several members of the public and one policeman, and when it was apparent that the safety of the Govind Shoe Mart, and of the public, and of the policemen themselves was seriously threatened.'

He stared at his interrogator, Ram Dhan, a short, dark, pockmarked man in his forties, who asked his questions – in standard Hindi but with a strong Brahmpuri accent – with his arms folded across his chest.

'Is it a fact,' continued the questioner, 'that on the same evening, the police beat up a large number of jatavs who were peacefully attempting to picket the Brahmpur Shoe Mart nearby?' Shri Ram Dhan was an Independent MLA from the scheduled castes, and he stressed the word 'jatavs'. A kind of indignant murmur rose from all around the House. The Speaker called for order, and the Home Minister stood up again.

'It is not a fact,' he stated, keeping his voice level. 'The police, being hard pressed by an angry mob, defended themselves and, in the course of this action, three people were injured. As for the honourable member's innuendo that the police singled out members of a particular caste from the mob or were especially severe because the mob consisted largely of members of that caste, I would advise him to be more just to the police. Let me assure him that the action would have been no different had the mob been constituted differently.'

Limpet-like, however, Shri Ram Dhan continued: 'Is it a fact that the honourable Home Minister was in constant touch with the local authorities of Brahmpur, in particular the District Magistrate and the Superintendent of Police?'

'Yes.' L.N. Agarwal looked upwards, having delivered himself of this single syllable and as if seeking patience, towards the great dome of white frosted glass through which the late morning light poured down on the Legislative Assembly.

'Was the specific sanction of the Home Minister taken

by the district authorities before making the lathi charge on the unarmed mob? If so, when? If not, why not?'

The Home Minister sighed with exasperation rather than weariness as he stood up again: 'May I reiterate that I do not accept the use of the words "lathi charge" in this context. Nor was the mob unarmed, since they used stones. However, I am glad that the honourable member admits that it was a mob that the police were facing. Indeed, from the fact that he uses the word in a printed, starred question, it is clear that he knew this before today.'

'Would the honourable Minister kindly answer the question put to him?' said Ram Dhan heatedly, opening his arms and clenching his fists.

'I should have thought the answer was obvious,' said L.N. Agarwal. He paused, then continued, as if reciting: 'The developing situation on the ground is sometimes such that it is often tactically impossible to foresee what will happen, and a certain flexibility must be left to the local authorities.'

But Ram Dhan clung on. 'If, as the honourable Minister admits, no such specific sanction was taken, was the honourable Home Minister informed of the proposed action of the police? Did he or the Chief Minister give their tacit approval?'

Once again the Home Minister rose. He glanced at a point in the dead centre of the dark green carpet that covered the well. 'The action was not premeditated. It had to be taken forthwith in order to meet a grave situation which had suddenly developed. It did not admit of any previous reference to Government.'

A member shouted: 'And what about the Chief Minister?'

The Speaker of the House, a learned but not normally very assertive man who was dressed in a kurta and dhoti, looked down from his high platform below the seal of Purva Pradesh – a great pipal tree – and said: 'These short-order starred questions are addressed specifically to the honourable Home Minister, and his answers must be taken to be sufficient.'

Several voices now rose. One, dominating the others, boomed out: 'Since the honourable Chief Minister is present in the House after his travels in other parts, perhaps he would care to oblige us with an answer even though he is not compelled by the Standing Orders to do so? I believe the House would appreciate it.'

The Chief Minister, Shri S.S. Sharma, stood up without his stick, leaned with his left hand on his dark wooden desk and looked to his left and right. He was positioned along the curve of the central well, almost exactly between L.N. Agarwal and Mahesh Kapoor. He addressed the Speaker in his nasal, rather paternal, voice, nodding his head gently as he did so: 'I have no objection to speaking, Mr Speaker, but I have nothing to add. The action taken – call it by what name the honourable members will – was taken under the aegis of the responsible Cabinet Minister.' There was a pause, during which it was not clear what the Chief Minister was going to add, if anything. 'Whom I naturally support,' he said.

He had not even sat down when the inexorable Ram Dhan came back into the fray. 'I am much obliged to the honourable Chief Minister,' he said, 'but I would like to seek a clarification. By saying that he supports the Home Minister, does the Chief Minister mean to imply that he approves of the policy of the district authorities?'

Before the Chief Minister could reply, the Home Minister quickly rose again to say: 'I hope that we have made ourselves clear on this point. It was not a case of prior approval. An inquiry was held immediately after the incident. The District Magistrate went into the matter fully and found that the very minimum force which was absolutely unavoidable was used. The Government regret that such an occasion should have arisen, but are satisfied that the finding of the District Magistrate is correct. It was accepted by practically all concerned that the authorities faced a serious situation with tact and due restraint.'

A member of the Socialist Party stood up. 'Is it true,' he asked, 'that it was on the prodding of members of the bania trading community to which he belongs that the honourable Home Minister' – angry murmurs rose from the Government benches – 'let me finish – that the Minister subsequently posted troops – I mean police – throughout the length and breadth of Misri Mandi?'

'I disallow that question,' said the Speaker.

'Well,' continued the member, 'would the honourable Minister kindly inform us on whose advice he decided on the placing of this threatening body of police?'

The Home Minister grasped the curve of hair under his cap and said: 'Government made its own decision, bearing the totality of the situation in mind. And in the event it has proved to be effective. There is peace at last in Misri Mandi.'

A babble of indignant shouts, earnest chatter and ostentatious laughter arose on all sides. There were shouts of 'What peace?' 'Shame!' 'Who is the DM to judge the matter?' 'What about the mosque?' and so on.

'Order! Order!' cried the Speaker, looking flustered as another member rose to his feet and said:

'Will the Government consider the advisability of creating machineries other than the interested district authorities for making inquiries in such cases?'

'I do not allow this question,' said the Speaker, shaking his head like a sparrow. 'Under Standing Orders questions making suggestions for action are not permissible and I am not prepared to allow them during Question Time.'

It was the end of the Home Minister's grilling on the Misri Mandi incident. Though there had been only five questions on the printed sheet, the supplementary questions had given the exchange the character almost of a cross-examination. The intervention of the Chief Minister had been more disturbing than reassuring to L.N. Agarwal. Was S.S. Sharma, in his wily, indirect way, trying to palm off full responsibility for the action onto his second-in-command? L.N. Agarwal sat down, sweating slightly, but he knew that he would have to be on his feet immediately again. And, though he prided himself on maintaining his calm in difficult circumstances, he did not relish what he would now have to face.

BEGUM ABIDA KHAN slowly stood up. She was dressed in a dark blue, almost black, sari, and her pale and furious face riveted the house even before she began to speak. She was the wife of the Nawab of Baitar's younger brother, and one of the leaders of the Democratic Party, the party that sought to protect the interests of the landowners in the face of the impending passage of the Zamindari Abolition Bill. Although a Shia, she had the reputation of being an aggressive protector of the rights of all Muslims in the new, truncated Independent India. Her husband, like his father, had been a member of the Muslim League before Independence and had left for Pakistan shortly afterwards. Despite the powerful persuasion and reproach of many relatives, she, however, had chosen not to go. 'I'll be useless there, sitting and gossiping. Here in Brahmpur at least I know where I am and what I can do,' she had said. And this morning she knew exactly what she wanted to do. Looking straight at the man whom she considered to be one of the less savoury manifestations of humankind, she began her questioning from her list of starred questions.

'Is the honourable Minister for Home Affairs aware that at least five people were killed by the police in the firing near Chowk last Friday?'

The Home Minister, who at the best of times could not stand the Begum, replied: 'Indeed, I was not.'

It was somewhat obstructive of him not to elaborate, but he did not feel like being forthcoming before this pale harridan.

Begum Abida Khan veered from her script. 'Will the honourable Minister inform us exactly what he is aware of?' she inquired acidly.

'I disallow that question,' murmured the Speaker.

'What would the honourable Minister say was the death toll in the firing in Chowk?' demanded Begum Abida Khan.

'One,' said L. N. Agarwal.

Begum Abida Khan's voice was incredulous: 'One?' she cried. 'One?'

'One,' replied the Home Minister, holding up the index finger of his right hand, as if to an idiot child who had difficulty with numbers or hearing or both.

Begum Abida Khan cried out angrily: 'If I may inform the honourable Minister, it was at least five, and I have good proof of this fact. Here are copies of the death certificates of four of the deceased. Indeed, it is likely that two more men will shortly –'

'I rise on a point of order, Sir,' said L.N. Agarwal, ignoring her and addressing the Speaker directly. 'I understand that Question Time is used for getting information from and not for giving information to Ministers.'

Begum Abida Khan's voice continued regardless: '– two more men will shortly be receiving such certificates of honour thanks to the henchmen of the honourable Minister. I would like to table these death certificates – these copies of death certificates.'

'I am afraid that that is not possible under the Standing Orders....' protested the Speaker.

Begum Abida Khan waved the documents around, and raised her voice higher: 'The newspapers have copies of them, why is the House not entitled to see them? When the blood of innocent men, of mere boys, is being callously shed –'

'The honourable member will not use Question Time to make speeches,' said the Speaker, and banged his gavel.

Begum Abida Khan suddenly pulled herself together, and once again addressed L.N. Agarwal.

'Will the honourable Minister kindly inform the House on what basis he came to the total figure of one?'

'The report was furnished by the District Magistrate, who was present at the time of the event.'

'By "present" you mean that he ordered the mowing down of these unfortunate people, is that not so?'

L.N. Agarwal paused before answering:

'The District Magistrate is a seasoned officer, who took whatever steps he considered the situation required. As the honourable member is aware, an inquiry under a more senior officer will shortly be made, as it is in all cases of an order to fire; and I suggest to her that we wait until such time as the report is published before we give vent to speculation.'

'Speculation?' burst out Begum Abida Khan. 'Speculation? Do you call this speculation? You should be – the honourable Minister' – she emphasized the word maananiya or honourable – 'the honourable Minister should be ashamed of himself. I have seen the corpses of two men with these very eyes. I am not speculating. If it were the blood of his own co-religionists that was flowing in the streets, the honourable Minister would not "wait until such time". We know of the overt and tacit support he gives that foul organization the Linga Rakshak Samiti, set up expressly to destroy the sanctity of our mosque –'

The House was getting increasingly excited under her oratory, inappropriate though it may have been. L.N. Agarwal was grasping his curve of grey hair with his right hand, tense as a claw, and – having cast his calm demeanour to the winds – was glaring at her at every scornful 'honourable'. The frail-looking Speaker made another attempt to stem the flow:

'The honourable member may perhaps need reminding that according to my Question List, she has three starred questions remaining.'

'I thank you, Sir,' said Begum Abida Khan. 'I shall come to them. In fact I shall ask the next one immediately. It is very germane to the subject. Will the honourable Minister of Home Affairs inform us whether prior to the firings in Chowk a warning to disperse was read out under Section 144 of the Criminal Procedure Code? If so, when? If not, why not?'

Brutally and angrily L.N. Agarwal replied:

'It was not. It could not have been. There was no time to do so. If people start riots for religious reasons and attempt to destroy temples they must accept the consequences. Or mosques, of course, for that matter –'

But now Begum Abida Khan was almost shouting. 'Riot?

Riot? How does the honourable Minister come to the conclusion that that was the intention of the crowd? It was the time of evening prayer. They were proceeding to the mosque –'

'From all reports, it was obvious. They were rushing forward violently, shouting with their accustomed zealotry, and brandishing weapons,' said the Home Minister.

There was uproar.

A member of the Socialist Party cried: 'Was the honourable Minister present?'

A member of the Congress Party said: 'He can't be everywhere.'

'But this was brutal,' shouted someone else. 'They fired at point-blank range.'

'Honourable members are reminded that the Minister is to answer his own questions,' cried the Speaker.

'I thank you, Sir –' began the Home Minister. But to his utter amazement and, indeed, horror, a Muslim member of the Congress Party, Abdus Salaam, who happened also to be Parliamentary Secretary to the Revenue Minister, now rose to ask: 'How could such a grave step – an order to fire – have been taken without either giving due warning to disperse or attempting to ascertain the intention of the crowd?'

That Abdus Salaam should have risen to his feet shocked the House. In a sense it was not clear where he was addressing the question – he was looking at an indeterminate point somewhere to the right of the great seal of Purva Pradesh above the Speaker's chair. He seemed, in fact, to be thinking aloud. He was a scholarly young man, known particularly for his excellent understanding of land tenure law, and was one of the chief architects of the Purva Pradesh Zamindari Abolition Bill. That he should make common cause with a leader of the Democratic Party – the party of the zamindars – on this issue, stunned members of all parties. Mahesh Kapoor himself was surprised at this intervention by his Parliamentary Secretary and turned around with a frown, not entirely pleased. The Chief Minister scowled. L.N. Agarwal was gripped with outrage and humiliation. Several members of the House were on their feet, waving their order papers, and no one, not even the Speaker, could be clearly heard. It was becoming a free-for-all.

When, after repeated thumps of the Speaker's gavel, a semblance of order was restored, the Home Minister, though still in shock, rose to ask:

'May I know, Sir, whether a Parliamentary Secretary to a Minister is authorized to put questions to Government?'

Abdus Salaam, looking around in bewilderment, amazed by the furore he had unwittingly caused, said: 'I withdraw.'

But now there were cries of: 'No, no!' 'How can you do that?' and 'If you won't ask it, I will'.

The Speaker sighed.

'As far as procedure is concerned, every member is at liberty to put questions,' he ruled.

'Why then?' asked a member angrily. 'Why was it done? Will the honourable Minister answer or not?'

'I did not catch the question,' said L.N. Agarwal. 'I believe it has been withdrawn.'

'I am asking, like the other member, why no one found out what the crowd wanted? How did the DM know it was violent?' repeated the member.

'There should be an adjournment motion on this,' cried another.

'The Speaker already has such a notice with him,' said a third.

Over all this rose the piercing voice of Begum Abida Khan: 'It was as brutal as the violence of Partition. A youth was killed who was not even part of the demonstration. Would the honourable Minister for Home Affairs care to explain how this happened?' She sat down and glared.

'Demonstration?' said L.N. Agarwal with an air of forensic triumph.

'Crowd, rather —' said the battling Begum, leaping up again and slipping out of his coils. 'You are not going to deny, surely, that it was the time of prayer? The demonstration – the demonstration of gross inhumanity, for that is what it was – was on the part of the police. Now will the honourable Minister not take refuge in semantics and deal with the facts.'

When he saw the wretched woman get up again, the Home Minister felt a stab of hatred in his heart. She was a thorn in his flesh and had insulted and humiliated him before the House and he now decided that, come what may, he was going to get back at her and her house – the family of the Nawab Sahib of Baitar. They were all fanatics, these Muslims, who appeared not to realize they were here in this country on sufferance. A calm dose of well-applied law would do them good.

'I can only answer one question at a time,' L.N. Agarwal said in a dangerous growl.

'The supplementary questions of the honourable member who asked the starred questions will take precedence,' said the Speaker.

Begum Abida Khan smiled grimly.

The Home Minister said: 'We must wait till the report is published. Government is not aware that an innocent youth was fired upon, let alone injured or killed.'

Now Abdus Salaam stood up again. From around the House outraged cries rose: 'Sit down, sit down.' 'Shame!' 'Why are you attacking your own side?'

'Why should he sit down?' 'What have you got to hide?' 'You are a Congress member – you should know better'.

But so unprecedented was the situation that even those who opposed his intervention were curious.

When the cries had died down to a sort of volatile muttering, Abdus Salaam, still looking rather puzzled, asked: 'What I have been wondering about during the course of this discussion is, well, why was a deterrent police force – well, maybe just an adequate police force – not maintained at the site of the temple? Then there would have been no need to fire in this panicky manner.'

The Home Minister drew in his breath. Everyone is looking at me, he thought. I must control my expression.

'Is this supplementary question addressed to the honourable Minister?' asked the Speaker.

'Yes, it is, Sir,' said Abdus Salaam, suddenly determined. 'I will not withdraw this question. Would the honourable Minister inform us why there was not a sufficient and deterrent police force maintained either at the kotwali or at the site of the temple itself? Why were there only a dozen men left to maintain law and order in this grievously disturbed area, especially after the contents of the Friday sermon at the Alamgiri Mosque became known to the authorities?'

This was the question that L.N. Agarwal had been dreading, and he was appalled and enraged that it had been asked by an MLA from his own party, and a Parliamentary Secretary at that. He felt defenceless. Was this a plot by Mahesh Kapoor to undermine him? He looked at the Chief Minister, who was waiting for his response with an unreadable expression. L.N. Agarwal suddenly realized that he had been on his feet for a long time, and wanted very badly to urinate. And he wanted to get out of here as quickly as possible. He began to take refuge in the kind of stonewalling that the Chief Minister himself often used, but to much shabbier effect than that master of parliamentary evasion. By now, however, he hardly cared. He was convinced that this was indeed a plot by Muslims and so-called secular Hindus to attack him – and that his own party had been infected with treason.

Looking with calm hatred first at Abdus Salaam, then at Begum Abida Khan, he said: 'I can merely reiterate – wait for the report.'

A member asked: 'Why were so many police diverted to Misri Mandi for a totally unnecessary show of force when they were really needed in Chowk?'

'Wait for the report,' said the Home Minister, glaring around the House, as if challenging the members to goad him further.

Begum Abida Khan stood up. 'Has the Government taken any action against the District Magistrate responsible for this unprovoked firing?' she demanded.

'The question does not arise.'

'If the much-anticipated report shows that the firing was uncalled for and irregular, does Government plan to take any steps in this regard?'

'That will be seen in due course. I should think it might.'

'What steps does Government intend to take?'

'Proper and adequate steps.'

'Has Government taken any such steps in similar situations in the past?'

'It has.'

'What are those steps that have been taken?'

'Such steps as were considered reasonable and proper.'

Begum Abida Khan looked at him as she would at a snake, wounded but still evading the final blow by twisting its head from side to side. Well, she was not done with him yet.

'Will the honourable Minister name the wards or neighbourhoods in which restrictions have now been placed with regard to the possession of cold steel? Have these restrictions been placed as the result of the recent firing? If so, why were they not placed earlier?'

The Home Minister looked at the pipal tree in the great seal, and said:

'Government presumes that the honourable member means by the phrase "cold steel" objects such as swords, daggers, axes, and similar weapons.'

'Household knives have also been wrested by the police from housewives,' said Begum Abida Khan in more of a jeer than a statement. 'Well, what are the neighbourhoods?'

'Chowk, Hazrat Mahal, and Captainganj,' said L.N. Agarwal.

'Not Misri Mandi?'

'No.'

'Although that was the site of the heaviest police presence?' persisted Begum Abida Khan.

'Police had to be shifted in large numbers to the real trouble spots –' began L.N. Agarwal.

347

He stopped abruptly, realizing too late how he had exposed himself by what he had started to say.

'So the honourable Minister admits –' began Begum Abida Khan, her eyes gleaming triumphantly.

'The Government admits nothing. The report will detail everything,' said the Home Minister, appalled by the confession she had elicited from him.

Begum Abida Khan smiled contemptuously, and decided that the reactionary, trigger-happy, anti-Muslim bully had just condemned himself out of his own mouth sufficiently for much further skewering to be productive. She let her questions taper away.

'Why were these restrictions on cold steel imposed?'

'In order to prevent crimes and incidents of violence.'

'Incidents?'

'Such as riots by inflamed mobs,' he cried out in weary rage.

'How long will these restrictions continue?' asked Begum Abida Khan, almost laughing.

'Till they are withdrawn.'

'And when does the Government propose to withdraw these restrictions?'

'As soon as the situation permits.'

Begum Abida Khan gently sat down.

There followed a notice for adjournment of the House in order to discuss the issue of the firing, but the Speaker disposed of this quickly enough. Adjournment motions were only granted in the most exceptional cases of crisis or emergency, where discussion could brook no delay; to grant them or not was in the Speaker's absolute discretion. The subject of the police firing, even had it been such a subject – which, to his mind, it was not – had been sufficiently aired already. The questions of that remarkable, almost unreinable woman had virtually become a debate.

The Speaker went on to the next items on the day's business: first, the announcement of bills passed by the state legislature that had received the assent of the Governor of the state or the President of India; next, the most important matter on the agenda for the entire session: the continuing debate on the Zamindari Abolition Bill.

But L.N. Agarwal did not stay to listen to discussions on the bill. As soon as the notice for an adjournment motion had been rejected by the Speaker, he fled – not directly across the well to the exit but along an aisle to the perimeter gallery, and then along the dark, wood-panelled wall. His tension and animus were palpable in the way he walked. He was unconsciously crushing his order papers in his hand. Several members tried to talk to him, to sympathize with him. He brushed them off. He walked unseeingly to the exit, and made straight for the bathroom.

5.8

L.N. AGARWAL undid the draw-string of his pyjamas and stood at the urinal. But he was so angry that he was unable to urinate for a while.

He stared at the long, white-tiled wall and saw in it an image of the packed chamber, the taunting face of Begum Abida Khan, the furrowed academic expression of Abdus Salaam, Mahesh Kapoor's uninterpretable frown, the patient but condescending look on the face of the Chief Minister as he had fumbled pathetically through the poisonous swamp of Question Time.

There was no one in the lavatory except a couple of sweepers, and they were talking to each other. A few words of their conversation broke in upon L.N. Agarwal's fury. They were complaining about the difficulties of obtaining grain even at the government ration shops. They talked casually, not paying any attention to the powerful Home Minister and very little attention to their own work. As they continued to talk, a feeling of unreality descended upon L.N. Agarwal. He was taken out of his own world, his own passions, ambitions, hatreds and ideals into a realization of the continuing and urgent lives of people other than himself. He even felt a little ashamed of himself.

The sweepers were now discussing a movie that one of them had seen. It happened to be *Deedar*.

'But it was Daleep Kumar's role – oh – it brought tears to my eyes – he always has that quiet smile on his lips even when singing the saddest songs – such a good-natured man – blind himself, and yet giving pleasure to the whole world –'

He began humming one of the hit songs from the movie – 'Do not forget the days of childhood. . . .'

The second man, who had not seen the movie yet, joined in the song – which, ever since the film had been released, was on almost everyone's lips.

He now said: 'Nargis looked so beautiful on the poster I thought I would see the movie last night, but my wife takes my money from me as soon as I get my pay.'

The first man laughed. 'If she let you keep the money, all she would see of it would be empty envelopes and empty bottles.'

The second man continued wistfully, trying to conjure up the divine images of his heroine. 'So, tell me, what was she like? How did she act? What a contrast – that cheap dancing girl Nimmi or Pimmi or whatever her name is – and Nargis – so high-class, so delicate.'

The first man grunted. 'Give me Nimmi any day, I'd rather live with her than with Nargis – Nargis is too thin, too full of herself. Anyway, what's the difference in class between them? She was also one of those.'

The second man looked shocked. 'Nargis?'

'Yes, yes, your Nargis. How do you think she got her first chance in the movies?' And he laughed and began to hum to himself again. The other man was silent and began to scrub the floor once more.

L.N. Agarwal's thoughts, as he listened to the sweepers talking, turned from Nargis to another 'one of those' – Saeeda Bai – and to the now commonplace gossip about her relationship with Mahesh Kapoor's son. Good! he thought. Mahesh Kapoor may starch his delicately embroidered kurtas into rigidity, but his son lies at the feet of prostitutes.

Though less possessed by rage, he had once again entered his own familiar world of politics and rivalry. He walked along the curved corridor that led to his room. He knew, however, that as soon as he entered his office, he would be set upon by his anxious supporters. What little calm he had achieved in the last few minutes would be destroyed.

'No – I'll go to the library instead,' he muttered to himself.

Upstairs, in the cool, quiet precincts of the library of the Legislative Assembly, he sat down, took off his cap, and rested his chin on his hands. A couple of other MLAs were sitting and reading at the long wooden tables. They looked up, greeted him, and continued with their work. L.N. Agarwal closed his eyes and tried to make his mind blank. He needed to establish his equanimity again before he faced the legislators below. But the image that came before him was not the blank nothingness he sought, but the spurious blankness of the urinal wall. His thoughts turned to the virulent Begum Abida Khan once more, and once more he had to fight down his rage and humiliation. How little there was in common between this shameless, exhibitionistic woman who smoked in private and screeched in public, who had not even followed her husband when he had left for Pakistan but had immodestly and spouselessly remained in Purva Pradesh to make trouble – and his own late wife, Priya's mother, who had sweetened his life through her years of selfless care and love.

I wonder if some part of Baitar House could be construed as evacuee property now that that woman's husband is living in Pakistan, thought L.N. Agarwal. A word to the Custodian, an order to the police, and let's see what I am able to do.

After ten minutes of thought, he got up, nodded at the two MLAs, and went downstairs to his room.

A few MLAs were already sitting in his room when he arrived, and several more gathered in the next few minutes as they came to know that he was holding court. Imperturbable, even smiling slightly to himself, L.N. Agarwal now held forth as he was accustomed to doing. He calmed

351

down his agitated followers, he placed matters in perspective, he mapped out strategy. To one of the MLAs, who had commiserated with his leader because the twin misfortunes of Misri Mandi and Chowk had fallen simultaneously upon him, L.N. Agarwal replied:

'You are a case in point that a good man will not make a good politician. Just think – if you had to do a number of outrageous things, would you want the public to forget them or remember them?'

Clearly the answer was intended to be 'Forget them,' and this was the MLA's response.

'As quickly as possible?' asked L.N. Agarwal.

'As quickly as possible, Minister Sahib.'

'Then the answer,' said L.N. Agarwal, 'if you have a number of outrageous things to do is to do them simultaneously. People will scatter their complaints, not concentrate them. When the dust settles, at least two or three out of five battles will be yours. And the public has a short memory. As for the firing in Chowk, and those dead rioters, it will all be stale news in a week.'

The MLA looked doubtful, but nodded in agreement.

'A lesson here and there,' went on L.N. Agarwal, 'never did anyone any harm. Either you rule, or you don't. The British knew that they had to make an example sometimes – that's why they blew the mutineers from cannons in 1857. Anyway, people are always dying – and I would prefer death by a bullet to death by starvation.'

Needless to say, this was not a choice that faced him. But he was in a philosophical mood.

'Our problems are very simple, you know. In fact, they all boil down to two things: lack of food and lack of morality. And the policies of our rulers in Delhi – what shall I say? – don't help either much.'

'Now that Sardar Patel is dead, no one can control Panditji,' remarked one young but very conservative MLA.

'Even before Patel died who would Nehru listen to?' said L.N. Agarwal dismissively. 'Except, of course, his great Muslim friend – Maulana Azad.'

He clutched his arc of grey hair, then turned to his personal assistant. 'Get me the Custodian on the phone.'

'Custodian – of Enemy Property, Sir?' asked the PA.

Very calmly and slowly and looking him full in the face, the Home Minister said to his rather scatterbrained PA: 'There is no war on. Use what intelligence God has given you. I would like to talk to the Custodian of Evacuee Property. I will talk to him in fifteen minutes.'

After a while he continued: 'Look at our situation today. We beg America for food, we have to buy whatever we can get from China and Russia, there's virtual famine in our neighbouring state. Last year landless labourers were selling themselves for five rupees each. And instead of giving the farmers and the traders a free hand so that they can produce more and store things better and distribute them efficiently, Delhi forces us to impose price controls and government godowns and rationing and every populist and unthought-out measure possible. It isn't just their hearts that are soft, it is their brains as well.'

'Panditji means well,' said someone.

'Means well – means well –' sighed L.N. Agarwal. 'He meant well when he gave away Pakistan. He meant well when he gave away half of Kashmir. If it hadn't been for Patel, we wouldn't even have the country that we do. Jawaharlal Nehru has built up his entire career by meaning well. Gandhiji loved him because he meant well. And the poor, stupid people love him because he means well. God save us from people who mean well. And these well-meaning letters he writes every month to the Chief Ministers. Why does he bother to write them? The Chief Ministers are not delighted to read them.' He shook his head, and continued: 'Do you know what they contain? Long homilies about Korea and the dismissal of General MacArthur. What is General MacArthur to us? – Yet so noble and sensitive is our Prime Minister that he considers all the ills of the world to be his own. He means well about Nepal and Egypt and God knows what else, and expects us to mean well too. He doesn't have the least idea of administration but he talks about the kind of food committees we should set up. Nor does he understand our society and our scriptures, yet he wants to overturn our family life and our family morals through his wonderful Hindu Code Bill. . . .'

L.N. Agarwal would have gone on with his own homily for quite a while if his PA had not said, 'Sir, the Custodian is on the line.'

'All right then,' said L.N. Agarwal, with a slight wave of his hand, which the others knew was a signal to withdraw. 'I'll see you all in the canteen.'

Left alone, the Home Minister talked for ten minutes to the Custodian of Evacuee Property. The discussion was precise and cold. For another few minutes the Home Minister sat at his desk, wondering if he had left any aspect of the matter ambiguous or vulnerable. He came to the conclusion that he had not.

He then got up, and walked rather wearily to the Assembly canteen. In the old days his wife used to send him a tiffin-carrier containing his simple food prepared exactly the way he liked it. Now he was at the mercy of indifferent cooks and their institutional cooking. There was a limit even to asceticism.

As he walked along the curved corridor he was reminded of the presence of the central chamber that the corridors circumscribed – the huge, domed chamber whose height and majestic elegance made almost trivial the frenetic and partisan proceedings below. But his insight did not succeed, except momentarily, in detaching his mind from this morning's events and the bitterness that they had aroused in him, nor did it make him regret in the least what he had been planning and preparing a few minutes ago.

5.9

THOUGH it had been less than five minutes since he had sent off the peon to fetch his Parliamentary Secretary, Mahesh Kapoor was waiting in the Legal Remembrancer's Office with great impatience. He was alone, as he had sent the regular occupants of the office scurrying about to get various papers and law-books.

'Ah, Huzoor has brought his presence to the Secretariat at last!' he said when he saw Abdus Salaam.

Abdus Salaam did a respectful — or was it ironical? — adaab, and asked what he could do.

'I'll come to that in a moment. The question is what you've done already.'

'Already?' Abdus Salaam was nonplussed.

'This morning. On the floor of the House. Making a kabab out of our honourable Home Minister.'

'I only asked —'

'I know what you only asked, Salaam,' said his Minister with a smile. 'I'm asking you why you asked it.'

'I was wondering why the police —'

'My good fool,' said Mahesh Kapoor fondly, 'don't you realize that Lakshmi Narayan Agarwal thinks I put you up to it?'

'You?'

'Yes, me!' Mahesh Kapoor was in good humour, thinking of this morning's proceedings and his rival's extreme discomfiture. 'It's exactly the kind of thing he would do — so he imagines the same of me. Tell me' — he went on — 'did he go to the canteen for lunch?'

'Oh, yes.'

'And was the Chief Minister there? What did he have to say?'

'No, Sharma Sahib was not there.'

The image of S.S. Sharma eating lunch seated traditionally on the floor at home, his upper body bare except for his sacred thread, passed before Mahesh Kapoor's eyes.

'No, I suppose not,' he said with some regret. 'So, how did he appear?'

'You mean Agarwal Sahib? Quite well, I think. Quite composed.'

'Uff! You are a useless informant,' said Mahesh Kapoor impatiently. 'Anyway, I've been thinking a little about this. You had better mind what you say or you'll make things difficult for both Agarwal and myself. At least restrain yourself until the Zamindari Bill has passed. Everyone needs everyone's cooperation on that.'

'All right, Minister Sahib.'

'Speaking of which, why have these people not returned yet?' asked Mahesh Kapoor, looking around the Legal Remembrancer's Office. 'I sent them out an hour ago.' This was not quite true. 'Everyone is always late and no one values time in this country. That's our main problem.... Yes, what is it? Come in, come in,' he continued, hearing a light knock at the door.

It was a peon with his lunch, which he usually ate quite late.

Opening his tiffin-carrier, Mahesh Kapoor spared half a moment's thought for his wife, who, despite her own ailments, took such pains on his behalf. April in Brahmpur was almost unbearable for her because of her allergy to neem blossoms, and the problem had become increasingly acute over the years. Sometimes, when the neem trees were in flower, she was reduced to a breathlessness that superficially resembled Pran's asthma.

She was also very upset these days by her younger son's affair with Saeeda Bai. So far, Mahesh Kapoor himself had not taken the matter as seriously as he would have had he realized the extent of Maan's infatuation. He was far too busy with matters that affected the lives of millions to have much time to go into the more irksome regions of his own family life. Maan would have to be brought to heel sooner or later, he thought, but for the moment he had other work to attend to.

'Have some of this: I suppose I've dragged you away from your lunch,' said Mahesh Kapoor to his Parliamentary Secretary.

'No, thank you, Minister Sahib, I'd finished when you sent for me. So do you think that everything is going well with the bill?'

'Yes, basically – at least on the floor, wouldn't you say? Now that it has come back from the Legislative Council with only a few minor changes, it shouldn't be difficult to get it re-passed in its amended form by the Legislative

Assembly. Of course, nothing is certain.' Mahesh Kapoor looked into his tiffin-carrier. After a while he went on: 'Ah, good, cauliflower pickle.... What really concerns me is what is going to happen to the bill later, assuming that it passes.'

'Well, legal challenges should not be much of a problem,' said Abdus Salaam. 'It's been well drafted, and I think it should pass muster.'

'You think so, do you, Salaam? What did you think about the Bihar Zamindari Act being struck down by the Patna High Court?' demanded Mahesh Kapoor.

'I think people are more worried than they need to be, Minister Sahib. As you know, the Brahmpur High Court does not have to follow the Patna High Court. It is only bound by the judgments of the Supreme Court in Delhi.'

'That may be true in theory,' said Mahesh Kapoor, frowning. 'In practice, previous judgments set psychological precedents. We have got to find a way, even at this late stage in the passage of the bill, of amending it so that it will be less vulnerable to legal challenge – especially on this question of equal protection.'

There was a pause for a while. The Minister had high regard for his scholarly young colleague, but did not hold out much hope that he would come up with something brilliant at short notice. But he respected his experience in this particular area and knew that his brains were the best that he could pick.

'Something occurred to me a few days ago,' said Abdus Salaam after a minute. 'Let me think about it further, Minister Sahib. I might have a helpful idea or two.'

The Revenue Minister looked at his Parliamentary Secretary with what might almost have been an amused expression, and said:

'Give me a draft of your ideas by tonight.'

'By tonight?' Abdus Salaam looked astonished.

'Yes,' said Mahesh Kapoor. 'The bill is going through its second reading. If anything is to be done, it must be done now.'

'Well,' said Abdus Salaam with a dazed look on his face,

'I had better go off to the library at once.' At the door he turned around and said, 'Perhaps you could ask the Legal Remembrancer to send me a couple of people from his drafting cell later this afternoon. But won't you need me on the floor this afternoon while the bill is being discussed?'

'No, this is far more important,' replied the Minister, getting up to wash his hands. 'Besides, I think you've caused enough mischief for one day on the floor of the House.'

As he washed his hands, Mahesh Kapoor thought about his old friend, the Nawab of Baitar. He would be one of those most deeply affected by the passage of the Zamindari Abolition Bill. His lands around Baitar in Rudhia District, from which he probably derived two-thirds of his income, would, if the act went into effect, be vested in the state of Purva Pradesh. He would not receive much compensation. The tenants would have the right to purchase the land they tilled, and until they did so their rents would go not into the coffers of the Nawab Sahib but directly into those of the Revenue Department of the State Government. Mahesh Kapoor believed, however, that he was doing the right thing. Although his was an urban constituency, he had lived on his own farm in Rudhia District long enough to see the immiserating effects of the zamindari system on the countryside all around him. With his own eyes he had seen the lack of productivity and the consequent hunger, the absence of investment in land improvement, the worst forms of feudal arrogance and subservience, the arbitrary oppression of the weak and the miserable by the agents and muscle-men of the typical landlord. If the lifestyle of a few good men like the Nawab Sahib had to be sacrificed for the greater good of millions of tenant farmers, it was a cost that had to be borne.

Having washed his hands, Mahesh Kapoor dried them carefully, left a note for the Legal Remembrancer, and walked over to the Legislative Building.

THE ancestral Baitar House, where the Nawab Sahib and his sons lived, was one of the most handsome buildings in Brahmpur. A long, pale yellow façade, dark green shutters, colonnades, high ceilings, tall mirrors, immensely heavy dark furniture, chandeliers, oil portraits of previous aristocratic denizens and framed photographs along the corridors commemorating the visits of various high British officials: most visitors to the huge house, surveying their surroundings, succumbed to a kind of gloomy awe – reinforced in recent days by the dusty and uncared-for appearance of those large sections of the mansion the former occupants of which had left for Pakistan.

Begum Abida Khan too used to live here once with her husband, the Nawab Sahib's younger brother. She spent years chafing in the women's quarters before she persuaded him to allow her more reasonable and direct access to the outside world. There she had proved to be more effective than him in social and political causes. With the coming of Partition, her husband – a firm supporter of that Partition – had realized how vulnerable his position was in Brahmpur and decided to leave. He went to Karachi at first. Then – partly because he was uncertain of the effect his settling in Pakistan might have on his Indian property and the fortunes of his wife, and partly because he was restless, and partly because he was religious – he went on to Iraq on a visit to the various holy shrines of the Shias, and decided to live there for a few years. Three years had passed since he had last returned to India, and no one knew what he planned to do. He and Abida were childless, so perhaps it did not greatly matter.

The entire question of property rights was unsettled. Baitar was not – like Marh – a princely state subject to primogeniture but a large zamindari estate whose territory lay squarely within British India and was subject to the Muslim personal law of inheritance. Division of the property upon death or dissolution of the family was possible, but for generations now there had been no effective division, and almost everyone had continued to live in the same rambling house in Brahmpur or at Baitar Fort in the countryside, if not amicably, at least not litigiously. And owing to the constant bustle, the visiting, the festivals, the celebrations, in both the men's and the women's quarters it had had a grand atmosphere of energy and life.

With Partition things had changed. The house was no longer the great community it had been. It had become, in many ways, lonely. Uncles and cousins had dispersed to Karachi or Lahore. Of the three brothers, one had died, one had gone away, and only that gentle widower, the Nawab Sahib, remained. He spent more and more of his time in his library reading Persian poetry or Roman history or whatever he felt inclined to on any particular day. He left most of the management of his country estate in Baitar – the source of most of his income – to his munshi. That crafty half-steward, half-clerk did not encourage him to spend much time going over his own zamindari affairs. For matters not related to his estate, the Nawab Sahib kept a private secretary.

With the death of his wife and his own increasing years the Nawab Sahib had become less sociable, more aware of the approach of death. He wanted to spend more time with his sons, but they were now in their twenties, and inclined to treat their father with affectionate distance. Firoz's law, Imtiaz's medicine, their own circle of young friends, their love affairs (of which he heard little) all drew them outside the orbit of Baitar House. And his dear daughter Zainab visited only rarely – once every few months – whenever her husband allowed her and the Nawab Sahib's two grandsons to come to Brahmpur.

Sometimes he even missed the lightning-like presence of Abida, a woman of whose immodesty and forwardness the Nawab Sahib instinctively disapproved. Begum Abida Khan, MLA, had refused to abide by the strictures of the zenana quarters and the constraints of a mansion, and was now living in a small house closer to the Legislative Assembly. She believed in being aggressive and if necessary immodest in fighting for causes she considered just or useful, and she looked upon the Nawab Sahib as utterly ineffectual. Indeed, she did not have a very high opinion of her own husband who had, as she thought, 'fled' Brahmpur at Partition in a state of panic and was now crawling around the Middle East in a state of religious dotage. Because her niece Zainab – of whom she was fond – was visiting, she did pay a visit to Baitar House, but the purdah she was expected to maintain irked her, and so did the inevitable criticism of her style of life that she faced from the old women of the zenana.

But who were these old women after all? – the repository of tradition and old affection and family history. Only two old aunts of the Nawab Sahib, and the widow of his other brother – no one else remained of that whole busy zenana. The only children in Baitar House were the two who were visiting, the six- and three-year-old grandchildren of the Nawab Sahib. They loved visiting Baitar House and Brahmpur because they found the huge old house exciting, because they could see mongooses sliding under the doors of locked and deserted rooms, because much was made of them by everyone from Firoz Mamu and Imtiaz Mamu to the 'old servitors' and the cooks. And because their mother seemed much happier here than at home.

*

The Nawab Sahib did not at all like to be disturbed when he was reading, but he made more than an exception for his grandsons. Hassan and Abbas were given a free run of the house. No matter what mood he was in, they lifted it; and even when he was sunk in the impersonal comfort of history, he was happy to be brought back to the present world, as long as it was personally through them. Like the rest of the house, the library too was running to seed. The magnificent collection, built up by his father and incorporating additions by the three brothers – each with his different tastes – was housed in an equally magnificent alcoved and high-windowed room. The Nawab Sahib, wearing a freshly starched kurta-pyjama – with a few small squarish holes in the kurta which looked a bit like moth-holes (but what moth would bite quite so squarely?) – was seated this morning at a round table in one of the alcoves, reading *The Marginal Notes of Lord Macaulay* selected by his nephew G.O. Trevelyan.

Macaulay's comments on Shakespeare, Plato and Cicero were as trenchant as they were discriminating, and the editor clearly believed that the marginalia of his distinguished uncle were well worth publishing. His own remarks were openly admiring: 'Even for Cicero's poetry Macaulay had enough respect to distinguish carefully between the bad and the less bad,' was one sentence that drew a mild smile from the Nawab Sahib.

But what, after all, thought the Nawab Sahib, is worth doing, and what is not? For people like me at least things are in decline, and I do not feel it worth my while consuming the rest of my life fighting politicians or tenants or silverfish or my son-in-law or Abida to preserve and maintain worlds that I find exhausting to preserve or maintain. Each of us lives in a small domain and returns to nothing. I suppose if I had a distinguished uncle I might spend a year or two collating and printing his marginal notes.

And he fell to musing about how Baitar House would eventually fall into ruin with the abolition of zamindari and the exhaustion of funds from the estate. Already it was becoming difficult, according to his munshi, to extract the standard rent from the tenants. They pleaded hard times, but underneath the pleas was the sense that the political equations of ownership and dependence were inexorably shifting. Among those who were most vocal against the Nawab Sahib were some whom he had treated with exceptional leniency, even generosity, in the past, and who found this difficult to forgive.

What would survive him? It occurred to him that although he had dabbled in Urdu poetry much of his life, he had never written a single poem, a single couplet, that would be remembered. Those who do not live in Brahmpur decry the poetry of Mast, he thought, but they can complete in their sleep many of the ghazals he has written. It struck him, with a start, that there had never been a truly scholarly edition of the poems of Mast, and he began to stare at the motes in the beam of sunlight that fell on his table.

Perhaps, he said to himself, this is the labour that I am best fitted for at this stage of things. At any rate, it is probably what I would most enjoy.

He read on, savouring the insight with which Macaulay unsparingly analysed the character of Cicero, a man taken over by the aristocracy into which he had been adopted, two-faced, eaten up by vanity and hatred, yet undoubtedly 'great'. The Nawab Sahib, who thought much of death these days, was startled by Macaulay's remark: 'I really think that he met with little more than his deserts from the Triumvirs.'

Despite the fact that the book had been dusted with a white preservative powder, a silverfish crawled out of the spine and scuttled across the band of sunlight on the round table. The Nawab Sahib looked at it for an instant, and wondered what had happened to the young man who had sounded so enthusiastic about taking charge of his library. He had said he would come over to Baitar House but that had been the last that the Nawab Sahib had heard of him – and it must have been at least a month ago. He shut the book and shook it, opened it again on a random page, and continued reading as if the new paragraph had led directly on from the previous one:

The document which he most admired in the whole collection of the correspondence was Caesar's answer to Cicero's message of gratitude for the humanity which the conqueror had displayed towards those political adversaries who had fallen into his power at the surrender of Corfinium. It contained (so Macaulay used to say) the finest sentence ever written:

'I triumph and rejoice that my action should have obtained your approval; nor am I disturbed when I hear it said that those whom I have sent off alive and free will again bear arms against me; for there is nothing which I so much covet as that I should be like myself, and they like themselves.'

The Nawab Sahib read the sentence several times. He had once hired a Latin tutor but had not got very far. Now he attempted to fit the resonant phrases of the English to what must have been the still more resonant phrases of the original. He sat in a reverie for a good ten minutes meditating on the content and manner of the sentence, and would have continued to do so had he not felt a tug at the leg of his pyjamas.

5.11

IT was his younger grandson, Abbas, who was tugging at him with both hands. The Nawab Sahib had not seen him come in, and looked at him with pleased surprise. A little behind Abbas stood his six-year-old brother Hassan. And behind Hassan stood the old servant, Ghulam Rusool.

The servant announced that lunch was waiting for the Nawab Sahib and his daughter in the small room adjoining the zenana quarters. He also apologized for allowing Hassan and Abbas into the library when the Nawab Sahib was reading. 'But Sahib, they insisted, and would not listen to reason.'

The Nawab Sahib nodded his approval and turned happily from Macaulay and Cicero to Hassan and Abbas.

'Are we eating on the floor or at the table today, Nana-jaan?' asked Hassan.

'It's just us – so we'll eat inside – on the rug,' replied his grandfather.

'Oh, good,' said Hassan, who got nervous when his feet were not on the ground.

'What's in that room, Nana-jaan?' asked three-year-old Abbas as they walked down a corridor past a room with a huge brass lock.

'Mongooses, of course,' said his elder brother knowledgeably.

'No, I mean inside the room,' Abbas insisted.

'I think we store some carpets in there,' said the Nawab

Sahib. Turning to Ghulam Rusool, he asked: 'What do we store in there?'

'Sahib, they say it has been two years since that room was locked. It is all on a list with Murtaza Ali. I will ask him and inform you.'

'Oh no, that's not necessary,' said the Nawab Sahib stroking his beard and trying to recall – for, to his surprise, it had slipped his mind – who used to use that particular room. 'As long as it's on a list,' he said.

'Tell us a ghost story, Nana-jaan,' said Hassan, tugging at his grandfather's right hand.

'Yes, yes,' said Abbas, who readily agreed with most of his elder brother's suggestions, even when he did not understand what was being suggested. 'Tell us a ghost story.'

'No, no,' said the Nawab Sahib. 'All the ghost stories I know are very frightening and if I tell you one you'll be so frightened you won't be able to eat your lunch.'

'We won't be frightened,' said Hassan.

'Not frightened,' said Abbas.

They reached the small room where lunch was awaiting them. The Nawab Sahib smiled to see his daughter, and washed his and his grandsons' hands in a small wash-basin with cool water from a nearby jug, and sat them down, each in front of a small thali into which food had already been served.

'Do you know what your two sons are demanding of me?' asked the Nawab Sahib.

Zainab turned to her children and scolded them.

'I told you not to disturb your Nana-jaan in the library, but the moment my back is turned you do what you like. Now what have you been asking for?'

'Nothing,' said Hassan, rather sullenly.

'Nothing,' repeated Abbas, sweetly.

Zainab looked at her father with affection and thought of the days when she used to cling onto his hands and make her own importunate demands, often using his indulgence to get around her mother's firmness. He was sitting on the rug in front of his silver thali with the same erect bearing that she remembered from her earliest childhood, but the thinness of the flesh on his cheekbones and the small square moth-holes on his immaculately starched kurta filled her with a sudden tenderness. It had been ten years since her mother had died – her own children only knew of her through photographs and stories – and those ten years of widowerhood had aged her father as twenty years would have done in the ordinary course of time.

'What are they asking for, Abba-jaan?' said Zainab with a smile.

'They want a ghost story,' said the Nawab Sahib. 'Just like you used to.'

'But I never asked for a ghost story at lunch,' said Zainab.

To her children she said, 'No ghost stories. Abbas, stop playing with your food. If you're very good maybe you'll get a story at night before you go to sleep.'

'No, now! Now –' said Hassan.

'Hassan,' said his mother warningly.

'Now! Now!' Hassan began crying and shouting.

The Nawab Sahib was quite distressed at his grandchildren's insubordination towards their mother, and told them not to speak in this way. Good children, he made it clear, didn't.

'I hope they listen to their father at least,' he said in mild rebuke.

To his horror he saw a tear roll down his daughter's cheek. He put his arm around her shoulder, and said, 'Is everything all right? Is everything all right there?'

It was the instinctive thing to say, but he realized as soon as he had said it that he should perhaps have waited until his grandchildren had finished their lunch and he was left alone with his daughter. He had heard indirectly that all was not well with his daughter's marriage.

'Yes, Abba-jaan. It's just that I think I'm a little tired.'

He kept his arm around her till her tears had ceased. The children looked bewildered. However, some of their favourite food had been prepared and they soon forgot about their mother's tears. Indeed, she too became involved in feeding them, especially the younger one, who was having trouble tearing the naan. Even the Nawab Sahib, looking at the picture the three of them made together, felt a little rush of painful happiness. Zainab was small, like her mother had been, and many of the gestures of affection or reproof that she made reminded him of those that his wife used to make when trying to get Firoz and Imtiaz to eat their food.

As if in response to his thoughts, Firoz now entered the room. Zainab and the children were delighted to see him.

'Firoz Mamu, Firoz Mamu!' said the children. 'Why didn't you have lunch with us?'

Firoz looked impatient and troubled. He placed his hand on Hassan's head.

'Abba-jaan, your munshi has arrived from Baitar. He wants to talk to you,' he said.

'Oh,' said the Nawab Sahib, not happy about this demand on his time when he would rather have been talking to his daughter.

'He wants you to come to the estate today. There is some crisis or other brewing.'

'What manner of crisis?' asked the Nawab Sahib. He did not relish the thought of a three-hour drive in a jeep in the April sun.

'You'd better speak to him,' said Firoz. 'You know how I feel about your munshi. If you think that I should come with you to Baitar, or go instead of you, that's all right. I don't have anything on this afternoon. Oh yes, I do have a meeting with a client, but his case isn't due to come up for a while, so I can postpone it.'

The Nawab Sahib got up with a sigh and washed his hands.

When he got to the ante-room where the munshi was waiting, he asked him brusquely what the matter was. Apparently, there were two problems, both brewing simultaneously. The main one was the perennial difficulty of realizing land-rent from the peasants. The Nawab Sahib did not like the strong-arm methods that the munshi was inclined to employ: the use of local toughs to deal with defaulters. As a result, collections had diminished, and the munshi now felt that the Nawab Sahib's personal presence at Baitar Fort for a day or two and a private talk with a couple of local politicians would help matters considerably. Normally, the sly munshi would have been unwilling to involve his master in the stewardship of his own estate, but this was an exception. He had even brought along a small local landlord to confirm that matters were troubled and required the Nawab Sahib's presence in the area immediately, not only on his own behalf but also because it would help the other landlords.

After a brief discussion (the other problem involved trouble at the local madrasa or school), the Nawab Sahib said: 'I have some things to do this afternoon. But I'll talk matters over with my son. Please wait here.'

Firoz said that on the whole he felt his father should go, if only to make sure that the munshi was not robbing him blind. He would come along as well and look at the accounts. They might well have to spend a night or two in Baitar, and he did not want his father to be by himself. As for Zainab, whom the Nawab Sahib was reluctant to leave 'alone in the house' as he put it, she was matter-of-fact about his departure, though sorry to see him go.

'But Abba-jaan, you'll be back tomorrow or the day after and I'm here for another week. Anyway, isn't Imtiaz due to return tomorrow? And please don't worry about me, I've lived in this house most of my life.' She smiled. 'Just because I'm now a married woman doesn't mean that I am less capable of taking care of myself. I'll spend my time gossiping in the zenana, and I'll even take over your duty of telling the children a ghost story.'

Though somewhat apprehensive – about what exactly he would not have been able to say – the Nawab Sahib acquiesced in what was obviously sound advice and, taking affectionate leave of his daughter and only forbearing from kissing his grandchildren because they were having an afternoon nap, left Brahmpur for Baitar within the hour.

EVENING came. Baitar House wore a deserted look. Half the house was unoccupied anyway, and servants no longer moved through the rooms at dusk, lighting candles or lamps or turning on electric lights. On this particular evening even the rooms of the Nawab Sahib and his sons and the occasionally occupied guest room were unlit, and from the road it would almost have seemed that no one lived there any longer. The only activity, conversation, bustle, movement took place in the zenana quarters, which did not face the road.

It was not yet dark. The children were asleep. It had been less difficult than Zainab had thought to distract them from the fact that their grandfather was not there to tell them the promised ghost story. Both of them were tired out from their previous day's journey to Brahmpur, although they had insisted the previous night on remaining awake till ten.

Zainab would have liked to settle down with a book, but decided to spend the evening talking to her aunt and great-aunts. These women, whom she had known from childhood, had spent their entire lives since the age of fifteen in purdah – either in their father's or in their husband's house. So had Zainab, although she considered herself, by virtue of her education, to have a wider sense of the world. The constraints of the zenana, the women's world that had driven Abida Khan almost crazy – the narrow circle of conversation, the religiosity, the halter on boldness or unorthodoxy of any kind – were seen by these women in an entirely different light. Their world was not busy with great concerns of state, but was essentially a human one. Food, festivals, family relations, objects of use and beauty, these – mainly for good but sometimes for ill – formed the basis, though not the entirety, of their interests. It was not as if they were ignorant of the great world outside. It was rather that the world was seen more heavily filtered through the interests of family and friends than it would be for a sojourner with more direct experience. The clues they received were more indirect, needing more sensitive interpretation; and so were those they gave out. For Zainab – who saw elegance, subtlety, etiquette and family culture as qualities to be prized in their own right, the world of the zenana was a complete world, even if a constrained one. She did not believe that because her aunts had met no men other than those of the family since they were young, and had been to very few rooms other than their own, they were as a result lacking in perspicacity about the world or understanding of human nature. She liked them, she enjoyed talking to them, and she knew what enjoyment they obtained from her occasional visits. But she was reluctant to sit and gossip with them on this particular visit to her father's house only because they would almost certainly touch upon matters that would hurt her. Any mention of her husband would remind her once again of the infidelities that she had only recently come to know of, and that caused her such startling anguish. She would have to pretend to her aunts that all was well with her, and even indulge in light banter about the intimacies of her family life.

They had been sitting and talking for only a few minutes when two panic-stricken young maidservants rushed into the room and, without making even the usual salutation, gasped out:

'The police – the police are here.'

They then burst into tears and became so incoherent that it was impossible to get any sense out of them.

Zainab managed to calm one of them down a little, and asked her what the police were doing.

'They have come to take over the house,' said the girl with a fresh bout of sobbing.

Everyone looked aghast at the wretched girl, who was wiping her eyes with her sleeve.

'Hai, hai!' cried an aunt in pitiable distress, and began weeping. 'What will we do? There is no one in the house.'

Zainab, though shocked at the sudden turn of events, thought of what her mother would have done if there had been no one – that is, no men – in the house.

After she had partially recovered from the shock, she shot a few quick questions at the maidservant:

'Where are they — the police? Are they actually in the house? What are the servants doing? And where is Murtaza Ali? Why do they want to take over the house? Munni, sit up and don't sob. I can't make any sense out of what you are saying.' She shook and consoled the girl alternately.

All that Zainab could ascertain was that young Murtaza Ali, her father's personal secretary, was standing at the far end of the lawn in front of Baitar House desperately trying to dissuade the police from carrying out their orders. The maidservant was particularly terrified because the group of policemen was headed by a Sikh officer.

'Munni, listen,' said Zainab. 'I want to talk to Murtaza.'

'But —'

'Now go and tell Ghulam Rusool or some other manservant to tell Murtaza Ali that I want to talk to him immediately.'

Her aunts stared at her, appalled.

'And, yes, take this note to Rusool to give to the Inspector or whoever it is who is in charge of the police. Make sure that it gets to him.'

Zainab wrote a short note in English as follows:

Dear Inspector Sahib,

My father, the Nawab of Baitar, is not at home, and since no legitimate action should be taken without intimating him first, I must ask you not to proceed further in this matter. I would like to speak to Mr Murtaza Ali, my father's personal secretary, immediately, and request you to make him available. I would also ask you to note that this is the hour of evening prayer, and that any incursion into our ancestral house at a time when the occupants are at prayer will be deeply injurious to all people of good faith.

Sincerely,
Zainab Khan

Munni took the note and left the room, still snivelling but

no longer panic-stricken. Zainab avoided her aunts' glances, and told the other girl, who had calmed down a little as well, to make sure that Hassan and Abbas had not been woken up by the commotion.

5.13

WHEN the Deputy Superintendent of Police who was in charge of the contingent that had come to take over Baitar House read the note, he flushed red, shrugged his shoulders, had a few words with the Nawab Sahib's private secretary, and – quickly glancing at his watch – said:

'All right, then, half an hour.'

His duty was clear and there was no getting around it, but he believed in firmness rather than brutality, and half an hour's delay was acceptable.

Zainab had got the two young maidservants to open the doorway that led from the zenana to the mardana, and to stretch a sheet across it. Then, despite the unbelieving 'tobas' and other pious exclamations of her aunts, she told Munni to tell a man-servant to tell Murtaza Ali to stand on the other side of it. The young man, crimson-faced with embarrassment and shame, stood close by the door which he had never imagined he would ever even approach in his lifetime.

'Murtaza Sahib, I must apologize for your embarrassment – and my own,' said Zainab softly in elegant and unornate Urdu. 'I know you are a modest man and I understand your qualms. Please forgive me. I too feel I have been driven to this recourse. But this is an emergency, and I know that it will not be taken amiss.'

She unconsciously used the first person plural rather than the singular that she was used to. Both were colloquially acceptable, but since the plural was invariant with respect to gender, it defused to some small extent the tension across the geographical line that lay between the mardana and zenana quarters, the breach of which had so shocked her aunts. Besides, there was implicit in the plural a mild sense of command, and this helped set a tone that enabled the exchange not merely of embarrassment – which was unavoidable – but of information as well.

In equally cultured but slightly ornate Urdu young Murtaza Ali replied: 'There is nothing to forgive, believe me, Begum Sahiba. I am only sorry that I was fated to be the messenger of such news.'

'Then let me ask you to tell me as briefly as you can what has happened. What are the police doing here in my father's house? And is it true that they wish to take over this house? On what grounds?'

'Begum Sahiba, I don't know where to begin. They are here, and they intend to take over this house as soon as they can. They were going to enter immediately but the DSP read your note and granted us half an hour's grace. He has an order from the Custodian of Evacuee Property and the Home Minister to take possession of all parts of the house that are not inhabited, in view of the fact that most of the former residents have now established residence in Pakistan.'

'Does this include entering the zenana?' said Zainab as calmly as she could.

'I do not know what it includes, Begum Sahiba. He said "all unoccupied portions."'

'How does he know that so much of the house is unoccupied?' asked Zainab.

'I am afraid, Begum Sahiba, that it is obvious. Partly, of course, it is common knowledge. I tried to persuade him that people were living here, but he pointed to the dark windows. Even the Nawab Sahib is not here at the moment. Nor the Nawabzadas.'

Zainab was silent for a moment. Then she said, 'Murtaza Sahib, I am not going to give up in half an hour what has belonged to our family for generations. We must try to contact Abida Chachi immediately. Her property too is at stake. And Kapoor Sahib, the Revenue Minister, who is an old friend of the family. You will have to do this, as there is no telephone in the zenana.'

'I will do so at once. I pray that I will get through.'

'I am afraid that you will have to forgo your regular prayers this evening,' said Zainab with a smile that could be heard in her voice.

'I fear I will have to,' replied Murtaza Ali, surprised that he too could smile at such an unhappy moment. 'Perhaps I should go now and try to get through to the Revenue Minister.'

'Send the car for him – no, wait –' said Zainab. 'It may be needed. Make sure it is standing by.'

She thought for a minute. Murtaza Ali felt the seconds ticking away.

'Who has the keys to the house?' asked Zainab. 'I mean to the empty rooms?'

'The zenana keys are with –'

'No, those rooms can't be seen from the road – they aren't important – I mean the mardana rooms.'

'I have some of them, some of them are with Ghulam Rusool, and some, I believe, have been taken by the Nawab Sahib to Baitar with him.'

'Now this is what you must do,' said Zainab quietly. 'We have very little time. Get all the menservants and the maidservants in this house to bring candles, torches, lamps, any kind of flame that we have in the house, and to light up a little of every room in this house that faces the road – you understand – even if it means entering rooms that you normally need permission to enter, and even if it means breaking a lock or a door here or there.'

It was a measure of Murtaza Ali's mind that he did not expostulate, but simply accepted the good – if desperate – sense of this measure.

'It must look from the road that the house is inhabited, even if the DSP has reason to believe it is not. He must be given an excuse to withdraw if he is inclined to, even if we do not actually make him believe it.'

'Yes, Begum Sahiba.' Murtaza was filled with admiration for this woman with the gentle voice whom he had never seen – nor ever would.

'I know this house like the back of my hand,' continued Zainab. 'I was born here, unlike my aunts. Even though now I am confined to this section, I am familiar with the other section from my childhood, and I know it has not changed much in structure. We are very short of time, and I plan to help personally in lighting the rooms. I know my father will understand, and it does not matter much to me if no one else does.'

'I beg you, Begum Sahiba,' said her father's private secretary, pain and dismay audible in his voice, 'I beg you do not do so. Arrange things in the zenana and get as many lamps and so on ready as you can so that they can be passed on to us on this side. But please stay where you are. I will see that everything is performed as you command. Now I must go, and I will send word within fifteen minutes about how things are going. God keep your family and this house in his protection.' With this he took his leave.

Zainab kept Munni with her, and told the other girl to help fetch and light the lamps, and take them across to the other side of the house. She then went back to her room and looked at Hassan and Abbas, who were still sleeping. It is your history, your inheritance, your world too that I am protecting, she thought, passing a hand through the younger one's hair. Hassan, usually so sullen, was smiling, and he had his arms wrapped around his younger brother. Her aunts were praying aloud in the next room.

Zainab closed her eyes, said the fatiha, and sat down exhausted. Then she remembered something her father had once said to her, reflected on its importance for a few seconds, and began to draft another letter.

She told Munni to wake up the boys and quickly dress them in their formal best – a small white kurta for Abbas, and a white angarkha for his elder brother. On their heads they were to wear white embroidered caps.

When, fifteen minutes later, Zainab had not heard from Murtaza Ali, she sent for him. On his arrival she asked him:

'Is it done?'

'Yes, Begum Sahiba, it is. The house looks as if it is lit. There is some light visible from every outside window.'

'And Kapoor Sahib?'

'I am afraid that I have not been able to get him on the phone, though Mrs Mahesh Kapoor has sent for him. He may be working late somewhere in the Secretariat. But no one is picking up the phone in his office.'

'Abida Chachi?'

'Her telephone appears to be out of order, and I have only just written her a note. Forgive me. I have been remiss.'

'Murtaza Sahib, you have already done far more than seemed possible to me. Now listen to this letter, and tell me how it can be improved.'

Very swiftly they went through the brief draft of the letter. It was in English, only seven or eight lines long. Murtaza Ali asked for a couple of explanations, and made a couple of suggestions; Zainab incorporated them and made a fair copy.

'Now, Hassan and Abbas,' she said to her sons, their eyes still full of sleep and wonderment at this unexpected game, 'you are to go with Murtaza Sahib and do everything he tells you to do. Your Nana-jaan will be very pleased with you when he comes back, and so will I. And so will Imtiaz Mamu and Firoz Mamu.' She gave each of them a kiss, and sent them to the other side of the screen, where Murtaza Ali took charge of them.

'They should be the ones to give him the letter,' said Zainab. 'Take the car, tell the Inspector – I mean the DSP – where you are going, and go at once. I do not know how to thank you for your help. If you had not been here we would certainly have been lost already.'

'I cannot repay your father's kindness, Begum Sahiba,' said Murtaza Ali. 'I will make sure that your sons come back within the hour.'

He walked down the corridor with a boy clutching each hand. He was too full of trepidation to say anything at first to either, but after he had walked for a minute towards the far end of the lawn where the police were standing, he said to the boys:

'Hassan, Abbas, do adaab to the DSP Sahib.'

'Adaab arz, DSP Sahib,' said Hassan in salutation.

Abbas looked up at his brother and repeated his words, except that his came out as 'Dipsy Sahib'.

'The Nawab Sahib's grandsons,' explained the private secretary.

The Deputy Superintendent of Police smiled warily.

'I am sorry,' he said to Murtaza Ali. 'My time is up and so is yours. The house may look as if it is lived in, but our information tells us otherwise, and we will have to investigate. We must do our duty. The Home Minister himself has instructed us.'

'I quite understand, DSP Sahib,' said Murtaza Ali. 'But may I beg you for a little more time? These two boys are carrying a letter which must be delivered before any action can be taken.'

The DSP shook his head. He held up his hand to indicate that enough was enough, and said: 'Agarwalji has told me personally that he will not entertain any petitions in this respect and that we are not to brook any delay. I am sorry. The decision can always be challenged or appealed later.'

'This letter is for the Chief Minister.'

The policeman stiffened slightly.

'What does this mean?' he said in a voice that was both irritated and bewildered. 'What does the letter say? What do you hope to achieve by this?'

Murtaza Ali said gravely:

'I cannot be expected to know the contents of a private and urgent letter between the daughter of the Nawab Sahib of Baitar and the Chief Minister of Purva Pradesh. Clearly it touches on this matter of the house, but about what it says it would be impertinent of me to speculate. The car, however, is ready, and I must escort these little messengers to Sharmaji's house before they lose their own. DSP Sahib, I hope you will wait for my return before you do anything sudden.'

The DSP, foiled for the moment, said nothing. He knew he would have to wait.

Murtaza Ali took his leave, gathered his charges and drove off in the Nawab Sahib's car.

Fifty yards outside the gates of Baitar House, however, the car came to a sudden halt and could not be re-started. Murtaza Ali told the driver to wait, walked back to the house with Abbas, deposited him with a servant, got out his bicycle and returned. He then propped a surprisingly unprotesting Hassan in front of him, and cycled off with him into the night.

5.14

WHEN they got to the Chief Minister's house fifteen minutes later, they were immediately admitted to his office, where he was working late.

After the usual salutations, they were asked to sit down. Murtaza Ali was sweating – he had been bicycling as fast as he could, considering the safety of his cargo. But Hassan looked cool and crisp in his fine white angarkha, if a little sleepy.

'Now to what do I owe this pleasure?'

The Chief Minister looked from the six-year-old boy to the Nawab Sahib's thirty-year-old secretary while nodding his head slightly from side to side as he sometimes did when tired.

Murtaza Ali had never met the Chief Minister in person. Since he had no idea how best to approach the matter, he simply said: 'Chief Minister Sahib, this letter will tell you everything.'

The Chief Minister looked over the letter only once, but slowly. Then in an angry and determined voice, nasal but with the unmistakable ring of authority, he said:

'Get me Agarwal on the phone!'

While the call was being connected, the Chief Minister ticked off Murtaza Ali for having brought the 'poor boy' with him so long past his bedtime. But it had clearly had an effect on his feelings. He would probably have had harsher things to say, reflected Murtaza Ali, if I had brought Abbas along as well.

When the call came through, the Chief Minister had a

few words with the Home Minister. There was no mistaking the annoyance in his voice.

'Agarwal, what does this Baitar House business mean?' asked the Chief Minister.

After a minute he said:

'No, I am not interested in all that. I have a good understanding of what the Custodian's job is. I cannot have this sort of thing going on under my nose. Call it off at once.'

A few seconds later he said, even more exasperatedly:

'No. It will not be sorted out in the morning. Tell the police to leave immediately. If you have to, put my signature on it.' He was about to put down the receiver when he added: 'And call me in half an hour.'

After the Chief Minister had put the phone down, he glanced at Zainab's letter again. Then he turned to Hassan and said, shaking his head a little:

'Go home now, things will be all right.'

5.15

BEGUM ABIDA KHAN (*Democratic Party*): I do not understand what the honourable member is saying. Is he claiming that we should take the government's word on this as on other matters? Does the honourable member not know what happened just the other day in this city – in Baitar House to be precise – where on the orders of this government, a gang of policemen, armed to the teeth, would have set upon the helpless members of an unprotected zenana – and, if it had not been for the grace of God –

The Hon'ble the Speaker: The honourable member is reminded that this is not germane to the Zamindari Bill that is being discussed. I must remind her of the rules of debate and ask her to refrain from introducing extraneous matter into her speeches.

Begum Abida Khan: I am deeply grateful to the honourable Speaker. This House has its own rules, but God too judges us from above and if I may say so without disrespect to this House, God too has his own rules and we will see which prevails. How can zamindars expect justice from this government in the countryside where redress is so distant when even in this city, in the sight of this honourable House, the honour of other honourable houses is being ravished?

The Hon'ble the Speaker: I will not remind the honourable member again. If there are further digressions in this vein I will ask her to resume her seat.

Begum Abida Khan: The honourable Speaker has been very indulgent with me, and I have no intention of troubling this House further with my feeble voice. But I will say that the entire conduct, the entire manner in which this bill has been created, amended, passed by the Upper House, brought down to this Lower House and amended drastically yet again by the government itself shows a lack of faith and a lack of responsibility, even integrity, with respect to its proclaimed original intent, and the people of this state will not forgive the government for this. They have used their brute majority to force through amendments which are patently mala fide. What we saw when the bill – as amended by the Legislative Council – was undergoing its second reading in this Legislative Assembly was something so shocking that even I – who have lived through many shocking events in my life – was appalled. It had been agreed that compensation was to be paid to landlords. Since they are going to be deprived of their ancestral means of livelihood, that is the least that we can expect in justice. But the amount that is being paid is a pittance – half of which we are expected, indeed enjoined, to accept in government bonds of uncertain date!

A member: You need not accept it. The treasury will be happy to keep it warm for you.

Begum Abida Khan: And even that bond-weakened pittance is on a graduated scale so that the larger landlords – many of whom have establishments on which hundreds of people depend – managers, relatives, retainers, musicians –

A member: Wrestlers, bullies, courtesans, wastrels –

Begum Abida Khan: – will not be paid in proportion to

the land that is rightfully theirs. What will these poor people do? Where will they go? The Government does not care. It thinks that this bill will be popular with the people and it has an eye on the General Elections that will be taking place in just a few months. That is the truth of the matter. That is the real truth and I do not accept any denials from the Minister of Revenue or his Parliamentary Secretary or the Chief Minister or anyone. They were afraid that the High Court of Brahmpur would strike down their graduated scale of payment. So what did they do at a late stage of the proceedings yesterday – at the very end of the second reading? Something that was so deceitful, so shameful, yet so transparent, that even a child would be able to see through it. They split up the compensation into two parts – a non-graduated so-called compensation – and a graduated so-called Rehabilitation Grant for zamindars – and passed an amendment late in the day to validate this new scheme of payment. Do they really think the court will accept that the compensation is 'equal treatment' for all – when by mere jugglery the Revenue Minister and his Parliamentary Secretary have transferred three-quarters of the compensation money into another category with a long and pious name – a category where there is blatantly unequal treatment of the larger landlords? You may be assured that we will fight this injustice while there is breath in our bodies –

A member : Or voice in our lungs.

The Hon'ble the Speaker : I would request members not to interrupt needlessly the speeches of other members.

Begum Abida Khan : But what is the use of my raising my voice for justice in a House where all we meet with is mockery and boorishness? We are called degenerates and wastrels but it is the sons of Ministers, believe me, who are the true proficients of dissipation. The class of people who preserved the culture, the music, the etiquette of this province is to be dispossessed, is to be driven through the lanes to beg its bread. But we will bear our vicissitudes with the dignity that is the inheritance of the aristocracy. This chamber may rubber-stamp this bill. The Upper Chamber may give it another cursory reading and rubber-stamp it. The President may sign it blindly. But the courts will vindicate us. As in our fellow-state of Bihar, this pernicious legislation will be struck down. And we will fight for justice, yes, before the bench and in the press and at the hustings — as long as there is breath in our bodies — and, yes, as long as there is voice in our lungs.

Shri Devakinandan Rai (Socialist Party): It has been very enlightening to be lectured to by the honourable member. I must confess that I see no likelihood of her begging for her bread through the lanes of Brahmpur. Perhaps for cake, but I doubt that too. If I had my way she would not beg for her bread, but she and those of her class would certainly have to work for it. This is what simple justice requires, and this is what is required also by the economic health of this province. I, and the members of the Socialist Party, agree with the honourable member who has just spoken that this bill is an election gimmick by the Congress Party and the government. But our belief is based on the grounds that this is a toothless bill, ineffectual and compromised. It does not go anywhere near what is needed for a thorough overhaul of agricultural relations in this province.

Compensation for the landlords! What? Compensation for the blood that they have already sucked from the limbs of a helpless and oppressed peasantry? Or compensation for their God-given right — I notice that the honourable member is in the habit of invoking God whenever His assistance is required to strengthen her weak arguments — their God-given right to continue to gorge themselves and their useless train of unemployed relations on the ghee of this state when the poor farmer, the poor tenant, the poor landless labourer, the poor worker can hardly afford half a sip of milk for his hungry children? Why is the treasury being depleted? Why are we writing ourselves and our children into debt with these promised bonds when this idle and vicious class of zamindars and taluqdars and landlords of all kinds should be summarily dispossessed — without any thought of compensation — of the lands that they are sitting on and have been sitting on for generations for the sole reason that they betrayed their country at the time of the Mutiny and were richly rewarded for their treason by the British? Is it just, Sir — is it reasonable that they should be awarded this compensation? The money that this government in its culpable so-called generosity is pouring into the laps of these hereditary oppressors should go into roads and schools, into housing for the landless and land reclamation, into clinics and agricultural research centres, not into the luxurious expenditure which is all that the aristocracy is accustomed to or capable of.

Mirza Amanat Hussain Khan (Democratic Party): I rise to a point of order, Sir. Is the honourable member to be permitted to wander off the subject and take up the time of the House with irrelevancies?

The Hon'ble the Speaker: I think he is not irrelevant. He is speaking on the general question of the relations between the tenants, the zamindars, and the government. That question is more or less before us and any remark which the honourable member now offers on that point is not irrelevant. You may like it or not, I may like it or not, but it is not out of order.

Shri Devakinandan Rai: I thank you, Sir. There stands the naked peasant in the hot sun, and here we sit in our cool debating rooms and discuss points of order and definitions of relevancy and make laws that leave him no better than before, that deprive him of hope, that take the part of the capitalist, oppressing, exploiting class. Why must the peasant pay for the land that is his by right, by right of effort, by right of pain, by right of nature, by right, if you will, of God? The only reason why we expect the peasant to pay this huge and unseemly purchase price to the treasury is in order to finance the landlord's exorbitant compensation. End the compensation, and there will be no need for a purchase price. Refuse to accept the notion of a purchase price, and any compensation becomes financially impossible. I have been arguing this point since the inception of the bill two years ago, and throughout the second reading last week. But at this stage of the proceedings what can I do? It is too late. What can I do but say to the treasury benches: you have set up an unholy alliance with the landlords and you are attempting to break the spirit of our people. But we will see what happens when the people realize how they have been cheated. The General Elections will throw out this cowardly and compromised government and replace it with a government worthy of the name: one that springs from the people, that works for the people and gives no support to its class enemies.

5.16

THE NAWAB SAHIB had entered the House during the earlier part of this last speech. He was sitting in the Visitor's Gallery, although, had he wished to, he would have been welcome in the Governor's Gallery. He had returned from Baitar the previous day in response to an urgent message from Brahmpur. He was shocked and embittered by what had happened and horrified that his daughter had had to face such a situation virtually on her own. His concern for her had been so much more patent than his pride in what she had done that Zainab had not been able to help smiling. For a long time he had hugged her and his two grandchildren with tears running down his cheeks. Hassan had been puzzled, but little Abbas had accepted this as a natural state of affairs and had enjoyed it all – he could tell that his grandfather was not at all unhappy to see them. Firoz had been white with anger, and it had taken all of Imtiaz's good humour when he arrived late that afternoon, to calm the family down.

The Nawab Sahib was almost as angry with his hornet of a sister-in-law as with L.N. Agarwal. He knew that it was she who had brought this visitation upon their heads. Then, when the worst was over, she had made light of the police action and was almost cavalier in her assumption that Zainab would have handled things with such tactical courage. As for L.N. Agarwal, the Nawab Sahib looked down onto the floor of the House, and saw him talking very civilly with the Revenue Minister, who had wandered over to his desk and was conferring with him on some point, probably floor management with respect to the impending and critical vote later this afternoon.

The Nawab Sahib had not had the opportunity to talk to his friend Mahesh Kapoor since his return, nor to convey his heart-felt thanks to the Chief Minister. He thought that he would do so after today's session in the Assembly was over. But another reason why he was present in the House today was that he realized – as did many others, for the press and public galleries were all crowded – that it was a historic occasion. For him, and for those like him, the impending vote was one that would – unless halted by the courts – spell a swift and precipitous decline.

Well, he thought fatalistically, it has to happen sooner or later. He was under no illusions that his class was a particularly meritorious one. Those who constituted it included not only a small number of decent men but also a large number of brutes and an even larger number of idiots. He remembered a petition that the Zamindars' Association had submitted to the Governor twelve years ago: a good third of the signatories had used their thumb-prints.

Perhaps if Pakistan had not come into existence, the landowners would have been able to parlay their way into self-preservation: in a united but unstable India each power-bloc might have been able to use its critical strength to maintain the status quo. The princely states, too, could have wielded their weight, and men such as the Raja of Marh might well have remained Rajas in fact as well as in name. The ifs and buts of history, thought the Nawab Sahib, form an insubstantial if intoxicating diet.

Since the annexation of Brahmpur by the British in the early 1850s the Nawabs of Baitar and other courtiers of the erstwhile royal house of Brahmpur had not even had the psychological satisfaction of serving the state, a satisfaction claimed by many aristocracies widely separated in space and time. The British had been happy to let the zamindars collect the revenue from land-rent (and were content in practice to allow them whatever they obtained in excess of the agreed British share) but for the administration of the state they had trusted no one but civil servants of their own race, selected in, partially trained in, and imported from England – or, later, brown equivalents so close in education and ethos as made no appreciable difference.

And indeed, apart from racial mistrust, there was, the Nawab Sahib was compelled to admit, the question of competence. Most zamindars – himself, alas, perhaps included – could hardly administer even their own estates and were fleeced by their munshis and money-lenders. For most of the landlords the primary question of management was not indeed how to increase their income but how to spend it. Very few invested it in industry or urban property. Some, certainly, had spent it on music and books and the fine arts. Others, like the present Prime Minister of Pakistan, Liaquat Ali Khan, who had been a good friend of the Nawab Sahib's father, had spent it to build up influence in politics. But for the most part the princes and landlords had squandered their money on high living of one kind or another : on hunting or wine or women or opium. A couple of images flashed irresistibly and unwelcomely across his mind. One ruler had such a passion for dogs that his entire life revolved around them : he dreamed, slept, woke, imagined, fantasized about dogs ; everything he could do was done to their greater glory. Another was an opium addict who was only content when a few women were thrown into his lap ; even then, he was not always roused to action ; sometimes he just snored on.

The Nawab of Baitar's thoughts continued to oscillate between the debate on the floor of the Assembly and his own meditations. At one point there was a brief intervention by L.N. Agarwal, who made a few amusing comments – at which even Mahesh Kapoor laughed. The Nawab Sahib stared at the bald head ringed with a horseshoe of grey hair and wondered at the thoughts that must be seething under that layer of flesh and bone. How could a man like this deliberately, indeed happily, cause so much misery to him and to those he held so dear? What satisfaction could it have given him that the relatives of someone who had worsted him in a debate would be dispossessed of the home in which they had spent the greater part of their lives?

It was now about half-past four, and there was less than half an hour before the division of votes. The final speeches were continuing and the Nawab Sahib listened with a somewhat wry expression as his sister-in-law circumscribed the institution of zamindari with a luminous purple halo.

Begum Abida Khan: For more than an hour we have been listening to speech after speech from the government benches, filled with the most odious self-congratulation. I did not think that I would wish to speak again, but I must do so now. I would have thought that it would be more appropriate to let those people speak whose death and burial you wish to preside over – I mean the zamindars, whom you wish to deprive of justice and redress and the means of livelihood. The same record has been going on and on for an hour – if it is not the Minister of Revenue it is some pawn of his who has been trained to sing the same song: His Master's Voice. I may tell you that the music is not very pleasant: it is monotonous without being soothing. It is not the voice of reason or reasonableness but the voice of majority power and self-righteousness. But it is pointless to speak further on this.

I pity this government that has lost its way and is trying to find a path out of the swamp of its own policies. They have no foresight, and they cannot, they dare not keep their eyes on the future. It is said that we should 'Beware of the day that is to come', and in the same way I say to this Congress government: 'Beware of the time that you are about to bring upon yourself and upon this country.' It is three years since we obtained Independence but look at the poor of the land: they have neither food to eat nor clothes to wear nor shelter to protect themselves from the sky. You promised Paradise and green gardens under which rivers flow, and gulled the people into believing that the cause of their pitiable condition was zamindari. Well, zamindari will go, but when your promises of these green gardens prove to be false, let us see then what the people say about you and do to you. You are dispossessing eight lakh people, and openly inviting communism. The people will soon find out who you are.

What are you doing that we did not do? You are not giving them the land, you are renting it out just as we did. But what do you care about them? We lived for generations together, we were like their fathers and grandfathers, they loved us and we loved them, we knew their temperament and they knew ours. They were happy with whatever we gave them, and we were happy with whatever they gave us. You have come between us and destroyed what was hallowed by the bonds of ancient emotion. And the crimes and oppressions you blame on us, what proof do these poor people have that you will be any better than you claim we are? They will have to go to the venal clerk and the gluttonous Sub-Divisional Officer, and they will be sucked dry. We were never like that. You have separated the nail from the flesh, and you are happy with the result....

As for compensation, I have said enough already. But is this decency, is this a just provision – that you should go to someone's shop and tell him: 'Give me this and this at such and such a price' and if he doesn't agree to sell it, you take it anyway? And then when he pleads with you at least to give him what you promised him, to turn around and you then say, 'Here is one rupee now, and the rest you will get in instalments over twenty-five years'?

You may call us all kinds of names and invent all manner of miseries for us – but the fact is that it is we zamindars who made this province what it is – who made it strong, who gave it its special flavour. In every field of life we have made our contribution, a contribution that will long outlive us, and that you cannot wipe away. The universities, the colleges, the traditions of classical music, the schools, the very culture of this place were established by us. When foreigners and those from other states in our country come to this province what do they see – what do they admire? The Barsaat Mahal, the Shahi Darvaza, the Imambaras, the gardens and the mansions that have come down to you from us. These things that are fragrant to the world you say are filled with the scent of exploitation, of rotting corpses. Are you not ashamed when you speak in this vein? When you curse and rob those who created this splendour and this beauty? When you do not give them enough compensation even to whitewash the buildings that are the heritage of this city and this state? This is the worst form of meanness, this is the grasping attitude of the village shopkeeper, the bania who smiles and smiles and grasps without any mercy –

The Hon'ble the Minister for Home Affairs (Shri L.N. Agarwal): I hope that the honourable member is not casting imputations upon my community. This is getting to be common sport in this House.

Begum Abida Khan: You understand very well what I am saying, you who are a master at twisting words and manipulating the law. But I will not waste my time arguing with you. Today you have made common cause with the Minister of Revenue in the shameful exploitation of a scapegoat class, but tomorrow will show you what such friendships of convenience are worth – and when you look around for friends everyone will have turned their face away from you. Then you will remember this day and what I have said, and you and your government will come to wish that you had behaved with greater justice and humanity.

There followed an extremely long-winded speech by a socialist member; and then the Chief Minister S.S. Sharma talked for about five minutes, thanking various people for their role in shaping this legislation – particularly Mahesh Kapoor, the Minister of Revenue, and Abdus Salaam, his Parliamentary Secretary. He advised the landowners to live in amity with their erstwhile tenants when the divestiture of their property took place. They should live together like brothers, he stated mildly and nasally. It was an opportunity for the landlords to show their goodness of heart.

They should think of the teachings of Gandhiji and devote their lives to the service of their fellow-men. Finally Mahesh Kapoor, the chief architect of the bill, got the chance to round off the debate in the House. But time was too short for him to say more than a few words:

The Hon'ble the Minister of Revenue (Shri Mahesh Kapoor): Mr Speaker, I had hoped that my friend from the socialist benches who talked so movingly of equality and a classless society and took the Government to task for producing an impotent and unjust bill, would be a just man himself and would confer some equality on me. It is the end of the last day. If he had taken a little less time for his speech I would have had a little more. As it is I now have barely two minutes to speak. He claimed that my bill was a measure created with the intention merely of preventing revolution – a revolution that he believes to be desirable. If that is so, I would be interested to see which way he and his party vote in a couple of minutes. After the honourable Chief Minister's words of thanks and advice – advice which I sincerely hope will be taken by the landlords – I have nothing to add except a few further words of thanks – to my colleagues in this section of the House and, yes, in that section too, who have made the passage of this bill possible, and to the officers of the Revenue Department and the Printing Department and the Law Department, in particular the drafting cell and the Office of the Legal Remembrancer. I thank them all for their months and years of assistance and advice, and I hope that I speak for the people of Purva Pradesh when I say that my thanks are not merely personal.

The Hon'ble the Speaker: The question before the House is that the Purva Pradesh Zamindari Abolition Bill of original date 1948 as passed by the Legislative Assembly, amended by the Legislative Council and further amended by the Legislative Assembly, be passed.

The motion was put and the House passed the bill by a large majority, consisting mainly of the Congress Party, whose numbers dominated the House. The Socialist Party had to vote, however reluctantly, in favour of the bill on the grounds that half a loaf was better than none, and despite the fact that it somewhat assuaged the hunger that would have allowed them to flourish. Had they voted against it they would never have lived it down. The Democratic Party voted against it unanimously, also as expected. The smaller parties and Independents voted predominantly for the bill.

Begum Abida Khan: With the permission of the Speaker I would like a minute's time to say something.

The Hon'ble the Speaker: I will give you a minute's time.

Begum Abida Khan: I would like to say on behalf of myself and the Democratic Party that the advice given by the pious and honourable Chief Minister to the zamindars – that they should maintain good relations with their tenants – is very valuable advice, and I thank him for it. But we would have maintained such excellent relations anyway regardless of his excellent advice, and regardless of the passage of this bill – this bill which will force so many people into poverty and unemployment, which will utterly destroy the economy and culture of this province, and which will at the same time grant not the least benefit to those who –

The Hon'ble the Minister of Revenue (Shri Mahesh Kapoor): Mr Speaker, what sort of occasion is this for speech-making?

The Hon'ble the Speaker: I gave her permission merely to make a short statement. I would request the honourable member –

Begum Abida Khan: As a result of its unjust passage by a brute majority we are left at this time with no other constitutional means of expressing our displeasure and sense of injustice other than to walk out of this House, which is a constitutional recourse, and I therefore call upon the members of my party to stage a walk-out to protest the passage of this bill.

The members of the Democratic Party walked out of the Assembly. There were a few hisses and cries of 'Shame!' but for the most part the Assembly was silent. It was the end of the day, so the gesture was symbolic rather than effective. After a few moments, the Speaker adjourned the House until eleven o'clock the next morning. Mahesh Kapoor gathered his papers together, looked up at the huge, frosted dome, sighed, then allowed his gaze to wander around the slowly emptying chamber. He looked across at the gallery and his eye caught that of the Nawab Sahib. They nodded at each other in a gesture of greeting that was almost entirely friendly, though the discomfort of the situation – not quite an irony – was lost on neither of them. Neither of them wished to talk to the other just yet, and each of them understood this. So Mahesh Kapoor continued to put his papers in order, and the Nawab Sahib, stroking his beard in thought, walked out of the gallery to look for the Chief Minister.

Part Six

ARRIVING at the Haridas College of Music, Ustad Majeed Khan nodded absently to a couple of other music teachers, grimaced with distaste at two female kathak dancers who were carrying their jangling anklets into a nearby practice room on the ground floor, and arrived at the closed door of his room. Outside the room, in casual disarray, lay three sets of chappals and one pair of shoes. Ustad Majeed Khan, realizing that this meant that he was forty-five minutes late, sighed a half-irritated and half-exhausted 'Ya Allah', took off his own peshawari chappals, and entered the room.

The room that he entered was a plain, rectangular, high-ceilinged box with not very much natural light. What few rays came in from outside were provided by a small skylight high on the far wall. On the wall to the left as he entered was a long cupboard with a rack where a number of tanpuras were resting. On the floor was a pale blue unpatterned cotton rug; this had been quite difficult to obtain, as most of the rugs available on the market had floral or other designs of one kind or another. But he had insisted on having a plain rug so that he would not be distracted in his music, and the authorities had very surprisingly agreed to find him one. On the rug facing him sat a short, fat young man whom he had never seen; the man stood up as soon as he entered. Facing away from him were seated a young man and two young women. They turned when the door opened, and immediately they saw it was him, got up respectfully to greet him. One of the women – it was Malati Trivedi – even bent down to touch his feet. Ustad Majeed Khan was not displeased. As she got up he said reprovingly to her:

'So you've decided to make a reappearance, have you? Now that the university is closed I suppose I can expect to see my classes fill up again. Everyone talks about their devotion to music but during examination time they disappear like rabbits into their burrows.'

The Ustad then turned to the stranger. This was Motu

Chand, the plump tabla player who as a rule accompanied Saeeda Bai. Ustad Majeed Khan, surprised to see someone whom he did not immediately recognize in place of his regular tabla player, looked at him sternly and said, 'Yes?'

Motu Chand, smiling benignly, said, 'Excuse me, Ustad Sahib, for my presumption. Your regular tabla player, my wife's sister's husband's friend, is not well and he asked me if I would stand in for him today.'

'Do you have a name?'

'Well, they call me Motu Chand, but actually –'

'Hmmh!' said Ustad Majeed Khan, picked up his tanpura from the rack, sat down and began to tune it. His students sat down as well, but Motu Chand continued standing.

'Oh-hoh, sit down,' said Ustad Majeed Khan irritably, not deigning to look at Motu Chand.

As he was tuning his tanpura, Ustad Majeed Khan looked up, wondering to which of the three students he would give the first fifteen-minute slot. Strictly speaking, it belonged to the boy, but because a bright ray from the skylight happened to fall on Malati's cheerful face Ustad Majeed Khan decided on a whim to ask her to begin. She got up, fetched one of the smaller tanpuras, and began to tune it. Motu Chand adjusted the pitch of his tabla accordingly.

'Now which raag was I teaching you – Bhairava?' asked Ustad Majeed Khan.

'No, Ustad Sahib, Ramkali,' said Malati, gently strumming the tanpura which she had laid flat on the rug in front of her.

'Hmmm!' said Ustad Majeed Khan. He began to sing a few slow phrases of the raag and Malati repeated the phrases after him. The other students listened intently. From the low notes of the raag the Ustad moved to its upper reaches and then, with an indication to Motu Chand to begin playing the tabla in a rhythmic cycle of sixteen beats, he began to sing the composition that Malati had been learning. Although Malati did her best to concentrate, she was distracted by the entrance of two more students –

both girls – who paid their respects to Ustad Majeed Khan before sitting down.

Clearly the Ustad was in a good mood once again; at one point he stopped singing to comment: 'So, you really want to become a doctor?' Turning away from Malati, he added ironically, 'With a voice like hers she will cause more heartache than even she will be able to cure, but if she wants to be a good musician she cannot give it second place in her life.' Then, turning back to Malati he said, 'Music requires as much concentration as surgery. You can't disappear for a month in the middle of an operation and take it up at will.'

'Yes, Ustad Sahib,' said Malati Trivedi with the suspicion of a smile.

'A woman as a doctor!' said Ustad Majeed Khan, musing. 'All right, all right, let us continue – which part of the composition were we at?'

His question was interrupted by a prolonged series of thumps from the room above. The bharatnatyam dancers had begun their practice. Unlike the kathak dancers whom the Ustad had glared at in the hall, they did not wear anklets for their practice session. But what they lost in tinkling distraction they more than compensated for in the vigour with which they pounded their heels and soles on the floor directly above. Ustad Majeed Khan's brows blackened and he abruptly terminated the lesson he was giving Malati.

The next student was the boy. He had a good voice and had put in a lot of work between lessons, but for some reason Ustad Majeed Khan treated him rather abruptly. Perhaps he was still upset by the bharatnatyam which sounded sporadically from above. The boy left as soon as his lesson was over.

Meanwhile, Veena Tandon entered, sat down, and began to listen. She looked troubled. She sat next to Malati, whom she knew both as a fellow-student of music and as a friend of Lata's. Motu Chand, who was facing them while playing, thought that they made an interesting contrast: Malati with her fair, fine features, brownish hair, and slightly amused green eyes, and Veena with her darker, plumper features, black hair, and dark eyes, animated but anxious.

After the boy came the turn of a cheerful but shy middle-aged Bengali woman, whose accent Ustad Majeed Khan enjoyed mimicking. She would normally come in the evenings, and at present he was teaching her Raag Malkauns. This she would sometimes call 'Malkosh' to the amusement of the Ustad.

'So you've come in the morning today,' said Ustad Majeed Khan. 'How can I teach you Malkosh in the morning?'

'My husband says I should come in the morning,' said the Bengali lady.

'So you are willing to sacrifice your art for your marriage?' asked the Ustad.

'Not entirely,' said the Bengali lady, keeping her eyes down. She had three children, and was bringing them up well, but was still incurably shy, especially when criticized by her Ustad.

'What do you mean, not entirely?'

'Well,' said the lady, 'my husband would prefer me to sing not classical music but Rabindrasangeet.'

'Hmmh!' said Ustad Majeed Khan. That the sickly-sweet so-called music of Rabindranath Tagore's songs should be more attractive to any man's ears than the beauty of classical khyaal clearly marked such a man as a buffoon. To the shy Bengali woman, the Ustad said in a tone of lenient contempt: 'So I expect he'll be asking you to sing him a "gojol" next.'

At his cruel mispronunciation the Bengali lady retreated entirely into a flustered silence, but Malati and Veena glanced at each other with amusement.

Ustad Majeed Khan, apropos of his earlier lesson, said: 'The boy has a good voice and he works hard, but he sings as if he were in church. It must be his earlier training in western music. It's a good tradition in its own way,' he went on tolerantly. Then, after a pause, he continued, 'But you can't unlearn it. The voice vibrates too much in the wrong kind of way. Hmm.' He turned to the Bengali woman: 'Tune the tanpura down to the "ma"; I may as well teach you your "Malkosh". One should not leave a raag half-taught even if it is the wrong time of day to sing it. But then I suppose one can set yogurt in the morning and eat it at night.'

Despite her nervousness, the Bengali lady acquitted herself well. The Ustad let her improvise a little on her own, and even said an encouraging 'May you live long!' a couple of times. If the truth be told, music mattered more to the Bengali lady than her husband and her three well-brought-up sons, but it was impossible, given the constraints of her life, for her to give it priority. The Ustad was pleased with her and gave her a longer lesson than usual. When it was over, she sat quietly to one side to listen to what was to follow.

What followed was Veena Tandon's lesson. She was to sing Raag Bhairava, for which the tanpura had to be re-tuned to 'pa'. But so distracted was she by various worries about her husband and her son that she began to strum it immediately.

'What raag are you studying?' said Ustad Majeed Khan, slightly puzzled. 'Isn't it Bhairava?'

'Yes, Guruji,' said Veena, somewhat perplexed herself.

'Guruji?' said Ustad Majeed Khan in a voice that would have been indignant if it had not been so astonished. Veena was one of his favourite pupils, and he could not imagine what had got into her.

'Ustad Sahib,' Veena corrected herself. She too was surprised that in addressing her Muslim teacher she had used the title of respect due to a Hindu one.

Ustad Majeed Khan continued: 'And if you are singing Bhairava, don't you think it would be a good idea to re-tune the tanpura?'

'Oh,' said Veena, looking down in surprise at the tanpura, as if it were somehow to blame for her own absence of mind.

After she had re-tuned it, the Ustad sang a few phrases of a slow alaap for her to imitate, but her performance was so unsatisfactory that at one point he said sharply to her: 'Listen. Listen first. Listen first, then sing. Listening is fifteen annas in the rupee. Reproducing it is one anna – it's the work of a parrot. Are you worried about something?' Veena did not think it right to speak of her anxieties before her teacher, and Ustad Majeed Khan continued: 'Why don't you strum the tanpura so that I can hear it? You should eat almonds for breakfast – that will increase your strength. All right, let's go on to the composition – Jaago Mohan Pyaare,' he added impatiently.

Motu Chand started the rhythmic cycle on the tabla and they began to sing. The words of the well-known composition lent stability to Veena's unsteady thoughts and the increasing confidence and liveliness of her singing pleased Ustad Majeed Khan. After a while first Malati, and then the Bengali woman got up to leave. The word 'gojol' flashed through the Ustad's mind and it dawned upon him where he had heard of Motu Chand before. Wasn't he the tabla player who accompanied the ghazals of Saeeda Bai, that desecrater of the holy shrine of music, the courtesan who served the notorious Raja of Marh? One thought led to another; he turned abruptly towards Veena and said, 'If your father, the Minister, is bent upon destroying our livelihood, at least he can protect our religion.'

Veena stopped singing and looked at him in bewildered silence. She realized that 'livelihood' referred to the patronage of the great rural landlords whose lands the Zamindari Abolition Bill was attempting to snatch away. But what the Ustad Sahib meant by a threat to his religion, she could not comprehend at all.

'Tell him that,' continued Ustad Majeed Khan.

'I will, Ustad Sahib,' said Veena in a subdued voice.

'The Congress-wallahs will finish Nehru and Maulana Azad and Rafi Sahib off. And our worthy Chief Minister and Home Minister will sooner or later suppress your father as well. But while he has some political life, he can do something to help those of us who depend on the likes of him for protection. Once they start singing their bhajans from the temple while we are at prayer, it can only end badly.'

Veena realized that Ustad Majeed Khan was referring to the Shiva Temple being constructed in Chowk, only a couple of lanes away from Ustad Majeed Khan's house.

After humming to himself for a few seconds the Ustad paused, cleared his throat and said, almost to himself: 'It is becoming unlivable in our area. Apart from Marh's madness, there is the whole insane business of Misri Mandi. It's amazing,' he went on: 'the whole place is on strike, no one ever works, and all they do is yell slogans and threats at each other. The small shoemakers starve and scream, the traders tighten their belts and bluster, and there are no shoes in the stores, no employment in the whole Mandi. Everyone's interests are harmed, yet no one will compromise. And this is Man whom God has made out of a clot of blood, and to whom he has given reason and discrimination.'

The Ustad finished his comment with a dismissive wave of his hand, a wave that implied that everything he had ever thought about human nature had been confirmed.

Seeing Veena look even more upset, an expression of concern passed over Majeed Khan's face. 'Why am I telling you this?' he said, almost in self-reproach. 'Your husband knows all this better than I do. So that's why you are distracted – of course, of course.'

Veena, moved though she was by this expression of sympathy from the normally unsympathetic Ustad, was silent, and continued to strum the tanpura. They resumed where they had left off, but it must have been obvious that her mind was not on the composition or the rhythmic patterns – the 'taans' – which followed. At one point, the Ustad said to her: 'You're singing the word "ga", "ga", "ga", but is that really the note "ga" you are singing? I think you have too much on your mind. You should leave such things with your shoes outside this room when you come in.'

He began to sing a complex series of taans, and Motu Chand, carried away by the pleasure of the music, started to improvise a pleasant filigree of rhythmic accompaniment on the tabla. The Ustad abruptly stopped.

He turned to Motu Chand with sarcastic deference. 'Please go on, Guruji,' he said.

The tabla player smiled embarrassedly.

'No, do go on, we were enjoying your solo,' continued Ustad Majeed Khan.

Motu Chand's smile became unhappier still.

'Do you know how to play a simple theka – the plain unornamented rhythmic cycle? Or are you in too high a circle of Paradise for that?'

Motu Chand looked pleadingly at Ustad Majeed Khan and said, 'It was the beauty of your singing that carried me away, Ustad Sahib. But I won't let it happen again.'

Ustad Majeed Khan looked sharply at him, but he had intended no impertinence.

After her lesson was over, Veena got up to leave. Normally she stayed as long as she could, but this was not possible today. Bhaskar had a fever and wanted her attention; Kedarnath needed cheering up; and her mother-in-law had just that morning made a hurtful comment on the amount of time she spent at the Haridas College of Music.

The Ustad glanced at his watch. There was still an hour before the noon prayer. He thought of the call to prayer which he heard every morning first from his local mosque and then at slightly staggered intervals from other mosques across the city. What he particularly liked in the morning call to prayer was the twice-repeated line that did not appear in the azaan later in the day: 'Prayer is better than sleep.'

Music too was prayer to him, and some mornings he would be up long before dawn to sing Lalit or some other early morning raag. Then the first words of the azaan, 'Allah-u-Akbar' – God is Great – would vibrate across the rooftops in the cool air and his ears would lie in wait for the sentence that admonished those who attempted to sleep on. When he heard it, he would smile. It was one of the pleasures of his day.

If the new Shiva Temple was built, the sound of the

muezzin's early cry would be challenged by that of the conch. The thought was unbearable. Surely something must be done to prevent it. Surely the powerful Minister Mahesh Kapoor – who was taunted by some in his party for being, like the Prime Minister Jawaharlal Nehru, almost an honorary Muslim – could do something about it. The Ustad began meditatively to hum the words of the composition that he had just been teaching the Minister's daughter – Jaago Mohan Pyaare. Humming it, he forgot himself. He forgot the room he was in and the students still waiting for their lessons. It was very far from his mind that the words were addressed to the dark god Krishna, asking him to wake up with the arrival of morning, or that 'Bhairava' – the name of the raag he was singing – was an epithet of the great god Shiva himself.

6.2

ISHAQ KHAN, Saeeda Bai's sarangi player, had been trying for several days to help his sister's husband – who was also a sarangi player – to get transferred from All India Radio Lucknow, where he was a 'staff artist', to All India Radio Brahmpur.

This morning too, Ishaq Khan had gone down to the AIR offices and tried his luck by talking to an assistant producer of music, but to no avail. It was a bitter business for the young man to realize that he could not even get to state his case properly to the Station Director. He did, however, state his case vociferously to a couple of musician friends he met there. The sun was warm, and they sat under a large and shady neem tree on the lawn outside the buildings. They looked at the cannas and talked of this and that. One of them had a radio – of a newfangled kind that could be operated by batteries – and they switched it on to the only station they could receive clearly, which was their own.

The unmistakable voice of Ustad Majeed Khan singing Raag Miya-ki-Todi filled their ears. He had just begun

403

singing and was accompanied only by the tabla and his own tanpura.

It was glorious music: grand, stately, sad, full of a deep sense of calm. They stopped gossiping and listened. Even an orange-crested hoopoe stopped pecking around the flowerbed for a minute.

As always with Ustad Majeed Khan, the clean unfolding of the raag occurred through a very slow rhythmic section rather than a rhythmless alaap. After about fifteen minutes he turned to a faster composition in the raag, and then, far, far too soon, Raag Todi was over, and a children's programme was on the air.

Ishaq Khan turned off the radio and sat still, deep more in trance than in thought.

After a while they got up and went to the AIR staff canteen. Ishaq Khan's friends, like his brother-in-law, were staff artists, with fixed hours and assured salaries. Ishaq Khan, who had only accompanied other musicians a few times on the air, fell into the category of 'casual artist'.

The small canteen was crowded with musicians, writers of programmes, administrators, and waiters. A couple of peons lounged against the wall. The entire scene was messy, noisy and cosy. The canteen was famous for its strong tea and delicious samosas. A board facing the entrance proclaimed that no credit would be given; but as the musicians were perennially short of cash, it always was.

Every table except one was crowded. Ustad Majeed Khan sat alone at the head of the table by the far wall, musing and stirring his tea. Perhaps out of deference to him, because he was considered something better than even an A-grade artist, no one presumed to sit near him. For all the apparent camaraderie and democracy of the canteen, there were distinctions. B-grade artists for instance would not normally sit with those of superior classifications such as B-plus or A – unless, of course, they happened to be their disciples – and would usually defer to them even in speech.

Ishaq Khan looked around the room and, seeing five

empty chairs ranged down the oblong length of Ustad Majeed Khan's table, moved towards it. His two friends followed a little hesitantly.

As they approached, a few people from another table got up, perhaps because they were performing next on the air. But Ishaq Khan chose to ignore this, and walked up to Ustad Majeed Khan's table. 'May we?' he asked politely. As the great musician was lost in some other world, Ishaq and his friends sat down at the three chairs at the opposite end. There were still two empty chairs, one on either side of Majeed Khan. He did not seem to register the presence of the new arrivals, and was now drinking his tea with both hands on the cup, though the weather was warm.

Ishaq sat at the other end facing Majeed Khan, and looked at that noble and arrogant face, softened as it appeared to be by some transient memory or thought rather than by the permanent impress of late middle age.

So profound had the effect of his brief performance of Raag Todi been on Ishaq that he wanted desperately to convey his appreciation. Ustad Majeed Khan was not a tall man, but seated either on the stage in his long black achkan – so tightly buttoned at the neck that one would have thought it would constrict his voice – or even at a table drinking tea, he conveyed, through his upright, rigid stance, a commanding presence; indeed, even an illusion of height. At the moment he seemed almost unapproachable.

If only he would say something to me, thought Ishaq, I would tell him what I felt about his performance. He must know we are sitting here. And he used to know my father. There were many things that the younger man did not like about the elder, but the music he and his friends had just listened to placed them in their trivial perspective.

They ordered their tea. The service in the canteen, despite the fact that it was part of a government organization, was prompt. The three friends began to talk among themselves. Ustad Majeed Khan continued to sip his tea in silence and abstraction.

Ishaq was quite popular in spite of his slightly sarcastic nature, and had a number of good friends. He was always willing to take the errands and burdens of others upon himself. After his father's death he and his sister had had to support their three young brothers. This was one reason why it was important that his sister's family move from Lucknow to Brahmpur.

One of Ishaq's two friends, a tabla player, now made the suggestion that Ishaq's brother-in-law change places with another sarangi player, Rafiq, who was keen to move to Lucknow.

'But Rafiq is a B-plus artist. What's your brother-in-law's grade?' asked Ishaq's other friend.

'B.'

'The Station Director won't want to lose a B-plus for a B. Still, you can try.'

Ishaq picked up his cup, wincing slightly as he did so, and sipped his tea.

'Unless he can upgrade himself,' continued his friend. 'I agree, it's a silly system, to grade someone in Delhi on the basis of a single tape of a performance, but that's the system we have.'

'Well,' said Ishaq, remembering his father who, in the last years of his life, had made it to A, 'it's not a bad system. It's impartial – and ensures a certain level of competence.'

'Competence!' It was Ustad Majeed Khan speaking. The three friends looked at him in amazement. The word was spoken with a contempt that seemed to come from the deepest level of his being. 'Mere pleasing competence is not worth having.'

Ishaq looked at Ustad Majeed Khan, deeply disquieted. The memory of his father made him bold enough to speak.

'Khan Sahib, for someone like you, competence is not even a question. But for the rest of us. . . .' His voice trailed off.

Ustad Majeed Khan, displeased at being even mildly contradicted, sat tight-lipped and silent. He seemed to be collecting his thoughts. After a while he spoke.

'You should not have a problem,' he said. 'For a sarangi-wallah no great musicianship is required. You don't need to be a master of a style. Whatever style the soloist has, you simply follow it. In musical terms it's actually a distraction.' He continued in an indifferent voice: 'If you want my help I'll speak to the Station Director. He knows I'm impartial – I don't need or use sarangi-wallahs. Rafiq or your sister's husband – it hardly matters who is where.'

Ishaq's face had gone white. Without thinking of what he was doing or where he was, he looked straight at Majeed Khan and said in a bitter and cutting voice:

'I have no objection to being called a mere sarangi-wallah rather than a sarangiya by a great man. I consider myself blessed that he has deigned to notice me. But these are matters about which Khan Sahib has personal knowledge. Perhaps he can elaborate on the uselessness of the instrument.'

It was no secret that Ustad Majeed Khan himself came from a family of hereditary sarangi players. His artistic strivings as a vocalist were bound up painfully with another endeavour: the attempt to dissociate himself from the demeaning sarangi tradition and its historical connection with courtesans and prostitutes – and to associate himself and his son and daughter with the so-called 'kalawant' families of higher-caste musicians.

But the taint of the sarangi was too strong, and no kalawant family wanted to marry into Majeed Khan's. This was one of the searing disappointments of his life. Another was that his music would end with himself, for he had never found a disciple whom he considered worthy of his art. His own son had the voice and musicianship of a frog. As for his daughter, she was musical all right, but the last thing that Ustad Majeed Khan wanted for her was that she should develop her voice and become a singer.

Ustad Majeed Khan cleared his throat but said nothing.

The thought of the great artist's treason, the contempt with which Majeed Khan, despite his own undoubted gifts, had treated the tradition that had given him birth continued to enrage Ishaq.

'Why does Khan Sahib not favour us with a response?' he went on, oblivious to his friends' attempts to restrain him. 'There are subjects, no matter how distanced he is today, on which Khan Sahib can illuminate our understanding. Who else has the background? We have heard of Khan Sahib's illustrious father and grandfather.'

'Ishaq, I knew your father, and I knew your grandfather. They were men who understood the meaning of respect and discrimination.'

'They looked at the worn grooves on their fingernails without feeling dishonoured,' retorted Ishaq.

The people at the neighbouring tables had stopped talking, and were listening to the exchange between the younger and the older man. That Ishaq, baited himself, was now doing the baiting, attempting to hurt and humiliate Ustad Majeed Khan, was painful and obvious. The scene was horrible, but everyone seemed to be frozen into immobility.

Ustad Majeed Khan said slowly and passionlessly: 'But they, believe me, would have felt dishonoured if they had been alive to see their son flirting with the sister of an employer, whose body his bow helps sell.'

He looked at his watch and got up. He had another performance in ten minutes. Almost to himself and with the utmost simplicity and sincerity, he said, 'Music is not a cheap spectacle – not the entertainment of the brothel. It is like prayer.'

Before Ishaq could respond he had started walking towards the door. Ishaq got up and almost lunged towards him. He was gripped by an uncontrollable spasm of pain and fury, and his two friends had to force him bodily down into his chair. Other people joined in, for Ishaq was well-liked, and had to be prevented from doing further damage.

'Ishaq Bhai, enough's been said.'

'Listen, Ishaq, one must swallow it – whatever our elders say, however bitter.'

'Don't ruin yourself. Think of your brothers. If he talks to the Director Sahib. . . .'

'Ishaq Bhai, how many times have I told you to guard your tongue!'

'Listen, you must apologize to him immediately.'

But Ishaq was almost incoherent:

'Never − never − I'll never apologize − on my father's grave − to that − to think, that such a man who insults the memory of his elders and mine − everyone creeps on all fours before him − yes, Khan Sahib, you can have a twenty-five-minute slot − yes, yes, Khan Sahib, you decide which raag you will sing − O God! If Miya Tansen were alive he would have cried to hear him sing his raag today − that God should have given him this gift −'

'Enough, enough, Ishaq....' said an old sitar player. Ishaq turned towards him with tears of hurt and anger:

'Would you marry your son to his daughter? Or your daughter to his son? Who is he that God is in his pocket? − he talks like a mullah about prayer and devotion − this man who spent half his youth in Tarbuz ka Bazaar −'

People began to turn away in pity and discomfort from Ishaq. Several of Ishaq's well-wishers left the canteen to try and pacify the insulted maestro, who was about to agitate the airwaves in his own great agitation.

'Khan Sahib, the boy didn't know what he was saying.'

Ustad Majeed Khan, who was almost at the door of the studio, said nothing.

'Khan Sahib, elders have always treated their youngers like children, with tolerance. You must not take what he said seriously. None of it is true.'

Ustad Majeed Khan looked at the interceder and said: 'If a dog pisses on my achkan, do I become a tree?'

The sitar player shook his head and said, 'I know it was the worst time he could have chosen − when you were about to perform, Ustad Sahib....'

But Ustad Majeed Khan went on to sing a Hindol of calm and surpassing beauty.

6.3

IT had been some days since Saeeda Bai had saved Maan from suicide, as he put it. Of course it was extremely unlikely – and his friend Firoz had told him so when he had complained to him of his lovelorn miseries – that that happy-go-lucky young man would have made any attempt even to cut himself while shaving in order to prove his passion for her. But Maan knew that Saeeda Bai, though hard-headed, was – at least to him – tender-hearted; and although he knew she did not believe that he was in any danger from himself if she refused to make love to him, he also knew that she would take it as more than a merely flattering figure of speech. Everything is in the saying, and Maan, while saying that he could not go on in this harsh world without her, had been as soulful as it was possible for him to be. For a while all his past loves vanished from his heart. The dozen or more 'girls of good family' from Brahmpur whom he had been in love with and who in general had loved him in return, ceased to exist. Saeeda Bai – for that moment at least – became everything for him.

And after they had made love, she became more than everything for him. Like that other source of domestic strife, Saeeda Bai too made hungry where most she satisfied. Part of it was simply the delicious skill with which she made love. But even more than that it was her nakhra, the art of pretended hurt or disaffection that she had learnt from her mother and other courtesans in the early days in Tarbuz ka Bazaar. Saeeda Bai practised this with such curious restraint that it became infinitely more believable. One tear, one remark that implied – perhaps, only perhaps implied – that something he had said or done had caused her injury – and Maan's heart would go out to her. No matter what the cost to himself, he would protect her from the cruel, censorious world. For minutes at a time he would lean over her shoulder and kiss her neck, glancing every few moments at her face in the hope of seeing her mood lift. And when it did, and he saw that same bright, sad smile that had so captivated him when she sang at Holi at Prem Nivas, he would be seized by a frenzy of sexual desire. Saeeda Bai seemed to know this, and graced him with a smile only when she herself was in the mood to satisfy him.

She had framed one of the paintings from the album of Ghalib's poems that Maan had given her. Although she had, as far as was possible, repaired the page that the Raja of Marh had ripped out of the volume, she had not dared to display that particular illustration for fear of exciting his further fury. What she had framed was 'A Persian Idyll', which showed a young woman dressed in pale orange, sitting near an arched doorway on a very pale orange rug, holding in her slender fingers a musical instrument resembling a sitar, and looking out of the archway into a mysterious garden. The woman's features were sharp and delicate, unlike Saeeda Bai's very attractive but unclassical, perhaps not even beautiful, face. And the instrument that the woman was holding – unlike Saeeda Bai's strong and responsive harmonium – was so finely tapered in the stylized illustration that it would have been entirely impossible to play it.

Maan did not care that the book might be considered damaged by having the painting thus plundered from its pages. He could not have been happier at this sign of Saeeda Bai's attachment to his gift. He lay in her bedroom and stared at the painting and was filled with a happiness as mysterious as the garden through the archway. Whether glowing with the immediate memory of her embraces or chewing contentedly at the delicate coconut-flavoured paan that she had just offered to him at the end of a small ornamented silver pin, it seemed to him that he himself had been led by her and her music and her affection into a paradisal garden, most insubstantial and yet most real.

'How unimaginable it is,' said Maan out loud rather dreamily, 'that our parents also must have – just like us –'

This remark struck Saeeda Bai as being in somewhat poor taste. She did not at all wish her imagination to be transported to the domestic love-making of Mahesh Kapoor – or anyone else for that matter. She did not know who her own father was: her mother, Mohsina Bai, had claimed not to know. Besides, domesticity and its standard concerns were not objects of fond contemplation for her. She had been accused by Brahmpur gossip of destroying several settled marriages by casting her lurid nets around hapless men. She said a little sharply to Maan:

'It is good to live in a household like I do where one does not have to imagine such things.'

Maan looked a little chastened. Saeeda Bai, who was quite fond of him by now and knew that he usually blurted out the first thing that came into his head, tried to cheer him up by saying:

'But Dagh Sahib looks distressed. Would he have been happier to have been immaculately conceived?'

'I think so,' said Maan. 'I sometimes think I would be happier without a father.'

'Oh?' said Saeeda Bai, who had clearly not been expecting this.

'Oh, yes,' said Maan. 'I often feel that whatever I do my father looks upon with contempt. When I opened the cloth business in Banaras, Baoji told me it would be a complete failure. Now that I have made a go of it, he is taking the line that I should sit there every day of every month of every year of my life. Why should I?'

Saeeda Bai did not say anything.

'And why should I marry?' continued Maan, spreading his arms wide on the bed and touching Saeeda Bai's cheek with his left hand. 'Why? Why? Why? Why? Why?'

'Because your father can get me to sing at your wedding,' said Saeeda Bai with a smile. 'And at the birth of your children. And at their mundan ceremony. And at their marriages, of course.' She was silent for a few seconds. 'But I won't be alive to do that,' she went on. 'In fact I sometimes wonder what you see in an old woman like me.'

Maan became very indignant. He raised his voice and said, 'Why do you say things like that? Do you do it just to get me annoyed? No one ever meant much to me until I met you. That girl in Banaras whom I met twice under heavy escort is less than nothing to me – and everyone thinks I must marry her just because my father and mother say so.'

Saeeda Bai turned towards him and buried her face in

his arm. 'But you must get married,' she said. 'You cannot cause your parents so much pain.'

'I don't find her at all attractive,' said Maan angrily.

'That will merely take time,' advised Saeeda Bai.

'And I won't be able to visit you after I'm married,' said Maan.

'Oh?' said Saeeda Bai in such a way that the question, rather than leading to a reply, implied the closure of the conversation.

6.4

AFTER a while they got up and moved to the other room. Saeeda Bai called for the parakeet, of whom she had become fond. Ishaq Khan brought in the cage, and a discussion ensued about when he would learn to speak. Saeeda Bai seemed to think that a couple of months would be sufficient, but Ishaq was doubtful. 'My grandfather had a parakeet who didn't speak for a whole year – and then wouldn't stop talking for the rest of his life,' he said.

'I've never heard anything like that,' said Saeeda Bai dismissively. 'Anyway, why are you holding that cage in such a funny way?'

'Oh, it's nothing really,' said Ishaq, setting the cage down on a table and rubbing his right wrist. 'Just a pain in my wrist.'

In fact it was very painful and had become worse during the previous few weeks.

'You seem to play well enough,' said Saeeda Bai, not very sympathetically.

'Saeeda Begum, what would I do if I didn't play?'

'Oh, I don't know,' said Saeeda Bai, tickling the little parakeet's beak. 'There's probably nothing the matter with your hand. You don't have plans to go off for a wedding in the family, do you? Or to leave town until your famous explosion at the radio station is forgotten?'

If Ishaq was injured by this painful reference or these

unjust suspicions, he did not show it. Saeeda Bai told him to fetch Motu Chand, and the three of them soon began to make music for Maan's pleasure. Ishaq bit his lower lip from time to time as his bow moved across the strings, but he said nothing.

Saeeda Bai sat on a Persian rug with her harmonium in front of her. Her head was covered with her sari, and she stroked the double string of pearls hanging around her neck with a finger of her left hand. Then, humming to herself, and moving her left hand onto the bellows of the harmonium, she began to play a few notes of Raag Pilu. After a little while, and as if undecided about her mood and the kind of song she wished to sing, she modulated to a few other raags.

'What would you like to hear?' she asked Maan gently.

She had used a more intimate 'you' than she had ever used so far – 'tum' instead of 'aap'. Maan looked at her, smiling.

'Well?' said Saeeda Bai, after a minute had gone by.

'Well, Saeeda Begum?' said Maan.

'What do you want to hear?' Again she used tum instead of aap and sent Maan's world into a happy spin. A couplet he'd heard somewhere came to his mind:

Among the lovers the Saki thus drew distinction's line,
Handing the wine-cups one by one: 'For you, Sir';
'Yours'; and 'Thine'.

'Oh, anything,' said Maan, 'Anything at all. Whatever you feel is in your heart.'

Maan had still not plucked up the courage to use 'tum' or plain 'Saeeda' with Saeeda Bai, except when he was making love, when he hardly knew what he said. Perhaps, he thought, she just used it absent-mindedly with me and will be offended if I reciprocate.

But Saeeda Bai was inclined to take offence at something else.

'I'm giving you the choice of music and you are returning the problem to me,' she said. 'There are twenty different things in my heart. Can't you hear me changing from raag to raag?' Then, turning away from Maan, she said:

'So, Motu, what is to be sung?'

'Whatever you wish, Saeeda Begum,' said Motu Chand happily.

'You blockhead, I'm giving you an opportunity that most of my audiences would kill themselves to receive and all you do is smile back at me like a weak-brained baby, and say, "Whatever you wish, Saeeda Begum." What ghazal? Quickly. Or do you want to hear a thumri instead of a ghazal?'

'A ghazal will be best, Saeeda Bai,' said Motu Chand, and suggested 'It's just a heart, not brick and stone,' by Ghalib.

At the end of the ghazal Saeeda Bai turned to Maan and said: 'You must write a dedication in your book.'

'What, in English?' asked Maan.

'It amazes me,' said Saeeda Bai, 'to see the great poet Dagh illiterate in his own language. We must do something about it.'

'I'll learn Urdu!' said Maan enthusiastically.

Motu Chand and Ishaq Khan exchanged glances. Clearly they thought that Maan was quite far gone in his fascination with Saeeda Bai.

Saeeda Bai laughed. She asked Maan teasingly, 'Will you really?' Then she asked Ishaq to call the maidservant.

For some reason Saeeda Bai was annoyed with Bibbo today. Bibbo seemed to know this, but to be unaffected by it. She came in grinning, and this re-ignited Saeeda Bai's annoyance.

'You're smiling just to annoy me,' she said impatiently. 'And you forgot to tell the cook that the parakeet's daal was not soft enough yesterday – do you think he has the jaws of a tiger? Stop grinning, you silly girl, and tell me – what time is Abdur Rasheed coming to give Tasneem her Arabic lesson?'

Saeeda Bai felt safe enough with Maan to mention Tasneem's name in his presence.

Bibbo assumed a satisfactorily apologetic expression and said:

'But he's here already, as you know, Saeeda Bai.'

'As I know? As I know?' said Saeeda Bai with renewed impatience. 'I don't know anything. And nor do you,' she added. 'Tell him to come up at once.'

A few minutes later Bibbo was back, but alone.

'Well?' said Saeeda Bai.

'He won't come,' said Bibbo.

'He won't come? Does he know who pays him to give tuition to Tasneem? Does he think his honour will be unsafe if he comes upstairs to this room? Or is it just that he is giving himself airs because he is a university student?'

'I don't know, Begum Sahiba,' said Bibbo.

'Then go, girl, and ask him why. It's his income I want to increase, not my own.'

Five minutes later Bibbo returned with a very broad grin on her face and said, 'He was very angry when I interrupted him again. He was teaching Tasneem a complicated passage in the Quran Sharif and told me that the divine word would have to take precedence over his earthly income. But he will come when the lesson is over.'

'Actually, I'm not sure I want to learn Urdu,' said Maan, who was beginning to regret his sudden enthusiasm. He didn't really want to be saddled with a lot of hard work. And he hadn't expected the conversation to take such a practical turn so suddenly. He was always making resolutions such as, 'I must learn polo' (to Firoz, who enjoyed introducing his friends to the tastes and joys of his own Nawabi lifestyle), or 'I must settle down' (to Veena, who was the only one in the family who was capable of ticking him off to some effect), or even 'I will not give swimming lessons to whales' (which Pran considered ill-judged levity). But he made these resolutions safe in the knowledge that their implementation was very far away.

By now, however, the young Arabic teacher was standing outside the door, quite hesitantly and a little disapprovingly. He did adaab to the whole company, and waited to hear what was required of him.

'Rasheed, can you teach my young friend here Urdu?' asked Saeeda Bai, coming straight to the point.

The young man nodded a little reluctantly.

'The understanding will be the same as with Tasneem,' said Saeeda Bai, who believed in getting practical matters sorted out quickly.

'That will be fine,' said Rasheed. He spoke in a somewhat clipped manner, as if he were still slightly piqued by the earlier interruptions to his Arabic lesson. 'And the name of the gentleman?'

'Oh yes, I'm sorry,' said Saeeda Bai. 'This is Dagh Sahib, whom the world so far knows only by the name of Maan Kapoor. He is the son of Mahesh Kapoor, the Minister. And his elder brother Pran teaches at the university, where you study.'

The young man was frowning with a sort of inward concentration. Then, fixing his sharp eyes on Maan he said, 'It will be an honour to teach the son of Mahesh Kapoor. I am afraid I am a little late already for my next tuition. I hope that when I come tomorrow we can fix up a suitable time for our lesson. When do you tend to be free?'

'Oh, he tends to be free all the time,' said Saeeda Bai with a tender smile. 'Time is not a problem with Dagh Sahib.'

6.5

ONE night, exhausted from marking examination papers, Pran was sleeping soundly when he was awakened with a jolt. He had been kicked. His wife had her arms around him, but she was sleeping soundly still.

'Savita, Savita – the baby kicked me!' said Pran excitedly, shaking his wife's shoulder.

Savita opened a reluctant eye, felt Pran's lanky and comforting body near her, and smiled in the dark, before sinking back to sleep.

'Are you awake?' asked Pran.

'Uh,' said Savita. 'Mm.'

'But it really did!' said Pran, unhappy with her lack of response.

'What did?' said Savita sleepily.

'The baby.'

'What baby?'

'Our baby.'

'Our baby did what?'

'It kicked me.'

Savita sat up carefully and kissed Pran's forehead, rather as if he were a baby himself. 'It couldn't have. You're dreaming. Go back to sleep. And I'll also go back to sleep. And so will the baby.'

'It did,' said Pran, a little indignantly.

'It couldn't have,' said Savita, lying down again. 'I'd have felt it.'

'Well it did, that's all. You probably don't feel its kicks any more. And you sleep very soundly. But it kicked me through your belly, it definitely did, and it woke me up.' He was very insistent.

'Oh, all right,' said Savita. 'Have it your way. I think he must have known that you were having bad dreams, all about chiasmus and Anna – whatever her name is.'

'Anacoluthia.'

'Yes, and I was having good dreams and he didn't want to disturb me.'

'Excellent baby,' said Pran.

'Our baby,' said Savita. Pran got another hug.

They were silent for a while. Then, as Pran was drifting off to sleep, Savita said:

'He seems to have a lot of energy.'

'Oh?' said Pran, half asleep.

Savita, now wide awake with her thoughts, was in no mood to cut off this conversation.

'Do you think he will turn out to be like Maan?' she asked.

'He?'

'I sense he's a boy,' said Savita in a resolved sort of way.

'In what sense like Maan?' asked Pran, suddenly remembering that his mother had asked him to talk to his brother about the direction of his life — and especially about Saeeda Bai, whom his mother referred to only as 'woh' — that woman.

'Handsome — and a flirt?'

'Maybe,' said Pran, his mind on other matters.

'Or an intellectual like his father?'

'Oh, why not?' said Pran, drawn back in. 'He could do worse. But without his asthma, I hope.'

'Or do you think he'll have the temper of my grandfather?'

'No, I don't think it was an angry sort of kick. Just informative. "Here I am; it's two in the morning, and all's well." Or perhaps he was, as you say, interrupting a nightmare.'

'Maybe he'll be like Arun   very dashing and sophisticated.'

'Sorry, Savita,' said Pran. 'If he turns out to be like your brother, I'll disown him. But he'll have disowned us long before that. In fact, if he's like Arun, he's probably thinking at this very moment: "Awful service in this room; I must speak to the manager so that I can get my nutrients on time. And they should adjust the temperature of the amniotic fluid in this indoor swimming pool, as they do in five-star wombs. But what can you expect in India? Nothing works at all in this damned country. What the natives need is a good solid dose of discipline." Perhaps that's why he kicked me.'

Savita laughed. 'You don't know Arun well enough,' was her response.

Pran merely grunted.

'Anyway, he might take after the women in this family,' Savita went on. 'He might turn out to be like your mother or mine.' The thought pleased her.

Pran frowned, but this latest flight of Savita's fancy was too taxing at two in the morning. 'Do you want me to get you something to drink?' he asked her.

'No, mm, yes, a glass of water.'

Pran sat up, coughed a little, turned towards the bedside

table, switched on the bedside lamp, and poured out a glass of cool water from the thermos flask.

'Here, darling,' he said, looking at her with slightly rueful affection. How beautiful she looked now, and how wonderful it would be to make love with her.

'You don't sound too good, Pran,' said Savita.

Pran smiled, and passed his hand across her forehead. 'I'm fine.'

'I worry about you.'

'I don't,' Pran lied.

'You don't get enough fresh air, and you use your lungs too much. I wish you were a writer, not a lecturer.' Savita drank the water slowly, savouring its coolness in the warm night.

'Thanks,' said Pran. 'But you don't get enough exercise either. You should walk around a bit, even during your pregnancy.'

'I know,' said Savita, yawning now. 'I've been reading the book my mother gave me.'

'All right, goodnight, darling. Give me the glass.'

He switched off the light and lay in the dark, his eyes still open. I never expected to be as happy as this, he told himself. I'm asking myself if I'm happy, and it hasn't made me cease to be so. But how long will this last? It isn't just me but my wife and child who are saddled with my useless lungs. I must take care of myself. I must take care of myself. I must not overwork. And I must get to sleep quickly.

And in five minutes he was in fact asleep again.

6.6

THE next morning a letter from Calcutta arrived in the post. It was written in Mrs Rupa Mehra's inimitable small handwriting, and went as follows:

Dearest Savita and Pran,

I have just a little while ago received your dear letter

and it is needless to say how delighted I am to get it. I was not expecting a letter from you Pran as I know you are working very hard and could hardly get any time to write letters so the pleasure of receiving it is even greater.

I am sure inspite of difficulties Pran dearest your dreams in the department will come true. You must have patience, it is a lesson I have learned in life. One must work hard and everything else is not in one's hands. I am blessed that my sweetheart Savita has such a good husband, only he must take care of his health.

By now the baby must be kicking even more and tears come into my eyes that I cannot be there with you my Savita to share the joy. I remember when you were kicking it was so gentle a kick and Daddy bless him was there and put his hand on my stomach and could not even feel it. Now my darlingest S, you are yourself to be a mother. You are so much in my thoughts. Sometimes Arun says to me you only care for Lata and Savita but it is not true, I care for all four of my children boys or girls and take an interest in all they do. Varun is so troubled this year in his maths studies that I am very worried for him.

Aparna is a sweetheart and so fond of her grandmother. I am often left with her in the evenings. Arun and Meenakshi go out and socialise, it is important for his job I know – and I am happy to play with her. Sometimes I read. Varun comes back very late from college, in the past he used to entertain her and that was good because children should not spend all their time with their ayahs, it can be bad for their upbringing. So now it has fallen to me and Aparna has grown so attached to me. Yesterday she said to her mother who had dressed up to go out to dinner: 'You can go, I don't care; if Daadi stays here I don't care two hoots.' Those were her exact words and I was so proud of her that at three years she could say so much. I am teaching her not to call me 'Grandma' but 'Daadi' but Meenakshi thinks if she does not learn correct English now when will she learn?

Meenakshi sometimes I find has moods, and then she stares at me and then Savita dearest I feel that I am not wanted in the house. I want to stare back but sometimes I start crying. I can't help it at all. Then Arun says to me, 'Ma, don't start the water-works, you are always making a fuss over nothing.' So I try not to cry, but when I think about your Daddy's gold medal the tears are there.

Lata is nowadays spending a lot of time with Meenakshi's family. Meenakshi's father Mr Justice Chatterji thinks highly of Lata I think, and Meenakshi's sister Kakoli is also fond of her. Then there are the three boys Amit and Dipankar and Tapan Chatterji, who all seem more and more strange to me. Amit says Lata should learn Bengali, it is the only truly civilised language in India. He himself as you know writes his books in English so why does he say that only Bengali is civilised and Hindi is not? I don't know, but the Chatterjis are an unusual family. They have a piano but the father wears a dhoti quite a lot in the evenings. Kakoli sings Rabindrasangeet and also western music, but her voice is not to my taste and she has a modern reputation in Calcutta. Sometimes I wonder how my Arun got married into such a family but all is for the best as I have my Aparna.

Lata I fear was very angry and hurt with me when we first came to Calcutta and also worried about her exam results and not like herself at all. You must telegram the results as soon as they come, no matter whether good or bad. It was that boy K of course and nothing else whom she met in Brahmpur and he was clearly a bad influence. Sometimes she made a bitter remark to me and sometimes only gave minimum answers to my questions, but can you imagine if I had let things go on in that way? I had no help or sympathy from Arun at all in this but now I have told him to introduce Lata to his covenanted and other friends and let us see. If only I could find a husband like Pran for my Lata, I would die contented. If Daddy had seen you Pran, he would have known that his Savita was in good hands.

One day I was so hurt that I said to Lata, it was all very well to have non-cooperation in Gandhiji's time against the British, but I am your own mother, and it is very stubborn of you that you are doing this. Doing what? she said – and it was so indifferent that I felt my heart had broken. My dearest Savita, I pray, if you have a daughter – although actually it is time for a grandson in the family – then she will not ever be so cold to you. But at other times, she forgets she is angry with me – and then she is quite affectionate until she remembers.

May God Almighty keep you well and happy to carry out all your plans. And soon in the Monsoon I will see you, D.V.

Lots and lots of love to both of you from me, Arun, Varun, Lata, Aparna and Meenakshi and a big hug and kiss as well. Don't worry about me, my blood sugar is all right.

From yours everloving Ma

P.S. Please give my love to Maan, Veena, Kedarnath and also Bhaskar and Kedarnath's mother and your own parents Pran (I hope the neem blossoms are less troublesome now) – and my father and Parvati – and of course to the Baby Expected. Also give my salaams to Mansoor and Mateen and the other servants. It is so hot in Calcutta but it must be worse in Brahmpur and in your condition Savita you must remain very cool and not go out in the sun or take unnecessary exercise. You must get plenty of rest. When in doubt about what to do, you must remember to do nothing. After the birth you will be busy enough, believe me, my dearest Savita, and you must conserve your strength.

6.7

THE reference to neem blossoms reminded Pran that he had not visited his mother in several days. Mrs Mahesh Kapoor had been even more badly affected this year by the

423

pollen of the neem trees than she usually was. Some days she could hardly breathe. Even her husband, who treated all allergies as if they were wilfully inflicted by the victims upon themselves, was forced to take some notice of his wife. As for Pran, who knew from experience what it felt like to struggle for breath, he thought of his mother with a feeling of sad helplessness – and with some anger towards his father who insisted that she remain in town in order to manage the household.

'Where should she go where there are no neem trees?' Mahesh Kapoor had said. 'Abroad?'

'Well, Baoji, perhaps to the south somewhere – or to the hills.'

'Don't be unrealistic. Who will take care of her there? Or do you think I should give up my work?'

There was no obvious answer to this. Mahesh Kapoor had always been dismissive of other people's illnesses and bodily pain, and had disappeared from town whenever his wife had been about to give birth. He could not stand 'the mess and the fuss and so on'.

Lately, Mrs Mahesh Kapoor had been much exercised by one issue which seemed to aggravate her condition. This was Maan's involvement with Saeeda Bai, and his loitering around in Brahmpur when he had work and other obligations in Banaras. When his fiancée's family sent an indirect inquiry through a relative about fixing a date for the marriage, Mrs Mahesh Kapoor had begged Pran to speak to him. Pran had told her that he had very little control over his younger brother. 'He only listens to Veena,' he had said, 'and even then he goes and does exactly as he pleases.' But his mother had looked so unhappy that he had agreed to talk to Maan. He had, however, put it off now for several days.

'Right,' said Pran to himself. 'I'll talk to him today. And it'll be a good opportunity to visit Prem Nivas.'

It was already too hot to walk, so they went by tonga. Savita sat smiling silently and – Pran thought – quite mysteriously. In fact she was merely pleased to be visiting her mother-in-law, whom she liked, and with whom she enjoyed discussing neem trees and vultures and lawns and lilies.

When they got to Prem Nivas they found that Maan was still asleep. Leaving Savita with Mrs Mahesh Kapoor, who looked a little better than before, Pran went off to wake his brother up. Maan was lying in his room with his face buried in his pillow. A ceiling fan was going round and round, but the room was still quite warm.

'Get up! Get up!' said Pran.

'Oh!' said Maan, trying to ward off the light of day.

'Get up! I have to talk to you.'

'What? Oh! Why? All right, let me wash my face.'

Maan got up, shook his head several times, examined his face in the mirror quite carefully, did a respectful adaab to himself when his brother was not watching and, after splashing some water upon himself, came back and lay down flat on the bed once more – but on his back.

'Who's told you to speak to me?' said Maan. Then, remembering what he had been dreaming about, he said, regretfully: 'I was having the most wonderful dream. I was walking near the Barsaat Mahal with a young woman – not so young really, but her face was unlined still –'

Pran started smiling. Maan looked a little hurt.

'Aren't you interested?' he asked.

'No.'

'Well, why have you come, Bhai Sahib? Why don't you sit down on the bed – it's much more comfortable. Oh yes,' he said, remembering: 'you've come to speak to me. Who has put you up to it?'

'Does someone have to have put me up to it?'

'Yes. You never proffer brotherly advice as a rule, and I can tell from your face that I am in for some proffering. All right, all right, go ahead. It's about Saeeda Bai, I suppose.'

'You're absolutely right.'

'Well, what's there to say?' said Maan, with a sort of happy hangdog look. 'I'm terribly in love with her. But I don't know if she cares for me at all.'

'Oh, you idiot,' said Pran affectionately.

'Don't make fun of me. I can't bear it. I'm feeling very low,' said Maan, gradually convincing himself of his romantic depression. 'But no one believes me. Even Firoz says –'

'And he's quite right. You're feeling nothing of the kind. Now tell me, do you really think that that kind of person is capable of loving?'

'Oh?' asked Maan. 'Why not?'

He thought back to the last evening that he had spent in Saeeda Bai's arms, and began to feel fuzzily amorous once more.

'Because it's her job not to,' replied Pran. 'If she fell in love with you it wouldn't be at all good for her work – or her reputation! So she won't. She's too hard-headed. Anyone with one good eye can see that, and I've seen her for three Holis in succession.'

'You just don't know her, Pran,' said his brother ardently.

This was the second time in a few hours that someone had told Pran that he just didn't understand someone else, and he reacted impatiently.

'Now listen, Maan, you're making a complete fool of yourself. Women like that are brought up to pretend they're in love with gullible men – to make their hearts light and their purses even lighter. You know that Saeeda Bai is notorious for this sort of thing.'

Maan just turned over onto his stomach and pressed his face into the pillow.

Pran found it very difficult to be righteous with his idiot of a brother. Well, I've done my duty, he thought. If I say anything further it'll have just the opposite reaction to what Ammaji wants.

He tousled his brother's hair and said: 'Maan – are you in difficulties with money?'

Maan's voice, slightly muffled by the pillow, said: 'Well, it isn't easy, you know. I'm not a client or anything, but I can't just go empty-handed. So, well, I've given her a few gifts. You know.'

Pran was silent. He did not know. Then he said: 'You haven't eaten into the money you came to Brahmpur to do

426

business with, have you, Maan? You know how Baoji would react if he came to know of that.'

'No,' said Maan, frowning. He had turned around again, and was looking up at the fan. 'Baoji, you know, said something sharp to me a few days ago – but I'm sure he doesn't really mind at all about Saeeda Bai. After all, he's had quite a lively youth himself – and, besides, he's invited her several times to sing at Prem Nivas.'

Pran said nothing. He was quite certain that his father was very displeased.

Maan went on: 'And just a few days ago I asked him for money – "for this and for that" – and he gave me quite a generous amount.'

Pran reflected that whenever his father was occupied with a piece of legislation or some other project, he hated being disturbed, and almost paid people off so as to be able to get on with his own work.

'So you see,' said Maan, 'there isn't a problem at all.' Having made the problem disappear, he went on: 'But where is my lovely bhabhi? I'd much rather be scolded by her.'

'She's downstairs.'

'Is she angry with me too?'

'I'm not exactly angry with you, Maan,' said Pran. 'All right, get ready and come down. She's looking forward to seeing you.'

'What's happening about your job?' asked Maan.

Pran made a gesture with his right hand which was the equivalent of a shrug.

'Oh, yes, and is Professor Mishra still furious with you?'

Pran frowned. 'He's not the sort of man who forgets little acts of kindness such as yours. Do you know, if you had been a student and did what you did at Holi, I might, as a member of the students' welfare committee, have had to recommend your expulsion.'

'Your students sound a very lively lot,' said Maan approvingly.

After a while he added, with a happy smile on his face: 'Do you know that she calls me Dagh Sahib?'

'Oh, really?' said Pran. 'Very charming. I'll see you downstairs in a few minutes.'

6.8

ONE evening after a longish day in the High Court, Firoz was on his way to the cantonment for some polo and a ride when he noticed his father's secretary, Murtaza Ali, bicycling down the road with a white envelope in his hand. Firoz halted the car and called out, and Murtaza Ali stopped.

'Where are you off to?' asked Firoz.

'Oh, nowhere, just within Pasand Bagh.'

'Who's that envelope for?'

'Saeeda Bai Firozabadi,' said Murtaza Ali rather reluctantly.

'Well, that's on my way. I'll drop it off.' Firoz looked at his watch. 'It shouldn't make me late.'

He reached out of the window to take the packet, but Murtaza Ali held back.

'It isn't any trouble at all, Chhoté Sahib,' he said, smiling. 'I must not palm off my duties on others. You are looking very well turned out in those new jodhpurs.'

'It's not a duty for me. Here –' And Firoz reached out once again for the packet. He reflected that it would provide him with the ostensibly innocent means to see that lovely girl Tasneem once more.

'I'm sorry, Chhoté Sahib, the Nawab Sahib was quite explicit that I deliver it.'

'That makes no sense to me,' said Firoz, now speaking in a somewhat patrician manner. 'I delivered the packet before – you let me take it to save you trouble when it was on my way – and I am capable of taking it again.'

'Chhoté Sahib, it is such a small matter, please let it be.'

'Now, good fellow, let me have the packet.'

'I cannot.'

'Cannot?' Firoz's voice became commandingly aloof.

'You see, Chhoté Sahib, the last time I did, the Nawab

Sahib was extremely annoyed. He told me very firmly that this was never to happen again. I must ask your forgiveness for my rudeness, but your father was so vehement that I dare not risk his displeasure again.'

'I see.' Firoz was perplexed. He could not understand his father's inordinate annoyance about this harmless matter. He had been looking forward to his game, but now his mood was spoilt. Why was his father behaving in this excessively puritanical way? He knew that it was not the done thing to socialize with singing girls, but what harm was there in simply delivering a letter? But perhaps that was not the problem at all.

'Let me get this clear,' he went on after a moment's thought. 'Was my father displeased that you had not delivered the packet or that I had delivered it?'

'That I could not say, Chhoté Sahib. I wish I understood it myself.' Murtaza Ali continued to stand politely beside his bicycle, holding the envelope firmly in one hand, as if he feared that Firoz might, on a sudden impulse, snatch it away from him after all.

'All right,' said Firoz and, with a curt nod at Murtaza Ali, drove on towards the cantonment.

It was a slightly cloudy day. Though it was only early evening, it was comparatively cool. On both sides of Kitchener Road stood tall gul-mohur trees in full orange bloom. The peculiar scent of the flowers, not sweet as such but as evocative as that of geraniums, was heavy in the air, and the light, fan-shaped petals were strewn across the road. Firoz decided to talk to his father when he got back to Baitar House, and this resolution helped him put the incident out of his mind.

He recalled his first glimpse of Tasneem and remembered the sudden and disturbing attraction he had felt for her – a sense that he had seen her before, somewhere 'if not in this life then in some earlier one'. But after a while, as he came closer to the polo grounds and smelt the familiar scent of horse dung and passed by the familiar buildings and waved to the familiar people, the game reasserted itself and Tasneem too faded into the background.

Firoz had promised to teach Maan a bit of polo this evening, and now he looked around for him at the club. In fact it would be more accurate to say that he had compelled a reluctant Maan to learn a little about the game. 'It's the best game in the world,' he had told him. 'You'll be an addict soon enough. And you have too much time on your hands.' Firoz had gripped Maan's hands in his own and had said: 'They're going soft from too much pampering.'

But Maan was nowhere to be seen at this moment, and Firoz glanced a little impatiently at his watch and at the lessening light.

6.9

A few minutes later, Maan came riding up towards him, doffed his riding cap in a cheerful gesture of greeting, and dismounted.

'Where were you?' asked Firoz. 'They're quite strict here about timing, and if we don't get to the wooden horse within ten minutes of the time for which we've reserved it, well, someone else will take it. Anyway, how did you manage to persuade them to allow you to ride one of their horses without being accompanied by a member?'

'Oh, I don't know,' said Maan. 'I just walked over and talked to one of the grooms for a few minutes, and he saddled up this bay for me.'

Firoz reflected that he should not have been too surprised: his friend had the knack of winging it in all kinds of unlikely situations through sheer insouciance. The groom must have taken it for granted that Maan was a fully-fledged member of the club.

With Maan uncomfortably astride the wooden horse, Firoz began his education. The light bamboo polo stick was put in Maan's right hand, and he was asked to point and swing it a few times for good measure.

'But this is no fun at all,' said Maan, after about five minutes.

'Nothing is fun in the first five minutes,' replied Firoz calmly. 'No, don't hold the stick that way – keep your arm straight – no, completely straight – that's right – yes, now swing it – just a half swing – good! – your arm should act like an extension of the stick itself.'

'I can think of one thing at least that's fun in the first five minutes,' said Maan with a slightly idiotic grin, heaving the stick around and losing his balance slightly.

Firoz surveyed Maan's posture coolly. 'I'm talking about anything requiring skill and practice,' he said.

'That requires a lot of skill and practice,' said Maan.

'Don't be flippant,' said Firoz, who took his polo seriously. 'Now just stay exactly as you are, and look at me. Notice that the line between my shoulders runs parallel to the spine of the horse. Aim for that position.'

Maan tried, but found it even more uncomfortable. 'Do you really think that everything that requires skill is painful at the beginning?' he asked. 'My Urdu teacher appears to take exactly the same view.' He rested the polo stick between his legs and wiped his forehead with the back of his right hand.

'Come now, Maan,' said Firoz, 'you can't say you're tired after just five minutes of this. I'm going to try you out with the ball now.'

'I am rather tired, actually,' said Maan. 'My wrist's hurting a little. And my elbow, and my shoulder.'

Firoz flashed him an encouraging smile and placed the ball on the ground. Maan swung his stick towards it and missed it entirely. He tried again and missed again.

'You know,' said Maan, 'I'm not at all in the mood for this. I'd rather be somewhere else.'

Firoz, ignoring him, said: 'Don't look at anything, just at the ball – just at the ball – nothing else – not at me – not at where the ball is going to go – not even at a distant image of Saeeda Bai.'

This last comment, instead of making Maan lose his swing entirely, actually resulted in a small impact as the mallet skimmed the top of the ball.

'Things aren't going all that well with Saeeda Bai, you

know, Firoz,' said Maan. 'She got very annoyed with me yesterday, and I don't know what it was I did.'

'What brought it on?' said Firoz, not very sympathetically.

'Well, her sister came in while we were talking and said something about the parrot looking as if he was exhausted. Well, it's a parakeet actually, but that's a sort of parrot, isn't it? So I smiled at her and mentioned our Urdu teacher and said that the two of us had something in common. Meaning, of course, that Tasneem and I did. And Saeeda Bai just flared up. She just flared up. It was half an hour before she would talk to me affectionately again.' Maan looked as abstracted as it was possible for him to look.

'Hmm,' said Firoz, thinking of how sharp Saeeda Bai had been with Tasneem when he had visited the house to deliver the envelope.

'It almost seemed as if she was jealous,' Maan went on after a pause and a few more shots. 'But why would someone as amazingly beautiful as her need to be jealous of anyone else? Especially her sister.'

Firoz reflected that he would never have used the words 'amazingly beautiful' of Saeeda Bai. It was her sister who had amazed him with her beauty. He could well imagine that Saeeda Bai might envy her freshness and youth.

'Well,' he said to Maan, a smile playing on his own fresh and handsome features, 'I wouldn't take it as a bad sign at all. I don't see why you're depressed about it. You should know by now that women are like that.'

'So you think jealousy is a healthy sign?' demanded Maan, who was quite prone to jealousy himself. 'But there must be something to feel jealous about, don't you think? Have you ever seen the younger sister? How could she even compare with Saeeda Bai?'

Firoz said nothing for a while, then made the brief comment: 'Yes, I've seen her. She's a pretty girl.' He didn't volunteer anything else.

But Maan, while hitting the ball ineffectually across the top, had his mind on Saeeda Bai again. 'I sometimes think she cares more for that parakeet than for me,' he said, frowning. 'She's never angry with him. I can't go on like this – I'm exhausted.'

The last sentence referred not to his heart but to his arm. Maan was expending a great deal of energy playing his shots, and Firoz appeared to enjoy seeing him huff and puff a little.

'How did your arm feel when you made that last shot?' he asked.

'It got quite a jolt,' said Maan. 'How long do you want me to go on?'

'Oh, till I feel you've had enough,' said Firoz. 'It's quite encouraging – you are making all the standard beginner's mistakes. What you just did was to top the ball. Don't do that – aim at a point at the bottom of the ball, and it'll rise very nicely. If you aim at the top, all the strength of the impact will be absorbed by the ground. The ball won't go far and, besides, you'll find as you did just now that your arm gets a sharp little shock.'

'I say, Firoz,' said Maan, 'how did you and Imtiaz learn Urdu? Wasn't it very difficult? I'm finding it impossible – all those dots and squiggles.'

'We had an old maulvi who came to the house especially to teach us,' said Firoz. 'My mother was very keen that we learn Persian and Arabic as well, but Zainab was the only one who got very far with those.'

'How is Zainab?' asked Maan. He reflected that though he had been a favourite of hers in childhood, he had not seen her for many years now – ever since she had disappeared into the world of purdah. She was six years older than him and he had adored her. In fact she had once saved his life in a swimming accident when he was six. I doubt I'll ever see her again, he thought to himself. How awful – and how strange.

'Don't use force, use strength –' said Firoz. 'Or hasn't your instructress taught you that?'

Maan aimed a gentle swipe at Firoz with his stick.

By now there were only about ten minutes of daylight left, and Firoz could see that Maan was not happy sitting on a merely wooden horse. 'Well, one last shot,' he said.

Maan pointed at the ball, made a light half-swing, and with one smooth, full, circular motion of his arm and wrist, hit the ball squarely in the centre. Pokk! The ball made a wonderful wooden sound, and flew up in a fine low parabola, passing over the net at the top of the pit.

Both Firoz and Maan were astonished.

'Good shot!' said Maan, very pleased with himself.

'Yes,' said Firoz. 'Good shot. Beginner's luck. Tomorrow we'll see if you can do that consistently. But now I'm going to get you to ride a real polo pony for a few minutes, and see if you can control the reins with the left hand alone.'

'Perhaps tomorrow,' said Maan. His shoulders were stiff and his back felt twisted, and he had had more than enough of polo. 'How about a ride instead?'

'I can see that, like your Urdu teacher, I'll have to teach you discipline before I teach you your subject,' said Firoz. 'Riding with one hand isn't hard at all. It's no more difficult than learning riding in the first place – or learning your alif-be-pe-te. If you try it now, you'll be in a better position tomorrow.'

'But I'm not very keen to try it today,' protested Maan. 'It's dark anyway, and I won't enjoy myself. Oh, all right, whatever you say, Firoz. You're the boss.'

He dismounted and put his arm around his friend's shoulder, and they walked towards the stables.

'The trouble with my Urdu teacher,' continued Maan, apropos of nothing immediate, 'is that he only wants to teach me the finer points of calligraphy and pronunciation, and I only want to learn how to read love poetry.'

'That's the trouble with the *teacher*, is it?' asked Firoz, holding his friend's polo stick to prevent retaliation. He was feeling cheerful again. Maan's company almost invariably did that to him.

'Well, don't you think I should have a say in the matter?' asked Maan.

'Perhaps,' said Firoz. 'If I thought you knew what was good for you.'

AFTER he got home, Firoz decided to have a word with his father. He was far less annoyed than he had been immediately after his exchange with Murtaza Ali, but just as puzzled as before. He had a suspicion that his father's private secretary was misinterpreting, or at least exaggerating, his father's words. What could his father have meant by issuing such a curious instruction? Did it apply to Imtiaz as well? If so, why was his father being so protective of them? What did he think his sons would be likely to go and do? Perhaps, Firoz felt, he should reassure him.

When he did not find his father in his room, he assumed that he had gone into the zenana to talk to Zainab, and decided not to follow him. It was just as well that he did not do so, because the Nawab Sahib was talking to her about a matter so personal that the presence of anyone else, even a beloved brother, would have put an abrupt end to the conversation.

Zainab, who had shown such courage when Baitar House was under siege by the police, was now sitting near her father and sobbing quietly with misery. The Nawab Sahib had his arm around her and there was an expression of great bitterness on his face.

'Yes,' he was saying softly, 'I have heard rumours that he goes out. But one should not take everything everyone says as true.'

Zainab said nothing for a while, then, covering her face in her hands, she said: 'Abba-jaan, I know it is true.'

The Nawab Sahib stroked her hair gently, thinking back to the days when Zainab was four years old and would come and sit on his lap whenever something troubled her. It was unbearably bitter to him that his son-in-law had, by his infidelities, injured her so deeply. He looked back at his own marriage, at the practical and gentle woman whom for many years he had hardly known, and who, late in their marriage and long after the birth of their three children, had entirely won his heart. All he said to Zainab was:

'Be patient like your mother. He will come around one day.'

Zainab did not look up, but she wondered that her father had invoked her mother's memory. After a while, her father added, almost as if he were speaking to himself:

'I came to realize her worth very late in life. God rest her soul.'

For many years now, the Nawab Sahib had visited his wife's grave as often as possible to read the fatiha over it. And indeed the old Begum Sahiba had been a most remarkable woman. She had put up with what she knew of the Nawab's own unsettled youth, had run much of the estate efficiently from behind the walls of her seclusion, had endured his later phases of piety (not as excessive, fortunately, as that of his younger brother), and had brought up her children and helped bring up her nephews and nieces with discipline and culture. Her influence on the zenana had been both diffuse and powerful. She had read; and, despite that, she had thought.

In fact, it was probably the books that she lent her sister-in-law Abida that had first planted a few scattered seeds of rebellion in that restless, chafing heart. Though Zainab's mother had no thoughts of leaving the zenana herself, it was only her presence that had made it bearable for Abida. When she died, Abida compelled her husband – and his elder brother the Nawab Sahib – by reason, cajolery, and threats of suicide (which she fully intended to carry out, and which they could see she did) to let her escape from what had become to her an intolerable bondage. Abida, the firebrand of the legislature, had little respect for the Nawab Sahib, whom she saw as weak and feckless, and who (again, as she saw it) had killed all desire in his wife ever to emerge from purdah. But she had great affection for his children: for Zainab, because her temperament was like her mother's; for Imtiaz, because his laughter and many of his expressions resembled hers; and for Firoz, whose long head and clear and handsome looks bore the imprint of his mother's face.

Hassan and Abbas were now brought in by the maidservant and Zainab kissed them a tearful goodnight.

Hassan, looking slightly sullen, said to his mother: 'Who's been making you cry, Ammi-jaan?'

His mother, smiling, hugged him to her and said, 'No one, sweetheart. No one.'

Hassan then demanded from his grandfather the ghost story that he had promised to tell them some nights earlier. The Nawab Sahib complied. As he was narrating his exciting and fairly bloodthirsty tale to the evident delight of the two boys, even the three-year-old, he reflected over the many ghost stories attached to this very house that he had been told in childhood by his own servants and family. The house and all its memories had been threatened with dissolution just a few nights ago. No one had been able to prevent the attack and it was a mere matter of grace or chance or fate that it had been saved. We are each of us alone, thought the Nawab Sahib; blessedly, we rarely realize this.

His old friend Mahesh Kapoor came to his mind and it struck him that in times of trouble it sometimes happened that even those who wanted to help were unable to. They might be tied down themselves for one reason or another; or else circumstances of expediency or some greater need could have kept them less involuntarily away.

6.11

MAHESH KAPOOR too had been thinking of his old friend, and with a sense of guilt. He had not received the emergency message from Baitar House on the night that L.N. Agarwal had sent the police to take possession of it. The peon whom Mrs Mahesh Kapoor had sent to find him had not been able to do so.

Unlike rural land (now threatened by the prospect of the abolition of zamindari), urban land and buildings were under no threat of appropriation at all – except if they fell into the hands of the Custodian of Evacuee Property.

Mahesh Kapoor had not thought it at all likely that Baitar House, one of the great houses of Brahmpur – indeed, one of the landmarks of the city – could be at risk. The Nawab Sahib continued to live there, his sister-in-law Begum Abida Khan was a powerful voice in the Assembly, and the grounds and gardens in the front of the house were well taken care of, even if many – or most – of the rooms inside were now empty and unused. He regretted that he had been too preoccupied to advise his friend to provide each room with at least the semblance of occupancy. And he felt very bad that he had not been able to intercede with the Chief Minister in order to help on the night of the crisis.

As it had turned out, Zainab's intercession had achieved all that Mahesh Kapoor could have hoped to. S.S. Sharma's heart had been touched, and his indignation against the Home Minister had been unfeigned.

The letter that Zainab had written to him had mentioned a circumstance that the Nawab Sahib had told her about some years previously; it had stuck in her memory. S.S. Sharma – the ex-Premier of the Protected Provinces (as the Chief Minister of Purva Pradesh was called before Independence) – had been held virtually incommunicado in a British prison during the Quit India Movement of 1942, and could do as little for his family as they could for him. At this time the Nawab Sahib's father had come to know that Sharma's wife was ill and had come to her to help. It was a simple matter of a doctor, medicines and a visit or two, but in those days not many, whether they believed in British rule or not, wished to be seen associating with the families of subversives. Sharma had in fact been Premier when the P.P. Land Tenancy Act of 1938 had been passed – an act that the Nawab Sahib's father had considered, correctly, to be the thin end of the wedge of more far-reaching land reform. Nonetheless, simple humanity and even a sense of admiration for his enemy had inspired this crucial assistance. Sharma had been deeply grateful for the kindness that his family had received in their hour of need, and when Hassan, the six-year-old great-grandchild of the man who had helped him then, had come to him with a letter requesting his help and protection, he had been very moved.

Mahesh Kapoor knew nothing of these circumstances, for neither party had wanted them known, and he had been astonished to hear of the Chief Minister's swift and unambiguous response. It made him feel even more strongly how ineffectual he himself had been. And when, after the passage of the Zamindari Bill in the Assembly, he had caught the Nawab Sahib's eye, something had held him back from going up to his friend – in order to commiserate, explain and apologize. Was it shame about his inaction – or simply the obvious immediate discomfort at the fact that the bill that he had just successfully steered through the House would, though there was no animus in it, injure the Nawab Sahib's interests as surely as the police action of the Home Minister?

Now still more time had passed, and the matter continued to prey on his mind. I must visit Baitar House this evening, said Mahesh Kapoor to himself. I cannot keep putting it off.

6.12

BUT meanwhile, this morning, there was work that needed to be done. A large number of people both from his constituency in Old Brahmpur and from elsewhere had gathered on the verandahs of Prem Nivas. Some of them were even milling around in the courtyard and wandering out into the garden. Mahesh Kapoor's personal secretary and personal assistants were doing what they could to control the crowd and regulate the flow of visitors into the small office that the Minister of Revenue maintained at home.

Mahesh Kapoor sat at a table in the corner of the office. The two narrow benches that ran along the walls were occupied by a variety of people: farmers, traders, minor politicians, suppliants of one kind or another. An old man, a teacher, sat on the chair that faced Mahesh Kapoor across the table. He was younger, but looked older than the Minister. He had been worn out by a lifetime of care. He was an old freedom fighter, who had spent many years in jail under the British, and had seen his family reduced to poverty. He had obtained a B.A. in 1921, and with a qualification like that in those days he might well have gone on to retire at the very highest levels of Government. But in the later Twenties he had left everything to follow Gandhiji, and this idealistic impulse had cost him dearly. When he was in jail, his wife, with no one to support her, had died of tuberculosis, and his children, reduced to eating other people's scraps, had suffered nearly fatal starvation. With the coming of Independence he had hoped that his sacrifice would result in an order of things closer to the ideals he had fought for, but he had been bitterly disappointed. He saw the corruption that had begun to eat into the rationing system and the system of government contracts with a rapacity that surpassed anything he had known under the British. The police too had become more overt in their extortions. What was worse was that the local politicians, the members of the local Congress Committees, were often hand in glove with the corrupt petty officials. But when the old man had gone to the Chief Minister, S.S. Sharma, on behalf of the people of his neighbourhood, to ask him to take action against specific politicians, that great figure had merely smiled tiredly and said to him:

'Masterji, your work, that of the teacher, is a sacred occupation. Politics is like the coal trade. How can you blame people if their hands and faces become a little black?'

The old man was now talking to Mahesh Kapoor, trying to persuade him that the Congress Party had become as shamefully vested in its interests and as shamefully oppressive in its rule as the British had ever been.

'What you, of all people, are doing in this party, Kapoor Sahib, I don't know,' he said in Hindi that had more of an

Allahabad than a Brahmpur accent. 'You should have left it long ago.'

The old man knew that everyone in the room could hear what he was saying but he did not care. Mahesh Kapoor looked at him directly and said:

'Masterji, the times of Gandhiji have gone. I have seen him at his zenith, and I have seen him lose his hold so completely that he was not able to prevent the Partition of this country. He, however, was wise enough to see that his power and his inspiration were not absolute. He once said that it was not he but the situation that held the magic.'

The old man said nothing for a few seconds. Then, his mouth working slightly at the edges, he said: 'Minister Sahib, what are you saying to me?'

The change in his mode of address was not lost on Mahesh Kapoor, and he felt slightly ashamed at his own evasion. 'Masterji,' he went on, 'I may have suffered in the old days, but I have not suffered as you have. It is not that I am not disenchanted with what I see around me. I just fear that I will be of less use outside the party than in it.'

The old man, half to himself, said: 'Gandhiji was right when he foresaw what would happen if the Congress Party continued after Independence as the party of Government. That is why he said that it should be disbanded and its members should dedicate themselves to social work.'

Mahesh Kapoor did not mince his words in response. He simply said: 'If all of us had done that, there would have been anarchy in the country. It was the duty of those of us who had had some experience in the provincial governments in the late Thirties to at least keep the administration going. You are right when you describe what is going on all around us. But if people like you, Masterji, and I were to wash our hands of this coal trade, you can imagine what kind of people would take over. Previously politics was not profitable. You languished in jail, your children starved. Now politics is profitable, and naturally the kind of people who are interested in making money are keen to join the game. If we move out, they move in. It is as simple as that. Look at all these people milling around,' he went on in a voice that did not carry beyond the old man's ears, embracing in a broad gesture of his hands the room, the verandahs and the lawn. 'I can't tell you how many of them are begging me to get them Congress Party tickets for the coming elections. And I know as well as you do that in the times of the British, they would have run a hundred miles before accepting such a mark of favour!'

'I was not suggesting that you move out of politics, Kapoor Sahib,' said the old man; 'just that you help to form another party. Everyone knows that Pandit Nehru often feels that Congress is not the right place for him. Everyone knows how unhappy he is about Tandonji becoming the Congress President through questionable means. Everyone knows that Panditji has almost lost his grip on his own party. Everyone knows that he respects you, and I believe that it is your duty to go to Delhi and help persuade him to leave. With Pandit Nehru and the less self-satisfied parts of Congress splitting off, the new party they form will have a good chance of winning the next elections. I believe that; indeed, if I did not believe that I would be in despair.'

Mahesh Kapoor nodded his head, then said: 'I will think deeply about what you have said, Masterji. I would not like to deceive you into thinking that I have not considered such matters before. But there is a logic to events, and a method to timing, and I will ask you to leave it at that.'

The old man nodded his head, got up, and walked away with an expression of undisguised disappointment on his face.

6.13

A number of other people, some individually, some in pairs, some in groups, and some in what could only be called throngs, spoke to Mahesh Kapoor during the morning and early afternoon. Cups of tea came from the kitchen and went back empty. Lunchtime came and went, and the

Minister Sahib remained energetic though unfed. Mrs Mahesh Kapoor sent word to him through a servant; he waved him impatiently away. She would never have dreamed of eating before her husband did, but her main concern was not that she was hungry but that he needed food and did not know it.

Mahesh Kapoor gave as patient an audience as he could to the people who were channelled his way. There were ticket-seekers and favour-seekers of all kinds, politicos of various shades of honesty and opinion, advisers, gossip-mongers, agents, assistants, lobbyists, MLAs and other colleagues and associates, local businessmen clad in nothing but a dhoti (yet worth lakhs of rupees) who were looking for a contract or information or simply to be able to tell people that they had been received by the Revenue Minister, good people, bad people, happy people, unhappy people (more of the latter), people who had just come to pay their respects because they were in town, people who had come to gape in open-mouthed awe and who took in nothing of what he was saying, people who wanted to pull him to the right, people who wanted to push him further towards the left, Congressmen, socialists, communists, Hindu revivalists, old members of the Muslim League who wanted admission into Congress, the indignant members of a deputation from Rudhia who were complaining about some decision made by the local Sub-Divisional Officer. As a Governor once wrote about his experience of popularly elected provincial governments in the late 1930s: 'nothing was too petty, too local, too palpably groundless' not to justify small local leaders appealing to politicians over the head of the district administration.

Mahesh Kapoor listened, explained, conciliated, tied matters together, disentangled others, wrote notes, issued instructions, spoke loudly, spoke softly, examined copies of sections of the new electoral rolls that were being revised for the coming General Elections, got angry and was extremely sharp with someone, smiled wryly at someone else, yawned at a third, stood up as a renowned lawyer came in, and asked that tea be served to him in more elegant china.

At nine o'clock he was explaining what he understood about the provisions of the Hindu Code Bill to farmers who were worried and resentful that their sons' right to their land would be shared by their daughters (and therefore their sons-in-law) under the laws of intestate succession under consideration by Parliament in Delhi.

At ten o'clock he was saying to an old colleague and lawyer: 'As for that bastard, do you think that he can get his way with me? He came into my office with a wad of money, trying to get me to soften a provision of the Zamindari Bill, and I was tempted to have him arrested – title or no title. He might have ruled Marh once, but he had better learn that other men rule Purva Pradesh. Of course I know that he and his kind will challenge the bill in court. Do you think we are not going to be ready ourselves? That is why I wanted to consult you.'

At eleven o'clock he was saying: 'The basic problem for me personally is not the temple or the mosque. The basic problem is how the two religions will get on with each other in Brahmpur. Maulvi Sahib, you know my views on this. I've lived here most of my life. Naturally there is mistrust: the question is how to overcome it. You know how it is. The rank and file of Congress opposes old Muslim Leaguers who wish to join Congress. Well, this is only to be expected. But Congress has had a long tradition of Hindu-Muslim collaboration, and, believe me, it is the obvious party to join. And as far as tickets are concerned, I am giving you my word that there will be fair representation for Muslims. You won't regret that we have no reserved seats or separate electorates. Yes, the nationalist Muslims, who have been with our party throughout their careers, will receive preference in this matter, but if I have anything to do with it there will be some room for others as well.'

At noon he was saying: 'Damodarji, that's a very handsome ring you have on your finger. How much is it worth?

Twelve hundred rupees? No, no, I'm pleased to see you, but as you can see' – he pointed to the papers piled on his desk with one hand and gestured towards the crowds with the other – 'I have much less time to talk to my old friends than I would wish....'

At one o'clock he was saying: 'Are you telling me that the lathi charge was necessary? Have you seen how these people live? And you have the gall to tell me that there should be some threat of further punitive action? Go and talk to the Home Minister, you'll find a more sympathetic audience. I am sorry – you can see how many people are waiting –'

At two o'clock he was saying: 'I suppose I have a little influence. I'll see what I can do. Tell the boy to come around to see me next week. Obviously, a lot will depend upon his exam results. No, no, don't thank me – and certainly don't thank me in advance.'

At three o'clock he was saying quietly: 'Look, Agarwal has about a hundred MLAs in his hand. I have about eighty. The rest are uncommitted, and will go wherever they sense victory. But I'm not going to think of mounting a challenge to Sharmaji. It's only if Panditji calls him to join the Central Cabinet in Delhi that the question of the leadership will come up. Still, I agree that there's no harm in keeping the issue alive – one has to remain in the public eye.'

At a quarter past three, Mrs Mahesh Kapoor came in, reproved the PAs gently, and pleaded with her husband to come and have lunch and lie down for a while. She herself was clearly still suffering from the residual neem blossoms, and her allergy was causing her to gasp a little. Mahesh Kapoor did not snap at her as he often did. He acquiesced and retired. People drifted away reluctantly and very gradually, and after a while Prem Nivas once more reverted from a political stage, clinic, and fairground to a private home.

After Mahesh Kapoor had eaten, he lay down for a short nap, and Mrs Mahesh Kapoor finally ate lunch herself.

AFTER lunch, Mahesh Kapoor asked his wife to read him
some passages from the *Proceedings of the P.P. Legislative
Council* that dealt with the debate on the Zamindari Bill
when it had first gone to the Upper House from the
Assembly. Since it was about to go there again with its
new encrustation of amendments, he wanted to regain his
sense of the possible obstacles it might face in that
chamber.

Mahesh Kapoor himself found it very difficult to read
the Purva Pradesh legislative debates of the last few years.
Some members took peculiar pride these days in couching
their speeches in a heavily Sanskritized Hindi which no one
in his right mind could understand. That, however, was
not the main problem. The real difficulty was that Mahesh
Kapoor was not very familiar with the Hindi – or Devana-
gari – script. He had been brought up at a time when boys
were taught to read and write the Urdu – or Arabic –
script. In the 1930s the *Proceedings of the Protected Provinces Legislative Assembly* were printed speech by speech
in English, Urdu, and Hindi – depending on the language
that the speaker wrote or spoke. His own speeches were
printed in Urdu, for instance, and so were the speeches of
a good many others. The English speeches he could of
course read without difficulty. But he tended to skip the
Hindi ones, as they made him struggle. Now, after Independence, the *Proceedings* were printed entirely in the
official language of the state, which was Hindi; Urdu
speeches too were printed in the Hindi script, and English
could only be spoken – and that, too, extremely rarely –
with the express permission of the Speaker of the House.
This was why Mahesh Kapoor often asked his wife to read
the debates out to him. She had been taught – like many
women at the time – to read and write under the influence
of the Hindu revivalist organization, the Arya Samaj, and
the script that she had been taught was, naturally enough,
the script of the ancient Sanskrit texts – and the modern
Hindi language.

Perhaps there was also an element of vanity or prudence in having his wife, rather than his personal assistants, read him these debates. The Minister did not wish the world at large to know that he could not read Hindi. As it happened, his PAs knew that he could not, but they were fairly discreet, and the word did not get around.

Mrs Mahesh Kapoor read in a rather monotonous voice, a bit as if she were chanting the scriptures. The pallu of her sari covered her head and a part of her face, and she did not look directly at her husband. Her breath was a little short these days, so she had to pause from time to time, and Mahesh Kapoor would become quite impatient. 'Yes, yes, go on, go on!' he would say whenever there was a longish pause, and she, patient woman that she was, would do so without complaint.

From time to time – usually between one debate and another, or as she reached for a different volume – she would mention something entirely outside the political sphere that had been on her mind. Since her husband was always busy, this was one of the few opportunities she got to talk to him. One such matter was that Mahesh Kapoor had not met his old friend and bridge partner Dr Kishen Chand Seth for some time.

'Yes, yes, I know,' said her husband impatiently. 'Go on, go on, yes, from page 303.' Mrs Mahesh Kapoor, having tested the water and found it too warm, was quiet for a while.

At the second opening she saw, she mentioned that she would like to have the Ramcharitmanas recited in the house some day soon. It would be good for the house and family in general: for Pran's job and health, for Maan, for Veena and Kedarnath and Bhaskar, for Savita's forthcoming baby. The ideal time, the nine nights leading up to and including the birthday of Rama, had gone by, and both her samdhins had been disappointed that she had not been able to persuade her husband to allow the recitation. At that time she could understand that he had been preoccupied with a number of things, but surely now –

She was interrupted abruptly. Mahesh Kapoor, pointing

his finger at the volume of debates, exclaimed: 'Oh, fortunate one —' (fortunate to have married him, that is) '— first recite the scriptures that I've asked you to recite.'

'But you promised that —'

'Enough of this. You three mothers-in-law can plot as much as you like, but I can't allow it in Prem Nivas. I have a secular image — and in a town like this where everyone is beating the drum of religion, I am not going to join in with the shehnai. Anyway, I don't believe in this chanting and hypocrisy — and all this fasting by saffron-clad heroes who want to ban cow slaughter and revive the Somnath Temple and the Shiva Temple and God knows what else.'

'The President of India himself will be going to Somnath to help inaugurate the new temple there —'

'Let the President of India do what he likes,' said Mahesh Kapoor sharply. 'Rajendra Babu does not have to win an election or face the Assembly. I do.'

Mrs Mahesh Kapoor waited for the next hiatus in the debates before venturing: 'I know that the nine nights of Ramnavami have gone, but the nine nights of Dussehra are still to come. If you think that in October —'

In her eagerness to convince her husband, she had begun to gasp a little.

'Calm down, calm down,' said Mahesh Kapoor, relenting slightly. 'We'll see all about that in due course.'

Even if the door was not exactly ajar, it had not been slammed shut, reflected Mrs Mahesh Kapoor. She retired from this subject with a sense that something, however slight, had been gained. She believed — though she would not have voiced the belief — that her husband was quite wrong-headed in divesting himself of the religious rites and ceremonies that gave meaning to life and donning the drab robes of his new religion of secularism.

At the next pause Mrs Mahesh Kapoor murmured tentatively: 'I have had a letter.'

Mahesh Kapoor clicked his tongue impatiently, dragged once again from his own thoughts down into the trivial vortices of domesticity. 'All right, all right, what is it that you want to talk about? Who is this letter from? What disaster am I in for?' He was used to the fact that his wife led these piecemeal conversations step by step and subject by subject from the most innocuous to the most troubling.

'It is from the Banaras people,' said Mrs Mahesh Kapoor.

'Hmmh!' said Mahesh Kapoor.

'They send their best wishes to everyone,' said Mrs Mahesh Kapoor.

'Yes, yes, yes! Get to the point. They realize no doubt that our son is too good for their daughter and want to call the whole thing off.'

Sometimes wisdom lies in not taking an ironical remark as ironical. Mrs Mahesh Kapoor said: 'No, quite the opposite. They want to fix the date as quickly as possible – and I don't know what to reply. If you read between the lines it seems that they even have some idea about – well, about "that". Why else would they be so concerned?'

'Uff-oh!' said Mahesh Kapoor impatiently. 'Do I have to hear about this from everyone? In the Assembly canteen, in my own office, everywhere I hear about Maan and his idiocy! This morning two or three people brought it up. Is there nothing more important in the world to talk about?'

But Mrs Mahesh Kapoor persevered.

'It is very important for our family,' she said. 'How can we hold our heads up in front of people if this goes on? And it is not good for Maan either to spend all his time and money like this. He was supposed to come here on business, and he has done nothing in that line. Please speak to him.'

'You speak to him,' said Mahesh Kapoor brutally. 'You have spoilt him all his life.'

Mrs Mahesh Kapoor was silent, but a tear trickled down her cheek. Then she rallied and said: 'Is it good for your public image either? A son who does nothing but spend his time with that kind of person? The rest of the time he lies down on his bed and stares up at the fan. He

449

should do something else, something serious. I don't have the heart to say anything to him. After all, what can a mother say?'

'All right, all right, all right,' said Mahesh Kapoor, and closed his eyes.

He reflected that the cloth business in Banaras was, under the care of a competent assistant, doing better in Maan's absence than it had been doing when he was there. What then was to be done with Maan?

At about eight o'clock that evening he was about to get into the car to visit Baitar House when he told the driver to wait. Then he sent a servant to see if Maan was in the house. When the servant told him that he was sleeping, Mahesh Kapoor said:

'Wake up the good-for-nothing fellow, and tell him to dress and come down at once. We are going to visit the Nawab Sahib of Baitar.'

Maan came down looking none too happy. Earlier in the day he had been exercising hard on the wooden horse, and now he was looking forward to visiting Saeeda Bai and exercising his wit, among other things.

'Baoji?' he said enquiringly.

'Get into the car. We're going to Baitar House.'

'Do you want me to come along?' asked Maan.

'Yes.'

'All right, then.' Maan got into the car. There was, he realized, no way to avoid being kidnapped.

'I am assuming you have nothing better to do,' said his father.

'No. . . . Not really.'

'Then you should get used to adult company again,' said his father sternly.

As it happened, he also enjoyed Maan's cheerfulness, and thought it would be good to take him along for moral support when he went to apologize to his old friend the Nawab Sahib. But Maan was less than cheerful at the moment. He was thinking of Saeeda Bai. She would be expecting him and he would not even be able to send her a message to say that he could not come.

AS they entered the grounds of Baitar House, however, he cheered up a little at the thought that he might meet Firoz. At polo practice Firoz had not mentioned that he would be going out for dinner.

They were asked to sit in the lobby for a few minutes. The old servant said that the Nawab Sahib was in the library, and that he would be informed of the Minister's arrival. After ten minutes or so, Mahesh Kapoor got up from the old leather sofa and started walking up and down. He was tired of twiddling his thumbs and staring at photographs of white men with dead tigers at their feet.

A few minutes more, and his patience was at an end. He told Maan to come with him, and walked through the high-ceilinged rooms and somewhat ill-lit corridors towards the library. Ghulam Rusool made a few ineffectual attempts at dissuasion, but to no effect. Murtaza Ali, who was hanging around near the library, was brushed aside as well. The Minister of Revenue with his son in tow strode up to the library door and flung it open.

Brilliant light blinded him for a moment. Not only the mellower reading lights but the great chandelier in the middle of the library had been lit. And at the large round table below – with papers spread out around them and even a couple of buff leather-bound law-books lying open before them – sat three other sets of fathers and sons: The Nawab Sahib of Baitar and Firoz; the Raja and Rajkumar of Marh; and two Bony Bespectacled Bannerji Barristers (as that famous family of lawyers was known in Brahmpur).

It would be difficult to say who was most embarrassed by this sudden intrusion.

The crass Marh snarled: 'Speak of the Devil.'

Firoz, though he found the situation uncomfortable, was pleased to see Maan and went up to him immediately to shake his hand. Maan put his left arm around his friend's shoulder and said: 'Don't shake my right hand – you've crippled it already.'

The Rajkumar of Marh, who was interested in young men more than in the jargon of the Zamindari Bill, looked at the handsome pair with a little more than approval.

The elder Bannerji ('P.N.') glanced quickly at his son ('S.N.') as if to say, 'I told you we should have had the conference in our chambers.'

The Nawab Sahib felt that he had been caught red-handed, plotting against Mahesh Kapoor's bill with a man whom he would normally have shunned.

And Mahesh Kapoor realized instantly that he was the least welcome intruder imaginable at this working conference – for it was he who was the enemy, the expropria-tor, the government, the fount of injustice, the other side.

It was, however, Mahesh Kapoor who broke the ice among the elder circle by going up to the Nawab Sahib and taking his hand. He did not say anything, but slowly nodded his head. No words of sympathy or apology were needed. The Nawab Sahib knew immediately that his friend would have done anything in his power to help him when Baitar House was under siege – but that he had been ignorant of the crisis.

The Raja of Marh broke the silence with a laugh:

'So you have come to spy on us! We are flattered. No mere minion but the Minister himself.'

Mahesh Kapoor said:

'Since I was not blinded by the vision of your gold number-plates outside, I could hardly have known you were here. Presumably, you came by rickshaw.'

'I will have to count my number-plates before I leave,' continued the Raja of Marh.

'If you need any help, let me send my son with you. He can count till two,' said Mahesh Kapoor.

The Raja of Marh had become red in the face. 'Was this planned?' he demanded of the Nawab Sahib. He was thinking that this could well be a plot by the Muslims and their sympathizers to humiliate him.

The Nawab Sahib found his voice. 'No, Your Highness, it was not. And I apologize to all of you, especially to you,

Mr Bannerji – I should not have insisted that we meet here.'

Since common interest in the impending litigation had thrown him together with the Raja of Marh anyway, the Nawab Sahib had hoped that by inviting the Raja to his own house he might get the chance to talk to him a little about the Shiva Temple in Chowk – or at least to create the possibility of a later talk. The communal situation among the Hindus and Muslims in Brahmpur was so troubling that the Nawab had swallowed his gorge and a little of his pride in order to help sort things out. The move had now backfired.

The elder of the Bony Bespectacleds, appalled by what had gone before, now said in a rather finicky voice: 'Well, I think we have already discussed the main lines of the matter, and can adjourn for the moment. I will inform my father by letter of what has been said by all sides, and I hope I can persuade him to appear for us in this matter if and when it is necessary.'

He was referring to the great G.N. Bannerji, a lawyer of legendary fame, acumen, and rapacity. If, as was now almost inevitable, the amended bill went through in the Upper House, obtained the President of India's signature, and became law, it would certainly be challenged in the Brahmpur High Court. If G.N. Bannerji could be persuaded to appear on behalf of the landlords, it would considerably improve their chances of having the act declared unconstitutional, and therefore null and void.

The Bannerjis took their leave. The younger Bannerji, though no older than Firoz, had a flourishing practice already. He was intelligent, worked hard, had cases shovelled his way by his family's old clients, and thought of Firoz as rather too languid for life at the Bar. Firoz admired his intelligence but thought him a prig, a little along the lines of his finicky father. His grandfather, the great G.N. Bannerji, however, was not a prig. Though he was in his seventies, he was as energetic erect on his feet in court as erect off his feet in bed. The huge, some would say unscrupulous, fees he insisted on before he accepted a case went to support a scattered harem of women; but he still succeeded in living beyond his means.

The Rajkumar of Marh was a basically decent and not bad-looking but somewhat weak young man who was bullied by his father. Firoz loathed the crude, Muslim-baiting Raja: 'black as coal with his diamond buttons and ear-tops'. His sense of family honour made him keep his distance from the Rajkumar as well. Not so Maan, who was inclined to like people unless they made themselves unlikable. The Rajkumar, quite attracted by Maan, and discovering that he was at a loose end these days, suggested a few things that they could do together, and Maan agreed to meet him later in the week.

Meanwhile the Raja of Marh, the Nawab Sahib, and Mahesh Kapoor were standing by the table in the full light of the chandelier. Mahesh Kapoor's eyes fell on the papers spread out on the table, but then, remembering the Raja's earlier jeer, he quickly turned his gaze away.

'No, no, be our guest, Minister Sahib,' sneered the Raja of Marh. 'Read away. And in exchange, tell me when exactly you plan to vest the ownership of our lands in your own pocket.'

'My own pocket?'

A silverfish scurried across the table. The Raja crushed it with his thumb.

'I meant, of course, the Revenue Department of the great state of Purva Pradesh.'

'In due course.'

'Now you are talking like your dear friend Agarwal in the Assembly.'

Mahesh Kapoor did not respond. The Nawab Sahib said: 'Should we move into the drawing room?'

The Raja of Marh made no attempt to move. He said, almost equally to the Nawab Sahib and the Minister of Revenue: 'I asked you that question merely from altruistic motives. I am supporting the other zamindars simply because I do not care for the attitude of the government – or political insects like you. I myself have nothing to lose. My lands are protected from your laws.'

'Oh?' said Mahesh Kapoor. 'One law for men and another for monkeys?'

'If you still call yourself a Hindu,' said the Raja of Marh, 'you may recall that it was the army of monkeys that defeated the army of demons.'

'And what miracle do you expect this time?' Mahesh Kapoor could not resist asking.

'Article 362 of the Constitution,' said the Raja of Marh, gleefully spitting out a number larger than two. 'These are our private lands, Minister Sahib, our own private lands, and by the covenants of merger that we rulers made when we agreed to join your India, the law cannot loot them and the courts cannot touch them.'

It was well known that the Raja of Marh had gone drunk and babbling to the dour Home Minister of India, Sardar Patel, to sign the Instrument of Accession by which he made over his state to the Indian Union, and had even smudged his signature with his tears – thus creating a unique historical document.

'We will see,' said Mahesh Kapoor. 'We will see. No doubt G.N. Bannerji will defend Your Highness in the future as ably as he has defended your lowness in the past.'

Whatever story lay behind this taunt, it had a signal effect.

The Raja of Marh made a sudden, growling, vicious lunge towards Mahesh Kapoor. Luckily he stumbled over a chair, and fell towards his left onto the table. Winded, he raised his face from among the law-books and scattered papers. But a page of a law-book had got torn.

For a second, staring at the torn page, the Raja of Marh looked dazed, as if he was uncertain where he was. Firoz, taking advantage of his disorientation, quickly went up to him, and with an assured arm led him towards the drawing room. It was all over in a few seconds. The Rajkumar followed his father.

The Nawab Sahib looked towards Mahesh Kapoor, and raised one hand slightly, as if to say, 'Let things be.' Mahesh Kapoor said, 'I am sorry, very sorry'; but both he and his friend knew that he was referring less to the immediate incident than to his delay in coming to Baitar House.

After a while, he said to his son: 'Come, Maan, let's go.' On the way out, they noticed the Raja's long black Lancia with its solid gold ingot-like licence-plates stamped 'MARH 1' lurking in the drive.

In the car back to Prem Nivas, each was lost in his own thoughts. Mahesh Kapoor was thinking that, despite his explosive timing, he was glad that he had not waited still longer to reassure his friend. He could sense how affected the Nawab Sahib had been when he had taken his hand.

Mahesh Kapoor expected that the Nawab Sahib would call him up the next day to apologize for what had happened, but not offer any substantial explanations. The whole business was very uncomfortable: there was a strange, unresolved air to events. And it was disturbing that a coalition – however volatile – of former enemies was coming into being out of self-interest or self-preservation against his long-nurtured legislation. He would very much have liked to know what legal weaknesses, if any, the lawyers had found in his bill.

Maan was thinking how glad he was that he had met his friend again. He had told Firoz that he would probably be stuck with his father the whole evening, and Firoz had promised to send a message to Saeeda Bai – and if necessary to take it there personally – to inform her that Dagh Sahib had been detained.

6.16

'NO; be careful; think.'

The voice was slightly mocking, but not without concern. It appeared to care that the task should be done well – that the neatly lined page should not become a record of shame and shapelessness. In a way, it appeared to care about what happened to Maan as well. Maan frowned, then wrote the character 'meem' again. It looked to him like a curved spermatozoon.

'Your mind isn't on the tip of your nib,' said Rasheed. 'If you want to make use of my time — and I am here at your service — why not concentrate on what you're doing?'

'Yes, yes, all right, all right,' said Maan shortly, sounding for a second remarkably like his father. He tried again. The Urdu alphabet, he felt, was difficult, multiform, fussy, elusive, unlike either the solid Hindi or the solid English script.

'I can't do this. It looks beautiful on the printed page, but to write it —'

'Try again. Don't be impatient.' Rasheed took the bamboo pen from his hand, dipped it in the inkwell, and wrote a perfect, dark blue 'meem'. He then wrote another below it: the letters were identical, as two letters rarely are.

'What does it matter, anyway?' asked Maan, looking up from the sloping desk at which he was sitting, cross-legged, on the floor. 'I want to read Urdu and to write it, not to practise calligraphy. Do I have to do this?' He reflected that he was asking for permission as he used to when he was a child. Rasheed was no older than he was, but had taken complete control of him in his role as a teacher.

'Well, you have put yourself in my hands, and I don't want you to start on shaky foundations. So what would you like to read now?' Rasheed inquired with a slight smile, hoping that Maan's answer would not be the predictable one once more.

'Ghazals,' said Maan unhesitatingly. 'Mir, Ghalib, Dagh....'

'Yes, well —' Rasheed said nothing for a while. There was tension in his eyes at the thought of having to teach ghazals to Maan shortly before going over passages of the Holy Book with Tasneem.

'So what do you say?' said Maan. 'Why don't we start today?'

'That would be like teaching a baby to run the marathon,' Rasheed responded after a few seconds, having found an analogy ridiculous enough to suit his dismay.

'Eventually, of course, you will be able to. But for now, just try that meem again.'

Maan put the pen down and stood up. He knew that Saeeda Bai was paying Rasheed, and he sensed that Rasheed needed the money. He had nothing against his teacher; in a way he liked his conscientiousness. But he rebelled against his attempt to impose a new infancy on him. What Rasheed was pointing out to him was the first step on an endless and intolerably tedious road; at this rate it would be years before he would be able to read even those ghazals that he knew by heart. And decades before he could pen the love-letters he yearned to write. Yet Saeeda Bai had made a compulsory half-hour lesson a day with Rasheed 'the little bitter foretaste' that would whet his appetite for her company.

The whole thing was so cruelly erratic, however, thought Maan. Sometimes she would see him, sometimes not, just as it suited her. He had no sense of what to expect, and it ruined his concentration. And so here he had to sit in a cool room on the ground floor of his beloved's house with his back hunched over a pad with sixty aliphs and forty zaals and twenty misshapen meems, while occasionally a few magical notes from the harmonium, a phrase from the sarangi, a strain of a thumri floated down the inner balcony and filtered through the door to frustrate both his lesson and him.

Maan never enjoyed being entirely by himself at the best of times, but these evenings, when his lesson was over, if word came through Bibbo or Ishaq that Saeeda Bai preferred to be alone, he felt crazy with unhappiness and frustration. Then, if Firoz and Imtiaz were not at home, and if family life appeared, as it usually did, unbearably bland and tense and pointless, Maan would fall in with his latest acquaintances, the Rajkumar of Marh and his set, and lose his sorrows and his money in gambling and drink.

'Look, if you aren't in the mood for a lesson today....' Rasheed's voice was kinder than Maan had expected, though there was rather a sharp expression on his wolf-like face.

'No, no, that's fine. Let's go on. It's just a question of self-control.' Maan sat down again.

'Indeed it is,' said Rasheed, reverting to his former tone of voice. Self-control, it struck him, was what Maan needed even more than perfect meems. 'Why have you got yourself trapped in a place like this?' he wanted to ask Maan. 'Isn't it pathetic that you should be sacrificing your dignity for a person of Saeeda Begum's profession?'

Perhaps all this was present in his three crisp words. At any rate, Maan suddenly felt like confiding in him.

'You see, it's like this –' began Maan. 'I have a weak will, and when I fall into bad company –' He stopped. What on earth was he saying? And how would Rasheed know what he was talking about? And why, even if he did, should he care?

But Rasheed appeared to understand. 'When I was younger,' he said, 'I – who now consider myself truly sober – would spend my time beating people up. My grandfather used to do so in our village, and he was a well-respected man, so I thought that beating people up was what made people look up to him. There were about five or six of us, and we would egg each other on. We'd just go up to some schoolfellow, who might be wandering innocently along, and slap him hard across the face. What I would never have dared to do alone, I did without any hesitation in company. But, well, I don't any more. I've learned to follow another voice, to be alone and to understand things – maybe to be alone and to be misunderstood.'

To Maan this sounded like the advice of a good angel; or perhaps a risen one. In his imagination's eye he saw the Rajkumar and Rasheed struggling for his soul. One was coaxing him towards hell with five poker cards, one beating him towards paradise with a quill. He botched another meem before asking:

'And is your grandfather still alive?'

'Oh yes,' said Rasheed, frowning. 'He sits on a cot in the shade and reads the Quran Sharif all day, and chases the village children away when they disturb him. And soon he will try to chase the officers of the law away too, because he doesn't like your father's plans.'

'So you're zamindars?' Maan was surprised.

Rasheed thought this over before saying: 'My grand-father was, before he divided his wealth among his sons. And so is my father and so is my, well, my uncle. As for myself –' He paused, appeared to look over Maan's page, then continued, without finishing his previous sentence, 'Well, who am I to set myself up in judgment in these matters? They are very happy, naturally, to keep things as they are. But I have lived in the village almost all my life, and I have seen the whole system. I know how it works. The zamindars – and my family is not so extra-ordinary as to be an exception to this – the zamindars do nothing but make their living from the misery of others; and they try to force their sons into the same ugly mould as themselves.' Here Rasheed paused, and the area around the corners of his mouth tightened. 'If their sons want to do anything else, they make life miserable for them too,' he continued. 'They talk a great deal about family honour, but they have no sense of honour except to gratify the promises of pleasure they have made to themselves.'

He was silent for a second, as if hesitating; then went on:

'Some of the most respected of landlords do not even keep their word, they are so petty. You might find this hard to believe but I was virtually offered a job here in Brahmpur as the curator of the library of one such great man, but when I got to the grand house I was told – well, anyway, all this is irrelevant. The main fact is that the system of landlords isn't good for the villagers, it isn't good for the countryside as a whole, it isn't good for the country, and until it goes. . . .' The sentence remained unfin-ished. Rasheed was pressing his fingertips to his forehead, as if he was in pain.

This was a far cry from meem, but Maan listened with sympathy to the young tutor, who appeared to speak out of some terrible pressure, not merely of circumstances.

Only a few minutes earlier he had been counselling care, concentration, and moderation for Maan.

There was a knock on the door, and Rasheed quickly straightened up. Ishaq Khan and Motu Chand entered.

'Our apologies, Kapoor Sahib.'

'No, no, you're quite right to enter,' said Maan. 'The time for my lesson is over, and I'm depriving Begum Sahiba's sister of her Arabic.' He got up. 'Well, I'll see you tomorrow, and my meems will be matchless,' he promised Rasheed impetuously. 'Well?' he nodded genially at the musicians, 'Is it life or death?'

But from Motu Chand's downcast looks he anticipated Ishaq Khan's words.

'Kapoor Sahib, I fear that this evening – I mean the Begum Sahiba asked me to inform you. . . .'

'Yes, yes,' said Maan, angry and hurt. 'Good. My deep respects to the Begum Sahiba. Till tomorrow, then.'

'It is just that she is indisposed.' Ishaq disliked lying and was bad at it.

'Yes,' said Maan, who would have been very much more concerned if he had believed in her indisposition. 'I trust that she will recover rapidly.' At the door he turned and added: 'If I thought it would do any good, I would prescribe her a string of meems, one to be taken every hour and several before she retires.'

Motu Chand looked at Ishaq for a clue, but Ishaq's face reflected his own perplexity.

'It's no more than she has prescribed for me,' said Maan. 'And, as you can see, I am flourishing as a result. My soul, at any rate, has avoided indisposition as successfully as she has been avoiding me.'

6.17

RASHEED was just picking up his books when Ishaq Khan, who was still standing by the door, blurted out:

'And Tasneem is indisposed as well.'

Motu Chand glanced at his friend. Rasheed's back was

towards them, but it had stiffened. He had heard Ishaq Khan's excuse to Maan; it had not increased his respect for the sarangi player that he had acted in this demeaning manner as an emissary for Saeeda Bai. Was he now acting as an emissary for Tasneem as well?

'What gives you that understanding?' he asked, turning around slowly.

Ishaq Khan coloured at the patent disbelief in the teacher's voice.

'Well, whatever state she is in now, she will be indisposed after her lesson with you,' he replied challengingly. And, indeed, it was true. Tasneem was often in tears after her lessons with Rasheed.

'She has a tendency to tears,' said Rasheed, sounding more harsh than he intended. 'But she is not unintelligent and is making good progress. If there are any problems with my teaching, her guardian can inform me in person – or in writing.'

'Can't you be a little less rigorous with her, Master Sahib?' said Ishaq hotly. 'She is a delicate girl. She is not training to become a mullah, you know. Or a haafiz.'

And yet, tears or no tears, reflected Ishaq painfully, Tasneem was spending so much of her spare time on Arabic these days that she had very little left for anyone else. Her lessons appeared to have redirected her even from romantic novels. Did he really wish her young teacher to start behaving gently towards her?

Rasheed had gathered up his papers and books. He now spoke almost to himself. 'I am no more rigorous with her than I am with' – he had been about to say 'myself' – 'with anyone else. One's emotions are largely a matter of self-control. Nothing is painless,' he added a little bitterly.

Ishaq's eyes flashed. Motu Chand placed a restraining hand on his shoulder.

'And anyway,' continued Rasheed, 'Tasneem has a tendency to indolence.'

'She appears to have lots of tendencies, Master Sahib.'

Rasheed frowned. 'And this is exacerbated by that half-witted parakeet which she keeps interrupting her work to feed or indulge. It is no pleasure to hear fragments of the Book of God being mangled in the beak of a blasphemous bird.'

Ishaq was too dumbstruck to say anything. Rasheed walked past him and out of the room.

'What made you provoke him like that, Ishaq Bhai?' said Motu Chand after a few seconds.

'Provoke him? Why, he provoked me. His last remark —'

'He couldn't have known that you had given her the parakeet.'

'Why, everyone knows.'

'He probably doesn't. He doesn't interest himself in that kind of thing, our upright Rasheed. What got into you? Why are you provoking everyone these days?'

The reference to Ustad Majeed Khan was not lost on Ishaq, but the subject was one he could hardly bear to think of. He said:

'So that owl book provoked you, did it? Have you tried any of its recipes? How many women has it lured into your power, Motu? And what does your wife have to say about your new-found prowess?'

'You know what I mean,' said Motu Chand, undeflected. 'Listen, Ishaq, there's nothing to be gained by putting people's backs up. Just now —'

'It's these wretched hands of mine,' cried Ishaq, holding them up and looking at them as if he hated them. 'These wretched hands. For the last hour upstairs it has been torture.'

'But you were playing so well —'

'What will happen to me? To my younger brothers? I can't get employment on the basis of my brilliant wit. And even my brother-in-law won't be able to come to Brahmpur to help us now. How can I show my face at the radio station, let alone ask for a transfer for him?'

'It's bound to get better, Ishaq Bhai. Don't distress yourself like this. I'll help you —'

This was of course impossible. Motu Chand had four small children.

'Even music means agony to me now,' said Ishaq Khan

463

to himself, shaking his head. 'Even music. I cannot bear to hear it even when I am not on duty. This hand follows the tune by itself, and it seizes up with pain. If my father had been alive, what would he have said if he had heard me speaking like this?'

6.18

'THE BEGUM SAHIBA was very explicit,' said the watchman. 'She is not seeing anyone this evening.'

'Why?' demanded Maan. 'Why?'

'I do not know,' said the watchman.

'Please find out,' said Maan, slipping a two-rupee note into the man's hand.

The watchman took the note and said: 'She is not well.'

'But you knew that before,' said Maan, a bit aggrieved. 'That means I must go and see her. She will be wanting to see me.'

'No,' said the watchman, standing before the gate. 'She will not be wanting to see you.'

This struck Maan as distinctly unfriendly. 'Now look,' he said, 'you have to let me in.' He tried to shoulder his way past the watchman, but the watchman resisted, and there was a scuffle.

Voices were heard from inside, and Bibbo emerged. When she saw what was happening, her hand flew to her mouth. Then she gasped out: 'Phool Singh – stop it! Dagh Sahib, please – please – what will Begum Sahiba say?'

This thought brought Maan to his senses, and he brushed down his kurta, looking rather shamefaced. Neither he nor the watchman was injured. The watchman continued to look entirely matter-of-fact about the whole incident.

'Bibbo, is she very ill?' asked Maan in vicarious pain.

'Ill?' said Bibbo. 'Who's ill?'

'Saeeda Bai, of course.'

'She's not in the least ill,' said Bibbo, laughing. Then, as she caught the watchman's eye, she added: 'At least not until half an hour ago, when she had a sharp pain around her heart. She can't see you – or anyone.'

'Who's with her?' demanded Maan.

'No one, that is, well, as I've just said – no one.'

'Someone is with her,' said Maan fiercely, with a sharp stab of jealousy.

'Dagh Sahib,' said Bibbo, not without sympathy, 'it is not like you to be like this.'

'Like what?' said Maan.

'Jealous. Begum Sahiba has her old admirers – she cannot cast them off. This house depends on their generosity.'

'Is she angry with me?' asked Maan.

'Angry? Why?' asked Bibbo blankly.

'Because I didn't come that day as I had promised,' said Maan. 'I tried – I just couldn't get away.'

'I don't think she was angry with you,' said Bibbo. 'But she was certainly angry with your messenger.'

'With Firoz?' said Maan, astonished.

'Yes, with the Nawabzada.'

'Did he deliver a note?' asked Maan. He reflected with a little envy that Firoz, who could read and write Urdu, could thereby communicate in writing with Saeeda Bai.

'I think so,' said Bibbo, a little vaguely.

'And why was she angry?' asked Maan.

'I don't know,' said Bibbo with a light laugh. 'I must go in now.' And she left Maan standing on the pavement looking very agitated.

Saeeda Bai had in fact been greatly displeased to see Firoz, and was annoyed at Maan for having sent him. Yet, when she received Maan's message that he could not come on the appointed evening, she could not help feeling disappointed and sad. And this fact too annoyed her. She could not afford to get emotionally attached to this light-hearted, light-headed, and probably light-footed young man. She had a profession to keep up, and he was definitely in the nature of a distraction, however pleasant. And so she began to realize that it might be a good thing if he stayed away for a while. Since she was entertaining a patron this evening, she had instructed the watchman to keep everyone else – and particularly Maan – away.

When Bibbo later reported to her what had happened, Saeeda Bai's reaction was irritation at what she saw as Maan's interference in her professional life: he had no claim on her time or what she did with it. But later still, talking to the parakeet, she said, 'Dagh Sahib, Dagh Sahib' quite a number of times, her expression ranging from sexual passion to flirtatiousness to tenderness to indifference to irritation to anger. The parakeet was receiving a more elaborate education in the ways of the world than most of his fellows.

*

Maan had wandered off, wondering what to do with his time, incapable of getting Saeeda Bai out of his mind, but craving some, any, activity that could distract him at least for a moment. He remembered that he'd said he would drop by to see the Rajkumar of Marh, and so he made his way to the lodgings not far from the university that the Rajkumar had taken with six or seven other students, four of whom were still in Brahmpur at the beginning of the summer vacation. These students – two the scions of other petty princedoms, and one the son of a large zamindar – were not short of money. Most of them got a couple of hundred rupees a month to spend as they liked. This would have been just about equal to Pran's entire salary, and these students looked upon their unwealthy lecturers with easy contempt.

The Rajkumar and his friends ate together, played cards together, and shared each other's company a good deal. Each of them spent fifteen rupees a month on mess fees (they had their own cook) and another twenty rupees a month on what they called 'girl fees'. These went to support a very beautiful nineteen-year-old dancing girl who lived with her mother in a street not far from the university. Rupvati would entertain the friends quite often, and one of them would stay behind afterwards. This way each of them got a turn once every two weeks by rotation.

On the other nights, Rupvati was free to entertain any of them or to take a night off, but the understanding was that she would have no other clients. The mother would greet the boys very affectionately; she was very pleased to see them, and often told them that she did not know what she and her daughter would have done if it hadn't been for their kindness.

Within half an hour of meeting the Rajkumar of Marh and drinking a fair amount of whisky, Maan had spilt out all his troubles on his shoulder. The Rajkumar mentioned Rupvati, and suggested that they visit her. Maan cheered up slightly at this and, taking the bottle with them, they began to walk in the direction of her house. But the Rajkumar suddenly remembered that this was one of her nights off, and that they would not be entirely welcome there.

'I know what we'll do. We'll visit Tarbuz ka Bazaar instead,' said the Rajkumar, hailing a tonga and pulling Maan onto it. Maan was in no mood to resist this suggestion.

But when the Rajkumar, who had placed a friendly hand on his thigh, moved it significantly upwards, he shook it away with a laugh.

The Rajkumar did not take this rejection at all amiss, and in a couple of minutes, with the bottle passing between them, they were talking as easily as before.

'This is a great risk for me,' said the Rajkumar, 'but because of our great friendship I am doing it.'

Maan began to laugh. 'Don't do it again,' he said. 'I feel ticklish.'

Now it was the Rajkumar's turn to laugh. 'I don't mean that,' he said. 'I mean that taking you to Tarbuz ka Bazaar is a risk for me.'

'Oh, how?' said Maan.

'Because "any student who is seen in an undesirable place shall be liable to immediate expulsion."'

The Rajkumar was quoting from the curious and detailed rules of conduct promulgated for the students of Brahmpur University. This particular rule sounded so vague and yet at the same time so delightfully draconian that the Rajkumar and his friends had learned it by heart and used to chant it in chorus to the lilt of the Gayatri Mantra whenever they went out to gamble or drink or whore.

6.19

THEY soon got to Old Brahmpur, and wound through the narrow streets towards Tarbuz ka Bazaar. Maan was beginning to have second thoughts.

'Why not some other night –?' he began.

'Oh, they serve very good biryani there,' said the Rajkumar.

'Where?'

'At Tahmina Bai's. I've been there once or twice when it's been a non-Rupvati day.'

Maan's head sank on his chest and he went off to sleep. When they got to Tarbuz ka Bazaar, the Rajkumar woke him up.

'From here we'll have to walk.'

'Not far?'

'No – not far. Tahmina Bai's place is just around the corner.'

They dismounted, paid the tonga-wallah, and walked hand in hand into a side alley. The Rajkumar then walked up a flight of narrow and steep stairs, pulling a tipsy Maan behind him.

But when they got to the top of the stairs they heard a confused noise, and when they had walked a few steps along the corridor they were faced with a curious scene.

The plump, pretty, dreamy-eyed Tahmina Bai was giggling in delight as an opium-eyed, vacant-faced, red-tongued, barrel-bodied, middle-aged man – an income tax clerk – was beating on the tabla and singing an obscene song in a thin voice. Two scruffy lower division clerks were lounging around, one of them with his head in her lap. They were trying to sing along.

The Rajkumar and Maan were about to beat a retreat, when the madam of the establishment saw them and bustled quickly towards them along the corridor. She knew who the Rajkumar was, and hastened to reassure him that the others would be cleared out in a couple of minutes.

The two loitered around a paan shop for a few minutes, then went back upstairs. Tahmina Bai, alone, and with a beatific smile on her face, was ready to entertain them.

First she sang a thumri, then – realizing that time was getting on – she fell into a sulk.

'Oh, do sing,' said the Rajkumar, prodding Maan to placate Tahmina Bai as well.

'Ye-es –' said Maan.

'No, I won't, you don't appreciate my voice.' She looked downwards and pouted.

'Well,' said the Rajkumar, 'at least grace us with some poetry.'

This sent Tahmina Bai into gales of laughter. Her pretty little jowls shook, and she snorted with delight. The Rajkumar was mystified. After another swig from his bottle, he looked at her in wonderment.

'Oh, it's too – ah, ah – grace us with some – hah, hah – poetry!'

Tahmina Bai was no longer in a sulk but in an ungovernable fit of laughter. She squealed and squealed and held her sides and gasped, the tears running down her face.

When she was finally capable of speech, she told them a joke.

'The poet Akbar Allahabadi was in Banaras when he was lured by some friends into a street just like ours. He had drunk quite a lot – just like you – so he leaned against a wall to urinate. And then – what happened? – a courtesan, leaning out from a window above, recognized him from one of his poetry recitals and – and she said –' Tahmina Bai giggled, then started laughing again, shaking from side to side. 'She said – Akbar Sahib is gracing us with his poetry!' Tahmina Bai began to laugh uncontrollably once more, and to Maan's fuddled amazement he found himself joining in.

But Tahmina Bai had not finished her joke, and went on:
'So when he heard her, the poet made this remark on the spur of the moment:

"Alas – what poor poetry can Akbar write
When the pen is in his hand and the inkpot upstairs?"'

This was followed by squeals and snorts of laughter. Then Tahmina Bai told Maan that she herself had something to show him in the other room, and led him in, while the Rajkumar took another couple of swigs.

After a few minutes she emerged, with Maan looking bedraggled and disgusted. But Tahmina Bai was pouting sweetly. She said to the Rajkumar: 'Now, I have something to show you.'

'No, no,' said the Rajkumar. 'I've already – no, I'm not in the mood – come, Maan, let's go.'

Tahmina Bai looked affronted, and said: 'Both of you are – are – very similar! What do you need me for?'

The Rajkumar had got up. He put an arm around Maan and they struggled towards the door. As they walked into the corridor they heard her say:

'At least have some biryani before you leave. It will be ready in a few minutes –'

Hearing no response from them, Tahmina Bai let fly:

'It might give you strength. Neither of you could grace me with your poetry!'

She began to laugh and shake, and her laughter followed them all the way down the stairs into the street.

6.20

EVEN though he had not done anything as such with her, Maan was feeling so remorseful about having visited such a low singing girl as Tahmina Bai that he wanted to go to Saeeda Bai's again immediately and beg her forgiveness. The Rajkumar persuaded him to go home instead. He took him to the gate of Prem Nivas and left him there.

Mrs Mahesh Kapoor was awake. When she saw Maan so drunk and unsteady she was very unhappy. Though she did not say anything to him, she was afraid for him. If his father had seen him in his present state he would have had a fit.

Maan, guided to his room, fell on his bed and went off to sleep.

The next day, contrite, he visited Saeeda Bai, and she was glad to see him. They spent the evening together. But she told him that she would be occupied for the next two days, and that he should not take it amiss.

Maan took it greatly amiss. He suffered from acute jealousy and thwarted desire, and wondered what he had done wrong. Even if he could have seen Saeeda Bai every evening, his days would merely have trickled by drop by drop. Now not only the days but the nights as well stretched interminably ahead of him, black and empty.

He practised a bit of polo with Firoz, but Firoz was busy during the days and sometimes even during the evenings with law or other work. Unlike the young Bespectacled Bannerji, Firoz did not treat time spent playing polo or deciding on a proper walking-stick as wasted; he considered these activities proper to the son of a Nawab. Compared to Maan, however, Firoz was an addict to his profession.

Maan tried to follow suit – to do a bit of purchasing and to seek a few orders for the cloth business in Banaras – but found it too irksome to pursue. He paid a visit or two to his brother Pran and his sister Veena, but the very domesticity and purposefulness of their lives was a rebuke to his own. Veena told him off roundly, asking him what kind of an example he thought he was setting for young Bhaskar, and old Mrs Tandon looked at him even more suspiciously and disapprovingly than before. Kedarnath, however, patted Maan on the shoulder, as if to compensate for his mother's coldness.

Having exhausted all his other possibilities, Maan began to hang around the Rajkumar of Marh's set and (though he did not visit Tarbuz ka Bazaar again) drank and gambled away much of the money that had been reserved for the business. The gambling – usually flush, but sometimes even poker, for which there was a recent craze among the more self-consciously dissolute students in Brahmpur – took place mainly in the students' rooms, but sometimes in informal gambling dens in private houses here and there in the city. Their drink was invariably Scotch. Maan thought of Saeeda Bai all the time, and declined a visit even to the beautiful Rupvati. For this he was chaffed by all his new companions, who told him that he might lose his abilities permanently for lack of exercise.

One day Maan, separated from his companions, was walking up and down Nabiganj in a lovesick haze when he bumped into an old flame of his. She was now married, but retained a great affection for Maan. Maan too continued to like her a great deal. Her husband – who had the unlikely nickname of Pigeon – asked Maan if he would join them for coffee at the Red Fox. But Maan, who would normally have accepted the invitation with alacrity, looked away unhappily and said that he had to be going.

'Why is your old admirer behaving so strangely?' said her husband to her with a smile.

'I don't know,' she said, mystified.

'Surely he's not fallen out of love with you.'

'That's possible – but unlikely. Maan Kapoor doesn't fall out of love with anyone as a rule.'

They let it go at that, and went into the Red Fox.

6.21

MAAN was not the only target of old Mrs Tandon's suspicions. Of late, the old lady, who kept tabs on everything, began to notice that Veena had not been wearing certain items of her jewellery: that though she continued to wear her in-laws' pieces, she had ceased to wear those that came from her parents. One day she reported this matter to her son.

Kedarnath paid no attention.

His mother kept at him, until eventually he agreed to ask Veena to put on her navratan.

Veena flushed. 'I've lent it to Priya, who wants to copy the design,' she said. 'She saw me wear it at Pran's wedding and liked it.'

But Veena looked so unhappy with her lie that the truth soon came out. Kedarnath discovered that running the household cost far more than she had told him it did; he, domestically impractical and often absent, had simply not noticed. She had hoped that by asking him for less household money she would reduce the financial pressure on his business. But now he realized that she had taken steps to pawn or sell her jewellery.

Kedarnath also learned that Bhaskar's school fees and books were already being supplied out of Mrs Mahesh Kapoor's monthly household money, some of which she diverted to her daughter.

'We can't have that,' said Kedarnath. 'Your father helped us enough three years ago.'

'Why not?' demanded Veena. 'Bhaskar's Nani is surely allowed to give him those, why not? It's not as if she's supplying us our rations.'

'There's something out of tune with my Veena today,' said Kedarnath, smiling a bit sadly.

Veena was not mollified.

'You never tell me anything,' she burst out, 'and then I find you with your head in your hands, and your eyes closed for minutes on end. What am I to think? And you are always away. Sometimes when you're away I cry to myself all night long; it would have been better to have a drunkard as a husband, as long as he slept here every night.'

'Now calm down. Where are these jewels?'

'Priya has them. She said she'd get me an estimate.'

'They haven't yet been sold then?'

'No.'

'Go and get them back.'

'No.'

'Go and get them back, Veena. How can you gamble with your mother's navratan?'

'How can you play chaupar with Bhaskar's future?'

Kedarnath closed his eyes for a few seconds.

'You understand nothing about business,' he said.

'I understand enough to know that you can't keep "over-extending" yourself.'

'Over-extension is just over-extension. All great fortunes are based on debt.'

'Well we, I know, will never be greatly fortunate again,' burst out Veena passionately. 'This isn't Lahore. Why can't we guard what little we have?'

Kedarnath was silent for a while. Then he said:

'Get the jewellery back. It's all right, it really is. Haresh's arrangement with the brogues is about to come through any day, and our long term problems will be solved.'

Veena looked at her husband very dubiously.

'Everything good is always about to happen, and everything bad always happens.'

'Now that's not true. At least in the short term something good has happened to me. The shops in Bombay have paid up at last. I promise you that that is true. I know I'm a bad liar, so I don't even attempt it. Now get the navratan back.'

'Show me the money first!'

Kedarnath burst out laughing. Veena burst into tears.

'Where's Bhaskar?' he asked, after she had sobbed for a bit and subsided into silence.

'At Dr Durrani's.'

'Good. I hope he stays there a couple of hours more. Let's play a game of chaupar, you and I.'

Veena dabbed at her eyes with her handkerchief.

'It's too hot on the roof. Your mother won't want her beloved son to turn black as ink.'

'Well, we'll play in this room, then,' said Kedarnath with decision.

*

Veena got the jewellery back late that afternoon. Priya was

not able to give her an estimate; with the witch hanging around the gossipy jeweller every minute of his previous visit, she had decided to subjugate urgency to discretion.

Veena looked at the navratan, gazing reminiscently at each stone in turn.

Early the same evening, Kedarnath went over with it to his father-in-law, and asked him to keep it in his custody at Prem Nivas.

'What on earth for?' asked Mahesh Kapoor. 'Why are you bothering me with these trinkets?'

'Baoji, it belongs to Veena, and I want to make sure she keeps it. If it's in my house, she might suddenly be struck with noble fancies and pawn it.'

'Pawn it?'

'Pawn it or sell it.'

'What madness. What's been going on? Have all my children taken leave of their senses?'

After a brief account of the navratan incident, Mahesh Kapoor said:

'And how is your business now that the strike is finally over?'

'I can't say it's going well – but it hasn't collapsed yet.'

'Kedarnath, run my farm instead.'

'No, but thank you, Baoji. I should be getting back now. The market must have opened already.' A further thought struck him. 'And besides, Baoji, who would mind your constituency if I decided to leave Misri Mandi?'

'True. All right. Fine. It's good that you have to go back because I have to deal with these files before tomorrow morning,' said Mahesh Kapoor inhospitably. 'I'll be working all night. Put it down here somewhere.'

'What – on the files, Baoji?' There was nowhere else on the table to place the navratan.

'Where else then – around my neck? Yes, yes, on that pink one: "Orders of the State Government on the Assessment Proposals". Don't look so anxious, Kedarnath, it won't disappear again. I'll see that Veena's mother puts the stupid thing away somewhere.'

LATER that night in the house where the Rajkumar and his friends lived, Maan lost more than two hundred rupees gambling on flush. He usually held onto his cards far too long before packing them in or asking for a show. The predictability of his optimism was fatal to his chances. Besides, he was entirely un-poker-faced, and his fellow-players had a shrewd idea of how good his cards were from the instant he picked them up. He lost ten rupees or more on hand after hand – and when he held three kings, all he won was four rupees.

The more he drank, the more he lost, and vice versa.

Every time he got a queen – or begum – in his hand, he thought with a pang of the Begum Sahiba whom he was allowed to see so rarely these days. He could sense that even when he was with her, despite their mutual excitement and affection, she was finding him less amusing as he became more intense.

After he had got completely cleaned out, he muttered in a slurred voice that he had to be off.

'Spend the night here if you wish – go home in the morning,' suggested the Rajkumar.

'No, no –' said Maan, and left.

He wandered over to Saeeda Bai's, reciting some poetry on the way and singing from time to time.

It was past midnight. The watchman, seeing the state he was in, asked him to go home. Maan started singing, appealing over his head to Saeeda Bai:

'It's just a heart, not brick and stone, why should it then
not fill with pain?
Yes, I will weep a thousand times, why should you
torture me in vain?'

'Kapoor Sahib, you will wake up everyone on the street,' said the watchman matter-of-factly. He bore Maan no grudge for the scuffle they had had the other night.

Bibbo came out and chided Maan gently. 'Kindly go

home, Dagh Sahib. This is a respectable house. Begum Sahiba asked who was singing, and when I told her, she was most annoyed. I believe she is fond of you, Dagh Sahib, but she will not see you tonight, and she has asked me to tell you that she will never see you in this state. Please forgive my impertinence, I am only repeating her words.'

'It's just a heart, not brick and stone,' sang Maan.

'Come, Sahib,' said the watchman calmly and led Maan gently but firmly down the street in the direction of Prem Nivas.

'Here, this is for you – you're a good man –' said Maan, reaching into his kurta pockets. He turned them inside out, but there was no money in them.

'Take my tip on account,' he suggested.

'Yes, Sahib,' said the watchman, and turned back to the rose-coloured house.

6.23

DRUNK, broke, and far from happy, Maan tottered back to Prem Nivas. To his surprise and rather unfocused distress, his mother was waiting up for him again. When she saw him, tears rolled down her cheeks. She was already overwrought because of the business with the navratan.

'Maan, my dear son, what has come over you? What has she done to my boy? Do you know what people are saying about you? Even the Banaras people know by now.'

'What Banaras people?' Maan inquired, his curiosity aroused.

'What Banaras people, he asks,' said Mrs Mahesh Kapoor, and began to cry even more intensely. There was a strong smell of whisky on her son's breath.

Maan put his arm protectively around her shoulder, and told her to go to sleep. She told him to go up to his room by the garden stairs to avoid disturbing his father, who was working late in his office.

But Maan, who had not taken in this last instruction, went humming off to bed by the main stairs.

'Who's that? Who's that? Is it Maan?' came his father's angry voice.

'Yes, Baoji,' said Maan, and continued to walk up the stairs.

'Did you hear me?' called his father in a voice that reverberated across half of Prem Nivas.

'Yes, Baoji,' Maan stopped.

'Then come down here at once.'

'Yes, Baoji.' Maan stumbled down the stairs and into his father's office. He sat down on the chair across the small table at which his father was sitting. There was no one in the office besides the two of them and a couple of lizards that kept scurrying across the ceiling throughout their conversation.

'Stand up. Did I tell you to sit down?'

Maan tried to stand up, but failed. Then he tried again, and leaned across the table towards his father. His eyes were glazed. The papers on the table and the glass of water near his father's hand seemed to frighten him.

Mahesh Kapoor stood up, his mouth set in a tight line, his eyes stern. He had a file in his right hand, which he slowly transferred to his left. He was about to slàp Maan hard across the face when Mrs Mahesh Kapoor rushed in and said:

'Don't – don't – don't do that –'

Her voice and eyes pleaded with her husband, and he relented. Maan, meanwhile, closed his eyes and collapsed back into the chair. He began to drift off to sleep.

His father, enraged, came around the table, and started shaking him as if he wanted to jolt every bone in his body.

'Baoji!' said Maan, awoken by the sensation, and began to laugh.

His father raised his right arm again, and with the back of his hand slapped his twenty-five-year-old son across the face. Maan gasped, stared at his father, and raised his hand to touch his cheek.

Mrs Mahesh Kapoor sat down on one of the benches that ran along the wall. She was crying.

'Now you listen, Maan, unless you want another of those — listen to me,' said his father, even more furious now that his wife was crying because of something he had done. 'I don't care how much of this you remember tomorrow morning but I am not going to wait until you are sober. Do you understand?' He raised his voice and repeated, 'Do you understand?'

Maan nodded his head, suppressing his first instinct, which was to close his eyes again. He was so sleepy that he could only hear a few words drifting in and out of his consciousness. Somewhere, it seemed to him, there was a sort of tingling pain. But whose?

'Have you seen yourself? Can you imagine how you look? Your hair wild, your eyes glazed, your pockets hanging out, a whisky stain all the way down your kurta –'

Maan shook his head, then let it droop gently on his chest. All he wanted to do was to cut off what was going on outside his head: this angry face, this shouting, this tingling.

He yawned.

Mahesh Kapoor picked up the glass and threw the water on Maan's face. Some of it fell on his own papers but he didn't even look down at them. Maan coughed and choked and sat up with a start. His mother covered her eyes with her hands and sobbed.

'What did you do with the money? What did you do with it?' asked Mahesh Kapoor.

'What money?' asked Maan, watching the water drip down the front of his kurta, one channel taking the route of his whisky stain.

'The business money.'

Maan shrugged, and frowned in concentration.

'And the spending money I gave you?' continued his father threateningly.

Maan frowned in deeper concentration, and shrugged again.

'What did you do with it? I'll tell you what you did with

it – you spent it on that whore.' Mahesh Kapoor would never have referred to Saeeda Bai in such terms if he had not been driven beyond the limit of restraint.

Mrs Mahesh Kapoor put her hands to her ears. Her husband snorted. She was behaving, he thought impatiently, like all three of Gandhiji's monkeys rolled into one. She would be clapping her hands over her mouth next.

Maan looked at his father, thought for a second, then said, 'No. I only brought her small presents. She never asked for anything more. . . .' He was wondering to himself where the money could have gone.

'Then you must have drunk and gambled it away,' said his father in disgust.

Ah yes, that was it, recalled Maan, relieved. Aloud he said, in a pleased tone, as if an intractable problem had, after long endeavour, suddenly been solved:

'Yes, that is it, Baoji. Drunk – gambled – gone.' Then the implications of this last word struck him, and he looked shamefaced.

'Shameless – shameless – you are behaving worse than a depraved zamindar, and I will not have it,' cried Mahesh Kapoor. He thumped the pink file in front of him. 'I will not have it, and I will not have you here any longer. Get out of town, get out of Brahmpur. Get out at once. I will not have you here. You are ruining your mother's peace of mind, and your own life, and my political career, and our family reputation. I give you money, and what do you do with it? – you gamble with it or spend it on whores or on whisky. Is debauchery your only skill? I never thought I would be ashamed of a son of mine. If you want to see someone with real hardships look at your brother-in-law – he never asks for money for his business, let alone "for this and for that". And what of your fiancée? We find a suitable girl from a good family, we arrange a good match for you – and then you chase after Saeeda Bai, whose life and history are an open book.'

'But I love her,' said Maan.

'Love?' cried his father, his incredulity mixed with rage. 'Go to bed at once. This is your last night in this house. I want you out by tomorrow. Get out! Go to Banaras or wherever you choose, but get out of Brahmpur. Out!'

Mrs Mahesh Kapoor begged her husband to rescind this drastic command, but to no avail. Maan looked at the two geckos on the ceiling as they scurried about to and fro. Then – suddenly – he got up with great resolution and without assistance, and said:

'All right. Goodnight! Goodnight! Goodnight! I'll go! I'll leave this house tomorrow.'

And he went off to bed without help, even remembering to take off his shoes before he fell off to sleep.

6.24

THE next morning he woke up with a dreadful headache, which, however, cleared up miraculously in a couple of hours. He remembered that his father and he had exchanged words, and waited till the Minister of Revenue had gone to the Assembly before he went to ask his mother what it was they had said to each other. Mrs Mahesh Kapoor was at her wits' end: her husband had been so incensed last night that he hadn't slept for hours. Nor had he been able to work, and this had incensed him further. Any suggestion of reconciliation from her had met with an almost incoherently angry rebuke from him. She realized that he was quite serious, that Maan would have to leave. Hugging her son to her she said:

'Go back to Banaras, work hard, behave responsibly, win back your father's heart.'

None of these four clauses appealed particularly to Maan, but he assured his mother that he would not cause trouble at Prem Nivas any longer. He ordered a servant to pack his things. He decided that he would go and stay with Firoz; or, failing that, with Pran; or, failing that, with the Rajkumar and his friends; or, failing that, somewhere else in Brahmpur. He would not leave this beautiful city or forgo the chance to meet the woman he loved because his disapproving, desiccated father told him so.

'Shall I get your father's PA to arrange your ticket to Banaras?' asked Mrs Mahesh Kapoor.

'No. If I need to, I'll do that at the station.'

After shaving and bathing he donned a crisp white kurta-pyjama and made his way a little shamefacedly towards Saeeda Bai's house. If he had been as drunk as his mother seemed to think he had been, he supposed that he must have been equally so outside Saeeda Bai's gate, where he had a vague sense of having gone.

He arrived at Saeeda Bai's house. He was admitted. Apparently, he was expected.

On the way up the stairs, he glanced at himself in the mirror. Unlike before, he now looked at himself quite critically. A white, embroidered cap covered his head; he took it off and surveyed his prematurely balding temples before putting it on again, thinking ruefully that perhaps it was his baldness that Saeeda Bai did not like. 'But what can I do about it?' he thought.

When she heard his step on the corridor, Saeeda Bai called out in a welcoming voice, 'Come in, come in, Dagh Sahib. Your footsteps sound regular today. Let us hope that your heart is beating as regularly.'

Saeeda Bai had slept over the question of Maan and had concluded that something had to be done. Though she had to admit to herself that he was good for her, he was getting to be too demanding of her time and energy, too obsessively attached, for her to handle easily.

When Maan told her about his scene with his father, and that he had been thrown out of the house, she was very upset. Prem Nivas, where she sang regularly at Holi and had once sung at Dussehra, had become a regular fixture of her annual calendar. She had to consider the question of her income. Equally importantly, she did not want her young friend to remain in trouble with his father. 'Where do you plan to go?' she asked him.

'Why, nowhere!' exclaimed Maan. 'My father has delusions of grandeur. He thinks that because he can strip a million landlords of their inheritance, he can equally easily order his son about. I am going to stay in Brahmpur — with friends.' A sudden thought struck him. 'Why not here?' he asked.

'Toba, toba!' cried Saeeda Bai, putting her hands to her shocked ears.

'Why should I be separated from you? From the town where you live?' He leaned towards her and began to embrace her. 'And your cook makes such delicious shami kababs,' he added.

Saeeda Bai might have been pleased by Maan's ardour, but she was thinking hard. 'I know,' she said, disengaging herself. 'I know what you must do.'

'Mmh,' said Maan, attempting to engage himself again.

'Do sit still and listen, Dagh Sahib,' said Saeeda Bai in a coquettish voice. 'You want to be close to me, to understand me, don't you?'

'Yes, yes, of course.'

'Why, Dagh Sahib?'

'Why?' asked Maan incredulously.

'Why?' persisted Saeeda Bai.

'Because I love you.'

'What is love – this ill-natured thing that makes enemies even of friends?'

This was too much for Maan, who was in no mood to get involved in abstract speculations. A sudden, horrible thought struck him: 'Do *you* want me to go as well?'

Saeeda Bai was silent, then she tugged her sari, which had slipped down slightly, back over her head. Her kohl-blackened eyes seemed to look into Maan's very soul.

'Dagh Sahib, Dagh Sahib!' she rebuked him.

Maan was instantly repentant, and hung his head. 'I just feared that you might want to test our love by distance,' he said.

'That would cause me as much pain as you,' she told him sadly. 'But what I was thinking was quite different.'

She was silent, then played a few notes on the harmonium and said:

'Your Urdu teacher, Rasheed, is leaving for his village in a few days. He will be gone for a month. I don't know how to arrange for an Arabic teacher for Tasneem or an

Urdu teacher for you in his absence. And I feel that in order to understand me truly, to appreciate my art, to resonate to my passion, you must learn my language, the language of the poetry I recite, the ghazals I sing, the very thoughts I think.'

'Yes, yes,' whispered Maan, enraptured.

'So you must go to the village with your Urdu teacher for a while – for a month.'

'What?' cried Maan, who felt that another glass of water had been flung in his face.

Saeeda Bai was apparently so upset by her own solution to the problem – it was the obvious solution, she murmured, biting her lower lip sadly, but she did not know how she could bear being separated from him, etc. – that in a few minutes it was Maan who was consoling her rather than she him. It was the only way out of the problem, he assured her: even if he had nowhere to live in the village, he would sleep in the open, he would speak – think – write – the language of her soul, he would send her letters written in the Urdu of an angel. Even his father would be proud of him.

'You have made me see that there is no other way,' said Saeeda Bai at length, letting herself be convinced gradually.

Maan noticed that the parakeet, who was in the room with them, was giving him a cynical look. He frowned.

'When is Rasheed leaving?'

'Tomorrow.'

Maan went pale. 'But that only leaves tonight!' he cried, his heart sinking. His courage failed him. 'No – I can't go – I can't leave you.'

'Dagh Sahib, if you are faithless to your own logic, how can I believe you will be faithful to me?'

'Then I must spend this evening here. It will be our last night together in a – in a month.'

A month? Even as he said the word, his mind rebelled at the thought. He refused to accept it.

'It will not work this evening,' said Saeeda Bai in a practical tone, thinking of her commitments.

'Then I won't go,' cried Maan. 'I can't. How can I? Anyway, we haven't consulted Rasheed.'

'Rasheed will be honoured to give you hospitality. He respects your father very much – no doubt because of his skill as a woodcutter – and, of course, he respects you very much – no doubt because of your skill as a calligrapher.'

'I must see you tonight,' insisted Maan. 'I must. What woodcutter?' he added, frowning.

Saeeda Bai sighed. 'It is very difficult to cut down a banyan tree, Dagh Sahib, especially one that has been rooted so long in the soil of this province. But I can hear your father's impatient axe on the last of its trunks. Soon it will be torn from the earth. The snakes will be driven from its roots and the termites burned with its rotten wood. But what will happen to the birds and monkeys who sang or chattered in its branches? Tell me that, Dagh Sahib. This is how things stand with us today.' Then, seeing Maan look crestfallen, she added, with another sigh: 'Come at one o'clock in the morning. I will tell your friend the watchman to make the Shahenshah's entry a triumphal one.'

Maan felt that she might be laughing at him. But the thought of seeing her tonight cheered him up instantly, even if he knew she was merely sweetening a bitter pill.

'Of course, I can't promise anything,' Saeeda Bai went on. 'If he tells you I am asleep, you must not make a scene or wake up the neighbourhood.'

It was Maan's turn to sigh:

> 'If Mir so loudly goes on weeping,
> How can his neighbour go on sleeping?'

But, as it happened, everything worked out well. Abdur Rasheed agreed to house Maan in his village and to continue to teach him Urdu. Mahesh Kapoor, who had been afraid that Maan might attempt to defy him by staying in Brahmpur, was not altogether displeased that he would not be going to Banaras, for he knew what Maan did not – that the cloth business was doing pretty well without him.

Mrs Mahesh Kapoor (though she would miss him) was glad that he would be in the charge of a strict and sober teacher and away from 'that'. Maan did at least receive the ecstatic sop of a last passionate night with Saeeda Bai. And Saeeda Bai heaved a sigh of relief tinged only slightly with regret when morning came.

A few hours later a glum Maan, fretting and exasperated at being so neatly pincered by his father and his beloved, together with Rasheed, who was conscious for the moment only of the pleasure of getting out of congested Brahmpur into the openness of the countryside, were on board a narrow-gauge train that swung in a painfully slow and halting arc towards Rudhia District and Rasheed's home village.

6.25

TASNEEM did not realize till Rasheed had gone how much she had enjoyed her Arabic lessons. Everything else she did was related to the household, and opened no windows onto a larger world. But her serious young teacher, with his insistence on the importance of grammar and his refusal to compromise with her tendency to take flight when faced with difficulties, had made her aware that she had within herself an ability for application that she had not known. She admired him, too, because he was making his own way in the world without support from his family. And when he refused to answer her sister's summons because he was explaining a passage from the Quran to her, she had greatly approved of his sense of principle.

All this admiration was silent. Rasheed had never once indicated that he was interested in her in any way other than as a teacher. Their hands had never touched accidentally over a book. That this should not have happened over a span of weeks spoke of deliberateness on his part, for in the ordinary innocent course of things it was bound to have occurred by chance, even if they had instantly drawn back afterwards.

Now he would be out of Brahmpur for a month, and Tasneem found herself feeling sad, far sadder than the loss of Arabic lessons would have accounted for. Ishaq Khan, sensing her mood, and the cause for it as well, tried to cheer her up.

'Listen, Tasneem.'

'Yes, Ishaq Bhai?' Tasneem replied, a little listlessly.

'Why do you insist on that "Bhai"?' said Ishaq.

Tasneem was silent.

'All right, call me brother if you wish – just get out of that tearful mood.'

'I can't,' said Tasneem. 'I'm feeling sad.'

'Poor Tasneem. He'll be back,' said Ishaq, trying not to sound anything but sympathetic.

'I wasn't thinking of him,' said Tasneem quickly. 'I was thinking that I'll have nothing useful to do now except read novels and cut vegetables. Nothing useful to learn –'

'Well, you could teach, even if not learn,' said Ishaq Khan, attempting to sound bright.

'Teach?'

'Teach Miya Mitthu how to speak. The first few months of life are very important in the education of a parakeet.'

Tasneem brightened up for a second. Then she said: 'Apa has appropriated my parakeet. The cage is always in her room, seldom in mine.' She sighed. 'It seems,' she added under her breath, 'that everything of mine becomes hers.'

'I'll get it,' said Ishaq Khan gallantly.

'Oh, you mustn't,' said Tasneem. 'Your hands –'

'Oh, I'm not as crippled as all that.'

'But it must be bad. Whenever I see you practising, I can see how painful it is from your face.'

'What if it is?' said Ishaq Khan. 'I have to play and I have to practise.'

'Why don't you show it to a doctor?'

'It'll go away.'

'Still – there's no harm in having it seen.'

'All right,' said Ishaq with a smile. 'I will, because you've asked me to.'

487

Sometimes when Ishaq accompanied Saeeda Bai these days it was all he could do not to cry out in pain. This trouble in his wrists had grown worse. What was strange was that it now affected both his wrists, despite the fact that his two hands – the right on the bow and the left on the strings – performed very different functions.

Since his livelihood and that of the younger brothers whom he supported depended on his hands, he was extremely anxious. As for the transfer of his brother-in-law: Ishaq had not dared to try to get an interview with the Station Director – who would certainly have heard about what had happened in the canteen and who would have been very unfavourably disposed towards him, especially if the great Ustad himself had made it a point to express his displeasure.

Ishaq Khan remembered his father saying to him, 'Practise at least four hours every day. Clerks push their pens in offices for longer than that, and you cannot insult your art by offering less.' Ishaq's father would sometimes – in the middle of a conversation – take Ishaq's left hand and look at it carefully; if the string-abraded grooves in the fingernails showed signs of recent wear, he would say, 'Good.' Otherwise he would merely continue with the conversation, not visibly but palpably disappointed. Of late, because of the sometimes unbearable pain in the tendons of his wrists, Ishaq Khan had been unable to practise for more than an hour or two a day. But the moment the pain let up he increased the regimen.

Sometimes it was difficult to concentrate on other matters. Lifting a cage, stirring his tea, opening a door, every action reminded him of his hands. He could turn to no one for help. If he told Saeeda Bai how painful it had become to accompany her, especially in fast passages, would he be able to blame her if she looked for someone else?

'It is not sensible to practise so much. You should rest – and use some balm,' murmured Tasneem.

'Do you think I don't want to rest – do you think it's easier for me to practise –'

'But you must use proper medicine: it is very unwise not to,' said Tasneem.

'Go and get some for me, then —' said Ishaq Khan with sudden and uncharacteristic sharpness. 'Everyone sympathizes, everyone advises, no one helps. Go – go –'

He stopped dead, and covered his eyes with his right hand. He did not want to open them.

He imagined Tasneem's startled face, her deer-like eyes starting with tears. If pain has made me so selfish, he thought, I will have to rest and restore myself, even if it means risking my work.

Aloud, after he had collected himself, he said: 'Tasneem, you will have to help me. Talk to your sister and tell her what I can't.' He sighed. 'I'll speak to her later. I cannot find other work in my present state. She will have to keep me on even if I cannot play for a while.'

Tasneem said, 'Yes.' Her voice betrayed that she was, as he had thought, crying silently.

'Please don't take what I said badly,' continued Ishaq. 'I'm not myself. I will rest.' He shook his head from side to side.

Tasneem put her hand on his shoulder. He became very still, and remained so even when she took it away.

'I'll talk to Apa,' she said, 'Should I go now?'

'Yes. No, stay here for a while.'

'What do you want to talk about?' said Tasneem.

'I don't want to talk,' said Ishaq. After a pause he looked up and saw her face. It was tear-stained.

He looked down again, then said: 'May I use that pen?'

Tasneem handed him the wooden pen with its broad split bamboo nib that Rasheed made her use for her calligraphy. The letters it wrote were large, almost childishly so; the dots above the letters came out like little rhombuses.

Ishaq Khan thought for a minute while she watched him. Then, drawing to himself a large sheet of lined paper – which she used for her exercises – he wrote a few lines with some effort, and handed them to her wordlessly even before the ink was dry:

Dear hands, that cause me so much pain,
When can I gain your use again?

When can we once again be friends?
Forgive me, and I'll make amends.

Never again will I enforce
My fiat, disciplined and coarse

Without consulting both of you
On any work we need to do,

Nor cause you seizure or distress
But win your trust through gentleness.

He looked at her while her lovely, liquid eyes moved from right to left, noticing with a kind of painful pleasure the flush that came to her face as they rested on the final couplet.

6.26

WHEN Tasneem entered her sister's bedroom, she found her sitting in front of the mirror applying kajal to her eyelids.

Most people have an expression that they reserve exclusively for looking at themselves in the mirror. Some pout, others arch their eyebrows, still others look superciliously down their noses at themselves. Saeeda Bai had a whole range of mirror faces. Just as her comments to her parakeet ran the gamut of emotions from passion to annoyance, so too did these expressions. When Tasneem entered, she was moving her head slowly from side to side with a dreamy air. It would have been difficult to guess that her thick black hair had just revealed a single white one, and that she was looking around for others.

A silver paan container was resting among the vials and phials on her dressing table and Saeeda Bai was eating a couple of paans laced with the fragrant, semi-solid tobacco known as kimam. When Tasneem appeared in the mirror and their eyes met, the first thought that struck Saeeda Bai was that she, Saeeda, was getting old and that in five years she would be forty. Her expression changed to one of melancholy, and she turned back to her own face in the mirror, looking at herself in the iris, first of one eye, then of the other. Then, recalling the guest whom she had invited to the house in the evening, she smiled at herself in affectionate welcome.

'What's the matter, Tasneem, tell me,' she said – somewhat indistinctly, because of the paan.

'Apa,' said Tasneem nervously, 'it's about Ishaq.'

'Has he been teasing you?' said Saeeda Bai a little sharply, misinterpreting Tasneem's nervousness. 'I'll speak to him. Send him here.'

'No, no, Apa, it's this,' said Tasneem, and handed her sister Ishaq's poem.

After reading it through Saeeda Bai set it down, and started toying with the only lipstick on the dressing table. She never used lipstick, as her lips had a natural redness which was enhanced by paan, but it had been given to her a long time ago by the guest who would be coming this evening, and to whom she was, in a mild sort of way, sentimentally attached.

'What do you think, Apa?' said Tasneem. 'Say something.'

'It's well expressed and badly written,' said Saeeda Bai, 'but what does it mean? He's not going on about his hands, is he?'

'They are giving him a lot of pain,' said Tasneem, 'and he's afraid that if he speaks to you, you'll ask him to leave.'

Saeeda Bai, remembering with a smile how she had got Maan to leave, was silent. She was about to apply a drop of perfume to her wrist when Bibbo came in with a great bustle.

'Oh-hoh, what is it now?' said Saeeda Bai. 'Go out, you wretched girl, can't I have a moment of peace? Have you fed the parakeet?'

'Yes, Begum Sahiba,' said Bibbo impertinently. 'But what shall I tell the cook to feed you and your guest this evening?'

Saeeda Bai addressed Bibbo's reflection in the mirror sternly:

'Wretched girl, you will never amount to anything — even after having stayed here so long you have not acquired the slightest sense of etiquette or discrimination.'

Bibbo looked unconvincingly penitent. Saeeda Bai went on: 'Find out what is growing in the kitchen garden and come back after five minutes.'

When Bibbo had disappeared, Saeeda Bai said to Tasneem:

'So he's sent you to speak to me, has he?'

'No,' said Tasneem. 'I came myself. I thought he needed help.'

'You're sure he hasn't been misbehaving?'

Tasneem shook her head.

'Maybe he can write a ghazal or two for me to sing,' said Saeeda Bai after a pause. 'I'll have to put him to some sort of work. Provisionally, at least.' She applied a drop of perfume. 'I suppose his hand works well enough to allow him to write?'

'Yes,' said Tasneem happily.

'Then let's leave it at that,' said Saeeda Bai.

But in her mind she was thinking about a permanent replacement. She knew she couldn't support Ishaq endlessly — or till some indefinite time when his hands decided to behave.

'Thank you, Apa,' said Tasneem, smiling.

'Don't thank me,' said Saeeda Bai crossly. 'I am used to taking all the world's troubles onto my own head. Now I'll have to find a sarangi player till your Ishaq Bhai is capable of wrestling with his sarangi again, and I also have to find someone to teach you Arabic —'

'Oh, no, no,' said Tasneem quickly, 'you needn't do that.'

'I needn't do that?' said Saeeda Bai, turning around to face not Tasneem's image but Tasneem herself. 'I thought you enjoyed your Arabic lessons.'

Bibbo had bounced back into the room again. Saeeda Bai looked at her impatiently and cried, 'Yes, yes, Bibbo? What is it? I told you to come back after five minutes.'

'But I've found out what's ripe in the back garden,' said Bibbo enthusiastically.

'All right, all right,' said Saeeda Bai, defeated. 'What is there apart from ladies' fingers? Has the karela begun?'

'Yes, Begum Sahiba, and there is even a pumpkin.'

'Well, then, tell the cook to make kababs as usual – shami kababs – and some vegetable of her choice – and let her make mutton with karela as well.'

Tasneem made a slight grimace, which was not lost on Saeeda Bai.

'If you find the karela too bitter, you don't have to eat it,' she said in an impatient voice. 'No one is forcing you. I work my heart out to keep you in comfort, and you don't appreciate it. And oh yes,' she said, turning to Bibbo again, 'let's have some phirni afterwards.'

'But there's so little sugar left from our ration,' cried Bibbo.

'Get it on the black market,' said Saeeda Bai. 'Bilgrami Sahib is very fond of phirni.'

Then she dismissed both Tasneem and Bibbo, and continued with her toilette in peace.

The guest whom she was expecting that evening was an old friend. He was a doctor, a general practitioner about ten years older than her, good-looking and cultivated. He was unmarried, and had proposed to her a number of times. Though at one stage he had been a client, he was now a friend. She felt no passion for him, but was grateful that he was always there when she needed him. She had not seen him for about three months now, and that was why she had invited him over this evening. He was bound to propose to her again, and this would cheer her up. Her refusal, being equally inevitable, would not upset him unduly.

She looked around the room, and her eyes fell on the framed picture of the woman looking out through an archway into a mysterious garden.

493

By now, she thought, Dagh Sahib will have reached his destination. I did not really want to send him off, but I did. He did not really want to go, but he did. Well, it is all for the best.

Dagh Sahib, however, would not have agreed with this assessment.

6.27

ISHAQ KHAN waited for Ustad Majeed Khan not far from his house. When he came out, carrying a small string bag in his hand, walking gravely along, Ishaq followed him at a distance. He turned towards Tarbuz ka Bazaar, past the road leading to the mosque, then into the comparatively open area of the local vegetable market. He moved from stall to stall to see if there was something that interested him. It was good to see tomatoes still plentiful and at a tolerable price so late in the season. Besides, they made the market look more cheerful. It was a pity that the season for spinach was almost over; it was one of his favourite vegetables. And carrots, cauliflowers, cabbages, all were virtually gone till next winter. Even those few that were available were dry, dingy, and dear, and had none of the flavour of their peak.

It was with thoughts such as these that the maestro was occupied that morning when he heard a voice say, respectfully:

'Adaab arz, Ustad Sahib.'

Ustad Majeed Khan turned to see Ishaq. A single glance at the young man was sufficient to remove the ease of his meditations and to remind him of the insults that he had had to face in the canteen. His face grew dark with the memory; he picked up two or three tomatoes from the stall, and asked their price.

'I have a request to make of you.' It was Ishaq Khan again.

'Yes?' The contempt in the great musician's voice was unmistakable. As he recalled, it was after he had offered his help to the young man in some footling matter that the whole exchange had occurred.

'I also have an apology to make.'

'Please do not waste my time.'

'I have followed you here from your house. I need your help. I am in trouble. I need work to support myself and my younger brothers, and I cannot get it. After that day, All India Radio has not called me even once to perform.'

The maestro shrugged his shoulders.

'I beg of you, Ustad Sahib, whatever you think of me, do not ruin my family. You knew my father and grandfather. Excuse any mistake that I may have made for their sakes.'

'That you may have made?'

'That I have made. I do not know what came over me.'

'I am not ruining you. Go in peace.'

'Ustad Sahib, since that day I have had no work, and my sister's husband has heard nothing about his transfer from Lucknow. I dare not approach the Director.'

'But you dare approach me. You follow me from my house –'

'Only to get the chance to speak to you. You might understand – as a fellow musician.' The Ustad winced. 'And of late my hands have been giving me trouble. I showed them to a doctor, but –'

'I had heard,' said the maestro dryly, but did not mention where.

'My employer has made it clear to me that I cannot be supported for my own sake much longer.'

'Your employer!' The great singer was about to walk on in disgust when he added: 'Go and thank God for that. Throw yourself on His mercy.'

'I am throwing myself on yours,' said Ishaq Khan desperately.

'I have said nothing for or against you to the Station Director. What happened that morning I shall put down to an aberration in your brain. If your work has fallen off, that is not my doing. In any case, with your hands, what do you propose to do? You are very proud of your long hours of practice. My advice to you is to practise less.'

495

This had been Tasneem's advice as well. Ishaq Khan nodded miserably. There was no hope, and since his pride had already suffered through his desperation, he felt that he could lose nothing by completing the apology he had begun and that he had come to believe he should make.

'On another matter,' he said, 'if I may presume on your further indulgence – I have been wishing for a long time to apologize for what I know is not forgivable. That morning, Ustad Sahib, the reason why I made so bold as to sit at your table in the canteen was because I had heard your Todi just a little earlier.'

The maestro, who had been examining the vegetables, turned towards him slightly.

'I had been sitting beneath the neem tree outside with those friends of mine. One of them had a radio. We were entranced, at least I was. I thought I would find some way of saying so to you. But then things went wrong, and other thoughts took over.'

He could not say any more by way of apology without, he felt, bringing in other matters – such as the memory of his own father, which he felt that the Ustad had demeaned.

Ustad Majeed Khan nodded his head almost imperceptibly by way of acknowledgment. He looked at the young man's hands, noticing the worn groove in the fingernail, and for a second he also found himself wondering why he did not have a bag to carry his vegetables home in.

'So – you liked my Todi,' he said.

'Yours – or God's,' said Ishaq Khan. 'I felt that the great Tansen himself would have listened rapt to that rendering of his raag. But since then I have never been able to listen to you.'

The maestro frowned, but did not deign to ask Ishaq what he meant by that last remark.

'I will be practising Todi this morning,' said Ustad Majeed Khan. 'Follow me after this.'

Ishaq's face expressed complete disbelief; it was as if heaven had fallen into his hands. He forgot his hands, his pride, the financial desperation that had forced him to speak to Ustad Majeed Khan. He merely listened as if in a dream to the Ustad's further conversation with the vegetable seller:

'How much are these?'

'Two-and-a-half annas per pao,' replied the vegetable seller.

'Beyond Subzipur you can get them for one-and-a-half annas.'

'Bhai Sahib, these are not the prices of Subzipur but of Chowk.'

'Very high, these prices of yours.'

'Oh, we had a child last year – since then my prices have gone up.' The vegetable seller, seated calmly on the ground on a bit of jute matting, looked up at the Ustad.

Ustad Majeed Khan did not smile at the vendor's quips. 'Two annas per pao – that's it.'

'I have to earn my meals from you, Sir, not from the charity of a gurudwara.'

'All right – all right –' And Ustad Majeed Khan threw him a couple of coins.

After buying a bit of ginger and some chillies, the Ustad decided to get a few tindas.

'Mind that you give me small ones.'

'Yes, yes, that's what I'm doing.'

'And these tomatoes – they are soft.'

'Soft, Sir?'

'Yes, look –' The Ustad took them off the scales. 'Weigh these ones instead.' He rummaged around among the selection.

'They wouldn't have gone soft in a week – but whatever you say, Sir.'

'Weigh them properly,' growled the Ustad. 'If you keep putting weights on one pan, I can keep putting tomatoes on the other. My pan should sink in the balance.'

Suddenly, the Ustad's attention was caught by a couple of cauliflowers which looked comparatively fresh, not like the stunted outriders of the season. But when the vegetable seller named the price, he was appalled.

'Don't you fear God?'

'For you, Sir, I have quoted a special price.'

497

'What do you mean, for me? It's what you charge everyone, you rogue, I am certain. Special price –'

'Ah, but these cauliflowers are special – you don't require oil to fry them.'

Ishaq smiled slightly, but Ustad Majeed Khan simply said to the local wit:

'Huh! Give me this one.'

Ishaq said: 'Let me carry them, Ustad Sahib.'

Ustad Majeed Khan gave Ishaq the bag of vegetables to carry, forgetful of his hands. On the way home he did not say anything. Ishaq walked along quietly.

At his door, Ustad Majeed Khan said in a loud voice: 'There is someone with me.' There was a sound of flustered female voices and then of people leaving the front room. They entered. The tanpura was in a corner. Ustad Majeed Khan told Ishaq to put the vegetables down and to wait for him. Ishaq remained standing, but looked about him. The room was full of cheap knick-knacks and tasteless furniture. There could not have been a greater contrast to Saeeda Bai's immaculate outer chamber.

Ustad Majeed Khan came back in, having washed his face and hands. He told Ishaq to sit down, and tuned the tanpura for a while. Finally, satisfied, he started to practise in Raag Todi.

There was no tabla player, and Ustad Majeed Khan began to sense his way around the raag in a freer, less rhythmic but more intense manner than Ishaq Khan had ever heard from him before. He always began his public performances not with a free alaap such as this but with a very slow composition in a long rhythmic cycle which allowed him a liberty that was almost, but not quite, comparable. The flavour of these few minutes was so startlingly different from those other great performances that Ishaq was enraptured. He closed his eyes, and the room ceased to exist; and then, after a while, himself; and finally even the singer.

He did not know how long he had been sitting there when he heard Ustad Majeed Khan saying:

'Now, you strum it.'

He opened his eyes. The maestro, sitting bolt upright, indicated the tanpura that was lying before him.

Ishaq's hands did not cause him any pain as he turned it towards himself and began to strum the four wires, tuned perfectly to the open and hypnotic combination of tonic and dominant. He assumed that the maestro was going to continue his practice.

'Now, sing this after me.' And the Ustad sang a phrase.

Ishaq Khan was literally dumbstruck.

'What is taking you so long?' asked the Ustad sternly, in the tone known so well to his students at the Haridas College of Music.

Ishaq Khan sang the phrase.

The Ustad continued to offer him phrases, at first brief, and then increasingly long and complex. Ishaq repeated them to the best of his ability, at first with unmusical hesitancy but after a while entirely forgetting himself in the surge and ebb of the music.

'Sarangi-wallahs are good at copying,' said the Ustad thoughtfully. 'But there is something in you that goes beyond that.'

So astonished was Ishaq that his hands stopped strumming the tanpura.

The Ustad was silent for a while. The only sound in the room was the ticking of a cheap clock. Ustad Majeed Khan looked at it, as if conscious for the first time of its presence, then turned his gaze towards Ishaq.

It struck him that possibly, but only just possibly, he may have found in Ishaq that disciple whom he had looked for now for years – someone to whom he could pass on his art, someone who, unlike his own frog-voiced son, loved music with a passion, who had a grounding in performance, whose voice was not displeasing, whose sense of pitch and ornament was exceptional, and who had that additional element of indefinable expressivity, even when he copied his own phrases, which was the soul of music. But originality in composition – did he possess that – or at least the germ of such originality? Only time would tell – months, perhaps years, of time.

'Come again tomorrow, but at seven in the morning,' said the Ustad, dismissing him. Ishaq Khan nodded slowly, then stood up to leave.

Part Seven

LATA saw the envelope on the salver. Arun's servant had brought the mail in just before breakfast and laid it on the dining table. As soon as she saw the letter she took in her breath sharply. She even glanced around the dining room. No one else had yet entered. Breakfast was an erratic meal in this household.

Lata knew Kabir's handwriting from the note that he had scribbled to her during the meeting of the Brahmpur Poetry Society. She had not expected him to write to her, and could not think how he had obtained her address in Calcutta. She had not wanted him to write. She did not want to hear from him or about him. Now that she looked back she saw that she had been happy before she had met him: anxious about her exams perhaps, worried about a few small differences she may have had with her mother or a friend, troubled about this constant talk of finding a suitable boy for her, but not miserable as she had been during this so-called holiday so suddenly enforced by her mother.

There was a paper-knife on the salver. Lata picked it up, then stood undecided. Her mother might come in at any moment, and – as she usually did – ask Lata whom the letter was from and what it said. She put the knife down and picked the letter up.

Arun entered. He was wearing a red-and-black striped tie over his starched white shirt, and was carrying his jacket in one hand and holding the *Statesman* in the other. He draped the jacket across the back of his chair, folded the newspaper to give him convenient access to the crossword, greeted Lata affectionately, and riffled through the post.

Lata wandered into the small drawing room that adjoined the dining room, got out a large volume on Egyptian mythology that no one ever read, and inserted her envelope in it. Then she returned to the dining room and sat down, humming to herself in Raag Todi. Arun frowned. Lata stopped. The servant brought her a fried egg.

Arun began whistling 'Three Coins in a Fountain' to himself. He had already solved several clues of the crossword puzzle while in the bathroom, and he filled in a few more at the breakfast table. Now he opened some of his mail, glanced through it and said:

'When is that damned fool going to bring me my bloody egg? I shall be late.'

He reached out for a piece of toast, and buttered it.

Varun entered. He was wearing the torn kurta-pyjama that he had obviously been sleeping in. 'Good morning. Good morning,' he said. He sounded uncertain, almost guilty. Then he sat down. When Hanif, the servant-cum-cook, came in with Arun's egg, he ordered his own. He first asked for an omelette, then decided on a scrambled egg. Meanwhile he took a piece of toast from the rack and buttered it.

'You might think of using the butter-knife,' growled Arun from the head of the table.

Varun had extracted butter from the butter-dish with his own knife to butter his toast. He accepted the rebuke in silence.

'Did you hear me?'

'Yes, Arun Bhai.'

'Then you would do well to acknowledge my remark with a word or at the very least a nod.'

'Yes.'

'There is a purpose to table manners, you know.'

Varun grimaced. Lata glanced sympathetically in his direction.

'Not everyone enjoys seeing the butter encrusted with crumbs from your toast.'

'All right, all right,' said Varun, driven to impatience. It was a feeble protest, and it was dealt with promptly.

Arun put down his knife and fork, looked at him, and waited.

'All right, Arun Bhai,' said Varun meekly.

He had been undecided as to whether to have marmalade or honey, but now decided on marmalade, since negotiating with the honey spoon was bound to bring reproof down on his head. As he spread the marmalade, he looked across at Lata, and they exchanged smiles. Lata's was a half-smile, very typical of her these days. Varun's was rather a twisted smile, as if he was not sure whether to be happy or despairing. It was the kind of smile that drove his elder brother mad and convinced him that Varun was a hopeless case. Varun had just got a Second in his mathematics B.A., and when he told his family the result, it was with exactly this kind of smile.

Soon after the term was over, instead of getting a job and contributing to expenses, Varun had, to Arun's annoyance, fallen ill. He was still somewhat weak, and started at loud sounds. Arun told himself that he really had to have a frank talk with his younger brother in the next week or so about how the world did not owe one a living, and about what Daddy would have said had he been alive.

Meenakshi came in with Aparna.

'Where's Daadi?' asked Aparna, looking around the table for Mrs Rupa Mehra.

'Grandma will be coming in a moment, Aparna precious,' said Meenakshi. 'She's probably reciting the Vedas,' she added vaguely.

Mrs Rupa Mehra, who recited a chapter or two from the Gita very early each morning, was in fact dressing.

As she came in, she beamed around the table. But when she noticed Aparna's golden chain, which Meenakshi in an unthinking moment had put around her neck, the smile died on her lips. Meenakshi was blithely unaware of anything being the matter, but Aparna asked a few minutes later:

'Why are you looking so sad, Daadi?'

Mrs Rupa Mehra finished chewing a bite of fried tomatoes on toast and said: 'I'm not sad, darling.'

'Are you angry with me, Daadi?' said Aparna.

'No, sweetheart, not with you.'

'Then with who?'

'With myself, perhaps,' said Mrs Rupa Mehra. She did not look at the medal-melter, but glanced across at Lata, who was gazing out of the window at the small garden.

Lata was more than usually quiet this morning, and Mrs Rupa Mehra told herself that she had to get the silly girl to snap out of this mood. Well, tomorrow there was a party at the Chatterjis, and, like it or not, Lata would have to go.

A car horn sounded loudly outside, and Varun flinched.

'I should fire that bloody driver,' said Arun. Then he laughed and added: 'But he certainly makes me aware when it's time to leave for the office. Bye, darling.' He swallowed a gulp of coffee and kissed Meenakshi. 'I'll send the car back in half an hour. Bye, Ugly.' He kissed Aparna and rubbed his cheek against hers. 'Bye, Ma. Bye, everyone. Don't forget, Basil Cox will be coming for dinner.'

Carrying his jacket over one arm and his briefcase in the other, he walked, rather, strode out to the little sky-blue Austin outside. It was never clear until the last moment whether Arun would take the newspaper with him to the office; it was part of the general uncertainty of living with him, just as were his sudden switches from anger to affection to urbanity. Today, to everyone's relief, he let the newspaper remain.

Normally Varun and Lata would both have made a grab for it, and today Varun was disappointed when Lata did not. The atmosphere had lightened since Arun's departure. Aparna now became the focus of attention. Her mother fed her incompetently, then called for the Toothless Crone to handle her. Varun read bits of the news to her, and she listened with a careful pretence at comprehension and interest.

All Lata could think of was when and where, in this household of two-and-a-half bedrooms and no privacy to speak of, she would find time and space to read her letter. She was thankful that she had been able to take possession of what (though Mrs Rupa Mehra would have disputed this) belonged to her alone. But as she looked out of the window towards the small, brilliantly green lawn with its white tracery of spider-lilies, she thought of its possible contents with a mixture of longing and foreboding.

MEANWHILE there was work to be done in preparation for the evening's dinner. Basil Cox, who would be coming over with his wife Patricia, was Arun's department head at Bentsen & Pryce. Hanif was dispatched to Jagubazaar to get two chickens, a fish, and vegetables, while Meenakshi – accompanied by Lata and Mrs Rupa Mehra – went off to New Market in the car, which had just returned from Arun's office.

Meenakshi bought her fortnightly stores – her white flour, her jam and Chivers Marmalade and Lyle's Golden Syrup and Anchor Butter and tea and coffee and cheese and clean sugar ('Not this dirty ration stuff') – from Baboralley, a couple of loaves of bread from a shop in Middleton Row ('The bread one gets from the market is so awful, Luts'), some salami from a cold store in Free School Street ('The salami from Keventers is dreadfully bland, I've decided never to go there again'), and half a dozen bottles of Beck's beer from Shaw Brothers. Lata tagged along everywhere, though Mrs Rupa Mehra refused to enter either the cold store or the liquor shop. She was astonished by Meenakshi's extravagance, and by the whimsical nature of some of her purchases ('Oh, Arun is bound to like that, yes, I'll take two,' said Meenakshi whenever the shopkeeper suggested something that he thought Madam would appreciate). All the purchases went into a large basket which a ragged little boy carried on his head and finally took to the car. Whenever she was accosted by beggars, Meenakshi looked straight through them.

Lata wanted to visit a bookshop on Park Street, and spent about fifteen minutes there while Meenakshi chafed impatiently. When she found that Lata hadn't in fact bought anything, she thought it very peculiar. Mrs Rupa Mehra was content to browse timelessly.

Upon their return home, Meenakshi found her cook in a flap. He was not sure about the exact proportions for the soufflé, and as for the hilsa, Meenakshi would have to instruct him about the kind of fire it needed to be smoked on. Aparna too was sulking because of her mother's absence. She now threatened to throw a tantrum. This was too much for Meenakshi, who was getting late for the canasta which she played with her ladies' club – the Shady Ladies – once a week, and which (Basil Cox or no Basil Cox) she could not possibly miss. She got into a flap herself and shouted at Aparna and the Toothless Crone and the cook. Varun locked himself in his small room and covered his head with a pillow.

'You should not get into a temper for nothing,' said Mrs Rupa Mehra unhelpfully.

Meenakshi turned towards her in exasperation. 'That's a big help, Ma,' she said. 'What do you expect me to do? Miss my canasta?'

'No, no, you will not miss your canasta,' said Mrs Rupa Mehra. 'That I am not asking you to do, Meenakshi, but you must not shout at Aparna like that. It is not good for her.' Hearing this, Aparna edged towards her grandmother's chair.

Meenakshi made an impatient sound.

The impossibility of her position suddenly came home to her. This cook was a real incompetent. Arun would be terribly, terribly angry with her if anything went wrong this evening. It was so important for his job too – and what could she do? Cut out the smoked hilsa? At least this idiot Hanif could handle the roast chicken. But he was a temperamental fellow, and had been known even to misfry an egg. Meenakshi looked around the room in wild distress.

'Ask your mother if you can borrow her Mugh cook,' said Lata with sudden inspiration.

Meenakshi gazed at Lata in wonder. 'What an Einstein you are, Luts!' she said, and immediately telephoned her mother. Mrs Chatterji rallied to her daughter's aid. She had two cooks, one for Bengali and one for western food. The Bengali cook was told that he would have to prepare dinner in the Chatterji household that evening, and the Mugh cook, who came from Chittagong and excelled in European food, was dispatched to Sunny Park within the half-hour. Meanwhile, Meenakshi had gone off for her canasta lunch with the Shady Ladies and had almost forgotten the tribulations of existence.

She returned in the middle of the afternoon to find a rebellion on her hands. The gramophone was blaring and the chickens were cackling in alarm. The Mugh cook told her as snootily as he could that he was not accustomed to being farmed out in this manner, that he was not used to working in such a small kitchen, that her cook-cum-bearer had behaved insolently towards him, that the fish and chickens that had been bought were none too fresh, and that he needed a certain kind of lemon extract for the soufflé which she had not had the foresight to provide. Hanif for his part was glaring resentfully, and was on the verge of giving notice. He was holding a squawking chicken out in front of him and saying: 'Feel, feel its breast – Memsahib – this is a young and fresh chicken. Why should I work below this man? Who is he to boss me around in my own kitchen? He keeps saying, "I am Mr Justice Chatterji's cook. I am Mr Justice Chatterji's cook."'

'No, no, I trust you, I don't need to –' cried Meenakshi, shuddering fastidiously and drawing back her red-polished fingernails as her cook pushed the chicken's feathers aside and offered its breast for her to assay.

Mrs Rupa Mehra, while not displeased at Meenakshi's discomfiture, did not want to jeopardize this dinner for the boss of her darling son. She was good at making peace between refractory servants, and she now did so. Harmony was restored, and she went into the drawing room to play a game of patience.

Varun had put on the gramophone about half an hour earlier and was playing the same scratchy 78-rpm record again and again: the Hindi film song 'Two intoxicating eyes', a song that no one, not even the sentimental Mrs Rupa Mehra, could tolerate after its fifth repetition. Varun had been singing the words to himself moodily and dreamily before Meenakshi returned. In her presence Varun stopped singing, but he continued to rewind the gramophone every few minutes and hum the song softly to

himself by way of accompaniment. As he put away the
spent needles one by one in the little compartment that
fitted into the side of the machine, he reflected gloomily on
his own fleeting life and personal uselessness.

Lata took the book on Egyptian mythology down from
the shelf, and was about to go into the garden with it
when her mother said:

'Where are you going?'

'To sit in the garden, Ma.'

'But it's so hot, Lata.'

'I know, Ma, but I can't read with this music going on.'

'I'll tell him to turn it off. All this sun is bad for your
complexion. Varun, turn it off.' She had to repeat her
request a few times before Varun heard what she was
saying.

Lata took the book into the bedroom.

'Lata, sit with me, darling,' said Mrs Rupa Mehra.

'Ma, please let me be,' said Lata.

'You have been ignoring me for days,' said Mrs Rupa
Mehra. 'Even when I told you your results, your kiss was
half-hearted.'

'Ma, I have not been ignoring you,' said Lata.

'You have, you can't deny it. I feel it – here.' Mrs Rupa
Mehra pointed to the region of her heart.

'All right, Ma, I have been ignoring you. Now please let
me read.'

'What's that you're reading? Let me see the book.'

Lata replaced it on the shelf, and said: 'All right, Ma, I
won't read it, I'll talk to you. Happy?'

'What do you want to talk about, darling?' asked Mrs
Rupa Mehra sympathetically.

'I don't want to talk. You want to talk,' Lata pointed out.

'Read your silly book!' cried Mrs Rupa Mehra in a
sudden temper. 'I have to do everything in this house, and
no one cares for me. Everything goes wrong and I have to
make peace. I have slaved for you all my life, and you
don't care if I live or die. Only when I'm burned on the
pyre will you realize my worth.' The tears started rolling
down her cheeks and she placed a black nine on a red ten.

Normally Lata would have made some dutiful attempt to console her mother, but she was so frustrated and annoyed by her sudden emotional sleight-of-hand that she did nothing. After a while, she took the book down from the shelf again, and walked into the garden.

'It will rain,' said Mrs Rupa Mehra, 'and the book will get spoiled. You have no sense of the value of money.'

'Good,' thought Lata violently. 'I hope the book and everything in it – and I too – get washed away.'

7.3

THE small green garden was empty. The part-time mali had gone. An intelligent-looking crow cawed from a banana tree. The delicate spider-lilies were in bloom. Lata sat down on the slatted green wooden bench in the shade of a tall flame-of-the-forest tree. Everything was rain-washed and clean, unlike in Brahmpur where each leaf had looked dusty and each blade of grass parched.

Lata looked at the envelope with its firm handwriting and Brahmpur postmark. Her name was followed immediately by the address; it was not 'care of' anybody.

She pulled out a hairpin and opened the envelope. The letter was only a page long. She had expected Kabir's letter to be effusive and apologetic. It was not exactly that.

After the address and date it went:

Dearest Lata,

Why should I repeat that I love you? I don't see why you should disbelieve me. I don't disbelieve you. Please tell me what the matter is. I don't want things to end in this way between us.

I can't think about anything except you, but I am annoyed that I should have to say so. I couldn't and I can't run off with you to some earthly paradise, but how could you have expected me to? Suppose I had agreed to your crazy plan. I know that you would then have discovered twenty reasons why it was impossible to carry it out. But perhaps I should have agreed anyway. Perhaps you would have felt reassured because I would have proved how much I cared for you. Well, I don't care for you so much that I'm willing to abdicate my intelligence. I don't even care for myself that much. I'm not made that way, and I do think ahead a bit.

Darling Lata, you are so brilliant, why don't you see things in perspective? I love you. You really owe me an apology.

Anyway, congratulations on your exam results. You must be very pleased – but I am not very surprised. You must not spend your time sitting on benches and crying in future. Who knows who might want to rescue you. Perhaps whenever you're tempted to do so, you can think of me returning to the pavilion and crying every time I fail to make a century.

Two days ago I hired a boat and went up the Ganges to the Barsaat Mahal. But, like Nawab Khushwaqt, I was so much grieved that my mind was upset, and the place was sordid and sad. For a long time I could not forget you though all possible efforts were made. I felt a strong kinship with him even though my tears did not fall fast and furious into the frangrant waters.

My father, though he is fairly absent-minded, can see that there is something the matter with me. Yesterday he said, 'It's not your results, so what is it, Kabir? I believe it must be a girl or something.' I too believe it must be a girl or something.

Well, now that you have my address why don't you write to me? I have been unhappy since you left and unable to concentrate on anything. I knew you couldn't write to me even if you wanted to because you didn't have my address. Well, now you do. So please do write. Otherwise I'll know what to think. And the next time I go to Mr Nowrojee's place I will have to read out some stricken verses of my own.

With all my love, my darling Lata,
Yours,
Kabir

FOR a long while Lata sat in a kind of reverie. She did not at first re-read the letter. She felt a great many emotions, but they pulled her in conflicting directions. Under ordinary circumstances the pressure of her feelings might have caused her to shed a few unselfconscious tears, but there were a couple of remarks in the letter which made that impossible. Her first sense was that she had been cheated, cheated out of something that she had expected. There was no apology in the letter for the pain that he must have known he had caused her. There were declarations of love, but they were not as fervent or untinged with irony as she had thought they would be. Perhaps she had given Kabir no opportunity to explain himself at their last meeting, but now that he was writing to her, he could have explained himself better. He had not addressed anything seriously, and Lata had above all wanted him to be serious. For her it had been a matter of life and death.

Nor had he given her much – or any – news of himself, and Lata longed for it. She wanted to know everything about him – including how well he had done in his exams. From his father's remark it was probable that he had not done badly, but that was not the only interpretation of his remark. It might simply have meant that with the results out, even if he had merely passed, one area of uncertainty had been closed as a possible explanation for his downcast – or perhaps merely unsettled –mood. And how had he obtained her address? Surely not from Pran and Savita? From Malati perhaps? But as far as she knew Kabir did not even know Malati.

He did not want to take any responsiblity for her feelings, that was clear. If anything it was she who – according to him – should be the one to apologize. In one sentence he praised her intelligence, in another he treated her like a dunce. Lata got the sense that he was trying to jolly her along without making any commitment to her beyond 'love'. And what was love?

Even more than their kisses, she remembered the morning when she had followed him to the cricket field and watched him practising in the nets. She had been in a trance, she had been entranced. He had leaned his head back and burst out laughing at something. His shirt had been open at the collar; there had been a faint breeze in the bamboos; a couple of mynas were quarrelling; it had been warm.

She read through the letter once again. Despite his injunction to her that she should not sit crying on benches, tears gathered in her eyes. Having finished the letter, she began, hardly conscious of what she was doing, to read a paragraph of the book on Egyptian mythology. But the words formed no pattern in her mind.

She was startled by Varun's voice, a couple of yards away.

'You'd better go in, Lata, Ma is getting anxious.'

Lata controlled herself and nodded.

'What's the matter?' he asked, noticing that she was – or had been – in tears. 'Have you been quarrelling with her?'

Lata shook her head.

Varun, glancing down at the book, saw the letter, and immediately understood who it was from.

'I'll kill him,' said Varun with timorous ferocity.

'There's nothing to kill,' said Lata, more angrily than sadly. 'Just don't tell Ma, please, Varun Bhai. It would drive both of us crazy.'

7.5

WHEN Arun came back from work that day, he was in excellent spirits. He had had a productive day, and he sensed that the evening was going to go off well. Meenakshi, her domestic crisis resolved, was no longer running around nervously; indeed, so elegantly collected was she that Arun could never have guessed she had been in the least distraught. After kissing him on the cheek and giving him the benefit of her tinkly laugh, she went in to change. Aparna was delighted to see her father and bestowed a few kisses on him too but was unable to convince him to do a jigsaw puzzle with her.

Arun thought that Lata looked a bit sulky, but then that was par for the course with Lata these days. Ma, well, Ma, there was no accounting for her moods. She looked impatient, probably because her tea had not come on time. Varun was his usual scruffy, shifty self. Why, Arun asked himself, did his brother have so little spine and initiative and why did he always dress in tattered kurta-pyjamas that looked as if they had been slept in? 'Turn off that bloody noise,' he shouted as he entered the drawing room and received the full power of 'Two intoxicating eyes'.

Varun, cowed down though he was by Arun and his bullying sophistication, occasionally raised his head, usually to have it brutally slashed off. It took time for another head to grow, but today it happened to have done so. Varun did turn off the gramophone, but his resentment smouldered. Having been subject to his brother's authority since boyhood, he hated it – and, in fact, all authority. He had once, in a fit of anti-imperialism and xenophobia, scrawled 'Pig' on two Bibles at St George's School, and had been soundly thrashed for it by the white headmaster. Arun too had bawled him out after that incident, using every possible hurtful reference to his pathetic childhood and past felonies, and Varun had duly flinched. But even while flinching before his well-built elder brother's attack, and expecting to be slapped by him at any moment, Varun thought to himself: All he knows how to do is to suck up to the British and crawl in their tracks. Pig! Pig! He must have looked his thoughts, for he did get the slap he expected.

Arun used to listen to Churchill's speeches on the radio during the War and murmur, as he had heard the English murmur, 'Good old Winnie!' Churchill loathed Indians and made no secret of it, and spoke with contempt of Gandhi, a far greater man than he could ever aspire to be; and Varun regarded Churchill with a visceral hatred.

'And change out of those crumpled pyjamas. Basil Cox will be coming within an hour and I don't want him to think I run a third-class dharamshala.'

'I'll change into cleaner ones,' said Varun sullenly.

'You will not,' said Arun. 'You will change into proper clothes.'

'Proper clothes!' mumbled Varun softly in a mocking tone.

'What did you say?' asked Arun slowly and threateningly.

'Nothing,' said Varun with a scowl.

'Please don't fight like this. It isn't good for my nerves,' said Mrs Rupa Mehra.

'Ma, you keep out of this,' said Arun, bluntly. He pointed in the direction of Varun's small bedroom – more a store-room than a bedroom. 'Now get out and change.'

'I planned to anyway,' said Varun, edging out of the door.

'Bloody fool,' said Arun to himself. Then, affectionately, he turned to Lata: 'So, what's the matter, why are you looking so down in the mouth?'

Lata smiled. 'I'm fine, Arun Bhai,' she said. 'I think I'll go and get ready as well.'

Arun went in to change too. About fifteen minutes before Basil Cox and his wife were due to arrive, he came out to find everyone except Varun dressed and ready. Meenakshi emerged from the kitchen where she had been doing some last minute supervising. The table had been laid for seven with the best glassware and crockery and cutlery, the flower arrangement was perfect, the hors-d'oeuvre had been tasted and found to be fine, the whisky and sherry and campari and so forth had been taken out of the cabinet, and Aparna had been put to bed.

'Where is he now?' demanded Arun of the three women.

'He hasn't come out. He must be in his room,' said Mrs Rupa Mehra. 'I do wish you wouldn't shout at him.'

'He should learn how to behave in a civilized household. This isn't some dhoti-wallah's establishment. Proper clothes indeed!'

Varun emerged a few minutes later. He was wearing a clean kurta-pyjama, not torn exactly, but with a button missing. He had shaved in a rudimentary sort of way after his bath. He reckoned he looked presentable.

Arun did not reckon so. His face reddened. Varun noticed it reddening, and – though he was scared – he was quite pleased as well.

For a second Arun was so furious he could hardly speak. Then he exploded.

'You bloody idiot!' he roared. 'Do you want to embarrass us all?'

Varun looked at him shiftily. 'What's embarrassing about Indian clothes?' he asked. 'Can't I wear what I want to? Ma and Lata and Meenakshi Bhabhi wear saris, not dresses. Or do I have to keep imitating the whiteys even in my own house? I don't think it's a good idea.'

'I don't care what you bloody well think. In my house you will do as I tell you. Now you change into shirt and tie – or – or –'

'Or else what, Arun Bhai?' said Varun, cheeking his brother and enjoying his rage. 'You won't give me dinner with your Colin Box? Actually, I'd much rather have dinner with my own friends anyway than bow and scrape before this box-wallah and his box-walli.'

'Meenakshi, tell Hanif to remove one place,' said Arun. Meenakshi looked undecided.

'Did you hear me?' asked Arun in a dangerous voice.

Meenakshi got up to do his bidding.

'Now get out,' shouted Arun. 'Go and have dinner with your Shamshu-drinking friends. And don't let me see you anywhere near this house for the rest of the evening. And let me tell you here and now that I won't put up with this sort of thing from you at all. If you live in this house, you bloody well abide by its rules.'

Varun looked uncertainly towards his mother for support.

'Darling, please do what he says. You look so much nicer in a shirt and trousers. Besides, that button is missing. These foreigners don't understand. He's Arun's boss, we must make a good impression.'

'He, for one, is incapable of making a good impression, no matter what he wears or does.' Arun put the boot in. 'I don't want him putting Basil Cox's back up, and he's perfectly capable of doing so. Now, Ma, will you stop these water-works? See – you've upset everyone, you blithering fool,' said Arun, turning on Varun again.

But Varun had slipped out already.

7.6

ALTHOUGH Arun was feeling more venomous than calm, he smiled a brave, morale-building smile and even put his arm around his mother's shoulder. Meenakshi reflected that the seating around the oval table looked a little more symmetrical now, though there would be an even greater imbalance between men and women. Still, it was not as if any other guests had been invited. It was just the Coxes and the family.

Basil Cox and his wife arrived punctually, and Meenakshi made small talk, interspersing comments about the weather ('so sultry, so unbearably close it's been these last few days, but then, this *is* Calcutta –') with her chiming laugh. She asked for a sherry and sipped it with a distant look in her eyes. The cigarettes were passed around; she lit up, and so did Arun and Basil Cox.

Basil Cox was in his late thirties, pink, shrewd, sound, and bespectacled. Patricia Cox was a small, dull sort of woman, a great contrast to the glamorous Meenakshi. She did not smoke. She drank quite rapidly however, and with a sort of desperation. She did not find Calcutta company interesting, and if there was anything she disliked more than large parties it was small ones, where she felt trapped into compulsory sociability.

Lata had a small sherry. Mrs Rupa Mehra had a nimbu pani.

Hanif, looking very smart in his starched white uniform, offered around the tray of hors-d'oeuvre: bits of salami and cheese and asparagus on small squares of bread. If the guests had not so obviously been sahibs – office guests – he might have allowed his disgruntlement with the turn of affairs in his kitchen to be more apparent. As it was, he was at his obliging best.

Arun had begun to hold forth with his usual savoir-faire and charm on various subjects: recent plays in London, books that had just appeared and were considered to be significant, the Persian oil crisis, the Korean conflict. The Reds were being pushed back, and not a moment too soon, in Arun's opinion, though of course the Americans, idiots that they were, would probably not make use of their tactical advantage. But then again, with this as with other matters, what could one do?

This Arun – affable, genial, engaging and knowledge-able, even (at times) diffident – was a very different crea-ture from the domestic tyrant and bully of half an hour ago. Basil Cox was charmed. Arun was good at his work, but Cox had not imagined that he was so widely read, indeed better read than most Englishmen of his acquaintance.

Patricia Cox talked to Meenakshi about her little pear-shaped earrings. 'Very pretty,' she commented. 'Where did you get them made?'

Meenakshi told her and promised to take her to the shop. She cast a glance in Mrs Rupa Mehra's direction, but noticed to her relief that she was listening, rapt, to Arun and Basil Cox. In her bedroom earlier this evening, Meenak-shi had paused for a second before putting them on – but then she had said to herself: Well, sooner or later Ma will have to get used to the facts of life. I can't always tread softly around her feelings.

Dinner passed smoothly. It was a full four-course meal: soup, smoked hilsa, roast chicken, lemon soufflé. Basil Cox tried to bring Lata and Mrs Rupa Mehra into the conversation, but they tended to speak only when spoken to. Lata's mind was far away. She was brought back with a start when she heard Meenakshi describing how the hilsa was smoked.

'It's a wonderful old recipe that's been in our family for ages,' said Meenakshi. 'It's smoked in a basket over a coal fire after it's been carefully de-boned, and hilsa is absolute hell to de-bone.'

'It's delicious, my dear,' said Basil Cox.

'Of course, the real secret,' continued Meenakshi knowledgeably – though she had only discovered this afternoon how it was done, and that too because the Mugh cook had insisted on the correct ingredients being supplied to him – 'the real secret is in the fire. We throw puffed rice on it and crude brown sugar or jaggery – what we in this country call "gur" –' (She rhymed it with 'fur'.)

As she prattled on and on Lata looked at her wonderingly.

'Of course, every girl in the family learns these things at an early age.'

For the first time Patricia Cox looked less than completely bored.

But by the time the soufflé came around, she had lapsed into passivity.

After dinner, coffee and liqueur, Arun brought out the cigars. He and Basil Cox talked a little about work. Arun would not have brought up the subject of the office, but Basil, having made up his mind that Arun was a thorough gentleman, wanted his opinion on a colleague. 'Between us, you know, and strictly between us, I've rather begun to doubt his soundness,' he said. Arun passed his finger around the rim of his liqueur glass, sighed a little, and confirmed his boss's opinion, adding a reason or two of his own.

'Mmm, well, yes, it's interesting that you should think so too,' said Basil Cox.

Arun stared contentedly and contemplatively into the grey and comforting haze around them.

Suddenly the untuneful and slurred notes of 'Two intoxicating eyes' were followed by the fumbling of the key in the front door. Varun, fortified by Shamshu, the cheap but effective Chinese spirits that he and his friends could just about afford, had returned to the fold.

Arun started as if at Banquo's ghost. He got up, fully intending to hustle Varun out of the house before he entered the drawing room. But he was too late.

Varun, tilting a little, and in an exceptional display of confidence, greeted everyone. The fumes of Shamshu filled the room. He kissed Mrs Rupa Mehra. She drew back. He trembled a little when he saw Meenakshi, who was looking even more dazzlingly beautiful now that she was so horror-struck. He greeted the guests.

'Hello, Mr Box, Mrs Box – er, Mrs Box, Mr Box,' he corrected himself. He bowed, and fumbled with the button-hole that corresponded to the missing button. The draw-string of his pyjamas hung out below his kurta.

'I don't believe we've met before,' said Basil Cox, looking troubled.

'Oh,' said Arun, his fair face beet-red with fury and embarrassment. 'This is, actually, this is – well, my brother Varun. He's a little, er – will you excuse me a minute?' He guided Varun with mildly suppressed violence towards the door, then towards his room. 'Not one word!' he hissed, looking with fury straight into Varun's puzzled eyes. 'Not one word, or I'll strangle you with my bare hands.'

He locked Varun's door from the outside.

He was his charming self by the time he returned to the drawing room.

'Well, as I was saying, he's a little – er, well, uncontrollable at times. I'm sure you understand. Black sheep and all that. Perfectly all right, not violent or anything, but –'

'It looked as if he'd been on a binge,' said Patricia Cox, suddenly livening up.

'Sent to try us, I'm afraid,' continued Arun. 'My father's early death and so on. Every family has one. Has his quirks: insists on wearing those ridiculous clothes.'

'Very strong, whatever it was. I can still smell it,' said Patricia. 'Unusual too. Is it a kind of whisky? I'd like to try it. Do you know what it is?'

'I'm afraid it's what's known as Shamshu.'

'Shamshu?' said Mrs Cox with the liveliest interest, trying the word out on her tongue three or four times. 'Shamshu. Do you know what that is, Basil?' She looked alive again. All her mousiness had disappeared.

'I don't believe I do, my dear,' said her husband.

'I believe it's made from rice,' said Arun. 'It's a Chinese concoction of some kind.'

'Would Shaw Brothers carry it?' asked Patricia Cox.

'I rather doubt it. It ought to be available in China-town,' said Arun.

In fact Varun and his friends did get it from China-town, from a hole-in-the-wall sort of place at eight annas a glass.

'It must be powerful stuff, whatever it is. Smoked hilsa and Shamshu – how marvellous to learn two entirely different things at dinner. One never does, you know,' Patricia confided. 'Usually, I'm bored as a fish.'

Bored as a fish? thought Arun. But by now Varun had started singing to himself inside his room.

'What a very interesting young man,' continued Patricia Cox. 'And he's your brother, you say. What is he singing? Why didn't he join us for dinner? We must have all of you around sometime soon. Mustn't we, darling?' Basil Cox looked very severely doubtful. Patricia Cox decided to take this for assent. 'I haven't had so much fun since I was at RADA. And you can bring a bottle of Shamshu.'

Heaven forbid, thought Basil Cox.

Heaven forbid, thought Arun.

7.7

THE guests were about to arrive at Mr Justice Chatterji's house in Ballygunge. This was one of the three or four grand parties that he took it upon himself to give at short notice during the course of the year. There was a peculiar mixture of guests for two reasons. First, because of Mr Justice Chatterji himself, whose net of friendship and ac-quaintance was very varied. (He was an absent-minded man, who picked up friends here and there.) Secondly, because any party of this kind was invariably treated by the whole Chatterji family as an opportunity to invite all their own friends as well. Mrs Chatterji invited some of hers, and so did their children; only Tapan, who had returned for his school holidays, was considered too young to tag on his own list of invitees to a party where there would be drinking.

Mr Justice Chatterji was not an orderly man, but he had produced five children in strict alternation of sex: Amit, Meenakshi (who was married to Arun Mehra), Dipankar, Kakoli, and Tapan. None of them worked, but each had an occupation. Amit wrote poetry, Meenakshi played canasta, Dipankar sought the Meaning of Life, Kakoli kept the telephone busy, and Tapan, who was only twelve or thirteen, and by far the youngest, went to the prestigious boarding-school, Jheel.

Amit, the poet, had studied Jurisprudence at Oxford, but having got his degree, had not completed, to his father's exasperation, what should have been easy enough for him to complete: his studies for the Bar at Lincoln's Inn, his father's old Inn. He had eaten most of his dinners and had even passed a paper or two, but had then lost interest in the law. Instead, on the strength of a couple of university prizes for poetry, some short fiction published here and there in literary magazines, and a book of poetry which had won him a prize in England (and therefore adulation in Calcutta) he was sitting pretty in his father's house and doing nothing that counted as real work.

At the moment he was talking to his two sisters and to Lata.

'How many do we expect?' asked Amit.

'I don't know,' said Kakoli. 'Fifty?'

Amit looked amused. 'Fifty would just about cover half your friends, Kuku. I'd say one hundred and fifty.'

'I can't abide these large parties,' said Meenakshi in high excitement.

'No, nor can I,' said Kakoli, glancing at herself in the tall mirror in the hall.

'I suppose the guest-list consists entirely of those invited by Ma and Tapan and myself,' said Amit, naming the three least sociable members of the family.

'Vereeeee funneeeee,' said (or, rather, sang) Kakoli, whose name implied the songbird that she was.

'You should go up to your room, Amit,' said Meenakshi, 'and settle down on a sofa with Jane Austen. We'll tell you when dinner is served. Or better still, we'll send it up to you. That way you can avoid all your admirers.'

'He's very peculiar,' said Kakoli to Lata. 'Jane Austen is the only woman in his life.'

'But half the bhadralok in Calcutta want him as a match for their daughters,' added Meenakshi. 'They believe he has brains.'

Kakoli recited:

> 'Amit Chatterji, what a catch!
> Is a highly suitable match.'

Meenakshi added:

> 'Why he has not married yet?
> Always playing hard to get.'

Kakoli continued:

> 'Famous poet, so they say.
> "Besh" decent in every way.'

She giggled.

Lata said to Amit: 'Why do you let them get away with this?'

'You mean with their doggerel?' said Amit.

'I mean with teasing you,' said Lata.

'Oh, I don't mind. It runs off my back like duck's water,' said Amit.

Lata looked surprised, but Kakoli said, 'He's doing a Biswas on you.'

'A Biswas?'

'Biswas Babu, my father's old clerk. He still comes around a couple of times a week to help with this and that, and gives us advice on life. He advised Meenakshi against marrying your brother,' said Kakoli.

In fact the opposition to Meenakshi's sudden affair and marriage had been wider and deeper. Meenakshi's parents had not particularly cared for the fact that she had married outside the community. Arun Mehra was neither a Brahmo, nor of Brahmin stock, nor even a Bengali. He came from a family that was struggling financially. To give the Chatterjis credit, this last fact did not matter very much to them, though they themselves had been more than affluent for generations. They were only (with respect to this objection) concerned that their daughter might not be able to afford the comforts of life that she had grown up with. But again, they had not swamped their married daughter with gifts. Even though Mr Justice Chatterji did not have an instinctive rapport with his son-in-law, he did not think that that would be fair.

'What does Biswas Babu have to do with duck's water?' asked Lata, who found Meenakshi's family amusing but confusing.

'Oh – that's just one of his expressions. I don't think it's very kind of Amit not to explain family references to outsiders.'

'She's not an outsider,' said Amit. 'Or she shouldn't be. Actually, we are all very fond of Biswas Babu, and he is very fond of us. He was my grandfather's clerk originally.'

'But he won't be Amit's – to his heart-deep regret,' said Meenakshi. 'In fact, Biswas Babu is even more upset than our father that Amit has deserted the Bar.'

'I can still practise if I choose to,' said Amit. 'A university degree is enough in Calcutta.'

'Ah, but you won't be admitted to the Bar Library.'

'Who cares?' said Amit. 'Actually, I'd be happy editing a small journal and writing a few good poems and a novel or two and passing gently into senility and posterity. May I offer you a drink? A sherry?'

'I'll have a sherry,' said Kakoli.

'Not you, Kuku, you can help yourself. I was offering Lata a drink.'

'Ouch,' said Kakoli. She looked at Lata's pale blue cotton sari with its fine chikan embroidery, and said: 'Do you know, Lata – pink is what would really suit you.'

Lata said: 'I'd better not have anything as dangerous as a sherry. Could I have some – oh, why not? A small sherry, please.'

Amit went to the bar with a smile and said: 'Do you think I might have two glasses of sherry?'

'Dry, medium or sweet, Sir?' asked Tapan.

Tapan was the baby of the family, whom everyone loved and fussed over, and who was even allowed an occasional sip of sherry himself. This evening he was helping at the bar.

'One sweet and one dry, please,' said Amit. 'Where's Dipankar?' he asked Tapan.

'I think he's in his room, Amit Da,' said Tapan. 'Shall I call him down?'

'No, no, you help with the bar,' said Amit, patting his brother on the shoulder. 'You're doing a fine job. I'll just see what he's up to.'

Dipankar, their middle brother, was a dreamer. He had studied economics, but spent most of his time reading about the poet and patriot Sri Aurobindo, whose flaccid mystical verse he was (to Amit's disgust) at present deeply engrossed in. Dipankar was indecisive by nature. Amit knew that it would be best simply to bring him downstairs himself. Left to his own devices, Dipankar treated every decision like a spiritual crisis. Whether to have one spoon of sugar in his tea or two, whether to come down now or fifteen minutes later, whether to enjoy the good life of Ballygunge or to take up Sri Aurobindo's path of renunciation, all these decisions caused him endless agony. A succession of strong women passed through his life and made most of his decisions for him, before they became impatient with his vacillation ('Is she really the one for me?') and moved on. His views moulded themselves to theirs while they lasted, then began to float freely again.

Dipankar was fond of making remarks such as, 'It is all the Void,' at breakfast, thus casting a mystical aura over the scrambled eggs.

Amit went up to Dipankar's room, and found him sitting on a prayer-mat at the harmonium, untunefully singing a song by Rabindranath Tagore.

'You had better come down soon,' Amit said in Bengali. 'The guests have begun to arrive.'

'Just coming, just coming,' said Dipankar. 'I'll just finish this song, and then I'll . . . I'll come down. I will.'

'I'll wait,' said Amit.

'You can go down, Dada. Don't trouble yourself. Please.'

'It's no trouble,' said Amit. After Dipankar had finished his song, unembarrassed by its tunelessness – for all pitches, no doubt, stood equal before the Void – Amit escorted him down the teak-balustraded marble stairs.

7.8

'WHERE'S Cuddles?' asked Amit when they were halfway down.

'Oh,' said Dipankar vaguely, 'I don't know.'

'He might bite someone.'

'Yes,' agreed Dipankar, not greatly troubled by the thought.

Cuddles was not a hospitable dog. He had been with the Chatterji family for more than ten years, during which time he had bitten Biswas Babu, several schoolchildren (friends who had come to play), a number of lawyers (who had visited Mr Justice Chatterji's chambers for conferences during his years as a barrister), a middle-level executive, a doctor on a house call, and the standard mixture of postmen and electricians.

Cuddles' most recent victim had been the man who had come to the door to take the decennial census.

The only creature Cuddles treated with respect was Mr

Justice Chatterji's father's cat Pillow, who lived in the next house, and who was so fierce that he was taken for walks on a leash.

'You should have tied him up,' said Amit.

Dipankar frowned. His thoughts were with Sri Aurobindo. 'I think I have,' he said.

'We'd better make sure,' said Amit. 'Just in case.'

It was good that they did. Cuddles rarely growled to identify his position, and Dipankar could not remember where – if at all – he had put him. He might still be ranging the garden in order to savage any guests who wandered onto the verandah.

They found Cuddles in the bedroom which had been set aside for people to leave their bags and other apparatus in. He was crouched quietly near a bedside table, watching them with shiny little black eyes. He was a small black dog, with some white on his chest and on his paws. When they had bought him the Chatterjis had been told he was an Apso, but he had turned out to be a mutt with a large proportion of Tibetan terrier.

In order to avoid trouble at the party, he had been fastened by a leash to a bedpost. Dipankar could not recall having done this, so it might have been someone else. He and Amit approached Cuddles. Cuddles normally loved the family, but today he was jittery.

Cuddles surveyed them closely without growling, and when he judged that the moment was ripe, he flew intently and viciously through the air towards them until the sudden restraint of the leash jerked him back. He strained against it, but could not get into biting range. All the Chatterjis knew how to step back rapidly when instinct told them Cuddles was on the attack. But perhaps the guests would not react so swiftly.

'I think we should move him out of this room,' said Amit. Strictly speaking, Cuddles was Dipankar's dog, and thus his responsibility, but he now in effect belonged to all of them – or, rather, was, accepted as one of them, like the sixth point of a regular hexagon.

'He seems quite happy here,' said Dipankar. 'He's a

living being too. Naturally he gets nervous with all this coming and going in the house.'

'Take it from me,' said Amit, 'he's going to bite someone.'

'Hmm. .... Should I put a notice on the door: Beware of Dog?' asked Dipankar.

'No. I think you should get him out of here. Lock him up in your room.'

'I can't do that,' said Dipankar. 'He hates being upstairs when everyone else is downstairs. He is a sort of lapdog, after all.'

Amit reflected that Cuddles was the most psychotic lapdog he had known. He too blamed his temperament on the constant stream of visitors to the house. Kakoli's friends of late had flooded the Chatterji mansion. Now, as it happened, Kakoli herself entered the room with a friend.

'Ah, there you are, Dipankar Da, we were wondering what had happened to you. Have you met Neera? Neera, these are my berruthers Amit and Dipankar. Oh yes, put it down on the bed,' said Kakoli. 'It'll be quite safe here. And the bathroom's through there.' Cuddles prepared for a lunge. 'Watch out for the dog – he's harmless but some-times he has moods. We have moods, don't we, Cuddlu? Poor Cuddlu, left all alone in the bedroom.

> Darling Cuddles, what to do
> When the house is such a zoo!'

sang Kakoli, then disappeared.

'We'd better take him upstairs,' said Amit. 'Come on.'

Dipankar consented. Cuddles growled. They calmed him down and took him up. Then Dipankar played a few soothing chords on the harmonium to reassure him, and they returned downstairs.

Many of the guests had arrived by now, and the party was in full swing. In the grand drawing room with its grand piano and grander chandelier milled scores of guests in full summer evening finery, the women fluttering and flattering and sizing each other up, the men engaging themselves in more self-important chatter. British and Indian, Bengali and non-Bengali, old and middle-aged and young, saris shimmering and necklaces glimmering, crisp Shantipuri dhotis edged with a fine line of gold and hand-creased to perfection, kurtas of raw off-white silk with gold buttons, chiffon saris of various pastel hues, white cotton saris with red borders, Dhakai saris with a white background and a pattern in the weave – or (still more elegant) a grey background with a white design, white dinner-jackets with black trousers and black bow-ties and black patent leather Derbys or Oxfords (each bearing a little reflected chandelier), long dresses of flowery-printed fine poplin chintz and finely polka-dotted white cotton organdy, even an off-the-shoulder silk dress or two in the lightest and most summery of silks: brilliant were the clothes, and glittering the people who filled them.

Arun, who considered it too hot for a jacket, was wearing a stylish cummerbund instead – a maroon monochrome sash with a shimmering pattern through the weave – and a matching bow-tie. He was talking rather gravely to Jock Mackay, a cheerful bachelor in his mid-forties who was one of the directors of the managing agency of McKibbin & Ross.

Meenakshi was dressed in a striking orange French chiffon sari and an electric blue backless choli tied on around her neck and waist with narrow cloth bands. Her midriff was gloriously exposed, around her long and fragrant neck was clasped a Jaipur enamel choker in blue and orange with matching bracelets on her arms, her already considerable height was enhanced by stiletto heels and a tall bun, large earrings dangled deliciously below her chin, the orange tika on her forehead was as huge as her eyes, and most striking and ornamental of all was her devastating smile.

She advanced towards Amit, exuding a fragrance of Shocking Schiaparelli.

But before Amit could greet her, he was accosted by a middle-aged, accusing woman with large, popping eyes whom he did not recognize. She said to him:

'I loved your last book but I can't say I understood it.'
She waited for a response.

'Oh – well, thank you,' said Amit.

'Surely that's not all you're going to say?' said the woman, disappointed. 'I thought poets were more articulate. I'm an old friend of your mother's though we haven't met for many years,' she added, irrelevantly. 'We go back to Shantiniketan.'

'Ah, I see,' said Amit. Although he did not much care for this woman, he did not move away. He felt he ought to say something.

'Well, I'm not so much of a poet now. I'm writing a novel,' he said.

'But that's no excuse at all,' said the woman. Then she added: 'Tell me, what is it about? Or is that a trade secret of the famous Amit Chatterji?'

'No, no, not really,' said Amit, who hated to talk about his current work. 'It's about a moneylender at the time of the Bengal Famine. As you know, my mother's family comes from East Bengal –'

'How wonderful that you should want to write about your own country,' said the woman. 'Especially after winning all those prizes abroad. Tell me, are you in India a lot?'

Amit noticed that both his sisters were standing near him now and listening in.

'Oh yes, well, now that I've returned I am here most of the time. I'm, well, in and out –'

'In and out,' repeated the woman wonderingly.

'Back and forth,' said Meenakshi helpfully.

'Off and on,' said Kakoli, who was incapable of restraint.

The woman frowned.

'To and fro,' said Meenakshi.

'Here and there,' said Kakoli.

She and Meenakshi started giggling. Then they waved to someone at the far side of the huge room, and instantly disappeared.

Amit smiled apologetically. But the woman was looking

at him angrily. Were the young Chatterjis trying to make fun of her?

She said to Amit: 'I am quite sick of reading about you.'

Amit said mildly: 'Mmm. Yes.'

'And of hearing about you.'

'If I weren't me,' said Amit, 'I would be pretty sick of hearing about myself.'

The woman frowned. Then, recovering, she said: 'I think my drink's finished.'

She noticed her husband hovering nearby, and handed him her empty glass, which was stained with crimson lipstick around the rim. 'But tell me, how do you write?'

'Do you mean –' began Amit.

'I mean, is it inspiration? Or is it hard work?'

'Well,' said Amit, 'without inspiration one can't –'

'I knew, I just knew it was inspiration. But without being married, how did you write that poem about the young bride?'

She sounded disapproving.

Amit looked thoughtful, and said: 'I just –'

'And tell me,' continued the woman, 'does it take you long to think of a book? I'm dying to read your new book.'

'So am I,' said Amit.

'I have some good ideas for books,' said the woman. 'When I was in Shantiniketan, the influence of Gurudeb on me was very deep ... you know – our own Rabindranath....'

Amit said, 'Ah.'

'It could not take you long, I know ... but the writing itself must be so difficult. I could never be a writer. I don't have the gift. It is a gift from God.'

'Yes, it seems to come –'

'I once wrote poetry,' said the woman. 'In English, like you. Though I have an aunt who writes Bengali poetry. She was a true disciple of Robi Babu. Does your poetry rhyme?'

'Yes.'

'Mine didn't. It was modern. I was young, in Darjeeling.

I wrote about nature, not about love. I hadn't met Mihir then. My husband, you know. Later I typed them. I showed them to Mihir. Once I spent a night in a hospital bitten by mosquitoes. And a poem came out suddenly. But he said, "It doesn't rhyme." '

She looked disapprovingly at her husband, who was hovering around like a cupbearer with her refilled glass.

'Your husband said that?' said Amit.

'Yes. Then I never had the urge again. I don't know why.'

'You've killed a poet,' said Amit to her husband, who seemed a good enough fellow.

'Come,' he continued to Lata, who had been listening to the last part of the conversation, 'I'll introduce you to a few people, as I promised. Excuse me for a minute.'

Amit had made no such promise, but it enabled him to get away.

7.9

'WELL, whom do you want to meet?' said Amit to Lata.

'No one,' said Lata.

'No one?' asked Amit. He looked amused.

'Anyone. How about that woman there with the red-and-white cotton sari?'

'The one with the short grey hair – who looks as if she's laying down the law to Dipankar and my grandfather?'

'Yes.'

'That's Ila Chattopadhyay. Dr Ila Chattopadhyay. She's related to us. She has strong and immediate opinions. You'll like her.'

Though Lata was unsure about the value of strong and immediate opinions, she liked the look of the woman. Dr Ila Chattopadhyay was shaking her finger at Dipankar and saying something to him with great and apparently affectionate vigour. Her sari was rather crushed.

'May we interrupt?' asked Amit.

'Of course you may, Amit, don't be stupid,' said Dr Ila Chattopadhyay.

'This is Lata, Arun's sister.'

'Good,' said Dr Ila Chattopadhyay, appraising her in a second. 'I'm sure she's nicer than her bumptious brother. I was telling Dipankar that economics is a pointless subject. He would have done far better to study mathematics. Don't you agree?'

'Of course,' said Amit.

'Now that you're back in India you must stay here permanently, Amit. Your country needs you – and I don't say that lightly.'

'Of course,' said Amit.

Dr Ila Chattopadhyay said to Lata: 'I never pay any attention to Amit, he always agrees with me.'

'Ila Kaki never pays any attention to anyone,' said Amit.

'No. And do you know why? It's because of your grandfather.'

'Because of me?' asked the old man.

'Yes,' said Dr Ila Chattopadhyay. 'Many years ago you told me that until you were forty you were very concerned about what people thought of you. Then you decided to be concerned about what you thought of other people instead.'

'Did I say that?' said old Mr Chatterji, surprised.

'Yes, indeed, whether you remember it or not. I too used to make myself miserable bothering about other people's opinions, so I decided to adopt your philosophy immediately, even though I wasn't forty then – or even thirty. Do you really not remember that remark of yours? I was trying to decide whether to give up my career, and was under a lot of pressure from my husband's family to do so. My talk with you made all the difference.'

'Well,' said old Mr Chatterji, 'I remember some things but not other things these days. But I'm very glad my remark made such a, such a, well, profound impression on you. Do you know, the other day I forgot the name of my last cat but one. I tried to recall it, but it didn't come to me.'

'Biplob,' said Amit.

'Yes, of course, and it did come back to me eventually. I had named him that because I was a friend of Subhas Bose – well, let me say I knew the family. ... Of course, in my position as a judge, a name like that would have to be, er –'

Amit waited while the old man searched for the right word, then helped him out.

'Ironic?'

'No, I wasn't looking for that word, Amit, I was – well, "ironic" will do. Of course, those were different times, mm, mm. Do you know, I can't even draw a map of India now. It seems so unimaginable. And the law too is changing every day. One keeps reading about writ petitions being brought up before the High Courts. Well, in my day we were content with regular suits. But I'm an old man, things must move ahead, and I must fall back. Now girls like Ila, and young people like you' – he gesticulated towards Amit and Lata – 'must carry things forward.'

'I'm hardly a girl,' said Dr Ila Chattopadhyay. 'My own daughter is twenty-five now.'

'For me, dear Ila, you will always be a girl,' said old Mr Chatterji.

Dr Ila Chattopadhyay made an impatient sound. 'Anyway, my students don't treat me like a girl. The other day I was discussing a chapter in one of my old books with a junior colleague of mine, a very serious young man, and he said, "Madam, far be it for me, not only as your junior but also as one who is appreciative of the situation of the book in the context of its time and the fact that you have not many years remaining, to suggest that –" I was quite charmed. Remarks like that rejuvenate me.'

'What book was that?' asked Lata.

'It was a book about Donne,' said Dr Ila Chattopadhyay. '*Metaphysical Causality*. It's a very stupid book.'

'Oh, so you teach English!' said Lata, surprised. 'I thought you were a doctor – I mean, a medical doctor.'

'What on earth have you been telling her?' said Dr Ila Chattopadhyay to Amit.

'Nothing. I didn't really get the chance to introduce you properly. You were telling Dipankar so forcefully that he should have dropped economics that I didn't dare to interrupt.'

'So I was. And so he should have. But where has he got to?'

Amit scanned the room cursorily, and noticed Dipankar standing with Kakoli and her babble-rabble. Dipankar, despite his mystical and religious tendencies, was fond of even foolish young women.

'Shall I deliver him back to you?' asked Amit.

'Oh, no,' said Dr Ila Chattopadhyay, 'arguing with him only upsets me, it's like battling a blancmange ... all his mushy ideas about the spiritual roots of India and the genius of Bengal. Well, if he were a true Bengali, he'd change his name back to Chattopadhyay – and so would you all, instead of continuing to cater to the feeble tongues and brains of the British.... Where are you studying?'

Lata, still a little shaken by Dr Ila Chattopadhyay's emphatic energy, said: 'Brahmpur.'

'Oh, Brahmpur,' said Dr Ila Chattopadhyay. 'An impossible place. I once was – no, no, I won't say it, it's too cruel, and you're a nice girl.'

'Oh, do go on, Ila Kaki,' said Amit. 'I adore cruelty, and I'm sure Lata can take anything you have to say.'

'Well, Brahmpur!' said Dr Ila Chattopadhyay, needing no second bidding. 'Brahmpur! I had to go there for a day about ten years ago to attend some conference or other in the English Department, and I'd heard so much about Brahmpur and the Barsaat Mahal and so on that I stayed on for a couple of extra days. It made me almost ill. All that courtly culture with its Yes Huzoor and No Huzoor and nothing robust about it at all. "How are you?" "Oh, well, I'm alive." I just couldn't stand it. "Yes, I'll have two florets of rice, and one drop of daal...." All that subtlety and etiquette and bowing and scraping and ghazals and kathak. Kathak! When I saw those fat women twirling around like tops, I wanted to say to them, "Run! Run! don't dance, run!"'

'It's a good thing you didn't, Ila Kaki, you'd have been strangled.'

'Well, at least it would have meant an end to my suffering. The next evening I had to undergo some more of your Brahmpuri culture. We had to go and listen to one of those ghazal singers. Dreadful, dreadful, I'll never forget it! One of those soulful women, Saeeda something, whom you couldn't see for her jewellery – it was like staring into the sun. Wild horses wouldn't drag me there again ... and all those brainless men in that silly northern dress, the pyjama, looking as if they'd just got out of bed, rolling about in ecstasy – or agony – groaning "wah! wah!" to the most abjectly self-pitying insipid verse – or so it seemed to me when my friends translated it. ... Do you like that sort of music?'

'Well, I do like classical music,' began Lata tentatively, waiting for Dr Ila Chattopadhyay to pronounce that she was completely misguided. 'Ustad Majeed Khan's performances of raags like Darbari, for instance. ...'

Amit, without waiting for Lata to finish her sentence, stepped swiftly in to draw Dr Ila Chattopadhyay's fire.

'So do I, so do I,' he said. 'I've always felt that the performance of a raag resembles a novel – or at least the kind of novel I'm attempting to write. You know,' he continued, extemporizing as he went along, 'first you take one note and explore it for a while, then another to discover its possibilities, then perhaps you get to the dominant, and pause for a bit, and it's only gradually that the phrases begin to form and the tabla joins in with the beat ... and then the more brilliant improvisations and diversions begin, with the main theme returning from time to time, and finally it all speeds up, and the excitement increases to a climax.'

Dr Ila Chattopadhyay was looking at him in astonishment. 'What utter nonsense,' she said to Amit. 'You're getting to be as fluffy as Dipankar. Don't pay any attention to him, Lata,' continued the author of *Metaphysical Causality*. 'He's just a writer, he knows nothing at all about literature. Nonsense always makes me hungry, I must get some food at once. At least the family serves dinner at a sensible hour. "Two florets of rice" indeed!' And, shaking her grey locks emphatically, she made for the buffet table.

Amit offered to bring some food on a plate to his grandfather, and the old man acquiesced. He sat down in a comfortable armchair, and Amit and Lata went towards the buffet. On the way, a pretty young woman detached herself from Kakoli's giggling, gossiping group, and came up to Amit.

'Don't you remember me?' she asked. 'We met at the Sarkars'.'

Amit, trying to work out when and at which Sarkars' they might have met, frowned and smiled simultaneously.

The girl looked at him reproachfully. 'We had a long conversation,' she said.

'Ah.'

'About Bankim Babu's attitude towards the British, and how it affected the form as opposed to the content of his writing.'

Amit thought: Oh God! Aloud he said: 'Yes ... yes. . . .'

Lata, though she felt sorry for both Amit and the girl, could not help smiling. She was glad she had come to the party after all.

The girl persisted: 'Don't you remember?'

Amit suddenly became voluble. 'I am so forgetful –' he said; '– and forgettable,' he added quickly, 'that I sometimes wonder if I ever existed. Nothing I've ever done seems to have happened. . . .'

The girl nodded. 'I know just what you mean,' she said. But she soon wandered away a little sadly.

Amit frowned.

Lata, who could tell that he was feeling bad for having made the girl feel bad, said:

'Your responsibilities don't end with having written your books, it seems.'

'What?' said Amit, as if noticing her for the first time. 'Oh yes, oh yes, that's certainly true. Here, Lata. Have a plate.'

ALTHOUGH Amit was not too conscientious about his general duties as a host, he tried to make sure that Lata at least was not left stranded during the evening. Varun (who might otherwise have kept her company) had not come to the party; he preferred his Shamshu friends. Meenakshi (who was fond of Lata and normally would have escorted her around) was talking to her parents during a brief respite in their hostly duties, describing the events in the kitchen yesterday afternoon with the Mugh cook and in the drawing room yesterday evening with the Coxes. She had had the Coxes invited this evening as well because she thought it might be good for Arun.

'But she's a drab little thing,' said Meenakshi. 'Her clothes look as if they've been bought off the hook.'

'She didn't look all that drab when she introduced herself,' said her father.

Meenakshi looked around the room casually and started slightly. Patricia Cox was wearing a beautiful green silk dress with a pearl necklace. Her gold-brown hair was short and, under the light of the chandelier, curiously radiant. This was not the mousy Patricia Cox of yesterday. Meenakshi's expression was not ecstatic.

'I hope things are well with you, Meenakshi,' said Mrs Chatterji, reverting for a moment to Bengali.

'Wonderfully well, Mago,' replied Meenakshi in English. 'I'm so much in love.'

This brought an anxious frown to Mrs Chatterji's face.

'We're so worried about Kakoli,' she said.

'We?' said Mr Justice Chatterji. 'Well, I suppose that's right.'

'Your father doesn't take things seriously enough. First it was that boy at Calcutta University, the, you know, the –'

'The commie,' said Mr Justice Chatterji benevolently.

'Then it was the boy with the deformed hand and the strange sense of humour, what was his name?'

'Tapan.'

'Yes, what an unfortunate coincidence.' Mrs Chatterji glanced at the bar where her own Tapan was still on duty. Poor baby. She must tell him to go to bed soon. Had he had time to snatch a bite to eat?

'And now?' asked Meenakshi, looking over at the corner where Kakoli and her friends were nattering and chattering away.

'Now,' said her mother, 'it's a foreigner. Well, I may as well tell you, it's that German fellow there.'

'He's very good-looking,' said Meenakshi, who noticed important things first. 'Why hasn't Kakoli told me?'

'She's quite secretive these days,' said her mother.

'On the contrary, she's very open,' said Mr Justice Chatterji.

'It's the same thing,' said Mrs Chatterji. 'We hear about so many friends and special friends that we never really know who the real one is. If indeed there is one at all.'

'Well, dear,' said Mr Justice Chatterji to his wife, 'you worried about the commie and that came to nothing, and about the boy with the hand, and that came to nothing. So why worry? Look at Arun's mother there, she's always smiling, she never worries about anything.'

'Bābā,' said Meenakshi, 'that's simply not true, she's the biggest worrier of all. She worries about everything – no matter how trivial.'

'Is that so?' said her father with interest.

'Anyway,' continued Meenakshi, 'how do you know that there is any romantic interest between them?'

'He keeps inviting her to all these diplomatic functions,' said her mother. 'He's a Second Secretary at the German Consulate General. He even pretends to like Rabindrasangeet. It's too much.'

'Darling, you're not being quite fair,' said Mr Justice Chatterji. 'Kakoli too has suddenly evinced an interest in playing the piano parts of Schubert songs. If we're lucky, we may even hear an impromptu recital tonight.'

'She says he has a lovely baritone voice, and it makes

her swoon. She will completely ruin her reputation,' said Mrs Chatterji.

'What's his name?' asked Meenakshi.

'Hans,' said Mrs Chatterji.

'Just Hans?'

'Hans something. Really, Meenakshi, it's too upsetting. If he's not serious, it'll break her heart. And if she marries him she'll leave India and we'll never see her again.'

'Hans Sieber,' said her father. 'Incidentally, if you introduce yourself as Mrs Mehra rather than as Miss Chatterji, he is liable to seize your hand and kiss it. I think his family was originally Austrian. Courtesy is something of a disease there.'

'Really?' breathed Meenakshi, intrigued.

'Really. Even Ila was charmed. But it didn't work with your mother; she considers him a sort of pallid Ravana come to spirit her daughter away to distant wilds.'

The analogy was not apt, but Mr Justice Chatterji, off the bench, relaxed considerably the logical rigour he was renowned for.

'So you think he might kiss my hand?'

'Not might, will. But that's nothing to what he did with mine.'

'What did he do, Baba?' Meenakshi fixed her huge eyes on her father.

'He nearly crushed it to pulp.' Her father opened his right hand and looked at it for a few seconds.

'Why did he do that?' asked Meenakshi, laughing in her tinkling way.

'I think he wanted to be reassuring,' said her father. 'And your husband was similarly reassured a few minutes later. At any rate, I noticed him open his mouth slightly when he was receiving his handshake.'

'Oh, poor Arun,' said Meenakshi with unconcern.

She looked across at Hans, who was gazing adoringly at Kakoli surrounded by her circle of jabberers. Then, to her mother's considerable distress, she repeated:

'He's very good-looking. Tall too. What's wrong with him? Aren't we Brahmos supposed to be very open-minded? Why shouldn't we marry Kuku off to a foreigner? It would be rather chic.'

'Yes, why not?' said her father. 'His limbs appear to be intact.'

Mrs Chatterji said: 'I wish you could dissuade your sister from acting rashly. I should never have let her learn that brutal language from that awful Miss Hebel.'

Meenakshi said: 'I don't think anything we say to one another has much effect. Didn't you want Kuku to dissuade me from marrying Arun a few years ago?'

'Oh, that was quite different,' said Mrs Chatterji. 'And besides, we're used to Arun now,' she continued unconvincingly. 'We're all one big happy family now.'

The conversation was interrupted by Mr Kohli, a very round teacher of physics who was fond of his drink, and was trying to avoid bumping into his reproving wife on his way to the bar. 'Hello, judge,' he said. 'What do you think of the verdict in the Bandel Road case?'

'Ah, well, as you know, I can't comment on it,' said Mr Justice Chatterji. 'It might turn up in my court on appeal. And really, I haven't been following it closely either, though everyone else I know appears to have been.'

Mrs Chatterji had no such compunctions, however. All the newspapers had carried long reports about the progress of the case and everyone had an opinion about it. 'It really is shocking,' she said. 'I can't see how a mere magistrate has the right –'

'A Sessions Judge, my dear,' interjected Mr Justice Chatterji.

'Yes, well, I don't see how he can possibly have the right to overturn the verdict of a jury. Is that justice? Twelve good men and true, don't they say? How dare he set himself up above them?'

'Nine, dear. It's nine in Calcutta. As for their goodness and truth –'

'Yes, well. And to call the verdict perverse – isn't that what he said – ?'

'Perverse, unreasonable, manifestly wrong and against

542

the weight of the evidence,' recited the bald-headed Mr Kohli with a relish he usually reserved for his whisky. His small mouth was half open, a little like that of a meditative fish.

'Perverse, unreasonably wrong and so on, well, does he have a right to do that? It is so – so undemocratic somehow,' continued Mrs Chatterji, 'and, like it or not, we live in democratic times. And democracy is half our trouble. And that's why we have all these disorders and all this bloodshed, and then we have jury trials – why we still have them in Calcutta when everyone else in India has got rid of them I really don't know – and someone bribes or intimidates the jury, and they bring in these impossible verdicts. If it weren't for courageous judges who set these verdicts aside, where would we be? Don't you agree, dear?' Mrs Chatterji sounded indignant.

Mr Justice Chatterji said, 'Yes, dear, of course. Well, there you are, Mr Kohli; now you know what I think. But your glass is empty.'

Mr Kohli, bewildered, said, 'Yes, I think I'll get another.' He looked quickly around to make sure the coast was clear.

'And please tell Tapan he should go to bed at once,' said Mrs Chatterji. 'Unless he hasn't eaten. If he hasn't eaten, he shouldn't go to bed at once. He should eat first.'

'Do you know, Meenakshi,' said Mr Justice Chatterji, 'that your mother and I were arguing with each other so convincingly one day last week that the next day by breakfast we had convinced ourselves of each other's points of view and argued just as fiercely as before?'

'What were you arguing about?' said Meenakshi. 'I miss our breakfast parliaments.'

'I can't remember,' said Mr Justice Chatterji. 'Can you? Wasn't it something to do with Biswas Babu?'

'It was something to do with Cuddles,' said Mrs Chatterji.

'Was it? I'm not sure it was. I thought it was – well,

anyway, Meenakshi, you must come for breakfast one day soon. Sunny Park is almost within walking distance of the house.'

'I know,' said Meenakshi. 'But it's so difficult to get away in the morning. Arun is very particular about things being just so, and Aparna is always so taxing and tedious before eleven. Mago, your cook really saved my life yesterday. Now I think I'll go and say hello to Hans. And who's that young man who's glowering at Hans and Kakoli? He's not even wearing a bow-tie.'

Indeed, the young man was virtually naked: dressed merely in a standard white shirt and white trousers with a regular striped tie. He was a college student.

'I don't know, dear,' said Mrs Chatterji.

'Another mushroom?' asked Meenakshi.

Mr Justice Chatterji, who had first coined the phrase when Kakoli's friends started springing up in profusion, nodded. 'I'm sure he is,' he said.

Halfway across the room, Meenakshi bumped into Amit, and repeated the question.

'He introduced himself to me as Krishnan,' said Amit. 'Kakoli knows him very well, it seems.'

'Oh,' said Meenakshi. 'What does he do?'

'I don't know. He's one of her close friends, he says.'

'One of her closest friends?'

'Oh no,' said Amit. 'He couldn't be one of her closest friends. She knows the names of those.'

'Well, I'm going to meet Kuku's Kraut,' said Meenakshi with decision. 'Where's Luts? She was with you a few minutes ago.'

'I don't know. Somewhere there.' Amit pointed in the direction of the piano, to a dense and voluble section of the crowd. 'By the way, watch your hands when watching Hans.'

'Yes, I know,' said Meenakshi. 'Daddy warned me too. But it's a safe moment. He's eating. Surely he won't set down his plate to seize my hand?'

'You can never tell,' said Amit darkly.

'Too delicious,' said Meenakshi.

MEANWHILE Lata, who was in the thickest part of the party, felt as if she was swimming in a sea of language. She was quite amazed by the glitter and glory of it all. Sometimes a half-comprehensible English wave would rise, sometimes an incomprehensible Bengali one. Like magpies cackling over baubles – or discovering occasional gems and imagining them to be baubles – the excited guests chattered on. Despite the fact that they were shovelling in a great deal of food, everyone managed to shovel out a great many words.

'Oh, no, no, Dipankar ... you don't understand – the fundamental construct of Indian civilization is the Square – the four stages of life, the four purposes of life – love, wealth, duty, and final liberation – even the four arms of our ancient symbol, the swastika, so sadly abused of late ... yes, it is the square and the square alone that is the fundamental construct of our spirituality ... you will only understand this when you are an old lady like me....'

'She keeps two cooks, that is the reason, no other. Truly – but you must try the luchis. No, no, you must have everything in the right order ... that is the secret of Bengali food....'

'*Such* a good speaker at the Ramakrishna Mission the other day; quite a young man but *so* spiritual ... Creativity in an Age of Crisis ... you really *must* go next week: he will be talking about the Quest for Peace and Harmony....'

'Everyone said that if I went down to the Sundarbans I'd see scores of tigers. I didn't even see a mosquito. Water, water everywhere – and nothing else at all. People are such dreadful liars.'

'They should be expelled – stiff exam or no stiff exam, is that a reason for snatching papers in the examination hall? These are commerce students of Calcutta University, mind you. What will happen to the economic order without discipline? If Sir Asutosh were alive today what would he say? Is this what Independence means?'

'Montoo is looking so sweet. But Poltoo and Loltoo are looking a little under par. Ever since their father's illness, of course. They say it is — that it is, you know ... well, liver ... from too much drink.'

'Oh, no, no, no, Dipankar — the elemental paradigm — I would never have said construct — of our ancient civilization is of course the Trinity ... I don't mean the Christian trinity, of course; all that seems so crude somehow — but the Trinity as Process and Aspect — Creation and Preservation and Destruction — yes, the Trinity, that is the elemental paradigm of our civilization, and no other....'

'Ridiculous nonsense, of course. So I called the union leaders in and I read them the riot act. Naturally it took a little straight talk for them to come into line again. Well, I won't say there wasn't a payment to one or two of the most recalcitrant of them, but all that is handled by Personnel.'

'That's not Je reviens — that's Quelque-fleurs — all the difference in the world. Not that my husband would know the difference. He can't even recognize Chanel!'

'Then I said to Robi Babu: "You are like a God to us, please give me a name for my child," and he consented. That is the reason why she is called Hemangini.... Actually, the name was not to my liking, but what could I do?'

'If the mullahs want war, they can have one. Our trade with East Pakistan has virtually come to a halt. Well, one happy side-effect is that the price of mangoes has come down! The Maldah growers had a huge crop this year, and they don't know what to do with them. ... Of course it's a transport problem too, just like the Bengal Famine.'

'Oh, no, no, no, Dipankar, you haven't got it at all — the primeval texture of Indian philosophy is that of Duality ... yes, Duality.... The warp and weft of our ancient garment, the sari itself — a single length of cloth which yet swathes our Indian womanhood — the warp and weft of the universe itself, the tension between Being and Non-being — yes, indubitably it is Duality alone that reigns over us here in our ancient land.'

'I felt like crying when I read the poem. They must be so proud of him. So proud.'

'Hello, Arun, where's Meenakshi?'

Lata turned around and saw Arun's rather displeased expression. It was his friend Billy Irani. This was the third time someone had spoken to him with the sole intention of finding out where his wife was. He looked around the room for her orange sari, and spied her near the Kakoli crowd.

'There she is, Billy, near Kuku's nest. If you want to meet her, I'll walk over with you and detach her,' he said.

Lata wondered for a second what her friend Malati would have made of all this. She attached herself to Arun as if to a life-raft, and floated across to where Kakoli was standing. Somehow or other Mrs Rupa Mehra, as well as an old Marwari gentleman clad in a dhoti, had infiltrated the crowd of bright young things.

The old gentleman, unconscious of the gilded youth surrounding him, was saying, rather fussily, to Hans:

'Ever since the year 1933 I have been drinking the juice of bitter gourds. You know bitter gourd? It is our famous Indian vegetable, called karela. It looks like this' – he gesticulated elongatedly – 'and it is green, and ribbed.'

Hans looked mystified. His informant continued:

'Every week my servant takes a seer of bitter gourd, and from the skin only, mark you, he will make juice. Each seer will yield one jam jar of juice.' His eyes squinted in concentration. 'What they do with the rest I do not care.'

He made a dismissive gesture.

'Yes?' said Hans politely. 'That makes me so interested.'

Kakoli had begun to giggle. Mrs Rupa Mehra was looking deeply interested. Arun caught Meenakshi's eye and frowned. Bloody Marwari, he was thinking. Trust them to make a fool of themselves in front of foreigners.

Sweetly oblivious of Arun's disapproval, the gourd-proponent continued:

'Then every morning for my breakfast he will give me one sherry glass or liqueur glass – so much – of this juice. Every day since 1933. And I have no sugar problems. I can

547

eat sweetmeats without anxiety. My dermatology is also very good, and all bowel movements are very satisfactory.'

As if to prove the point he bit into a gulab-jamun which was dripping with syrup.

Mrs Rupa Mehra, fascinated, said: 'Only the skin?' If this was true, diabetes need no longer interpose itself between her palate and her desires.

'Yes,' said the man fastidiously. 'Only the skin, like I have said. The rest is a superfluity. Beauty of bitter gourd is only skin deep.'

7.12

'ENJOYING yourself?' Jock Mackay asked Basil Cox as they wandered out onto the verandah.

'Well, yes, rather,' said Basil Cox, resting his whisky precariously on the white cast-iron railing. He felt light-headed, almost as if he wanted to balance on the railings himself. The fragrance of gardenias wafted across the lawn.

'First time I've seen you at the Chatterjis. Patricia's looking ravishing.'

'Thanks ... she is, isn't she? I can never predict when she's going to have a good time. Do you know, when I had to come out to India, she was most unwilling. She even, well. . . .'

Basil, moving his thumb gently across his lower lip, looked out into the garden, where a few mellow golden globes lit up the underside of a huge laburnum tree covered with grape-like clusters of yellow flowers. There appeared to be a hut of sorts under the tree.

'But you're enjoying it here, are you?'

'I suppose so. . . . Puzzling sort of place, though. . . . Of course, I've been here less than a year.'

'What do you mean?'

'Well, what's that bird for instance that was singing a moment ago – pu-puuuuuu-pu! pu-puuuuu-pu! higher and higher. It certainly isn't a cuckoo and I rather wish it was.

Disconcerting. And I find all these lakhs and crores and annas and pice quite confusing still. I have to re-calculate things in my head. I suppose I'll get used to it all with time.' From the expression on Basil Cox's face it didn't look likely. Twelve pence to the shilling and twenty shillings to the pound was infinitely more logical than four pice to the anna and sixteen annas to the rupee.

'Well, it is a cuckoo, as a matter of fact,' said Jock Mackay, 'it's the hawk-cuckoo — or brainfever bird ... didn't you know that? It's hard to believe, but I've got so used to it that I miss it when I'm back home on leave. The song of the birds I don't mind at all, what I can't abide is the dreadful music Indian singers make ... awful wailing stuff. ... But do you know the question that disconcerted me most of all when I first came here twenty years ago and saw all these beautiful, elegantly dressed women?' Jock Mackay cheerfully and confidingly jerked his head towards the drawing room. 'How do you fuck in a sari?'

Basil Cox made a sudden movement, and his drink fell over into a flowerbed. Jock Mackay looked faintly amused.

'Well,' said Basil Cox, rather annoyed, 'did you find out?'

'Everyone makes his own discoveries sooner or later,' said Jock Mackay in an enigmatic manner. 'But it's a charming country on the whole,' he continued expansively. 'By the end of the Raj they were so busy slitting each other's throats that they left ours unslit. Lucky.' He sipped his drink.

'Well, there doesn't seem to be any resentment — quite the opposite, if anything,' said Basil Cox after a while, looking over into the flowerbed. 'But I wonder what people like the Chatterjis really think of us. ... After all, we're still quite a presence in Calcutta. We still run things here — commercially speaking, of course.'

'Oh, I shouldn't worry if I were you. What people think or don't think is never very interesting,' said Jock Mackay. 'Horses, now, I often wonder what they're thinking. ...'

'Well, I had dinner with their son-in-law the other day —

yesterday, as a matter of fact – Arun Mehra, he works with us – oh, of course, you know Arun – and suddenly his brother tumbles in, drunk as a lord and singing away – and reeking of some fearsome Shimsham fire-water – well, I'd never in a hundred years have guessed that Arun had a brother like that. And dressed in crumpled pyjamas!'

'No, it is puzzling,' agreed Jock Mackay. 'I knew an old ICS chap, Indian, but pukka enough, who, when he retired, renounced everything, became a sadhu and was never heard of again. And he was a married man with a couple of grown-up children.'

'Really?'

'Really. But a charming people, I'd say: face-flattering, back-biting, name-dropping, all-knowing, self-praising, law-mongering, power-worshipping, road-hogging, spittle-hawking. ... There were a few more items to my litany once, but I've forgotten them.'

'You sound as if you hate the place,' said Basil Cox.

'Quite the contrary,' said Jock Mackay. 'I wouldn't be surprised if I decided to retire here. But should we go back in? I see you've lost your drink.'

7.13

'DON'T think of anything serious before you are thirty,' young Tapan was being advised by the round Mr Kohli, who had managed to free himself of his wife for a few minutes. He had his glass in his hand, and looked like a large, worried, almost disconsolate teddy-bear in a slow hurry; his huge dome – a phrenological marvel – glistened as he leaned over the bar; he half closed his heavily lidded eyes and half opened his small mouth after he had delivered himself of one of his bon mots.

'Now, Baby Sahib,' said the old servant Bahadur firmly to Tapan, 'Memsahib says you must go to bed at once.'

Tapan began laughing.

'Tell Ma I'll go to bed when I'm thirty,' he said, dismissing Bahadur.

'People are stuck at seventeen, you know,' continued Mr Kohli. 'That's where they imagine themselves ever afterwards — always seventeen, and always happy. Not that they're happy when they're actually seventeen. But you have some years to go still. How old are you?'

'Thirteen — almost.'

'Good — stay there, that's my advice,' suggested Mr Kohli.

'Are you serious?' said Tapan, suddenly looking more than a little unhappy. 'You mean things don't get any better?'

'Oh, don't take anything I say seriously,' said Mr Kohli. He paused for a sip. 'On the other hand,' he added, 'take everything I say more seriously than what other adults say.'

'Go to bed at once, Tapan,' said Mrs Chatterji, coming up to them. 'What's this you've been saying to Bahadur? You won't be allowed to stay up late if you behave like this. Now pour Mr Kohli a drink, and then go to bed at once.'

7.14

'OH, no, no, no, Dipankar,' said the Grande Dame of Culture, slowly shaking her ancient and benevolent head from side to side in pitying condescension as she held him with her dully glittering eye, 'that's not it at all, not Duality, I could never have said Duality, Dipankar, oh dear me, no — the intrinsic essence of our being here in India is a Oneness, yes, a Oneness of Being, an ecumenical assimilation of all that pours into this great subcontinent of ours.' She gestured around the drawing room tolerantly, maternally. 'It is Unity that governs our souls, here in our ancient land.'

Dipankar nodded furiously, blinked rapidly, and gulped his Scotch down, while Kakoli winked at him. That's what she liked about Dipankar, thought Kakoli: he was the only serious younger Chatterji, and because he was such a gentle, accommodating soul, he made the ideal captive listener for any purveyors of pabulum who happened to stray into the irreverent household. And everyone in the family could go to him when they wanted unflippant advice.

'Dipankar,' said Kakoli, 'Hemangini wants to talk to you, she's pining away without you, and she has to leave in ten minutes.'

'Yes, Kuku, thanks,' said Dipankar unhappily, and blinking a little more than usual as a result. 'Try to keep her here as long as you can ... we were just having this interesting discussion.... Why don't you join us, Kuku?' he added desperately. 'It's all about how Unity is the intrinsic essence of our being....'

'Oh, no, no, no, no, Dipankar,' said the Grande Dame, correcting him a trifle sadly, but still patiently: 'Not Unity, not Unity, but Zero, Nullity itself, is the guiding principle of our existence. I could never have used the term intrinsic essence – for what is an essence if it is not intrinsic? India is the land of the Zero, for it was from the horizons of our soil that it rose like a vast sun to spread its light on the world of knowledge.' She surveyed a gulab-jamun for a few seconds. 'It is the Zero, Dipankar, represented by the Mandala, the circle, the circular nature of Time itself, that is the guiding principle of our civilization. All this' – she waved her arm around the drawing room once more, taking in, in one slow plump sweep the piano, the bookcases, the flowers in their huge cut-glass vases, the cigarettes smouldering at the edges of ashtrays, two plates of gulab-jamuns, the glittering guests, and Dipankar himself – 'all this is Non-Being. It is the Non-ness of things, Dipankar, that you must accept, for in Nothing lies the secret of Everything.'

7.15

THE Chatterji Parliament (including Kakoli, who normally found it difficult to wake up before ten) was assembled for breakfast the next day.

All signs of the party had been cleared away. Cuddles had been unleashed upon the world. He had bounded around the garden in delight, and had disturbed Dipankar's meditations in the small hut that he had made for himself in a corner of the garden. He had also dug up a few plants in the vegetable garden that Dipankar took so much interest in. Dipankar took all this calmly. Cuddles had probably buried something there, and after the trauma of last night merely wanted to reassure himself that the world and the objects in it were as they used to be.

Kakoli had left instructions that she was to be woken up at seven. She had to make a phone call to Hans after he came back from his morning ride. How he managed to wake up at five – like Dipankar – and do all these vigorous things on a horse she did not know. But she felt that he must have great strength of will.

Kakoli was deeply attached to the telephone, and monopolized it shamelessly – as she did the car. Often she would burble on for forty-five minutes on end and her father sometimes found it impossible to get through to his house from the High Court or the Calcutta Club. There were fewer than ten thousand telephones in the whole of Calcutta, so a second phone would have been an unimaginable luxury. Ever since Kakoli had had an extension installed in her room, however, the unimaginable had begun to appear to him almost reasonable.

Since it had been a late night, the old servant Bahadur, who usually performed the difficult task of waking the unwilling Kuku and placating her with milk, had been told to sleep late. Amit had therefore taken on the duty of waking his sister.

He knocked gently on her door. There was no response. He opened the door. Light was streaming through the window onto Kakoli's bed. She was sleeping diagonally across the bed with her arm thrown across her eyes. Her pretty, round face was covered with dried Lacto-calamine, which, like papaya pulp, she used to improve her complexion.

Amit said, 'Kuku, wake up. It's seven o'clock.'

Kakoli continued to sleep soundly.

'Wake up, Kuku.'

Kakoli stirred slightly, then said what sounded like 'choo-moo'. It was a sound of complaint.

After about five minutes of trying to get her to wake up, first by gentle words and then by a gentle shake or two of the shoulders, and being rewarded with nothing but 'choo-moo', Amit threw a pillow rather ungently over her head.

Kakoli bestirred herself enough to say: 'Take a lesson from Bahadur. Wake people up nicely.'

Amit said, 'I don't have the practice. He has probably had to stand around your bed ten thousand times murmuring, "Kuku Baby, wake up; wake up, Baby Memsahib," for twenty minutes while you do your "choo-moo".'

'Ungh,' said Kakoli.

'Open your eyes at least,' said Amit. 'Otherwise you'll just roll over and go back to sleep.' After a pause he added, 'Kuku Baby.'

'Ungh,' said Kakoli irritably. She opened both her eyes a fraction, however.

'Do you want your teddy-bear? Your telephone? A glass of milk?' said Amit.

'Milk.'

'How many glasses?'

'A glass of milk.'

'All right.'

Amit went off to fetch her a glass of milk.

When he returned he found that she was sitting on the bed, with the telephone receiver in one hand and Cuddles tucked under the other arm. She was treating Cuddles to a stream of Chatterji chatter.

'Oh you beastie,' she was saying; 'oh you beastly beastie – oh you ghastly, beastly beastie.' She stroked his head with the telephone receiver. 'Oh you vastly ghastly mostly beastly beastie.' She paid no attention to Amit.

'Do shut up, Kuku, and take your milk,' said Amit

irritably. 'I have other things to do than wait on you, you know.'

This remark struck Kakoli with novel force. She was well-practised in the art of being helpless when there were helpful people around.

'Or do you want me to drink it for you as well?' added Amit gratuitously.

'Go bite Amit,' Kakoli instructed Cuddles. Cuddles did not comply.

'Shall I set it down here, Madam?'

'Yes, do.' Kakoli ignored the sarcasm.

'Will that be all, Madam?'

'Yes.'

'Yes what?'

'Yes, thank you.'

'I was going to ask for a good-morning kiss, but that Lacto-calamine looks so disgusting I think I'll defer it.'

Kakoli surveyed Amit severely. 'You are a horrible, insensitive person,' she informed him. 'I don't know why women swoooooon over your poetry.'

'That's because my poetry is so sensitive,' said Amit.

'I pity the girl who marries you. I reeeeeally pity her.'

'And I pity the man who marries you. I reeeeeally pity him. By the way, was that my future brother-in-law you were going to call? The nutcracker?'

'The nutcracker?'

Amit held out his right hand as if shaking it with an invisible man. Slowly his mouth opened in shock and agony.

'Do go away, Amit, you've spoilt my mood completely,' said Kakoli.

'What there was to spoil,' said Amit.

'When I say anything about the women you're interested in you get very peeved.'

'Like who? Jane Austen?'

'May I make my phone call in peace and privacy?'

'Yes, yes, Kuku Baby,' said Amit, succeeding in being both sarcastic and placatory, 'I'm just going, I'm just going. See you at breakfast.'

555

THE Chatterji family at breakfast presented a scene of cordial conflict. It was an intelligent family where everyone thought of everyone else as an idiot. Some people thought the Chatterjis obnoxious because they appeared to enjoy each others' company even more than the company of others. But if they had dropped by at the Chatterjis for breakfast and seen them bickering, they would probably have disliked them less.

Mr Justice Chatterji sat at the head of the table. Though small in size, short-sighted, and fairly absent-minded, he was a man of some dignity. He inspired respect in court and a sort of obedience even in his eccentric family. He didn't like to talk more than was necessary.

'Anyone who likes mixed fruit jam is a lunatic,' said Amit.

'Are you calling me a lunatic?' asked Kakoli.

'No, of course not, Kuku, I'm working from general principles. Please pass me the butter.'

'You can reach for it yourself,' said Kuku.

'Now, now, Kuku,' murmured Mrs Chatterji.

'I can't,' protested Amit. 'My hand's been crushed.'

Tapan laughed. Kakoli gave him a black look, then began to look glum in preparation for a request.

'I need the car today, Baba,' said Kuku after a few seconds. 'I have to go out. I need it for the whole day.'

'But Baba,' said Tapan, 'I'm spending the day with Pankaj.'

'I really must go to Hamilton's this morning to get the silver inkstand back,' said Mrs Chatterji.

Mr Justice Chatterji raised his eyebrows. 'Amit?' he asked.

'No bid,' said Amit.

Dipankar, who also declined transport, wondered aloud why Kuku was looking so wistful. Kuku frowned.

Amit and Tapan promptly began an antiphonal chant.

'We look before and after, and pine for what is –'

'NOT!'

'Our sincerest laughter with some pain is –'

'FROT!'

'Our sweetest songs are those that tell of saddest –'

'THOT!' cried Tapan jubilantly, for he hero-worshipped Amit.

'Don't worry, darling,' said Mrs Chatterji comfortingly; 'everything will come out all right in the end.'

'You don't have any idea what I was thinking of,' countered Kakoli.

'You mean who,' said Tapan.

'You be quiet, you amoeba,' said Kakoli.

'He seemed a nice enough chap,' ventured Dipankar.

'Oh no, he's just a glamdip,' countered Amit.

'Glamdip? Glamdip? Have I missed something?' asked their father.

Mrs Chatterji looked equally mystified. 'Yes, what is a glamdip, darling?' she asked Amit.

'A glamorous diplomat,' replied Amit. 'Very vacant, very charming. The kind of person whom Meenakshi used to sigh after. And talking of which, one of them is coming around to visit me this morning. He wants to ask me about culture and literature.'

'Really, Amit?' asked Mrs Chatterji eagerly. 'Who?'

'Some South American ambassador – from Peru or Chile or somewhere,' said Amit, 'with an interest in the arts. I got a phone call from Delhi a week or two ago, and we fixed it up. Or was it Bolivia? He wanted to meet an author on his visit to Calcutta. I doubt he's read anything by me.'

Mrs Chatterji looked flustered. 'But then I must make sure that everything is in order –' she said. 'And you told Biswas Babu you'd see him this morning.'

'So I did, so I did,' agreed Amit. 'And so I will.'

'He is not just a glamdip,' said Kakoli suddenly. 'You've hardly met him.'

'No, he is a good boy for our Kuku,' said Tapan. 'He is so shinsheer.'

This was one of Biswas Babu's adjectives of high praise. Kuku felt that Tapan should have his ears boxed.

'I like Hans,' said Dipankar. 'He was very polite to the man who told him to drink the juice of bitter gourds. He does have a good heart.'

'O my darling, don't be heartless.
Hold my hand. Let us be partless,'

murmured Amit.

'But don't hold it too hard,' laughed Tapan.

'Stop it!' cried Kuku. 'You are all being utterly horrible.'

'He is good wedding bell material for our Kuku,' continued Tapan, tempting retribution.

'Wedding bell? Or bedding well?' asked Amit. Tapan grinned delightedly.

'Now, that's enough, Amit,' said Mr Justice Chatterji before his wife could intervene. 'No bloodshed at breakfast. Let's talk about something else.'

'Yes,' agreed Kuku. 'Like the way Amit was mooning over Lata last night.'

'Over Lata?' said Amit, genuinely astonished.

'Over Lata?' repeated Kuku, imitating him.

'Really, Kuku, love has destroyed your brain,' said Amit. 'I didn't notice I was spending any time with her at all.'

'No, I'm sure you didn't.'

'She's just a nice girl, that's all,' said Amit. 'If Meenakshi hadn't been so busy gossiping and Arun making contacts I wouldn't have assumed any responsibility for her at all.'

'So we needn't invite her over unnecessarily while she's in Calcutta,' murmured Kuku.

Mrs Chatterji said nothing, but had begun to look anxious.

'I'll invite whoever I like over,' said Amit. 'You, Kuku, invited fifty-odd people to the party last night.'

'Fifty odd people,' Tapan couldn't resist saying.

Kuku turned on him severely.

'Little boys shouldn't interrupt adult conversations,' she said.

Tapan, from the safety of the other side of the table, made a face at her. Once Kuku had actually got so incensed she had chased him around the table, but usually she was sluggish till noon.

'Yes,' Amit frowned. 'Some of them were very odd, Kuku. Who is that fellow Krishnan? Dark chap, south Indian, I imagine. He was glaring at you and your Second Secretary very resentfully.'

'Oh, he's just a friend,' said Kuku, spreading her butter with more than usual concentration. 'I suppose he's annoyed with me.'

Amit could not resist delivering a Kakoli-couplet:

> 'What is Krishnan in the end?
> Just a mushroom, just a friend.'

Tapan continued:

> 'Always eating dosa-iddly,
> Drinking beer and going piddly!'

'Tapan!' gasped his mother.

Amit, Meenakshi and Kuku, it appeared, had completely corrupted her baby with their stupid rhyming.

Mr Justice Chatterji put down his toast. 'That's enough from you, Tapan,' he said.

'But Baba, I was only joking,' protested Tapan, thinking it unfair that he should have been singled out. Just because I'm the youngest, he thought. And it was a pretty good couplet too.

'A joke's a joke, but enough's enough,' said his father. 'And you too, Amit. You'd have a better claim to criticizing others if you did something useful yourself.'

'Yes, that's right,' added Kuku happily, seeing the tables turning. 'Do some serious work, Amit Da. Act like a useful member of society before you criticize others.'

'What's wrong with writing poems and novels?' asked Amit. 'Or has passion made you illiterate as well?'

'It's all right as an amusement, Amit,' said Mr Justice Chatterji. 'But it's not a living. And what's wrong with the law?'

'Well, it's like going back to school,' said Amit.

'I don't quite see how you come to that conclusion,' said his father dryly.

'Well,' said Amit, 'you have to be properly dressed – that's like school uniform. And instead of saying "Sir" you say "My Lord" – which is just as bad – until you're raised to the bench and people say it to you instead. And you get holidays, and you get good chits and bad chits just like Tapan does: I mean judgments in your favour and against you.'

'Well,' said Mr Justice Chatterji, not entirely pleased by the analogy, 'it was good enough for your grandfather and for me.'

'But Amit has a special gift,' broke in Mrs Chatterji. 'Aren't you proud of him?'

'He can practise his special gifts in his spare time,' said her husband.

'Is that what they said to Rabindranath Tagore?' asked Amit.

'I'm sure you'll admit there's a difference between you and Tagore,' said his father, looking at his eldest son in surprise.

'I'll admit there's a difference, Baba,' said Amit. 'But what's the relevance of the difference to the point I'm making?'

But at the mention of Tagore, Mrs Chatterji had entered a mode of righteous reverence.

'Amit, Amit,' she cried, 'how can you think of Gurudeb like that?'

'Mago, I didn't say –' began Amit.

Mrs Chatterji broke in. 'Amit, Robi Babu is like a saint. We in Bengal owe everything to him. When I was in Shantiniketan, I remember he once said to me –'

But now Kakoli joined forces with Amit.

'Please, Mago, really – we've heard enough about Shantiniketan and how idyllic it is. I know that if I had to live there I'd commit suicide every day.'

'His voice is like a cry in the wilderness,' continued her mother, hardly hearing her.

'I'd hardly say so, Ma,' said Amit. 'We idolize him more than the English do Shakespeare.'

'And with good reason,' said Mrs Chatterji. 'His songs come to our lips – his poems come to our hearts –'

'Actually,' said Kakoli, '*Abol Tabol* is the only good book in the whole of Bengali literature.

> The Griffonling from birth
> Is indisposed to mirth.
> To laugh or grin he counts a sin
> And shudders, "Not on earth."

Oh, yes, and I like *The Sketches of Hutom the Owl*. And when I take up literature, I shall write my own: *The Sketches of Cuddles the Dog*.'

'Kuku, you are a really shameless girl,' cried Mrs Chatterji, incensed. 'Please stop her from saying these things.'

'It's just an opinion, dear,' said Mr Justice Chatterji, 'I can't stop her from holding opinions.'

'But about Gurudeb, whose songs she sings – about Robi Babu –'

Kakoli, who had been force-fed, almost from birth, with Rabindrasangeet, now warbled out to the tune of a truncated 'Shonkochero bihvalata nijere apoman':

> 'Robi Babu, R. Tagore, O, he's such a bore!
> Robi Babu, R. Tagore, O, he's such a bore!
> O, he's su-uch a bore.
> Such a, such a bore.
> Such a, such a bore,
> O, he's such a, O, he's such a, O, he's such a bore.
> Robi Babu, R. Tagore, O, he's such a bore!'

'Stop! Stop it at once! Kakoli, do you hear me?' cried Mrs Chatterji, appalled. 'Stop it! How dare you! You stupid, shameless, shallow girl.'

'Really, Ma,' continued Kakoli, 'reading him is like trying to swim breaststroke through treacle. You should hear Ila Chattopadhyay on your Robi Babu. Flowers and moonlight and nuptial beds. . . .'

'Ma,' said Dipankar, 'why do you let them get to you? You should take the best in the words and mould them to your own spirit. That way, you can attain stillness.'

Mrs Chatterji was unsoothed. Stillness was very far from her.

'May I get up? I've finished my breakfast,' said Tapan.

'Of course, Tapan,' said his father, 'I'll see about the car.'

'Ila Chattopadhyay is a very ignorant girl, I've always thought so,' burst out Mrs Chatterji. 'As for her books – I think that the more people write, the less they think. And she was dressed in a completely crushed sari last night.'

'She's hardly a girl any more, dear,' said her husband. 'She's quite an elderly woman – must be at least fifty-five.'

Mrs Chatterji glanced with annoyance at her husband. Fifty-five was hardly elderly.

'And one should heed her opinions,' added Amit. 'She's quite hard-headed. She was advising Dipankar yesterday that there was no future in economics. She appeared to know.'

'She always appears to know,' said Mrs Chatterji. 'Anyway, she's from your father's side of the family,' she added irrelevantly. 'And if she doesn't appreciate Gurudeb she must have a heart of stone.'

'You can't blame her,' said Amit. 'After a life so full of tragedy anyone would become hard.'

'What tragedy?' asked Mrs Chatterji.

'Well, when she was four,' said Amit, 'her mother slapped her – it was quite traumatic – and then things went on in that vein. When she was twelve she came second in an exam. . . . It hardens you.'

'Where did you get such mad children?' Mrs Chatterji asked her husband.

'I don't know,' he replied.

'If you had spent more time with them instead of going to the club every day, they wouldn't have turned out this way,' said Mrs Chatterji in a rare rebuke; but she was overwrought.

The phone rang.

'Ten to one it's for Kuku,' said Amit.

'It's not.'

'I suppose you can tell from the kind of ring, hunh, Kuku?'

'It's for Kuku,' cried Tapan from the door.

'Oh. Who's it from?' asked Kuku, and poked her tongue out at Amit.

'Krishnan.'

'Tell him I can't come to the phone. I'll call back later,' said Kuku.

'Shall I tell him you're having a bath? Or sleeping? Or out in the car? Or all three?' Tapan grinned.

'Please, Tapan,' said Kuku, 'be a sweet boy and make some excuse. Yes, say I've gone out.'

Mrs Chatterji was shocked into exclaiming: 'But, Kuku, that's a barefaced lie.'

'I know, Ma,' said Kuku, 'but he's so tedious, what can I do?'

'Yes, what can one do when one has a hundred best friends?' muttered Amit, looking mournful.

'Just because nobody loves you —' cried Kuku, stung to fierceness.

'Lots of people love me,' said Amit, 'don't you, Dipankar?'

'Yes, Dada,' said Dipankar, who thought it best to be simply factual.

'And all my fans love me,' added Amit.

'That's because they don't know you,' said Kakoli.

'I won't contest that point,' said Amit; 'and, talking of unseen fans, I'd better get ready for His Excellency. Excuse me.'

Amit got up to go, and so did Dipankar; and Mr Justice Chatterji settled the use of the car between the two main claimants, while keeping Tapan's interests in mind as well.

ABOUT fifteen minutes after the Ambassador was due to arrive at the house for their one hour talk, Amit was informed by telephone that he would be 'a little late'. That would be fine, said Amit.

About half an hour after he was due to arrive, Amit was told that he might be a little later still. This annoyed him somewhat, as he could have done some writing in the meantime. 'Has the Ambassador arrived in Calcutta?' he asked the man on the phone. 'Oh, yes,' said the voice. 'He arrived yesterday afternoon. He is just running a little late. But he left for your house ten minutes ago. He should be there in the next five minutes.'

Since Biswas Babu was due to arrive soon and Amit did not want to keep the family's old clerk waiting, he was irritated. But he swallowed his irritation, and muttered something polite.

Fifteen minutes later, Señor Bernardo Lopez arrived at the door in a great black car. He came with a lively young woman whose first name was Anna-Maria. He was extremely apologetic and full of cultural goodwill; she on the other hand was brisk and energetic and extracted a pocket-book from her handbag the moment they sat down.

During the flow of his ponderous and gentle words, all slowly weighed, deliberated and qualified before they could be expressed, the Ambassador looked everywhere but at Amit: he looked at his teacup, at his own flexed or drumming fingers, at Anna-Maria (to whom he nodded reassuringly), and at a globe in a corner of the room. From time to time he would smile. He pronounced 'very' with a 'b'.

Caressing his pointed bald head nervously and gravely, and conscious of the fact that he was an inexcusable forty-five minutes late, he attempted to come straight to the point:

'Well, Mr Chatterji, Mr Amit Chatterji, if I may make so bold, I am often called upon in my official duties, as you know, being Ambassador and so on, which I have been for about a year now – unfortunately, with us it is not permanent, or indeed definite; there is an element of, I might even say, or it would perhaps not be unfair to say (yes, that is better put, if I might be allowed to praise myself for a locution in another language) that there is an element of arbitrariness in it, in our stay in a particular place, I mean; unlike you writers who ... but anyway, what I meant was that I would like to put to you one question directly, which is to say, forgive me, but as you know I have arrived here forty-five minutes in tardiness and have taken up forty-five minutes of your good time (of your good self, as I notice some say here), partly because I set out very tardily (I came here directly from a friend's home here in this remarkable city, to which I hope you will come some time when you are more at leisure – or to Delhi needlessly – by which I mean rather, needless to say, to our own home – though you must of course tell me if I am imposing myself on you) but I asked my secretary to inform you of that (I hope he did, yes?), but partly because our driver led us to Hazra Road, a, I understand, very natural mistake, because the streets are almost parallel and close to each other, where we met a gentleman who was kind enough to redirect us to this beautiful house – I speak as an appreciator of not just the architecture but the way you have preserved its atmosphere, its perhaps ingenuity, no, ingenuousness, even virginity – but as I said I am (to come to the point) late, and indeed forty-five, well, what I must now ask you as I have asked others in the course of my official duties, although this is by no means an official duty but one entirely of pleasure (though I indeed do have something to ask of you, or rather, ask you about), I have to ask you as I ask other officials who have schedules to keep, not that you are official, but, well, a busy man: do you have any appointment after this hour that you have allotted me, or can we perhaps exceed ... yes? Do I make myself clear?'

Amit, terrified that he might have to face more of this, said hastily: 'Alas, Your Excellency will forgive me, but I have a pressing engagement in fifteen minutes, no, forgive me, five minutes now, with an old colleague of my father's.'

'Tomorrow then?' asked Anna-Maria.

'No, alas, I am going to Palashnagar tomorrow,' said Amit, naming the fictitious town in which his novel was set. He reflected that this was no more than the truth.

'A pity, a pity,' said Bernardo Lopez. 'But we still have five minutes, so let me ask simply this, a long puzzlement to me: What is all this about "being" and birds and boats and the river of life – that we find in Indian poetry, the great Tagore unexcluded? But let me say in qualification that by "we" I mean merely we of the West, if the South may be subsumed in the West, and by "find" I mean that which is as if to say that Columbus found America which we know needed no finding, for there were those there for whom "finding" would be more insulting than superfluous, and of course by Indian poetry, I mean such poetry as has been made accessible to us, which is to say, such as has been traduced by translation. In that light, can you enlighten me? Us?'

'I will try,' said Amit.

'You see?' said Bernardo Lopez with mild triumph to Anna-Maria, who had put down her notebook. 'The unanswerables are not unanswerable in the lands of the East. Felix qui potuit rerum cognoscere causas, and when it is true of a whole nation, it makes one marvel the more. Truly when I came here one year ago I had a sense –'

But Bahadur now entered, and informed Amit that Biswas Babu was waiting for him in his father's study.

'Forgive me, Your Excellency,' said Amit, getting up, 'it appears as though my father's colleague has arrived. But I shall give earnest thought to what you have said. And I am deeply honoured and grateful.'

'And I, young man, though young here is merely to say that the earth has gone around the sun less often since your inception, er, conception, than mine (and is that to say anything at all?), I too will bear in mind the result of this confabulation, and consider it "in vacant or in pensive mood", as the Poet of the Lake has chosen to express it. Its intensity, the urgings I have felt during this brief interview, which have led me upwards from nescience to science – yet is that in truth an upward movement? Will time even tell us that? Does time tell us anything at all? – such I will cherish.'

'Yes, we are indebted,' said Anna-Maria, picking up her notebook.

As the great black car spirited them away, no longer running behind time, Amit stood on the porch step waving slowly.

Though the fluffy white cat Pillow, led on a leash by his grandfather's servant, crossed his field of vision, Amit did not follow it with his eyes, as he normally did.

He had a headache, and was in no mood to talk to anyone. But Biswas Babu had come specially to see him, probably to make him see sense and take up the law again, and Amit felt that his father's old clerk, whom everyone treated with great affection and respect, should not be required to sit and cool his heels longer than necessary – or rather, shake his knees, which was a habit with him.

7.18

WHAT made matters slightly uncomfortable was that though Amit's Bengali was fine and Biswas Babu's spoken English was not, he had insisted – ever since Amit had returned from England 'laden with laurels' as he put it on speaking to him almost exclusively in English. For the others, this privilege was only occasional; Amit had always been Biswas Babu's favourite, and he deserved a special effort.

Though it was summer, Biswas Babu was dressed in a coat and dhoti. He had an umbrella with him and a black bag. Bahadur had given him a cup of tea, which he was stirring thoughtfully while looking around at the room in which he had worked for so many years – both for Amit's father and for his grandfather. When Amit entered, he stood up.

After respectful greetings to Biswas Babu, Amit sat down at his father's large mahogany desk. Biswas Babu was sitting on the other side of it. After the usual questions about how everyone was doing and whether either could perform any service for the other, the conversation petered out.

Biswas Babu then helped himself to a small amount of snuff. He placed a bit in each nostril and sniffed. There was clearly something weighing on his mind but he was reluctant to bring it up.

'Now, Biswas Babu, I have an idea of what has brought you here,' said Amit.

'You have?' said Biswas Babu, startled, and looking rather guilty.

'But I have to tell you that I don't think that even your advocacy is going to work.'

'No?' said Biswas Babu, leaning forward. His knees started vibrating rapidly in and out.

'You see, Biswas Babu, I know you feel I have let the family down.'

'Yes?' said Biswas Babu.

'You see, my grandfather went in for it, and my father, but I haven't. And you probably think it is very peculiar. I know you are disappointed in me.'

'It is not peculiar, it is just late. But you are probably making hail while the sun shines, and sowing oats. That is why I have come.'

'Sowing oats?' Amit was puzzled.

'But Meenakshi has rolled the ball, now you must follow it.'

It suddenly struck Amit that Biswas Babu was talking not about the law but about marriage. He began to laugh.

'So it is about this, Biswas Babu, that you have come to talk to me?' he said. 'And you are speaking to me about the matter, not to my father.'

'I also spoke to your father. But that was one year ago, and where is the progress?'

Amit, despite his headache, was smiling.

Biswas Babu was not offended. He told Amit:

'Man without life companion is either god or beast.

568

Now you can decide where to place yourself. Unless you are above such thoughts. . . .'

Amit confessed that he wasn't.

Very few were, said Biswas Babu. Perhaps only people like Dipankar, with his spiritual leanings, were able to renounce such yearnings. That made it all the more imperative that Amit should continue the family line.

'Don't believe it, Biswas Babu,' said Amit. 'It is all Scotch and sannyaas with Dipankar.'

But Biswas Babu was not to be distracted from his purpose. 'I was thinking about you three days ago,' he said. 'You are so old – twenty-nine or more – and are still issueless. How can you give joy to your parents? You owe to them. Even Mrs Biswas agrees. They are so proud of your achievement.'

'But Meenakshi has given them Aparna.'

Obviously a non-Chatterji like Aparna, and a girl at that, did not count for much in Biswas Babu's eyes. He shook his head and pursed his lips in disagreement.

'In my heart-deep opinion –' he began, and stopped, so that Amit could encourage him to continue.

'What do you advise me to do, Biswas Babu?' asked Amit obligingly. 'When my parents were keen that I should meet that girl Shormishtha, you made your objections known to my father, and he passed them on to me.'

'Sorry to say, she had tinted reputation,' said Biswas Babu, frowning at the corner of the desk. This conversation was proving more difficult than he had imagined it would. 'I did not want trouble for you. Enquiries were necessary.'

'And so you made them.'

'Yes, Amit Babu. Now maybe about law you know best. But I know about early life and youth. It is hard to restrain, and then there is danger.'

'I am not sure I understand.'

After a pause Biswas Babu went on. He seemed a little embarrassed, but the consciousness of his duty as an adviser to the family kept him going.

'Of course it is dangerous business but any lady who

cohabits with more than one man increases risks. It is but natural,' he added.

Amit did not know what to say, as he had not got Biswas Babu's drift.

'Indeed, any lady who has the opportunity to go to second man will know no limits,' Biswas Babu remarked gravely, even sadly, as if admonishing Amit in a muted way.

'In fact,' he ruminated, 'though not admitted in our Hindu society, lady is more excited than man as a rule, I will have to say. That is why there should not be too much difference. So that lady can cool down with man.'

Amit looked startled.

'I mean,' continued Biswas Babu, 'difference in age of course. That way they are commenstruate. Otherwise of course an older man is cool in later years when his wife is in the prime of lusty life and there is scope for mischief.'

'Mischief,' echoed Amit. Biswas Babu had never talked in this vein to him before.

'Of course,' thought Biswas Babu aloud, glancing in a melancholy way at the rows of law-books around him, 'that is not true in all cases. But you must not leave it till you are more than thirty. Do you have headache?' he asked, concerned, for Amit looked as if he was in pain.

'A slight headache,' said Amit. 'Nothing serious.'

'An arranged marriage with a sober girl, that is the solution. And I will also think about a helpmeet for Dipankar.'

They were both quiet for a minute. Amit broke the silence.

'Nowadays people say that you should choose your own life-partner, Biswas Babu. Certainly, poets like myself say that.'

'What people think, what people say, and what people do are two different things,' said Biswas Babu. 'Now I and Mrs Biswas are happily married for thirty-four years. Where is the harm in an arrangement like that? Nobody asked me. One day my father said it is fixed.'

'But if I find someone myself –'

Biswas Babu was willing to compromise. 'Good. But then there should be enquiries also. She should be a sober girl from –'

'– from a good family?' prompted Amit.

'From a good family.'

'Well-educated?'

'Well-educated. Saraswati gives better blessings in long run than Lakshmi.'

'Well, now I have heard the whole case, I will reserve judgment.'

'Do not reserve it too long, Amit Babu,' said Biswas Babu with an anxious, almost paternal, smile. 'Sooner or later you will have to cut Gordon's knot.'

'And tie it?'

'Tie it?'

'Tie the knot, I mean,' said Amit.

'Surely you must then also tie the knot,' said Biswas Babu.

7.19

LATER that evening, in the same room, Mr Justice Chatterji, who was wearing a dhoti-kurta rather than his black tie of the previous evening, said to his two elder sons:

'Well, Amit – Dipankar – I've called you here because I have something to say to both of you. I've decided to speak to you alone, because your mother gets emotional about things, and that doesn't really help. It's about financial matters, our family investments and property and so on. I've continued to handle these affairs so far, for more than thirty years in fact, but it puts a heavy burden on me in addition to all my other work, and the time has come for one or the other of you to take over the running of that side of things.... Now wait, wait' – Mr Justice Chatterji held up a hand – 'let me finish, then both of you will have the chance to speak. The one thing I will not change is my decision to hand things over. My burden of work – and this is true of all my brother judges – has increased very

571

considerably over the last year, and, well, I am not getting any younger. At first I was simply going to tell you, Amit, to manage things. You are the eldest and it is, strictly speaking, your duty. But your mother and I have discussed the whole issue at length, and we have taken your literary interests into account, and we now agree that it does not have to be you. You have studied law – whether or not you are practising it – and Dipankar, you have a degree in economics. There are no better qualifications for managing the family properties – now, wait a second, Dipankar, I have not finished – and both of you are intelligent. So what we have decided is this. If you, Dipankar, put your degree in economics to some use instead of concentrating on the – well, the spiritual side of things, well and good. If not, I am afraid, Amit, that the job will fall to you.'

'But, Baba –' protested Dipankar, blinking in distress, 'economics is the worst possible qualification for running anything. It's the most useless, impractical subject in the world.'

'Dipankar,' said his father, not very pleased, 'you have studied it for several years now, and you must have learned something – certainly more than I did as a student – about how economic affairs are handled. Even without your training I have – in earlier days with Biswas Babu's help, and now largely without it – somehow managed to deal with our affairs. Even if, as you claim, a degree in economics doesn't help, I do not believe it can actually be a hindrance. And it is new to my ears to hear you claim that impractical things are useless.'

Dipankar said nothing. Nor did Amit.

'Well, Amit?' asked Mr Justice Chatterji.

'What should I say, Baba?' said Amit. 'I don't want you to have to keep on doing this work. I suppose I hadn't realized quite how time-consuming it must be. But, well, my literary interests aren't just interests, they are my vocation – my obsession, almost. If it was a question of my own share of the property, I would just sell it all, put the money in a bank, and live off the interest – or, if that wasn't enough, I'd let it run down while I kept working at my novels and my poems. But, well, that isn't the case. We can't jeopardize everyone's future – Tapan's, Kuku's, Ma's, to some extent Meenakshi's as well. I suppose I'm glad that there's at least the possibility that I might not have to do it – that is, if Dipankar –'

'Why don't we both do a bit, Dada?' asked Dipankar, turning towards Amit.

Their father shook his head. 'That would only cause confusion and difficulties within the family. One or the other.'

Both of them looked subdued. Mr Justice Chatterji turned to Dipankar and continued: 'Now I know that you have your heart set on going to the Pul Mela, and, for all I know, after you have submerged yourself in the Ganga a few times, it might help you decide things one way or another. At any rate, I am willing to wait for a few more months, say, till the end of this year, for you to mull over matters and make up your mind. My view of it is that you should get a job in a firm – in a bank, preferably; then all of this would probably fall comfortably into the kind of work you'll be doing anyway. But, as Amit will tell you, my views of things are not always sound – and, whether sound or not, are not always acceptable. But, well, if you don't agree, then, Amit, it will have to be you. Your novel will take at least another year or two to complete, and I cannot wait that long. You will have to work on your literary activities on the side.'

Neither brother looked at the other.

'Do you think I am being unjust?' asked Mr Justice Chatterji in Bengali, with a smile.

'No, of course not, Baba,' said Amit, trying to smile, but only succeeding in looking deeply troubled.

7.20

ARUN MEHRA arrived at his office in Dalhousie Square not long after 9.30. The sky was black with clouds and the rain was coming down in sheets. The rain swept across the vast façade of the Writers' Building, and added its direct contribution to the huge tank in the middle of the square.

'Bloody monsoon.'

He got out of the car, leaving his briefcase inside and protecting himself with the *Statesman*. His peon, who had been standing in the porch of the building, started when he saw his master's little blue car. It had been raining so hard that he had not seen it until it had almost stopped. Agitated, he opened the umbrella and rushed out to protect the sahib. He was a second or two late.

'Bloody idiot.'

The peon, though several inches shorter than Arun Mehra, contrived to hold the umbrella over the sacred head as Arun sauntered into the building. He got into the lift, and nodded in a preoccupied manner at the lift-boy.

The peon rushed back to the car to get his master's briefcase, and climbed the stairs to the second floor of the large building.

The head office of the managing agency, Bentsen & Pryce, more popularly known as Bentsen Pryce, occupied the entire second floor.

From these surroundings, officials of the company controlled their share of the trade and commerce of India. Though Calcutta was not what it had been before 1912 – the capital of the Government of India – it was, nearly four decades later and nearly four years after Independence, indisputably the commercial capital still. More than half the exports of the country flowed down the silty Hooghly to the Bay of Bengal. The Calcutta-based managing agencies such as Bentsen Pryce managed the bulk of the foreign trade of India; they controlled, besides, a large share of the production of the goods that were processed or manufactured in the hinterland of Calcutta, and the services, such as insurance, that went into ensuring their smooth movement down the channels of commerce.

The managing agencies typically owned controlling interests in the actual manufacturing companies that operated the factories, and supervised them all from the Calcutta head office. Almost without exception these agencies were still owned by the British, and almost without exception the executive officers of the managing agencies near Dalhousie Square – the commercial heart of Calcutta – were white. Final control lay with the directors in the London office and the shareholders in England – but they were usually content to leave things to the Calcutta head office so long as the profits kept flowing in.

The web was wide and the work both interesting and substantial. Bentsen Pryce itself was involved in the following areas, as one of its advertisements stated:

Abrasives, Air Conditioning, Belting, Brushes, Building, Cement, Chemicals and Pigments, Coal, Coal Mining Machinery, Copper & Brass, Cutch & Katha, Disinfectants, Drugs & Medicines, Drums and Containers, Engineering, Handling Materials, Industrial Heating, Insurance, Jute Mills, Lead Pipes, Linen Thread, Loose Leaf Equipment, Oils inc. Linseed Oil Products, Paints, Paper, Rope, Ropeway Construction, Ropeways, Shipping, Spraying Equipment, Tea, Timber, Vertical Turbine Pumps, Wire Rope.

The young men who came out from England in their twenties, most of them from Oxford or Cambridge, fell easily into the pattern of command that was a tradition at Bentsen Pryce, Andrew Yule, Bird & Company, or any of a number of similar firms that considered themselves (and were considered by others to be) the pinnacle of the Calcutta – and therefore Indian – business establishment. They were covenanted assistants, bound by covenant or rolling contract to the company. At Bentsen Pryce, until a few years ago, there had been no place for Indians in the company's European Covenanted Service. Indians were slotted into the Indian Covenanted Service, where the levels of both responsibility and remuneration were far lower.

Around the time of Independence, under pressure from the government and as a concession to the changing times, a few Indians had been grudgingly allowed to enter the cool sanctum of the inner offices of Bentsen Pryce. As a result, by 1951 five of the eighty executives in the firm (though so far none of the department heads, let alone directors) were what could be called brown-whites.

All of them were extraordinarily conscious of their exceptional position, and none more so than Arun Mehra. If ever there was a man enraptured by England and the English it was he. And here he was, hobnobbing with them on terms of tolerable familiarity.

The British knew how to run things, reflected Arun Mehra. They worked hard and they played hard. They believed in command, and so did he. They assumed that if you couldn't command at twenty-five, you didn't have it in you. Their fresh-faced young men came out to India even earlier; it was hard to restrain them from commanding at twenty-one. What was wrong with this country was a lack of initiative. All that Indians wanted was a safe job.

Bloody pen-pushers, the whole lot of them, Arun said to himself as he surveyed the sweltering clerical section on his way to the air-conditioned executive offices beyond.

He was in a bad mood not only because of the foul weather but because he had solved only about a third of the *Statesman* crossword puzzle, and James Pettigrew, a friend of his from another firm, with whom he exchanged clues and solutions by phone most mornings, would probably have solved most of them by now. Arun Mehra enjoyed explaining things, and did not like having things explained to him. He enjoyed giving the impression to others that he knew whatever was worth knowing, and he had virtually succeeded in giving himself the same impression.

7.21

THE morning mail was sorted out by Arun's department head Basil Cox with the help of a couple of his principal lieutenants. This morning about ten letters had been marked out to Arun. One of them was from the Persian

Fine Teas Company, and he looked it over with particular interest.

'Would you take down a letter, Miss Christie?' he said to his secretary, an exceptionally discreet and cheerful young Anglo-Indian woman, who had grown accustomed to his moods. Miss Christie had at first been resentful of the fact that she had been allocated to an Indian rather than a British executive, but Arun had charmed and patronized her into accepting his authority.

'Yes, Mr Mehra, I'm ready.'

'The usual heading. Dear Mr Poorzahedy, We have received your description of the contents of the shipment of tea – take down the particulars from the letter, Miss Christie – to Teheran – sorry, make that Khurramshahr and Teheran – that you wish us to insure from auction in Calcutta to arrival by customs bond to consignee in Teheran. Our rates, as before, are five annas per hundred rupees for the standard policy, including SR&CC as well as TPND. The shipment is valued at six lakhs, thirty-nine thousand, nine hundred and seventy rupees, and the premium payable will be – would you work that out, Miss Christie? – thank you – yours sincerely, and so on.... Wasn't there a claim from them about a month ago?'

'I think so, Mr Mehra.'

'Hmm.' Arun pointed his hands together under his chin, then said: 'I think I'll have a word with the burra babu.'

Rather than call the head clerk of the department into his office, he decided to pay him a visit. The burra babu had served in the insurance department of Bentsen Pryce for twenty-five years and there was nothing about the nuts and bolts of the department that he did not know. He was something like a regimental sergeant-major, and everything at the lower levels passed through his hands. The European executives never dealt with anyone but him.

When Arun wandered over to his desk, the burra babu was looking over a sheaf of cheques and duplicates of letters, and telling his underlings what to do. 'Tridib, you handle this one,' he was saying; 'Sarat, you make out this invoice.' It was a muggy day, and the ceiling fans were rustling the high piles of paper on the clerks' desks.

Seeing Arun, the burra babu stood up. 'Sir,' he said.

'Do sit down,' said Arun casually. 'Tell me, what has been happening lately with Persian Fine Teas? On the claims side, I mean.'

'Binoy, tell the claims clerk to come here with the claims ledger.'

After Arun, who was dressed in his suit, as was appropriate to (and unavoidable for) one of his position, had spent a sweaty but enlightening twenty minutes with the clerks and ledgers, he returned to the chilled sanctum of his office and told Miss Christie to hold off typing the letter he had dictated.

'Anyway, it's Friday,' he said. 'It can wait, if necessary, till Monday. I won't be taking calls for the next fifteen minutes or so. Oh yes, and I won't be in this afternoon either. I have a lunch appointment at the Calcutta Club and then I have to visit that damned jute factory at Puttigurh with Mr Cox and Mr Swindon.'

Mr Swindon was from the jute department, and they were going to visit a factory that another company wished to insure against fire. Arun could not see the sense of visiting a particular jute factory, when the insurance for all such factories was clearly based on a standard tariff that depended upon very little other than the process of manufacture used. But Swindon had apparently told Basil Cox that it was important to look over the plant, and Basil had asked Arun to accompany him.

'All a waste of time if you ask me,' said Arun. Friday afternoon by tradition at Bentsen Pryce usually meant a long, leisurely meal at the club followed by a round of golf and possibly a token appearance at the office around closing time. The week's work was effectively over by Thursday afternoon. But, upon reflection, Arun thought it possible that by asking him to help with a matter of Fire Insurance when his normal duties fell under Marine Insurance, Basil Cox was attempting to groom him for wider responsibilities. In fact, now that he considered it, a number of matters of General Insurance had also been marked out to him lately. All this could only mean that the powers above approved of him and his work.

Cheered by this thought, he knocked at Basil Cox's door.

'Come in. Yes, Arun?' Basil Cox gestured to a chair, and, taking his hand off the mouthpiece of the phone, continued: 'Well, that's excellent. Lunch then, and – yes, we'll both look forward to seeing you ride. Bye.'

He turned to Arun and said: 'I do apologize, dear boy, for nibbling away at your Friday afternoon. But I wonder if I can make up for it by inviting you and Meenakshi to the races at Tolly tomorrow as our guests.'

'We'd be delighted,' said Arun.

'I was talking to Jock Mackay. It appears he's riding in one of the races. It might be rather fun to see him. Of course, if the weather keeps up, they'll be swimming their horses round the track.'

Arun permitted himself a chuckle.

'I didn't know he'd be riding tomorrow. Did you?' said Basil Cox.

'No, I can't say I did. But he rides often enough,' said Arun. He reflected that Varun, the racing fiend, would have known not only that Jock Mackay was riding, but in which race he would be riding, on what horse, with what handicap and at what probable odds. Varun and his Shamshu friends usually bought a provisional or kutcha racing form the moment it appeared on the streets on Wednesday, and from then until Saturday afternoon would think about and discuss little else.

'And now?' Basil Cox prompted Arun.

'It's about the tariffs for Persian Fine Teas. They want us to insure another shipment.'

'Yes. I marked that letter out to you. Purely routine, isn't it?'

'I'm not so sure.'

Basil Cox stroked his lower lip with his thumb and waited for Arun to go on.

'I don't think our claims experience with them is so good,' said Arun.

'Well, that's easily checked.'

'I've already done so.'

'I see.'

'Claims are a hundred and fifty-two per cent of premiums if you take the last three years. Not a happy situation.'

'No, no, indeed,' said Basil Cox, considering. 'Not a happy situation. What do they usually claim for? Pilferage, I seem to recall. Or is it rainwater damage? And didn't they have a claim for taint once? Leather in the same hold as tea or something like that.'

'Rainwater damage was another company. And taint we disallowed after getting a report from Lloyds, our claims settlement agents on the spot. Their surveyors said that taint was minimal, even though the Persians appear to judge their tea more by fragrance than by flavour. It's pilferage that has really harmed them. Or, rather, us. Skilful pilferage at the customs warehouse in Khurram-shahr. It's a bad port, and for all we know the customs authorities may be in on it.'

'Well, what is the premium at present? Five annas?'

'Yes.'

'Put it up to eight annas.'

'I'm not sure that would work,' said Arun. 'I could call upon their agent in Calcutta and do that. But I don't think he'd take kindly to it. He once mentioned that even our five anna rate was barely competitive with what Commercial Union was willing to insure them for. We would very likely lose them.'

'Well, do you have anything else to suggest?' said Basil Cox with a rather tired smile. From experience he knew that Arun very likely did have something else to suggest.

'As it happens, I do,' said Arun.

'Ah,' said Basil Cox, pretending surprise.

'We could write to Lloyds and ask them what steps had been taken to prevent or reduce pilferage from the customs warehouse.'

Basil Cox was rather disappointed but did not say so.

'I see. Well, thank you, Arun.'

But Arun had not finished.

'And we could offer to reduce the premium.'

'Reduce it, did you say?' Basil Cox raised both eyebrows.

'Yes. Just remove the Theft, Pilferage and Non-Delivery clause. They can have everything else: the standard policy of fire, storm, leakage, piracy, forced jettison and so on, plus Strike, Riot and Civil Commotion, rainwater damage, even taint, whatever they want. All on very favourable terms. But no TPND. That they can insure with someone else. They obviously have very little incentive to protect their cargo if we fork out their claims every time someone decides to drink their tea for them.'

Basil Cox smiled. 'It's an idea. Let me think about it. We'll talk about it in the car this afternoon on the way to Puttigurh.'

'There's one other matter, Basil.'

'Could it wait till the afternoon too?'

'Actually, one of our friends from Rajasthan is coming to see me in an hour and it has to do with him. I should have brought it up earlier, but I thought it could wait. I didn't know he was so eager to have a quick response.'

This was a stock euphemism for a Marwari businessman. The grasping, enterprising, canny, energetic and above all ungentlemanly traits of that community were intensely distasteful to the leisured and gentlemanly sahibs of the managing agencies. The managing agency might borrow a great deal of money from a certain kind of Marwari businessman, but the chairman would not dream of inviting him to his club, even if it were one to which Indians were admitted.

But in this case it was the Marwari businessman who wanted Bentsen Pryce to finance him. His suggestion, in brief, was this: his house wanted to expand into a new line of operations, but he wanted Bentsen Pryce to invest in this expansion. In return, he would give them whatever insurance business arose from the new operations.

Arun, swallowing his own instinctive distaste for the community, and reminding himself that business was business, put the matter to Basil Cox as objectively as he could. He forbore from mentioning that this was no more than what one British firm did for another in the regular way of business. He knew that his boss was not unaware of that fact.

Basil Cox did not ask him for his advice. He looked at a point beyond Arun's right shoulder for a disconcertingly long time, then said:

'I don't like it – it smells a bit Marwari to me.'

By his tone he implied that it was a species of sharp practice. Arun was about to speak when he added:

'No. It's definitely not for us. And Finance, I know, would not like it at all. Let's leave it at that. So I'll see you at two-thirty?'

'Right,' said Arun.

When he got back to his room, he wondered how he would put things to his visitor, and what reasons he could adduce to defend the decision. But he did not need to. Mr Jhunjhunwala took the decision surprisingly well. When Arun told him that his company couldn't go ahead with the proposal, Mr Jhunjhunwala did not ask him to explain himself. He merely nodded, then said in Hindi – implying an awful complicity, it seemed to Arun, a complicity of one Indian with another – 'You know, that's the trouble with Bentsen Pryce: they won't take something on unless there's a bit of a smell of the English in it.'

7.22

AFTER Mr Jhunjhunwala had gone, Arun phoned Meenakshi to say that he would be back from work fairly late that evening, but that they should still plan to go for cocktails at the Finlays' at about seven-thirty. He then answered a couple of other letters, and finally settled back to his crossword.

But before he could solve more than two or three more clues, the phone rang. It was James Pettigrew.

'Well, Arun, how many?'

'Not many, I'm afraid. I've just begun to look at it.'

This was an outright lie. Apart from straining every brain-cell he could while sitting on the toilet, Arun had frowned at the crossword over breakfast and even scribbled the letters of possible anagrams underneath the clues while being driven to work. Since his handwriting was illegible, even to himself, this usually didn't help him much.

'I won't ask you if you got "that confounded pane in the neck".'

'Thanks,' said Arun. 'I'm glad you give me credit for an IQ of at least eighty.'

'And "Johnson's rose"?'

'Yes.'

'How about "Knife a gentleman buys in Paris"?'

'No — but since you're obviously eager to tell me, why don't you put both of us out of our agony?'

'Machete.'

'Machete?'

'Machete.'

'I'm afraid I don't quite see how —'

'Ah, Arun, you'll have to learn French some day,' said James Pettigrew infuriatingly.

'Well, what didn't you get?' asked Arun with ill-masked irritation.

'Very little, as it happens,' said the obnoxious James.

'So you've solved it all, have you?' said Arun.

'Well, not exactly, not exactly. There are a couple that are still troubling me a little.'

'Oh, just a couple?'

'Well, perhaps a couple of couples.'

'For example?'

'"Musician who sounds rapacious", five letters, third letter T, fifth letter R.'

'Luter,' said Arun promptly.

'Aaah, that's got to be right. But I always thought the right word was lutanist or perhaps lutist.'

583

'Does the L give you any help in the other direction?'

'Er ... let's see ... yes, it does. That must be "Belfry". Thank you.'

'Don't mention it,' said Arun. 'As it happens, I had a linguistic advantage with that one.'

'How so?' said James.

'The word "loot" comes from Hindi.'

'So it does, so it does,' said James Pettigrew. 'Anyway,' he continued, 'it seems that I've won the Ashes three to two, and you owe me lunch sometime next week.'

He was referring to their weekly crossword stakes that ran from Monday to Friday. Arun grunted his admission of defeat.

*

While this conversation, devoted largely to the peculiarities of words, and not entirely pleasing to Arun Mehra, was taking place, another telephone conversation, also dealing with the peculiarities of words, was taking place, which, had he been aware of it, would have pleased Arun Mehra even less.

Meenakshi: Hello.

Billy Irani: Hello!

Meenakshi: You sound different. Is there anyone in the office with you?

Billy: No. But I wish you wouldn't call me at the office.

Meenakshi: It's so difficult for me to call at other times. But everyone happens to be out this morning. How are you?

Billy: I'm in fine, er, fettle.

Meenakshi: That makes you sound like a sort of stallion.

Billy: Are you sure you're not thinking of fetlock?

Meenakshi: Silly Billy! Of course not. Fetlock is the hair somewhere. It's what you catch a horse by, I think. I think it's the part of the mane at the base of the neck. Hair equals lock.

Billy: Well then, tell me, how can you sprain a fetlock

or break one? You keep hearing of a horse having to be shot because it's broken a fetlock. By the way, are you going to the races tomorrow at Tolly?

Meenakshi: Yes, as it happens. Arun just called me from the office. Basil Cox has invited us. So will I see you there?

Billy: I'm not sure I'm going tomorrow. But we're all meeting this evening aren't we, for cocktails at the Finlays' – and then dinner and dancing somewhere?

Meenakshi: But I won't get a chance to say a word to you – what with Shireen guarding you like an emerald egg, and Arun – and my sister-in-law.

Billy: Your sister-in-law?

Meenakshi: She's quite nice; she needs to be brought out a bit, though. I thought we'd throw her in with Bish, and see how they get along.

Billy: And did you call me an emerald egg?

Meenakshi: Yes. You are rather like an emerald egg. And that brings me to the point. Arun is going to be out in Puttigurh or somewhere until seven o'clock or so. What are you doing this afternoon? I know it's Friday, so don't say you're working.

Billy: Actually, I have lunch first, then a game of golf.

Meenakshi: What? In this weather? You'll be swept out to sea. So let's meet – for tea and so on.

Billy: Well – I'm not sure all this is such a good idea.

Meenakshi: Let's go to the zoo. It'll be pouring with rain so we won't meet the usual good citizen. We'll meet a horse – or a zebra and we'll ask him if he's sprained his hair or his neck. I'm so funny, aren't I?

Billy: Yes, hilarious. Well, I'll meet you at four-thirty. At the Fairlawn Hotel. For tea.

Meenakshi: For tea and so on.

Billy [rather reluctantly]: And so on. Yes.

Meenakshi: At three o'clock.

Billy: Four o'clock.

Meenakshi: Four o'clock. Four o'clock. Perhaps you were thinking of forelock when you said fetlock.

Billy: Perhaps I was.

Meenakshi: Or foreskin.

Billy: I wouldn't grab a horse by that.

Meenakshi: Silly Billy! But what is a fetlock then?

Billy: Look up a dictionary – and tell me this afternoon. Or show me.

Meenakshi: Naughty.

Billy [with a sigh]: You're far naughtier than I am, Meenakshi. I don't think this is at all a good idea.

Meenakshi: Four o'clock then. I'll take a taxi. Bye.

Billy: Bye.

Meenakshi: I don't love you a bit.

Billy: Thank God.

7.23

WHEN Meenakshi returned from her assignation with Billy, it was half past six, and she was smiling contentedly. She was so pleasant to Mrs Rupa Mehra that it quite unsettled her, and she asked Meenakshi if something was the matter. Meenakshi assured her that nothing at all was the matter.

Lata couldn't decide what to wear for the evening. She entered the drawing room carrying a light pink cotton sari, a part of which she had draped over her shoulder. 'What do you think of this, Ma?' she said.

'Very nice, darling,' said Mrs Rupa Mehra, and fanned a fly away from Aparna's sleeping head.

'What nonsense, Ma, it's absolutely awful,' said Meenakshi.

'It is not at all awful,' said Mrs Rupa Mehra defensively. 'Pink was your father-in-law's favourite colour.'

'Pink?' Meenakshi started laughing. 'He liked wearing pink?'

'On me. When I wore it!' Mrs Rupa Mehra was angry. Meenakshi had changed from nice to nasty in an instant. 'If you don't have any respect for me, at least have respect for my husband. You have no sense of proportion. Going off gallivanting to New Market and leaving Aparna for the servants to take care of.'

'Now, Ma, I'm sure pink looked lovely on you,' said Meenakshi in a conciliatory manner. 'But it's absolutely the wrong thing for Luts's complexion. And for Calcutta, and for the evening, and for this kind of society. And cotton just won't do. I'll see what Luts has and help her choose something that will make her look her best. We'd better hurry, Arun will be home at any moment, and then we won't have time for anything. Come on, Luts.'

And Lata was taken in hand. She was finally dressed in one of Meenakshi's deep blue chiffon saris which happened to go with one of her own blue blouses. (She had to tuck the sari in considerably more than Meenakshi, since she was a few inches shorter.) A peacock brooch of light blue, dark blue and green enamel, also belonging to Meenakshi, pinned her sari to her blouse. Lata had never worn a brooch in her life, and had to be scolded by Meenakshi into it.

Meenakshi next overruled the tight bun into which Lata usually coiled her hair. 'That style looks simply too prim, Luts,' said her mentor. 'It really isn't flattering to you. You have to leave it open.'

'No, I can't do that,' protested Lata. 'It just isn't proper. Ma would have a fit.'

'Proper!' exclaimed Meenakshi. 'Well, let's at least soften up the front of it so that you don't look so schoolmarmish.'

Finally, Meenakshi marched Lata off to the dressing-table in her bedroom, and put the final touches to her face with a bit of mascara. 'This will make your eyelashes look longer,' she said.

Lata fluttered her eyelashes experimentally. 'Do you think they'll fall like flies?' she asked Meenakshi, laughing.

'Yes, Luts,' said Meenakshi. 'And you must keep smiling. Your eyes really do look appealing now.'

And when she looked at herself in the mirror, Lata had to admit they did.

'Now what perfume would suit you?' said Meenakshi aloud to herself. 'Worth seems about right for you.'

But before she could come to a final decision, the

doorbell rang impatiently. Arun was back from Puttigurh. Everyone hopped around and danced attendance on him for the next few minutes.

When he was ready, he became frustrated that Meenakshi was taking so long. When she did finally emerge, Mrs Rupa Mehra stared at her in outrage. She was wearing a sleeveless, low-cut, magenta blouse in open-back choli style, with a bottle-green sari of exquisitely fine chiffon.

'You can't wear that!' gasped Mrs Rupa Mehra, making what in the Mehra family were known as big-big eyes. Her glance veered from Meenakshi's cleavage to her midriff to her entirely exposed arms. 'You can't, you – you can't. It is even worse than last night at your parents' house.'

'Of course I can, Maloos dear, don't be so old-fashioned.'

'Well? Are you finally ready?' asked Arun, looking pointedly at his watch.

'Not quite, darling. Would you close the clasp on my choker for me?' And Meenakshi with a slow, sensuous gesture passed her hand across her neck just below her thick gold choker.

Her mother-in-law averted her eyes.

'Why do you allow her to wear this?' she asked her son. 'Can't she wear a decent blouse like other Indian girls?'

'Ma, I'm sorry, we're getting late,' said Arun.

'One can't tango in a dowdy choli,' said Meenakshi. 'Come, Luts.'

Lata gave her mother a kiss. 'Don't worry, Ma, I'll be fine.'

'Tango?' said Mrs Rupa Mehra in alarm. 'What is tango?'

'Bye, Ma,' said Meenakshi. 'Tango. A dance. We're going to the Golden Slipper. Nothing to worry about. There's just a large crowd and a band and dancing.'

'Abandoned dancing!' Mrs Rupa Mehra could hardly believe her ears.

But before she could think of anything to say the little sky-blue Austin had started off on the first leg of the night's revels.

COCKTAILS at the Finlays' was a hubbub of chatter. Everyone stood around talking about the 'monsoonish' weather, which had struck earlier than usual this year. Opinion was divided as to whether today's tremendous rains were monsoonal or pre-monsoonal. Golf had been quite impossible this afternoon, and though the races at Tollygunge were very rarely cancelled owing to the weather (after all, it was known as the Monsoon Racing Season to distinguish it from the winter one), if the rains were as heavy tomorrow as they had been today, the ground might be complete slush and the going too difficult for the horses. English county cricket too played a large part in the conversation, and Lata heard more than she might have wished to about Denis Compton's brilliant batting and his left arm spinners, and how superbly he was doing as captain of Middlesex. She nodded in agreement wherever necessary, her mind on a different cricketer.

About a third of the crowd was Indian: executives of managing agencies like Arun, with a smattering of civil servants, lawyers, doctors and army officers. Unlike in Brahmpur, which she had just been visiting in her thoughts, in this stratum of Calcutta society – even more obviously than at the Chatterjis' – men and women mixed freely and unselfconsciously. The hawk-nosed hostess, Mrs Finlay, was very kind to her and introduced her to a couple of people when she noticed her standing by herself. But Lata felt ill at ease. Meenakshi, on the other hand, was in her element, and her laughter could be heard from time to time tinkling above the general mash of sociable noise.

Arun and Meenakshi were both floating a few inches above the ground by the time they and Lata drove over from Alipore to Firpos. The rain had stopped a couple of hours earlier. They drove by the Victoria Memorial, where the ice-cream and jhaal-muri sellers provisioned the couples and families who had come out for a stroll in the comparative cool of the evening. Chowringhee was uncrowded.

Even at night the broad and spacious frontage of the street presented an impressive appearance. To the left a few late trams plied along the edge of the Maidan.

At the entrance to Firpos, they met Bishwanath Bhaduri: a dark, tall young man of about Arun's age with a square-set jaw and hair combed neatly back. He bent at the waist when introduced to Lata, and told her that he was Bish, and that he was charmed.

They waited for Billy Irani and Shireen Framjee for a few minutes. 'I told them we were leaving the party,' said Arun. 'Why the hell haven't they appeared?'

Perhaps responding to his importunity, they appeared within seconds, and after they had been introduced to Lata – there had been no time for Arun and Meenakshi to make the necessary introductions at the Finlays' once they had got caught up in small talk – they all went up together to the restaurant, and were shown to the table they had reserved.

Lata found the food at Firpos delicious and the talk of Bishwanath Bhaduri glitteringly insipid. He mentioned that he had happened to be in Brahmpur at the time of her sister Savita's wedding, to which he had gone with Arun. 'A lovely bride – one felt like snatching her away from the altar oneself. But of course not as lovely as her younger sister,' he added suavely.

Lata stared at him incredulously for a second or two, then looked at the rolls, imagining them into pellets.

'I suppose the shehnai should have been playing "Here Comes the Bride",' she could not resist saying as she looked up again.

'What? Er, hum, yes?' said Bish, nonplussed. Then he added, glancing at a neighbouring table, that what he liked about Firpos was that you could see 'the world and their wife' here.

Lata reflected that her remark had clearly run off his back like duck's water. And at the thought of that phrase, she began to smile.

Bishwanath Bhaduri, for his part, found Lata puzzling but attractive. At least she looked at him while she talked.

Most Calcutta girls in his set spent half their time looking around to see who else was at Firpos.

Arun had decided that Bish would be a good possibility for Lata, and had told her that he was an 'up-and-coming young fellow'.

Now Bish was telling Lata about his passage to England:

'One feels discontented and searches about for one's soul.... One feels homesick at Aden and buys one's post-cards at Port Said. ... One does a certain sort of job and gets used to it. ... Back in Calcutta one sometimes imagines that Chowringhee is Piccadilly. ... Of course, sometimes when one is on tour, one misses one's connections. ... One stops at a railway station and finds nothing behind it – and spends the night with the coolies snoring on the platform....' He picked up the menu again. 'I wonder whether I should have something sweet ... one's Bengali tooth, you know....'

Lata began to wish that he were up-and-going.

Bish had begun to discuss some matter in his department in which he had acquitted himself particularly well.

'... and of course, not that one wants to take personal credit for it, but the upshot of it all was that one secured the contract, and one has been handling the business ever since. Naturally' – and here he smiled smoothly at Lata – 'there was considerable disquiet among one's competitors. They couldn't imagine how one had swung it.'

'Oh?' said Lata, frowning as she tackled her peach melba. 'Was there? Was the disquiet considerable?'

Bishwanath Bhaduri shot her a quick glance of – not dislike exactly but, well, disquiet.

Shireen wanted to dance at the 300 Club, but was overruled, and they all went to the Golden Slipper in Free School Street instead, where it was livelier if less exclusive. The bright young things sometimes believed in slumming it.

Bish, perhaps sensing that Lata had not taken to him, made an excuse and disappeared after dinner.

'See you anon,' were his parting words.

Billy Irani had been remarkably quiet throughout the evening, and he did not appear to want to dance at all – not even fox-trots and waltzes. Arun made Lata dance a waltz with him despite her protests that she did not know how to dance at all. 'Nonsense,' said Arun affectionately. 'You do, you just don't know it.' He was right; she quickly got the hang of it, and enjoyed it too.

Shireen forced Billy onto his feet. Later, when the orchestra struck up an intimate number, Meenakshi requisitioned him. When they returned to the table Billy was blushing furiously.

'Look at him blush,' said Meenakshi delightedly. 'I think he likes holding me close. He was pressing me so close to his broad chest with his strong, golf-playing arms that I could feel his heart thump.'

'I was not,' said Billy indignantly.

'I wish you would,' said Meenakshi with a sigh. 'I nurture a secret lust for you, you know, Billy.'

Shireen laughed. Billy glared fiercely at Meenakshi and blushed even more furiously.

'That's enough nonsense,' said Arun. 'Don't embarrass my friend – or my younger sister.'

'Oh, I'm not embarrassed, Arun Bhai,' said Lata, though she was amazed all right by the tenor of the conversation.

But what amazed Lata most of all was the tango. At about one-thirty in the morning, by which time the two couples were fairly high, Meenakshi sent a note to the band-leader, and five minutes later he struck up a tango. Since very few people knew how to tango, the couples on the floor stood around looking a little perplexed. But Meenakshi went straight up to a man dressed in a dinner-jacket who was sitting with some friends at a table across the room – and enchanted him onto the floor. She did not know him but she recognized him as a wonderful dancer whom she had once seen in action before. His friends prodded him on as well. Everyone cleared the floor for them, and without even any initial discomfiture, they paced and twirled and froze together in swift, jerky, stylized movements with such erotic control and abandon that very soon the entire night-club was cheering them on. Lata felt her own heart beating faster. She was fascinated by Meenakshi's brazenness and dazzled by the play of light on the gold choker round her neck. Clearly Meenakshi was right; one couldn't tango in a dowdy choli.

They stumbled out of the night-club at two-thirty, and Arun shouted: 'Let's go – let's go to Falta! The waterworks – a picnic – I'm hungry – kababs at Nizam's.'

'It's getting rather late, Arun,' said Billy. 'Perhaps we should call it a night. I'll drop Shireen and –'

'No nonsense – I'm master of ceremonies,' insisted Arun. 'You get into my car. We'll all go – no, into the back – I'll sit with this pretty girl in the front – no, no, no, Saturday tomorrow – and we'll all go now – at once – we'll all go and have breakfast at the airport – airport picnic – all to the airport for breakfast – bloody car won't start – oh, wrong key.'

Off zoomed the little car through the streets, with Arun at the shaky helm, Shireen sitting with him in front, and Billy squashed between the two other women at the back. Lata must have appeared very nervous, because Billy patted her hand kindly once. A little later, she noticed that Billy's other hand was interlocked with Meenakshi's. She was surprised, but – after the torrid tango – not suspicious; she assumed that that was how things were done when one went for a drive in this kind of society. But she hoped for the sake of their common safety that the same sort of thing was not going on in the front seat.

Although there was no broad and direct road to the airport, even the narrower streets of North Calcutta were deserted at this hour, and driving was not intrinsically difficult. Arun roared along, blowing his horn loudly from time to time. But suddenly a child rushed out from behind a cart straight into their path. Arun swerved wildly, narrowly missed hitting it, and came to a halt before a lamp-post.

Luckily neither child nor car was damaged. The child disappeared as suddenly as it had appeared.

Arun got out of the car in a black fury and started

shouting into the night. There was a piece of smouldering rope hanging from the lamp-post for people to light their biris with, and Arun started pulling it as if it were a bell-rope. 'Get up – get up – all of you – all of you bastards –' he shouted at the entire neighbourhood.

'Arun – Arun – please don't,' said Meenakshi.

'Bloody idiots – can't control their children – at three in the bloody morning –'

A few destitute people, sleeping in their rags on the narrow pavement next to a pile of rubbish, stirred themselves.

'Do shut up, Arun,' said Billy Irani. 'You'll cause trouble.'

'You trying to take charge, Billy? – No good – good fellow, but not much there –' He turned his attention to the unseen enemy, the breeding, stupid masses. 'Get up – you bastards – can't you hear me?' He followed this up with a few other Hindi swear-words, since he could not speak Bengali.

Meenakshi knew that if she said anything, Arun would snap at her.

'Arun Bhai,' said Lata as calmly as she could. 'I'm very sleepy, and Ma will be worried about us. Let's go home now.'

'Home? Yes, let's go home.' Arun, startled by this excellent suggestion, smiled at his brilliant sister.

Billy was about to suggest that he drive, then thought better of it.

When he and Shireen were dropped off near his car, he was in a thoughtful mood, though he said nothing except to wish everyone goodnight.

Mrs Rupa Mehra was sitting up late for them. She was so relieved to hear the car drive up that when they came in she could not at first speak.

'Why are you up at this hour, Ma?' said Meenakshi, yawning.

'I will get no sleep tonight at all thanks to your selfishness,' said Mrs Rupa Mehra. 'Soon it will be time to get up.'

'Ma, you know we always come back late when we go dancing,' said Meenakshi. Arun had meanwhile gone into the bedroom, and Varun too, who had been woken up at two by his alarmed mother and forced to sit up with her, had seized the opportunity and slunk away to bed.

'Yes, you can behave as irresponsibly as you like when you are gallivanting around by yourselves,' said Mrs Rupa Mehra. 'But not when you have my daughter with you. Are you all right, darling?' she asked Lata.

'Yes, Ma, I had a good time,' said Lata, yawning as well. She remembered the tango and began to smile.

Mrs Rupa Mehra looked doubtful. 'You must tell me everything you did. What you ate, what you saw, whom you met, what you did.'

'Yes, Ma. Tomorrow,' said Lata with another yawn.

'All right,' conceded Mrs Rupa Mehra.

7.25

LATA woke up almost at noon the next day with a headache that did not improve when she had to give a recitation of the previous night's events. Both Aparna and Mrs Rupa Mehra wanted to know about the tango. After she had absorbed the details of the dance, the scarily precocious Aparna wanted reassurance, for some reason, on one particular point:

'So Mummy tangoed and everyone clapped?'

'Yes, sweetheart.'

'Daddy also?'

'Oh yes. Daddy clapped too.'

'Will you teach me to tango?'

'I don't know how to tango,' said Lata. 'But if I did, I would.'

'Does Uncle Varun know how to tango?'

Lata tried to visualize Varun's terror if Meenakshi had tried to prise him away from a table onto the dance floor. 'I doubt it,' she said. 'Where is Varun anyway?' she asked her mother.

'He went out,' said Mrs Rupa Mehra shortly. 'Sajid and Jason turned up, and they disappeared.'

Lata had only met these two Shamshu friends once. Sajid had a cigarette that hung down, literally hung down with no apparent means of support, from the left side of his lower lip. What he did for a living she did not know. Jason frowned toughly when speaking to her. He was an Anglo-Indian, and had been in the Calcutta police before he had been thrown out a few months earlier for sleeping with another Sub-Inspector's wife. Varun knew both of them from St George's. Arun shuddered to think that his own alma mater could have produced such seedy characters.

'Isn't Varun studying at all for the IAS?' asked Lata. The other day Varun had been talking about sitting for the civil service exams later in the year.

'No,' said Mrs Rupa Mehra with a sigh. 'And there's nothing I can do. He does not listen to his mother any more. When I say anything to him, he just agrees with me and then goes off with his friends an hour later.'

'Perhaps he's not cut out for the administrative service,' suggested Lata.

But her mother would have none of that.

'Studying is a good discipline,' she said. 'It needs application. Your father used to say that it does not matter what you study. As long as you study hard, it improves the mind.'

By that criterion, the late Raghubir Mehra should have been proud of his younger son. Varun, Sajid and Jason were at that moment standing in the two-rupee enclosure at the Tollygunge race-track, cheek by jowl with what Arun would have considered the riffraff of the solar system, studying with intense concentration the pukka or final version of the racing form for the afternoon's six races. They were hoping that they would thereby improve, if not their mind, at least their economic situation.

Normally they would not have invested the six annas that it cost to buy a pukka racing form, and would – with the help of the handicap list and information about cancellations – have simply pencilled in changes on the provisional form that they had bought on Wednesday. But Sajid had lost it.

A thin, warm rain was falling all over Calcutta, and the Tollygunge race-course was slushy. The discontented horses being walked around the paddock were being eyed keenly from all sides through the drizzle. The Tolly had gymkhana racing, not turf racing, unlike the Royal Calcutta Turf Club, whose monsoon season began more than a month later. This meant that professional jockeys were not compulsory, and there were plenty of gentleman-jockeys and even one or two ladies who rode in the races. Since the riders were sometimes quite heavy, the handicap on the horses too started at a heavier level.

'Heart's Story has 11 stones 6 pounds on her,' said Jason glumly. 'I would have bet on her, but –'

'So what?' said Sajid. 'She's used to Jock Mackay, and he can out-ride anyone on this track. He'll use up a good part of that 11 stones odd, and that's live weight, not lead pellets. It makes a difference.'

'It makes no difference. Weight is weight,' said Jason. His attention was caught by a strikingly attractive European woman of middle age, who was talking to Jock Mackay in low tones.

'My God – that's Mrs DiPiero!' said Varun, in a voice half fascinated, half terrified. 'She's dangerous!' he added with admiration.

Mrs DiPiero was a merry widow who usually did well at the races by gleaning tips from knowledgeable sources, in particular from Jock Mackay, who was reputed to be her lover. She often bet a few thousand rupees on a single race.

'Quick! Follow her!' said Jason, though the direction of his intentions only became clear when she went to the bookies and he turned his attention from her figure to the chalk markings on the blackboards which the bookies were rapidly rubbing out and re-marking. She was placing her bets in such a low voice that they could not hear her. But the bookies' notations told their own tale. They were changing their odds in the wake of her heavy betting. Heart's Story had come down from 7-to-1 to 6-to-1.

'That's it!' said Sajid languorously. 'I'm betting on that one.'

'Don't be too hasty,' said Jason. 'Obviously he'd praise his own horse.'

'But not at the cost of her displeasure. He must know it's undervalued at the odds.'

'Mmm,' intervened Varun. 'One thing worries me.'

'What?' said Sajid and Jason simultaneously. Varun's interventions were usually to the point in racing matters. He was a true but cautious addict.

'It's the rain. The heavily handicapped horses suffer the most when the ground is so wet. And 11 stones 6 pounds is about the heaviest handicap you can get. I think they penalized that mare because her rider held her back three weeks ago in the finishing straight.'

Sajid disagreed. His cigarette bobbed up and down as he spoke. 'It's a short race,' he said, 'Handicap doesn't matter all that much in a short race. I'm going to bet on her anyway. You two can do as you please.'

'What do you say, Varun?' said Jason, undecided.

'Yes. OK.'

They went to buy their tickets from the tote rather than the bookies, since a couple of two-rupee tickets each was all they could afford. Besides, the bookies' odds on Heart's Story had now come down to 5-to-1.

They returned to their enclosure and stared out at the rainy course in a state of uncontainable excitement.

It was a short race, only five-eighths of a mile. The starting point, on the other side of the course, was invisible because of the rain and the distance, especially from their lowly position, so far below the members' enclosure. But the thundering sound of the horses' hooves and their indistinct, swift movement through the blurred wall of rain had them shouting and screaming. Varun was almost foaming at the mouth with excitement and yelling: 'Heart's Story! Come on, Heart's Story!' at the top of his lungs. At the end all he could manage was:

'Heart! Heart! Heart! Heart!'

He was grasping Sajid's shoulder in an ecstasy of uncertainty.

The horses emerged round the bend for the final straight. Their colours and the colours of their riders became more distinct – and it became clear that the green-and-red colours of Jock Mackay on the bay were to the fore, closely followed by Anne Hodge on Outrageous Fortune. She made a valiant effort to spur him on for a last effort. Exhausted by the churned earth around his ankles – his fetlocks perhaps – he gave up the struggle when it seemed certain that he would succeed: just twenty yards from the finishing line.

Heart's Story had won by a length-and-a-half.

There were groans of disappointment and screams of delight all around them. The three friends went wild with excitement. Their winnings swelled in their imaginations to vast proportions. They might have won as much as fifteen rupees each! A bottle of Scotch – why even think of Shamshu? – was only fourteen rupees.

Joy!

All they had to do now was to wait for the white cone to go up, and to collect their winnings.

A red cone went up with the white.

Despair.

There had been an objection. 'Number seven has objected to Number two crossing,' said someone nearby.

'How can they tell in all that rain?'

'Of course they can tell.'

'He'd never do it to her. These are gentlemen.'

'Anne Hodge wouldn't lie about something like that.'

'This Jock chap is very unscrupulous. He'll do anything to win.'

'These things can happen by mistake as well.'

'By mistake!'

The suspense was unbearable. Three minutes passed. Varun was gasping with emotion and stress, and Sajid's cigarette was quivering. Jason was trying to look tough and unconcerned, and failing dismally. When the red cone slowly went down, confirming the result of the race, they embraced each other as if they were long-lost brothers, and went off immediately to collect their earnings – and to place their bets on the next race.

'Hello! Varun isn't it?' She pronounced it Vay-roon.

Varun swung around and stared at Patricia Cox, dressed elegantly in an airy white cotton dress and carrying a white umbrella which doubled as a parasol. She was not looking mousy at all, but rather cat-like in fact. She too had just won on Heart's Story.

Varun's hair was wild, his face red; the racing form in his hands was crushed; his shirt was wet with rain and sweat. Jason and Sajid were flanking him. They had just received their winnings and were jumping up and down.

Miraculously, however, Sajid's cigarette had not been dislodged, and was hanging down from his lip as supportlessly as ever.

'Heh, heh,' laughed Varun nervously, looking this way and that.

'How delightful to meet you again,' said Patricia Cox with unmistakable pleasure.

'Erh, eh, heh, heh,' said Varun. 'Hum. Er.' He couldn't remember her name. Box? He looked undecided.

'Patricia Cox,' said Patricia Cox helpfully. 'We met that evening at your house after dinner. But I suppose you've forgotten.'

'No, er, no, heh, heh!' laughed Varun weakly, looking for escape.

'And I suppose these are your Shamshu friends,' she continued with approval.

Jason and Sajid, who had been looking on astonished, now gaped at Patricia Cox, then turned questioningly and a little threateningly towards Varun.

'Heh, heh,' bleated Varun pathetically.

'Do you have any recommendations for the next race?' asked Patricia Cox. 'Your brother's here as our guest. Would you like to –'

'No – no – I have to go –' Varun found his voice at last,

and almost fled from the hall without even laying a bet on the next race.

When Patricia Cox returned to the members' enclosure she said brightly to Arun: 'You didn't tell me your brother would be here. We didn't know he was keen on the races. We would have invited him too.'

Arun stiffened. 'Here? Oh yes, here. Yes, sometimes. Of course. Rain's let up.'

'I'm afraid he doesn't like me much,' continued Patricia Cox sadly.

'He's probably afraid of you,' said Meenakshi perceptively.

'Of me?' Patricia Cox found this difficult to believe.

During the next race, Arun found it impossible to concentrate on the track. While everyone else around him was (with some restraint) cheering on the horses, his eyes, as if of their own accord, strayed downwards. Beyond the path from the paddock to the track was the exclusive (and exclusively European) Tollygunge Club where, now that the rain had stopped, a few members were having tea on the lawn and watching the races at leisure. And here, where Arun was sitting as a guest of the Coxes, was the balancing social pinnacle of the members' enclosure.

But in between the two, in the two-rupee enclosure, stood Arun's brother, sandwiched between his two disreputable companions, and so caught up in the excitement of the next race that he had forgotten his traumatic meeting of a few minutes ago and was jumping up and down, red in the face and screaming words that were unintelligible from this distance but were almost certainly the name of the horse on which he had laid, if not his bet, his heart. He looked almost, but not quite, unrecognizable.

Arun's nostrils quivered slightly and after a few seconds he looked away. He told himself that he had better start being his brother's keeper – for that beast, once out of its cage, could do no end of damage to the equilibrium of the universe.

MRS RUPA MEHRA and Lata were continuing their conversation. From Varun and the IAS they had moved on to Savita and the baby. Though not yet a reality, in Mrs Rupa Mehra's mind the baby was already a professor or a judge. Needless to say, it was a boy.

'I have had no news from my daughter for a week. I am very upset with her,' said Mrs Rupa Mehra. When she was with Lata, Mrs Rupa Mehra referred to Savita as 'my daughter', and vice versa.

'She's fine, Ma,' said Lata reassuringly. 'Or you would certainly have heard.'

'And to be expecting in this heat!' said Mrs Rupa Mehra, implying that Savita should have timed it better. 'You were also born in the monsoon,' she told Lata. 'You were a very difficult birth,' she added, and her eyes glistened with emotion.

Lata had heard about her own difficult birth a hundred times before. Sometimes when her mother was angry with her she flung this fact at her accusingly. At other times, when she was feeling especially fond of her, she mentioned it as a reminder of how precious to her Lata had always been. Lata had also heard a number of times about the tenacious grip she had as a baby.

'And poor Pran. I hear it has not yet rained in Brahmpur,' continued Mrs Rupa Mehra.

'It has, Ma, a little.'

'Not proper rain – just a droplet or two here and there. It is still so dusty, and terrible for his asthma.'

Lata said: 'Ma, you shouldn't worry about him. Savita keeps a careful eye on him, and so does his mother.' She knew, however, that it was no use. Mrs Rupa Mehra thrived on worrying. One of the marvellous by-products of Savita's marriage was a whole new family to worry about.

'But his mother herself is not well,' said Mrs Rupa Mehra triumphantly. 'And, talking of which, I have been feeling like visiting my homoeopath.'

If Arun had been present, he would have told his mother that all homoeopaths were charlatans. Lata merely said:

'But do those little white pills do you any good, Ma? I think it's all faith-healing.'

'What is wrong with faith?' asked Mrs Rupa Mehra. 'In your generation no one believes in anything.'

Lata did not defend her generation.

'Except in having a good time and staying out till four in the morning,' added Mrs Rupa Mehra.

Lata, to her own surprise, laughed.

'What is it?' her mother demanded. 'Why are you laughing? You weren't laughing two days ago.'

'Nothing, Ma, I was just laughing, that's all. Can't I laugh once in a while?' She had stopped laughing, though, having suddenly thought of Kabir.

Mrs Rupa Mehra ignored the general point, and homed in on the particular.

'But you were laughing for some reason. There must be a reason. You can tell your mother.'

'Ma, I'm not a baby, I'm allowed to have my own thoughts.'

'For me, you will always be my baby.'

'Even when I'm sixty?'

Mrs Rupa Mehra looked at her daughter in surprise. Although she had just visualized Savita's unborn child as a judge, she had never visualized Lata as a woman of sixty. She attempted to now, but the thought was too daunting. Luckily, another intervened.

'God will have taken me away long before then,' she sighed. 'And it is only when I am dead and gone and you see my empty chair that you will appreciate me. Now you are hiding everything from me, as if you don't trust me.'

Lata reflected, painfully, that she did not in fact trust her mother to understand much of what she felt. She thought of Kabir's letter, which she had transferred from the book on Egyptian mythology to a writing pad at the bottom of her suitcase. Where had he got her address from? How often did he think of her? She thought again of the flippant tone of his letter and felt a rush of anger.

Perhaps it wasn't really flippant, though, she said to herself. And perhaps he had been right in suggesting that she hadn't given him much of a chance to explain himself. She thought of their last meeting – it seemed very long ago – and of her own behaviour: it had bordered on the hysterical. But for her it had been her whole life and for him probably no more than a pleasant early-morning outing. He clearly had not expected the intensity of her outburst. Perhaps, Lata admitted, perhaps he could not have been expected to expect it.

As it was, her heart ached for him. It was him and not her brother whom she had, in her imagination, been dancing with last night. And she had dreamed about him in her sleep this morning, strangely enough reciting his letter to her in a declamation contest for which she was one of the judges.

'So why were you laughing?' said Mrs Rupa Mehra.

Lata said: 'I was thinking about Bishwanath Bhaduri and his ridiculous comments last night at Firpos.'

'But he is covenanted,' her mother pointed out.

'He told me I was more beautiful than Savita, and that my hair was like a river.'

'You are quite pretty when you put your mind to it, darling,' said her mother reassuringly. 'But your hair was in a bun, wasn't it?'

Lata nodded and yawned. It was past noon. Except when studying for her exams, she rarely felt so sleepy so late in the day. Meenakshi was the one who usually yawned – yawned with decided elegance whenever it suited the occasion.

'Where's Varun?' Lata asked. 'I was supposed to look through the *Gazette* with him – it's got details about the IAS exams. Do you think he's gone to the races too?'

'You are always saying things to upset me, Lata,' exclaimed Mrs Rupa Mehra with sudden indignation. 'I have so many troubles, and then you say things like this. Races. No one cares about my troubles, they are always thinking about their own.'

'What troubles, Ma?' said Lata unsympathetically. 'You

are well taken care of, and everyone who knows you loves you.'

Mrs Rupa Mehra looked at Lata sternly. Savita would never have asked such a brutal question. In fact, it was more in the nature of a comment or even judgment than a question. Sometimes, she said to herself, I don't understand Lata at all.

'I have plenty of troubles,' said Mrs Rupa Mehra in a decided manner. 'You know them as well as I do. Look at Meenakshi and how she handles the child. And Varun and his studies – what will happen to him – smoking and drinking and gambling and all that? And you don't get married – isn't that a trouble? And Savita, expecting. And Pran with his illness. And Pran's brother: doing all those things and people talking about it all over Brahmpur. And Meenakshi's sister – people are talking about her also. Do you think I don't have to listen to these things from people? Just yesterday Purobi Ray was gossiping about Kuku. So these are my troubles, and now you've upset me even more. And I am a widow with diabetes,' she added, almost as an afterthought. 'Isn't that a trouble?'

Lata admitted that the last would count as a true trouble.

'And Arun shouts, which is very bad for my blood pressure. And today Hanif has taken a day off, so I am expected to do everything myself, even make tea.'

'I'll make it for you, Ma,' said Lata. 'Would you like some now?'

'No, darling, you're yawning, you go and rest,' said Mrs Rupa Mehra, suddenly accommodating. By offering to make tea, Lata had as good as made it for her.

'I don't want to rest, Ma,' said Lata.

'Then why are you yawning, darling?'

'Probably because I've slept too much. Would you like some tea?'

'Not if it's too much trouble.'

Lata went to the kitchen. She had been brought up by her mother 'not to give trouble but to take trouble'. After her father's death, they had lived for a number of years in the house – and therefore in a sense on the charity, however graciously bestowed – of friends, so it was natural that Mrs Rupa Mehra should have been concerned about giving trouble either directly or because of her children. A great deal in the personality of all four children could be traced to these years. The sense of uncertainty and the consciousness of obligation to others outside the family had had its effect on them. Savita had been affected least of all, it seemed; but then with Savita one sometimes got the impression that her kindness and gentleness had come to her as a baby, and that no circumstances of mere environment could have greatly altered them.

'Was Savita sunny even as a baby?' asked Lata a few minutes later when she returned with the tea. Lata knew the answer to her question not only because it was part of Mehra folklore but because there were plenty of photographs to attest to Savita's sunniness: baby pictures of her wolfing down quarter-boiled eggs with a beatific grin, or smiling in her infant sleep. But she asked it anyway, perhaps in order to put her mother in a better mood.

'Yes, very sunny,' said Mrs Rupa Mehra. 'But, darling, you have forgotten my saccharine.'

7.27

A little later Amit and Dipankar dropped by in the Chatterji car, a large white Humber. They could tell that Lata and her mother were slightly surprised to see them.

'Where's Meenakshi?' asked Dipankar, looking around slowly. 'Nice spider-lilies outside.'

'She's gone with Arun to the races,' said Mrs Rupa Mehra. 'They are determined to catch pneumonia. We were just having a cup of tea. Lata will make another pot.'

'No, really, it isn't necessary,' said Amit.

'That's all right,' said Lata with a smile. 'The water's hot.'

'How like Meenakshi,' said Amit, a bit irked and a bit amused. 'And she said it would be fine to drop by this afternoon. I suppose we'd better be going. Dipankar has some work at the library of the Asiatic Society.'

'You can't do that,' said Mrs Rupa Mehra hospitably. 'Not without having tea.'

'But didn't she even tell you we'd be coming?'

'No one ever tells me anything,' said Mrs Rupa Mehra automatically.

'Setting off without a brolly,
Meenee-haha goes to Tolly,'

remarked Amit.

Mrs Rupa Mehra frowned. She always found it difficult to hold a coherent conversation with any of the younger Chatterjis.

Dipankar, having looked around once more, asked: 'Where's Varun?'

He liked talking to Varun. Even when Varun was bored, he was too nervous to object, and Dipankar construed his silence as interest. Certainly he was a better listener than anyone in Dipankar's own family, who became impatient when he talked about the Skein of Nothingness or the Cessation of Desire. When he had talked about the latter subject at the breakfast table, Kakoli had listed his girlfriends seriatim and stated that she saw no marked Deceleration, let alone Cessation, in his own life so far. Kuku did not see things in the abstract, thought Dipankar. She was still trapped on the plane of contingent actuality.

'Varun's gone out too,' said Lata, returning with the tea. 'Should I tell him to phone you when he returns?'

'If we are to meet, we will meet,' said Dipankar thoughtfully. He then walked into the garden, though it was still drizzling and his shoes would get muddy.

Meenakshi's brothers! thought Mrs Rupa Mehra.

Since Amit was sitting in silence, and Mrs Rupa Mehra abhorred silence, she asked after Tapan.

'Oh, he's very well,' said Amit. 'We've just dropped him and Cuddles at a friend's place. They have a lot of dogs, and Cuddles, oddly enough, gets along with them.'

'Oddly enough' was right, thought Mrs Rupa Mehra. Cuddles had flown through the air on their first meeting and tried to bite her. Luckily, he had been tied to the leg of the piano, and had remained just out of range. Meanwhile Kakoli had continued to play her Chopin without missing a beat. 'Don't mind him,' she had said, 'he means well.' Truly a mad family, reflected Mrs Rupa Mehra.

'And dear Kakoli?' she asked.

'She's singing Schubert with Hans. Or rather, she's playing, he's singing.'

Mrs Rupa Mehra looked stern. This must be the boy whom Purobi Ray had mentioned in connection with Kakoli. Most unsuitable.

'At home, of course,' she said.

'No, at Hans' place. He came to fetch her. A good thing too, otherwise Kuku would have beaten us to the car.'

'Who is with them?' asked Mrs Rupa Mehra.

'The spirit of Schubert,' replied Amit casually.

'For Kuku's sake you *must* be careful,' said Mrs Rupa Mehra, startled as much by his tone as by what he had said. She simply could not understand the Chatterjis' attitude to the risks their sister was running. 'Why can't they sing in Ballygunge?'

'Well, for a start, there's often a conflict between the harmonium and the piano. And I can't write in that din.'

'My husband wrote his railway inspection reports with four children shouting all around him,' said Mrs Rupa Mehra.

'Ma, that's not the same thing at all,' said Lata. 'Amit's a poet. Poetry's different.'

Amit shot her a grateful glance, even though he wondered whether the novel he was engaged on – or even poetry – was different from inspection reports to quite the extent that she imagined.

Dipankar came in from the garden, fairly wet. He did, however, wipe his feet on the mat before he entered. He was reciting, indeed, chanting, a passage from Sri Aurobindo's mystic poem *Savitri*:

'Calm heavens of imperishable Light,
Illumined continents of violet peace,
Oceans and rivers of the mirth of God
And griefless countries under purple suns. ...'

He turned towards them. 'Oh, the tea,' he said, and fell to wondering how much sugar he ought to have.

Amit turned to Lata. 'Did you understand that?' he asked.

Dipankar fixed a look of gentle condescension upon his elder brother. 'Amit Da is a cynic,' he said, 'and believes in Life and Matter. But what about the psychical entity behind the vital and physical mentality?'

'What about it?' said Amit.

'You mean you don't believe in the Supramental?' asked Dipankar, beginning to blink. It was as if Amit had questioned the existence of Saturday – which, as a matter of fact, he was capable of doing.

'I don't know if I believe in it or not,' said Amit. 'I don't know what it is. But it's all right – no, don't – don't tell me.'

'It's the plane on which the Divine meets the individual soul and transforms the individual to a "gnostic being",' explained Dipankar with mild disdain.

'How interesting,' said Mrs Rupa Mehra, who from time to time wondered about the Divine. She began to feel quite positive about Dipankar. Of all the Chatterji children he appeared to be the most serious-minded. He blinked a lot, which was disconcerting, but Mrs Rupa Mehra was willing to make allowances.

'Yes,' said Dipankar, stirring a third spoon of sugar into his tea. 'It is below Brahma and sat-chit-ananda, but acts like a conduit or conductor.'

'Is it sweet enough?' asked Mrs Rupa Mehra with concern.

'I think so,' said Dipankar with an air of appraisal.

Having found a listener, Dipankar now expanded into several channels that interested him. His interests in mysticism were wide-ranging, and included Tantra and the

609

worship of the Mother-Goddess besides the more conceptual 'synthetic' philosophy he had just been expounding. Soon he and Mrs Rupa Mehra were chatting happily about the great seers Ramakrishna and Vivekananda. Half an hour later it was Unity, Duality, and the Trinity, on which Dipankar had recently had a crash-course. Mrs Rupa Mehra was trying her best to keep up with Dipankar's free flow of ideas.

'It all comes to a climax in the Pul Mela at Brahmpur,' said Dipankar. 'That is when the astral conjunctions are most powerful. On the night of the full moon of the month of Jeth the gravitational pull of the moon will act with full force upon all our chakras. I don't believe in all the legends, but one can't deny science. I will be going this year, and we can immerse ourselves in the Ganga together. I have already booked my ticket.'

Mrs Rupa Mehra looked doubtful. Then she said:
'That is a good idea. Let us see how things turn out.'

She had just recalled with relief that she would not be in Brahmpur at the time.

7.28

AMIT, meanwhile, was talking to Lata about Kakoli. He was telling Lata about her latest beau, the German nutcracker. Kuku had even got him to paint a diplomatically unsuitable Reichsadler above her bathtub. The tub itself had been painted inside and out with turtles, fish, crabs and other watery creatures by Kuku's more artistic friends. Kuku loved the sea, especially at the delta of the Ganges, the Sundarbans. And fish and crabs reminded her of delicious Bengali dishes, and enhanced the wallowing luxuriousness of her bath.

'And your parents didn't object?' asked Lata, recalling the stateliness of the Chatterji mansion.

'My parents may mind,' said Amit, 'but Kuku can twist my father around her little finger. She's his favourite. I think even my mother is jealous of the way he indulges her. A few days ago there was talk of letting her have a telephone of her own rather than just an extension.'

Two telephones in one home seemed utterly extravagant to Lata. She asked why they were necessary, and Amit told her about Kakoli's umbilical linkage to the telephone. He even imitated her characteristic greetings for her A-level, B-level and C-level friends. 'But the phone holds such magic for her that she will readily desert an A-level friend who's taken the trouble to visit her in order to talk to a C-level friend for twenty minutes if he happens to be on the line.'

'I suppose she's very sociable. I've never seen her alone,' said Lata.

'She is,' said Amit.

'Does she mean to be?'

'What do you mean?'

'Is it of her own volition?'

'That's a difficult question,' said Amit.

'Well,' said Lata, picturing the good-humouredly giggling Kakoli surrounded by a large crowd at the party, 'she's very nice, and attractive, and lively. I'm not surprised people like her.'

'Mmm,' said Amit. 'She doesn't call people on the phone herself, and ignores messages that come when she's out of the house, so she doesn't show a lot of volition as such. And yet she's always on the phone. They always call back.'

'So she's, well, passively volitional.' Lata looked rather surprised at her own phrase.

'Well, passively volitional – in a lively way,' said Amit, thinking this was an odd way to describe Kuku.

'My mother's getting along well with your brother,' said Lata, with a glance towards them.

'Looks like it,' said Amit with a smile.

'And what sort of music does she like?' asked Lata. 'I mean Kuku.'

Amit thought for a second. 'Despairing music,' he said.

Lata waited for him to elaborate, but he didn't. Instead he said, 'And what kind of music do you like?'

'I?' said Lata.

'You,' said Amit.

'Oh, all sorts. I told you I liked Indian classical music. And don't tell your Ila Kaki, but the one time I went to a ghazal concert, I enjoyed it. And you?'

'All sorts as well.'

'Does Kuku have any reason for liking despairing music?' asked Lata.

'Well, I'm sure she's suffered her share of heartbreak,' said Amit rather callously. 'But she wouldn't have found Hans if someone else hadn't broken her heart.'

Lata looked curiously at Amit, perhaps almost sternly. 'I can hardly believe you're a poet,' she said.

'No. Nor can I,' said Amit. 'Have you read anything by me?'

'No,' said Lata. 'I was sure there'd be a copy of your book in this house, but –'

'And are you fond of poetry?'

'Very fond.'

There was a pause. Then Amit said:

'What have you seen of Calcutta so far?'

'Victoria Memorial and Howrah Bridge.'

'That's all?'

'That's all.'

It was Amit's turn to look stern.

'And what are you doing this afternoon?' he asked.

'Nothing,' said Lata, surprised.

'Good. I'll show you a few places of poetic interest. We've got the car, which is good. And there are a couple of umbrellas in the car – so we won't get wet when we walk around the cemetery.'

But even though it was 'just Amit', as Lata pointed out, whom she would be going out with, Mrs Rupa Mehra unreasonably insisted on someone accompanying them. Amit for Mrs Rupa Mehra was merely Meenakshi's brother – and not a risk in any sense of the word. But, well, he was a young man, and for form's sake it was important that someone be with them, so that they would not be seen alone together. On the other hand, Mrs Rupa Mehra was prepared to be fairly flexible as to who the chaperon could be. She herself was certainly not going to walk around with them in the rain. But Dipankar would do.

'I can't go with you, Dada,' said Dipankar. 'I have to go to the library.'

'Well, I'll phone Tapan at his friend's place and see what he has to say,' said Amit.

Tapan agreed on the condition that Cuddles could accompany them – on a leash of course.

Since Cuddles was nominally Dipankar's dog, his sanction was required as well. This he readily gave.

And so, on a warm, rainy Saturday afternoon, Amit, Lata, Dipankar (who would go with them as far as the Asiatic Society), Tapan and Cuddles went for a drive and a walk with the acquiescence of Mrs Rupa Mehra, who was relieved that Lata was at last behaving more like her normal self again.

7.29

WHEN the mass of the British left India at Independence, they left behind them a great number of pianos, and one of them, a large, black, tropicalized Steinway, stood in the drawing room of Hans Sieber's apartment in Queens Mansions. Kakoli was seated at it and Hans was standing behind her, singing from the same score that she was playing from, and feeling extremely happy although the songs that he was singing were extremely gloomy.

Hans adored Schubert. They were singing through *Winterreise*, a snow-bound song-cycle of rejection and dejection that ends in madness. Outside, the warm Calcutta rain came down in sheets. It flooded the streets, gurgled down the inadequate drainage system, poured into the Hooghly, and finally flowed down into the Indian Ocean. In an earlier incarnation it could well have been the soft German snow that had whirled around the memory-haunted traveller, and in a later one it might well become part of the icy brook into whose surface he had carved his initials and those of his faithless beloved. Or possibly even his hot tears that threatened to melt all the snow of winter.

Kakoli had not at first been ecstatic about Schubert, her tastes running more to Chopin, whom she played with heavy rubato and gloom. But now that she was accompanying Hans' singing she had grown to like Schubert more and more.

The same was true about her feeling for Hans, whose excessive courtliness had at first amused her, then irked her, and now reassured her. Hans, for his part, was as smitten by Kuku as any of her mushrooms had ever been. But he felt that she took him lightly, only returning one in three of his calls. If he had known of her even poorer rate of return with other friends, he would have realized how highly she valued him.

Of the twenty-four lieder in the song-cycle they had now arrived at the last song but one, 'The Mock Suns'. Hans was singing this cheerfully and briskly. Kuku was dragging the pace on the piano. It was a tussle of interpretation.

'No, no, Hans,' said Kakoli when he leaned over and turned the page to the final song. 'You sang that too fast.'

'Too fast?' said Hans. 'I felt the accompaniment was not very brisk. You wanted to go slower, yes? "Ach, meine Sonnen seid ihr nicht!"' He dragged it out. 'So?'

'Yes.'

'Well, he is mad, Kakoli, you know.' The real reason why Hans had sung the song so energetically was Kuku's perfect presence.

'*Almost* mad,' said Kuku. 'In the next song he goes quite mad. You can sing that as fast as you like.'

'But that last song must be very slow,' said Hans. 'Like this —' And he played out what he meant with his right hand in the treble reaches of the piano. His hand touched Kuku's for a second at the end of the first line. 'There, you see, Kakoli, he is resigned to his fate.'

'So he's suddenly stopped being mad?' said Kakoli. What nonsense, she thought.

'Maybe he is mad and resigned to his fate. Mixed.'

Kuku tried it, and shook her head. 'I'd go to sleep,' she said.

'So now, Kakoli, you think "The Mock Suns" must be slow and "The Organ-grinder" must be fast.'

'Exactly.' Kakoli liked it when Hans spoke her name; he pronounced the three syllables with equal weight. Very rarely did he call her Kuku.

'And I think "The Mock Suns" must be fast and "The Organ-grinder" must be slow,' continued Hans.

'Yes,' said Kuku. How dreadfully incompatible we are, she thought. And everything should be perfect – just perfect. If it wasn't perfect it was awful.

'So each of us thinks that one song must be fast and one slow,' said Hans with triumphant logic. This seemed to prove to him that, given an adjustment or two, he and Kakoli were unusually compatible.

Kuku looked at Hans' square and handsome face, which was glowing with pleasure. 'You see,' said Hans, 'most times I hear it, people sing both slow.'

'Both slow?' said Kuku. 'That would never do.'

'No, never do,' said Hans. 'Shall we take it again from there with slower tempo, like you suggest?'

'Yes,' said Kakoli. 'But what on earth does it mean? Or in the sky? The song, I mean.'

'There are three suns,' explained Hans, 'and two go and then one is left.'

'Hans,' said Kakoli. 'I think you are very lovable. And your subtraction is accurate. But you haven't added to my understanding.'

Hans blushed. 'I think the two suns are the girl and her mother, and he himself is the third.'

Kakoli stared at him. 'Her mother?' she said incredulously. Perhaps Hans had too stodgy a soul after all.

Hans looked doubtful. 'Maybe not,' he admitted. 'But who else?' He reflected that the mother had appeared somewhere in the song-cycle, though much earlier.

'I don't understand it at all. It's a mystery,' said Kakoli. 'But it's certainly not the mother.' She sensed that a major

615

crisis was brewing. This was almost as bad as Hans'
dislike of Bengali food.

'Yes?' said Hans. 'A mystery?'

'Anyway, Hans, you sing very well,' said Kuku. 'I like it
when you sing about heartbreak. It sounds very professional. We must do this again next week.'

Hans blushed once more, and offered Kakoli a drink.
Although he was expert at kissing the hands of married
women, he had not kissed Kakoli yet. He did not think she
would approve of it; but he was wrong.

7.30

WHEN they got to the Park Street Cemetery, Amit and Lata
got out of the car. Dipankar decided he'd wait in the car
with Tapan, since they were only going to be a few
minutes and, besides, there were only two umbrellas.

They walked through a wrought-iron gate. The cemetery
was laid out in a grid with narrow avenues between
clusters of tombs. A few soggy palm trees stood here and
there in clumps, and the cawing of crows interspersed with
thunder and the noise of rain. It was a melancholy place.
Founded in 1767, it had filled up quickly with European
dead. Young and old alike – mostly victims of the feverish
climate – lay buried here, compacted under great slabs and
pyramids, mausolea and cenotaphs, urns and columns, all
decayed and greyed now by ten generations of Calcutta
heat and rain. So densely packed were the tombs that it
was in places difficult to walk between them. Rich, rain-
fed grass grew between the graves, and the rain poured
down ceaselessly over it all. Compared to Brahmpur or
Banaras, Allahabad or Agra, Lucknow or Delhi, Calcutta
could hardly be considered to have a history, but the
climate had bestowed on its comparative recency a desolate
and unromantic sense of slow ruin.

'Why have you brought me here?' asked Lata.

'Do you know Landor?'

'Landor? No.'

'You've never heard of Walter Savage Landor?' asked Amit, disappointed.

'Oh yes. Walter Savage Landor. Of course. "Rose Aylmer, whom these watchful eyes."'

'Wakeful. Well, she lies buried here. As does Thackeray's father and one of Dickens' sons, and the original for Byron's *Don Juan*,' said Amit, with a proper Calcuttan pride.

'Really?' said Lata. 'Here? Here in Calcutta?' It was as if she had suddenly heard that Hamlet was the Prince of Delhi. 'Ah, what avails the sceptred race!'

'Ah, what the form divine!' continued Amit.

'What every virtue, every grace!' cried Lata with sudden enthusiasm.

'Rose Aylmer, all were thine.'

A roll of thunder punctuated the two stanzas.

'Rose Aylmer, whom these watchful eyes —' continued Lata.

'Wakeful.'

'Sorry, wakeful. Rose Aylmer, whom these wakeful eyes —'

'May weep, but never see,' said Amit, brandishing his umbrella.

'A night of memories and sighs,'

'I consecrate to thee.'

Amit paused. 'Ah, lovely poem, lovely poem,' he said, looking delightedly at Lata. He paused again, then said: 'Actually, it's "A night of memories and of sighs".'

'Isn't that what I said?' asked Lata, thinking of nights — or parts of nights that she herself had recently spent in a similar fashion.

'No. You left out the second "of".'

'A night of memories and sighs. Of memories and of sighs. I see what you mean. But does it make such a difference?'

'Yes, it makes a difference. Not all the difference in the world but, well, a difference. A mere "of"; conventionally permitted to rhyme with "love". But she is in her grave, and oh, the difference to him.'

They walked on. Walking two abreast was not possible, and their umbrellas complicated matters among the cluttered monuments. Not that her tomb was so far away – it was at the first intersection – but Amit had chosen a circuitous route. It was a small tomb capped by a conical pillar with swirling lines; Landor's poem was inscribed on a plaque on one side beneath her name and age and a few lines of pedestrian pentameter:

> What was her fate? Long, long before her hour,
> Death called her tender soul by break of bliss
> From the first blossoms, from the buds of joy;
> Those few our noxious fate unblasted leaves
> In this inclement clime of human life.

Lata looked at the tomb and then at Amit, who appeared to be deep in thought. She thought to herself: he has a comfortable sort of face.

'So she was twenty when she died?' said Lata.

'Yes. Just about your age. They met in the Swansea Circulating Library. And then her parents took her out to India. Poor Landor. Noble Savage. Go, lovely Rose.'

'What did she die of? The sorrow of parting?'

'A surfeit of pineapples.'

Lata looked shocked.

'I can see you don't believe me, but oh, 'tis true, 'tis true,' said Amit. 'We'd better go back,' he continued. 'They will not wait for us – and who can wonder? You're drenched.'

'And so are you.'

'Her tomb,' continued Amit, 'looks like an upside-down ice-cream cone.'

Lata said nothing. She was rather annoyed with Amit.

After Dipankar had been dropped off at the Asiatic Society, Amit asked the driver to take them down Chowringhee to the Presidency Hospital. As they passed the Victoria Memorial he said:

'So the Victoria Memorial and Howrah Bridge is all you know and all you need to know of Calcutta?'

'Not all I need to know,' said Lata. 'All I happen to know. And Firpos and The Golden Slipper. And the New Market.'

Tapan greeted this news with a Kakoli-couplet:

'Cuddles, Cuddles, gentle dog,
Go and bite Sir Stuart Hogg.'

Lata looked mystified. Since neither Tapan nor Amit explained the reference, she went on: 'But Arun has said we'll go for a picnic to the Botanical Gardens.'

'Under the spreading banyan tree,' said Amit.

'It's the biggest in the world,' said Tapan, with a Calcutta chauvinism equal to his brother's.

'And will you go there in the rains?' said Amit.

'Well, if not now, then at Christmas.'

'So you'll be back at Christmas?' asked Amit, pleased.

'I think so,' said Lata.

'Good, good,' said Amit. 'There are lots of concerts of Indian classical music in winter. And Calcutta is very pleasant. I'll show you around. I'll dispel your ignorance. I'll expand your mind. I'll teach you Bangla!'

Lata laughed. 'I'll look forward to it,' she said.

Cuddles gave a blood-curdling growl.

'What's the matter with you now?' asked Tapan. 'Will you hold this for a second?' he asked Lata, handing her the leash.

Cuddles subsided into silence.

Tapan bent down and looked carefully at Cuddles' ear.

'He hasn't had his walk yet,' said Tapan. 'And I haven't had my milkshake.'

'You're right,' said Amit. 'Well, the rain's let up. Let's just look at the second great poetic relic and then we'll go out onto the Maidan and the two of you can get as muddy as you like. And on the way back we'll stop at Keventers.' He continued, turning to Lata: 'I was thinking of taking you to Rabindranath Tagore's house in North Calcutta, but it's quite far and a bit slushy and it can wait for another day. But you haven't told me if there's anything particular that you'd like to see.'

'I'd like to see the university area some day,' said Lata. 'College Street and all that. But nothing else really. Are you sure you can spare the time?'

'Yes,' said Amit. 'And here we are. It was in that small building there that Sir Ronald Ross discovered what caused malaria.' He pointed to a plaque affixed to the gate. 'And he wrote a poem to celebrate it.'

Everyone got down this time, though Tapan and Cuddles took no interest in the plaque. Lata read it through with a great deal of curiosity. She was not used to the comprehensible writings of scientists, and did not know what to expect.

> This day relenting God
> Hath placed within my hand
> A wondrous thing; and God
> Be praised. At his command,
> Seeking his secret deeds
> With tears and toiling breath,
> I find thy cunning seeds
> O million-murdering death.
> I know this little thing
> A myriad men will save.
> O death where is thy sting
> And victory, O grave?

Lata read it a second time. 'What do you think of it?' asked Amit.

'Not much,' said Lata.

'Really? Why?'

'I'm not sure,' said Lata. 'I just don't. "Tears and toiling", "million-murdering" – it's too alliterative. And why should "God" be allowed to rhyme with "God"? Do you like it?'

'Well, yes, in a way,' said Amit. 'I do like it. But equally I can't defend that feeling. Perhaps I find it moving that a Surgeon-Major should write so fervently and with such religious force about something he'd done. I like the quaint chiasmus at the end. Ah, I've just created a pentameter,' he said, pleased.

Lata was frowning slightly, still looking at the plaque, and Amit could see she was not convinced.

'You're quite severe in your judgment,' he said with a smile. 'I wonder what you'd say about my poems.'

'Maybe some day I'll read them,' said Lata. 'I can't imagine the kind of poetry you write. You seem so cheerful and cynical.'

'I'm certainly cynical,' said Amit.

'Do you ever recite your poetry?'

'Almost never,' said Amit.

'Don't people ask you to?'

'Yes, all the time,' said Amit. 'Have you listened to poets reading their work? It's usually awful.'

Lata thought back to the Brahmpur Poetry Society and smiled broadly. Then she thought again of Kabir. She felt confused and sad.

Amit saw the swift change of expression on her face. He hesitated for a few seconds, wanting to ask her what had brought it about, but before he could do so she asked, pointing to the plaque:

'How did he discover it?'

'Oh,' said Amit, 'he sent his servant to get some mosquitoes, then got the mosquitoes to bite him – his servant, that is – and when he got malaria soon afterwards, Ross realized that it was mosquitoes that caused it. O million-murdering death.'

'Almost a million and one,' said Lata.

'Yes, I see what you mean. But people have always treated their servants strangely. Landor of the memories and sighs once threw his cook out of a window.'

'I'm not sure I like Calcutta poets,' said Lata.

7.31

AFTER the Maidan and the milkshake, Amit asked Lata if she had time for a cup of tea at his house before returning home. Lata said she did. She liked the fertile turmoil of that house, the piano, the books, the verandah, the large garden. When Amit asked that tea for two be sent up to his room, the servant Bahadur, who took a proprietorial interest in Amit, asked him if there was someone else to drink it with him.

'Oh no,' said Amit, 'I'm going to drink both cups myself.'

'You mustn't mind him,' said Amit later, when Bahadur had looked at Lata appraisingly as he set the tea-tray down. 'He thinks that I plan to marry everyone I have tea with. One or two?'

'Two please,' said Lata. She continued mischievously, since the question was riskless: 'And do you?'

'Oh, not so far,' said Amit. 'But he doesn't believe it. Our servants haven't given up trying to run our lives. Bahadur has seen me staring at the moon at odd hours, and wants to cure me by getting me married within the year. Dipankar has been dreaming of surrounding his hut with papaya and banana plants, and the mali has been lecturing him about herbaceous borders. The Mugh cook almost gave notice because Tapan, when he came back from boarding-school, insisted on eating lamb chops and mango ice-cream for breakfast for a whole week.'

'And Kuku?'

'Kuku drives the driver cuckoo.'

'What a crazy family you are,' said Lata.

'On the contrary,' said Amit, 'We're a hotbed of sanity.'

7.32

WHEN Lata returned home towards evening Mrs Rupa Mehra did not ask her for a detailed account of where she had been and what she had seen. She was too distressed to do so. Arun and Varun had had a grand flare-up, and the smell of combustion was still thick in the air.

Varun had returned to the house with his winnings in his pocket. He was not drunk yet, but it was clear where his windfall was going to go. Arun had told him he was irresponsible; he should contribute the winnings to the family kitty and never go to the race-track again. He was wasting his life, and didn't know the meaning of sacrifice and hard work. Varun, who knew that Arun had been at the races himself, had told him what he could do with his advice. Arun, purple-faced, had ordered him to get out of the house. Mrs Rupa Mehra had wept and pleaded and acted as an exacerbating intermediary. Meenakshi had said she couldn't live in such a noisy family and had threatened to go back to Ballygunge. She was glad, she said, that it was Hanif's day off. Aparna had started bawling. Even her ayah had not been able to pacify her.

Aparna's bawling had calmed everyone down, perhaps even made them feel a little ashamed. Now Meenakshi and Arun had just left for a party, and Varun was sitting in his small half-room, muttering to himself.

'I wish Savita was here,' said Mrs Rupa Mehra. 'Only she can control Arun when he is in one of his moods.'

'It's good she isn't here, Ma,' said Lata. 'Anyway, Varun's the one I'm more worried about. I'm going to see how he is.' It seemed to her that her advice to him in Brahmpur had been futile.

When she knocked at his door and entered, she found him sprawled on the bed with the *Gazette of India* lying open in front of him.

'I've decided to improve myself,' Varun said in a nervous manner, looking this way and that. 'I'm going through the rules for the IAS exams. They're to be held this September, and I haven't even begun studying. Arun Bhai thinks I'm irresponsible, and he's right. I'm terribly irresponsible. I'm wasting my life. Daddy would have been ashamed of me. Look at me, Luts, just look at me. What am I?' He was growing more and more agitated. 'I'm a bloody fool,' he concluded, with the Arun-like condemnation pronounced in an Arun-like tone of dismissal. 'Bloody fool!' he repeated for good measure. 'Don't you think so too?' he asked Lata hopefully.

'Shall I make you some tea?' asked Lata, wondering why he, in the manner of Meenakshi, had called her 'Luts'. Varun was far too easily led.

Varun looked gloomily at the Pay Scales, the lists of Optional and Compulsory Papers, the Standard and Syllabus of the Examinations, even the List of Scheduled Castes.

'Yes. If you think that's best,' he said at last.

When Lata came back with the tea, she found him plunged into renewed despair. He had just read the paragraph on the Viva Voce:

> The candidate will be interviewed by a Board who will have before them a record of his/her career. He/she will be asked questions on matters of general interest. The object of the interview is to assess his/her suitability for the Service for which he/she is entered, and in framing their assessment the Board will attach particular importance to his/her intelligence and alertness, his/her vigour and strength of character and his/her potential qualities of leadership.

'Read this!' said Varun. 'Just read this.' Lata picked up the *Gazette* and began to read it with interest.

'I don't have a chance,' continued Varun. 'I have such a poor personality. I don't make a good impression on anyone. I don't make an impression at all. And the interview counts for 400 marks. No. I may as well accept it. I'm not fit for the civil service. They want people with qualities of leadership – not fifth-class bloody fools like me.'

'Here, have some tea, Varun Bhai,' said Lata.

Varun accepted with tears in his eyes. 'But what else can I do?' he asked her. 'I can't teach, I can't join a managing agency, all the Indian business firms are family-run, I don't have the guts to set up in business on my own – or to get the money to do so. And Arun shouts at me all the time. I've been reading *How to Win Friends and Influence People*,' he confided. 'To improve my personality.'

'Is it working?' asked Lata.

'I don't know,' said Varun. 'I can't even judge that.'

'Varun Bhai, why didn't you listen to what I told you that day at the zoo?' asked Lata.

'I did. I'm going out with my friends now. And see where that has led me!' said Varun.

There was a pause. They sipped tea silently together in the little room. Then Lata, who had been scanning the *Gazette*, sat up with sudden indignation. 'Listen to this,' she said. "For the Indian Administrative Service and the Indian Police Service the Government of India may not select a woman candidate who is married and might require a woman to resign from the service in the event of her marrying subsequently."'

'Oh,' said Varun, who was not sure what was wrong with that. Jason was, or had been, a policeman, and Varun wondered whether any woman, married or not, should be permitted to do his kind of brutal work.

'And it gets worse,' continued Lata. "For the Indian Foreign Service a woman candidate is eligible only if she is unmarried or a widow without encumbrances. If such a candidate is selected, she will be appointed on the express condition that she might be called upon to resign the service on marriage or re-marriage."'

'Without encumbrances?' said Varun.

'That means children, I suppose. Presumably you can be a widower with encumbrances and handle both your family life and your work. But not if you're a widow. ... I'm sorry, I've taken over the *Gazette*.'

'Oh, no, no, you read it. I've suddenly remembered I must go out. I promised.'

'Promised whom?' said Lata. 'Sajid and Jason?'

'No, not exactly,' said Varun shiftily. 'Anyway, a promise is a promise and never should be broken.' He laughed weakly; he was quoting one of his mother's adages. 'But I'll tell them that I can't see them any more. I'm too busy studying. Will you talk to Ma for a little while?'

'While you slip out?' said Lata. 'No fears.'

'Please, Luts, what can I say to her? She's bound to ask me where I'm going.'

'Tell her you're going to get disgustingly drunk on Shamshu.'

'It won't be Shamshu today,' said Varun, cheering up.

After he had left, Lata went to her room with the *Gazette*. Kabir had said that he wanted to sit for the IFS exams after he had got his degree. She had no doubt that if he got to that stage, he would do well in the interview. He certainly had leadership qualities and vigour. She could imagine what a good impression he would make on the Board. She could picture his alertness, his open smile, the ready way in which he would admit to not knowing something.

She looked through the rules, wondering which optional subjects he might select. One was described simply as: 'World History. 1789 to 1939.'

Once more she wondered whether she should reply to his letter, and once more she wondered what she could possibly say. She looked idly down the list of optionals till her eye fell on an item a few lines further on. At first it puzzled her, then it made her laugh, and finally it helped somewhat to restore her equilibrium. It read as follows:

Philosophy. The subject covers the history and the theory of Ethics, Eastern and Western, and includes moral standards and their application, the problems of moral order and progress of Society and the State, and theories of punishment. It includes also the history of Western Philosophy and should be studied with special reference to the problems of space, time and causality, evolution and value and the nature of God.

'Child's play,' said Lata to herself, and decided to go and talk to her mother, who was sitting alone in the next room. All of a sudden she began to feel quite light-headed.

7.33

MY sweet Rat, my sweetest sweetest Rat,

I dreamed of you all last night. I woke up twice and each time it was from a dream of you. I don't know why you insist on coming into my mind so often, and inflicting memories and sighs on me. I was determined after our last meeting not to think of you, and your letter annoys me still. How can you write so coolly when you know what you mean to me and what I thought I meant to you?

I was in a room – at first it was a dark room with no way out. After a while a window appeared, and I saw a sundial through it. Then, somehow, the room was lit, and there was furniture in it – and before I knew it, it was the room at 20 Hastings Road, complete with Mr Nowrojee and Shrimati Supriya Joshi and Dr Makhijani, but, strangely enough, there was no door anywhere, so I assumed that they must have climbed in through the window. And how had I come in myself? Anyway, before I could puzzle all this out, a door did appear just where it should have been, and someone knocked at it – casually, but impatiently. I knew it was you – though I've never heard you knock on a door, in fact we've only met out of doors except that once – and, yes, also at Ustad Majeed Khan's concert. I was convinced it was you, and my heart started beating so fast I could hardly bear it, I was looking forward to seeing you so much. Then it turned out to be someone else, and I breathed a sigh of relief.

Dearest Kabir, I am not going to mail this letter, so you needn't worry about my becoming passionately fond of you and disturbing all your plans for the Indian Foreign Service and Cambridge and the rest of it. If you think I was unreasonable, well, perhaps I was, but I've never been in love before and it is certainly an unreasonable feeling too – and one that I never want to feel again for you or for anyone.

I read your letter sitting among spider-lilies, but all I could think about was gul-mohur flowers at my feet, and your telling me that I'd forget about all my troubles in five years. Oh, yes, and shaking kamini flowers out of my hair and crying.

The second dream – well, why don't I tell you, since it won't reach your eyes anyway. We were lying together by ourselves on a boat far away from both shores, and you were kissing me, and – oh, it was absolute bliss. Then later you got up and said, 'I've got to go now and swim four lengths; if I do, our team will win the match, and if I don't it won't,' and you left me alone in the boat. My heart sank, but you were quite determined to leave. Luckily the boat didn't sink, and I rowed it alone to the shore. I think I have finally got rid of you. At least I hope I have. I have decided to remain a spinster without encumbrances, and to devote my time to thinking about space, time and causality, evolution and value and the nature of God.

So God speed, sweet prince, sweet Rat-prince, and may you emerge near the dhobi-ghat, safe but bedraggled and do brilliantly in life.

> With all my love too, my darling Kabir,
> Lata.

Lata folded the letter into an envelope, and wrote Kabir's name on it. Then, instead of writing his address, she wrote his name here and there on the envelope a few more times for good measure. Then she drew a stamp on the corner of the envelope ('Waste not, want not') and marked it 'Postage Due'. Finally, she tore the whole thing into tiny pieces and began crying.

If I achieve nothing else in life, thought Lata, I shall at least have turned into one of the World's Great Neurotics.

7.34

AMIT asked Lata to lunch and tea the next day at the Chatterjis.

'I thought I'd ask you over so that you could see us Brahmos at our clannish best,' he said. 'Ila Chattopadhyay, whom you met the other day, will be there, as will an aunt and uncle on my mother's side and all their brood. And of course now you're part of the clan by marriage.'

So the next day at Amit's house they sat down to a

traditional Bengali meal, unlike the party fare of the previous week. Amit assumed that Lata had eaten this sort of food before. But when she saw a small helping of karela and rice – and nothing else – in front of her, she appeared so surprised that he had to tell her that there were other courses coming.

It was odd, thought Amit, that she shouldn't have known. Before Arun and Meenakshi had got married, though he himself had been in England, he knew that the Mehras had been invited once or twice to the Chatterjis'. But perhaps it hadn't been to this sort of meal.

Lunch had begun a little late. They had waited for Dr Ila Chattopadhyay, but had eventually decided to eat because the children were hungry. Amit's uncle Mr Ganguly was an extremely taciturn man whose energies went entirely into eating. His jowls worked vigorously, swiftly, almost twice a second, and only occasionally pausing, while his mild, bland, bovine eyes looked at his hosts and fellow-guests who were doing the talking. His wife was a fat, highly emotional woman who wore a great deal of sindoor in her hair and had a very large bindi of equally brilliant red in the middle of her forehead. She was a shocking gossip and in between extracting fine fishbones from her large paan-stained mouth she impaled the reputations of all her neighbours and any of her relatives who were not present. Embezzlement, drunkenness, gangsterism, incest: whatever could be stated was stated and whatever could not be was implied. Mrs Chatterji was shocked, pretended to be even more shocked than she was, and enjoyed her company greatly. The only thing that worried her was what Mrs Ganguly would say about their family – especially about Kuku – once she had left the house.

For Kuku was behaving as freely as she always did, encouraged by Tapan and Amit. Soon Dr Ila Chattopadhyay turned up ('I am such a stupid woman, I always forget lunch timings. Am I late? Stupid question. Hello. Hello. Hello. Oh, you again? Lalita? Lata? I never remember names') and things became even more boisterous.

629

Bahadur announced that there was a phone call for Kakoli.

'Tell whoever it is that Kuku will take it after lunch,' said her father.

'Oh, Baba!' Kuku turned a liquid gaze on her father.

'Who is it?' Mr Justice Chatterji asked Bahadur.

'That German Sahib.'

Mrs Ganguly's intelligent, pig-like eyes darted from face to face.

'Oh, Baba, it's Hans. I must go.' The 'Hans' was pleadingly elongated.

Mr Justice Chatterji nodded slightly, and Kuku leapt up and ran to the phone.

When Kakoli returned to the table, everyone except the children turned towards her. The children were consuming large quantities of tomato chutney, and their mother was not even reproving them, so keen was she to hear what Kuku was going to say.

But Kuku had turned from love to food. 'Oh, gulab-jamun,' she said, imitating Biswas Babu, 'and the chumchum! And mishti doi. Oh – the bhery mhemory makesh my shallybhery juishes to phlow.'

'Kuku.' Mr Justice Chatterji was seriously displeased.

'Sorry, Baba. Sorry. Sorry. Let me join in the gossip. What were you talking about in my absence?'

'Have a sandesh, Kuku,' said her mother.

'So, Dipankar,' said Dr Ila Chattopadhyay. 'Have you changed your subject yet?'

'I can't, Ila Kaki,' said Dipankar.

'Why not? The sooner you make the move the better. There isn't a single decent human being I know who is an economist. Why can't you change?'

'Because I've already graduated.'

'Oh!' Dr Ila Chattopadhyay appeared temporarily floored. 'And what are you going to do with yourself?'

'I'll decide in a week or two. I'll think things out when I'm at the Pul Mela. It'll be a time for appraising myself in the spiritual and intellectual context.'

Dr Ila Chattopadhyay, breaking a sandesh in half, said:

'Really, Lata, have you ever heard such unconvincing pre-varication? I've never understood what "the spiritual con-text" means. Spiritual matters are an utter waste of time. I'd rather spend my time listening to the kind of gossip your aunt purveys and that your mother pretends to suffer through than go to something like the Pul Mela. Isn't it very dirty?' she turned to Dipankar. 'All those millions of pilgrims crowded along a strip of sand just under the Brahmpur Fort? And doing – doing everything there.'

'I don't know,' said Dipankar. 'I've never been. But it's supposed to be well organized. They even have a District Magistrate allocated especially for the great Pul Mela every sixth year. This year's a sixth year, so bathing is especially auspicious.'

'The Ganges is an absolutely filthy river,' said Dr Ila Chattopadhyay. 'I hope you don't propose to bathe in it.... Oh, do stop blinking, Dipankar, it ruins my concentration.'

'If I bathe,' said Dipankar, 'I'll wash away not only my own sins but those of six generations above me. That might even include you, Ila Kaki.'

'God forbid,' said Dr Ila Chattopadhyay.

Turning to Lata, Dipankar said: 'You should come too, Lata. After all, you're from Brahmpur.'

'I'm not really from Brahmpur,' said Lata, with a glance at Dr Ila Chattopadhyay.

'Where are you from, then?' asked Dipankar.

'Nowhere now,' said Lata.

'Anyway,' continued Dipankar earnestly, 'I think I've convinced your mother to come.'

'I doubt it,' said Lata, smiling at the thought of Mrs Rupa Mehra and Dipankar guiding each other through the Pul Mela crowds and the labyrinths of time and causality. 'She won't be in Brahmpur at the time. But where will you live in Brahmpur?'

'On the sands – I'll find a place in someone's tent,' said Dipankar optimistically.

'Don't you know anyone in Brahmpur?'

'No. Well, Savita, of course. And there's an old Mr

Maitra who's related to us somehow, whom I met once as a child.'

'You must look up Savita and her husband when you get there,' said Lata. 'I'll write and tell Pran you'll be coming. You can always stay with them if the sand runs out. And it's useful anyway to have an address and phone number in a strange town.'

'Thank you,' said Dipankar. 'Oh, there's a lecture at the Ramakrishna Mission tonight on Popular Religion and its Philosophical Dimensions. Why don't you come? It's bound to cover the Pul Mela.'

'Really, Dipankar, you are more of an idiot than I thought,' said Dr Ila Chattopadhyay to her nephew. 'Why am I wasting my time on you? Don't you waste your time on him either,' she advised Lata. 'I'm going to talk to Amit. Where is he?'

Amit was in the garden. He had been forced by the children to show them the frog-spawn in the lily pond.

7.35

THE hall was almost full. There must have been about two hundred people, though Lata noticed that there were only about five women. The lecture, which was in English, started on time, at seven o'clock. Professor Dutta-Ray (who had a bad cough) introduced the speaker, informing the audience of the young luminary's biography and credentials, and continuing for a few minutes to speculate about what he would say.

The young speaker stood up. He did not look at all like someone who had been, as the professor had stated, a sadhu for five years. He had a round, anxious face. He was wearing a well-starched kurta and dhoti, and there were two pens in the pocket of his kurta. He did not speak about Popular Religion and its Philosophical Dimensions, though he did mention the Pul Mela once, elliptically, as 'this great concourse that will be assembling on the banks of the Ganga to lave itself in the light of the full moon'.

For the most part he treated the patient audience to a speech of exceptional banality. He soared and veered over a vast terrain, and assumed that his droppings would make an intelligible pattern.

Every few sentences, he stretched his arms out in a gentle, all-inclusive gesture as if he were a bird spreading its wings.

Dipankar looked rapt, Amit bored, Lata perplexed.

The speaker was now in full flight: 'Humanity must be made incarnate in the present ... shatter the horizons of the mind ... the challenge is interior ... birth is a remarkable thing ... the bird feels the vast quivering of the leaf ... a certain relation of sacrality can be maintained between the popular and the philosophical ... an open-ended mind through which life can flow, through which one can hear the birdsong, the impulse of space-time.'

Finally, an hour down the line, he came to the Great Question:

'Can humanity even tell where a newer inspiration will emerge? Can we penetrate those great darknesses within ourselves where symbols are born? I say that our rites, call them popular if you will, do penetrate this darkness. The alternative is the death of the mind, and not "re-death" or punarmrityu, which is the first reference to "re-birth" in our scriptures, but ultimate death, the death of ignorance. Let me then emphasize to you all' – he stretched his arms out towards the audience – 'that, let objectors say what they will, it is only by preserving the ancient forms of sacrality, however perverse, however superstitious they may seem to the philosophical eye, that we can maintain our elementality, our ethos, our evolution, our very essence.' He sat down.

'Our egg-shells,' said Amit to Lata.

The audience applauded guardedly.

But now the venerable Professor Dutta-Ray, who had introduced the speaker so paternally at first, got up and, shooting glances of undisguised hostility at him, proceeded to demolish what he saw as the theories he had just propounded. (It was clear that the Professor saw himself as one of the 'objectors' referred to in the speech.) But were there any theories in the speech at all? There was certainly a tenor, but it was difficult to demolish a tenor. At any rate, the Professor tried to, his voice, mild at first, rising to this hoarse-throated battlecry:

'Let us not deceive ourselves! For whilst it may often be the case that the theses are intrinsically plausible, they are by the same token impossible to substantiate or refute with more than illustrative evidence; indeed, it is in practice difficult to know whether they come into the orbit of reference of the key question, which, although it may well shed light on the tendency, can scarcely tell us whether an answer can be couched convincingly in terms of what might broadly be called its evolving patterns; in this perspective, then, though admittedly the theory may appear – to the ignorant eye – well-founded, it is not compelling as an analysis of the basic difficulty, which traces to considerations we must descry elsewhere; to be quite specific, its failure to explain must make it seem irrelevant even if it does not, as it were, actually refute it; but to stipulate this is to remove the underpinnings of the entire analytical framework, and the most pertinent and cogent argument must be abandoned.'

He looked with triumph and malice at the speaker before continuing: 'As a broad generalization, one might tentatively hazard a guess therefore, that, all other things being equal, one should not make particular generalizations when general particularizations are equally available – and available to far less idle effect.'

Dipankar was looking shocked, Amit bored, Lata puzzled.

Several people in the audience wanted to ask questions, but Amit had had enough. Lata was willingly, and Dipankar unwillingly, drawn out of the hall. She was feeling slightly dizzy, and not only because of the rarefied abstractions she had just breathed. It had been hot and stuffy inside.

For a minute or two none of them spoke. Lata, who had noticed Amit's boredom, expected him to show his annoyance, and Dipankar to expostulate. Instead, Amit merely said:

'When faced with something like that, if I am caught short without paper and pencil, I amuse myself by taking any word that the speaker has used – like "bird" or "cloth" or "central" or "blue" – and try to imagine different varieties of them.'

'Even words like "central"?' asked Lata, amused by the idea.

'Even those,' said Amit. 'Most words are fertile.'

He felt in his pocket for an anna, and bought a small, fragrant garland of fresh white bela flowers from a vendor. 'Here,' he said, giving it to Lata.

Lata, very pleased, said 'Thank you,' and after inhaling its fragrance with a delighted smile, put it unselfconsciously in her hair.

There was something so pleasing, natural and unpretentious about her gesture that Amit found himself thinking: She may be more intelligent than my sisters, but I'm glad she's not as sophisticated. She's the nicest girl I've met for a long time.

Lata for her part was thinking how much she liked Meenakshi's family. They brought her out of herself and her stupid, self-created misery. In their company it was possible to enjoy, after a fashion, even such a lecture as she had just sat through.

7.36

MR JUSTICE CHATTERJI was sitting in his study. In front of him lay a half-completed judgment. On his desk stood a black-and-white photograph of his parents, and another of himself, his wife, and their five children that had been taken many years ago by a fashionable Calcutta studio. Kakoli, wilful child, had insisted on including her teddy-bear; Tapan had been too small at the time to have had an articulate will at all.

The case involved the confirmation of the death sentence

on six members of a gang of dacoits. Such cases caused Mr Justice Chatterji a great deal of pain. He did not like criminal work at all, and looked forward to being re-allocated civil work, which was both more intellectually stimulating and less distressing. There was no question that these six men had been found guilty according to law and that the sentence of the Sessions Judge was not unreasonable or perverse. And so Mr Justice Chatterji knew that he would not set it aside. Not all of them may have intended specifically to cause the death of the men they were robbing but, under the Indian Penal Code, in a case of dacoity-cum-murder each criminal was severally liable for the act.

This was not a case for the Supreme Court. The High Court at Calcutta was the last effective court of appeal. He would sign the judgment, and so would his brother judge, and that, for these men, would be the end. One morning a few weeks down the line, they would be hanged in Alipore Jail.

Mr Justice Chatterji looked at the photograph of his family for a minute or two, and then around his room. Three of the walls were lined with the buff-coloured half-calf or deep blue bindings of law-books: the *Indian Law Reports*, the *All India Reporter*, the *Income Tax Reports*, the *All England Law Reports*, *Halsbury's Laws*, a few textbooks and books on general jurisprudence, the *Constitution of India* (just over a year old) and the various codes and statutes with their commentaries. Though the Judges' Library at the High Court now provided him with any books he might need, he still continued to subscribe to the journals he had always subscribed to. He did not wish to cut off the series, partly because he liked on occasion to write his judgments at home, partly because he continued to hope that Amit would follow in his footsteps – just as he had followed in his own father's footsteps, down to choosing for himself and later for his son the same Inn to qualify from.

It was not absence of mind that had made Mr Justice Chatterji evade his duties as a host this afternoon, nor the fat gossip, nor the noise made by her children, whom he was in fact quite fond of. It was the gossip's husband, Mr Ganguly, who had suddenly – after a prolonged silence throughout lunch – begun on the verandah to talk about his favourite great man – Hitler: six years dead but still revered by him like a god. In his monotonous voice, chewing his thoughts like cud, he had begun the kind of monologue that Mr Justice Chatterji had heard from him twice before: how even Napoleon (another great Bengali hero) did not come up to Hitlerian standards, how Hitler had helped Netaji Subhas Chandra Bose when he wanted to fight the dreadful British, how atavistic and admirable a force the Indo-Germanic bond was, and how terrible it was that the Germans and the British would within a month be officially terminating the state of war that had existed between them since 1939. (Mr Justice Chatterji thought that it was high time, but did not say so; he refused to get drawn into what was essentially a soliloquy.)

Now that Kakoli's 'German Sahib' had been mentioned over lunch, this man had expressed his gratification at the possibility that the 'Indo-Germanic bond' might become manifest even in his own family. Mr Justice Chatterji had listened for a while with amiable disgust; he had then made a polite excuse, got up, and not returned.

Mr Justice Chatterji had nothing against Hans. He liked what little he had seen of him. Hans was handsome and well-dressed and in every sense presentable, and he behaved with amusing if aggressive politeness. Kakoli liked him a great deal. In time he would probably even learn not to mangle people's hands. What Mr Justice Chatterji could not abide, however, was the syndrome just exemplified by his wife's relative – a combination that was by no means uncommon in Bengal: the mad deification of the patriot Subhas Bose who had fled to Germany and Japan and later established the Indian National Army to fight the British; the eulogization of Hitler and Fascism and violence; the denigration of all things British or tainted with 'pseudo-British liberalism'; and resentment bordering on contempt

637

for the sly milksop Gandhi who had dispossessed Bose of the presidentship of the Congress Party which he had won by election many years before. Netaji Subhas Chandra Bose was a Bengali, and Mr Justice Chatterji was certainly as proud of being a Bengali as of being an Indian, but he – like his father, 'old Mr Chatterji' – was profoundly grateful that the likes of Subhas Bose had never succeeded in ruling the country. His father had much preferred Subhas Bose's quieter and equally patriotic brother Sarat, also a lawyer, whom he had known and, after a fashion, admired.

If this fellow wasn't related to my wife, he would be the last person I'd ruin my Sunday afternoon with, thought Mr Justice Chatterji. Families contain far too great a range of temperament – and, unlike acquaintances, they can't be dropped. And we'll continue to be related till one of us drops dead.

Such thoughts on death, such overviews of life were more appropriate to his father, who was nearly eighty, than to himself, thought Mr Justice Chatterji. But the older man seemed so content with his cat and his leisured reading of Sanskrit classics (literary, not religious ones) that he hardly seemed to think of mortality or the passage of time. His wife had died after they had been married ten years, and he had very rarely mentioned her after that. Did he think about her any more often these days? 'I like reading those old plays,' he had said to his son a few days ago. 'King, princess, maidservant – whatever they thought then is still true now. Birth, awareness, love, ambition, hate, death, all the same. All the same.'

With a start Mr Justice Chatterji realized that he himself did not think very often of his wife. They had met at one of those – what were they called, those special festivals for young people held by the Brahmo Samaj, where teenagers and so on could get to meet? – Jubok Juboti Dibosh. His father had approved of her, and they had got married. They got on well; the house ran well; the children, eccentric though they were, were not bad as children went. He spent the earlier part of his evenings at the club. She very rarely complained about this; in fact, he suspected that she did not mind having the early evening to herself and the children.

She was there in his life, and had been there for thirty years. He would doubtless miss her if she wasn't. But he spent more time thinking about his children – especially Amit and Kakoli, both of whom worried him – than about her. And this was probably true of her as well. Their conversations, including the recent one that had resulted in his ultimatum to Amit and Dipankar, were largely child-bound: 'Kuku's on the phone the whole time, and I never know who she's speaking with. And now she's taken to going out at odd hours, and evading my questions.' 'Oh, let her be. She knows what she's doing.' 'Well, you know what happened to the Lahiri girl.' And so it would start. His wife was on the committee of a school for the poor and was involved in other social causes dear to women, but most of her aspirations centred on her children's welfare. That they should be married and well settled was what, above all, she desired.

She had been greatly upset at first by Meenakshi's marriage to Arun Mehra. Predictably enough, once Aparna was born she had come around. But Mr Justice Chatterji himself, though he had behaved with grace and decency in the matter, had felt increasingly rather than decreasingly uneasy about the marriage. For a start, there was Arun's mother, who was, in his mind, a peculiar woman – overly sentimental and liable to make much of nothing. (He had thought that she was not a worrier, but Meenakshi had filled him in with her version of the matter of the medals.) And there was Meenakshi, who sometimes displayed glints of a cold selfishness that even as a father he could not completely blind himself to; he missed her, but their breakfast parliaments, when she lived at home, had been more seriously acrimonious than they now were.

Finally, there was Arun himself. Mr Justice Chatterji respected his drive and his intelligence, but not much else. He seemed to him to be a needlessly aggressive man and a rank snob. They met at the Calcutta Club from time to time, but never found anything much to say. Each moved in his separate cluster at the club, clusters suited to their difference of age and profession. Arun's crowd struck him as gratuitously boisterous, slightly unbefitting the palms and the panelling. But perhaps this was just the intolerance of age, thought Mr Justice Chatterji. The times were changing beneath him, and he was reacting exactly as everyone – king, princess, maidservant – had reacted to the same situation.

But who would have thought that things would have changed as much and as swiftly as they had. Less than ten years ago Hitler had England by the throat, Japan had bombed Pearl Harbour, Gandhi was fasting in jail while Churchill was inquiring impatiently why he was not yet dead, and Tagore had just died. Amit was involved in student politics and in danger of being jailed by the British. Tapan was three and had almost died of nephritis. But in the High Court things were going well. His work as a barrister became increasingly interesting as he grappled with cases based on the War Profits Act and the Excess Income Act. His acuity was undiminished and Biswas Babu's excellent filing system kept his absent-mindedness in check.

In the first year after Independence he had been offered judgeship, something that had delighted his father and his clerk even more than himself. Though Biswas Babu knew that he himself would have to find a new position, his pride in the family and his sense of the lineal fitness of things had made him relish the fact that his employer would now be followed around, as his father before him had been, by a turbaned servitor in red, white and gold livery. What he had regretted was that Amit Babu was not immediately ready to step into his father's practice; but surely, he had thought, that would not be more than a couple of years away.

7.37

THE bench that Mr Justice Chatterji had joined, however, was very different from the one he had imagined – even a few years earlier – that he might be appointed to. He got up from his large mahogany desk and went to the shelf that held the more recent volumes of the *All India Reporter* in their bindings of buff, red, black and gold. He took down two volumes – *Calcutta* 1947 and *Calcutta* 1948 – and began comparing the first pages of each. As he compared them he felt a great sadness for what had happened to the country he had known since childhood, and indeed to his own circle of friends, especially those who were English and those who were Muslim.

For no apparent reason he suddenly thought of an extremely unsociable English doctor, a friend of his, who (like him) would escape from parties given in his own house. He would claim a sudden emergency – perhaps a dying patient – and disappear. He would then go to the Bengal Club, where he would sit on a high chair and drink as many whiskies as he could. The doctor's wife, who threw these huge parties, was fairly eccentric herself. She would go around on a bicycle with a large hat, from under which she could see everything that went on in the world without – or so she imagined – being recognized. It was said of her that she once arrived for dinner at Firpos with some black lace underwear thrown around her shoulders. Apparently, vague as she was, she had thought it was a stole.

Mr Justice Chatterji could not help smiling, but the smile disappeared as he looked at the two pages he had opened for comparison. In microcosm those two pages reflected the passage of an empire and the birth of two countries from the idea – tragic and ignorant – that people of different religions could not live peaceably together in one.

With the red pencil that he used for notations in his law-books, Mr Justice Chatterji marked a small 'x' against those names in the 1947 volume that did not appear in 1948, just one year later. This is what the list looked like when he had done:

CALCUTTA HIGH COURT
1947

The Hon'ble   Sir   Arthur Trevor Harries, Kt., Bar-at-law.

"   "   Roopendra Kumar Mitter, Kt., M.Sc., M.L. (Actg.).

PUISNE JUDGES

x   The Hon'ble   Sir   Nurul Azeem Khundkar, Kt., B.A. (Cantab.), LL.B., Bar-at-law.

x   "   "   Norman George Armstrong Edgley, Kt., M.A., I.C.S., Bar-at-law.

    "   Dr   Bijan Kumar Mukherjee, M.A., D.L.

    "   Mr   Charu Chandra Biswas, C.I.E., M.A., B.L.

x   "   "   Ronald Francis Lodge, B.A. (Cantab.), ICS

x   "   "   Frederick William Gentle, Bar-at-law.

    "   "   Amarendra Nath Sen, Bar-at-law.

    "   "   Thomas James Young Roxburgh, C.I.E., B.A., I.C.S., Bar-at-law.

x   "   "   Abu Saleh Mohamed Akram, B.L.

    "   "   Abraham Lewis Blank, M.A., I.C.S., Bar-at-law.

    "   "   Sudhi Ranjan Das, B.A., LL.B. (Lond.), Bar-at-law.

x   "   "   Ernest Charles Ormond, Bar-at-law.

    "   "   William McCornick Sharpe, D.S.O., B.A., I.C.S.

    "   "   Phani Bhusan Chakravartti, M.A., B.L.

    "   "   John Alfred Clough, Bar-at-law.

x   "   "   Thomas Hobart Ellis, M.A. (Oxon.), I.C.S.

    "   "   Jogendra Narayan Mazumdar, C.I.E., M.A., B.L., Bar-at-law.

x	The Hon'ble	Mr	Amir-Ud-din Ahmad, M.B.E., M.A., B.L.
x	"	"	Amin Ahmad, Bar-at-law.
	"	"	Kamal Chunder Chunder, B.A. (Cantab.), I.C.S., Bar-at-law.
	"	"	Gopendra Nath Das, M.A., B.L.

There were a few more names at the bottom of the 1948 list, his own included. But half the English judges and all the Muslim judges had gone. There was not a single Muslim judge in the Calcutta High Court in 1948.

For a man who in his friendships and acquaintance looked upon religion and nationality as both significant and irrelevant, the changing composition of the High Court was a cause for sadness. Soon, of course, the British ranks were further depleted. Now only Trevor Harries (still the Chief Justice) and Roxburgh remained.

The appointment of judges had always been a matter of the greatest importance for the British, and indeed (except for a few scandals such as in the Lahore High Court in the Forties) the administration of justice under the British had been honest and fairly swift. (Needless to say, there were plenty of repressive laws, but that was a different, if related, matter.) The Chief Justice would sound a man out directly or indirectly if he felt that he was a fit candidate for the bench, and if he indicated that he was interested, would propose his name to the government.

Occasionally, political objections were raised by the government, but in general a political man would not be sounded out in the first place, nor – if he were sounded out by the Chief Justice – would he be keen to accept. He would not want to be stifled in the expression of his views. besides, if another Quit India agitation came along, he might have to pass a number of judgments that to his own mind would be unconscionable. Sarat Bose, for instance, would not have been offered judgeship by the British, nor would he have accepted if he had been.

After the British left, matters did not greatly change,

particularly in Calcutta, which continued to have an Englishman as Chief Justice. Mr Justice Chatterji considered Sir Arthur Trevor Harries to be a good man and a good Chief Justice. He now recalled his own 'interview' with him when, as one of the leading barristers of Calcutta, he had been asked to visit him in his chambers.

As soon as they were both seated, Trevor Harries had said: 'If I may, Mr Chatterji, I'll come straight to the point. I would like to recommend your name for judgeship to the government. Would this be acceptable to you?'

Mr Chatterji had said: 'Chief Justice, this is an honour, but I am afraid I must decline.'

Trevor Harries had been rather taken aback. 'Might I ask why?'

'I hope you do not mind if I am equally direct,' had been Mr Chatterji's reply. 'A junior man was appointed before me two years ago, and his comparative competence could not have been the reason.'

'An Englishman?'

'As it happens. I am not speculating about the reason.'

Trevor Harries had nodded. 'I believe I know whom you are referring to. But that was done by another Chief Justice – and I thought the man was your friend.'

'Friend he is, and I'm not talking about the friendship. But the question is one of principle.'

After a pause, Trevor Harries had continued: 'Well, I, like you, will not speculate about the correctness of that decision. But he was a sick man, and his time was running out.'

'Nevertheless.'

Trevor Harries had smiled. 'Your father made an excellent judge, Mr Chatterji. Just the other day I had occasion to quote a 1933 judgment of his on the question of estoppel.'

'I shall tell him so. He will be most pleased.'

There had been a pause. Mr Chatterji had been about to get up when the Chief Justice, with the slightest suspicion of a sigh, had said:

'Mr Chatterji, I respect you too much to wish to, well,

tilt the scales of your judgment in this matter. But I don't mind confessing my disappointment that you wish to decline. I dare say you realize that it is difficult for me to make up the loss of so many good judges at such short notice. Pakistan and England have each claimed several judges of this court. Our workload is increasing steadily, and what with the constitutional work that will be upon us soon, we will need the best new judges we can get. It is in this light that I have asked you to join, and it is in this light that I would like to ask you to reconsider your decision.' He had paused before continuing. 'May I take the liberty of asking you at the end of this coming week if your mind is still unchanged? If so, my regard will remain unchanged, but I will not trouble you further on this point.'

Mr Chatterji had gone home with no intention of changing his mind or of consulting anyone else on the matter. But while talking to his father, he had happened to mention what the Chief Justice had said about the 1933 judgment. 'What did the Chief Justice want to see you about?' his father had asked. And the story had come out.

His father had quoted a line of Sanskrit to him, to the effect that the best ornament for knowledge was humility. He had said nothing at all about duty.

Mrs Chatterji came to know about it because her husband carelessly left a little slip of paper near his bed before he went to sleep, which read: 'CJ Fri 4:45 (?) re J'ship.' When he woke up the next morning he found her quite cross. Again the facts came out. His wife said: 'It'll be much better for your health. No late night conferences with juniors. A much more balanced life.'

'My health's fine, dear. I thrive on the work. And Orr, Dignams have a pretty good sense of how many cases they should brief me in.'

'Well, I like the thought of your wearing a wig and scarlet robes.'

'I'm afraid we only wear scarlet robes when trying criminal cases on the original side. And no wig. No, there's much less sartorial splendour in it these days.'

'Mr Justice Chatterji. It sounds just the thing.'

'I'm afraid I shall turn into my father.'

'You could do worse.'

How Biswas Babu came to know of it was a complete mystery. But he did. One evening in his chambers Mr Chatterji was dictating an opinion to him when Biswas Babu addressed him unconsciously as 'My Lord'. Mr Chatterji sat up. 'He must have slipped back into the past for a bit,' he thought, 'and have imagined that I'm my father.' But Biswas Babu looked so startled and guilty at his slip that he gave himself away. And, having given himself away, he hastily added, shaking his knees swiftly: 'I am so pleased, although prematurely, Sir, to administer my felici –'

'I'm not taking it, Biswas Babu,' said Mr Chatterji, very sharply, and in Bengali.

So shocked was his clerk that he quite forgot himself. 'Why not, Sir?' he replied, also in Bengali: 'Don't you want to do justice?'

Mr Chatterji, displeased, collected himself and continued to dictate his opinion. But Biswas Babu's words had a slow but profound effect on him. He had not said, 'Don't you want to be a judge?'

What a lawyer did was to fight for his client – his client, right or wrong – with all the intelligence and experience he could summon. What a judge could do was to weigh matters with equity, to decide what was right. He had the power to do justice, and it was a noble power. When he met the Chief Justice at the end of the week, Mr Chatterji told him he would be honoured if his name was submitted to the government. A few months later he was sworn in.

*

He enjoyed his work, though he did not mix a great deal with his brethren. He had a wide circle of friends and acquaintances, and he did not, as some judges did, distance himself from them. He had no ambition to become Chief Justice or to go to the Supreme Court in Delhi. (The

Federal Court and appeal to the Privy Council had ceased to exist.)

Apart from everything else, he liked Calcutta too much to uproot himself. He found his uniformed and turbaned servitor irksome and slightly ridiculous, unlike one of his brother judges, who insisted on being trailed by him even when he went to buy fish in the market. But he did not mind being addressed as My Lord or even, by certain barristers, as M'Lud.

Most of all he enjoyed what Biswas Babu, for all his own love of pomp and display, had known would be at the core of his satisfaction: the dispensation of justice within the law. Two cases that he had recently tried illustrated this. One was a case under the Preventive Detention Act of 1950 by which a labour organizer who was Muslim had been detained without being informed of the grounds of his detention except in the broadest terms. One of several such allegations was that he was an agent for Pakistan, although no proof of this was adduced. Another bald and sweeping statement, impossible to rebut, was that he was fomenting public strife. The vagueness and uncertainty of the allegations induced Mr Justice Chatterji and his colleague on the division bench to set aside the order on the basis of Article 22 clause 5 of the Constitution.

In another recent case, when an appeal against conviction for conspiracy of one accused was successful but his single co-accused had not – possibly because of poverty – filed an appeal against his own conviction, Mr Justice Chatterji and a fellow judge had themselves issued a Rule on the State to show cause why the conviction and sentence on the co-accused should not also be set aside. This suo motu ruling had led to a great deal of complex jurisdictional wrangling, but finally the court had decided that it was within its inherent jurisdiction to pass a proper order when a manifest injustice was being perpetrated.

Even in the case at present before him, though it gave Mr Justice Chatterji no pleasure to confirm sentences of death, he felt that he was doing what was just. His judgment was clearly thought out and robustly expressed. But he was considerably worried by the fact that in the first draft of his judgment he had named five of the dacoits and missed out the sixth. This was just the kind of potential disaster that the careful housekeeping of Biswas Babu was always saving him from in his lawyering days.

For a moment his mind turned to Biswas Babu. He wondered how he was and what he was doing. The sound of Kuku at the piano wafted through the open door of his study. He remembered what she had said at lunch about shallybhery juishes. Then he had been annoyed, now he was amused. Biswas Babu's written legal English may have been sharp and economical (except for the occasional misplaced article), but his general English was a thing of tortuous beauty. And one could hardly expect the high-spirited Kuku not to be alive to its expressive possibilities.

7.38

BISWAS BABU, as it happened, was at that very moment with his friend and fellow clerk, the burra babu of the insurance department of Bentsen Pryce. They had been friends for over twenty years now, and Biswas Babu's adda or den had slowly cemented this relationship. (When Arun had married Meenakshi it was almost as if their families had suddenly found themselves allied.) The burra babu would visit Biswas Babu's house most evenings; here a number of old companions would gather to talk about the world or simply to sit around, drinking tea and reading the newspapers with an occasional comment. Today some of them were thinking of going to a play.

'So it seems that your High Court building has been struck by lightning,' ventured one man.

'No damage, no damage,' said Biswas Babu. 'The main problem is the refugees from East Bengal who have begun to camp in the corridors.' No one here referred to it as East Pakistan.

'The Hindus there are being terrified and driven out.

Every day one reads in the *Hindustan Standard* of Hindu girls being kidnapped –'

'Ay, Ma' – this was addressed to Biswas Babu's youngest granddaughter, a girl of six – 'tell your mother to send some more tea.'

'One quick war, and Bengal will be united once again.'

This was considered so stupid that no one responded.

For a few minutes there was contented silence.

'Did you read that article where Netaji's air-crash death was contradicted? It appeared two days ago –'

'Well, if he's alive, he's not doing much to prove it.'

'Naturally he has to lie low.'

'Why? The British have gone.'

'Ah – but he has worse enemies among those left behind.'

'Who?'

'Nehru – and all the others,' ended the proponent darkly if lamely.

'I suppose you think Hitler is alive as well?' This elicited a chuckle all around.

'When is your Amit Babu getting married?' asked someone of Biswas Babu after a pause. 'All Calcutta is waiting.'

'Let Calcutta wait,' said Biswas Babu and returned to his newspaper.

'It is your responsibility to do something – "by hooks and by crooks" as they say in English.'

'I have done enough,' said Biswas Babu with stylized weariness. 'He's a good boy, but a dreamer.'

'A good boy – but a dreamer! Oh, let's have that son-in-law joke again,' said someone to Biswas Babu and the burra babu.

'No, no –' they both demurred. But they were easily enough prevailed upon by the others to act it out. Both of them enjoyed acting, and this skit was only a few lines long. They had acted it half a dozen times before, and to the same audience; the adda, normally so torpid, was given to occasional theatricality.

The burra babu walked around the room, examining the

produce in a fish market. Suddenly he saw his old friend. 'Ah, ah, Biswas Babu,' he exclaimed joyfully.

'Yes, yes, borro babu – it has been a long time,' said Biswas Babu, shaking out his umbrella.

'Congratulations on your daughter's engagement, Biswas Babu. A good boy?'

Biswas Babu nodded his head vigorously. 'He's a good boy. Very decent. Well, he eats an onion or two sometimes, but that's all.'

The burra babu, clearly shocked, exclaimed: 'What? Does he eat onions every day?'

'Oh no! Not every day. Far from it. Only when he has had a few drinks.'

'But drinking! Surely he doesn't drink often.'

'Oh no!' said Biswas Babu. 'By no means. Only when he's with women of an evening. . . .'

'But women – what! – and does this happen regularly?'

'Oh no!' exclaimed Biswas Babu. 'He can't afford to visit prostitutes so often. His father is a retired pimp, and destitute, and the boy can only sponge off him once in a while.'

The adda greeted this performance with cheers and laughter. It whetted their appetite for the play they would be going to see later in the evening at a local North Calcutta venue – the Star Theatre. The tea soon came in, together with a few delicious lobongolotikas and other sweets prepared by Biswas Babu's daughter-in-law; and for a few minutes everyone fell appreciatively silent except for a few tongue-clicks and comments of enjoyment.

7.39

DIPANKAR sat on the little rug in his room with Cuddles on his lap, and dispensed advice to his troubled siblings.

Whereas no one dared to interrupt Amit while he was working, or for fear that he might be working, on his immortal prose or verse, it was open season on Dipankar's time and energy.

They came in for specific advice, or sometimes just to talk. There was something pleasantly and zanily earnest about Dipankar which was very reassuring.

Although Dipankar was utterly indecisive in his own life – or perhaps for that very reason – he was quite good at throwing out useful suggestions into the lives of others.

Meenakshi dropped in first with a question about whether it was possible to love more than one person – 'utterly, desperately, and truly'. Dipankar talked the matter over with her in strictly unspecific terms, and came to the conclusion that it certainly was possible. The ideal, of course, was to love everyone in the universe equally, he said. Meenakshi was far from convinced of this but felt much better for having talked it over.

Kuku came in next with a specific problem. What was she to do with Hans? He couldn't bear Bengali food, he was a worse philistine even than Arun, who refused to eat fish-heads, even the most delicious bits, the eyes. Hans had not taken to fried neem leaves (he found them too bitter, just imagine, said Kuku), and she did not know if she could really love a man who didn't like neem leaves. More importantly, did he really love her? Hans might have to be discarded yet, for all his Schubert and Schmerz.

Dipankar reassured her that she could, and that he did. He mentioned that tastes were tastes, and that, if she recalled, Mrs Rupa Mehra had once thought Kuku herself a barbarian because she had spoken slightingly of the dussehri mango. As for Hans, Dipankar suspected that he was in for an education. Sauerkraut would soon be replaced by the banana flower, and stollen and sachertorte by lobongolotikas and ladycannings; and he would have to adapt, and accept, and appreciate, if he was to remain Kakoli's most-favoured mushroom; for if everyone else was putty in his firmly-grasping hands, he was certainly putty in hers.

'And where will I go and live?' asked Kuku, beginning to sniff. 'In that freezing, bombed-out country?' She looked around Dipankar's room, and said, 'You know what's lacking on that wall is a picture of the Sundarbans. I'll paint you one. ... I hear it rains all the time in Germany, and people spend their whole lives shivering, and if Hans and I quarrel, I can't just walk home like Meenakshi.'

Kakoli sneezed. Cuddles barked. Dipankar blinked and continued.

'Well, Kuku, if I were you —'

'You didn't bless me,' protested Kakoli.

'Oh, sorry, Kuku, bless you.'

'Oh, Cuddles, Cuddles, Cuddles,' said Kuku, 'no one loves us, no one at all, not even Dipankar. No one cares if we get pneumonia and die.'

Bahadur entered. 'A phone call for Baby Memsahib,' he said.

'Oh,' said Kuku, 'I must flee.'

'But you were discussing the direction of your life,' protested Dipankar mildly. 'You don't even know who's called — it couldn't possibly be that important.'

'But it's the phone,' said Kuku and, having delivered herself of this complete and ineluctable explanation, did indeed flee.

Next came Dipankar's mother, not to take, but to give advice.

'Ki korchho tumi, Dipankar? ...' she began, and continued to upbraid him quietly, while Dipankar continued to smile pacifically. 'Your father is so worried ... and I also would like you to settle down ... family business ... after all, we are not going to live for ever ... responsibility ... father's getting old ... look at your brother, only wants to write poetry, and now these novels, thinks he is another Saratchandra ... you are our only hope ... then your father and I can rest in peace.'

'But, Mago, we still have some time left to settle the matter,' said Dipankar, who always deferred whatever he could and left the rest undecided.

Mrs Chatterji looked uncertain. When Dipankar was small, whenever Bahadur asked him what he wanted to eat for breakfast, he would just look up and shake his head in one way or another, and Bahadur, understanding intuitively what was required, would turn up with a fried egg or an omelette or whatever, which Dipankar would eat quite happily. The family had been filled with wonderment. Perhaps, Mrs Chatterji now thought, no mental message had ever passed between them at all, and Bahadur merely represented Fate making its offerings to a Dipankar who decided nothing but accepted everything.

'And even among girls, you don't decide,' continued Mrs Chatterji. 'There's Hemangini, and Chitra, and . . . it's as bad as Kuku,' she ended sadly.

Dipankar had rather chiselled features, not like the milder, more rounded, features of the large-eyed Amit, who fitted Mrs Chatterji's Bengali idea of good looks. She always thought of Dipankar as a sort of ugly duckling, was fiercely ready to protect him against accusations of angularity and boniness, and was amazed when women of the younger generation, all these Chitras and Hemanginis, babbled on about how attractive he was.

'None of them is the Ideal, Mago,' said Dipankar. 'I must continue to search for the Ideal. And for Unity.'

'And now you are going to this Pul Mela in Brahmpur. It is so inappropriate for a Brahmo, praying to the Ganga and taking dips.'

'No, Ma, not at all —' said Dipankar seriously. 'Even Keshub Chunder Sen anointed himself with oil and dipped himself three times in the tank in Dalhousie Square.'

'He did not!' said Mrs Chatterji, shocked by Dipankar's apostasy.

The Brahmos, who believed in an abstract and elevated monotheism, or were supposed to, simply did not go about doing that sort of thing.

'He did, Mago. Well, I'm not sure it was Dalhousie Square,' Dipankar conceded. 'But, on the other hand, I think it was four dips, not three. And the Ganga is so much holier than a stagnant tank. Why, even Rabindranath Tagore said about the Ganga. . . .'

'Oh, Robi Babu!' exclaimed Mrs Chatterji, her face transfigured with muted ecstasy.

The fourth to visit Dipankar's clinic was Tapan.

Cuddles at once jumped out of Dipankar's lap and onto

Tapan's. Whenever Tapan's trunk was packed for him to go to school, Cuddles would become almost desperate, would sit on the trunk to prevent its removal, and would be inconsolably ferocious for a week afterwards.

Tapan stroked Cuddles' head and looked at the shiny black triangle formed by his eyes and nose.

'We'll never shoot you, Cuddles,' he promised. 'Your eyes have no whites at all.'

Cuddles wagged his bristly tail in wholehearted approval.

Tapan looked a bit troubled and seemed to want to talk about something, but wasn't very articulate about what he wanted to say. Dipankar let him ramble on for a bit. After a while Tapan noticed a book about famous battles on Dipankar's topmost shelf, and asked to borrow it. Dipankar looked at the dusty book in astonishment – it was a remnant of his unenlightened days – and got it down.

'Keep it,' he told Tapan.

'Are you sure, Dipankar Da?' asked Tapan gratefully.

'Sure?' asked Dipankar, beginning to wonder whether such a book would really be good for Tapan to keep. 'Well, I'm not really sure. When you've read it, bring it back, and we'll decide what to do with it then . . . or later.'

Finally, just as he was about to begin meditating, Amit wandered by. He had been writing all day and looked tired.

'Are you certain I'm not disturbing you?' he asked.

'No, Dada, not at all.'

'You're quite certain?'

'Yes.'

'Because I wanted to discuss something with you – something that it's quite impossible to discuss with Meenakshi or Kuku.'

'I know, Dada. Yes, she's quite nice.'

'Dipankar!'

'Yes; unaffected,' said Dipankar, looking like an umpire indicating a batsman out; 'intelligent,' he continued, like Churchill signalling victory; 'attractive –', he went on, now representing the trident of Shiva; 'Chatterji-compatible,' he murmured, like the Grande Dame emphasizing the four aims of life; 'and Beastly to Bish,' he added finally, in the stance of a benevolent Buddha.

'Beastly to Bish?' asked Amit.

'So Meenakshi told me a little while ago, Dada. Apparently, Arun was quite put out and refuses to introduce her to anyone else. Arun's mother is distraught, Lata is secretly elated, and – oh yes – Meenakshi – who thinks there's nothing wrong with Bish except that he's insufferable – is taking Lata's side. And incidentally, Dada, Biswas Babu, who has heard of her, thinks she is just my type! Did you tell him about her?' asked Dipankar unblinkingly.

'No,' said Amit, frowning. 'I didn't. Perhaps Kuku did – the chatterbox. What a gossip you are, Dipankar, don't you do any work at all? I wish you'd do what Baba says, and get a proper job and handle all these wretched family finances. It would kill both me and my novel if I had to. Anyway, she's not your type in the least, and you know it. Go and find your own Ideal.'

'Anything for you, Dada,' said Dipankar sweetly, and lowered his right hand in gentle blessing.

7.40

MANGOES arrived for Mrs Rupa Mehra from Brahmpur one afternoon, and her eyes gleamed. She had had enough of the langra mango in Calcutta, which (though it was acceptable) did not remind her of her childhood. What she longed for was the delicate, delectable dussehri, and the season for dussehris was, she had thought, over. Savita had sent her a dozen by parcel post a few days earlier, but when the parcel had arrived, apart from three squashed mangoes at the top, there were only stones underneath. Clearly someone in the Post Office had intercepted them. Mrs Rupa Mehra had been as distressed by the wickedness of man as by her own sense of deprivation. She had given up hope of dussehris for this season. And who knows if I'll be alive next year? she thought to herself dramatically –

and somewhat unreasonably, since she was still several years short of fifty. But now here was another parcel with two dozen dussehris, ripe but not over-ripe, and even cool to the touch.

'Who brought them?' Mrs Rupa Mehra asked Hanif. 'The postman?'

'No, Memsahib. A man.'

'What did he look like? Where was he from?'

'He was just a man, Memsahib. But he gave me this letter for you.'

Mrs Rupa Mehra looked at Hanif severely. 'You should have given it to me at once. All right. Bring me a plate and a sharp knife, and wash two mangoes.' Mrs Rupa Mehra pressed and sniffed a few and selected two. 'These two.'

'Yes, Memsahib.'

'And tell Lata to come in from the garden and eat a mango with me at once.'

Lata had been sitting in the garden. It had not been raining, though there was a slight breeze. When she came in, Mrs Rupa Mehra read out the whole of Savita's accompanying letter.

... but I said I could imagine how disappointed you must be feeling, Ma darling, and we ourselves were so sad because we had chosen them so carefully and with so much affection, judging each one to ensure that it would be ripe in six days' time. But then a Bengali gentleman who works in the Registrar's Office told us how to get around the problem. He knows an attendant who works in the air-conditioned bogey of the Brahmpur-Calcutta Mail. We gave him ten rupees to take the mangoes to you, and we hope that they have arrived – safe and cool and complete. Please do tell me if they have arrived in time. If so we might be able to manage another batch before the season is over because we will not have to choose half-ripe mangoes as we had to for the parcel post. But Ma, you must also be very careful not to eat too many because of your blood sugar.

Arun should also read this letter, and monitor your intake. . . .

Mrs Rupa Mehra's eyes filled with tears as she read the letter out to her younger daughter. Then she ate a mango with great gusto, and insisted that Lata eat one as well.

'Now we will share another one,' said Mrs Rupa Mehra.

'Ma, your blood sugar –'

'One mango will make no difference.'

'Of course it will, Ma, and so will the next, and so will the next. And don't you want to make them last till the next parcel comes?'

The discussion was cut short by the arrival of Amit and Kuku.

'Where's Meenakshi?' asked Amit.

'She's gone out,' said Mrs Rupa Mehra.

'Not again!' said Amit. 'I had hoped to see her. By the time I heard she had come to see Dipankar, she'd gone. Please tell her I called. Where's she gone?'

'To the Shady Ladies,' said Mrs Rupa Mehra, frowning.

'What a pity,' said Amit. 'But it's nice to see you both.' He turned to Lata and said: 'Kuku was just going off to Presidency College to see an old friend, and I thought that perhaps we might go along together. I remember you wanted to visit that area.'

'Yes!' said Lata, happy that Amit had remembered. 'May I go, Ma? Or do you need me for something this afternoon?'

'That is all right,' said Mrs Rupa Mehra, feeling liberal. 'But you must have some mangoes before you go,' she continued hospitably to Amit and Kuku. 'These have just come from Brahmpur. Savita has sent them. And Pran – it is so good when one's child gets married to such a thoughtful person. And you must also take some home with you,' she added.

When Amit, Kuku and Lata had gone, Mrs Rupa Mehra decided to cut another mango. When Aparna woke up after her nap, she was fed a slice. When Meenakshi came back from the Shady Ladies, having played a few successful games of mah-jongg, the letter from Savita was read out to her, and she was told to eat a mango.

'No, Ma, I really can't – it's not good for my figure – and it will ruin my lipstick. Hello, Aparna darling – no, don't kiss Mummy just yet. Your lips are all sticky.'

Mrs Rupa Mehra was confirmed in her opinion that Meenakshi was extremely odd. To steel yourself against mangoes showed a degree of iciness that was almost inhuman.

'Amit and Kuku enjoyed them.'

'Oh, what a pity I missed meeting them.' Meenakshi's tone implied relief.

'Amit came specially to see you. He's come several times, and you've always been out.'

'I doubt it.'

'What do you mean?' said Mrs Rupa Mehra, who did not enjoy being contradicted, least of all by her daughter-in-law.

'I doubt he came to see me. He very rarely visited us before you came from Brahmpur. He's quite content living in his own dreamworld of characters.'

Mrs Rupa Mehra frowned at Meenakshi but was silent.

'Oh, Ma, you're so slow on the uptake,' continued Meenakshi. 'It's clearly Luts whom he's interested in. I've never seen him behave with any kind of consideration towards a girl before. And it's no bad thing either.'

'No bad thing either,' repeated Aparna, testing out the phrase.

'Be quiet, Aparna,' said her grandmother sharply. Aparna, too astonished to be hurt by a rebuke from this everloving quarter, kept quiet but continued to listen intently.

'That's not true, that is simply not true. And don't give either of them any ideas,' said Mrs Rupa Mehra, shaking her finger at Meenakshi.

'I'll give them no ideas that they don't have already,' was the cool response.

'You are a mischief-maker, Meenakshi, I won't have it,' said Mrs Rupa Mehra.

'My dear Ma,' said Meenakshi, amused. 'Don't fly off the handle. Neither is it mischief, nor have I made it. I'd just accept things as they come.'

'I have no intention of accepting things as they come,' said Mrs Rupa Mehra, the unsavoury vision of sacrificing yet another of her children on the altar of the Chatterjis making her flush with indignation. 'I will take her back to Brahmpur at once.' She stopped. 'No, not to Brahmpur. Somewhere else.'

'And Luts will traipse after you obediently?' said Meenakshi, stretching her long neck.

'Lata is a sensible and a good girl, and she will do as I tell her. She is not wilful and disobedient like girls who think they are very modern. She has been well brought up.'

Meenakshi stretched back her head lazily, and looked first at her nails and then at her watch. 'Oh, I have to be somewhere in ten minutes,' she said. 'Ma, will you look after Aparna?'

Mrs Rupa Mehra silently conveyed her irked consent. Meenakshi knew too well that her mother-in-law would be pleased to look after her only grandchild.

'I'll be back by six-thirty,' said Meenakshi. 'Arun said he'd be a little late at the office today.'

But Mrs Rupa Mehra was annoyed, and did not respond. And behind her annoyance a slow panic was beginning to build and take hold of her.

7.41

AMIT and Lata were browsing among the innumerable bookstalls of College Street. (Kuku had gone to meet Krishnan at the Coffee House. According to her he needed to be 'appeased', though to her irritation Amit did not ask what she meant by that.)

'One feels so bewildered among all these millions of books,' said Lata, astonished that several hundred yards of a city could actually be given over to nothing but books – books on the pavement, books on makeshift bookshelves out in the street, books in the library and in Presidency College, first-, second-, third- and tenth-hand books, everything from technical monographs on electroplating to the latest Agatha Christie.

'I feel so bewildered among these millions of books, you mean.'

'No, I do,' said Lata.

'What I meant,' said Amit, 'was "I", as opposed to "one". If you meant the general "one", that would be fine. But you meant "I". Far too many people say "one" when they mean "I". I found them doing it all the time in England, and it'll survive here long after they've given up that idiocy.'

Lata reddened but said nothing. Bish, she recalled, referred to himself exclusively and incessantly as 'one'.

'It's like "thrice",' said Amit.

'I see,' said Lata.

'Just imagine if I were to say to you: "One loves you," Amit went on. Or worse still, "One loves one." Doesn't that sound idiotic?'

'Yes,' Lata admitted with a frown. She felt he was sounding a bit too professional. And the word 'love' reminded her unnecessarily of Kabir.

'That's all I meant,' said Amit.

'I see,' said Lata. 'Or, rather, one sees.'

'I see one does,' said Amit.

'What is it like to write a novel?' asked Lata after a pause. 'Don't you have to forget the "I" or the "one" – ?'

'I don't know exactly,' said Amit. 'This is my first novel, and I'm in the process of finding out. At the moment it feels like a banyan tree.'

'I see,' said Lata, though she didn't.

'What I mean is,' continued Amit, 'it sprouts, and grows, and spreads, and drops down branches that become trunks or intertwine with other branches. Sometimes branches die. Sometimes the main trunk dies, and the structure is held up by the supporting trunks. When you go to the Botanical Garden you'll see what I mean. It has its own life – but so do the snakes and birds and bees and lizards and termites that live in it and on it and off it. But then it's also like the Ganges in its upper, middle and lower courses – including its delta – of course.'

'Of course,' said Lata.

'I have the feeling,' said Amit, 'that you're laughing at me.'

'How far have you got so far with writing it?' she said.

'I'm about a third of the way.'

'And aren't I wasting your time?'

'No.'

'It's about the Bengal Famine, isn't it?'

'Yes.'

'Do you have any memory of the famine yourself?'

'I do. I remember it only too well. It was only eight years ago.' He paused. 'I was somewhat active in student politics then. But do you know, we had a dog even then, and fed it well.' He looked distressed.

'Does a writer have to feel strongly about what he writes?' asked Lata.

'I haven't the least idea,' said Amit. 'Sometimes I write best about the things I care about least. But even that's not a consistent rule.'

'So do you just flounder and hope?'

'No, no, not exactly.'

Lata felt that Amit, who had been so open, even expansive, a minute ago, was resisting her questioning now, and she did not press it further.

'I'll send you a book of my poems sometime,' said Amit. 'And you can form your own opinion about how much or how little I feel.'

'Why not now?' asked Lata.

'I need time to think of a suitable inscription,' said Amit. 'Ah, there's Kuku.'

7.42

KUKU had performed her errand of appeasement. Now she wanted to go home as quickly as possible. Unfortunately, it had begun to rain once more, and soon the warm rain was battering down on the roof of the Humber. Rivulets of brown water began running down the sides of the street. A little further there was no street at all, just a sort of shallow canal, where traffic in the opposite direction created waves that shook the chassis of the car. Ten minutes later the car was trapped in a flash flood. The driver inched forward, trying to keep to the middle of the road, where the camber created a slightly higher level. Then the engine died.

With Kuku and Amit to talk to in the car, Lata did not fret. It was very hot, though, and beads of perspiration formed on her forehead. Amit told her a bit about his college days and how he had begun writing poetry. 'Most of it was terrible, and I burned it,' he said.

'How could you have done that?' asked Lata, amazed that anyone could burn what must have been written with so much feeling. But at least he had burned it and not simply torn it up. That would have been too matter-of-fact. The thought of a fire in the Calcutta climate was odd too. There was no fireplace in the Ballygunge house.

'Where did you burn the poems?' she asked.

'In the wash-basin,' interjected Kuku. 'He nearly burned the house down too.'

'It was awful poetry,' said Amit by way of extenuation. 'Embarrassingly bad. Self-indulgent, dishonest.'

> 'Poetry I don't desire
> I will immolate with fire,'

said Kuku.

> 'All my sorrow, all my pain:
> Ashes flowing down the drain,'

continued Amit.

'Aren't there any Chatterjis who don't make flippant couplets?' asked Lata, unaccountably annoyed. Weren't

662

they ever serious? How could they joke about such heart-breaking matters?

'Ma and Baba don't,' said Kuku. 'That's because they've never had Amit as an elder brother. And Dipankar's not quite as skilled as the rest of us. It comes naturally to us, like singing in a raag if you've heard it often enough. People are astonished we can do it, but we're astonished Dipankar can't. Or only once a month or so, when he has his poetic periods. . . .

> Rhyming, rhyming so precisely –
> Couplets, they are coming nicely,'

gurgled Kakoli, who churned them out with such appalling frequency that they were now called Kakoli-couplets, though Amit had started the trend.

By now most of the motor traffic had come to a halt. A few rickshaws were still moving, the rickshaw-wallahs waist-deep in the flood, their passengers, laden with packages, surveying the watery brown world around them with a kind of alarmed satisfaction.

In due course the water subsided. The driver looked at the engine, examined the ignition wire, which was moist, and wiped it with a piece of cloth. The car still wouldn't start. Then he looked at the carburettor, fiddled a bit here and there, and murmured the names of his favourite goddesses in correct firing sequence. The car began to move.

By the time they got back to Sunny Park it was dark.

'You have taken your own sweet time,' said Mrs Rupa Mehra sharply to Lata. She glared at Amit.

Amit and Lata were both surprised by the hostility of their reception.

'Even Meenakshi has returned before you,' continued Mrs Rupa Mehra. She looked at Amit, and thought: Poet, wastrel! He has never earned an honest rupee in his life. I will not have all my grandchildren speaking Bengali! Suddenly she remembered that the last time Amit had dropped Lata home, she had had flowers in her hair.

Looking at Lata, but presumably addressing both of

663

them – or perhaps all three of them, Kuku included – she continued: 'You have put up my blood pressure and my blood sugar.'

'No, Ma,' said Lata, looking at the fresh mango peels on the plate. 'If your blood sugar has gone up it's because of all those dussehris you've been eating. Now please don't have more than one a day – or at most two.'

'Are you teaching your grandmother to suck eggs?' asked Mrs Rupa Mehra, glowering.

Amit smiled. 'It was my fault, Ma,' he said. 'The streets were flooded not far from the university, and we got caught.'

Mrs Rupa Mehra was in no mood to be friendly. What was he smiling for?

'Is your blood sugar very high?' asked Kakoli quickly.

'Very high,' said Mrs Rupa Mehra with distress and pride. 'I have even been having karela juice, but it has no effect.'

'Then you must go to my homoeopathic doctor,' said Kakoli.

Mrs Rupa Mehra, diverted from her attack, said, 'I already have a homoeopath.'

But Kakoli insisted that her doctor was better than anyone else. 'Doctor Nuruddin.'

'A Mohammedan?' said Mrs Rupa Mehra doubtfully.

'Yes. It happened in Kashmir, when we were on holiday.'

'I am not going to Kashmir,' said Mrs Rupa Mehra decidedly.

'No, he cured me here. His clinic is here, in Calcutta. He cures people of everything – diabetes, gout, skin troubles. I had a friend who had a cyst on his eyelid. He gave him a medicine called thuja, and the cyst dropped right off.'

'Yes,' agreed Amit energetically. 'I sent a friend of mine to a homoeopath, and her brain tumour disappeared, and her broken leg mended, and though she was barren she had twins within three months.'

Both Kuku and Mrs Rupa Mehra glared at him. Lata looked at him with a smile of mixed reproof and approval.

'Amit always makes fun of what he can't understand,' said Kuku. 'He clubs homoeopathy together with astrology. But even our family doctor has slowly become convinced of the effectiveness of homoeopathy. And ever since my terrible problem in Kashmir I am a complete convert. I believe in results,' continued Kuku. 'When something works I believe in it.'

'What problem did you have?' asked Mrs Rupa Mehra eagerly.

'It was the ice-cream in a hotel in Gulmarg.'

'Oh.' Ice-cream was one of Mrs Rupa Mehra's weaknesses too.

'The hotel made its own ice-cream. On the spur of the moment I ate two scoops.'

'And then?'

'Then – then it was terrible.' Kuku's voice reflected her trauma. 'I had an awful throat. I was given some allopathic medicine by the local doctor. It suppressed the symptoms for a day, then they came back again. I couldn't eat, I couldn't sing, I could hardly speak, I couldn't swallow. It was like having thorns in my throat. I had to think before I decided to say something.'

Mrs Rupa Mehra clicked her tongue in sympathy.

'And my sinuses were blocked completely.' Kuku paused, then went on:

'Then I had another dose of medicine. And again it suppressed the condition, but it came back again. I had to be sent to Delhi and flown back to Calcutta. After dose number three, my throat was inflamed, my sinuses and nose were both infected, I was in a terrible state. My aunt, Mrs Ganguly, suggested Dr Nuruddin. "Try him and see," she told my mother. "What's the harm?"'

The suspense, for Mrs Rupa Mehra, was unbearable. Stories involving ailments were as fascinating for her as murder mysteries or romances.

'He took my history, and asked me some strange questions. Then he said: "Take two doses of pulsetilla, and come back to me." I said: "Two doses? Just two doses? Will that be enough? Not a regular course?" He said:

'Inshallah, two doses should be enough.' And it was. I was cured. The swelling disappeared. My sinuses cleared up completely and the thing never recurred. Allopathic treatment would have required puncturing and draining the sinuses to relieve an endemic complaint – which is what it would have become if I hadn't gone to Dr Nuruddin; and you can stop laughing, Amit.'

Mrs Rupa Mehra was convinced. 'I'll go with you to see him,' she said.

'But you mustn't mind his strange questions,' said Kakoli.

'I can handle myself in all situations,' said Mrs Rupa Mehra.

When they had left, Mrs Rupa Mehra said pointedly to Lata:

'I am very tired of Calcutta, darling, and it is not good for my health. Let us go to Delhi.'

'What on earth for, Ma?' said Lata. 'I'm beginning to have a good time here. And why so suddenly?'

Mrs Rupa Mehra looked closely at her daughter.

'And we have all those mangoes to eat still,' laughed Lata. 'And we have to make sure that Varun studies a little.'

Mrs Rupa Mehra looked severe. 'Tell me –' she began, then stopped. Surely Lata could not be pretending the innocence that was written so plainly on her face. And if she wasn't, why put ideas into her head?

'Yes, Ma?'

'Tell me what you did today.'

This was more in the line of Mrs Rupa Mehra's daily questioning, and Lata was relieved to see her mother behaving more in character. Lata had no intention of being torn away from Calcutta and the Chatterjis. When she thought how unhappy she had been when she had first come here, she felt grateful to that family – and most of all to the comfortable, cynical, considerate Amit – for the way they had absorbed her into their clan – almost as a third sister, she thought.

Meanwhile Mrs Rupa Mehra was also thinking about

the Chatterjis, but in less charitable terms. Meenakshi's remarks had made her panic.

I will go to Delhi, by myself if necessary, she was thinking. Kalpana Gaur will have to help me to find a suitable boy at once. Then I will summon Lata. Arun is completely useless. Ever since his marriage he has lost all feeling for his own family. He introduced Lata to this Bishwanath boy, and since then he has done nothing further. He has no sense of responsibility for his sister. I am all alone in the world now. Only my Aparna loves me. Meenakshi was sleeping, and Aparna was with the Toothless Crone. Mrs Rupa Mehra had her granddaughter transferred immediately to her own arms.

7.43

THE rain had delayed Arun as well. When he returned home he was in a black temper.

Without more than a grunt apiece for his mother, sister and daughter, he marched straight into the bedroom. 'Damned swine, the whole lot of them,' he announced. 'And the driver too.'

Meenakshi surveyed him from the bed. She yawned:

> 'Arun, darling, why such fury?
> Have a chocolate made by Flury.'

'Oh, stop that moronic Blabberji blather,' shouted Arun, setting down his briefcase and laying his damp coat across the arm of a chair. 'You're my wife. You can at least pretend to be sympathetic.'

'What happened, darling?' said Meenakshi, composing her features into the required emotion. 'Bad day at the office?'

Arun closed his eyes. He sat down on the edge of the bed.

'Tell me,' said Meenakshi, her long, elegant, red-nailed fingers slowly loosening his tie.

Arun sighed. 'This bloody rickshaw-wallah asked me for three rupees to take me across the road to my car. Across the road,' he repeated, shaking his head in disgust and disbelief.

Meenakshi's fingers stopped. 'No!' she exclaimed, genuinely shocked. 'I hope you didn't agree to pay.'

'What could I do?' asked Arun. 'I wasn't going to wade knee-deep through water to get to my car – or risk the car crossing the flooded section of the road and stalling. He could see that – and he was smirking with the pleasure of having a sahib by the balls. "It's your decision," he said. "Three rupees." Three rupees! When normally it would be two annas at the most. One anna would have been a fairer price – it was no more than twenty steps. But he could see there was no other rickshaw in sight and that I was getting wet. Bloody profiteering swine.'

Meenakshi glanced at the mirror from the bed and thought for a moment. 'Tell me,' she said, 'what does Bentsen Pryce do when there's a temporary shortage of, oh, jute in the world market and the price goes up? Don't they put up their prices to whatever level the market will bear? Or is that only a Marwari practice? I know that's what goldsmiths and silversmiths do. And vegetable sellers. I suppose that was what the rickshaw-wallah was doing too. Perhaps I shouldn't have been shocked after all. Or you.'

She had forgotten her intention to be sympathetic. Arun looked at her, injured, but saw, despite himself, the unpleasantly forceful logic of her words.

'Would you like to do my job?' he demanded.

'Oh no, darling,' said Meenakshi, refusing to take offence. 'I couldn't bear to wear a coat and tie. And I wouldn't know how to dictate letters to your charming Miss Christie. ... Oh, by the way, some mangoes came from Brahmpur today. And a letter from Savita.'

'Oh.'

'And Ma, being Ma, has been glutting away at them without regard for her diabetes.'

Arun shook his head. As if he didn't have troubles

enough already. His mother was incorrigible. Tomorrow she'd complain that she wasn't feeling well, and he'd have to take her to the doctor. Mother, sister, daughter, wife: he suddenly felt trapped – a whole bloody household of women. And the feckless Varun to boot.

'Where's Varun?'

'I don't know,' said Meenakshi. 'He hasn't returned, and he hasn't called. I don't think he has, anyway. I've been taking a nap.'

Arun sighed.

'I've been dreaming about you,' lied Meenakshi.

'You have?' asked Arun, mollified. 'Let's –'

'Oh, later, don't you think, darling?' said Meenakshi coolly. 'We have to go out this evening.'

'Isn't there any bloody evening when we don't go out?' asked Arun.

Meenakshi shrugged, as if to say that most of the engagements were not of her making.

'I wish I were a bachelor again.' Arun had said it without meaning to.

Meenakshi's eyes flamed. 'If you want to be like that –' she began.

'No, no, I don't mean it. It's just this bloody stress. And my back's playing up again.'

'I don't find Varun's bachelor life all that admirable,' said Meenakshi.

Nor did Arun. He shook his head again, and sighed. He looked exhausted.

Poor Arun, thought Meenakshi. 'Tea – or a drink, darling?' she said.

'Tea,' said Arun. 'Tea. A nice cup of tea. A drink can wait.'

7.44

VARUN had not yet returned because he was busy gambling and smoking in Sajid's house in Park Lane, a street that was seedier than it sounded. Sajid, Jason, Varun and a few other friends were sitting on Sajid's huge bed upstairs, and playing flush: starting from one anna blind, two annas seen. Today, as on a few other occasions, they were joined by Sajid's downstairs tenants, Paul and his sister Hortense. Hortense (referred to by Sajid and his friends among themselves as 'Hot-Ends') was sitting on the lap of her boyfriend (a ship's purser) and playing on his behalf from that position. The stakes had risen to four annas blind, eight annas seen – the maximum they ever allowed themselves. Everyone was jittery, and people were packing in their hands left and right. Eventually only Varun, who was extremely nervous, and Hot-Ends, who was extremely calm, were left.

'Just Varun and Hortense alone together,' said Sajid. 'It'll really hot up now.'

Varun flushed deep red and almost dropped his cards. It was common knowledge among the friends (but not to Hortense's boyfriend the purser) that Paul – who was otherwise unemployed – pimped for his sister whenever her boyfriend was out of town. God knows where he went to get his customers, but he would sometimes come back late in the evening with a businessman in a taxi, and stand, smoking Rhodes Navy Cut, at the foot of the stairs or outside on the steps while Hortense and her client got on with it.

'A royal flush,' said Jason, referring to Varun's expression.

Varun, trembling with nervous tension and glancing at his cards for reassurance, whispered, 'I'll stay in.' He put an eight-anna coin in the kitty, which now contained almost five rupees.

Hot-Ends, without glancing at her cards, or at anyone, and with as blasé an expression as she could manage, wordlessly pushed another eight annas into the pool. Her boyfriend moved his finger up and down the hollow of her throat, and she leaned back.

Varun, his tongue passing nervously over his lips and his eyes glazed with excitement, staked another eight annas. Hot-Ends, looking straight at him this time, and holding his frightened and fascinated glance with her own, said, as huskily as possible: 'Oh you greedy boy! You just want to take advantage of me. Well, I'll give you what you want.' And she put another eight annas into the kitty.

Varun could bear it no longer. Weak with suspense and terrified by what her hand might reveal, he asked for a show. Hot-Ends had a King, Queen and Jack of spades. Varun almost collapsed with relief. He had an Ace, King and Queen of diamonds.

But he looked as shattered as if he had lost. He begged his friends to excuse him and let him go home.

'Not a chance!' said Sajid. 'You can't just make a packet and disappear. You have to fight to keep it.'

And Varun promptly lost all his winnings (and more) over the next few games. Everything I do goes wrong, he thought to himself as he returned home in the tram. I am a useless person – useless – and a disgrace to the family. Thinking of how Hot-Ends had looked at him, he began to get nervous again, and wondered if more trouble was not in store for him if he continued to associate with his Shamshu friends.

7.45

THE morning that Mrs Rupa Mehra was about to leave for Delhi, the Mehra family was sitting at the breakfast table. Arun as usual was doing the crossword. After a while he looked at a few other pages.

'You could at least talk to me,' said Mrs Rupa Mehra. 'I am leaving today, and you are hiding behind your newspaper.'

Arun looked up. 'Listen to this, Ma,' he said. 'Just the thing for you.' And he read out an advertisement from the paper in a sarcastic voice:

'Diabetes cured in Seven Days. No matter how severe or longstanding, Diabetes can be completely cured by VENUS CHARM, the very latest Scientific Discovery.

Some of the main symptoms of this disease are Abnormal thirst and hunger, Excess sugar in urine and Itching etc. In its serious form it causes Carbuncles, Boils, Cataract and other complications. Thousands have escaped from the gallows of death by using VENUS CHARM. The very next day it eradicates sugar and normalises specific gravity. Within 2 or 3 days you will feel more than half cured. No dietary restrictions. Price per phial of 50 tablets 6 rupees 12 annas. Postage free. Available from Venus Research Laboratory (N.H.) Post Box 587. Calcutta.'

Mrs Rupa Mehra had begun weeping silently. 'I hope you never get diabetes,' she said to her elder son. 'Make as much fun of me as you like now, but –'

'But when you are dead and gone – the pyre – the empty chair – yes, yes, we know the rest,' continued Arun rather brutally.

His back had been acting up the previous night, and Meenakshi had not been satisfied with his performance.

'Shut up, Arun Bhai!' said Varun, his face white and twitching with anger. He went to his mother and put his arm around her shoulder.

'Don't speak to me like that,' said Arun, getting up and advancing menacingly towards Varun. "Shut up"? Did you say "Shut up" to me? Get out at once. Get out!' He was working himself into a fit of rage. 'Get out!' he bellowed once more.

It was unclear whether he wanted Varun out of the room, the house or his life.

'Arun Bhai, really –' protested Lata indignantly.

Varun flinched, and retreated to the other side of the table.

'Oh do sit down, both of you,' said Meenakshi. 'Let's have breakfast in peace.'

Both of them sat down. Arun glared at Varun, Varun glared at his egg.

'And he won't even provide me with a car to get to the station,' continued Mrs Rupa Mehra, reaching into her black bag for a handkerchief. 'I have to depend on the charity of strangers.'

'Really, Ma,' said Lata, putting her arm around her mother and kissing her. 'Amit is hardly a stranger.'

Mrs Rupa Mehra's shoulders became tense.

'You also,' she said to Lata. 'You have no care for my feelings.'

'Ma!' said Lata.

'You will be gallivanting around merrily. Only my darling Aparna will be sorry to see me go.'

'Ma, do be reasonable. Varun and I will be going with you to the homoeopath's and then to the station. And Amit will be here in fifteen minutes with the car. Do you want him to see you in tears?'

'I don't care what he sees or does not see,' said Mrs Rupa Mehra with a snappish edge to her voice.

Amit arrived on time. Mrs Rupa Mehra had washed her face, but her nose was still red with emotion. When she said goodbye to Aparna, both of them began to cry. Luckily Arun had already left for work, so he could not make unhelpful comments from the sidelines.

*

Dr Nuruddin, the homoeopath, was a middle-aged man with a long face, a jovial manner, and rather a drawl-like voice. He greeted Mrs Rupa Mehra warmly, obtained her general particulars and her medical history, looked at her blood sugar charts, talked for a minute or two about Kakoli Chatterji, stood up, sat down again, and then embarked upon a disconcerting line of questioning.

'You have reached menopause?'

'Yes. But why –'

'Yes?' asked Dr Nuruddin, as of a fractious child.

'Nothing,' said Mrs Rupa Mehra meekly.

'Do you find yourself easily irritable, upset?'

'Doesn't everyone?'

Dr Nuruddin smiled. 'Many people do. Do you, Mrs Mehra?'

'Yes. This morning at breakfast –'

'Tears?'

'Yes.'

'Do you sometimes feel extreme sadness? Abject despair, uncompromising melancholy?'

He pronounced these as one would medical symptoms like itching or intestinal pain. Mrs Rupa Mehra looked at him in perplexity.

'Extreme? How extreme?' she faltered.

'Any answer you can give me will be helpful.'

Mrs Rupa Mehra thought before replying: 'Sometimes I feel very despairing. Whenever I think of my late husband.'

'Are you thinking of him now?'

'Yes.'

'And are you in despair?'

'Not just now,' confessed Mrs Rupa Mehra.

'What are you feeling just now?' asked Dr Nuruddin.

'How peculiar all this is.'

Translated, this meant: 'That you are mad. And so am I, for putting up with these questions.'

Dr Nuruddin touched the eraser on his pencil to the tip of his nose before asking: 'Mrs Mehra, do you think my questions are not pertinent? That they are impertinent?'

'Well –'

'I assure you that they are very pertinent for understanding your condition. In homoeopathy we try to deal with the whole system, we do not merely confine ourselves to the physical side. Now tell me, do you suffer from loss of memory?'

'No. I always remember the names and birthdays of friends, and other important things.'

Dr Nuruddin wrote something down on a small pad. 'Good, good,' he said. 'And dreams?'

'Dreams?'

'Dreams.'

'Yes?' asked Mrs Rupa Mehra in bewilderment.

'What dreams do you have, Mrs Mehra?'

'I don't remember.'

'You don't remember?' he responded with genial scepticism.

'No,' said Mrs Rupa Mehra, gritting her teeth.

'Do you grind your teeth in your sleep?'

'How do I know? I'm sleeping. What does all this have to do with my diabetes?'

Dr Nuruddin continued jovially: 'Do you ever wake up thirsty at night?'

Mrs Rupa Mehra, frowning, replied: 'Yes, quite often. I keep a jug of water by my bedside.'

'Do you feel more tired in the morning or in the evening?'

'In the morning, I think. Until I do my recitations from the Gita. Then I feel stronger.'

'Are you fond of mangoes?'

Mrs Rupa Mehra stared at Dr Nuruddin across the table: 'How do you know?' she demanded.

'It was only a question, Mrs Mehra. Does your urine smell of violets?'

'How dare you?' cried Mrs Rupa Mehra, outraged.

'Mrs Mehra, I am trying to help you,' said Dr Nuruddin, laying his pencil down. 'Will you answer my questions?'

'I will not answer such questions. My train is leaving from Howrah in under an hour. I have to go.'

Dr Nuruddin took down his copy of the *Materia Medica* and opened it to the relevant page. 'You see, Mrs Mehra,' he said, 'I am not conjuring up these symptoms out of my head. But even the strength of your resistance to my questions has been helpful to me in my diagnosis. Now I have only one further question.'

Mrs Rupa Mehra tensed up. 'Yes?' she asked.

'Do the tips of your fingers ever itch?' asked Dr Nuruddin.

'No.' said Mrs Rupa Mehra, and breathed a deep sigh.

Dr Nuruddin stroked the bridge of his nose with his two index fingers for a minute, then wrote out a prescription, and handed it to his dispensing assistant, who began to grind various materials up into a white powder, which he distributed into twenty-one tiny paper packets.

'You will not eat onions or ginger or garlic, and you will

take one small packet of powder before each meal. At least half an hour before each meal,' said Dr Nuruddin.

'And this will improve my diabetes?'

'Inshallah.'

'But I thought you would give me those small pills,' protested Mrs Rupa Mehra.

'I prefer powders,' said Dr Nuruddin. 'Come back in seven days, and we will see –'

'I am leaving Calcutta. I won't be back for months.'

Dr Nuruddin, not quite so jovially, said: 'Why didn't you tell me?'

'You didn't ask me. I'm sorry, Doctor.'

'Yes. And where are you going to?'

'To Delhi, and then to Brahmpur. My daughter Savita is expecting,' confided Mrs Rupa Mehra.

'When will you be in Brahmpur?'

'In a week or two.'

'I don't like to prescribe for long periods,' said Dr Nuruddin, 'but there doesn't seem to be much choice.' He spoke to his assistant before continuing: 'I am giving you medicines for two weeks. You must write to me at this address after five days, telling me how you are feeling. And in Brahmpur you must visit Dr Baldev Singh. Here is his address. I will write him a note about you later today. Please pay and collect your medicines at the front. Goodbye, Mrs Mehra.'

'Thank you, Doctor,' said Mrs Rupa Mehra.

'Next,' called Dr Nuruddin cheerfully.

7.46

MRS RUPA MEHRA was unusually quiet on the way to the station. When asked by her children how the appointment with the doctor had gone she said: 'It was peculiar. You can tell Kuku that.'

'Are you going to follow his prescription?'

'Yes,' said Mrs Rupa Mehra. 'I was not brought up to waste money.' She sounded as if she was irritated by their presence.

Throughout a long traffic jam on Howrah Bridge, while precious minutes ticked by, and the Humber inched its way forward through a raucous, horn-blowing, yelling, deafening throng of buses, trams, taxis, cars, motorcycles, carts, rickshaws, bicycles and – above all – pedestrians, Mrs Rupa Mehra, who would normally have been in a desperate, bangle-clutching panic, hardly seemed to be aware that her train would be leaving in less than fifteen minutes.

Only after the traffic had miraculously got moving and she was ensconced with all her suitcases in her compartment and had had a good chance to look at the other passengers did Mrs Rupa Mehra's natural emotions re-assert themselves. Kissing Lata with tears in her eyes she told her that she had to take care of Varun. Kissing Varun with tears in her eyes, she told him that he had to take care of Lata. Amit stood a little apart. Howrah Station with its crowds and smoke and bustle and blare and all-pervasive smell of decaying fish was not his favourite place in the world.

'Really, Amit, it was very nice of you to let us have the car,' said Mrs Rupa Mehra, attempting to be gracious.

'Not at all, Ma, it happened to be free. Kuku, by some miracle, hadn't reserved it.'

'Yes. Kuku,' said Mrs Rupa Mehra, suddenly flustered. Though she was in the habit of telling people that she was invariably called Ma and that she liked it, she was not happy at present to hear herself thus addressed by Amit. She looked at her daughter with alarm. She thought of Lata when she had been as old as Aparna. Who could have thought she would have grown up so quickly?

'Give my best love to your family,' she said to Amit in a voice that carried very little conviction.

Amit was puzzled by what seemed to be – but perhaps he had only imagined it? – an undercurrent of hostility. What, he wondered, had happened at the homoeopath's to upset Lata's mother? Or was she upset with him?

On the way back home, all of them agreed that Mrs Rupa Mehra had been in a most peculiar mood.

Amit said: 'I feel I've done something to upset your mother. I should have brought you back on time that evening.'

Lata said: 'It isn't you. It's me. She wanted me to go with her to Delhi, and I didn't want to go.'

Varun said: 'It's because of me. I know it. She looked so unhappy with me. She can't bear to see me waste my life. I've got to turn over a new leaf. I can't disappoint her again. And when you see me going back to my old ways, Luts, you have to get angry with me. Really angry. Shout at me. Tell me I'm a damn fool and have no leadership qualities. None!'

Lata promised to do so.

Also available in paperback

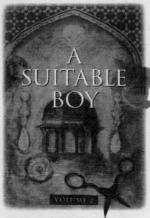

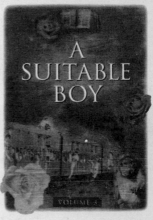

A SUITABLE BOY
Volume 2

ISBN 0–316–78152–5
Price $7.99

A SUITABLE BOY
Volume 3

ISBN 0–316–78151–7
Price $7.99